THE EVELYN ANTHONY OMNIBUS

By the same author

The Assassin
The Legend
The Malaspiga Exit
The Occupying Power
The Persian Ransom
The Poellenberg Inheritance
The Return
The Silver Falcon
The Tamarind Seed
The Grave of Truth
The Defector
The Avenue of the Dead
Albatross
The Company of Saints
Voices of the Wind
The House of Vandekar
The Scarlet Thread
The Relic

Historical romances

Imperial Highness
Curse Not the King
Far Fly the Eagles
Anne Boleyn
Elizabeth
Charles the King
Clandara
The Heiress
Valentina
Anne of Austria
Victoria

THE EVELYN ANTHONY OMNIBUS

The Poellenberg Inheritance,
The Occupying Power,
The Grave of Truth

Evelyn Anthony

HUTCHINSON

London Sydney Auckland Johannesburg

© Evelyn Anthony 1991

The right of Evelyn Anthony to be
identified as Author of this work as been asserted
by Evelyn Anthony in accordance with the
Copyright, Designs and Patents Act, 1988

All rights reserved

This Omnibus edition first published in 1991 by Hutchinson

Random Century Group Ltd
20 Vauxhall Bridge Road, London SW1V 2SA

Random Century Australia (Pty) Ltd
20 Alfred Street, Milsons Point, Sydney, NSW 2061, Australia

Random Century New Zealand Ltd
PO Box 40–086, Glenfield, Auckland 10, New Zealand

Random Century South Africa (Pty) Ltd
PO Box 337, Bergvlei, 2012, South Africa

Incorporating

THE POELLENBERG INHERITANCE
First published in 1972 by Hutchinson and Co (Publishers) Ltd
second impression 1972
third impression 1976
fourth impression 1979
reissued 1986
© Evelyn Anthony 1972

THE OCCUPYING POWER
First published in 1973 by Hutchinson and Co (Publishers) Ltd
second impression 1973
third impression 1974
fourth impression 1978
fifth impression 1981
reissued 1986
© Evelyn Anthony 1973

THE GRAVE OF TRUTH
First published in 1979 by Hutchinson and Co (Publishers) Ltd
reissued 1987
© Evelyn Anthony 1979

BRITISH LIBRARY CATALOGUING–IN–PUBLICATION DATA

Anthony, Evelyn
  The Evelyn Anthony omnibus: 'The Poellenberg
  Inheritance', 'The Occupying Power', 'The Grave of
  Truth'. – Reissue
  I. Title

  823[F]

  ISBN 0–09–175056–3

Set in Sabon by Falcon Typographic Art Ltd
Printed and bound in Great Britain by Clays Ltd, St Ives PLC

THE
POELLENBERG INHERITANCE

I

It took fifteen minutes exactly to walk from his apartment in the Avenida de Infanta to the corner of the Calle del Rey to buy the papers. In winter, even when the weather was bitterly cold and there was snow on the streets of Madrid, he came to the store at the same time, collected the English, French and German newspapers and went home to spend the afternoon reading them. He never bothered with the Italian Press. They had turned coward during the war and joined the Allies. He had never forgiven them. It was May and the sunshine gilded the city; in a few weeks the temperature would rise and the atmosphere would become stifling. By the end of June he went away to the Costa Del Sol for a two weeks' holiday. He had been in Switzerland for ten years, living a miserable existence in near poverty, unable to work at any but the most menial jobs, supported by funds from the organisation which had helped him escape. Then he was found a job in Spain, and life improved gradually, as the risk of discovery diminished and he applied himself to the engineering work in which he was engaged. Now, twenty-five years after his flight from Germany, he was a well-paid executive with the original company, living in a flat in Madrid. In Spain he was known as Paul Weiss. He had few friends; one Spanish family whom he sometimes visited, and two German couples, both expatriate but much younger. He maintained no link with the past now except one. The apartment was on the third floor of a modern block; he disdained the elevator, and always used the stairs. All his life he had emphasised physical fitness. He never lost an opportunity to take exercise. Inside his flat he went into the kitchen and made himself coffee; this he brought into the small living room and settled down to read the papers during the four hours' siesta which closed everything in Spain from two till six.

The idea of wasting an afternoon sleeping was too ridiculous to be considered. He began with the French papers first, reading every item; occasionally he exclaimed under his breath. Then the English papers followed. On the inside page of the *Daily Express*, he saw the photograph and the report of the divorce. He read it carefully the first and then the second time. He folded the paper back, and stared at the photograph. James Stanley's Wife Wins Divorce. He would never have read the item, because scandals didn't interest him, but the face in the photograph was large and clearly taken from a studio portrait. It was his own face, and the face of his mother and a sister who had been killed in a bombing raid during the war. He held the paper and his hands shook. Paula Stanley was granted a decree nisi on account of her husband's adultery with a Mrs Fiona Harper. Then the account of the proceedings followed, and a write-up about her husband and his career as a racing driver. He had the name that made news. James Stanley, the hero of the international circuits, wealthy amateur who challenged the world's professionals at the world's most dangerous sport. There was a photograph of him taken by a low-slung racing car, one arm flung across the bonnet, the other cradling a silver cup. The face was indistinct, and the caption mentioned some triumph at Le Mans. He picked up his coffee and tried to drink it. Then he read the story again, to make sure. The racing driver and his exploits occupied nine-tenths of the report. The few facts given about his wife were bald and vaguely unsympathetic. She was twenty-eight. He had a pencil out by now and was underlining sections. The age was right. There were no children of the marriage, and her address was given in full. She was formerly Paula Ridgeway, and the marriage had lasted five years. Ridgeway. That was the right name too. The name of the man his wife had married after the war. The organisation had kept him informed of his family's situation immediately after Germany's defeat. He had heard about the confiscation of his property and the occupation of his home by British staff officers. And then his wife's re-marriage. To a Major Ridgeway. They had left Germany, taking his daughter with them, and until that afternoon twenty-five years later, he had never heard of them again. He went to the desk, where he kept his files and business correspondence for work at home, and cut out the article and the photograph. Inside his breast pocket he carried a wallet, and in the wallet a small yellow snapshot. Everything else which identified him had been destroyed. This one photograph he had kept. It had travelled through the nightmare of the Russian retreat with him; he had taken it out at night, with fingers so stiff with cold that they could hardly hold it, and kissed it. It showed a little girl, a leggy child of three years old, in a party dress with a lace collar, her brown hair tied back with a bow. It was frayed round the edges and a crack ran diagonally across it. He laid the snapshot beside the newspaper photograph; the resemblance was slight, probably only visible to someone who was looking for it; he recognised that. But the family likeness in the woman was unmistakable. It was a Bronsart face, high cheek-boned, light-eyed, with hair that grew back from a wide forehead, exactly as his own had done. He stood back from the desk. After twenty-five years. After resigning himself to a permanent loss, to taking out his treasured memory, faded and petrified like the little snapshot, and contenting himself with that, the impossible had happened. He had found his daughter again. And the dream he had dreamed for her in the last year before disaster overwhelmed his country could now become reality. Love, as he often said, died quickly enough between men and women. Marriage was a convenience and sentiment a trap. But the love of a father for his child transcended everything. That, and his love for his country, were what distinguished human emotion from the weak and the carnal. He had never loved Paula's mother; he had adored his child with single-minded passion, with tenderness, with fanatical pride. She was his flesh, his blood, she had his eyes, so distinctively blue that they had hindered his escape; she aroused in him a protectiveness normally found in women towards their young. She was the only human being with whom his emotions had ever been involved. Because of her, he sat down again and made the first telephone call to Switzerland in five years. It was only to be used in emergency. He knew it still operated because any change would have been notified. He knew who would answer, because they had served together and fought together, and through the offices of this one man, he had escaped. He asked for the number and waited. When the call came through he said only one sentence. 'This is the General. I am flying to Switzerland tomorrow; meet me at Zurich airport between six and seven. I need your help.'

Paula Stanley was in the bath when the telephone rang. Since she had left her husband, she lived alone; she waited, hoping the caller would ring off, but the bell persisted. She got out of the hot water, wrapped a towel around herself and went through to the bedroom. Her feet left wet marks on the carpet; she looked down and grimaced. James, her husband, had always been untidy. He threw his clothes on the floor, dropped his ash indiscriminately, flung his papers into the corner when he had finished reading them, and refused to submit to any kind of domestic routine. All his concentration and discipline had gone into his racing career. Perhaps it was the very carelessness with which he approached ordinary life which had attracted her when they first met. He hadn't given a damn about anything. He was deliberately unconventional. He spent money on nonsense, and forgot about mundane demands like electricity bills; he would stay up all night going from one night club to the next, picking up friends and strangers, surrounded by admiring spongers, dragging Paula, bewildered and impressed, along with him. Her own life had always been rigid; it was governed by routine since her childhood, by a strict boarding school and a mother whose principal dislike was being asked for, or expected to do, anything connected with her daughter. Paula had lived within narrow confines. Meeting a man like James Stanley was like being permanently drunk. The inhibitions vanished, the obligations of normality disintegrated, and there was a frightening sense of liberation. It hadn't lasted. The euphoria was temporary, the liberty became, after marriage, a worse constriction of freedom than she had ever known. He declined all responsibilities; he picked up the details of their married life and dropped them into her lap, with the injunction to take care of it because he couldn't be distracted when he was racing. The fact that girls and drink and disorder weren't considered distractions made no impression as an argument. When Paula remonstrated he simply disappeared. His cars were his life; the excitement, the concentration, the publicity and adulation were all that mattered. She had often wondered why he married her at all. She had refused to go to bed with him when they first met; she was too ashamed to admit that at twenty-three she was still a virgin, and the existence of such a freak never suggested itself to him. He had wanted her and been unable to get her. So, typically impulsive and without responsibility, he had asked her to marry him, and in a blaze of flashbulbs and screaming fans, they had rushed to the registry office and out again. Sexually, it had not been a success. Paula didn't know exactly when he had begun his infidelities, but an instinctive fear of being hurt dictated that she ask no questions and investigate nothing, however flimsy his excuses. And so for five years they had lived, James projecting his unattractive free-wheeling image for the imitation of his fans, both on and off the racing track, and Paula waiting uncertainly for something to happen. When it did it was typical of her husband. He had begun a publicised affair with one woman and confessed in a burst of boyish candour, that he was in love with another. One was a close friend of Paula's, who had twice accompanied them on holiday, but the object of his immediate affections was unknown, one of the crowd of speed-mad girls who surrounded the racing heroes. Paula had packed her suitcase the same day and moved out. Their divorce had been granted only a month ago.

She put the receiver to her ear.

'Hello?'

'Is that Mrs Stanley?' It was a man's voice, with a foreign accent.

'Yes, speaking. Who is that?'

'My name is Black. But you don't know me. I would like to come and see you.'

Paula hesitated. It was five-thirty and she was getting ready to go down to her mother for the weekend.

'Why do you want to see me?' she asked. 'What can I do for you?'

'I just want to come and talk to you,' the voice said. 'Don't be alarmed, Mrs Stanley. I am not a crank. I have something very important to tell you. Something which is to your advantage.'

'What do you mean? Are you a solicitor?'

Which she realised at once was immaterial because there was no one to die and leave her money. Her mother was her only relative.

'No, Mrs Stanley. I am not a solicitor. I am a friend of your father's. When can I come?'

'What do you mean, a friend of my father's – my father is dead.'

'I know that; does the name Poellenberg mean anything to you?'

'Not a thing. I've never heard of it.' For a moment she was tempted to hang up. The towel was slipping and she was cold.

'Let me come and see you and I will explain,' the voice said. 'But don't mention it to anyone. Don't mention Poellenberg. Can I come tomorrow morning?'

'No,' Paula said. 'I'm going away for the weekend. Why mustn't I mention this to anyone – what's all the mystery about, Mr Black?'

'I will explain when I see you,' he said. 'I will explain everything then, but you will have to trust me. On Monday morning, at ten o'clock.'

'I go to my office at ten,' she said. 'Wait a minute, let me think – why don't you come there? About eleven-thirty?'

'Will we be able to speak in private?'

'Certainly. Nobody will disturb me. One moment, tell me one thing – you say you're a friend of my father's . . .'

'I will come to your office on Monday at half past eleven,' the voice cut in. 'I know the address. Goodbye, Mrs Stanley. I look forward to meeting you.'

The line clicked. He had rung off. Paula put the phone down and stood shivering, holding the towel round her. Of course she wasn't afraid. That was what James always said about her, 'Nothing would scare you, sweetheart, you're a real tough little Hun.' It was a remark that wounded, assuming, as it did, that she was able to take care of herself and consequently he was free of obligation. Even if he were right, that epithet, Hun, always rubbed raw. It was not as if she had been to Germany since her childhood or even spoke the language. James had made the accident of blood into a genetic crime. She had been born in Germany, but she left it as a child, and the Englishman her mother married had adopted her legally and given her his name. Paula went back and let the tepid water out of the bath. She dried herself and stood for a moment before the mirror, examining the naked body for defects. There were none visible; she was young, firm, slenderly built, with an attractive face framed in smooth brown hair. Only the eyes were different. They were blue, but of an extraordinary colour. She went back into her bedroom and dressed in trousers, sweater and jacket. Her weekend case was packed. She looked at the telephone again. What an extraordinary call. A complete stranger ringing out of the unknown, claiming to have news of great importance for her, claiming to have known the dead father she could not remember. It was odd, but Paula realised suddenly that this was what had made her agree to a meeting. He had known her father. Who was he, this Mr Black, with an accent that came from her unknown homeland across the Rhine? The voice was that of an old man, and if he had known her father the General, then he must be well into his sixties. She locked the flat door behind her and went into her car. As it started up, her thoughts were far from the traffic that choked her route out through the City of London, through the East End and on to the Newmarket road. She knew the route by heart; she had travelled down to her stepfather's house in Essex for the last eight years, since she had left home at twenty to live and work in London alone. Alone. It was the operative word to describe the best part of her life. Five years of that dismal marriage, after a childhood which was spent playing gooseberry to two adults who only wanted to be left alone with each other. Now that she was truly independent, free of family ties and without James to nag about neglecting them so he could go off on his own, Paula paid infrequent visits to the house in Essex. They didn't miss her when she stayed away. They were pleased to see her in a distant way, and kind, prepared to let her share their warmth and smugness in each other's company. The result was to drive her out of the house as quickly as good manners would permit.

But her mother was sixty, although she didn't look it, and sometimes Paula's conscience jabbed. On those occasions she gave up her weekend with friends in London or declined another invitation to go away, and invited herself down to the farm.

It was a handsome lath and plaster Essex house, sixteenth century in the most part, with an eighteenth-century wing, which her stepfather's ancestor had built.

Brigadier Gerald Ridgeway, DSO, MC. She could remember that rosy complexioned face, with the brisk gingery moustache and the hearty voice, bending over her from what seemed a gigantic height. He used to smell of leather and cologne. He had always been kind, but it was a stiff relationship, with bouts of false bonhomie which embarrassed Paula even when she was very young. Children have an instinct for what is assumed, and she knew that her stepfather didn't really love her, that he was only making an effort.

So there was no relationship; she didn't hate him as she might have done if his attitude towards her had been more positive. She accepted him as part of her life, and accepted also that she had lost her mother to him as inevitably as if she had died, like the General. She didn't remember the General. She knew he was dead, and her mother had answered her questions about him with obvious resentment at being expected to explain. Paula hadn't pursued the subject. Her mother indicated her displeasure and Paula, even though nearly grown up, withdrew from the contest.

The man called Black knew her father. She was clear of the traffic and beyond the bottleneck at Epping; Paula pressed down on the accelerator and the little car gathered speed. He had insisted upon secrecy; what was the name he had mentioned? – Poellenberg. Paula shrugged as she drove. It meant nothing to her. What was it, a name, a place – what was its significance. In an hour and a half she had turned into the drive and pulled up at the entrance. It was June, and the front of the low-built house was covered with yellow climbing roses. The Brigadier was a keen gardener; he had interested her mother in the art, and Paula remembered her astonishment at seeing that elegant figure down on its knees with a garden trowel, grubbing in a flower bed.

Two black labradors came bounding out of the door, barking and leaping up to welcome her. Dogs, roses, the Women's Institute, a distinguished retired soldier as her adoring husband – this was the role in which her mother had elected to live the rest of her life. She came through the door after the labradors, a tall, thin woman in muted tweeds, old but still beautiful with the agelessness of fine aristocratic bone structure, the blue eyes filled with vitality.

They were not the same colour as Paula's; that astonishing blue was the General's legacy.

'Paula, dear . . .' She gave her daughter a kiss on the cheek. 'You're early; did you have a good journey down?'

'Rather a lot of traffic,' Paula said. 'How are you, Mother? You're looking very well.'

'I am, dear. But your poor father's got a cold. Come inside, and push those naughty dogs down, they'll ruin your clothes.'

She always referred to the Brigadier as 'your father'. It was quite unselfconscious; Paula was sure her mother would have been horrified to know how deeply she resented it.

Inside, the house was furnished with comfort and elegance; they spent their time in a small panelled study filled with her stepfather's collection of military books; the pictures and furniture were exactly in character with the owner. Very English, slightly shabby, valuable but understated. There was nothing in this country gentleman's home to remind Paula of the dimly remembered gilt and stucco palace where she had lived until the age of four years. That was a confused and fading memory, unaided by photographs or any of the normal souvenirs of another life. It was as if her mother had decided to erase the first thirty years before she had met and married Gerald Ridgeway.

She had succeeded in what she set out to do, as indeed she succeeded in everything. A German-born baroness, widow of a man who had risen to the rank of general fighting the Allies, she now played a leading part in the village life, looked up to and respected in the area. She had succeeded as an army officer's wife under the most difficult post-war conditions. Even her husband's ultra-conservative military family had ended by accepting the beautiful young German into their circle. Paula was offered a drink and she sat down; one of the labradors had settled beside her and was pressed against her knee. It should have made her feel at home, relaxed and at ease, her mother sitting opposite, talking about the latest village news, the dusk deepening outside. Instead, its effect upon Paula was to make her feel strange and isolated. It was not part of her, however much it had been superimposed upon her. Unlike her mother, she had not adopted the protective colouring of an alien country and an alien culture.

As a result she had no country and no affiliations, but it was not possible to miss what one had never known. Or at least it was difficult to blame the sense of restlessness and vacuity upon that deprivation. If Paula was unhappy, she did not know whom to blame or how to define what she needed. She was merely aware of a condition within herself, which had always existed. This she accepted.

'If you don't mind, dear,' Mrs Ridgeway said, 'I've made your father stay in bed; I don't want him to take any risks with that cold. The last one was on his chest. It made him quite ill.'

'Of course I don't mind,' Paula said. 'I'll go up and say hello to him later. By the way, Mother, I'm glad we're on our own tonight. I want to talk to you.'

'Oh? What about?' There was the same guarded look on her mother's face, an instant letting down of shutters, whenever Paula attempted any intimacy.

'I hope there's no more trouble with James.'

'It's nothing to do with James,' Paula said.

'You know we were very upset about that,' her mother said. 'It's such a final step, breaking up a marriage.'

'Sleeping with my best friend was a pretty final step,' Paula said. 'Not to mention the little bird he wanted to marry. I suppose I might have taken one of them but I'm sorry, Mother, both was just too much. Besides, we weren't in love with each other. It was bound to come sooner or later.'

'I could never imagine leaving my husband,' Mrs Ridgeway said. 'Whatever he did.'

'But he didn't do anything, did he?' Paula countered. 'He's adored you all your married life, so how would you know what you'd do if you had a rotten husband, for instance.'

The beautiful, ageing face was like a mask. The coldness struck at Paula suddenly and made her angry. How would her mother know anything about the problems of being married to a man who neglected you, avoided responsibility, and only made love when he felt like it? She had been loved and spoiled by one man with an obsessive passion for her. All they had ever wanted was to be alone together, to share their bed and their life without the encumbrances of a child, who seemed always standing in the shadows, looking on.

'Anyway, I don't want to talk about James. I had a very curious telephone call tonight. A man rang up and said his name was Black and he was a friend of my father. He asked to see me.'

Now there was a faint colour in the face opposite; it tinged the fine white skin, as if her mother were blushing. Paula saw the change from impassive disapproval to outright alarm. The mouth opened for a second; she thought her mother was going to say something. But the moment passed. Now it really was a mask, the colour was fading, leaving a grey pallor, the eyes were bright with wariness watching her daughter like an intruding stranger.

'I don't understand.' The voice was cold, angry. 'I know no one connected with us called Black. It sounds like a practical joke.'

'It wasn't,' Paula insisted. 'I'm quite sure it was perfectly genuine. Mr Black. He sounded German. Mother, please don't go out of the room, I want to ask you about this!'

'There is nothing to ask.' Mrs Ridgeway was standing, poised to walk out. 'I advise you to have nothing to do with this man, whoever he is. I know your father would say the same.'

Now Paula was standing too. 'He's not my father. He's your husband, but he's nothing to me. Let's leave him out of it for once. I want to talk about my *real* father. Don't walk out on me, Mother. What are you afraid of?'

'I refuse to be bullied,' her mother said. 'I have nothing to discuss with you about your father. He was killed in Russia, and you never even knew him. I suspect you've been building up some fiction about him in your mind. My advice to you is not to make a fool of yourself. As for Mr Black, it's probably a hoax or else some unpleasant creature with a kink about telephoning women living alone. I think you'd be extremely foolish to have anything to do with it. That's all I have to say.'

'He mentioned something,' Paula said. 'Poellenberg. That was what he said. He asked me if I knew what it meant. By the look on your face, Mother, it seems to mean something to you.'

'I'm going upstairs,' her mother said. 'I'm going to your father.'

'Stop calling him my father.' Paula burst out with it, the suppressed anger of a lifetime exploding in that angry cry. 'He's my bloody step-father and I didn't choose him! Go up to him and leave me. That's what you've always done!'

She dropped back into the chair and began to cry. Immediately the labrador leaned its black muzzle on her knee. She heard the door close as her mother left the room.

There was a long silence. One of the dogs moved round the room and then resumed its place by its mistress's empty chair. Paula cried for some time. It was a luxury in which she had refused to indulge, even when her marriage disintegrated. She had been unable to feel pain in such clear definition as she did at that moment, sitting alone in the study where she had grown up and always felt a stranger. After a time she became calm. She looked round her, and fought down a sudden impulse to run out of the room and the house and drive straight back to her flat. In the quiet she could hear sounds above; boards were creaking as if someone were walking up and down, but the house was built with the solidity of centuries and no voices could be heard. They must be talking up there, her mother and the Brigadier. He would be in their double bed, nursing his cold; Paula could imagine him in a dressing-gown with a silk handkerchief tucked into the neck. She had never hated him. At that moment it was her mother she hated with all the bitterness of a rejected child. She had dismissed Paula all her life, turning aside her quest for affection as she had done her questions. She had dismissed her father as if Paula had no right to think of him at all, as if his death were a reason for complete oblivion. It was as if he had never existed.

Damn her. Damn them both. She heard herself say the words aloud. She had an identity of her own, and her father was part of that identity. They had no right to deny him to her. But the expression on her mother's face was frigid with resistance. It was as if Paula had brought up some forbidden subject, something which was under an unspoken ban. She had denied knowing Black, and Paula had believed her. But the peculiar name, Poellenberg, that had meant something. It was as if her daughter had suddenly struck her in the face. It was useless to go upstairs and demand to be answered. If she faced her mother and stepfather, they would combine together as they always had, and she would retire from them in defeat.

They didn't want to discuss her father. The General, Paul Bronsart, dead and buried in the Russian wastes around Stalingrad; they had laid his ghost and enjoyed their association without any sense of guilt, so long as he and what he represented were effaced from memory. It was such a pity she had been born, Paula thought angrily. That must have made it difficult for her mother to forget that she was the widow of a distinguished German soldier. She had fraternised with the invader within months of his death. They had been living in their old house in the Platzburg outside Munich when the Allied forces entered the city and the company commander billeted himself and six of his officers in their home. Paula had heard the story from her mother in snatches over the years, a sentence here and there and once a sentimental recital of how the Brigadier, then a young major, had discovered the mistress of the mansion living in the freezing attics with a sick little girl. It had all been very touching, and Paula remembered how they had reached across and held hands while they talked about it. Her mother had married him, and fled the ruins of Germany to make a new life for herself, cocooned by the adoration of her English husband. They were inseparable, smug, completely wrapped up in each other. The inference was very plain to Paula. Whatever her father was like, his wife couldn't have cared for him at all.

Paula got up and lit a cigarette. She felt tired and angry, trapped in the house at least for that evening, a criminal waiting in the room below while her mother stayed upstairs to be comforted. The clock in the hall outside struck eight o'clock, and at the last chime the door opened and her mother stood there.

'Aren't you coming for dinner? We're waiting.'

He must have got up and come down to support her.

Two against one again.

'I'm not hungry,' Paula said. 'I've got a headache, I think I'll just go to bed, if you don't mind.'

Mrs Ridgeway came into the room. Her daughter noticed that she had changed out of her tweeds into a long black skirt and blouse. She looked very pale and handsome.

'Paula, you've been crying! I haven't seen you cry since you were a child. Do come and have some dinner with us. Do let us forget this stupid quarrel.' She came and put a hand on Paula's arm. She looked concerned.

'I don't want to quarrel,' Paula said. 'I'm sorry I swore at you, Mother.'

'That's all right, dear. Just promise me you'll forget all about that telephone call. Have nothing to do with it. It will be better for all of us.'

'Why? Can you just answer me that? Why will it be better?'

'Because there's nothing to be gained by bringing up the past.' The look was firm, determined to overcome resistance. She had made her gesture and now she was demanding her price. Surrender. Now do what I want and forget the whole thing.

Paula shrugged and stubbed out the cigarette. Her stepfather detested anyone smoking during meals. 'That's not much of an answer, Mother. But I can see it's the only one you're going to give me, so don't let's argue. I'll have dinner and then I will go to bed early.' She opened the door and her mother went ahead without answering. Paula heard her stepfather coughing in the dining room.

Nothing was mentioned the next day. Paula slept late. and drove her mother to the village for some shopping. Everything seemed normal and peaceful. The Brigadier had been friendly and in good spirits the night before, but Paula was not deceived. All was not what it appeared. In spite of the people invited to drinks, the determined bonhomie of her stepfather, who was thick and spluttering with his cold and the grim dignity of her mother, Paula knew that their calm was a façade. Their glances at each other were apprehensive; their attitude tense and worried. The telephone call was never mentioned again. It was tacitly understood that she would do as her mother wanted and ignore the caller. But they weren't sure of this, and that disturbed them. Paula spun out the day and a half till she could leave with decency. At the door they came out to say goodbye, accompanied by the dogs. It occurred to Paula that only the animals were sorry to see her go.

'Goodbye, dear.' Her mother brushed her cold lips against her face.

'Goodbye, Paula.' Gerald Ridgeway had his arm linked with his wife's; he smiled at her and waved. There was a strained, unhappy look about his mouth under the ginger moustache. He looked miserable and unwell. She got into the car, wound down the window and waved to them. 'Goodbye, thanks for the weekend; it was a lovely rest. Take care of yourself, Gerald, don't stay out in the cold.'

All the clichés of departure, the trite little phrases of farewell expected from a stranger. It was the coldest leave-taking she could remember, and it suddenly hurt so much she couldn't wait to start the car and drive away.

And then it didn't seem to matter. The next day was Monday and her appointment with Black was only a few hours away. For the first time she would be able to discover about the other half of herself. She had forgotten that the caller had something important to tell her; she had forgotten about Poellenberg, that mysterious word which had drained the blood from her mother's face till she looked like a corpse. Paula wasn't thinking of anything but the excitement of discovery and the hunger to know, so that if Providence were merciful, she would be able to love, even if it were a memory passed on to her at second hand.

Eric Fisher's plane landed at Munich airport at three-thirty. It was a warm afternoon, and the sun beat down upon the tarmac, making him sweat. Fisher was used to flying; he regarded it as a good opportunity to sleep. He was bored by the routine, the pre-lunch snacks, the rattling drinks trolley, the bland hostesses who looked so unreal he was tempted to put it to the test by pinching a round bottom in a tight skirt.

So he settled into his seat, even for a short trip like the flight from London to Munich and went straight to sleep till they landed.

He knew Munich slightly, and was looking forward to spending a day and a night there, revisiting old places known from the early days of the Cold War, when he had been a journalist. He supposed that his business could be accomplished within a couple of hours and he would have the rest of the time free. The clients were paying all expenses and he had booked himself into the Hoffburger, which was the city's best hotel. Outside Customs, he paused. He was expecting to be met. A man in dark brown chauffeur's livery came towards him and gave a military salute. Fisher noticed with surprise that he wore old-fashioned leather boots and polished leggings.

'Herr Fisher?'

'Yes.'

'Her Highness's car is just outside. Your bag, if you please. Follow me this way, sir.'

With pleasure, Fisher thought, threading a way through the crowd. Nothing so crumby as a common taxi. Her Highness's very own awaited. He grinned, enjoying himself. This was the sort of client he preferred. The car was an enormous Mercedes, shining black with silver-grey upholstery and a large coat-of-arms painted on the doors. He got into the back seat; he felt tempted to give a regal wave to the porters left outside on the pavement.

The drive took thirty-five minutes; Fisher timed it just for something to do. Scenery didn't interest him. He took a case of cigarettes out of his pocket and lit one. The glass screen separating his compartment from the front slid down; without turning his head the chauffeur spoke.

'Excuse me, Herr Fisher, but her Highness dislikes cigarette smoke in the car. Would you mind not smoking? I am very sorry but her orders are strict.'

'Anything you say.' Fisher stubbed it out. Her Highness sounded as if she might be hell on wheels. But then money, rank and power seldom improved human nature. Especially when they were inherited along with an armament empire in a country where feudality was deeply ingrained in the people. The Germans had a passion for rank and authority. He could tell that the chauffeur despised him because he was casually dressed and his attitude was like his clothes.

With a different breed of passenger he wouldn't have mentioned the no smoking rule. He'd have cleaned and aired the car and never said a word. Fisher knew his Germans. They were the only race in the world he really disliked. He spoke the language fluently, as he did French and Italian. He liked to think of himself as completely unacademic, but he despised the English attitude which refused to learn any language on the assumption that if you shouted, foreigners understood. He had worked as correspondent for a major midlands newspaper for five years, and then he had met Dunston, who was working for Interpol on a smuggling ring who were spiriting gold out of Western Europe into the East in return for a supply of pure opium. It had been a nasty case, with several murders and an abduction thrown in; Fisher joined the hunt on behalf of his newspaper, and by the time it was over and the ring dispersed, he and the man from Interpol had become good friends. It was Dunston who contacted him a year later and put a proposition to him over drinks in London. Dunston had left Interpol and set up on his own as a private detective. He had the skill and the police contacts, but he needed a partner. Fisher had impressed him. He was, Dunston said, a natural bloodhound. And one of the best sources of information in the world was the Press, to which he had the entrée. To start with the money wouldn't amount to much, but if they were successful, the sky could be the limit.

Fisher had no dependents; both his parents were dead and he had no intention of getting married. He could take the chance and see what happened. Within six years the Dunston Fisher Agency was the biggest private investigating service in Europe, with offices in every capital and a staff of a hundred operators. Now Dunston sat in the head office in London, and Fisher only undertook the biggest assignments, where the fees ran into thousands. The letter from the Princess Margaret Von Hessel had been addressed to Dunston, but Dunston was on holiday in Portugal. A cheque for a thousand pounds had been enclosed with the letter, as an inducement to take the case without delaying. Fisher had cabled back immediately, saying he was coming in his partner's place, and before he left for Germany, he had investigated the family. The name was famous enough. Steel, coal, armaments, property; millions and millions before both wars and a new fortune made since the end of the last. Blood which could be traced to the Bavarian kings, and to several European royal families, now dispossessed or extinct. A title granted by Frederick the Great. Castles in Germany, a vast property in East Prussia which the Communists had overrun, a villa at Cap Ferrat which had not been used for twenty years. A passion for the vicious concentration camp dog, the dobermann pinscher. And at its head the princess, aged seventy-six, the mother of two sons. Widowed in the last war when her husband died of a heart attack. Even before he arrived at the house itself, Fisher was expecting something formidable.

The car turned in through wrought-iron gates, surmounted by the heraldic boar of the Von Hessel crest. The house was enormous, a

square stuccoed building, painted washed pink. Flowers were growing in ornamental tubs round a paved courtyard big enough to have
taken half a dozen of the Mercedes. Trees enclosed the garden, but he
glimpsed vast lawns and formal beds; the whole place gave an illusion
of being in the depth of the countryside instead of within five miles of
Munich's centre.

He got out, the chauffeur preceding him. A butler in uniform, brass
buttoned tail-coat, white cotton gloves, opened the front door, took
his hat away, and made a small bow, asking him to follow. The
main hall of the house was like a church. It was doiminated by a
huge, hideous Victorian stained-glass window at one end; the ceiling
disappeared upward in painted clouds and bibulous fauns pursuing
naked nymphs. The scent of flowers was overpowering; there were
huge bowls and urns filled with them, and it gave the hall a funereal
smell. The furniture was heavy mahogany, massively carved, uphol-
stered in velvet. A ten-foot gilt mirror gave Fisher a sudden glimpse
of himself, standing dwarfed and uncertain in the ugly, overpowering
surroundings with the light from the stained glass window making
bloody patterns over him.

'This way, please,' the butler said. He opened a door and Fisher
stepped through. It was like walking into the sunlight. The room was
large and painted white. The colours were yellow and green and the
sunshine poured into it from three floor-length windows. Three people
waited for him like figures in a stage set; the centre one was sitting,
very upright, her back to the light, holding a cane in one hand. Behind
her two other figures were silhouetted, standing sentinel either side of
the sofa.

'Your Highnesses, Herr Fisher.' He heard the butler's voice and then
the click of the door closing. He walked forward into the room, across
an Aubusson carpet covered in green and golden flowers woven in
garlands from the centre, and stopped in front of the sofa. The Princess
Von Hessel held out her hand, palm downwards. Fisher looked her in
the eye and shook it firmly.

'How do you do, Mr Fisher. Let me present my sons.'

Seventy-six. She looked about fifty; there wasn't a white hair on her
head, and the face was like a predator bird's, beaked nose, taut skin,
dark eyes bright and unblinking, with a yellow circle round the iris.
Formidable wasn't the word. But he hadn't kissed her hand. He felt
comforted by that.

'My eldest son Prince Heinrich. My second son Prince Philip. Please
sit down.'

He took his eyes off the woman and examined the sons. The younger
attracted his attention first because he was extremely handsome, in his
late thirties, and very blond. He looked out of place beside the South

German darkness of his mother and his elder brother. The elder was very like the Princess. He had the same birdlike face, but the sharp lines of character and pride were blurred, the contours sagged and the dark eyes were sunk in puffs of flesh. He stood very upright, shoulders well back and one hand, with a big gold crested ring on the last finger, rested on the back of the sofa.

'Did you have a good journey?' That was the younger son, Philip.

'Fine, thanks.' They were all speaking English. Fisher would have preferred to converse in German but there seemed no way of changing over. He decided to take the initiative before the old woman did. He suspected that the sons were not expected to contribute much.

'You didn't say very much about this investigation in your letter, Princess.' He had no intention of calling her Your Highness, like a bloody footman. His hostility was rising with every minute. He resented the imperious stare, the arrogance which was quite unselfconscious. 'You mentioned the recovery of some property, but that's all.'

'I thought it best to wait until you were here and we could discuss the details privately. I believe one should keep these things out of correspondence, Mr Fisher. As a family, we have learned to be cautious.'

'Would you like to give me the details now?' Fisher suggested. He was in need of a cigarette, but he remembered the chauffeur's warning. The inhibition made him even more irritable than the deprivation. Who the hell did she think she was, that he couldn't have a cigarette when he wanted one . . .

'As you know.' The Princess began what he suspected was a prepared speech. She had folded her hands and settled in her seat. He recognised the symptoms of rehearsal. 'As you know, the Nazis conducted a systematic policy of looting art treasures during the war. They confiscated pictures, jewellery, *objets d'art* and every kind of valuable; I had the misfortune to go to Goering's house and see the result of this disgraceful pillage for myself. The houses of all the high-ranking Nazi officials were stocked with other people's property. They stole from some of my dearest friends in France, for example. The property was recovered after the war and returned to them in a deplorable state. It was in Berlin and the house was shelled by the Russians. There was a magnificent Titian which was ripped to pieces by shrapnel. It was very sad.'

Fisher sat still. It was going to be a long speech. Her eldest son shifted his position behind the sofa. Fisher noticed that he gripped the back of it so hard that his knuckles were taut against the skin. Unrelaxed, that was Prince Heinrich. Finding it a strain standing at attention like a dutiful soldier behind the general's chair . . .

'All this you know, Mr Fisher, as I said before. What you probably don't know is that these creatures stole equally from their fellow Germans. There are many old families in this country who were looted as if they were enemies. A lorry with SS troopers just pulled up outside the door, and loaded everything from a list which had probably been made when some senior official was a guest in the house. It was infamous, and I could quote you several cases.'

'And is that what happened to you?' Fisher interrupted. He wasn't interested in the vicissitudes suffered by those who wined and dined the members of the Nazi hierarchy. The woes of the aristocracy seldom moved him to compassion.

'No, it was not,' she answered. 'We were too important to be treated in that way. My husband had a certain amount of influence with people like Goering, for instance. He was a dreadful gangster but he had come from a gentle family and it was possible to trust his word. We were not harmed in any way.'

'But something was stolen from you.'

'Yes. Stolen. Taken out of Schloss Würtzen, our house in the Rhineland. I must tell you, Mr Fisher, I had given up any hope of recovering it until I read this in the newspaper. Philip, get the cutting of the *Allegemeine Zeitung*, will you? It is in the second drawer of my bureau, on the left.'

Fisher watched the son move across the room. By contrast with the rigid figure of his elder brother he was pleasant to watch. He walked like a human being. He even looked across at Fisher and smiled as he handed his mother a newspaper cutting. She held it out and Fisher took it. He read it quickly; he showed no sign of surprise. Impassivity was part of the job. But if this tied in with the Princess's desire to recover her stolen property, that thousand pound cheque was just confetti. He gave the cutting back to her.

'It's only a report,' he said. 'There've been a lot like it.'

'Not for this man,' she said. 'He's been accounted dead since 1945. Believe me, Mr Fisher, we made our own enquiries after the war, and they all said the same. Dead. Positively identified and buried. Now this report says he was seen in Paris, walking down a street in broad daylight.'

'I presume this means he's the thief,' Fisher said.

'It does.' She nodded. The eyes reminded him of something but he couldn't think what. Some kind of bird. And certainly no domestic pet. It was the circle of yellow round the darkbrown iris. 'He stole the Poellenberg Salt from us, Mr Fisher. It's never been found, and if he's alive he's the only person who knows where it is hidden. That is why I've sent for you. I want you to find him.'

Mr Black was a small man. Paula was behind her desk when he was shown in, and she was surprised to find that he was a head shorter than she was. She had expected someone tall.

But Black was thin and small-boned; he took off a dark felt hat and his hair was completely white, brushed back from a wide forehead. It was a Slavic face, high cheek-boned, with heavy-lidded grey eyes and a narrow mouth.

Paula held out her hand and he made a little bow and kissed it. It was not a real kiss, just an upper-class German gesture where the lips never made contact.

'How do you do, Mr Black,' she said. 'Please come and sit down.'

'How do you do, Mrs Stanley. Thank you. Over here?'

She pointed to one of the two modern armchairs which furnished her office. It was a cheerful room, the walls covered with Paula's own fabric designs. This room and what it represented was a very important part of her life. During the latter part of her marriage to James, her career as a designer had provided self-respect.

'What can I do for you?' she said. 'Have a cigarette?'

'No, thank you, I don't smoke. Mrs Stanley, I have something very important to tell you, but I think I should explain myself a little first.'

'You said something on the phone,' Paula said. 'You mentioned knowing my father. I'd like you to tell me about him. Please.'

'What do you want to know?' he asked her. 'I served under him for three years and I was also his friend. And his devoted admirer. He was a great man, Mrs Stanley. I hope you realise that.' The grey eyes were dilated; his stare made her uncomfortable. 'A very great man. I was with him and I know. You resemble him very much, did you know that?'

'No,' Paula said slowly. 'I didn't know.'

'You have his eyes,' Black said. 'The moment I came into the room, it was like seeing the General again. He was very proud of you; he carried a photograph of you in his wallet. He used to show it round. You don't remember him, do you?'

'No,' she said. 'I was too small. I haven't even a photograph of him. I don't even know what he looked like.'

'Ah,' he said slowly. 'Your mother married again, didn't she – to an English officer? Yes, I heard about it. She would prefer to forget the General. They both would. You didn't tell her I had telephoned, did you?'

'Yes,' Paula admitted. It seemed pointless to lie. There was a fanatical look about him which disturbed her. For a small man, white-haired and frail, he was rather frightening. She had never met anyone like him before, and she couldn't have described why she was afraid. Then he smiled, and his face became gentle again.

'I am not criticising her, please don't misunderstand. She was always charming to me,' he said. 'Things were very difficult after the war. We had to survive as best we could. It's a pity you don't remember your father. He was very fond of you. Very fond.'

'I didn't know that,' Paula said. 'I've never been told anything about him.'

'He loved you,' Black said. He leaned a little forward in his chair, his hands clasped tightly on his knees. 'He loved you as no man has ever loved a child. He told me in the last months before the end, that if he was killed his only regret would be leaving you. He felt your mother would be able to take care of herself.'

'She did,' Paula said. She was surprised by the sensation of bitterness. 'She married and got out.'

'She was very fortunate. Most of the prominent families lost everything, apart from the unlucky ones in the East, who were taken away by the Russians and never seen again. Many of us committed suicide. I chose to live, Mrs Stanley. And I have a question to ask you. A very important question.'

'What is it?' The pale-green eyes were glittering at her. It struck Paula suddenly that what made the little man frightening was the unhinged expression which came and went on his face. She found herself gripping the arms of her chair. 'What question, Mr Black?'

'Would you like your father to be alive or dead?'

'There is no question of what I would like,' she said. Now she was frightened. He looked completely crazy. 'My father has been dead for twenty-five years. He was killed in Russia.'

'A lot of people were said to be killed in Russia.' He smiled and his look was sly. 'Or in Berlin during the final Russian advance. But supposing he had escaped, by some miracle – how would you feel, Mrs Stanley?'

'I don't know,' Paula said. 'I'm sorry, I can't take any of this seriously. I know my father is dead, and that's all there is to it.' She raised her wrist and looked at her watch. 'Mr Black, I have an appointment in a few minutes . . .'

'I understand,' he said. 'You want to get rid of me. Very well, Mrs

Stanley. But I promised your father I would give you a message, and I must keep my word. The General's money and properties were confiscated after the war. He guessed this would happen; he guessed we would be defeated. So he put something away for you, Mrs Stanley. Something very, very precious. Does the name Poellenberg mean anything to you?'

'No,' Paula said. 'Nothing. I've never heard of it.'

'In the sixteenth century,' Mr Black said gently, 'there was a Count von Poellenberg who married a niece of the Medicis. They were married in Florence, and part of the bride's dowry was at the wedding feast. Benvenuto Cellini had made it. It was the wonder of the city, Mrs Stanley. A salt, a marvel made of solid gold and covered with jewels, made by the greatest goldsmith the world has ever seen. A huge ornament, so heavy it took a man to lift it. And it was known afterwards as the Poellenberg Salt. For four hundred years it was one of the treasures of Germany. Then during the war it was given to your father.'

'Given?'

'Given,' Black repeated. He said the word with emphasis. 'The General accepted it as a gift. He had done the owners a favour and they wanted to show their gratitude. They knew he was a man of taste, a connoisseur. They gave him the Poellenberg Salt. And he bequeathes it to you.'

'I don't believe you,' she said. 'I don't believe any of this. Either you're trying to hoax me, Mr Black, or you should see a doctor.'

He got out of his chair. He looked at her and there was something cold and authoritative about him, an echo of the past when he had been young.

'You don't believe me?'

'No, I'm afraid I don't. The whole story is too fantastic. I don't know why you've come here, and I shan't take it any further if you'll please leave now. If you bother me again with this sort of thing, Mr Black, I shall go to the police.'

The little man stood up. 'I told the General this might be your reaction.' His expression was contemptuous. 'He believed in your love for him; more than he trusted me. He wouldn't tell me where the Salt was hidden. But he gave me this clue to give you. Paris, 25th June 1944. Tante Ambrosine and her nephew Jacquot. If you want the Poellenberg Salt, without your father, then you will have to solve this little riddle. If you want both of them, then you can get in touch through me. I will telephone once more. I leave the day after tomorrow.'

'I don't believe you.' Paula got up. 'I think you're mentally unbalanced, coming here with a story like this. There's no such thing as a

Poellenberg Salt, and all that nonsense about a riddle and my father being alive. If he was alive he would have come to find me himself!'

'You don't know very much about him, do you, Mrs Stanley? You can believe me or not, as you like. But I have told the truth. Think about it. You may change your mind. Good morning.'

His heels came together with a click and he bowed. Before Paula could move he had gone out of the office.

The reference room at the British Museum smelt of must. The attendant looked up at Paula and shook his head. 'Never heard of it, miss. Look in the section on Cellini; you'll find a book listing all his known works, some of 'em are illustrated. Then there's the *European Treasures, the History of Gold and Silverwork, Art Treasures of the Renaissance*. Try Cellini first; if it's a major piece by him it ought to be in there.' Paula got out two volumes and sat down at one of the long reference tables. A scattered group of students and two elderly men were reading and making notes. It was her lunch-time, and she had been telling herself all the way from her office, what a fool she was being, wasting a lovely summer's day on a wild goose chase to prove a harmless lunatic in the wrong. Of course Black was an eccentric; perhaps he had known her father or been in the army with him. That part she was inclined to believe, probably, as she suspected afterwards, because she wanted to hear about her father, whereas she didn't in the least want to hear about a hidden treasure made by Benvenuto Cellini. It was obviously a figment of the old man's sick imagination. She was disappointed and angry, and she assured herself that she was setting out to prove the whole story was nonsense. There would be no Poellenberg Salt, made of gold and covered with jewels. It was just fantasy.

It was illustrated in the last third of the book on Cellini's work. It was photographed in colour, detailed as being thirty-six inches high, set with a hundred and eighteen diamonds, eighty-three rubies, a hundred and five sapphires and twenty-five Baroque pearls of large size. Brought to the Poellenberg family as part of Adela de Medici's dowry. Now in the possession of the Prince of Von Hessel at Schloss Würtzen in the Rhineland. Paula sat looking at it.

All right. There was a Poellenberg Salt. That part was true. But it belonged to a prince, not to her father. Then she turned to the front of the book. It was dated from before the war. Black must have seen it somewhere, perhaps in a museum, or in a magazine illustration, and woven the whole crazy story round it. Just because one thing was true, it lent no credence to the rest. Of course the Salt was still in the possession of the Bavarian prince, Von Hessel. She had remembered the name. What she really needed was an up-to-date book on Cellini, not something written forty years ago. Something which could identify and place the Salt in its present ownership. She replaced the book and began to search among the shelves. Then she chided herself for being ridiculous. She was behaving as if there might be some truth in the old man's fairy story. She looked at her watch and told herself it was late and she should go.

But towards the end of the shelf there was a recent volume on Great Art Treasures of Europe. She took it down and turned to the index. Poellenberg, page 187. It was illustrated again, gleaming and glittering in colour. The figures of nymphs and centaurs intertwined round a rock basin hollowed out of solid gold to take the salt. A massive collection of gems glittered round the base and in the leaves of a spreading golden tree which surmounted the whole.

The figures were so beautifully moulded that they could have moved. There was a paragraph written under the photograph giving the same history as the book on Cellini but in less detail. The last sentence seemed to enlarge as she started reading. 'Tragically the Poellenberg Salt was among the art treasures looted by the Nazis during the war and its whereabouts have never been discovered.' Paula shut the book and put it back on the shelf. It was heavy and her arm ached. He must have read about that too. She walked out of the room; the attendant called softly after her, 'Find anything, miss?'

'Yes, thank you,' Paula said. Outside it was sunny and warm; she had left her car round the corner of Bedford Square. She walked towards it slowly. It was all lies. The man was mad, unbalanced. He had looked mad at times during that meeting. Then why had the name Poellenberg upset her mother? She had been hiding away from that question, because it somehow made sense of what Black had said. Her mother had heard of it and not just as a national possession.

Looted by the Nazis during the war. Given, the sinister little man had said, biting on the word. Given out of gratitude. If you want to find it go to Paris, ask for somebody called Tante Ambrosine and her nephew Jacquot. June 25th 1944.

What was the truth? Had her father really owned the Salt and hidden it? Was there any use asking her mother, trying to force the forbidden subject out into discussion — Paula started the car and swung into the traffic. Just supposing it were true — just suppose for a moment the strange visitor was telling the truth that morning. Her father was still alive and had hidden a priceless art treasure ... At first it had all seemed to be nonsense; fantasy was the word which described it. But now there were enough facts to cast credibility upon the rest. She didn't even know where to find Black. And her mother wouldn't help. Why would it be better to leave the past alone? Paula had demanded that over the weekend and the answer came back to her. Because there was nothing to be gained from it. Now she saw that answer for what it was: not only a cliché but a lie. If there was nothing to be gained perhaps there was something to be lost. Lost to her mother and the Brigadier in their cosy life from which the General's daughter had been excluded. Just supposing the most important part of Black's story were a fact and not the delusion she had first believed it – supposing her father were not dead, supposing he were only missing and her mother had lied, contracting a bigamous marriage to rescue herself . . .

No wonder she wouldn't want the matter raised, no wonder she preferred to keep consistent silence about the past. Now some of it was beginning to make sense. What a fool she had been to dismiss Black. How hasty and arrogant, to call him a liar or a madman and let him go with nothing but a promise to contact her before he left. Back in her office Paula tried to work, but concentration was impossible. The facts she had read about the Poellenberg Salt chased round her brain. It had been looted by the Nazis. That part did not accord with Black, who insisted that it was a gift. And her father was an army general, not a Nazi. Perhaps this cast doubts on Black's story – perhaps she was building insane hopes upon something which was only a delusion after all. By five o'clock her head was aching, and she had wasted the afternoon; everything she had done would have to be thrown away. She had a date for dinner that evening; the prospect of making conversation with the man who had invited her, was only one degree better than spending the evening alone waiting for the hours to pass until Black might telephone again. If he didn't she would be left with an insoluble mystery which could never be answered. Tante Ambrosine and her nephew Jacquot. It sounded like a nursery rhyme. And a rhyme which she would never try to solve in terms of any hidden treasure. Because from the confusion and doubt which assailed her, one fact had emerged, taking precedence over everything else. If any part of Black's story were true then all that concerned her was the possibility of coming face to face with her father at last.

'I wish you wouldn't go to London.' Mrs Ridgeway had never nagged or frustrated her husband when he wanted to do something. Only her intense concern for his health would have made her repeat herself so often during the morning. He still had the cough, and he looked pale and puffy under the eyes. He had made up his mind to go to London and see Paula and nothing she could say would stop him.

'Your cold is so bad. That trip on Monday morning made it worse,' she said. 'You know the doctor told you to stay in bed; going on a train journey could make you very ill! Why must you go up again?'

'I'm much better,' the Brigadier said. 'The pain's gone and those pills have done the trick. Don't fuss about me, darling, it's not necessary. What's much more important is to stop this damned nonsense with Paula. I know you haven't had a night's sleep since she came down.'

'You won't be able to do anything,' his wife said. 'I tried, I appealed to her to leave it alone, but she's determined. She wants to dig up the past. And she'll be more sorry than anyone else when it all comes to light!' Her husband came and put his arm around her. He kissed the pale brow and held her close to him.

'Not as sorry as you and I,' he said gently. 'We have everything to lose. Your peace of mind, your happiness; that's what matters to me. I know what this means to you. I couldn't give a tinker's curse for myself, but I can't bear to see you unhappy. I never could, you know that. We've made our lives, my darling, and nobody's going to come in and start ruining our last years on any pretext. I like Paula, she's a good girl. I think she's messed up her life, leaving James and going off on her own, but that's her business. The General and everything connected with him is our business – I'm going to see her and make her drop it. And don't you worry. Promise me, you won't worry.'

'I'll try,' his wife said. 'But it's like a nightmare. After all these years – why should anyone contact her, why should anyone even mention the Poellenberg Salt!'

'That's what I'll find out,' the Brigadier said. His breath caught and he coughed. 'I'll go and see Paula; I'll even frighten her if I have to. But I promise you, sweetheart, you won't have to worry. Now I must go, or I'll miss the train. I'll be back after tea.' He kissed her again and she went to the car to see him drive away. He was a gentle man; his gentleness had attracted her from the first, that odd mixture of diffidence and kindliness which she knew now was so typically English.

The General was not a gentle type; diffidence was not within his comprehension. Fanatical, disciplined, courageous, and completely without feeling as far as she could ascertain in the thirteen years they had been married. He had behaved towards her with scrupulous correctness and complete indifference. They had existed together rather than lived. In the beginning he had made love to her to satisfy his impulses and to beget children. He had not been cruel, or unduly inconsiderate, but only after she had been married for some months to Gerald Ridgeway had she realised what this relationship could mean between two people. The General had wanted sons; she had borne him one daughter. The only inconsistent thing she had ever known about him was his reaction to the child and its sex. She had expected disappointment and reproaches. Instead he had astounded her by his attachment to the little girl. He was a grim, forbidding man of whom she had always been afraid. She hadn't been sure whether the sight of him cradling the baby and crooning to it repelled her or increased her nervousness. But something jealous and primeval stirred in her nature, some buried instinct of resentment for the response called forth by another female from the male upon whom she had made no sentimental impression at all. She had hated the child, and suppressed the hatred, as she had done with her feeling for her husband. When they married he was young and splendid, with a glamour peculiar to the élite of the day. He was a handsome man who attracted women, all the more because of his cool, unapproachable attitude towards them. To the masochistic yearnings of her women friends he was a godlike challenge. To his wife he was a ruthless, cold-hearted stranger with whom she was forced to share her life. She had ended by hating him; she hated his child, because he loved it so extravagantly, and as it grew it was the carbon copy of him. She turned back into the house and sighed. Gerald's chest was still infected. He had gone to London to a club committee meeting on Monday. He should never have got out of bed and gone a second time to see Paula; she shouldn't have rushed upstairs that first night when Paula told her about Black and burdened him with everything. But the habit of dependence upon him was too strong. She relied upon him for everything and he had never disappointed her. She loved him with the intensity of an obsessional, introverted personality, to whom emotional security had finally been given. She would have done anything in the world for Gerald Ridgeway and he would have done anything for her.

The room in the cheap hotel where Black was staying was in darkness when he opened the door. He never left a light on; for twenty-five years he had lived on the pittance allotted him, scraping a casual living, doing menial jobs and moving on. He had lived like a nomad, always alone, collecting a monthly pension from the fund, which kept him at subsistence level. In return he acted as telephone liaison for others. Often in the early years he had debated whether life was worth living under these conditions. As he had told Paula, many of his comrades had chosen to die rather than suffer the consequences of defeat. But Black had an instinct for survival. Hope persisted in him, though he had long forgotten in what, or for what. Merely to wake and see the sun, to move about freely in the world. This was enough, and the years had dimmed and distorted his memories. Now he lived through them, withdrawing a little more each day from reality into that golden past when he and his kind had possessed the world. It was a world in which beautiful women moved, submissive and smiling, hanging on the arms of men in uniform; where champagne was drunk and music played. The houses were palaces, the beds were thrones, the cars were huge and sleek, with outriders. It was a soldier's paradise, and even the destruction of the enemy, with its attendant horrors, had a Wagnerian magnificence that made it poetry to watch so many dying, by the light of such a fire.

He spent the day in St. James's Park, feeding the birds. He had bought some sandwiches, and sat by the water's edge. throwing crumbs to the sparrows and coaxing them on to his hand. A group of children had surrounded him watching. Black liked children; he gave them pieces of bread and showed them how to hold it still to tempt the fluttering assault of the sparrows. He smiled and talked a little to them, enjoying his day in the sunshine. He had been married, with a son and daughter. Both were dead. His daughter had been killed in an air raid on the Berlin hospital where she was nursing, and his son had died in Poland. He had divorced his wife in the early part of the war, and even now he never thought about her. After the last child she had been sterilised, and it was impossible for Black to remain married to her. It set a bad example to the younger officers. She had taken his decision very badly, especially since the court awarded him the custody of both their children, and he decided it was better if she did not contact them. There had been great bitterness and reproach on her side.

He had forgotten about his dead son and daughter now. So many had died. So much had dissolved in ash and disintegrated in blast. He had dozed in the sunshine on his seat. He had kept his promise; it made him happy to think that after all these years, he had been able to be of service to the General.

The resemblance between father and daughter was extraordinary. She had the same blue eyes, so bright and piercing. The women used to go mad about the General because of those eyes. He was a handsome man; impressive, with a natural swagger to him. No matter who he was with, the General always stood out. Truly, Black had loved him. There was nobody he admired more. The General had befriended him, taken him into his confidence. They had fought in the last campaign in Russia together, when the Red wave crashed against them and rolled on towards the Fatherland. There had been death and destruction during those last months. Black had a dream even now, where he walked through a passage and the walls were built of the dead. It wasn't a nightmare which frightened him. It was just a dream. He had lived through the reality and emerged sane, determined and skilful enough to survive. The years of exile had unhinged him a little: the loneliness taught him to talk aloud to himself; people in the streets stared after him as he walked along. He had admired the General's daughter. She had spirit, like her father. She had received him well, until she spoilt it all at the end by refusing to believe and telling him he ought to see a doctor. That was the mother coming out. The stupid mother, concerned only for her own survival, trying to stand apart from the

General and his work. He had recognised the General immediately at Zürich airport; he was older and his hair was completely white, but he carried himself with the same arrogance, he stood unbent by the years; when he took off the tinted glasses for a moment his remarkable eyes were as blue as he remembered. Schwarz was not a homosexual, but he admitted to himself that there was something stronger than normal allegiance in his attitude towards the General. It had always been so; he had conceived hero-worship for the man when he began to serve him as ADC. The General personified the idea by which Black lived; all Germans ought to look and act as he did. Black had followed him like a dog, and the General had honoured him with his confidence and occasional marks of favour which might be interpreted as friendship. He had got the General out when the war was ending, because he had been chosen by the organisation as one of its key men. He had taken the General through Germany and into Switzerland and then been ordered to leave him and vanish out of sight himself. Since he had never disobeyed an order, Black had done what he was told. Twice in the twenty-odd years that followed, he had spoken to the General; on both occasions it was to answer a request for fresh papers and a new place to live. Black had procured the papers and made the arrangements. He had heard nothing of the General since, and as the number of men living in disguise was diminishing, he had less to do for the organisation. Time had weakened him and shifted his equilibrium until it was delicately balanced.

He lived now for the simple pleasures of existing, like spending the day in the park in London and feeding the birds with English children hanging round his knee. His meeting with the General had induced a powerful upsurge of old feelings; he had shaken his hand and wiped tears from his eyes. They had gone to have a meal together and to Black it was like a dream in which the past had swung back as if time were a pendulum. He had listened to the General and promised to do as he asked.

He accepted the General's money, and repeated the curious clue which he was to give the General's daughter. Black had sensed, although he was too proud to put it into words that what the General really wanted was to establish a contact with his daughter. But even if she rejected him, his love for her had provided the means of her finding the Poellenberg Salt. Black had seen it once; it was the most beautiful thing he had ever imagined. Too beautiful, too rich with jewels and gold. The possession of such a thing would be beyond him. He would have melted it down and taken out the priceless stones. Only a man of the General's stature could have owned such an object. He understood that the General hadn't trusted him with a plain message; he accepted that caution. He hoped, because he knew it was what the

General also wanted, that the girl would come out on the side of her father and ask to be taken to him direct. He hoped but without much conviction. The idea of her disappointing her father made Black angry. He would telephone her the next day, before he left. He hadn't delayed after he left her office. He had sent the General a telegram. 'Contact has been made and your instructions carried out.' The General had flown to Paris and remained there, waiting. He wanted to be near in case his daughter came. It had seemed an unnecessary risk, but then Black didn't dare to argue. Paris was closer than Switzerland. Closer to what — Black put the thought away from him. The Poellenberg Salt was not his concern. Had the General told him to go and recover it, he would have done so without thought of personal gain. He opened the door and switched on the light. There was a gas ring and a gas fire; he filled a tin kettle and put it on to heat for some coffee. He had just made a large mug when he heard somebody knocking gently on the door.

'Heinrich, let me in!' The Princess banged on the door panel with the handle of her stick. She rapped once, twice. 'Open the door! I know what you're doing!'

There was a shuffling sound from the other side, a heavy lurch against the wood and the noise of a key being twisted the wrong way. When the door did open, Heinrich, Prince Von Hessel stood leaning on the door jamb. His mother walked past him and turned round.

'Close that and get out of sight. I don't want a servant to walk by and see you in that disgusting state!'

'I am not in a disgusting state,' her son said. 'I am a little drunk, but that is all. You knew I would be, Mother, why did you come in?'

'Because I want to talk to you,' she said. 'Go and sit down before you fall over.'

She herself sat stiffly in an armchair; she was a woman who had never slouched in her life. She looked at her eldest son with a mixture of distaste and despair. 'Couldn't you have waited till that detective was out of the house? Couldn't you control yourself for just one day and night?'

'I didn't have to be there,' Prince Heinrich said reasonably. He made his way across the room, picking a path across the carpet as if it were strewn with rocks.' He sat down on the end of his bed.

'This business is nothing to do with me. I've told you; I'll have no part in it.'

'You had a part in it,' she said fiercely. 'If it weren't for you . . . Ach, what is the use of reproaching you? What is the use of talking to you at all?'

'Don't let me keep you, Mother. I shan't be down to dinner.'

She looked at him. 'Philip could search this room. We could smash every bottle you've got hidden.'

'You could have me committed,' he said. 'That would be more sensible. If you take my bottles away, Mother, I only get more. Why can't you leave me to get drunk in peace? It isn't much to ask. I don't bother you, I keep to myself.'

'Except when you're driving.' The Princess's voice rose. 'Then you take your car and kill some wretched child, and who has to pay the parents and silence the police? Your family! Always your family . . .'

'You didn't want the scandal,' he said. He shrugged. 'I don't even remember an accident.'

'How could you. You were unconscious over the wheel, stinking of brandy. Philip could hardly get you out of the car.'

'Being a Von Hessel has its uses.' He laughed at her, his mouth wide in a drunken grin, his eyes taunting. 'There's nothing we can't buy, is there? Even the parents were calling you Highness and bowing and scraping when you paid them off! Go down and deal with your detective, Mother. Get Philip to impress him. I don't matter, so long as you have Philip.'

'If he sees you drunk,' the Princess said, 'if he asks questions or gets curious, this whole thing could blow up in our faces. I saw him watching you in the drawing room. You were swaying on your feet, I could feel it!'

He shrugged again, spreading his hands. 'If you say so. Why don't you leave it alone? Why try to dig the dead out of their graves? It's a mistake, and you'll be sorry. You and my brother, who is always right, of course. But not this time. This time it's a mistake.'

'I'm not digging out the dead, I'm trying to make sure they're still buried. If he's dead, then we can rest in peace. If he's alive . . .'

'Yes,' her son said. The drunken grin was a leer. There was hatred in the look he gave her. She didn't see it, her own gaze was distant, fiercely concentrated upon something else. 'Yes, suppose that newspaper was right. What are you going to do about it, Mother? You can't buy *him* off. He has the Salt. What are you going to do then?'

The Princess turned round to him; slowly she rose from the chair, supporting herself on the cane. 'I am going to get it back,' she said. 'That's all I will say. I want you to stay here and not come down tonight. Fisher is with your brother in the library, looking at some of our records. He mustn't see you, and I want the key of your room. Give it to me.'

'It's in the lock. Take it, Mother. Lock me up like a naughty boy. I'm in my fifty-second year, but you can lock me in my room if you like. I have a bottle to occupy me, and I shan't batter the door down to get out.'

'Make sure you don't,' his mother said. 'Finish your bottle. I don't care what you do so long as the world never knows what you are.'

She took the key and went out. He heard her turn it and saw the handle move from the other side to make sure. He opened the cupboard by the bed and took a full bottle of cognac from the chamber-pot compartment. There was an empty one standing at the back of the recess. He poured some into his water glass and raised it to the door. 'Prosit, Mother,' he said. 'Let's hope he really is alive. By God, he'll be a match for you!'

Fisher caught the early morning plane. He had paid off his taxi cab and was walking through to the departure lounge when he felt a touch on his arm. He turned and saw Prince Philip Von Hessel.

'Good morning.' He looked very handsome; he had a charming, frank smile. In spite of his disinclination to unbend towards any of them, Fisher had found himself liking the younger son. 'I hoped I'd be able to catch you. Have we time for a cup of coffee?'

Fisher looked at his watch. 'I should think so. Let's go through to the lounge.' People turned to look after them, and Fisher knew it was the other man who was attracting their attention. He was very tall and he moved with purpose, fast but without hurrying. The majority of people travelling, scurried, anxious about the time, about their luggage, about the flight. This superior German wouldn't be discountenanced by anything. Fisher followed and let him order. The smile was still there, but a shade less bright. Perhaps, Fisher thought, he's not quite as invulnerable as he appears. Something has brought him here at this God awful hour, and it's not to have coffee and wave me goodbye.

'I wanted to talk to you alone,' the Prince said. 'That's why I came.'

'Go ahead.' Fisher offered him a cigarette.

'Do you think it's possible this man is still alive?'

'I don't know. I shouldn't have said so; your mother seemed certain you had covered all angles after the war, but a lot of them did slip through. I couldn't answer that till I've done some digging around myself. What do you think?'

'I think we should drop the whole business.' The Prince leaned forward. 'So does my brother. The Poellenberg Salt has gone for ever. It's a terrible loss but compared to other people we were lucky. We have survived.'

'That's putting it mildly,' Fisher said. Philip Von Hessel laughed.

'My mother is a very determined woman. When my father died during the war she ran the business, the factories, the estates, everything. She's remarkable; we owe everything to her. But this time, Herr Fisher, I think she's going too far. She has an obsession about the Salt.

She wants it back; I know her, I know how tenacious she is. She'd accepted its loss as a fact, and then she saw that newspaper with the report of him being seen in Paris, and the whole thing was reopened. It's become an obsession.'

'What are you trying to say, Prince?' Fisher finished his coffee. There was an announcement over the tannoy.

'I'm trying to suggest that you cut this investigation short. Your fee will be met, Herr Fisher. You won't lose by it. Humour my mother for a time, but don't take this assignment seriously. It's a waste of time. He is dead. That report from Paris was just nonsense, I'm convinced of it. Would you do that?'

Fisher stood up. 'No,' he said. 'One thing is essential in my kind of business, Prince Philip, and that's integrity to the employer. Your mother engaged us to find this man if he's alive and to get back the Poellenberg Salt. And that is what I'm going to try to do. If he is dead, and that report was nonsense, then you've nothing to worry about. That was my flight. I've got to go. Thanks for the coffee.'

The Prince stood up. 'It was my pleasure. Goodbye, have a good journey.'

Fisher went through to the departure lounge to board his plane. The Von Hessels thought he was returning to England. In fact he was on his way to the Interpol headquarters at Bonn. That was the place to make enquiries about General Paul Heinrich Bronsart. They would have the complete dossier on him there.

Three days later Fisher walked into Paula Stanley's office.

He had a preference for blondes; redheads he avoided, he disliked the freckles and the temperament that went with the hair; brunettes he could take or leave.

He was unprepared for the combination of her colouring and her astonishing eyes. It gave him a shock, because his photographic mind registered instantly that they were listed among the General's distinguishing marks. She got up and came to shake hands with him. He caught a drift of expensive scent; she had a firm grip, which he liked. Limp handshakes from either sex always repelled him. Pretty. Very pretty indeed, smartly dressed, upper class, didn't look German, but on closer inspection wasn't typically English either. He sat down in the chair once taken by Black, and produced his cigarette case. He had given the name of a French manufacturing company when he made the appointment. People were none too pleased to give interviews to private detectives. He was prepared to be thrown out when he revealed himself.

'What can I do for you, Mr Fisher?' A pleasant voice, an attractive smile. It would very soon be wiped away when he produced his identification card. There was no point in wasting time. He walked over and put the Agency wallet on her desk. His photograph was on it.

'I'm sorry, Mrs Stanley. I'm here under false pretensions. I'm from the Dunston Fisher Investigating Agency. I'm making enquiries for a client and I hoped you might be able to help.'

Paula looked up at him. 'You said you were from Levée Freres,' she said. 'If this is the normal way of getting in to see people, Mr Fisher, I don't think much of it.'

'I'm sorry,' he apologised. 'But you wouldn't have given me an appointment otherwise. People are very cagey with investigators. It makes our life that much more difficult.'

'I feel very sorry for you,' she said coldly. 'Now either you can tell me very quickly what you want, or you can leave. I have exactly five minutes to spare.'

'Make it ten.' Fisher grinned at her. 'And stop looking so angry. It won't take very long and it might even interest you. You're General Paul Bronsart's daughter, aren't you?'

'Yes.' By God, he said to himself, that had hit her where it hurt.

'I plan to talk to your mother, but as you're in London I thought I'd come and see you first.'

'Why?' Paula kept her voice calm: she put her hands below the level of the desk. The man had sharp eyes, they ranged over everything, noting detail, storing it away. She didn't know why she was nervous or why he mustn't see it. 'I never knew my father. He was killed in the war. What is the enquiry about?'

Fisher made a snap decision. His friend at Interpol Bonn, had emphasised this point. 'If the bastard is alive, and coming out of cover, he'll go to the daughter, if he goes to anyone. The mother's remarried, he won't contact her. The daughter could be the key. If there's anything in it at all . . .'

'The enquiry,' Fisher said, 'is on behalf of German clients, and I'm not allowed to give their name. They want to trace your father.'

'But I told you,' Paula said. 'He's dead. He was killed in Russia in 1944.'

'Mrs Stanley.' Fisher got up. 'I don't want to raise any hopes on your part, but it's just possible that he's alive. Would you let me give you lunch and I can tell you about it? It's a long story, and you only have five minutes.'

An hour later they were sitting side by side at the Caprice. It was Fisher's favourite restaurant; he was well known there and was given a banquette table, close to a large party where a famous theatrical knight was holding court. It gave Paula something to look at; the first few moments when they met in the bar had been difficult. Fisher had tried talking, but she found herself unable to make conversation.

'Marvellous looking man, isn't he?' Fisher said. 'I saw him play Othello, and it was the greatest thing I've ever seen on the stage. Did you see it?'

'Yes,' Paula said. She and James had gone. She remembered that they had enjoyed the evening. She hadn't thought of James for a long time. She wished desperately that he were with her now. There was something about this man sitting beside her which made her uncomfortable. He was tough. That was it; she recognised the elusive quality for what it was. He had nice manners, he was attractive in a rough-hewn way, he had authority and a sense of humour, but he was fundamentally a rough, tough man from a completely different world. Nothing in existence would have persuaded her to lunch with him except that one phrase. 'It's just possible he's still alive.'

She had got over the initial shock; her hands were quite steady, she lit cigarettes and the lighter flame didn't tremble; she ordered a Tom Collins before lunch and watched the famous actor giving a performance for the benefit of the restaurant. Fisher sat beside her, drinking Scotch and soda, letting her take time to relax. She looked strained and he felt rather sorry for her. He wondered exactly how much she knew about her father, and felt instinctively that from the way she talked it was the minimum. Killed in Russia in 1944. Full stop. He had spent two hours reading through the file at Bonn, making notes, reaching back into the past, looking at old photographs.

Many of them showed the father of the girl, whose elbow was touching his at that moment. A good-looking, impressive man, splendidly uniformed. Was it possible she knew anything beyond the fact of a soldier father killed in battle – he didn't think so. He gave her the menu and suggested the restaurant's speciality.

'Would you like to eat first,' he said, 'and then we can get down to business? There's no reason not to enjoy a good lunch.'

'I'm not very hungry,' Paula said. 'I'd rather talk now. Please tell me, Mr Fisher, what is this all about?'

'Can I ask you a couple of questions first? I'm not being difficult, but it will help me to explain if I know how much you're in the picture. Your mother has remarried, hasn't she?'

'Yes; soon after the war ended. She married an Englishman called Ridgeway, he was billeted in our house. I was about three and a half at the time. I never knew my father, he was away fighting.'

'Did your mother talk about him to you – what did she tell you about him?'

'Practically nothing,' Paula said. 'She's not a confiding type of person. You'll see that when you try asking her questions yourself.'

'If you can help me enough I may not have to bother her,' Fisher said.

'I hope you won't,' she answered. 'It'll upset her very much. She never wants to discuss my father. I think she'd rather pretend he never existed at all. Anyway that's the attitude she's always taken with me.'

'So she told you nothing; he was a general in the German army and he was killed. On the retreat from Stalingrad, I believe.'

'If you say so.' Paula lit another cigarette; she had chain smoked since they sat down.

'You don't like your mother much, do you?' Fisher said suddenly.

'That's a very personal remark.'

'I'm sorry. It wasn't relevant; just an observation. So that's all you know? Nothing about his war record, who his friends were, any family left living?'

'No, nothing.' She hesitated. It was humiliating to admit such total ignorance. He wanted information from her, she wanted to get it back. She had never wanted anything so much in her life. 'Wait a minute, I do know of somebody. There was an officer who served under him in the Germany army. He called himself Black.'

'Black?' Fisher said. 'That's funny. He had an aide de camp whose name was Albrecht Schwarz. How do you know this?'

'Because this man Black came to see me last week,' Paula said.

Fisher didn't twitch a muscle. He even sipped at his drink before he said anything.

'Black came to see you? Here in England?'

Albrecht Schwarz, anglicised to Black. There was a companion file on him, twice as thick as the General's. He was marked disappeared, presumed killed in Berlin during the Russian bombardment of the city. Schwarz, Jesus Christ. He changed his mind and finished the Scotch. He looked into her face. It was pale but innocent. There was nothing in those beautiful blue eyes.

'Yes, he came to the office. Actually I thought he was a bit eccentric.'

Eccentric. Oh, just possibly, Fisher said to himself. Just possibly he had bad dreams at night. 'Why did he come and see you?'

'Just to introduce himself.'

That was a lie and Fisher knew it because she glanced away and wouldn't look at him. He wished for a moment that he was still a journalist. What a trail this could turn out to be. Albrecht Schwarz turning up in England. If *he* had come through alive . . .

The first course came. Paula began to eat it; she felt taut and unhungry. He had ordered a good wine and she drank some of it.

'Did he talk about your father?'

'Yes. He said what a wonderful person he was.' Paula spoke quietly.

'He said he carried a photograph of me in his wallet. You may think this silly, Mr Fisher, but I was rather touched by the idea.'

'I don't think it's silly at all. Was that all? There wasn't any hint that his death wasn't certain – that he might have got away?'

'Yes, there was, as a matter of fact. But Black was eccentric, as I said. I didn't really believe him.'

'I see. Where is this Mr Black, or Schwarz? I ought to go and see him.'

'I don't know,' Paula said. 'He just came into my office, and then walked out again. He didn't leave any address and I forgot to ask him. I told you, he was a little – odd, I can't explain it. He said he would ring me again but I've heard nothing from him since. To be honest, I rather doubted that he knew my father at all, he seemed so strange. Rather a frightening little man.'

'Little?' Fisher prompted. There was a photograph of the General reviewing an armoured corps, with Schwarz walking behind him.

'Yes, quite short. About five foot six, I should think.'

'That tallies,' Fisher said. 'If I got a photograph for you you'd recognise him, wouldn't you – even though it was taken years ago?'

'Oh, I should think so. He had a rather distinctive face. You could advertise for him.'

'Yes,' he said, 'Yes, I suppose I could.' The idea made him smile in irony. He had already been advertised for, but the man had no sense of propriety. He had just kept quiet and never answered. He was really feeling sorry for Paula Stanley now. The trouble was that his excitement kept getting in the way. 'Here, have some more wine. Is there anything else you can think of? Anything to help me? You've been marvellous so far.'

'Nothing,' Paula said. 'Do you mind if I don't finish this – I'm really not hungry. It was delicious, but I just can't manage any more. Now it's your turn, Mr Fisher. I want to know everything, I want to know exactly why you said my father might just be alive.'

He faced the anxious look, and thought how pretty she was when she was worried. 'Two months ago there was a newspaper report in Germany that he'd been seen in Paris. It appeared in the *Allgemeine Zeitung*, and was reprinted in all the major European newspapers through A.P. My clients saw it, and wanted an investigation.'

'Seen in Paris? But that's impossible! That could mean Black was right!'

'It certainly could,' Fisher agreed. 'It seemed pretty definite. It has to be looked into; anyway, that's what I'm being paid for.'

'Who said they saw him in Paris? And who is employing you?'

He had the photostat copy of the original cutting in his briefcase. It was a Frenchwoman who had made the claim. And she insisted that she knew. She recognised the General; she knew him by the eyes . . .

'Somebody said they knew him during the occupation and saw him walking down a Paris street. They tried to catch up with him but he disappeared in the crowd. As for the second question, I can't answer that. Not without the client's permission.' He couldn't quite imagine the Princess giving it. He had promised to go back in a month and make a personal report on his progress. He was looking forward to seeing the younger son's face when he heard this latest development.

Why in hell had he been so anxious to have the affair dropped cold? And why hadn't the eldest, the heir and head of the family, said one bloody word during the interview, except shift from foot to foot and hold on to the back of the sofa as if he was frightened of falling over? Fisher had been too busy in Bonn to ask the questions. Now they came back to him, prompted by Paula's question. He felt awkward at holding out on her, but as he had said to the smiling, persuasive Prince when he tried to double-cross his mother, in his business, integrity to the client was all important. It was the profession's one claim to respectability.

'Mr Fisher, you know some of the details about my father. Would you tell me about him – everything you know. I'd be very grateful.'

Fisher signalled the waiter. 'Nothing else?'

Paula shook her head. 'No thanks. Just coffee.'

'Two black coffees. When you say everything I know, you don't want a history from start to finish, do you? – I mean you know all that of course. You want to know where he was killed. If he was.'

She wanted to hear it all, but shame prevented her from asking. Shame at not knowing. She felt like a foundling. More and more she judged her mother for that damnable reticence which had closed her out. James always said she was uptight and disorientated. He liked long, medical sounding words and the description irritated her. But if what he said was true, she knew who to blame for it.

'Just the end,' she said. 'Where it was, and how it was supposed to have happened.'

'In a village outside Cracow, during the final German retreat in '44. Let me light that for you. You're smoking like a chimney, Mrs Stanley. Don't you know it's bad for you? Anyway, your father's HQ was in this place; it has a hopeless name I couldn't begin to pronounce, but he and his staff were there, including our friend Schwarz, or Black. He had taken up quarters in the police station, some kind of brickbuilt house. These Polish places were pretty small and primitive and most of them had been occupied and fought over during the original campaign. I imagine conditions were pretty rough at the time; the Russians were chasing hell out of the German army, and the fighting was not exactly Queensberry rules.

'Anyway on 23rd November a massive Russian bombardment began over the area. The house where your father was living was hit and everyone in it was killed. Apparently a body was found wearing his decorations but otherwise unidentifiable. Half a dozen survivors of the battle swore that the General had been in the house in conference with his staff at the time. Nobody got out alive. The bodies were buried on the spot. Your mother must have been notified of his death in action. I can't understand why she wouldn't tell you this.'

Paula ignored the question. 'One thing puzzles me,' she said.

'What's that?'

'Why was anything reported in all the papers? Why should anyone bother about whether my father was alive or not after all these years? It seems very odd.'

'He was a very important man,' Fisher said. 'He had the Knights Cross of the Iron Cross, and every other decoration you can think of; he was one of Germany's glamour soldiers.' He had a mental picture of the faded photograph in the Bonn file. The hard, clean cut face under the distinctive peaked cap, the pattern of gold braid and the unmistakable lightning flashes on the collar. He must have looked pretty good in his prime, a perfect specimen of the Wagnerian superman. He smiled at Paula.

'There's nothing more intriguing than the dead coming back to life,' he said kindly. 'Naturally it aroused interest.'

'Do you believe it, Mr Fisher?' she asked him. 'Do you think it's possible?'

'You'd like it to be, wouldn't you?'

'Wouldn't you? If you had never known one of your parents?'

'I don't know,' Fisher said. 'I didn't know either of mine very well. They died when I was a kid. But I made out. I wouldn't let it worry you. If I find anything out, I'll let you know; just privately, between friends.'

'That's very kind of you,' Paula said. In spite of her first reaction she was beginning to like him. He looked different when he smiled; she felt that he was not normally as nice as he was being to her. 'Will you promise?'

'If you'll have dinner with me this week,' Fisher said. 'I'll give you a full report. Just in case you want me before, here's my address and you can get a message to me at this number. It's a calling service. How about Thursday for dinner. I thought I might motor down and see your mother and stepfather on Wednesday. Can I come and pick you up at about eight?'

'I haven't said I'd go,' Paula said. 'This isn't more investigating, is it? I've nothing more to tell you.'

'No, this is strictly pleasure from my point of view.' Fisher paid the bill. 'And as I said, I'll give you a progress report – free. I usually charge blood money for this sort of thing. You will have dinner, won't you?'

'All right. I live at 28 Charlton Square. Flat 2. I warn you, you won't get anything out of my mother and stepfather. I tried to bring it up myself and I got absolutely nowhere.'

'Perhaps I'm a little tougher to deal with,' he said pleasantly. 'Anyway, we'll see. Come on, I'll put you in a taxi. Are you going back to your office?'

They stood outside on the warm pavement; the sky was clouding over with the advent of a summer shower.

'Yes, of course. I have to do some work.' She held out her hand. 'Goodbye; thank you for lunch.'

'I have to do some work too,' Fisher replied. He liked the way she did her hair; it curled round her head, not too short, but soft and casual, taking its own shape. He had never liked brown hair before. But with those eyes, she couldn't fail. 'See you Thursday,' he said. He helped her into a cab and turning, walked back down the street to find his car.

He wondered what the mother would be like. He had seen her in one of the photographs too; a tall, a very good-looking woman, with blonde hair plaited round her head, fox furs trailing from her shoulders, shaking hands with her husband's boss.

He wondered about the English husband. What kind of man had he been to pick her up and marry her, knowing what he must have known? Perhaps there was a beautiful love story being lived out in the serenity of the Essex countryside. Perhaps the attractive girl he had just left was the changeling, cursed with her heredity, even though she didn't know it. Fisher doubted that. Blood wasn't thicker than water; heredity without environment didn't make sense to him. What did make sense was the appearance of a man who was obviously the General's ADC, a man accounted dead for twenty odd years, and his contacting of Paula Stanley with hints that the General was still alive. He would wire Bonn for a photocopy of Schwarz's picture just to confirm it, but the coincidence was already too close. Schwarz had been anglicised to Black; he had claimed to have served under the General.

Why had he contacted Paula Stanley? Why, after all these years, had the little bastard risked disclosing himself? Just to effect a reunion – to drop hints and test her reaction? It sounded unlikely. She had described him as eccentric. Maybe this would account for the lack of caution. But nothing would persuade Fisher that he had found her and introduced himself without a purpose. And whatever the purpose was, she hadn't told Fisher about it. His invitation to dinner was not entirely motivated by her attractiveness. There was something he had to know, and somehow he had to make her tell him. Seeing the parents was a formality he couldn't neglect; but if there was a lead anywhere, and he had begun to feel a strange conviction that there was, then it would be found through Paula Stanley.

3

'I tried to telephone your office, my dear, but you hadn't come back from lunch. So I thought I'd just pop round.'

Paula had opened the flat door and found her stepfather standing there. He looked embarrassed, and then cheerful. He had a permanent air of bonhomie which Paula found extremely depressing. 'What a nice surprise, Gerald. Come in and have a drink.' He had sat in the little drawing room, made the same soothing remarks about the decorations as he had done on his last visit, and fidgeted until she could have screamed at him to get to the point and stop going round in circles of small talk. When it came out, it was unusually simple, as if the effort to approach her with tact had exhausted him.

'I had to come and see you, Paula. Your mother's very worried.'

'Oh? I'm sorry to hear that. What about?' She knew before he said it. She knew exactly what was worrying her mother and why the Brigadier had left his comfortable nest in Essex and made the trip to London.

'She's not been sleeping,' he explained. 'I made her go to the doctor yesterday. You told her something that upset her. Something to do with your father.'

'That's right, I did. I said a friend of his had asked to see me. She didn't want me to; we had a row about it last weekend. I know she told you about it, Gerald. She's never kept anything secret from you. And you want to know what I did, isn't that it?'

'Yes, put like that, I suppose it is.' The false cheerfulness had been sloughed off; he looked a worried old man, deep creases between his brows, a resentful expression on his face. 'What did you do, Paula? Did you take your mother's advice? Or did you see this man?'

'I saw him,' Paula said. 'Last Monday, in my office. We talked about my father and he told me quite a lot about him.'

'Oh, Christ.' The Brigadier put his head in his hands. 'Why couldn't you have left it alone? If you knew what an agony your mother's gone through . . .'

'I don't know anything about my mother,' she said coldly. 'She's never confided in me. She's never talked to me or told me anything. She's kept me at a distance all my life. And why do you say Christ like that? Why shouldn't I hear about my father!'

His face had reddened; he straightened up in his chair and glared at her.

'Because of what it means to her! She deserves to be left in peace now. Don't you realise how old she is?'

'What's that got to do with it? It's not as if she loved my father! She's never cared for anyone but you. Don't tell me she can't stand the painful memories – it's over twenty-five years ago. I'm sorry, Gerald, but I have a right to know about the other side of my family.'

'Even at her expense?'

'But why should it be at her expense?' Paula demanded. 'What is there to hide?' He didn't answer. He heaved himself out of the chair and faced her.

'Paula, if I asked you to drop this and not ask questions, would you do it?'

'No, Gerald, I wouldn't. I'm sorry. Give me a reason, one reason why and I might listen. But I'm not making an arbitrary promise to anyone.'

'I can't understand you,' the Brigadier said. 'We did our best for you. Your mother . . .'

'I don't want to talk about Mother,' Paula said. 'You did your best for me, Gerald, and I appreciate it. I wasn't your child. You haven't had a visitor by any chance?'

'What do you mean, what kind of visitor?'

'A private detective. If you and Mother don't like the past being dug up then I'm afraid you're not going to like this. There's been a report that my father was seen in Paris. He may be alive after all.' To her surprise there was no reaction of astonishment or alarm. He looked at her and nodded.

'We saw it,' he said. 'But thank God it wasn't true.'

'My God!' Paula said. 'It didn't occur to either of you to mention this to me? It was only my father who might have come back, that's all! I can excuse you, Gerald, but I'll never forgive her. How could she have hidden it from me? How could she have been so cruel!'

'How much did this man Black tell you about him?' It was an unexpected question.

'He said he was a wonderful person, that he loved me very much. Oh,' she said bitterly, 'I know what the trouble is – I've always known. Father was a Nazi general, he fought for Hitler, and you and she don't want it mentioned. You're smug and English and it wouldn't look good at the Women's Institute if it got round she was the widow of one of those Nazi beasts we heard so much about. I've been stuffed full of atrocities and concentration camps! I knew what a Bloody Hun was before I was old enough to realise I was one myself – Mother's a coward, she doesn't want to own up to her country or to me! That's why she's never liked me; I tied her to Father and to Germany. Without me she could have been just Mrs bloody Gerald Ridgeway.'

'You don't know what you're talking about.' Her stepfather had drawn himself up; she had never seen him look so angry. 'And don't you dare speak about your mother like that! I hope you'll never have to know what she went through, but you're too stupid and prejudiced against her to appreciate it if you did. I'm going home now.

'Any detective who comes near my house will be told to clear off pretty quickly. If he's chasing that story about your father being seen in Paris, he's wasting his time. He's dead, Paula, and all I can tell you is to be thankful for it!'

He walked out of the room and she heard her front door bang. She sat down and lit a cigarette. It was the first quarrel she had ever had with her stepfather. He wasn't a cruel man, or remotely unfair, but he was incapable of seeing her point of view, of appreciating anything but the feelings of his wife. Paula had said the unspoken grievances of years. She had brought the sense of shame endured through her adolescence into the open. She had grown up to realise that she was a member of a race whose crimes against humanity were an outrage to civilised societies everywhere. The marauding hordes of twelfth-century Mongolia were likened to her people. Genocide. Ten million Jews. Two million gypsies. Men and women and children being mowed down in France, Italy, Poland, the Low Countries. Horror piled upon horror. Names associated with unspeakable infamy. Dachau. Belsen. Buchenwald. Her name had been changed to Ridgeway when she was a child. So nobody would know what she was, a German and the child of a German general.

The only person who could have assuaged that awful loneliness and calmed the sense of guilt was her mother. And she had brought down a curtain of silence that nothing Paula did had been able to tear open. She went and poured herself a drink, which was unusual. She was naturally abstemious and she never drank alone. She brushed her hair and powdered her face; it was pale and her eyes looked tired. All her life she had been looking at that face reflected in mirrors without being able to identify it to herself. James had accused her of being a stranger; he was probably right. She had never come out of the inner shell into the cold winds of the world. It must have made her uncomfortable to live with. For the first time she understood why he had been unfaithful. Her best friend was a warm, affectionate woman, not particularly pretty but with an attractive laugh. James had liked her, and the inevitable happened. She didn't know about the younger girl and she didn't care. She brushed her hair again, and thought suddenly that she had forgiven James. She was quite calm about it; she poured another drink and went to the telephone to ring and tell him so, when the front door bell rang. Paula looked at her watch. It was nine o'clock. She had forgotten about dinner; she had forgotten about everything in her immersion in the past. When she opened the door she found Fisher outside.

'It's not Thursday,' she said. 'You're two days early.'

'Let me come in,' he said. 'I came right round when I saw the papers.'

'What papers?' She walked after him down the hall; her own newspaper was still in the downstairs lobby. She had forgotten to collect it.

In the sitting room Fisher waited; she came towards him. 'It's Black,' he said. 'So I came round.'

The newspaper was in his hand. She took it from him. The black headline faded out of focus. There was a photograph of a face she knew, a face with high cheekbones and eyes fixed in a narrow stare. Then the heading came at her again. Murdered man identified as War Criminal.

Fisher let her read, watching her face. He had been shaken himself when he opened the paper in a pub outside Shepherd Market. It was an old haunt and he was meeting a friend from his journalist days. He left the pub without leaving a message. It wasn't just the picture and the discovery that Albrecht Schwarz had been found murdered. It was the story printed underneath.

Paula suddenly began to read aloud.

'Albrecht Schwarz, alias Black, alias Winter, resident in Switzerland with a Swiss passport for the past fifteen years, was one of the small band of notorious war criminals wanted for multiple murder in the Ukraine and for his part in the infamous massacre of the population of the Polish village of Darienne during the German withdrawal in 1944.' She lowered the paper and looked at Fisher. She seemed dazed. 'Come and sit down and I'll get you a drink,' Fisher said. She didn't move. She was reading the paper again, her lips moving. He found the whisky and poured a stiff measure. The soda syphon hissed; it was empty. It occurred to Fisher that empty syphons and a lack of things like tonic water or matches were hallmarks of women who lived alone. Fisher swore and decided she might as well have the drink straight. He gave her the glass and made her sit beside him.

'You look upset,' he said suddenly. 'This has been quite a shock to you.'

'I can't believe it,' Paula said. 'He was sitting in my office – a funny little old man, with white hair. I thought he was crazy! Mr Fisher, I don't understand what's happening. I've just had my stepfather up here shouting at me because I'd seen Black, telling me I was hurting my mother and hadn't any right to go digging up the past – why haven't I? If my father is alive, why can't I find him?'

'Hadn't you better ask yourself why he hasn't come forward?' Fisher said gently. 'Why did he have to send Black, – why's he been lying low for all these years?'

Paula put down the glass. 'What do you mean? Are you trying to tell me he's done something criminal?'

'I don't know,' Fisher said. 'Interpol have a record of him, as they did everybody on the top Nazi level. Your father wasn't in the Wehrmacht. He was a general in the SS.'

'Why didn't you tell me?' Paula asked.

'Because my job was to get information out of you,' Fisher said. 'And anyway you seemed so keen on the idea of him I didn't want to point it out. Look, I've got an idea. Have you eaten dinner yet?'

'No.' Paula shook her head. 'And after this I'm not hungry.'

'You never are,' Fisher remarked. 'The time I took you out to lunch you left everything on the plate. I'm going to take you out tonight, Mrs Stanley, and if you don't want to eat you don't have to. And you don't have to talk about any of this either. This is going to be strictly pleasure and not business. Go and get a coat and put some powder on your nose.'

'I don't want to go anywhere,' Paula said. 'If you want a drink I can give it to you here.'

'I can't do without soda,' Fisher insisted. 'And you're fresh out of it. Go and get that coat. Hurry up.'

He lit a cigarette while he waited for her. She looked shaken and he was quite certain that if he took her at her word, she would sit in the flat and cry after he had left. He felt like an evening out; he had nothing to celebrate; rather, the murder of Schwarz was a first-class check to his investigations. So he might as well celebrate that. But what he really wanted was to get Paula Stanley out of the flat. When she came back into the room he got up. 'You look terrific,' he said. 'And that's how you're going to feel in a little while from now. I know just the place for both of us tonight. Come on.'

They drove into the centre of London, down past the Houses of Parliament, where a light burned in the clock tower of Big Ben to show that the House was sitting, on down Whitehall and round Trafalgar Square, where Nelson surveyed the city from his column and the pigeons roosted peacefully on the official buildings in spite of all efforts to dislodge them. The fountains shot water jets into the air, and the tourists wandered round the basins, clustered on the steps, enjoying the warmth of the evening. Up Piccadilly, past the Circus with its neon lights and sad little groups of addicts already assembling in a queue at the all-night chemist for their supplies.

They swung into Berkeley Square.

'Where are we going?' Paula asked.

'Annabels,' Fisher answered. 'Soft lights, very loud music, and plenty to look at.' He gave the car key to the doorman. 'Put it somewhere for me, will you.'

The doorman saluted and smiled. Fisher had a very big expense account on his company. Apart from his share in the profits. He could afford the best night club in London. Paula had never been there. Better-class night clubs were not James' idea of fun, and professionally she didn't move in that kind of circle.

The men who took her out were the type who chose discreet, folksy little places where the food was good. They went into the bar, which was exactly like the study in a rich man's country house. The walls were covered with sporting cartoons, prints, and valuable pictures. There was an open fire with an old-fashioned wire guard in front of it; leather sofas, a specially woven tartan carpet. A few yards beyond, the restaurant was a dark cavern filled with music. It was still early for the club, and there were very few people there.

Fisher didn't take her to the bar; it was too public. People sat there in order to be seen. They went straight to a table.

He ordered champagne for them both. He reached over and held her hand. It was cold.

'I can't go on calling you Mrs Stanley,' he said. 'It seems indecent in a place like this. My name is Eric.'

'Call me Paula.' She looked down at her hand in his. He had strong hands with thick powerful wrists, where dark hairs grew. His hand was warm and it gripped.

'Why did you bring me here?'

'To take you out of yourself. Drink up. Don't you like champagne?'

'Yes. Why are you doing all this for me? Why should you bother?'

'You've got a thing about this, haven't you?' Fisher said. He was leaning close to her; he could smell her scent and her hand was warmer.

'Why shouldn't someone care about you? You must have had a lot of men.'

'One husband,' she said. 'Who left me for another woman. Two other women to be honest. He said I wasn't much good at it.'

'Good at what? Sex? Or being married. They're not the same thing, I understand.'

'Good at either,' Paula answered. She drank some of the champagne. 'I was too reserved. Too wrapped up in myself. I thought he was hell too, so I suppose it was equal. And you're wrong about the men. The only ones who ever fell for me were thoroughly off beat.'

'I've never liked conventional women,' Fisher said. 'Maybe that's why I've never married. Apart from leading a slightly disorganised life.'

'Why did you choose it? Nobody ever meets a private detective.'

'Now, now,' Fisher said. 'We're not all sleazy little men in macs, poking into hotel bedrooms. We have a very big agency. We deal with all sorts of problems.'

Like missing Nazi treasure. Odd items like a Benvenuto Cellini masterpiece worth millions. Things like that. He looked down at her and smiled.

'You're feeling better, aren't you? Not quite so shaken.'

'Not quite.' He felt the hand inside his give a slight pressure. It roused a pang of excitement in him.

'Tell me some more about yourself. You're a bachelor and a detective. Were you in the police?'

'I was a journalist,' he said, 'for about five years. It was great fun, lots of travel, quite a bit of excitement. Then I met this chap called Dunston, he was in Interpol. We worked on a gold smuggling racket together in West Berlin, and we liked each other very much. He's not like me, much more of a solid type. Wife and three children. I didn't see him for quite a time, then one day he looked me up. He'd left Interpol and started his own investigating service. He asked me to join him. So I did and here I am. More champagne?'

'I couldn't,' she protested.

'Oh yes you could. It won't hurt you. Anything more you want to know about me?'

'I can't think of anything. Except what you won't tell me. Why you're looking for my father and who's employing you.'

'I tell you what,' Fisher said cheerfully. 'You tell me why Schwarz really came to see you and I'll answer your questions. Now I am going to take you for a dance. We came here to forget about all that.'

She got up. 'I can't forget it, Eric. I can't think of anything else.'

'You *are* going to forget about it. Just for tonight. Tomorrow I shall bully the hell out of you to get the answers, but not tonight. This is a nice slow tune. Come on.'

Paula didn't dance with him, she clung; his arm supported her, his body warmed hers as he pressed her against him. The dance floor was small and it was full of people twined around each other. Some of the couples jigged and gesticulated; the discotheque switched from the slow beat to a fast rhythm, playing at ear-splitting pitch.

Fisher ignored the tempo and went on holding her against him. She didn't move or respond to his pressure; his intention had been to cushion her against the shock and he had succeeded. Too bloody well, he thought, and permitted a laugh at his own expense. She was extra-ordinarily attractive; he had known many women who could claim to be more beautiful or more obviously sexy, but Paula Stanley was having a profound effect upon him. The fact that she was completely unaware of it, and was doing nothing to contribute to it, made Fisher even more disturbed. She rested her head on his shoulder and danced with her eyes closed.

Fisher made an effort. 'Back to the table,' he said. 'I'm thirsty.' The club was now uncomfortably full; beautiful women in expensive evening dresses, smart young girls in velvet dungarees and pure silk shirts, escorts of all ages came drifting through to dance. Fisher settled behind his table and took hold of Paula's hand.

'You are feeling better, aren't you?'

'Better or high, I'm not sure which,' she said. 'Did I thank you for doing this for me?'

'You did,' Fisher said. 'This is about the fourth time. And I'm not going to repeat it again, but it's a pleasure. Drink up.'

'If I do,' she said,' I'll go to sleep.'

'That won't matter,' Fisher said. 'You'll feel pretty nasty in the morning, but the worst will be over by then. One more dance to keep your eyes open, and then I'll take you home.'

As soon as he met her, Fisher had decided that she had the most unusual eyes he had ever seen.

The colour was indescribable; it was the vulnerable expression in them which was worrying him. She looked as if she were easy to hurt. Fisher wasn't used to this after a life spent in the company of assorted female toughs, good for a screw, a booze-up and a laugh. Paula Stanley was not his type at all.

He spent another fifteen minutes holding her tight on the dance floor wishing he could go to bed with her, and then he drove her home.

Outside her flat he stopped, leaned across and opened the car door.

'I'm not being a gentleman and seeing you in,' he said, 'because I'm a bit high myself, and I can't promise to behave unless you get out pretty quickly.'

Paula turned to him.

'If you want to come up with me, you can. I don't mind.'

'Thanks.' Fisher bowed his head. 'Thanks very much. But I don't go for the lamb to the slaughter routine. You're not fit for anything but a good night's sleep. Ask me up another time and you'll be surprised what happens!'

'You can phone me tomorrow,' Paula said. She slid out of the car and stood on the pavement. In spite of what he had said, Fisher got out with her.

'Have you got your keys?'

'Yes. I shan't go into the office. And I'll answer whatever you like if you call me tomorrow. I owe you that for what you've done tonight. Goodnight, Eric. And thanks again.'

He watched her go through the front door; he waited in the car until he saw the light in her window go on.

She had asked him up and he had refused. He couldn't believe it. He had spent the evening wanting her so much it hurt, and then behaved like a gentleman. Something very suspect, he decided, very odd indeed, was happening to him in his old age.

Margaret Von Hessel was alone with her younger son. They were drinking coffee in the enormous conservatory that ran down the south side of the house. Every variety of hothouse plant was growing round them; the Princess could remember exactly the same atmosphere in her grandmother's day. Humid closeness, and the pervading tropical scents. She sat in a tall wicker chair, and her son Philip arranged the cushions behind her. She looked up at him and patted his hand. He reminded her so much of her side of the family. Whereas her son Heinrich was a pure Von Hessel of the Würtzen branch. Weak, degenerate, a drunkard; useless to God or man.

Women and gambling had been the old Prince's occupations; his great empire ran itself, wealth bred wealth without his making any effort, and he had married more. Margaret was his second cousin. She had not loved the Prince; love was not part of the settlement.

But fidelity in public, above all, the maintenance of the family's image, were duties which the young Princess fulfilled from the start of her marriage. She had been a handsome girl, tall and well developed in the style which her generation admired. She was a most envied young woman in her own circle.

The Prince was young and his appearance was distinguished; if he showed little humour or animation this was not regarded as a cause for criticism. Pride and their past sat like a mantle on the shoulders of the Von Hessel family.

His wife was treated with the awe accorded minor royalty, her jewels, clothes and cars, her villa in France where Royalty frequently stayed, the Grimm's fairy tale schloss on top of a mountain, the Berlin town house, shooting lodges, and art treasures which would have graced any museum in the world – all these things were part of Margaret Von Hessel's daily life. Living with a man who contracted a venereal disease within a year of their wedding, who spent every night gambling with his friends or dining with one of his many mistresses, was the hidden part of her existence.

She had borne the humiliation, the disgust he inspired in her, and the loneliness of her youth with silent fortitude. She was a Von Hessel, and eight hundred years of tradition helped sustain her. She occupied herself with charities, with taking a personal interest in the running of her houses. and with compiling a detailed inventory of the treasures in the family's possession. And that was when her passion for the Poellenberg Salt developed. They spent part of every year at the Schloss Würtzen, a medieval castle built by an ancestor in the thirteenth century and extensively modernised by her husband's grandfather. The Salt was displayed in the main dining hall. It was not protected; it stood on the enormous oak table exactly as it had done for hundreds of years, shining with ineffable beauty in the lofty hall, its magnificent jewels like beacons when the lights were lit. Margaret could look at it for hours, absorbed in the poetic lines of its figures. touching the tremulous golden leaves of the central tree with a finger to make the branches move. There was a ruby as big as a large pebble; she loved to stare into its heart, where a tiny reflection of her own face was discernible. It was said to have belonged to Lorenzo the Magnificent. The faces of the nymphs fascinated her equally; there was a sly sensuality in the golden eyes and round the curving lips, more subtle than the sexual leering of the muscular male figures. It seemed impossible, but every female face was different. The master had painted portraits in metal, each a likeness to a real woman. Margaret loved the Salt; her feeling towards it was so personal that she resented anybody even touching it. It was as if the whole unbelievable creation had been made for her alone, for another bride to look at and fondle, after Eleanor de Medici who had been dead for five hundred years. Her husband found this obsession with an inanimate object quite abnormal, and he said as much. The exquisite beauty of form, the harmony in the jewels which prevented so much opulence from ever being vulgar, none of this appealed to him. He preferred flesh and blood women to the cold nakedness of golden nymphs. But if it amused his wife to gloat, then he had no objection. He objected very seldom to anything she did. She had borne him one son, and he forgot her existence thereafter. She could spend what she wished, travel where she chose, surround herself with her own friends and amusements, while he enjoyed life in his own way. He took no interest in his son either; that was the mother's province.

And as the boy grew up Margaret detected the same traits in him as in his father. He was stupid; even as a baby he lacked initiative, content to sit and play with his fists, sucking and chewing until his nurse put him into gloves. His eyes had the Von Hessel glaze of indifference to life. He made little progress at lessons. His tutors said frankly he was bored. At school he showed an aptitude for sport, and being who he was, his academic failings were overlooked. He was a failure whose family name protected him, and nothing his mother could say or do could light any gleam of ambition or enthusiasm in him. The more she criticised the less he reacted. He was found dead drunk in his room at the age of fourteen. He was a member of the Hitler Youth, which his father had insisted he become with the idea that the discipline would do him good. Margaret had objected bitterly but there was nothing she could do. Her husband had to be obeyed. He talked of discipline, when what he meant was politics. They were immensely powerful and rich, but even so they didn't dare to flout the growing power of the dictator who controlled the country. Friendship with the Nazi hierarchy wasn't required of people like them; but it was unwise to deviate in public. So Heinrich was enrolled in the Hitler Jugend and dressed up in the uniform. After a year he was privately expelled for being drunk. He was sent to a clinic in Austria under another name, surrounded by servants and a bodyguard to keep away the curious. He came back apparently cured but within six months the bouts began again. He smashed the furniture in his room, and there was a short spell in a nursing-home before another cure was tried, this time in Switzerland. It was the beginning of a pattern which was repeated over the next ten years. He grew up with his public Von Hessel image; a typical German aristocrat, heir to an immense empire of armaments, steel, coal, and allied industries, one of the most eligible bachelors in the world. Heinrich showed no interest in women. He had a permanent, passionate love affair with alcohol, and his world was bounded by the possibility and availability of drink. There was no contact between him and his father, who quite calmly declared him useless and gave no more thought to him. His only concern was to prevent the secret being known, to protect the family name. All the influence which his incredible wealth could exert was employed to keep Heinrich's misdemeanours out of the newspapers. There was gossip among their friends. His frequent absences caused a rumour that he was subject to mental breakdown. He was said to be a homosexual, because there were no women in his life. When war broke out he was eighteen. The Prince made him a director of the armament factory in the Ruhr, and he was exempted from military service. It was the only time in their long married life that Margaret had felt sorry for her husband. They spent the evening together, which was a rare occurrence, and he said quite simply that it was the most miserable day of his life.

'My son isn't even fit to serve his Fatherland. He has to hide while his friends go out to fight. And he's the last of us. Our family dies out with a drunken degenerate who can't be trusted not to disgrace himself. Which is my fault, not yours. We must have more children.'

His wife had suspected his sterility, when he ceased to cohabit with her. His syphilis was cured but its after-effects were permanent. There had been nothing she could say, yet he seemed to expect an answer.

The silence had grown between them. Finally it was the Prince who broke it. 'If you found a lover, I should not object, provided he was of our blood, I thought I should tell you this. Now I'm going to bed.'

And two years later, in 1942, her son Philip, the child of her one love affair, was born. She had met his father during a visit to Berlin. He was a Luftwaffe pilot, seven years younger than herself, a gay and charming young man, the son of her own second cousin. They shared the same Von Hessel blood, the same traditions. Together they would keep the line unsullied.

She had known he would be killed; there was a sense of impermanence about him which broke her heart. The child she carried was born after his death in action over the English Channel. It was baptised in the chapel at Schloss Würtzen in the font where ten generations of the family had been christened.

Philip Friedrich Augustus Franz, Prince Von Hessel, the bastard son of a dead man. The Princess stood in the chapel and accepted the congratulations of their friends. Her husband stood beside her. Nothing was ever said, it was never acknowledged that Philip was not his child. But he was content; the family had a second heir, the name would continue in spite of Heinrich. And by the same unspoken attitude he let his wife understand that there must be no more lovers.

'Philip,' Margaret said, 'I know I'm right. What that Englishman said on the telephone convinces me that we are getting near.'

'Did you know there was a daughter?' Philip asked.

'Yes,' his mother said. 'There was one child, I had forgotten what the sex was. It was clever of Fisher to make contact with her so quickly. He says he's sure she knows something but that unless he reveals our interest in the case she won't tell him what it is. I gave my permission, because we have to know what Schwarz came to tell her.'

'Mother,' Philip said, 'Mother, is there any use trying to persuade you to call a halt, even now? You know how I feel about it; you know what Heinrich feels.'

'Heinrich has no right to feel anything,' she said angrily. 'If it wasn't for him we wouldn't have lost the Salt.'

'One man is dead,' her son said slowly. 'Beaten to death, after all these years. Who killed him? Is there any connection between his death and that report about Bronsart being seen in Paris – Mother, I think we're opening up something that should never be disturbed at all! Supposing that he is alive; now that we know Schwarz escaped and stayed in hiding all those years, it's possible that Bronsart did the same. And if he's coming into the open, he's certain to be caught. If he comes to trial the whole story could come out! Please, Mother darling.' He reached out and held her hand. There was a deep love and sympathy between them. 'Please stop while there's still time. Forget the Salt. Other people lost great treasures; what does it matter now, besides the other risk!'

'It matters to me.' The proud eyes blazed in memory. 'It matters to me that one of the most beautiful objects in the world was taken from us by a ruthless parvenu, seized and hidden so that he could creep out one day and claim it. No, Philip, I'm going to get it back! If he lives, he'll lead us to it. And it's coming back to the place where it belongs. It's ours, my son. One day it will be yours; you know that. You know that you'll own everything, be responsible for all our interests. The Poellenberg Salt belongs to you.'

'And Heinrich?' her son asked quietly. 'You talk as if he didn't exist. I wish you wouldn't.'

'You have a kind heart,' she said. 'You find something to pity about him. I find nothing. There is no excuse for what he became. He's a degenerate; he has no will, no feelings, no interest in anything but lying in a coma of drink. He's my son, but the day he dies, I shall not shed a tear. Also he hates you, Philip. You know he does.'

'That's because you've always loved me,' he said. 'And you've shown it. I don't blame him.'

'He'll die,' the Princess said. 'His liver is rotted, his health is getting worse. One day he just won't recover. The doctors have made this clear to me for some time. And when that comes, you will be the head of the family, and I can retire and become an old woman, doing gross point in my armchair.' She squeezed his hand and smiled. The memory of his father was very clear. Whenever Philip laughed it was as if the man she loved had come back from the grave. It would all be his. Millions, power, prestige, a great future in a Germany already counting high in the councils of the world which it had almost conquered. And the Salt belonged to him.

'If Bronsart lives,' she said suddenly, 'we will have our treasure back. If he died in the retreat, then it is lost to us. So it rests with Fate, my son. Fate will decide what happens next.'

'It wasn't Fate that killed Schwarz,' her son said.

'No,' she agreed. 'It could have been a thief that he disturbed, the papers said so. It could have been a quarrel. Or it could have been the General, come back to close his mouth. That, my darling, is what I think, and what I believe Fisher thinks also. Now we have to wait and see what comes from the daughter. Just imagine being the child of such a man! Come, it's time we went inside. I have to telephone Brükner about the extension to the Verbegan plant.'

'I have the most terrible hangover,' Paula said into the telephone. 'Otherwise I'm all right. How about you?'

Fisher sounded cheerful. 'I'm fine. You said you weren't working today. How about lunch?'

'I've changed my mind.' Paula spoke with her eyes closed. Her head was pounding. 'I have some things to do and I've got to get some letters written and sent off. I could have dinner this evening, or better still, come here and I'll cook something. We've got to talk.'

'You haven't changed your mind about that, then,' Fisher said. 'I'm glad. We need each other in this. Anyway, at the moment I need you, and I can give you the information you wanted. Shall I come at about eight?'

'Make it seven-thirty. I'll get my own back on you and give you a drink.' She sounded as if she were smiling. He was sorry she refused an earlier meeting. He was anxious to get on and get the information; he had spoken to the Princess at eight o'clock that morning and extracted permission to reveal her identity and the purpose of his enquiry. He was impatient to get on with his investigation, to start on a serious hunt for Bronsart, but no action was possible without exhausting Paula as a source. Another reason, which in the morning light he wasn't so eager to recognise, was a desire to see her again.

Her father was a Nazi general, a member of the infamous murder squads which had spread Hitler's terror throughout Europe. No wonder the mother had played it down. Fisher could see her point. But it had been a cruel and selfish attitude to take in regard to her daughter. Some hint should have been given, some warning that her father was not the hero figure that the girl had obviously tried to create out of nothing. Besides, the mother had been married to him. She knew what he was and what he was doing. The wives of all the top men were singing the same song after the war. We didn't know; we weren't told, our place was in the home. Fisher called that excuse a lot of balls. Their estates were staffed by foreign slave labour, their homes were filled with other people's treasures, the furs and jewels that arrived back from France and the Low Countries were the property of captured Jews who'd tried to buy their lives. Fisher had no sympathy for Mrs Ridgeway. She had baled out after the war, with a well-heeled Englishman as a protector. If he felt sorry for anyone it was Paula, who had been left as an appendage all her life.

He felt a vindictive impulse to go down to Essex that day and stir the pair of them up. Why should the girl be the only one to answer questions . . .?

'I'm going down to pay your mother a visit,' he said. 'I'll tell you about it tonight.'

'She must have seen about Black in the papers,' Paula said. 'I expect she's terrified she'll be connected.'

'Why the hell should she be?' He said it irritably. 'She's Mrs Ridgeway, that is all anyone knows about her. She can go on hiding. Black's murder was on TV last night, on the news. So she can't frig about pretending she doesn't know anything to me.'

'You'd be surprised,' Paula said. 'You don't know my mother. She never even telephoned me.'

'To hell,' he said. 'What do you care? I phoned you, didn't I? Don't be greedy, wanting all the attention. You go and take something for that hangover and I'll be with you at seven-thirty. And don't work too hard today.'

'I won't,' Paula promised. 'I feel so awful I can't. I haven't thanked you for last night. It was very kind of you.'

'We'll do it again,' he said. 'I liked it too.'

She put down the telephone and got out of bed. Her headache was a dull pain that throbbed; aspirins would stop it. She made tea and took two tablets.

The night before seemed distant and unreal. She couldn't believe that she had invited him up. She must have been drunk. She had never asked a man up to her flat after two meetings in her life. Since parting from her husband she had not spent a night with any one, or thought of doing so.

But this rather ugly man had woken something in her. In spite of the feeling of malaise it was still there. It was like having something to hold on to when one was swimming in a limitless sea. There was a man and contact had been made between them. Only a transitory contact, a brief meeting, but for the moment it was enough. She went into the sitting room; the paper with Black's photograph was lying on the floor. She picked it up and read the inside story. Her father was an SS general. She had never been able to picture him in detail; she had no photograph, no memento to prove that he had ever existed. But out of her imagination she had fashioned an image; it was a soldier, it wore the German general's uniform she had once found in a reference book of uniforms she had consulted as a girl, it had her bright blue eyes, because her mother had once remarked on them to Gerald Ridgeway, and Paula had been listening. 'Of course she has his eyes. That makes her look like him.' And Paula had examined herself in the glass afterwards and tried to visualise him. The image was a shadow, but she borrowed for it, from books and things she heard over the years. The German army weren't responsible for the atrocities. They were gentlemen. The best fighting soldiers in the world. The old officer caste hated the Nazis. Her father had been a man like those men, who were spoken of with respect by their enemies. She could be proud of him. Even though her mother was so patently ashamed.

She bathed and dressed; she felt numbed. One part of her had spoken to Fisher with every appearance of normality; she had smiled and made a joke, responded to his cheerfulness; even looked forward to seeing him that night.

But apart from this there was a cold, suspended personality, almost a second entity, watching the other going through the motions as if it were a stranger. And now, with the paper in her hand, the two sides fused, and she thought with surprise that she was no longer Paula Ridgeway but Paula Bronsart.

She had an identity at last. Not the competent divorcee with a career of her own and an independent life, with a mother and stepfather safely in the background, but a German living in an alien country. The shadow had a substance; there was the smell of fire and death, the echo of a brazen trumpet in a vast arena where the people gathered to pay homage. Reality had come with knowledge. And now she had to live with it and with herself. She went to the outer hall, her bag and gloves in her hand and paused before the mirror on the wall. She looked like him. There was no likeness to her aristocratic mother, whose background really was the conservative old German army. She was Paul Bronsart's daughter; whatever he had been, she was part of it. A phrase returned to her. Flesh of my flesh, bone of my bone. He had taken her photograph in his hands and shown it to Black, to others. He had established a bond between himself and the child who had never known him and it had stretched from the past, holding her to his memory. Whatever he had done and whatever he was as a human being, nothing could separate them. He had put something away for her, planning for long after his death. If he *were* dead, and not in hiding somewhere. He had hidden one of the greatest art treasures in the world so that she might have the evidence of his love. But she didn't want the Poellenberg Salt. Paula opened the front door and stepped out. She didn't want his treasure. If it were within human possibility, regardless of the past, she knew that all she wanted was to find him.

Paula's mother was crying. She sat on the chintz sofa in the pleasant sitting room, with her husband's arms around her, weeping. 'Don't, darling.' He kept repeating it. 'Don't upset yourself! After what I said to him he won't come back!'

It had been an ugly interview. Fisher's attitude was aggressive from the start. He hadn't made an appointment, he had just called, finding the Brigadier out and his wife in the garden. There was nothing Mrs Ridgeway could do but ask him inside, and there the ruthless cross-examination had begun. She wasn't as tough a proposition as Fisher had imagined. But then, he reminded himself, she wasn't dealing with her own daughter. He had thrown the paper with Black's photograph in front of her and asked her to identify him.

She had been shocked and pale, but she kept her head. She had tried to lie, but at the first denial Fisher sprang. 'In March 1938 you married Colonel Paul Heinrich Bronsart of the SS at the town hall in Potsdam, the wedding reception was at your father's home, Shrievenburg, you had four hundred guests and you spent your honeymoon in Denmark. Shall I go on, or would you be kind enough to answer my questjons now?' She had given in then. Nothing about her reminded him of Paula and he was relieved. The photograph was Albrecht Schwarz, and he had served as ADC to her husband.

'You knew he was coming to see your daughter, didn't you?'

'I would prefer not to say any more till my husband gets back.'

'You knew an ex-Nazi war criminal was on the loose and prowling round your daughter and you never said a word about it? You never even warned her – didn't you think it might be dangerous?'

'I begged her not to see him.' She had spoken with sudden passion and Fisher knew there wouldn't be any more stalling till the Brigadier's return.

'She refused to listen to either of us. She's extremely obstinate; there was nothing I could do to stop her!'

'Except tell her the truth.' Fisher sneered. 'Instead of leaving her to find it out for herself. I was with her yesterday when she read that paper, Mrs Ridgeway. I saw her face. It ought to haunt you.'

She had tried to turn him out, threatening to ring the police. Fisher invited her to do so; he also reminded her that they might like to ask a few questions when they knew of Black's connection with her family.

'What I really came for,' Fisher said, 'was to get two answers to two simple questions. Give me those, Mrs Ridgeway, and I won't bother you. First, did your husband ever discuss escaping if Germany lost the war?'

She had looked at him with bitterness, almost with contempt.

'If you had ever known my husband you wouldn't ask that,' she said. 'No one would have dared to mention the word defeat. Or escape. Also we detested each other; he wouldn't have discussed anything with me.'

'Okay.' Fisher lit a cigarette. 'So you got the official notification of his death. You never doubted it?'

'Never. And I don't now.'

'What did he do with the Poellenberg Salt?'

She turned to him, astonishment distorting her face.

'He had it, didn't he?'

'Yes,' she admitted. 'It vanished. I don't know where he put it; I wouldn't have asked.'

'And you would swear to that, Mrs Ridgeway?'

There was a movement behind Fisher.

'Swear to what? What the hell's going on?' It was the Brigadier. The exchange between them was short; there was no doubt in Fisher's mind that the old man would bring the police to the house and have him ejected. He had no legal right to force himself upon them or to demand any answers and he had bluffed the woman. He didn't try to bluff her husband. Ridgeway was blazing with anger; as if to make it worse his wife suddenly dissolved into tears and Fisher thought he was going to lose his head and throw a punch at him. 'Get out of here, you bloody snooper – you try and come here again and bother my wife and I'll take a horsewhip to you!' Fisher had left; his last sight was of the man cradling the woman in his arms. There was nothing he wouldn't do to protect her; Fisher filed that observation away. Paula hadn't exaggerated when she said they were devoted to each other. It must have been pretty solitary living alongside them. When he arrived at Paula's flat that evening he brought a bottle of Riesling. He thought she looked rather pale; her hair was brushed back and the blue eyes were very vivid in the artificial lights. 'Hello,' Fisher said. He had an odd feeling when she smiled at him. 'I'm sorry I'm a bit late. The traffic up was terrible.'

'You're not late,' Paula said. 'Come in.' He gave her the wine.

'Something pretty good from your country,' he said gently. She looked at him.

'Good things have come out of it, haven't they?' she said quietly. 'I've been trying to think of as many of them as I can today. Beethoven, Mozart, Rhine wines, Goethe, Mann – I couldn't think of any scientist except Von Braun. Come and sit down, Eric. I'll get you a drink.'

'Whisky, please,' he said. He watched her walking to the drinks laid out on a side table. She moved without any trace of self-consciousness, no hip swinging to call attention to a very good figure. And from the front she looked like a woman instead of a flat-chested boy. Fisher approved of that too. He brought his mind back to his business.

'I went down to Essex,' he said. He gave her a cigarette; she sat beside him on the sofa. 'I got nothing but an identification of Black as Schwarz. And one important admission, but I'll come to that in a minute.'

'How was my mother?' The voice was cold. 'She's still never contacted me. Oddly enough I'm not even hurt any more.'

'I'm glad to hear it,' Fisher said. 'She was extremely upset. Cried her eyes out, as the saying goes.'

'I can't imagine her crying,' Paula said. 'I don't think I've ever seen it. Go on.'

'Your stepfather came bounding in looking like a furious St. Bernard, threatening to call the police and give me a good horse-whipping! It must have had its funny side, but I felt he meant every word. I left them in each other's arms. Incidentally, she said one thing. She said she and your real father hated the sight of each other.'

'I see. That may account for the way she's avoided me,' Paula said. 'It must be a nuisance being saddled with a child by someone you hated. I always suspected it. What was the other thing she told you?'

'In a minute,' Fisher said. 'I promised to tell you who my employer is, didn't I? I got the permission this morning, before I phoned you. It's the Princess Von Hessel. You know who I mean – the armament family.'

'I know the name,' Paula said. 'How very extraordinary this is. And they want you to find my father?'

'That's the idea. You see he took something from them during the war and they want it back.' He had put personal considerations aside; he was a professional and he was watching her. She faced him without guile.

'I know what it is,' she said. 'That was why Black came to see me. He told me about it and I didn't believe him. I thought he was crazy. It's the Poellenberg Salt, isn't it?'

'Yes,' Fisher said. 'Yes, it is. And your father did have it. Your mother said so. Paula, what did Black tell you? This could solve the whole thing!'

She extended her hand, turning the cigarette between her fingers. 'He said my father had hidden it. He said he had hidden it to give to me.' She raised her eyes to Fisher. 'I suppose that makes a difference.'

He kept his surprise under control. 'It could do, only you don't have any legal right to it,' he said. 'It was stolen.'

'Black said it was a gift. He emphasised that. He said he had promised my father to find me and give me the clue to where it was.'

'Are you going to tell me that clue?'

'I don't want the Salt,' she said. 'I looked it up – it's belonged to that family for hundreds of years. I'd like to give it back to them. But it's only a clue. Black said my father didn't trust him with the whole secret. He was certain that my father was alive. The message he gave me doesn't make any sense at all.'

'For Christ's sake,' Fisher said. 'What was it?'

'Paris, 25th June, 1944. Tante Ambrosine and her nephew Jacquot. That was all. It sounds gibberish to me.'

'Your father was no fool,' Fisher said grimly. 'He knew what he was doing. That message must make sense. Paris, 25th June, 1944. Tante Ambrosine and her nephew Jacquot. I'll just have to find out what it means.'

'We'll both have to find out,' Paula said quietly. 'By the way, what would happen if my father were found alive now?'

'He'd be extradited to West Germany and put on trial. He was a big man in the Nazi party. They'd find something to charge him with.'

'But if you find the Poellenberg Salt, that will be enough for you, won't it? You won't have to look for him?'

'No,' Fisher said, 'I won't. My clients want the Salt, that's all.'

'They can have it,' Paula said. 'And that's a promise. Because I believe Black; I believe my father owned it legally and it's mine. But I'll give it back on one condition.'

'That I lay off looking for your father?'

'No. That you help me to find him, if he's still alive.'

Fisher hesitated. 'You really mean this? You know what you're doing?'

'Not really,' Paula said. 'I'm still confused. I'm still looking for something and I haven't found it.'

'Does it have to be a father?' Fisher asked her.

'I don't know that either. He must be an old man now; I've been thinking about it all day, thinking of what he was and what kind of man he must have been. An SS general. I've grown up with the idea of the bogey men in the black uniforms. But I want to find him. I want to see him for myself. That's as far as I can go at the moment. I've helped you and I trust you to help me. It's not your job to expose him but it's mine to help him if he's still alive. I want to search with you, Eric. And even if the Salt is legally mine I'll hand it back. Is that a bargain?'

'All right.'

She turned and held her hand out to him. He thought she was crazy and he wanted to say so. He also wanted to kiss her, which was nothing to do with Nazi generals or hidden masterpieces. He had expected almost any development but this one. He had undertaken to find the Poellenberg Salt and she wanted to find the General. So for good or evil they were in it together. He took her hand and shook it. He went on holding it for a few moments until she drew it away.

'All right,' he said again. 'It's a bargain. Next stop is Paris.'

'Well,' Dunston said, 'so you're off to Paris. Lucky you.'

'I'll be busy,' Fisher said. 'Don't tell me you've still got the musical hall Englishman's idea of Paris, all tits and Folies Bergere! I've got a lousy assignment and you're welcome to take it over any time you like!'

'No thanks,' Dunston laughed. They were sitting in a public house down the street from their office; Fisher had ordered beer and Dunston had a double whisky on the counter in front of him. In Fisher's opinion he drank too much. He was a tall, thickset man, with bushy black hair and eyebrows, a genial ugliness redeemed by splendid white teeth. He laughed very easily, showing them off. He had a pretty little wife and three children; he was a lot cleverer than his cheery personality indicated. On his own admission, he was no gentleman, and he professed a passion for making money. 'No trips to Europe for me at the moment,' he said. 'I'm up to my balls in work right here. How do you think it's going?'

'Don't know,' Fisher said. 'My guess is the General is alive and hiding out. Everything points to it. My second guess is that when he does show up, if he does, he'll make for his daughter. From what I've heard, he was crazy about her as a kid. And he's apparently made contact now through Schwarz. So he's still interested in her. And he wants her to find this Salt. From the point of view of our clients, that does worry me. From what Schwarz said to her, she seems to think she's got a legal claim to it. So there could be quite a fight over the bloody thing. Of course she's saying now she'll give it back to them.'

'That's all very well till she sees it,' Dunston said. 'I've heard those generous gestures taken back before. You've told Princess Von Hessel about this?'

'I sent her a long report. Personally, I think Mrs Stanley might keep her word. She's a funny sort of girl, not the usual grabber at all.'

'Oh?' Dunston's bushy eyebrows lifted and the spectacular teeth appeared. 'First time I've heard you giving a bird a good character reference. Taking her to Paris with you, aren't you? I suppose that'll go down on the expense account . . .'

'I'm not taking her, she's coming.' Fisher answered rather sharper than he intended. Dunston's grin irritated him.

'Have fun.'

'Get stuffed. Have another whisky?'

'So long as you're paying. When do you leave for Gay Paree?'

'Tomorrow morning. We're staying at the Odile; that shouldn't break the expense account. I'll be in touch with you to let you know how things are going. I wish I knew what the hell it means. Tante Ambrosine and her nephew Jacquot.'

'Try the telephone directory,' Dunston suggested. 'It could be a restaurant. Suppose some poor bloody foreigner was told to find the Great American Disaster, what do you think he'd make of that? Tante Ambrosine and her nephew – could be anything. You've checked round about?'

'I got straight through to Joe Daly at Reuters in Paris,' Fisher said. 'It meant nothing to him either. It's got nothing to do with any contemporary pop Paris "scene" or he'd have known it. Anyway, we'll see what happens when we get there. My first move will be to check on whoever thought they saw Bronsart.'

'I'm off to Manchester this afternoon.' Dunston stretched a little. He was very powerfully built.

'No wonder you're so narky about Paris.' Now it was Fisher's turn to laugh. 'You won't get into much mischief there.'

'No, but I might make some money for us. Nice little five hundred guinea fee for a background check. Rich daddy with silly bitch daughter who wants to marry the little pouf who does her hair. If I can get some real dirt on him for Daddy to show darling daughter, I might even get a bonus. I'm off now. Good luck with Aunty Ambrosine.'

'Thanks.' Fisher nodded to him. At the door Dunston turned and waved again. They got on very well together; as men they were completely different in type; they proceeded in different ways on an investigation. Fisher used intuition and took risks, Dunston was methodical, unswerving and possessed a remarkable instinct for anything crooked. Their friendship was not deep but they spent odd evenings together and never seriously disagreed. Fisher enjoyed his company. He could be extremely vulgar and very funny. He paid the bill and left to go back to his office. Outside Dunston hailed a taxi. Inside he leaned back and lit a menthol cigarette. His choice of the brand was an idiosyncrasy which Fisher sometimes used against him. He couldn't give up smoking but he had a morbid horror of lung cancer. Fisher was going off to Paris with Mrs Stanley. Well, well, Dunston said to himself. He'd picked himself up a piece of crumpet on the way; trust him. He never passed up a chance to get a slice. Fisher didn't think much of women; Dunston knew that. He always chose the same type. They were all loose and hard, and good looking. There had never been a snowball's chance in hell of Fisher falling for any of them. If he bothered with a woman it was to lay her and for nothing else. He was curious about this Mrs Stanley. She was divorced from Jimmy Stanley, and everyone who read the newspapers knew what a high-powered little playboy he was; always firing on all six cylinders. So she was probably the same type as Fisher's usual, but a better-class edition. And she claimed a legal title to the Poellenberg Salt. Dunston had looked it up, and the photograph of it had been enough. People murdered for a thing like that. She wouldn't give it back. If it was hers, by any unsuspected twist, she'd hang on and fight for it till the blood ran. And that was probably why he was going, not to Manchester, as he had told Fisher, but to Germany, at the urgent and secret request of the Princess Von Hessel.

'Get in, Mr Dunston. We are going for a drive.'

The rear door was held open for him by the chauffeur; he had a glimpse of a woman sitting in the seat, her face pale and grim. He got in and sat beside her.

'I am Princess Von Hessel,' she said. She spoke in German to the chauffeur, and then pressed a knob on the arm of the seat. The glass partition slid up and closed them off from the front of the car.

'It's very kind of you to meet me,' Dunston said. He wasn't quite sure how to address her. The size of the car, the uniformed chauffeur and the patrician arrogance of the woman beside him had shaken his self-confidence. He wouldn't have been ill at ease if he were dealing with the newly rich. But a face like Princess Von Hessel's was the result of centuries of aristocratic breeding and power.

'I didn't come to meet you,' she said. 'I came to have our interview. That's why we are going for a drive. You know my original letter was addressed to you?'

'Fisher showed it to me,' Dunston said. 'I was in Portugal, on holiday. I followed your instructions. I didn't tell him I was coming over here. I presume that you're not satisfied with him, is that it?'

'He was not the man I wanted,' she said. 'But since I've got him, he can continue his enquiries. He's made a lot of progress in a very short time.'

'Then may I ask,' Dunston said, 'why you sent for me?'

The Princess glanced at him; there was something in the eyes which made him wary; he had a faultless instinct for the unexpected, and he knew, by blind intuition, that the interview was not going to be what it seemed.

'You spent quite a time in Germany five years ago, didn't you, Mr Dunston? When you were with Interpol.'

'Yes. I know the country very well.'

'And your last assignment was breaking up a gold smuggling ring, I believe?'

Now Dunston's skin was crawling. 'That's right. You've made quite an investigation of the investigators.'

'Naturally. I always prefer to know what I am dealing with. And what I discovered convinced me that you were just the man I needed. It was unfortunate that Mr Fisher came instead of you. It appears he is of honest character.' She turned towards him and smiled; it was an expression of amused contempt. 'You have gone red, Mr Dunston. Please don't be insulted. Taking offence is a luxury which I don't believe you can afford.'

'I don't know what you're trying to say,' Dunston began angrily. 'But if you're suggesting, Princess Von Hessel, that there's anything wrong . . .'

'How much money did you take from the smuggling ring to slow up that investigation?'

The question caught him in mid speech. He stopped and floundered. She went on, still smiling and implacable. 'You left Interpol under a suspicion of accepting a bribe. Nothing could be proved against you, but you had no future after that episode. The sum mentioned was a miserable ten thousand pounds. Perhaps not so miserable to you in those days, but surely a contemptible amount by present standards. I wouldn't insult you by offering anything so paltry.'

Dunston took out a packet of cigarettes. He was sweating.

'Put those away, please. I object to smoking; it's a disgusting habit!'

For a moment Dunston hesitated. His composure had been shattered by her direct attack. He felt naked, sitting in the car with the old woman staring him out, the intangible force of her authority browbeating his will. Slowly he closed the packet and put it back in his pocket. 'All right,' he said quietly. 'You've got some proposition for me. It must be pretty shady or you wouldn't have brought up that old rumour. And it was just a rumour. There wasn't any truth in it; but the damage was done. I cut my losses and left.'

'Mr Dunston,' the Princess said, 'if you convince me of your moral probity I won't be able to put any proposition to you. Luckily, I know that you began your detective business with a sum of capital which wasn't there before. So I am sure you took the bribe and that you are a man who has a price. Shall I go on, or are you going to persist in this little fiction about yourself?'

'There's never any harm,' he said, 'in listening.'

'Good. You know the facts about our loss of the Poellenberg Salt; you know as much as Fisher knows, is that correct?'

'He keeps me briefed,' Dunston answered. 'You want it back and you believe that General Bronsart is alive and can lead you to it.'

'Exactly. I am determined to recover it.' For a moment she glanced out of the window, frowning. 'Determined. Nothing will stop me. But there are complications. Mr Fisher is not aware of them.'

'Too honest?' Dunston asked her. He was recovering himself now.

'Much too honest. My younger son tried to persuade him to go behind my back and drop the case and he refused.'

'Why should your son do that? Doesn't he want the Salt back?'

'He's not prepared to take the risk,' she said. 'I am. I am prepared to risk anything and to do anything. That's why I've sent for you.'

'What are the complications?'

'The General has a legal right to it,' she said quietly. 'It was moral theft but he took it legally. For reasons which don't concern you, we can never have a public fight about its ownership.'

'He's not in a position to fight,' Dunston said. 'He's a wanted criminal. He can never come into the open.'

'No.' Princess Von Hessel turned right round and faced him. 'No, but his daughter can. I wanted somebody to find the General and the Salt, and then remove him.'

'I see,' Dunston said; he nodded slowly at her. 'I'm getting it now. But you hadn't reckoned on the daughter.'

'Exactly.'

'When you say "remove",' Dunston sounded casual, 'what do you mean by that?'

'Just what you think I mean,' she said coldly. 'Dispose of; kill, if you prefer plain language. I want the General dead, unable to talk or make trouble if by any chance he is arrested.'

'And the daughter? She could claim the Salt and get away with it. That's the real trouble, isn't it?'

'Yes,' she said. 'Once she came into it everything changed. Mr Dunston, I will pay two hundred and fifty thousand pounds into a numbered bank account in Switzerland. Fifty thousand on account, as a retainer, and the rest later. But I want the Poellenberg Salt and I don't want anyone alive to claim it.

'Christ,' Dunston said softly. He pursed up his lips and whistled, but no sound came. 'You're asking for a murder. You're asking me to kill that girl.'

'I'm asking you to kill them both,' she said. 'And I'm paying you a quarter of a million pounds. Think of the money, Mr Dunston. Think how rich you'll be. You don't have to give your answer now. Just think about it.'

'You're taking a hell of a risk, trusting me with this. What's to stop me going to the police and telling them the whole story?'

'Nothing but your common sense,' she retorted. 'Nobody would believe you; you have no witnesses, no proof. On the other hand you have the chance to be a very rich man. I believe you'll make the right choice.'

'I believe I might,' Dunston said. 'But only if you double it. And that's my answer. Half a million, and I'll take care of them both. You'll have the Salt and there won't be any Mrs Stanley round to make counter claim.'

'If I agree to double the money, you'll do it?'

'We can shake hands on it now,' Dunston said.

'Very well. Half a million.'

'By the way,' he said. 'Just what did the General have on you to make you give it to him?'

Again her slow, contemptuous smile appeared.

'If you knew that, Mr Dunston, your life wouldn't be any safer than Mrs Stanley's is at the moment. Now we will take you back to the airport.'

4

Paris in July was full of tourists; the heat was not as intense as it would be in August, when the Parisians fled their city, but there seemed a preponderance of English and American faces among the crowds sauntering along the elegant boulevards and parading up and down the Champs Elysées.

Paula noticed the numbers of Germans wandering about and going into the expensive shops. She felt no sense of identity with them; they were strangers, speaking the harsh language which she had never learnt. Fisher had booked them into a comfortable middle group hotel near the Madelon; their rooms were not adjoining but they were on the same floor. They had dinner together in the hotel restaurant the first evening, and Fisher came to the door of her bedroom with her. He pulled her close and kissed her. She put her arms round his neck, but she didn't repeat that earlier invitation. She went inside and closed the door, leaving him in the corridor.

The next morning Fisher went to the offices of the Sûreté. He suggested that Paula amuse herself for an hour or so and that they would meet for lunch.

'What are you going to the police for? How can they help us . . . ?'

'They can tell me the name and address of the woman who thought she identified your father. Let's get her out of the way before we start trying to find out who Tante Ambrosine and Jacquot are. That's going to be the real problem. You go and buy yourself a hat and meet me at the Tour D'Argent at one o'clock. I'll buy you lunch and tell you what happened. And don't get picked up, will you?'

'Why not — it might be fun.' She had smiled at him, her eyes with a gentle warmth in their depth. He hadn't seen her look at him like that before.

'Because I wouldn't like it,' Fisher said. He laid a hand on her shoulder. 'From now on, Mrs Stanley, you're with me.'

He saw a detective inspector after half an hour of refusing to accept the blocking tactics of a junior officer, who was determined not to help a 'flic amateur anglais'. The senior police officer was a fat man of middle age, chewing on the stem of a very blackened pipe. He greeted Fisher without enthusiasm. Fisher showed his card, explained that he was working for private clients in Germany and asked for the name and address of the woman who thought she saw the former SS General Bronsart in the street.

'Why don't you look up the newspaper files instead of troubling us?'

'Because it says a Madame Brevet, and gives no further information,' Fisher answered. 'How many hundred people of that name are there in Paris, monsieur?'

'About five, maybe more. You could have placed an advertisement in the newspapers. Offer a reward and you'd have every Brevet in France running to give you information. We have other things to do, you know.'

'So the officer outside explained,' Fisher replied. 'Less politely than you. I appreciate that this is a nuisance for you, but it only takes a moment to consult your files. And if you would be kind enough to tell me your conclusions in the business . . .'

The Detective Inspector shrugged. He looked as if he were bored by life, as much as by people like Fisher who made demands upon his time. 'I will get the file. I can't offer you a cigarette, I only smoke this.' He waved the revolting pipe.

'Thanks, I have my own.' Fisher took out a packet. He knew the French and liked them; he had worked in Paris for nearly two years and grown to love the city and its citizens. They were usually described as the most insular, hard-headed people in the world, who would see you dead before they did you a favour. Taken in the right way, with allowances made for mood and suspicion, they were obliging, hospitable and kind. The Inspector proved this by settling down to a long discussion of the Bronsart case and showing Fisher everything in the Sûreté file upon him. Having complained of the waste of his time, he spent over an hour with Fisher, smoking and going over his memories of the war.

'We followed the lead at once,' he said. 'Nothing would please us more than to find that bastard still alive and able to face justice. He was here in Paris for six months. I could show you the graves of men and women who were executed at Fresnes by his personal order. Humble citizens who had done nothing but be caught on the streets by his murder squads, looking for hostages.

'But the woman didn't make any sense, Monsieur Fisher. She babbled on, insisting she had seen him, but it was nothing. Just a face in a crowd. Just her imagination. He's dead, I'm sure of it. But there is the address if you want to prove it for yourself.'

Fisher got up and the two shook hands. 'I agree with you,' he said. 'But I have to earn my fee.'

'Make it a fat one,' the policeman advised him. 'They are all the same. Boche. Make them pay.'

Fisher saw Paula walking along the street as he arrived in a cab outside the restaurant. The sun was shining and he felt happy. It was a strange sensation, powerfully connected with the presence of the girl who was coming up to him, waving, one hand holding a wide-brimmed felt hat on her head. Fisher was not a coward; he would have faced anything physical. But the implication of Paula Stanley and the way his heart kept jumping every time he saw her, required a different kind of courage and he didn't have it yet. He took her arm and guided her to the table. The waiters recognised him and there was an animated exchange in French. Paula sat down and watched him. His hair was on end, where he had brushed his hand over it; it was a habit she had noticed when he was concentrating. He was not a good-looking man and nothing could be done to make him suave and Establishment. He had the kind of body that resented anything but the most casual clothes, and a face that was wary in expectation of trouble. But with her he was gentle; she felt his sexuality whenever they made contact. When he kissed he showed it, and when he handled her on trivial excuses like getting out of taxis or going into a lift.

He took a grip of her and she could feel the proprietary attitude which was so clearly male. 'From now on you're with me.' James would never have said or thought such a thing. He had never been responsible for her in five years. Fisher had taken control of everything from the moment they left England. And it would need all her resolution to resist a final appropriation of herself.

'What happened?'

He grinned at her over a glass of Cinzano.

'I got the name and address of the woman. But it's a dead end; they looked into it and found nothing. I'm half inclined to suggest we hire a car and drive through the Bois this afternoon and give the whole thing a miss for today. What do you say to that?'

'I'd rather see the woman,' Paula said. 'I want to get it over, one way or another. And you won't find the Salt for the Von Hessels by driving through the woods with me.'

'A day never made any difference. Besides, I'm not all that enthusiastic for my employers. I'm inclined to agree with the Inspector this morning. They're real Boche. Sorry, I shouldn't have said that. I didn't mean it.'

'Oh yes, you did,' Paula said. 'But I don't mind. I'm sure they're awful. I remember reading an article in *Time*, I think it was, all about their money and how they'd come back after the war. Can you tell me about them? Don't look like that, I know you didn't mean anything by calling them Boche. I'm not that silly.'

'I'm glad,' he said. He reached out and took her hand. He was relieved to feel her fingers grip in return. 'I'm a clumsy bastard. You know I wouldn't say anything to upset you. All right, the Von Hessels. The mother is the interesting one; she's just like a bird, something like a cross between an eagle and a peregrine falcon. About as feminine and inviting, I should say. Tough, arrogant, clever – runs the whole show. She didn't exactly treat me like dirt, but she showed that's what she thought of me. There are two sons, the old man died during the war. The eldest must be in his fifties; he was very odd. There was something about him I couldn't figure out at all. I had half an hour's interview with her and he never said a word. He just stood there like a dummy.'

'Probably frightened to speak with a mother like that,' Paula said. 'They sound ghastly.'

'They are,' he said. 'But the younger son was less so. Quite pleasant in fact, very good looking if you like the blond superman type. Now, he spoke up and seemed quite sure of himself. She must have really taken the guts out of the elder son. It was a very funny set-up. The house was a nightmare; I thought I was in church when I first went inside. Stained glass windows, potted palms. And everything the size of a cathedral. You could write a good play about a set-up like that, only nobody would believe it. They'd say it was too far-fetched. Here come the crevettes. I hope you're hungry.'

'I am.' Paula smiled at him. 'Your description is marvellous; but I forgot you were a journalist. And you speak perfect French.'

'I'm a talented man,' he said. 'Why don't you take off that hat? I can't see your face.'

'Oh, don't you like it? I took your advice and bought it this morning. I think it's very smart!'

'I think so too, but I like looking at you. You're a very pretty sight, don't you know that?'

'If you say so.'

'I do. Put it on the seat beside me and get on with your crevettes, they're delicious. You sure you wouldn't rather go driving with me this afternoon?'

'I'm sure,' Paula said. 'Let's go and see the woman; please.'

'All right, we'll go. But tonight we will have dinner somewhere special. And we'll make a pact; we won't talk about your father or the Poellenberg Salt.'

'What will we talk about then?'

'Ourselves,' Fisher said. 'I shall tell you the story of my life and I want to hear all about that nice husband of yours. Incidentally, he must have been a shit.'

'He wasn't too bad,' she said. 'I'm not very easy to live with either.'

'So far,' Fisher wiped his mouth with a napkin, 'I haven't found you difficult.'

He had hired a car that morning and they drove. There was a fleet of boats travelling down the Seine, carrying merchandise and tourists. A huge coal barge floated past them, a solitary dog standing sentinel in the bows. The streets they drove through became shabbier and dirtier; refuse and prowling cats cluttered the narrow pavements; washing hung festooned out of the windows. It took forty-five minutes of crawling through the traffic in the narrow roads to reach the place where Madame Brevet lived.

It was a crumbling apartment building, the walls scrofulous with peeling plaster, the front door hanging ajar. They went into the dark hall and were assailed by a smell of cooking and cats' urine. Up one flight of wooden stairs, they knocked at another door.

It was a young woman who opened it and stood blocking their way; she carried a fat little two-year-old baby on her arm.

'Madame Brevet?' Fisher said.

'I'm Madame Brevet.' She was about twenty-five. 'I think,' he said politely, 'that we want your mother-in-law. Could we speak with her for a minute? It will be worth her while to see us, madame.'

'What do you want?' The woman hadn't moved. She had a tired, sullen face with small dark eyes that stared at them suspiciously. Her look at Paula was distinctly hostile.

'Information,' Fisher said. He held out a fifty-franc note. 'Would you ask Madame Brevet to see us?'

The daughter-in-law took the money; she gave the baby a comforting jiggle as it began to whimper, fingers stuffed in its mouth. 'You can see her,' she said. 'But you won't get much sense out of her. She drives me crazy, monsieur. She had the police round here a while ago. Come in.' She stepped back and they went into a room which was crowded with furniture and dominated by a large scrubbed wooden table. The smell of cooking was overpowering, so was the heat, for the windows were shut and a big kitchen stove was alight in the corner. An old woman, white haired and dressed in frowzy black, was sitting in an armchair by the stove.

'There's some people to see you. What's your name, monsieur?'

Fisher came forward to the armchair; a lined white face looked up at him and a hand came out. 'I am Monsieur Fisher and this lady is Madame Stanley. We are from England, madame, and we wanted to ask you a few questions. Would you be kind enough to answer for us?'

The eyes were hooded in loose skin; they had a filmy look associated with age. 'What questions do you want to ask? I'll do my best, but my memory is not as it was. She tells me I forget everything.' The old woman jerked her head towards the younger woman.

'And you do,' was the retort. 'You drive me crazy the way you forget.'

'Madame Brevet,' Fisher began. 'Not long ago you were walking down the Rue D'Auvergne and you thought you saw a man. A German officer who used to be in Paris during the war. Do you remember?'

For a moment there was absolute blankness. Paula moved a step nearer; it was useless, just as the police had said. The old woman was senile, she couldn't be relied upon for anything. The white head turned from Fisher to her and back again.

'What German officer?' she said.

'The one you said you saw!' Her daughter-in-law couldn't contain herself. 'Jesus, you had the newspapers and the flics running all over us with that story! What do you mean, what German officer – stupid old cow!'

'General Bronsart,' Fisher said. 'You thought you saw him in the Rue D'Auvergne. Can you tell us about it?'

'Ah, my God,' the old woman cried out. Suddenly her eyes were bright, her face alive with excitement. 'That devil – I saw him, monsieur! I saw him as clear as I see you, walking down the same side of the street; it was him and I knew him, even though it must be twenty years . . .'

'Thirty is more like it,' the younger woman said acidly. 'Get something right, can't you. Old cow,' she repeated.

'And you're certain it was him?' Paula stepped forward; she felt stifled with heat and anxiety. Her father's life hung by the thread of this old woman's credibility.

'Of course it was, I recognised him, I knew him!'

'When did you last see the General?' Fisher asked her.

'Eh? I told you, a little while ago, I forget exactly when, but a little while . . .'

'When you saw him again,' Fisher prompted, 'had he changed very much? Wasn't he much older? How was he dressed, madame?'

She raised her head and looked at him. The expression was blurred.

'In black, of course. They all wore black uniforms.'

'I told you,' her daughter-in-law said. 'That's all the police got out of it. But do you know, she went to the station round here and reported seeing this man! Can you imagine it? The crazy old cow.' She shook her head and humped the baby from one shoulder to the other.

'I don't think this is any good,' Fisher said to Paula. He took her by the arm. 'I'm sorry, but I think it was just a fantasy, reliving the past. We'd better go.'

'Yes,' Paula said. The atmosphere in the little room was thick with heat and human odours. She felt sick. It had been a failure, and only now, faced with total disappointment, did she realise how much she had relied upon this interview.

The heat was suffocating. She took a deep breath and pulled off her hat.

There was a high, fierce little scream. The old woman was out of her chair and on her feet. One gnarled hand was in the air, balled into a fist.

'The eyes!' she shrieked. 'That's how I knew him! He was an old man and his hair was white, but I knew those eyes! And you have them – you have the same eyes as that swine who murdered my son!'

'Yes,' Paula said quietly. 'I am afraid I have. I am General Bronsart's daughter.'

With two quick steps the old Madame Brevet had reached her. With a forward jerk of her head, she spat into Paula's face.

'Heinrich, where do you think this will end? If you interfere in this you can only do harm. Harm to Mother and to all of us!'

'I should like to do Mother harm,' Prince Heinrich said. 'It's time somebody injured her for a change. You will be here to hold her hand, why shouldn't I go to Paris? Are you suggesting that you'll miss me?'

His brother made a gesture of impatience. 'You'll get into trouble,' he said. 'You force me to say these things. You'll get drunk and it will be in the newspapers. Why can't you stay here – or go up to the schloss, if you're bored.'

'A drunkard is never bored,' Heinrich Von Hessel said. 'Or lonely. He swallows consolation for all his ills. I hate the schloss. I spent three months shut up there with a male nurse who used to punch me black and blue when nobody was looking.

'But then nobody would have cared – so long as the family name wasn't damaged. And what a great name it is, eh? Making millions out of armaments, employing slave labour, financing the Nazis.' He laughed out loud. 'I'm going to Paris, and I shall stand with a placard round my neck saying who I am, and I shall piss in the street!' His brother went out and the door banged. The Prince went over to the window; his mother's car had just driven up in the courtyard. In a few moments she and Philip would have a family conclave and discuss what best to do about him.

Their trouble was, he thought, that provided he stayed within some bounds of sobriety, there wasn't much they could do. His last severe bout was only two months away; the accident with the car had happened before that. He had recovered and was soaking at a steady rate. He staggered, so to speak, but didn't fall. And unless he fell, there was no restriction his family could place upon him. He had a private fortune, inherited under a family trust which his father had been unable to break, and he couldn't be certified insane and put away without the scandal coming out.

That had always been his safeguard and it still was. He could move about with freedom and thereby torment his mother with suspense and fear. And he had told his brother Philip that he meant to go to Paris, partly for the pleasure of alarming him and partly from a sense of irresponsible curiosity. He had a juvenile habit of listening in to telephone conversations and looking in other people's drawers. He spied on his mother with a sharp degree of drunken cunning, as he had spied on her all his life, partly for self-protection and partly from malice because he knew himself to be excluded. He had discovered that Fisher was in Paris and that he had the General's daughter with him. And during the night when he woke up to have a drink, the idea came to him of going there and making himself known. It would convulse his mother and cause his upright brother many anxious hours. They couldn't stop him. He could take his valet with him, who had acted as a private nurse for twenty years, and book in at the Ritz Hotel. He need never leave his suite unless he felt inclined. Or he could amuse himself by meddling, by indulging one of his infrequent bouts of self-assertion, like ordering a Ferrari motor-car and driving it himself while drunk.

He had no recollection of killing the child. He remembered nothing till he woke up in his own bed and saw his mother standing near him, looking much older. They had bribed and cajoled him out of a charge of manslaughter and kept the newspaper coverage to the minimum. He had accepted what was done, at the same time resenting it because it placed him under obligation, and gratitude was not within his capability. He hadn't been on a trip for months; when Philip suggested he was bored he had denied it, but he realised that it must be true. He was tired of his surroundings, inhibited by his family's presence; required to be on parade, as on the occasion when the detective came and he had stood behind the sofa, trying not to sway about and then locked in his bedroom because they were afraid he might stumble downstairs; at other times banished out of sight with the discreet connivance of his valet. He liked his valet; there was an understanding between them. Prince Heinrich paid his salary and gave him extra money when he felt in a good mood. The valet took orders from the Princess in a crisis, but from day to day he set out to please the Prince. He had made up his mind. He was drunk as usual but by no means incapable. He was going to Paris. He rang for his valet, gave him the news and instructed him to pack.

Downstairs his mother and his brother Philip were in conference as he had imagined. 'I won't allow it,' the Princess said. 'God knows what he'll do when he gets there; imagine the Ritz if he has one of those drunken rages and begins to smash things!'

'He won't do that,' Philip tried to comfort her. 'The clinic cured him of those impulses. He simply drinks now, Mother. I tried to persuade him not to go but you know how obstinate he becomes if you argue with him.'

'You're too soft,' the Princess said angrily. 'You always plead and make excuses for him! I'm going to have him put away – I've borne enough from him! I'll get him certified and committed. Then we can have peace!'

'You can't do that,' her son said quietly. 'Heinrich's not mad; you can't do that to him. I won't agree to it. And you know it would leak out. We've covered him all his life, and you said yourself he hasn't long. You mustn't think of that solution. It's impossible.'

The fierce glare turned on him like a light beam. She looked old and cruel with anger. 'Nothing is impossible to us,' she said. 'As we have proved once already. It came to the Von Hessels and the might of Adolf Hitler's Gestapo and we survived. Never say to me that something can't be done.'

'At a price, Mother. But the days for paying it are over too. We have power and we have money. We no longer have the right to abuse either of them. The old world permitted it, the new one won't, whatever you think. We hid the killing of that child because we set the parents up for life and moved them five hundred miles away to Frankfurt. But we can't put Heinrich into a lunatic asylum and hope to get away with it. He has trustees, and he's nominally head of the family. You don't want the scandal over the Salt to destroy us; this would be almost as bad.'

'You have the new conscience, don't you, my son?' She sneered at him, standing at her full height, with the force of her patrician contempt for ordinary moral standards beating against him. 'You talk like a bourgeois. You forget who we are.'

'I could never do that,' Philip reminded her. 'I have lived and breathed the importance of this family from the moment I was born. I've watched you ruling our empire, Mother, and I've accepted all my obligations. But the times have changed, and even we can't put them back to what we were. We're powerful, yes, but we're no longer the feudal barons of before the war. We can't dispose exactly as we like, even of our own blood. Society won't tolerate us if we try, and I'm very anxious not to put it to the test.'

'That's not your reason for protecting that drunken maniac.' The Princess turned on him. 'It's weakness!' She was so angry with him for this determined thwarting of her will, that she was capable of saying anything to punish him. She loved him, as she had loved his father, but she loved her power of domination more than anything else. He was a Von Hessel, but he was of weaker stuff, with a silly conscience and a set of tepid morals that filled her with disgust. The temptation to tell him so, came upon her, but she conquered it. Only a fool pulls down the house because a door squeaks.

'He's a danger and he's bad,' she said coldly. 'I've always known he would bring some dreadful tragedy upon us. Let him go to Paris, then. Let him meddle, let him blunder drunkenly into this hornet's nest, with Fisher and that woman. It is your responsibility if anything goes wrong.' She turned her back on him and walked out of the room. Prince Philip watched her as she left. His mother's anger lasted for days; she would ignore him until he came and abjectly apologised. She was a woman who, when she once established contact, never let go. He felt her influence even when they were separated, the force of her affection, the pull of her willpower.

And he admired her for the superhuman strength of character that had kept the Hessel factories in the face of government attempts to seize them, that had fought the accusations of Nazi sympathy and gathered the loyalty of thousands of workers to herself. She was like iron; the rock upon which he had leaned since his infancy; the old Prince died when he was still a little boy.

She hated his brother Heinrich, as only a woman of that determined cast can hate a weakling of whom she fails to rid herself. It would have surprised her to know that the feeling was returned; she thought the sodden, drink-distorted personality of her son incapable of a coherent emotion or of a sensibility that could be wounded. And if she had admitted it, Philip knew she wouldn't have cared. Heinrich had disappointed her; he embodied everything she most despised. Lack of self-control, whether it was lying in a coma with his own vomit on the floor beside the bed, or flying into violent trantrums when he broke the furniture or drove a car at lethal speed on the wrong side of the road. He had a keeper, a valet who was trained to clean up after him, and nurse him, armed with a hypodermic when he fell into DTs. He lived with them and yet he had an entity and freedom which his mother had been powerless to take away from him. He seldom baulked her, but when he did, as on this occasion when he had decided to go to Paris, its effect upon her was alarming. Her solutions were the sweeping variety that suggest themselves to those with too much power. Put him away. Shut him up forever. But the terms of an old trust formed by her sons' great-grandfather made this impossible to do without the maximum publicity. Philip wondered whether his brother understood the factors that had saved him, or whether he would capitalise still further to embarrass his family if he did realise. In any case it didn't matter. What did matter was this intention to go to Paris and involve himself in Fisher's activities. He would attract attention, because their name was like honey to a swarm of bees where the world press was concerned. Heinrich would be followed and photographed, and the old rumours of his illness resurrected, to be followed by veiled suggestions what their exact cause might have been. Nervous breakdowns. Tuberculosis. That had covered a six-month stay in a Swiss clinic after a violent outburst which luckily took place in the Schloss Würtzen, far enough from the public eye to be disguised. Unmarried. The world's most eligible bachelor. The wealthiest recluse who seldom left his hotel suite.

Philip had seen the press cutting his mother kept of the reports over the years during the early days of the war when Heinrich had got loose in Europe, for the second time. The efforts of his valet had brought him home without a major breakdown, or the disclosure of his real malady. Alcoholic degeneracy. He had said Henrich wasn't mad. Clinically this could be argued. He was the result of centuries of overbreeding, an unhappy genetic accident which he, Philip, had escaped. Knowledge of his own good fortune made him guilty in relation to his brother. He insisted to his mother that it could have been his burden instead of Heinrich's to carry through life the sins and intermarriages of his ancestors. He sighed, and pushed the blond hair back from his forehead. It too was a genetic gesture, from the father who had died in a blazing Stuka over the English Channel. If Heinrich was determined to go, then he had better follow him. That might placate his mother, and give them some safeguard against the future. Because the future could turn very dark if the detective's latest report was right.

In his opinion, and he had been very emphatic on the telephone, the newspaper report of a month ago had been correct. The General was still alive.

'Darling, why don't you sit down and relax? I've brought the newspapers, it's a lovely afternoon.' The Brigadier looked up anxiously at his wife. She wore slacks and gardening gloves; her face was lined and tired. Overhead the sun was burning in an empty sky; the scent of roses was strong in the still air, birds perched in the beautiful old medlar tree beside their garden chairs and sang.

It was a dreamlike English summer afternoon, too hot to work, a time for peace and silence, for reading the Sunday papers and waking afterwards from a light doze to drink tea and eat home-made cake. This had been their idyll for many years; their lives had passed in uninterrupted calm and mutual compatibility. They gardened, they read, they talked and held hands like lovers, which, in spite of their ages, they still were. Their life together had been good. It was an almost biblical phrase which the Brigadier enjoyed using to describe something entirely satisfactory in the sight of God and man. He held out his hand to her and she obeyed him, sitting at his side. She leaned back and closed her eyes. In repose her face was beautiful; it had a purity of feature that delighted him as much as the day he first saw it, in a freezing attic in her own home, that enormous stuccoed house in Munich which his commanding officer had commandeered. She had been a young woman then, frightened and hostile, facing an enemy intruder who had come up the back stairs and been a witness to her humiliation and despair. She had been burning pieces of broken furniture in the grate to keep herself and Paula warm. The child was in bed and coughing miserably. Gerald Ridgeway would never forget that first meeting with his wife. He had fallen in love immediately, and for the first time in his life. There was a nice, conventional English girl at home whom he expected to marry one day; she disappeared from possibility as soon as he saw the German woman's sculptured face, and flinched at the tragedy in her eyes. He had loved her from the first moment of their encounter, and his intensity of feeling had not diminished. She didn't sleep well; she was restless and sad. The serenity which was their greatest achievement had disappeared.

'Darling,' he said. 'Do stop worrying. It's all over now.'

'I don't believe it,' Magda Ridgeway said. 'I lie awake, thinking it will all come out, that the world will know and wherever we go, people will point us out. How do you think our friends would feel if they knew who I was – who my husband had been?'

'It's a long time ago,' he said. 'Nobody cares now.'

'Our generation cares,' she said. 'They fought in that war, they were part of it all. The stain will never be washed away for them. It can never be washed away for me.'

'You mustn't say that.' He turned to her quickly. 'You had nothing to do with what happened!'

'I was married to him for ten years.' His wife spoke slowly as if it were an effort. 'I entertained those creatures in my home, I lived with the spoils he took from families who were shipped away and murdered. I was part of it all, Gerald. I lived with death, I lay in its arms and I bore it a child. That was the most horrible part – that obsession with the child.' She shivered. 'Without pity, without one human feeling for anyone or anything, and yet when it came to the baby he was besotted! Do you know, he used to spend hours in the nursery, playing with her? Sitting by the cot, watching every movement, holding her hand in his fingers. When I went upstairs I'd hear him talking away to her, crooning and humming like a woman. If she cried, he would rush to the nursery and shout at the nurse – I was nauseated by it. I tell you, I found it so horrible that I couldn't go near her myself. And he knew this. He was very angry with me because I didn't love her.

But I couldn't; she was his. Whenever she looked at me they were his eyes. I felt as if I'd given birth to a monster; that was why he loved her, because she was the image of him. Poor Paula – I just couldn't help it. And in my heart I've never really got over that early feeling. It makes me very guilty.'

'You've been a wonderful mother,' her husband retorted. 'Don't talk nonsense. I'm afraid she's just been spoilt, that's all. And losing James has made a difference. She's soured. It's nothing to do with you, my sweetheart. And you can stop thinking about Bronsart and the past. He's dead, and so is that man Black. There's nothing to connect you.'

'I remember Black so well,' she said. 'Albrecht Schwarz, a little man, very dapper in his uniform. He adored the General; he followed him like a shadow. I remember him standing in the room when they first brought the Poellenberg Salt to the house, and my husband laughing. "How do you like your table centre?" That's what he said to me. I knew where it came from; I'll never forget the shame. My father and the Von Hessels' grandfather were friends. I ran out of the room, and do you know what he did? He brought Paula down out of her cot and showed it to her! "It's for her," he said to me afterwards. "She touched it and she laughed. She liked it! So she shall have it – my gift to her!" Not long after that it was taken away and I never saw it again. I never asked what he had done with it, I didn't want to know. He was like a madman, things were going so badly for us in the war. He was worse than I had ever known him. He talked of going to fight in Russia with his SS divison and wiping every Russian off the earth. I used to pray he'd go and never come back. And that prayer was granted. Do you know, that's when I believed in God?'

'I know,' the Brigadier said. 'You told me. And he is dead, and nobody can bring him back whatever Paula does.'

'And the Salt? What did Black tell her – why has she gone to Paris?'

'I don't know,' he admitted, 'but I am sure it will all come to nothing. You have no real reason to worry.'

His wife looked at him. He too looked tired and fresh lines had appeared round the eyes and mouth. She brought his hand up to her lips and kissed it.

'This has put years on to you,' she said sadly. 'I have only one fear. One terrible fear and I can't get rid of it. What if that devil *is* alive?'

'He isn't,' Gerald Ridgeway said. 'But if the impossible turned up and he had escaped – we'll face it, as we've faced everything, my darling. Together. And don't you worry. Whatever comes out of all this, I will protect you.'

*

'By God,' Fisher said. 'Look at this – Heinrich Von Hessel is here! He's staying at the Ritz!'

He passed the newspaper to Paula; they were having breakfast in the dining room of their hotel. It was a morning ritual which had never appealed to Fisher. Sitting up and eating at an early hour had bored him and he eschewed the habit as a waste of time. Now he looked forward to going down and waiting for Paula to come in; after the first few mornings he went to her room and they came down together. He could see by the hotel management's attitude that they were thought to be lovers. He only wished they had been right.

There was a bizarre horror about what had happened that clung to them when they left the old woman. Paula kept rubbing her cheek though the spittle had long disappeared. She shivered, in spite of Fisher's arm around her. It was an unnerving experience, crude and physically disgusting. Hate had come up and spat in her face. Fisher blamed himself for having taken her there. But if he hadn't he would have gone away like the men from the Sûreté, believing the old woman to be suffering from senile delusions.

Senile she was, and mentally confused. But for that moment the fog of age had cleared from her mind. There was no doubt about the reaction when she saw Paula, or that angry scream. 'He was an old man with white hair – but I knew him by the eyes . . .' The man was still alive. He was old and his hair was white, but he had the same distinctive eyes and she had known him. She had remembered with the clarity of her maternal grief, the face of the man who had sentenced her son to death.

Shrieking and fighting to get at Paula, the old woman had brought back the terror of the last phase of the war. Through her, Paula had been shown her father walking among a crowd of cowed and frightened men, dragged off the Paris streets as hostages, coldly selecting victims with a movement of his riding crop. In this way he had sentenced Madame Brevet's son to death, watched by the distracted, weeping mother, who had gone to the prison in search of her son. There was no ban on relatives going to look for missing sons and husbands. It spread the news through the city when there were witnesses to the executions. Through her words the figure of the General rose like a devil in the squalid little room, dressed in his sinister black, pitiless and inhuman, sending the shrinking boy to the firing squad. She had looked into his face and she had yelled, and cursed him. And she had seen that face again in a crowded street twenty-five years later, and remembered it. If Fisher and her daughter-in-law hadn't held her, she would have attacked Paula with her nails. On the drive back Paula said nothing. Alone in the hotel Fisher put his arms round her.

'That was terrible for you,' he said. 'I wish to Christ I hadn't taken you.'

'It was so real,' Paula said. 'She made it so real; I could see it happening.'

'I'm going to get you a drink,' Fisher said. 'You're shaking. Go and sit down.'

'I suppose,' Paula said slowly, 'that I suspected it. When I heard he was SS and on the wanted list, I knew he'd done this kind of thing. But it didn't sink into me. I knew it, but I couldn't believe it. Do you understand that?'

'I think so. Here, drink this. Come and sit with me.'

'She made me see it,' Paula said. Fisher had his arm round her. She didn't seem aware of it. She went on talking, looking ahead, holding the glass of brandy in both hands. 'The more she screamed and struggled to get at me, the more I could see her in the prison yard, begging and pleading with them not to take her son. And my father standing there, pointing with his stick . . .'

'All right,' Fisher said. 'Now that you know it, now that you've accepted it, do you still want to find him? Are you quite sure?'

'Yes.' Paula turned to him for the first time. 'Yes, I have to find him. Nothing can alter that. He's my father, he's part of me. Whatever he's like, whatever he did, I have to see him face to face. I have to hear his side.'

'But then what?' Fisher asked her. 'Isn't it better to keep the illusion? How will you feel if he turns out to be the kind of man that old woman talked about today – a soulless bastard, or half cracked like you said Schwarz was – you've got to think what may be at the end of this.'

'If he's sick,' Paula said, 'I shall take care of him. That would be the easiest of all. If he needs me, I'm his daughter. He's been in hiding for all these years; he must have paid for what he did.'

'And you could forgive him?'

'I want to,' she said. 'I want to find him and have him put his arms around me. I know you think I'm crazy, but that's what I want. When I was a child I used to watch my mother and Gerald going off together, and think if only my father could walk through the door or up the garden, and come and take me away with him. I created him, Eric, because I had nothing else. Now I know he's real and everything in me is crying out to find him. To see him and touch him. To make the dream into a reality.'

'And you're prepared to find that it's a nightmare?' Fisher asked her.

'I don't think it will be,' she said. 'I don't think anything he's done will matter to me. I don't think I'll care.'

'I see,' Fisher said. He got up and poured himself a drink. 'I love you, Paula.' He spoke quietly, watching her. 'I know I'm not much of a substitute but couldn't you make do with me instead?'

Paula shook her head. He looked unhappy and strained. It occurred to her suddenly that she had hurt him.

'No, darling. It's not the same thing. I'd never be happy with you if I walked away from him now. Our turn will come when this is over.'

'It may never be over,' Fisher said. 'He may take you away from me for ever.'

'I don't believe that,' she said. 'But till I see him, I can't promise. You will go on helping me, won't you?'

'That was our bargain,' Fisher said. 'And I'll keep to it, if that's what you want. But don't expect me to be happy about it. Don't expect me to see you run into your father's arms and give three bloody cheers.'

'I won't,' she said. 'But just remember this. I love you too.' She had gone up to him and kissed him, and nothing more was said. When he came to bring her down to breakfast in the morning, he appeared relaxed, but he looked tired and tense, as if he hadn't slept well. On the way to the lift she took his arm. Reading *Le Monde* a little later over the breakfast table, Fisher had seen the news of Prince Heinrich's arrival.

'Now,' he said, 'why the hell has he come here? I cabled the mother about you coming to Paris. I suppose he wants to check up. There's one thing I won't have, and that's the client breathing down my neck.' He folded up the paper and threw it down. 'I shall go and pay the gentleman a call and make that clear.'

Twenty minutes after he applied at the reception desk, Fisher was shown up to the Prince's suite. The hotel had been unco-operative when he asked to have a message sent up. The Prince was not to be disturbed. Fisher suggested aggressively that they had better put it to the test. Reluctantly the reception spoke to the deputy manager, who referred it higher still. Finally Fisher was taken up to the first floor by a page boy.

At the door of suite F/G the boy left him. He knocked and a minute later a man in the dark coat and trousers of a personal valet opened it and speaking in very bad French, invited him inside. Fisher spoke briskly in German. The valet bowed. His Highness was expecting him; if he would wait in the sitting room for a few moments.

It was a charming little room, the walls lined with beautiful eighteenth-century boiserie, its colour scheme and pictures were in the same period. It was delicate, restful, and unlike the usual decorated suites found even in a hotel of the Ritz renown. Fisher heard the door open behind him. Heinrich Von Hessel was in a silk dressing gown, with dark trousers underneath. He wore a white silk muffler round his throat and he reminded Fisher of a character in a Noël Coward comedy. He advanced stiffly into the room; his legs seemed difficult to bend, and held out his hand. Fisher took it.

'Good morning,' the Prince said. It was the first time he had spoken; it was a deep voice, with a guttural English accent.

'Good morning, sir. I saw your arrival in the paper this morning and I thought I should have a word with you. Did you have a good flight?'

'Excellent,' the Prince said. 'Very smooth.' He lowered himself into one of the dainty little French armchairs. Fisher had noticed a tremor in his hand when he shook it. He moved with the uncertainty of someone who was either very old or very delicate. Yet his physique was above average. He was tall, powerfully built, bigger in proportion than Fisher. He didn't look in the least like a man suffering from any infirmity. But there was a deliberation about the way he spoke and handled himself that struck Fisher as abnormal. As abnormal as the position taken behind his mother's sofa on that first afternoon.

'I find flying agreeable,' he said. 'Very relaxing.' He seemed to be looking for something, his eyes glanced round the room and came back to Fisher with an expression of abstraction. Fisher produced his cigarettes.

'May I offer you one?' He was more conventional in his approach to the son than he had been to the mother. There was no attempt to overwhelm or impress; he looked what he was, an immensely rich, pampered man, with nice manners and no desire to impose himself upon anyone. He looked through Fisher rather than at him.

'I would like a cigarette, thank you. Do you speak German, Mr Fisher? Ach, Josef . . .' At that moment the valet came into the room. He carried a large glass in a silver holder on a salver. There was a look on the Prince's face that made Fisher pause before he answered. It was satisfied, secretive. He took the glass with both hands. On an impulse Fisher lied. 'No,' he said.

'Ah.' The Prince nodded. He looked round and spoke to his valet in their own language. 'Bring me another brandy in fifteen minutes. And don't keep me waiting again.' He smiled at Fisher. 'This is my little indulgence. Cold tea. Would you like some coffee?'

'No thank you.' For a second Fisher almost asked for the same as his host, then he decided that jokes were not in order, even private ones. He watched the Prince take a deep swallow. He cradled the glass in both hands as if he were afraid he might drop it; or it might be snatched away from him. Cold tea.

Christ, Fisher murmured inside, brandy at ten-thirty in the morning. And another one in fifteen minutes. So that was what it was all about – that was the wooden walk and the glazed aristocratic stare. The Prince was stiff drunk.

'I enjoy aeroplanes,' he remarked. 'Flying is very pleasant.' Fisher didn't answer, he was so surprised he forgot to light his cigarette. Now the details began to make sense. He watched the man opposite to him and saw the big body sinking downward in the seat, the hands with their alcoholic tremor gripping the glass of brandy like an animal's claws. For no reason that he could explain, Fisher suddenly felt sorry for him. The eyes were wretched.

'How is the Princess?' Fisher asked. He couldn't think of anything else to say. Talking seriously to someone in that state was out of the question.

'My mother is well,' the Prince said. He took another swallow. 'She is a very active woman for her age. She dislikes flying. I like it. I find it relaxing.'

Fisher recognised the single-mindedness of the alcoholic. He was likely to repeat the remark about flying every few minutes. 'And Prince Philip?'

'He is on his way over here. He decided to come because I came. They are afraid I will interfere with you, Mr Fisher. They want the Poellenberg Salt very badly.'

'Your brother doesn't,' Fisher said. 'He came out to the airport when I visited you and tried to persuade me not to take the case too seriously. Don't you want it found either?'

'Not very much.' The Prince put down his precious glass, and with some difficulty negotiated a cigarette out of a box. Fisher got up and lit it for him. The stench of brandy was unmistakable; he must have been pumped full to ignite so quickly on one drink. He glanced down and looked at his watch. The time for another refill must be near.

'Why don't you want it back, sir?' Fisher asked him.

'Why should I?' He gestured with the cigarette. 'We have enough. My mother has one of the finest Raphaels in the world in her bedroom. Why do we need any more? We have enough treasures to worry about. But she is determined, Mr Fisher. My mother always gets what she wants, you know. Sometimes she does what Philip asks but never what I ask. You know I am head of our family?'

'Yes,' Fisher said. The Prince was not just drunk; he was the product of a permanent alcoholic condition. That was the meaning behind the tag of 'a recluse, subject to ill health'. He was pickled to the brain cells and must have been for years. Anything he said would be irresponsible. No wonder his brother was following him. To keep visitors away. And yet if he hadn't overheard that exchange between the master and the servant, if he hadn't seen for himself the valet come in with another glass and the same pantomime repeated, he might not have guessed. Which proved how deep seated the Prince's sickness was. The genuine alcoholic is permanently drunk. It's only on occasions that they fall about and give themselves away. And that was where the valet and the family influence would raise a shield to hide him from the world. Poor bastard, Fisher thought suddenly. Poor sick, lonely bastard, killing himself by inches. I bet that bloody mother would be glad to see him dead.

'I am the head of the family,' Prince Heinrich repeated. 'But they don't listen to me. How will my mother feel if Bronsart tells the truth? How will she like that?'

'He can't tell anything if he's dead.' Fisher was going slowly. The sad pouched eyes looked at him and there was a glint of something humorous in them. But it was gallows humour.

'He isn't dead, is he? I heard them talking. You don't think so, Mr Fisher. Men like him don't die, they live for ever. To plague and torment. She'll be sorry. He was the only one who beat my mother, do you know that? Most unusual. She always gets her way. But not with him.' He fingered his empty glass. 'I never liked him, Mr Fisher, even before it happened. But he got the better of her. Would you be good enough to give me a light – I can't find my lighter.'

Fisher held his lighter flame to the trembling cigarette end. The hand was steadier now, but the heavy head was bobbing on the neck.

'What truth could he tell, if he is alive? What happened between him and your family, sir?'

'I can't tell you that,' the Prince said. 'No, that cannot be told. Besides, I have forgotten the details. In the end one forgets everything. But if you find him and you try to get the Salt back, it will all come out. My mother knows that. Has she asked you to kill him yet?'

Fisher went back to his seat. He took a cigarette and lit it himself. 'No,' he said. 'She hasn't. And it won't do her any good if she does.'

'She will ask you.' The watch was being consulted again. He seemed as calm as when they were discussing his flight in from Munich. 'She will have to ask you, and you will say yes. Nobody says no to her for long.' He smiled at Fisher; as a young man he must have been handsome in a ponderous way. 'Josef, you are two minutes late. Ach, Mr Fisher, perhaps you would like a drink? I only take tea.'

'No thank you.' Fisher got up. One detail was nagging at him. He refused to take that last suggestion seriously. The man was crazy with drink. He would have said anything. Why in hell had they let him appear at all?

'If you and your brother didn't want the Salt to be found, why didn't your mother see me alone?'

'Because I am the head of the family. People are always saying they don't see me. She wanted you to know that there was nothing wrong. Once a newspaper said I was dead. I had to go to the opera with her that night. I hate opera. Philip was there because she relies on him. You see?'

'I see,' Fisher said. He didn't see at all. With the erratic insight of his kind the Prince seemed to sense this.

'She's going to need you if the General is still alive', he said. 'So you had to see me, Mr Fisher. She won't be pleased that I've talked to you.'

'I don't have to tell her,' Fisher said. He held out his hand and the Prince released his glass of brandy and shook it.

'I'd be obliged,' he said. 'Good morning, Mr Fisher. Thank you for calling on me.'

As Fisher left the suite, he heard the voice raised from the romantic little sitting room. 'Josef! Josef!'

'Tante Ambrosine and nephew Jacquot,' Fisher said. 'Jacquot, Paris, 25th June, 1944. That's all we have to go on. That and the fact that I'm certain your father is still alive and in this city. The point is, my darling, where do we start looking and for what?'

They were holding hands in the car, parked under the trees in an avenue of the Bois de Boulogne. He had given her lunch and then taken her for the drive out of Paris to the peace and beauty of the famous woods where the Kings of France had hunted game and the fashionable used to parade in their carriages until the outbreak of the First World War. Now it was a place for trippers, for coach parties eating sweets and throwing ice-cream wrappers in the grass, with the echo of the centuries returning as a group of riders trotted by.

Fisher had told her about Prince Heinrich. Paula had surprised him by her attitude. 'So he's a drunk,' she said. 'That's not such a terrible secret; surely they don't have to go to all this trouble covering his tracks if that's all it is. There must be something more.' Fisher didn't answer for some moments. The simplicity of what she said was obvious. There must be something more. And of course there was. There was the secret which concerned the Poellenberg Salt and General Bronsart of the SS for example. 'Has she asked you to kill him yet?' He hadn't told Paula about that remark. He refused to take it seriously, and yet it had begun to worry him. Why hadn't the Princess called in Interpol? With her influence she could have instigated a full enquiry into the report of Bronsart's reappearance and got further through official channels than she could hope to do using a detective agency, however competent. Why make a secret of the Salt, why not publicise it, offer a huge reward for information? This was the normal course to take in her position, but she hadn't taken it. She needed secrecy; there was always a shame attached to the wish for a private investigation. Whatever the circumstances which gave Bronsart his treasure, they didn't reflect credit upon the Von Hessels and the Prince had let that much out during their conversation. And so little credit did the family derive from the affair, that both the sons were ready to forgo the priceless heirloom which was lost, rather than court discovery. It was intriguing and a little sinister.

But until he could begin to trace the Salt through the General's message to Paula, Fisher hadn't a hope of solving anything.

'Jacquot,' he repeated. 'Who the hell is Jacquot?'

'What about the date?' Paula said. 'That means something too. June 1944. What happened in Paris in June 1944?'

'A hell of a lot,' Fisher answered. 'D Day for instance. There must be thousands of incidents which could be relevant, but which one and where to start?'

'Why not start with my father?' Paula suggested. 'If he hid the Poellenberg Salt, it must have been then. Otherwise the message makes no sense at all. And I'm certain Black didn't know any more. My father told him just enough but he didn't trust even him with the whole secret. Why don't we start with that date?'

'You ought to join the firm,' Fisher said. He slipped his arm round her and kissed her. 'Get out and let's walk,' he said. 'I've had an idea.'

They made their way through the wood on a bridle path; the sun dappled the ground at their feet and glimmered through the leaves overhead. It was cool and still. 'What's the idea?' Paula asked him. He held her close against him as they walked.

'I'm going to try and knock out two birds at the same time,' he said. 'I'm bothered to hell by those Von Hessels. The more I think of it, the less I like to feel I'm working in the dark. The Princess didn't tell me half the truth and what I got out of that poor drunken sod this morning didn't reassure me either.

'He's the black sheep, and as you say, it must be more than drink. So I'm going to do a little investigating of the Von Hessels for myself. I'm going to call an associate in Bonn and see what they can dig up. Especially in 1944, because I'm assuming that you're right and your father hid the Salt that year. I'm also assuming that that's when he got hold of it. So let's find out what the Von Hessels were doing at the time. Especially Prince Heinrich; he must have been serving in the army about then.'

'What about the other part, Tante Ambrosine and Jacquot?'

'I had quite a chat with that chap from the Sûreté the other day.' Fisher lit the usual two cigarettes and handed one to her. 'I'll take a chance and go to see him. He remembered your father pretty clearly. I've a feeling he was in Paris round that time too. It's just a chance he might have heard those names. Or he could think of someone I could contact who might know. It's all loose ends but it's the best I can do at the moment. Why the frown – what are you thinking?'

'You don't suppose my father has been living here, in France, for all these years?'

'Not a chance,' Fisher said. 'Far too well known; remember the old woman only saw him once and she remembered him. He was a famous man in his day; he couldn't have lain low anywhere in occupied Europe. Most of them got to South or Central America through that underground organisation of theirs. Code name Odessa – did you know that? They had it all organised with the usual efficiency, when it became obvious the war was going to be lost. My guess is your father holed up in Switzerland or Spain, ditto our friend Black, and that's why he's been able to come here and Black could get to England. He'd been living in Switzerland under a phoney passport for a long time.'

'So why has my father come back to Paris?'

'Because he knew Black was going to deliver his message,' Fisher said. 'So your father comes to Paris. To wait for you. Isn't that obvious? Didn't you realise that was what it meant?'

'No.' Paula had stopped on the pathway. She pulled free of Fisher and stood alone. 'No, I didn't think of that. You mean he's looking for me? We're looking for each other?'

'That's what I think.' She made no move to take his arm again; she just stood there with the sunshine catching her brown hair, alone in the middle of the wood. Fisher didn't like the reaction.

'He'll be somewhere near the Salt, that's my guess. So if we find one we're almost certain to find the other. Or perhaps not; perhaps he just wants to make sure you get it.'

'That's a terrible risk to take,' she said slowly. 'Tell me something truthfully. Do you think he killed Black?'

'I don't know.' Fisher didn't lie to her. There was no intimacy between them now. She had completely withdrawn.

'He might have done. Destroying the link when it had served its purpose. But I'm not sure. I can't honestly answer you.'

'He must be mad if he did. I don't believe it.'

'Not necessarily mad. Death didn't mean much to people like him. It was often the logical solution to a problem. Personally I don't think there's a connection. Don't worry about it. I'm sure it wasn't your father.'

'If he is looking for me,' Paula said, 'he won't come near me if I'm with you, will he? He wouldn't dare.'

'Well, I *am* with you,' Fisher said; he was beginning to feel angry. 'So that's too bloody bad, isn't it?'

'It gives me the most extraordinary feeling to think he might be near me.' She didn't seem to notice his irritation. 'It's getting cool, let's walk back to the car.'

'All right,' Fisher said. 'We'll take a drive through the Bois and then go back. I might invite the man at the Sûreté to have a drink with me. Then we'll have dinner out somewhere. How about Maxims? Would you like that?'

'Yes. That would be nice.'

The silence that developed between them lasted all the way back to the hotel. Fisher didn't come into her room with her; Paula said she was tired and wanted a bath. He could meet his Sûreté contact and have drinks with him; she would be ready at eight or a little after. Fisher put both hands on her shoulders.

'What's the matter with you?'

'Nothing,' Paula said simply. 'I was just thinking of something else, that's all.'

'Do me a favour in the next couple of hours,' Fisher said. He jabbed her playfully on the chin, but his smile was strained. 'Think about me. I'll come back around eight.' He kissed her and went along to his room to telephone.

The first call was to Bonn; they had an arrangement with an agency there; they kept a small staff of half a dozen skilled operators, three of whom were former members of the West German police force, and a woman who had worked for three years with the German Intelligence Service. He wanted information on the Von Hessels. The answer was reserved; it was not easy to get anything except unfounded scandal about the Von Hessels. They were well protected. All right, Fisher had said sharply, let's have the unfounded scandal as well as the society column crap. And where was Prince Heinrich during '43 '44? There must be a record of his war service; that would make nice reading for the beleaguered German population, knowing the big industrial giants were out there fighting for the survival of the Fatherland.

He ordered himself a drink before he looked up the number of the Sûreté office and called the detective inspector. The response was hesitant; it was almost four o'clock, and the inspector had promised to be home early. Fisher offered to come down to the office, but suggested that a drink on the way home might be more pleasant. Finally there was a grudging acceptance. They arranged to meet at a small bistro round the corner from the Sûreté office.

It was a brightly painted place, with a record player in one corner and plastic-topped tables. Fisher looked round with distaste, regretting the garlic smells, checked cloths and comfortable fustiness of the usual French bistro. To his horror the machine was belting out a noisy pop music selection. The inspector was already seated in a corner, his eyes closed, his pipe in his mouth with a thin plume of foul smoke issuing out of it.

Fisher went over, sat down and enquired what his guest would like to drink.'

'A Pression, thank you.' The inspector's name was Foulet, and he shook hands with Fisher across the table. They exchanged remarks upon the weather; Fisher said he had spent the afternoon in the Bois, and Foulet nodded, remarking that it was a beautiful spot. There had been a hideous sexual murder committed there only six weeks ago, and the criminal was still at liberty. Woods attracted madmen, he observed. Some psychiatrist had suggested that it was a return to primeval conditions, in which the retarded mentality felt at home. Personally he believed the assailant chose it because it was a place favoured by young girls out walking, or riding alone. The victim had been on a horse, dragged off it and horribly mutilated. Fisher decided to interrupt before he was given the anatomical details. The police, the law and the medical profession were all akin in the one vice; they found their own activities the only source of conversation. He headed Foulet off homicide by offering him another beer.

'I went to see Madame Brevet,' he said.

'Oh?' The inspector's pipe came out of his mouth for a moment.

'She was gaga, just as you said. A waste of time. But thanks for the help you gave me.'

'It was nothing. We've had a dozen reports about Bronsart since that one. They were all the same; cranks.'

'Were you in Paris when he was here?' Fisher asked. He had intended bringing the conversation round to the General without letting the police know that the old woman had not been mistaken. He had also decided to tell the inspector part of the truth.

'I was,' the Frenchman said. He took the pipe out again and drank some of his beer. 'He was here in '42 on a tour of inspection; I was a youngster then, I'd come back from the army after 1940, been demobilised and gone into the police. I thought it was the safest place to be, and also that I might get a chance to work against the Boche. The Wehrmacht were in control of Paris at that time; those SS swine were longing to get a foot in and bring the Gestapo with them but the army held them off. There was great jealousy between the two branches, you know that – it wasn't that those Prussians were humane, they shot as many hostages as the Gestapo when the trouble really started, but they looked on the SS as upstarts, not bred to be officers and gentlemen. Merde – how I hated them! But the worst of them was nothing compared to that bastard. When he came back he was not just picking faults with the army people. He had power, Monsieur Fisher, and he used it.'

'And when did he come back?'

'In May 1944. He spent three months here in Paris. The Gestapo and the SS were established in force. Why are you so interested in this man?'

'I told you I was privately employed to try and find him.' Fisher ordered a third beer and a Campari for himself. 'If he's dead, that's only part of it. He stole a valuable work of art from my client during the war and they are trying to get it back. The Nazis hid hoards of treasures all over Europe; this man Bronsart left some kind of clue with a relative, which my clients got hold of – I'm trying to figure out what it meant.'

'And this is a very valuable art treasure?'

'Pretty well priceless,' Fisher said. 'Tell me, Inspector Foulet, does the name Tante Ambrosine and her nephew Jacquot mean anything to you?'

He shook his head. 'No, nothing. Tante Ambrosine, Jacquot. It could mean anything; everybody lived by pseudonyms in those days. I'm afraid I can't help you. Is that all of your clue?'

'June 25th, Paris, 1944. That's all there is.'

'Hmm. Well, he was here at that time. I can vouch for that. From May till the end of July. I know because all the districts were alerted for security. He was one of the most hated men in France; by the end of June every Resistance leader had promised to kill him. But they couldn't get near. He moved with an army of SS. I saw him once or twice at Fresnes. He used to go down there to watch the execution of hostages. I've seen women weeping, going on their knees, begging him for the life of a husband, a son . . .'

Fisher was beginning to wish he would stop. He kept seeing the look on Paula's face in the Bois, the light in her eyes, as if she were seeing something or someone far away.

'He had no pity,' the inspector said.

'I was told that.'

'No pity,' Foulet repeated. 'Some of them were sadists; they got real pleasure from the things that were done. And there were Frenchmen among them, don't let us forget that. The Vichy militia were worse than the Gestapo. But Bronsart was above that. He was just inhuman. Tante Ambrosine. Jacquot.' Again he shook his head. 'I can't help you, Monsieur Fisher. It means nothing to me.'

'Thank you anyway,' Fisher said. 'At least you've established one thing; Bronsart was here in June that year. That's something.'

He decided to walk back to the hotel; it was a warm evening and Paris was preparing for the night and its activities. The streets were filled with slow-moving crowds. Fisher found himself staring at faces as he passed. Somewhere in the teeming mass, in some part of that city, the man he wanted was alive and waiting. Waiting for what? For his daughter to solve the riddle passed to her after a lapse of nearly thirty years. To see her recover the Poellenberg Salt as a silent watcher in the shadows, then to disappear for ever. Fisher didn't think so. His instincts rejected this romantic supposition. Men like Bronsart didn't efface themselves from selfless motives. This man was old by now; Madame Brevet, shrieking her hate and grievance, had talked of him as old with white hair. But the burning blue eyes were not dimmed by time, nor was the tenacity and toughness diminished which had kept him alive. The General was in the same city as Paula, and if they couldn't understand the meaning of that message and find the Poellenberg Salt, then they would never find the General. Which, in the interests of his own happiness with the woman he loved, might be the best of all solutions.

5

The receptionist at the Ritz Hotel saw a shadow fall across his counter and he put down his pen and looked up. A tall man, white haired and distinguished, wearing tinted glasses against the hot glare outside, stood in front of him.

The receptionist had a sharply tuned sense of a guest's social status; he could scent wealth and titles, even in the most unobtrusive.

The man was well dressed in a lightweight grey suit, a plain silk shirt and a dark tie; he held himself like a soldier, and before he spoke the receptionist reckoned that he was a German. It was something about the cut of the hair, and the set of the shoulders.

'Good afternoon. I wish to book a suite.' He spoke in French.

The man behind the desk shook his head.

'I regret, monsieur, there aren't any suites available. We are fully booked. I can offer you – one moment, please.' He opened his register and looked quickly through. 'I can offer you a double room and the usual private bathroom. But not until the day after tomorrow.'

'I wanted the suite on the first floor,' the tall man said. 'I am not interested in a room. How long is the suite booked for? I am not in an immediate hurry.'

'I can't say,' the receptionist answered. 'The present occupant hasn't given any date for leaving.'

'And who is the present occupant?'

'I'm sorry, monsieur, I can't say that.'

'Is the Prince Heinrich Von Hessel in the hotel?'

'Yes.' The receptionist was very guarded now. 'He is staying here.'

'And you cannot tell me if he is in the suite.'

'I'm sorry,' he said again. 'I am not allowed to give anyone information about him. All I can tell you is that the suite is occupied and I have no idea when it will be vacant. If monsieur is not in a hurry, I have a very nice suite on the second floor which I can offer in ten days' time.'

'I'm afraid that will not do. The Prince Von Hessel is an old friend of mine. Would you be good enough to connect me to his room.'

'Certainly, monsieur. If you will go into the cubicle over there, number six, I will put the call through the switchboard.'

The General walked across the foyer and into the little soundproofed
cubicle. Coolly, he lit a cigarette. Without meaning to, the pompous
little Frenchman had given him the information. If Von Hessel had
been staying in another room, he would have denied his presence in
the suite the General specifically mentioned. He now knew where he
was. The idea of the telephone call had come to him in the last few
seconds while he spoke to the receptionist. He had come into the hotel
without any plan in mind except to check up on the Prince and set
a certain anxiety at rest. He had read the account of Von Hessel's
arrival in Paris, and the idea of him staying there at that particular
time had begun to suggest more than coincidence. He knew all about
Heinrich. He smiled a little to himself as he waited in the cubicle.
He had known him many years ago; the screen of rich recluse didn't
protect him from the General. In fact he could remember the time when
he had seen him last, swaying drunkenly with his mother beside him,
ashen-faced and trembling, rounding like a tigress on her son because
he was demeaning himself by crying. The General had enjoyed that
scene, not because he relished the misery of the unhappy alcoholic but
because it occasioned the humiliation of the most arrogant woman he
had ever known. So proud and disdainful of the outside world and
everybody in it. He knew that she tolerated him and his kind because
she dared not do anything else, but that she hated and despised them.
The General had endured her freezing condescension and the repeated
snubbing of his wife, whose birth was irreproachable, but he had been
revenged at last.

He knew Heinrich better perhaps than anyone outside his family;
he wondered whether the Prince were capable at this stage of even
remembering. But the roots of fear went deep; he would remember if
the General mentioned certain things. The telephone rang beside him;
he picked up the receiver and spoke into it in German.

'Prince Von Hessel?'

He recognised the throaty voice immediately. It hadn't changed over
the twenty-five years since he'd last heard it.

'Yes. This is Heinrich Von Hessel. Who is that?'

'Ah,' said the General. 'Now listen very carefully to me.' A few
moments later he put the telephone down, lit another cigarette and
walked down the lounge to one of the armchairs. He chose one which
had a view of the lift, and sat down in it, one leg crossed over the other,
perfectly relaxed.

Fisher had been out since lunch-time, going through the old press-
cuttings of *France Soir*, whose editor had been a friend of his.

It was a long and tedious task on a hot day; the files smelt dusty and
the bright strip lighting in the filing room had given him a headache.

There was enough material about the General to occupy him for more than two hours. His first visit to Paris had been in 1942; there was a picture and a short piece about him visiting the military Governor of the city, General Von Stulpnagle. It was a poor photograph, taken from a distance. By 1944 the scant references to him flying to different parts of France had become a steady flow of propaganda hand-outs, which the French newspapers were obliged to print. There were items about him attending the opera, spending the weekend with some of the notorious collaborators, and finally taking charge of the situation in June 1944 when there was a serious outbreak of sabotage.

This was what Fisher wanted to find out; the exact duration of the General's stay in Paris, and whether there was an item which could account for his choice of the 25th of that month. But there he had met failure. There was nothing. He handed back the files and returned to the hotel. As he crossed the foyer he glanced at the notice-board and saw something white in his room slot.

There were in fact two messages, both telephone calls. One was from Prince Heinrich Von Hessel, who had called twice in fifteen minutes. The other was from Inspector Foulet. The Prince had phoned in more than an hour ago. Foulet's call was more recent. Fisher had known a number of drunks and they all followed the same type of routine. If the Prince had made up his mind to telephone, he would do so again and again. But the call from Inspector Foulet might be very important.

He looked at his watch; it was nearly five. Foulet might be in his office still. But the switchboard at the Sûreté said that the Inspector had left the building and advised him to try again tomorrow.

Fisher swore. He dialled the Ritz.

The valet Josef answered. Fisher asked for the Prince. Josef sounded worried, his English was very bad indeed as he tried to explain.

The Prince was not in the hotel. He, Josef, had gone out for a moment on a private errand, leaving the Prince settled comfortably in his sitting room with a television programme (and a bottle of brandy, Fisher said to himself), and when the valet returned, the Prince had gone out. He was very anxious but as he had no idea where the Prince had gone, there was nothing he could do but wait.

Fisher said that the Prince had tried to telephone him twice, had Josef any idea what he wanted? No, the answer came quickly, no, he didn't know anything except that the Prince had a telephone call which seemed to disturb him, and he began trying to contact Fisher after that. Fisher decided it was some alcoholic foible and told the valet not to worry. He would telephone again in an hour and see if the Prince had returned. He went upstairs to find Paula, and forgot about him.

Heinrich Von Hessel came down in the lift and walked carefully across the hotel vestibule. He had found his hat and walking stick. The hall porter sprang forward to open the doors, and asked whether his Highness wished a taxi. The Prince hesitated; the bright sunlight in the street hurt his eyes, people were hurrying past him, the effect was confused and he had an impulse to turn back and resume the shelter of the hotel. He wasn't used to the outside world without Josef there to cushion the impact for him. But the hotel wasn't shelter. That was why he had left it. Josef had gone out; when he discovered that, he had panicked at the thought of being alone in his suite after that call. His first reflex was to try and get Fisher. But there was no reply, and he had sat by the telephone, muddled and becoming increasingly afraid, while the hotel operator tried to reach him.

Josef had given him a lot to drink because he sensed that his master was upset, and the Prince had not intimated his intention to go out. He had done so as a consequence of finding himself alone. Now the porter was beside him, asking about a taxi. The Prince had no idea where he wanted to go.

He shook his head, said 'No, thank you,' and began walking slowly away towards the Place de la Concorde. He was a distinguished-looking man, and people stared after him; he walked stiffly and with the deliberation of the unsober, holding his walking stick in the right hand, not knowing where he was going to or why he should feel safer in the street. Normally Josef answered the telephone; he had been sitting by it, having a drink and watching the racing programme on the television in a pleasant haze, when the phone rang and he picked it up. It hadn't been a long call, and he had only spoken twice. The first time he announced himself in answer to a question, and the second time he had asked who his caller was. But no reply was given. The message was brief. If you want to go on living, get out of the Ritz. Today. That was all. No more and no less than an ultimatum, and then silence. The Prince had replaced the receiver and spent some moments looking at it in surprise. He hadn't been frightened until a little later, when he thought about it. That was when he tried to enlist Fisher. Fisher was a detective; he would know how to deal with threats. From past experience the Prince was conditioned never, under any circumstances, to go near the police. He had a hearty dislike of them after the accident in which the child so foolishly ran in front of his car. The fact that it was mounting the pavement at the time had escaped his attention. He distrusted the police; they were only interested in nailing some scandal on his family. He never considered calling them. And because Josef was a servant, he didn't confide in him either. He merely demanded more to drink and felt comforted by the fact that Josef was in the suite and could afford protection. But after the second abortive attempt to find Fisher, he grew restless and called for the valet. That was when he found himself alone, and for the first time he was overcome by an irrational panic. The charming little suite seemed unpleasantly quiet. His bedroom, the bathroom, the sitting room, all assumed a sinister aspect as if something were about to happen. He had been told to leave the Ritz immediately, or something *would* happen. So he had seized a hat and his stick and left.

Now his fear had subsided. The sunshine was bright, but not too warm as it was late in the afternoon; he found it agreeable to walk. He had always liked Paris; he had better memories of France than of places like Switzerland and Denmark, where he had spent a long time in a particularly unpleasant clinic before the war. He had hated the Danes ever since; the Swiss he regarded as jailors but amenable to rank and money, so life was not made too uncomfortable for him under their care. Paris was his favourite city; he felt quite calm and in a nostalgic mood. A walk would do him good; he would show his displeasure very clearly to Josef when he went back to the hotel. It had only been a telephone call, and he shouldn't have taken it seriously. No harm could have come to him. He had forgotten what had frightened him. *The voice*. He was walking up towards the Champs Elysées when he suddenly stopped. A man bumped into him from behind. The Prince removed his hat and apologised. The man swore at him and hurried on. There was a café immediately opposite; he crossed the street. He sat down, placed his cane and hat upon a chair, and signalled the waiter.

He needed a drink. The need had to be satisfied. Then the panic would go away and he wouldn't feel anything. He drank two cognacs straight down, and lit a cigarette. It was a pleasant place from which to watch the crowds walk by. Two more drinks followed, and he had forgotten why he needed them. He had forgotten about the telephone call. It was growing dark, and lights were glittering along the central avenue, as the shops and cafés prepared for the evening trade. There was a dusty smell, with the fumes of petrol mixed with the human scents and the odours of cooking, which were coming through to him from the kitchen. He thought that he might eat something, but there was no hurry. He smoked again, and the waiter, who by this time was hovering near his table, came at once and brought another drink. Heinrich had spent two months in Paris just before the war; he had made the trip with his paternal grandmother, a stately old lady who took a floor of the Ritz Hotel to accommodate herself and her staff of maids, hairdresser and nurse.

She had been kind to Heinrich, whose illness she didn't understand. He had liked her; love was too strong a word to describe any of his emotions. He had never loved. Not really loved . . . He existed, and he drank to make that condition easier. He had gone to Paris with the

old Princess, and found a special kind of happiness. A very special kind.
He thought of it then, with the sights and smells of the city crowding
memories back upon him. They were disjointed and distorted, but they
had reality at their core. He fingered his glass of brandy and smiled
into the distance. The waiters were watching him and whispering. He
was very drunk indeed; he lifted the glass as if his right arm were a
crane negotiating a huge load. His cigarette burned unnoticed in the
ashtray, and there was a glaze over his eyes as he looked ahead of him.
The waiters were taking bets on when he would keel over. It grew dark;
the cars racing up the Champs Elysées were a stream of flashing lights;
the Prince sat on, stiff as a waxwork, swallowing drinks. He raised his
hand and clicked his fingers when he wanted more. Somewhere in his
brain a signal warned him feebly that it was time he went home.

They got him to his feet; he took some minutes finding his wallet,
and trying to extract a note. A man at the next table, who had been
reading a newspaper, got up, paid his bill and came round. He looked
sympathetic.

'I'll get him to a taxi,' he said. 'I'll see him home. Poor devil, I had
a brother like this once.' He picked up the hat and the cane, and took
Prince Heinrich by the arm. 'All right,' he said. 'Take my arm and lean
on me.'

They didn't find a taxi. The Prince struggled to extricate himself.
He felt he was able to walk alone, and he resented being guided. He
got his arm free, but immediately he staggered, thrown off balance.
It was held again and he submitted. They were walking by the Seine,
making a slow progress. They didn't speak. Couples passed them
strolling with their arms round each other. The Prince had no idea
of the time; stars glittered overhead, reflected in the black water of the
Seine. The reflections danced and twinkled in the tide. A boat glided
past them, its port and starboard lights preceding it like eyes in the
water. They had stopped, and the man had taken his support away.

'Now,' the General said. 'Why are you here?'

The Prince looked at him, dazed and unable to focus. 'I wish to go
home. My hotel – back to my hotel.'

'You shall go when you've answered me. Why have you come to
Paris – why have they let you come back here?'

The Prince grinned suddenly. He had no idea of what he was
doing by the river answering questions. He didn't recognise the
man who asked them, who had suddenly taken his supporting
arm away just when the Prince most needed it. His mind registered nothing but the last thing he had heard. He thought of his
mother.

'She couldn't stop me,' he said. 'They don't want me interfering.
But I am the head of the family. I have a right to know.'

'That is correct,' the General said. 'I hope you make yourself a nuisance.'

'I don't want the Salt back,' the Prince mumbled. 'I told my mother to leave it alone. But you know her. She always gets her way.' He swayed and clutched clumsily at his companion.

'Oh yes,' the General said softly. 'I know her. But she doesn't always get her way. What do you mean about the Salt? It's gone; it's lost to you.'

'She thinks she may find it.' Prince Heinrich gave a bark of laughter. 'She thinks that Bronsart is alive. I hope he is, I hope he is. Do you know something? He's the only man who ever frightened her. Do you know that?'

'Oh yes,' the General nodded. 'I know that. When are you going home?'

'I'm not,' the Prince said. 'I like Paris. It has happy memories for me. Very happy memories. I'm staying where I am. I may stay here for ever. Why should I go home . . .? I want to go now. My legs are tired.'

'You are a tired man, I can see that,' the General said.

'It is kind of you to take me back to my hotel.' Prince Heinrich raised his head and peered at him.

'It is a pleasure. Shall we go now?'

'Yes. Yes, let us go now.' They were walking below the parapet on the dark bank of the river.

'And you are quite sure you mean to stay in Paris? Wouldn't you be safer somewhere else than in the Ritz?'

'No, no. We have a detective. He is looking for the Salt. He will take good care of me. I thought I telephoned him . . . I want to go now. Why don't we go?'

'We are going,' the General said. 'But separate ways.' There was nobody in sight; the river was empty of traffic. He stepped back a pace and struck the Prince full on the jaw. Before the body buckled and fell down, he had caught it, and was supporting the weight. The General heaved and pushed, and suddenly he stepped away. There was a splash and drops of water spattered the pavement and spotted the front of his jacket. He brushed them away and went to the side. There was nothing to be seen but a turbulence in the water and a circle of bursting air bubbles. Even if he hadn't stunned him, the Prince was too drunk to swim. The General looked down and saw his walking stick, lying where the Prince had dropped it. He left it there, and walked away, crossing to the other side of the road. As he waited for a taxi to come by, he lit himself a cigarette. Now when he next enquired, the suite at the Ritz would not be occupied.

The next telephone call that came for Fisher was from Prince Philip

Von Hessel with the news that his brother had walked out of his hotel and disappeared.

By the next morning the newspapers carried the story, and on their front pages there was a photograph of the Prince's silver-mounted cane lying on the pavement by the riverside.

'It's so horrible,' Paula said. 'It's the second death.'

'I know,' Fisher said. He held her hand; she looked very pale and unhappy. He hated to see it.

'I know it is. It's getting creepy. Listen, darling, I've been thinking. I know you won't like the idea, but all the same I think it's not a bad one. I want you to go home to London.'

'No!' Paula turned to him immediately. 'I knew you were going to say that! Why should I go home? We made a bargain and you promised.'

'I did,' he agreed. 'I promised to help you find your father. But I'm not sure now it's a very good idea. Be a good girl and give it up. Let me get on with it and find the bloody Salt, if I can. And if I can't then it's too bad and the Von Hessels can have their deposit back, as far as I'm concerned. I just don't want you mixed up in this. I don't like the way it's shaping up at all.'

'I'm not going back to London,' Paula said. 'I'm not giving up now. You said you loved me; I told you what this means to me. If you go back on me now I'll never forgive you.'

'You know bloody well I can't risk that,' he said. 'As for loving you, hasn't it struck you that this is just a bit one sided? I know how you feel about your father, but I'm not so sure how you feel about me.'

'You ought to be,' she said. 'I've told you. I love you too. It's only that I have to do this first!'

'I wonder,' Fisher said slowly. 'I wonder if you're not fooling yourself. Maybe there's no room for anyone else in your life but this phantom you've created. There is a name for it, you know.'

'I know.' Paula got up. 'And as I told you before, I don't care. I've got to have the chance to judge for myself. Otherwise I'll live for the rest of my life with the things that old woman told me! Can't you understand at all?'

'No,' Fisher said. 'Honestly I can't. All I know is that I'm not enough for you, and I find that very hard to take. It's a funny thing; you're the first woman I've ever cared a damn about. Are you going to marry me, or has that got to be put on the waiting list too?'

'Oh, don't let's quarrel.' She came and put her arms around him. 'Please don't say things like this to me. I know it's difficult for you, but try to be patient. How can I say I'll marry you at this moment? My life is in chaos, I've only been divorced a few weeks and now I'm going to find my father after thinking he was dead since I was a child. You're not being reasonable.'

'No, I suppose I'm not,' he said. He put his arm around her, and kissed her gently on the mouth. 'I'm so bloody scared of losing you, that's my trouble.'

'You needn't be,' Paula said. 'I need you too. And I'm probably going to need you even more before it's finished. I've never known anyone like you. I've never known anyone who wanted to fight the battles for me. All my life I've been pushed out to fend for myself; and women hate that. I did it, but I hated it. With you I know it'll be different. You're a real man, darling, that's why I love you. And you're probably the first one I've ever met.'

'And the last, if I have any say in it, Fisher said. 'You wouldn't like to prove what you've just said?'

'How?'

'By letting me make love to you.'

'Will it convince you?'

'I don't know,' he said. He pressed her round the waist. 'But I think it would certainly help.' She didn't answer, she stood against him, feeling the tension in his body, letting him open her mouth and explore while his hands stroked her back and picked at the fastening of her dress. It was a different kind of love-making to James's, her husband. It was more forceful, yet controlled. Fisher knew what he was doing; he took the initiative at once and never let it go. He brought her to the bedroom and went on kissing her; he didn't say anything, none of the superlatives she had heard about how great she was and what a swinging trip they were going to make together. He didn't talk at all. He used his body to arouse her, to confuse and compel her, and he gave the act of love a significance which Paula had never known could exist. For the first time she felt dignified by sex instead of used. When it was over he looked down at her.

'I love you,' he said. 'And nobody and nothing is going to take you away from me. Never forget that.'

'I won't,' Paula whispered. 'And after this, there isn't anything that could.' For the rest of that night Fisher believed her. But by the morning, when he woke and left her sleeping, he had already begun to doubt.

At eleven o'clock he arrived at the Sûreté office and asked for Superintendent Foulet. The Superintendent was very busy; he looked harassed and not very pleased to see Fisher; then his expression changed. He asked him to sit down.

'You must excuse me,' he said. 'I have very little time. This Von Hessel case is driving me mad. Why should someone as rich as that want to jump in the Seine? Poor little girls and penniless students, but not that Boche, with his millions!'

'I knew him,' Fisher said. 'And I may be able to provide an explanation. Analyse the contents of his stomach and you'll find enough alcohol to drown anyone. He didn't jump in, Superintendent, he fell in!'

'You are sure of this?'

'Dead sure. Princess Von Hessel is the client I am working for.' He saw the older man's jaw slip.

'The Von Hessels? They want to find the war criminal? Is that why the Prince was here . . .?'

'Partly,' Fisher answered. 'And partly to meddle. I don't think he knew what he was doing half the time. Poor bastard, what a lousy way to die!'

'Not at all.' The Frenchman's eyes were hostile. 'There's nothing to pity about him or any of them. The Von Hessels are just a gang of millionaire criminals, guilty of everything the Nazis did. Slave labour, collaborating to the limit, growing fat on German victims. Don't waste your sympathy on any Von Hessel. They are all the same. All bad.'

'If you say so,' Fisher said. 'I just take their money and do my job. And speaking of that, you were kind enough to telephone me.'

'Ah yes, so I did. It was about your question – Tante Ambrosine and Jacquot.'

Fisher was on the edge of the chair. 'Yes? You've found them?'

'Oh no.' The Superintendent shook his head and frowned. 'I don't work miracles. The names are a mystery to me; but I have a friend you might go and see. He worked in the Resistance during the war and he operated in Paris when Bronsart was here. He might be able to think of something. I wrote down the name and address; one moment while I find it.'

He passed a sheet off a memo pad to Fisher. 'You will get on well, I think,' Foulet said. 'He's an old friend of mine, a most remarkable man. He used to be a hard line Communist and he ran the most successful Reseau in the central Paris area. He's mellowed now; politics have sickened him, like most of us. But he could be helpful to you if anyone could. Would you excuse me now? That telephone has never stopped ringing all the morning and I have a lot of paperwork.'

Fisher thanked him. He stopped in the street outside and reread the name and address. Albert Lebrun, and the number of a house in 16th arrondissement. For an ex-Communist, it was an exceedingly smart place to live. He put the paper in his wallet and drove to the Ritz Hotel to see Prince Philip. The Princess was flying in later that day, and it was planned to take Prince Heinrich's body back to Germany for burial. He wondered whether the family might not be too concerned with the scandal to want to look for anything, even Cellini's masterpiece.

And that was the first thing the Prince said to him after he had expressed his sympathy.

'I want this stopped,' Philip Von Hessel said. 'I want you to accept a cheque from me, Mr Fisher, which will cover all your expenses and leave a substantial sum in compensation for the time we have wasted. I tried to persuade my mother to drop this investigation but I failed; now I know she will be glad to forget the whole affair.'

'Do you have her instructions to do this?' Fisher asked. 'Written instructions, I mean.'

'No,' the Prince said. 'She is too upset about my brother to be worried at the moment. But you can take my word for it.'

'Unfortunately I can't,' Fisher said. 'I thought I'd made this plain to you before. I'm working for your mother and if she wants it dropped I'll be happy to oblige. For personal reasons, Prince Von Hessel, I'm anything but anxious to find either General Bronsart or the Poellenberg Salt. But I have my responsibility to my client. Please don't try and offer me money again, because I shall walk right out of here if you do. I'm not amenable to bribes.'

For a moment the Prince looked at him; suddenly he made a gesture.

'Mr Fisher, please sit down and listen to me. Forget that you are working for my mother. I want to talk to you as one man to another. Mine is an old and honourable family; during the war we lost our good name and we did things of which I am personally deeply ashamed. What would have happened to us if we had refused to go with the Nazis can be argued several ways. I'm not prepared to judge my parents because I wasn't old enough to know the issues, and it's easy to criticise in retrospect. But I want to make up for the past. I want to re-establish my family as a force for good in the destiny of my country. This is my life's work, if you like to put it in rather dramatic terms. And the Poellenberg Salt can destroy everything I mean to do. Now that my brother Heinrich is dead I am in a position to do it. My mother still has the power but she is old, and I can persuade her to hand over to me. I can build something constructive out of our resources. Call off the investigation. I'm asking you as a personal favour to me. Not for money, if that offends you, but for much greater, more important reasons. Leave this thing alone.'

For a moment Fisher was tempted. It sounded very sentimental and noble; real tears-to-the-eye stuff. It would have been easier if he could have dismissed the Prince's appeal as a piece of emotional blackmail, but he was genuine. He meant what he said, with the passionate idealism which was yet another contradictory facet of his race. But

Fisher also had his ethics, and they were not to be discarded, for the salvation of the Von Hessel soul.

He stood up. 'I'm sorry,' he said. 'I told you, dropping the case would suit me just as much as it would you. But I can't do it. Not unless I get instructions from your mother. If she asks my opinion I'll advise her to forget about it. But that's all I can do.'

'Thank you,' Prince Philip said. He didn't look as if he were grateful; he rang the bell by the fireplace. A servant in livery appeared.

'Show Mr Fisher out,' he said.

'I'm sorry about your son,' Dunston said.

'Thank you.' The Princess's voice was brisk. She showed no inclination to discuss the matter.

'Why have you telephoned me?'

'I received a letter from Switzerland,' Dunston said. 'You've made the first payment. Thanks very much. I thought I'd let you know I'm getting ready to take action on that business we talked about. I'll have to go and spy out the land a bit, meet the person concerned, you understand.'

'So long as it's successfully concluded I don't care what your methods are,' the Princess said. 'But your partner is very confident; I hope you prove to be as efficient in your conduct of our business.'

'Oh, don't worry,' Dunston said. 'When it comes to a fee like that, you'll get the very best I have to offer.'

'What do you intend to do now?'

'I'm going over there. I want to be on the spot.'

'Good. I don't think we should be in touch again. When you've completed your part, the bill will be settled in full. Goodbye, Mr Dunston.'

'Goodbye.' He hung up, and for a moment sat looking at the telephone. There had been times in the past two weeks when he had woken in the night and wondered whether he could do what he had promised, even for the huge fortune involved. Dunston didn't suffer from scruples, or from a sensitive imagination. No ghosts would haunt his conscience, no guilty qualm allay his enjoyment of a leisured, wealthy life. He would never look back. But in the still hours of the early morning, he considered the problem and pondered the means. He had killed once before in the exercise of his police duties, and the experience had left him quite unmoved. He had a low opinion of human beings and an even lower sense of their value in the scheme of life. He had an affinity with the dishonest, due, he supposed, to his long association with crime and criminals. It was known that in some cases the dirt of law-breaking tended to rub off on those engaged in its suppression. The bent policeman was a familiar phenomenon;

Dunston's acceptance of the bribe from a front man for the smuggling ring was the logical progression of his attitude towards his work. It hadn't been too difficult. Ten thousand pounds was a lot of money. And what he was asked to do was simple. He had delayed operations, and once quietly suppressed evidence. In retrospect his action had been foolish. He had jeopardised his career for insufficient gain, and after he left Interpol with the question mark above his character, he made up his mind never to take a chance again. He had run his agency with scrupulous honesty, assisted by the rigid attitude of Fisher to anything which wasn't according to the rules.

But what he was going to do now was in a very different league from taking money and obstructing an investigation. This was murder. He said the word aloud to himself during his night-time meditations. He had to kill a woman in such a way that no blame could ever attach itself to him. Or to anyone. Which meant her death must be an accident. He liked the sound of the word. It conjured up scenes of cars leaping over cliffs, of trains thundering towards a hurtling body, of windows high above the ground. However he got rid of Paula Stanley, it mustn't look like murder. Because he was a professional and he knew that once an investigation started, no matter how carefully the killer plotted his course, the chances of discovery were higher than those of getting clear away with it. One difficulty presented itself, and that also worried him. Fisher's involvement with the girl. He had to find out just how close they were, he had to go to Paris and begin by watching the victim and noting her routine. This was the first step towards the ultimate goal of isolating her for death. It wasn't going to be easy; he knew the odds and he hadn't tried to minimise the risks. But balanced against all was that enormous sum of money. The first payment was a fortune in itself and that was safe in Switzerland in an account of which he had the number. The final sum would take him and his family anywhere in the world, without the need to think about money ever again. He could buy a villa in Portugal, where they had spent such a good holiday. A motor yacht. Any kind of car he fancied. There would be some fancy jewellery for his wife, who was a good girl and solid as a rock with the children and any amount of women to be had on the side. It would be a golden world for them all. He picked up his office telephone and began making the arrangements to go to Paris.

Fisher arrived at the Lebruns' address and found an elegant private house, with a charming eighteenth-century façade. A maid opened the front door and showed him to a first-floor drawing room. Fisher had been trying hard to reconcile Foulet's description of the man as a hard line Communist with the exclusive area and expensive house; the sight of a Modgliani hanging on the wall didn't help. It was a long room, discreetly lit by ceiling spotlights which were directed on the pictures, and the pictures, even to Fisher's disinterested eye, were very good indeed. It was a modern room, subdued and comfortable, with a hint of an art gallery about it, there were several large pieces of avant garde sculpture.

'Monsieur Fisher,' the maid said. A woman got up from a long white leather armchair and came towards him, holding out her hand.

'Good evening,' she said. 'I am Madame Jenarski. Albert won't be a moment. Please sit down. What can I offer you to drink?'

She was somewhere in the fifties, dark haired, with black eyes that glittered like coals, a handsome face which had been beautiful in her youth. She was superbly dressed, and she wore a gold and ruby pin in the shape of a tiger on one shoulder. Rich; very rich indeed. The scent she used cost five pounds an ounce.

She smiled at him; there was a gleam of gold in her mouth. She was not a Frenchwoman; Fisher made a guess and came up with Greek.

He sat down, and accepted a glass of whisky. She offered him a cigarette out of a small gold box. He made a remark about the weather. She sat opposite to him and smiled.

'Why do you want to see Albert, Monsieur Fisher? His friend Jean Foulet said you would be coming. I hope it's nothing that will worry him.'

'I hope so too, madame,' Fisher said. 'But I'm making an investigation and I hope he can help me.'

'Something to do with the war? Not with the camp, I hope. I can't let you talk to him about that. It upsets him too much.'

'No.' Fisher shook his head. He admired her directness.

'I am not concerned with any camp. I presume you mean he was a prisoner.'

'He was in Dachau for eight months,' she said. 'When you see him you will understand what was done to him there. People have tried to interview him, wanting to write his life story – you know the sort of thing. It would be too much for him, to be asked questions about that time. It took me five years to get him as well as he is, Monsieur Fisher.'

'You look after him, I understand.' Fisher decided to clarify the position. 'Is he an invalid?'

'No,' she answered. 'He can walk now, thank God. I took him to the best specialists in Europe to see what could be done. The Germans crippled him, you see. He suffered terribly. When I found him after the war he was in a hospital for incurables, dying of loneliness and despair. It was so fortunate for me that I heard where he was.'

'And for him too,' Fisher said. The black eyes burned at him.

'No, for me. He saved my life during the war. I loved him then, when he was the great Resistance hero with every Boche in Paris looking for him, and I love him better now than I did then. Caring for him has been my privilege, monsieur.'

'Thank you for telling me about it. I won't worry him, I promise you.'

'I'm sure you won't.' The smile appeared and she was charming again. 'He will be glad to see you. He likes visitors.'

When the door opened they both got up; the man who came through it was on two sticks, one leg grotesquely twisted up. He was almost bald, with a seamed and wrinkled skin that made him look very old. He wore a patch over his right eye. Fisher came forward and introduced himself.

Madame Jenarski had come to Lebrun's side and slipped an arm round him. 'Come and sit down, Albert. I have been entertaining Monsieur Fisher for you. I will get you a drink.'

Fisher didn't begin a conversation. He let the old man settle in a chair and accept the drink first. Then it was he who spoke.

'What can I do to help you?' he asked. 'Jean Foulet told me a little about you. You're a private detective, aren't you?'

'Yes,' Fisher said. 'I can't go into any details of my job, as I'm sure you'll understand, but very briefly I'm interested in the career of a General Bronsart, who was SS commander in Paris around June 1944.'

Lebrun had pale grey eyes, at least the one remaining looked that colour; it was sunk deep in his head. Fisher thought suddenly how difficult it was to judge emotion in a man without the guide of two good eyes.

'I knew of him,' Lebrun said. 'What interests you about him, monsieur?'

'He stole an art treasure,' Fisher said. He felt that without some amplification on his part, the old man and the Greek woman would refuse to tell him anything. 'It's original owners are anxious to get it back. There are one or two pretty flimsy clues and one of them is a man's name. Inspector Foulet thought it might mean something to you.'

'He told me,' Lebrun said. 'Tante Ambrosine and her nephew Jacquot. Isn't that it? You want to know its significance.'

'Yes,' Fisher said. 'Yes, I do. It's very important. Who are Tante Ambrosine and Jacquot?'

It was all so simple, without effort on his part. He asked the question and suddenly, unexpectedly, there was an answer.

'Tante Ambrosine was the code name for my Reseau during the war,' Lebrun said. 'And Jacquot was the code name of a member of it. But there is nothing he can do to help you, Monsieur Fisher.

He is dead. He was shot by personal order of General Bronsart that June.'

The room was silent; none of them moved. Then Fisher said quietly, 'Goddamn it. I was afraid of something like that. How well did you know him, sir? Why should Bronsart use his name in connection with hidden loot . . . ?'

'Why did the General have him shot? He was a humble man, very young and unimportant. He was arrested and not even questioned. Then they executed him the next day. His mother told me how it happened. Now you tell me there is a connection with some hidden treasure . . .' The single eye switched from Fisher to Madame Jenarski.

'What do you think, Madeleine?'

'I think it is all very fascinating.' She smiled at him, tenderness softening her face. 'Hidden treasure – fascinating,' she repeated.

'Poor little Jacquot; I can't see what he could have had to do with such a thing. I remember him well.' She turned to Fisher. 'You see, he worked for Albert, as I did. Although I'm not French, I was in Paris when they invaded Greece, my country. So I met Albert and became one of his couriers. He didn't think very much of me in those days – he didn't approve of the rich. Did you, my darling?'

Lebrun shook his head, the scalp glistened under the spotlight above him. 'No. I did not. But I tried to redeem you, didn't I? I was a fervent Communist, you see, Monsieur Fisher, and I hoped to save Madeleine's soul in spite of her money. I still do, even though I am fortunate enough to live on it.' He laughed and she joined in.

'And there's nothing else you can tell me about Jacquot?'

'Nothing.' They both seemed to shake their heads in unison.

'He was a courier for me,' Lebrun said. 'A quiet, simple young man, loyal and a good patriot. He was captured by a piece of bad luck; he was picked up in the street in a Gestapo swoop for hostages. They took the poor devils to Fresnes Prison to hold them for a few days before they shot them. Jacquot was brought out the following morning, picked out at a parade by the General and executed minutes later. I got all the information I could from others in Fresnes. They said Jacquot was away during the night but came back without a mark on him. And when they questioned you, monsieur, believe me, they left marks.' He put up a hand and touched his eye patch. Madame Jenarski got up suddenly. She looked at Fisher.

'Thank you for coming to see us,' she said. 'I'm sorry we haven't been able to help more. I will see you out.'

Fisher shook Lebrun's hand. Close to, he could see some horrible scar tissue at the edge of the eye patch. Down in the front hall, the Greek woman turned to him and held out her hand.

'I saw a report in the newspapers some month or so back,' she said. 'Bronsart was reported seen. It was a curious coincidence. It was poor Jacquot's mother who thought she saw him.'

'Thank for your sympathy.' The Princess was sitting, her back as straight as a steel rod, dressed from head to toe in black, her eyes undimmed by any sign of weeping. Fisher had come the morning after her arrival to make his report. He had offered his sympathy as a formality and she accepted it curtly, as if she despised him for wasting both their time. Looking into the hard face, the features accentuated by the black dress and a chiffon scarf of the same colour, Fisher remembered the blurred features of her dead son, with the lurking wretchedness in the eyes, and felt sorry for him all over again. 'It is a disgusting business,' she said suddenly. 'I was besieged with photographers when I arrived. Reporters have been hiding in the hotel. I warned the management that if one intruder got near me, I should move immediately to the Crillon!'

She had taken up quarters in the Ritz on the floor below her son Philip. 'To drown in the Seine,' she said. 'It's unbelievable. It's such a vulgar thing to happen to us, Mr Fisher. If my son had died in any other way I could have faced it with more equanimity!'

Fisher could well imagine it. She made so little pretence of being sorry that it was grotesque. He felt his dislike of her increasing in ratio to his pity for the unhappy alcoholic whose passing was so little lamented. 'I went to see Prince Heinrich,' he said. The steely glance shot at him.

'Why did you do that?'

'I wanted to make a report.' Fisher couldn't resist it. 'I must tell you, Princess, that I thought he had been drinking.' The remark was prompted by sheer middle-class malice; that was how Fisher analysed the motive to himself. He wanted to see the arrogant bitch wilt a little. Her mouth actually curled – with contempt for whom? – Fisher couldn't be sure it wasn't for his effort to score off her.

'My son did drink from time to time,' she said coolly. 'But he held it like a gentleman. And that is all that matters. What progress have you made?'

'Not very much since I last checked with you,' he said. 'I've traced one man who seemed to be a vital part of it, but he's dead. I'm afraid this could bring us to a dead stop.'

'Why should it? You are sure the General is alive – I agree with you – his daughter has been contacted, all that remains is to solve the riddle he set for her.'

'The dead man was part of that riddle,' Fisher said. 'I'd hoped he was alive and could supply us with some answers. But he's dead, and it was done by the General's personal order.' As soon as he said it, the irrationality was obvious. He wondered how he could have missed seeing it before, when he spoke to Lebrun. But as soon as he left them he had joined Paula and that drove everything else out of his mind. It didn't take the Princess long to see what had eluded him.

'Bronsart must have known he gave a dead man as part of his clue, so his being dead is not important. What must matter is something else about him. Really, Mr Fisher, what am I paying for?'

'That,' he said slowly, 'is what I've been wanting to ask you. Which is the most important to you, Princess Von Hessel – finding the Poellenberg Salt or getting our hands on the General?'

'The Salt,' she said; the answer was a little too quick. 'That's what I engaged you to find. If you find the man who stole it from us, well and good! I don't understand your question.'

'Both your sons have tried to dissuade me from going on with it,' Fisher said. 'Your eldest son talked of a scandal. I want to know what's behind this, what you haven't told me. I don't like working in the dark.'

'My eldest son drank,' she said sharply. 'Sometimes his imagination wandered away from the facts. I've no idea what he was talking about.'

'Your second son said the same.' Fisher wasn't going to back down now. 'There's nothing unreliable about him.'

'Philip came and talked this nonsense to you? I don't believe it!'

'Twice,' he said. 'He came to the airport to see me off after my first interview, and the day before yesterday in this very hotel, he as good as ordered me to throw my hand in.'

'I see.' The eyes were narrow, watchful. 'And what did you reply, Mr Fisher?'

'I said I was employed by you and didn't take instructions from him or anyone else. If you said to drop it, I would, but not otherwise.'

'I appreciate your loyalty.' It was a sneer, and Fisher reddened. 'You did the right thing; disregard everything my son Philip says to you. I'll deal with his objections.'

'I'd rather you dealt first with mine.' That stopped her; she moved abruptly in her chair.

'I don't have to deal with anything with you,' she said. 'You're being paid. That's all you need expect from me.'

'I want the truth,' Fisher said. 'You can stuff the money unless you tell me what the General had over you that you gave him the Poellenberg Salt.'

She took it well, he had to grant her that; she didn't betray herself by a single flicker. She glared at Fisher. 'What do you want, more money? Is that what this quest for truth is all about? Don't try and fool with me; I know what your profession is – once removed from the criminal classes!'

Fisher didn't answer. He got up and walked to the door. Her voice rose above its normal pitch.

'Mr Fisher! How dare you walk out!'

He turned at the door. 'That poor devil was married, wasn't he?' He spoke quite calmly. 'What was the matter with her – why did you have to hide it up?'

'Come back, please.' She offered the invitation in a normal way, but now there were two red patches on her face, and both hands festooned with diamond rings, were clutching the chair arms.

'Please,' she repeated. 'Sit down and let us both be reasonable. We won't gain anything by losing our tempers.'

Fisher didn't move. 'I'm not losing mine,' he said. 'And you haven't answered my question.'

'Why should I answer it?' She rounded on him bitterly. 'Who are you to pry into my family and try to confront me!'

'You've just told me, once removed from the criminal classes. What are you afraid of – blackmail? You needn't be. But I want the truth or I won't go on with the case. There happens to be an innocent person involved apart from you.'

'I see.' The Princess stood up; she seemed taller than Fisher remembered. 'Very well. Come away from the door and I will tell you what you want to know. How did you find out about my son's marriage?'

'There was a report in a Swiss newspaper in 1943. The Prince was said to have got married secretly in Paris, during a trip over here. I had my office check it out and they discovered a similar report in a local French paper. He was married in a small village about twenty-eight kilometres from Paris, wasn't he?'

'Yes.' She spat the word out. 'But how did you find out? – There are no records.'

'I know that,' Fisher said. 'My operator spoke to the Mayor of the village, and he remembered the Prince simply because there was such a fuss about it afterwards, and his records were removed and returned with the entry taken out. So he couldn't tell us anything about the marriage except confirm that it took place, because he officiated.'

She made a gesture with her hand. 'You must be very stupid if you can't guess,' she said. 'She was a Jewess. Heinrich was completely irresponsible; he was always unreliable. My fool of a mother-in-law took a fancy to him and insisted on having him travel with her. And that is when he married this girl, while he was staying in Paris with his grandmother.'

She moved across the room and took a handkerchief out of her handbag. 'You can imagine what that would have meant to us, in the middle of the war. It was hushed up, we separated them and brought him home, but we failed to keep the secret. Bronsart discovered it, and you can understand now why he was able to take the Poellenberg Salt.'

'In return for his silence?'

'Precisely. And you can appreciate why I am determined to get it back!'

'What happened to your daughter-in-law?'

She seemed to wince at the title. 'I have no idea. She was just an adventuress who had her schemes frustrated. She disappeared after we took Heinrich home.'

'It can't have been very easy being Jewish at that time.'

'It was before the German persecution of the Jews in France,' the Princess said. 'That came later. I expect she had escaped by then. Most of them did. It doesn't concern me now.'

'I see,' Fisher said. 'Thank you for telling me.'

'If this becomes generally known,' she said quietly, 'I shall make it a personal issue between you and me, Mr Fisher. And believe me, neither you nor your detective agency would win.'

'I can believe it,' he said. 'Don't worry, nobody will know your son married a Jewish girl and you dragged him home to Germany and left her to fend for herself.'

'If we hadn't,' the Princess said. 'If that had come to Hitler's notice, my son would have been sent to a concentration camp. And we could have lost our factories. We did what had to be done because of the circumstances at the time. You may disapprove but you have no right. You were not there, and you can't judge. I had to protect my son.'

'I can see that,' Fisher said. 'I'll keep you in close touch with everything that happens. And I'd be obliged if you'd get your son Prince Philip off my back. I don't want any more calls from him telling me to lay off.'

'You will go on working for me?' she demanded. 'You will get the Salt back?'

'I said I would,' Fisher answered. 'And even though I'm only a common Englishman and pretty near being a crook on your reckoning, I always keep my word. Good morning to you.'

When the door closed, she stood looking at it for a moment. Then she went to the telephone and asked for her son Philip's suite. Her right foot tapped an impatient rhythm while she waited.

'Philip? I've just seen Fisher.'

'What did he say?' The voice sounded anxious through the receiver.

'He wanted to know the truth,' the Princess said. 'You fool, you only aroused his curiosity by trying to go behind my back! This isn't your affair and I forbid you to interfere!'

'I'm sorry,' her son said. 'I thought it was for the best, Mother. What did you tell him?'

'He had found out about the marriage. I confirmed it. That was all.'

'And he was satisfied with that?'

'Yes. Please God he won't look any further.'

6

'She's dead,' the young woman said. The child was balanced on her hip, greedily sucking its fingers; she stared at Fisher with hostility, holding the door half shut.

'I'm sorry. When did it happen?'

'The day after you came here,' the woman said. 'The excitement was too much for her; she went on raving after you left – I blessed you and your lady friend, I can tell you! Then she just went to pieces, the next afternoon she had a heart attack and that was the end of it. Thank God!' She rolled her eyes upwards. 'I ought to thank you – I thought she'd live for ever, the old cow . . .'

'Then perhaps you could help me?' Fisher was desperate to keep the door open; one hand was in his coat pocket holding a wad of notes. The woman looked at him, suspicion closing her face against him.

'Help with what? Not that old wartime stuff again?'

'Your brother-in-law Jacquot, the one who was shot by the Germans . . .' he said. 'I want to know about him.'

'There's nothing I can tell you.' She shrugged, dislodging the baby's fist from its mouth. 'Christ, monsieur, my husband was six years old when it happened. I wasn't even born! The old cow told you all there was to know. He got himself caught like a fool, meddling with what wasn't his business, I daresay, and the Germans did for him. Always talking about him, she was, raving on and on. She drove me crazy; thank God she's gone. Old cow.'

Fisher brought his hand out of his pocket without anything in it. He gave the young Madame Brevet a look of disgust.

'I expect your mother-in-law's glad too,' he said. 'Living with you can't have been much fun for her.' He turned and walked away; she was shouting abuse after him. At the end of the shabby street he said out loud to himself, 'Hell's teeth, now what?'

The only source of personal information about Jacquot was gone; he had been full of hope when he left the hotel to see Madame Brevet that morning.

He was ready to exercise patience, to spend hours with the old lady if necessary, until he could dredge up something about her son which might make sense of the General's inclusion of his name. Now hope was gone. The door which appeared to be opening had slammed shut; added to which his partner Dunston had phoned early that morning to say that he had to make a trip to France on another case and intended stopping over in Paris. Fisher liked Dunston, but he didn't want him intruding at that moment, booming on about the Von Hessels, putting his foot in it about Paula. Most of all he didn't want Dunston meeting her, eyeing her up and down and making his bar-room jokes to Fisher afterwards. Now he had another reason for resenting Dunston's visit. He had come to a complete dead end. He had pinned his hopes upon the old lady; the senile have a happy facility for the past, whereas the present confuses them. He had memories of an old aunt in a dreary home near Brighton, who could talk with amazing clarity about the First World War but didn't know which day of the week it was. He thought of the vixen-faced daughter-in-law, and swore. Jacquot was as clear in his mother's mind as if he had met his brutal death on the day before. She could have answered questions, Fisher was certain of that. But he had come too late. With her death there was nobody left to ask about Jacquot. He searched through his pockets for the cigarettes; there was only one left in his packet, and when he tried to light it, he found a split in the paper. He swore again and threw it away. He saw a tobacconist's on the other side of the road, and crossed over.

Three children were playing a game with coloured chalks on the pavement; they were hopping from foot to foot among the chalked-out squares, calling to each other and laughing. Fisher sidestepped them and went inside the shop.

It was dark and the air was stale; there was a woman inside, counting out money, and a man waited behind the counter. He wore a soiled shirt, collarless and open at the neck, showing thick black hairs like creeper at the base of his throat; his moustache was bushy and stained yellow at the ends. He looked up at Fisher as his customer handed her coins across the counter.

'Monsieur?'

'Forty Gauloise.' Fisher found his money; the man scooped up the coins with a horny workman's hand; instead of turning away he peered at Fisher for a moment.

'Excuse me,' he said, 'but you are a friend of Madame Brevet?' He spoke hurriedly, as if he had been waiting to get it out since Fisher came into the shop. The question took him unawares.

'Which Madame Brevet?'

The man jabbed with his thumb out of the window.

'Not that bitch. The old lady; I heard the other one shouting after you. I saw you standing at the front door. She wouldn't let you in, eh?'

'No,' Fisher said. 'I came to see her mother-in-law. She told me she was dead. I was sorry to hear about it.'

'Don't be sorry.' The shopkeeper leaned over the counter; garlic and sour wine sighed over Fisher. 'It was a mercy that she died. For ten years she lived in that house with that vixen, nag, nag, nag at her all the time. Always calling her dirty names, never a kind word. It broke our hearts, monsieur, to see the poor woman go to pieces as she did. Just for the want of a little kindness in her old age. And what a woman she used to be!'

'Oh?' Fisher had been about to turn and go. He wasn't in the mood for a back-street gossip. 'You knew her well? '

'She lived in this street all her life,' the man said. 'We went through the war together, her family and mine. One never forgets something like that!'

'No.' Fisher came and leaned against the counter; he took out the Gauloise and offered one. 'No, I'm sure you don't. Then you must have known her son, too.'

'I'm glad to meet you,' Dunston said. He shook hands with Paula. Fisher hadn't been pleased to see Dunston; he didn't listen to Dunston's alleged reason for being in the city, which was a fictitious client with a business problem. He had tried very hard to avoid Dunston meeting Paula, but Dunston refused to be put off. He was genial and thick skinned, and finally he won. They met in the lounge of their hotel, and immediately he gave Fisher credit for good taste. The girl was certainly attractive. He appraised her quickly. Good figure, nice legs, pretty face with marvellous eyes. He shook hands with her and smiled, showing his bright white teeth. Pity it had to be her. But still. He took them both to the bar of the Tour de France for a drink, and set out to get as much information as he could. He thought Fisher looked hung up over something; probably she hadn't gone to bed with him yet. He kept watching her. Dunston didn't like it. He had never seen Fisher behave like this with anyone before. He was deeply hooked by this one. Which might prove to be a bloody nuisance He hadn't reckoned on having to fool Fisher, but now this factor couldn't be ignored. The bloody fool was mad about her. And she, so cool and gentle, with her upper-class manners and her elegant clothes – how did she feel towards him? Dunston made small talk about the city and the weather for the first half an hour, and watched them very closely. He couldn't decide about her. He couldn't be sure how she felt about Fisher or how closely she was involved. And this could be important. If he were going to set something up for her, she had to be alone, and he had to be sure that she would walk into his situation without suddenly referring to anyone else. He decided to play it along and see what happened.

'Now tell me.' He leaned forward towards her. 'How do you feel about finding this treasure, Mrs Stanley?'

'Not very enthusiastic,' Paula said. 'I've said all along to Eric, that if we do find it, and I do have a legal claim, I don't intend to keep it. The original owners can have it back.'

'That's very noble of you,' he said. 'Mind you, you might change your mind when you actually saw it! I don't think I'd give it up in a hurry!' He laughed and looked across at Fisher.

'And what do you do all day, while our boy here is out playing Sherlock Holmes?'

'She comes with me,' Fisher interjected. He wouldn't have put it past Dunston to try and make a date. He found the steady grin and the flickering eyes up and down Paula so offensive that he could hardly keep his temper. He had never imagined he could dislike Dunston. Now he could have taken him by the collar and told him to keep his dirty looks to himself.

'Does she? Everywhere?'

'No, of course not,' Paula said. 'I do quite a lot of sightseeing, and I'm afraid I shop. Paris is a terrible place for spending money.'

'And that reminds me,' Dunston said. 'I must look round for something nice for Betty. That's my wife — maybe you'd come along with me one day and help me choose a dress — I've got her size.'

'I'd be delighted,' Paula said.

'How long do you expect to be here?' Fisher asked. He didn't want Paula going shopping with him; he didn't want her going anywhere with anyone. He caught himself up with surprise. His latent jealousy had surfaced until he was sullen and suspicious when they were apart.

The fact that they were lovers had not improved the relationship for Fisher; it had transformed his uncertainty about her into an obsession. The more he made love to her and she responded, the more he wanted her to relinquish the search for her father, and the deeper his resentment when she showed no sign of doing so. He should have filled the vacuum in her life; he couldn't accept that there was any need for the fantasy of a neglected child, if she were really in love with him. He looked across at her, talking to Dunston whom he had expected her to find objectionable, and was irritated that she was smiling. Why the hell should he ask her to go shopping for a present for his dreary wife . . . ?

'How long are you staying?' He repeated the question.

'I don't know,' Dunston said. 'Depends on how the sleuthing goes. I shan't hurry back though; it's very pleasant here. You'll be staying to the end of the business, Mrs Stanley?'

'Yes,' Paula said. She avoided Fisher's look. 'I'm staying.'

'In for the kill,' Dunston said and laughed. He turned slightly towards Fisher. 'Since it's all in the family, how near are you to finding it?'

'I'm going to England,' Fisher said. He reached across and took Paula's hand; he didn't care what Dunston thought. 'I need to see Paula's mother just once more. And then we start digging.'

'Literally?'

'Figuratively, I think,' Fisher answered Dunston. He felt Paula's fingers stiff and unresponsive in his grasp. He hadn't mentioned the trip to England before; he found it difficult to discuss the progress of the search with her now. Every forward move was a move towards the General and, however hard he strove as a lover, Fisher had no surety that in a confrontation Paula would choose him and not her father. In his darker moods, he would have bet on the General every time.

'You mean you've solved the little riddle about Aunty Ambrosine?'

'It was a code name for a Resistance group,' Fisher explained. This much he had told Paula. 'Jacquot was the name for a courier in the group. I managed to get enough information about him to make sense of most of it. The last bit, your mother may be able to fill in.' He addressed Paula and squeezed her hand, asking for forgiveness. She responded and for the moment Fisher relaxed. Dunston ordered them another drink. The subject changed to Dunston's business in Paris, and Paula withdrew from the discussion. She sat holding Fisher's hand, looking at both of them and wondering what they had ever had in common. The moody, possessive man beside her was a different breed of human being. The other was cheerful and self-confident; she applied that elusive word 'breezy' to him and it was an apt description. Nothing would bother Dunston, whereas the more she knew Fisher the more complicated she discovered him to be. Sexual surrender hadn't satisfied him; he conducted what could only be termed a war when they went to bed, a campaign of calculated seduction which was designed to dominate her completely. And the tragic truth, which she could never let him see, was that his success in one field ensured his failure in another. Paula would not be sensually dominated; her body and emotions were interdependent; she was not yet ready to surrender both to Fisher, even though she loved him. And she did love him; she insisted upon that. She needed to love him in order to deny his constant assertion that she didn't. When he left her at night she often cried. It could have been a happy, fulfilling relationship, so different from the one she had experienced in her marriage, but his possessiveness and insecurity were ruining it for both of them. She should have warned him, but she couldn't. He was too strong for her and at the same time too vulnerable. She felt unhappy and confused, but still determined. Fisher was not enough to fill the wasted years; he couldn't answer the question which had to be answered if she were ever to know peace or independence of spirit. What manner of man was her father, the General? Was he the inhuman brute of old Madame

Brevet's wild denunciation, or the tender father of a little girl, doting and sentimental?

Fisher couldn't forgive this hunger to know. He saw it as a personal slight, a proof that she was still free of him and able to choose something else. And she was free; with her hand imprisoned in his, Paula felt a desperate need of that liberty of choice, of the freedom to see her whole life in true perspective once. She had been alone too long and independence had been thrust upon her. Now a man had come into her life who wanted her to give herself completely. She couldn't do it. She gently withdrew her hand on the pretext of lighting a cigarette. Dunston was speaking to her again.

'Are you going back to England to see your mother too, Mrs Stanley?'

'No,' Paula said. 'I'm not. I'm staying here.'

'And when are you going?' he asked Fisher.

'Tuesday,' Fisher said. 'I'll only be away one night.'

'Oh well.' Dunston's smile beamed at both of them. 'In that case Mrs Stanley could come and help me with my shopping. That would be great. All right by you, Eric?'

'Why not.' Fisher was surly. 'If Paula wants to . . .'

'And don't you worry,' Dunston said happily. 'I'll take good care of her while you're away. Now let's go and eat some dinner. I'm starving.'

Paula was sitting in the lounge of the hotel; she had taken a chair facing the entrance and as soon as the tall, fair man walked through the door and stood, looking round, she knew that this must be Philip Von Hessel. She had the opportunity to study him while he paused, looking round the room to see which of the lone women she might be. He was one of the best-looking men she had ever seen; he held himself with an arrogant grace that was without self-consciousness. So did a man look, with a hundred million and an ancient title to buttress his personality. Added to which were the advantages of youth and that Wagnerian face. He caught Paula's glance, and moved towards her. She got up and came to meet him, holding out her hand. 'Prince Von Hessel?'

'Yes. Mrs Stanley . . .'

He took her hand and kissed it, bowing a little. The telephone call had been such a surprise that when he asked her to meet him for a few minutes, in Fisher's absence, Paula hadn't been able to think of an excuse. He had sounded older on the telephone, very precise and rather grave, like many foreigners who spoke good English but were out of practice.

The reality was very different. He took a seat beside her, offered her a cigarette and asked if he might order her a drink. He smiled, and Paula felt an impact of charm. She realised that except for her mother, this was the first of her countrymen that she had ever met.

But she had forgotten Schwarz, with the bright eyes that burned at her, sitting hunched up in her office. He had been German too, like the handsome young man sitting at her side.

'I hope you'll forgive me for intruding myself on you,' the Prince said. 'I had hoped to talk to Mr Fisher, but I have also been anxious to meet you. When the hotel said you were in, it seemed too good an opportunity to miss.'

Paula noticed that he wore a black tie. 'I'm very glad to meet you,' she said. 'May I say how sorry I am about what happened to your brother?'

'Thank you.' Philip Von Hessel looked down. 'My mother is here; we are taking my brother's body home as soon as the formalities are completed. Have you been to Germany, Mrs Stanley?'

Paula changed the subject gladly. 'No, never. I shall do one day, but my mother left at the end of the war and she's never been back.'

'A number of people have cut themselves off because of the past,' he said. 'Even people like your mother, who were only innocent bystanders. I think it is a pity. Do you mind my saying this?'

'Not at all,' Paula answered. 'I was brought up to be ashamed of what I was, without ever being told the reason. Now at least I know it.'

'You are not responsible for the past either,' he said gently. 'No more am I, Mrs Stanley. Your father committed crimes, well, so did my family. We are just becoming acceptable to the civilised world, both ourselves and our nation. Because, of course, they need us. So don't feel too guilty. We are not so black and the rest of the world white, I assure you.'

Paula looked at him. 'My father stole a family treasure from you' she said. 'But you're not bitter – you can talk about him so calmly. I think it's very admirable of you. And I'm glad to meet you, Prince Von Hessel, because I have something to say to you.'

'Please,' he said. The expression in his eyes was gentle. 'You don't have to say anything to me.'

'But I want to.' Paula turned towards him. 'It's possible that I have a legal claim to the Poellenberg Salt. I don't know if this is true, but if by any chance it is, I want you to know that as far as I'm concerned the Salt belongs to your family. I shall hand it over to you immediately.'

'That is a very generous thing to say,' he said. 'I appreciate it deeply. But do you know how valuable it is?'

'I know,' Paula said. 'It couldn't be priced. But that's not my concern. It was taken from you; by whatever means within the law, it was morally illegal, I'm sure of that. And you must have it back. I just wanted to tell you this. There won't be any difficulties or wrangling about ownership. It's your property.'

'Mrs Stanley.' He spoke quietly, twisting the broad gold signet ring upon his little finger. 'I repeat, that is the most generous thing I've ever heard. But can I ask you something?'

'Yes,' Paula said. 'Ask me whatever you like.'

'If you don't want the Poellenberg Salt,' he said, 'will you use your influence with Mr Fisher to call off the search? It's terribly important to me. I don't want it found, Mrs Stanley. I don't ever want to see it again. I can't make any impression on him, or my mother. I shall continue to try with her if you could possibly talk to him.'

'Why don't you want it?' Paula asked. 'It's one of the treasures of the world. Why wouldn't you have it back?'

'I can't tell you that,' he said seriously. 'So please don't ask me. I know I have no right to say this, because I'm only a stranger to you, but you must believe me when I tell you that it is a bloodstained thing, and it's better left wherever your father hid it. Please; would you do this for me?'

He had nice eyes, as he talked he had leaned across and laid his hand on her arm. Suddenly it moved down and closed upon hers. It gave her a shock to feel its warmth. Slowly she shook her head.

'I can't do that,' she said. 'It's just not possible. I'm not with Eric Fisher to find the Poellenberg Salt, I'm here looking for my father. If I find it, I believe I'll find him. I can't help you, Prince Philip. I only wish I could.'

'I see,' he said. He took his hand away. 'I'm sorry, I became emotional. I didn't know this, or I wouldn't have asked you.'

'I don't expect anyone to understand,' Paula said. 'Anyway, nobody does. I never knew him. I told you, I was brought up to be ashamed of being his child, ashamed of being German. My name was changed, my nationality, everything. And then I was told about him. He began to take shape for me. Nobody ever loved me, Prince Philip; forgive me if I'm being emotional now, but it's true. My mother didn't and my husband didn't. Now someone does, but I'm afraid it's come too late. I need my father. I need to see him and judge him for myself. He's a war criminal, and he's been on the run for nearly thirty years. And whatever he's done I must be the only person in the world who cares about him. Or would help him. That's why there's nothing I can do.'

'I understand,' the Prince said quietly. 'I too would feel the same; it is our German blood. We all have a strong sense of family. For your sake I hope you find him – without the Salt. The irony is, only one person wants it. My mother. It has become an obsession with her.'

'Why did you say it was bloodstained?' Paula said. 'What did you mean?'

'I can't explain that either,' Philip Von Hessel said. 'Mrs Stanley, would you do me a favour?'

'If I can,' Paula answered.

'Would you have dinner with me before I go back to Germany? I promise not to talk about the Salt.'

'That's very nice of you.' Paula stood up. She held out her hand and he kissed it, touching her fingers with his mouth. 'I could tell you about your country,' he said quietly. 'We have much to be ashamed of, but also much in which we can take pride. It would give me great pleasure. Say you will come.'

'I will,' Paula answered. 'I shall be alone on Tuesday evening. Perhaps we can meet then.'

'I have an engagement for Tuesday,' Philip said. 'But I shall cancel it. I will come here at eight. Goodbye, Mrs Stanley. Or better still, *auf wiedersehen.*'

The garden in Essex was a kaleidoscope of roses. The formal rose garden was one of the sights of the district; the Ridgeways had been persuaded to open the gardens for charity, and on a blazing July afternoon a crowd of well over a hundred were walking through the trees and lawns, wandering alongside the wide herbaceous border which was the loving work of Paula's mother. The Brigadier hovered on the perimeter, pausing to answer questions about the various plants and some of the rarities in the small walled enclave which he tended himself. Gardening was a passion, taken up as a hobby in the years following his retirement and developed into an absorbing pastime in which his wife shared with as much enthusiasm.

He could see her walking among the roses, smiling and talking to the visitors; he felt a pang of pride and love as he watched her, cool in a pastel linen dress, her grey blonde hair shining in the sunlight, as beautiful and dignified in old age as she had been as a young woman.

There was nothing he would not do or had not done to preserve that air of calm serenity, to see her smile and pass through life untroubled by care. She had suffered too much to endure even a moment's disquiet or a qualm of pain. She had given him a love and contentment which he had never imagined to be within the grasp of a man as simple as himself. The debt could never be repaid except by a lifetime of care and protectiveness. It made him happy just to be alive and act as a buffer between her and life. He was answering a middle-aged couple's enquiries about a miniature specie clematis which rioted in shades of purple and white along the edge of an old red brick wall, when the cook, who had worked for them since they moved into the house, came down the path towards him.

There was a telephone call for him; he excused himself and went towards the house, walking slowly in the heat, wondering which of their friends had been inconsiderate enough to call on a day when they were open to the public. The local Red Cross was the Ridgeways' favourite charity and it benefited every year from this particular occasion.

The line crackled, with the atmospherics peculiar to English rural telephone systems.

'Brigadier Ridgeway?'

'Yes. Who is it?'

'Eric Fisher; Dunston and Fisher detective agency. I came to see you and your wife about two weeks ago.'

The Brigadier held the receiver closer to his ear. 'Who? I'm sorry, the line is bad.' He hadn't wanted to hear the name, his denial was instinctive. The words were repeated. This time he couldn't pretend to himself, there was no escape. He swore, one hand over the mouthpiece.

'I've nothing to say to you.' He raised his voice. 'And you've chosen a very inconvenient time to telephone.'

'I'm coming to England tomorrow,' the voice said. 'I want to come and see you. It's very important. You know Paula's with me.'

'I know,' Ridgeway said. 'What my step-daughter does is her own affair. It's nothing to do with us.'

'It's very much to do with you. I have to talk to you and her mother. Will you see me?'

'No.' The Brigadier was shouting down the telephone. 'No, certainly not. I won't have you here bothering my wife!'

'There's a strong possibility that she's not legally married to you.' He could hear Fisher clearly now, the crackling on the line had stopped and the awful words might have been spoken in the room.

'I'm pretty sure that General Bronsart is alive. I think you'd better see me. I'll fly over tomorrow morning and drive straight down.'

'Go to hell!' He rammed the telephone down and stood there looking at it as if it had displayed a malevolent life of its own. Slowly he sank to a chair, an old man whose knees were trembling. His legs were the only part of him to show the sign of age; that and the weakness in his chest which worried his wife every time he caught a cold. He put his hands over his face and his head dropped.

'Oh my God,' he said. 'Oh my God, my God.' Outside in the bright sunshine the couple who had been waiting for him to come back, gave up and decided to walk on.

*

Philip Von Hessel faced his mother; she was sitting up in bed, the breakfast tray across her knees. It was a brilliant morning, and the room was full of sunlight. Paris was emptying as the summer advanced; there were few Parisians left. The tourist crowds abounded, making the city an alien place. The Ritz was full of Americans, which annoyed the Princess, who found their accents and their ubiquitous presence in the hallowed places of the European aristocracy particularly irksome. She glanced at her handsome son and her expression softened. Of all the human beings with whom she had made contact in her long life, she loved Philip the best. No qualm of sentiment for her dead son had troubled her mind. She was a relic of an age when grief was regarded as an indulgence, the luxury of the inferior classes whose women shrouded their heads in their aprons and cried. Marriage with the Prince Von Hessel had withered any sensibilities she might have had in her youth. She held out her hand to Philip; he bent and kissed her.

'You're sure you don't want me with you?' he said.

'No, it's better you stay here. Fisher will be away in England for a day and a night. The funeral will take place privately; I shall give it out that you're ill. You must be here in case he comes back with something decisive. He seemed very confident on the telephone.'

'There will be photographers at the airport,' Philip said. 'There are half a dozen hanging round the entrance already.'

'The authorities have promised that we shall get away without being bothered,' she said. 'As soon as it is over, I shall fly back. In the meantime I leave it in your hands. I feel it will all turn out for the best for us. Promise me you won't worry. This will be the end of a long and troublesome period for our family. From now on it will be up to you to expunge the past and build up what I have preserved. I know you'll do it.'

'I will,' he promised. 'You have my word.'

She thought how much he resembled his father, that gallant airman who had come so briefly and decisively into her life. Power, wealth, world influence. She leaned against the pillows, a little tired with the onset of emotion, yet mellow in her triumph that in spite of everything she had succeeded, and through her son, the future would be safe. For a moment their hands clasped. 'My son,' she said gently. 'I'm very proud of you.'

7

It was mid afternoon when Fisher's car drove up to the front door of the Ridgeways' house. He got out and the labradors came leaping up to investigate him, barking a welcome. Fisher didn't like dogs; he could honestly say that it was his only fear, that instinctive recoil from the leap and the bared teeth. He swore at them and they went backwards, puzzled and hurt. It was some moments before the door opened, and then it was the Brigadier who stood facing him.

'I told you not to come,' he said.

'I know,' Fisher answered quietly. 'But I have to see you. I'm not trying to be difficult or upset anyone. I told the truth on the phone. It's very important.'

The older man turned away, leaving the door open. Within the shadowy hall he turned.

'All right, come in then. My wife's waiting.'

Paula's mother was in the drawing room; she looked tense and there were shadows under her eyes. Fisher saw a resemblance to Paula in the way she stood, and the carriage of her head. He should have felt distaste for what he was going to do but he didn't. They had had their life together, these two, standing with their arms linked, united against him as they had been against her daughter.

'My husband told me what you said,' she began. 'Why do you say my first husband is alive? What proof have you?'

'He was seen in Paris,' Fisher said. 'That newspaper report was right. I interviewed the woman. She remembered the General, and she had good reason to; he ordered her son's execution. She saw him in a street and then he disappeared.' He saw Paula's mother clutch at the Brigadier's arm.

'I'm certain he's alive,' Fisher said. 'And in the circumstances you'd be well advised to help me get this business over. If the police pick him up, I imagine you'd find it rather embarrassing.'

'We married in good faith,' Ridgeway said stiffly. 'My wife was told he was killed in action. No blame can be attached to her.'

'It's no use, Gerald,' Mrs Ridgeway said suddenly. 'He knows what we have to fear. Public knowledge of my past, isn't that right? The wife of a war criminal, a woman who was arrested when the allied troops marched into Munich and held for weeks in prison. You didn't know that part, did you, Mr Fisher? I was the wife of a man who consorted with Hitler. I was spat upon, abused, humiliated – accused of complicity in my husband's crimes, denounced for having slave labour in my house. If one thing could have been proved against me I'd have been sent to prison for years! When they let me go home to my child, there was a screaming mob, howling and spitting at me outside the gates – I was almost broken; I thought of suicide. Then Gerald found me, burning the furniture in the grate to keep myself and Paula warm, without enough food to eat, too ashamed to go out and beg for it like the rest of the German civilians. I hated my first husband; he was a cruel and heartless brute and I thanked God when I heard he was dead! But I was the only one who could be punished for what he had done. I suffered, Mr Fisher; it's taken all these years of living with a man like my husband to make me forget it. If I have to live through that shame again, I shall die. So there's no point in your talking about "embarrassment" and trying to frighten us. We know what we have to fear. The loss of our friends, the glare of publicity. Can't you see it? "War criminal's wife discovered in Essex village. Brigadier committed bigamy during the war." My God, embarrassed! This means the ruin of our lives. We're respected and liked here; Gerald has had a distinguished career; we've lived happily and decently for nearly thirty years. If you want to ask me questions, I shall answer them. But understand that nothing you can do or say can frighten me now. No, darling,' she turned to her husband. 'Let me do this. We can't go on hiding. We will always have each other.'

'One moment,' the Brigadier interrupted, speaking to Fisher. 'One moment; before my wife says anything to you I want to ask a question. If you find the General, what do you propose to do?'

'Nothing,' Fisher said. 'I'm looking for the Poellenberg Salt, I'm not interested in catching war criminals. In fact, Mrs Ridgeway, as things have turned out, I'm as anxious to keep him under cover as you are. You know Paula's looking for him? She's got an obsession about him; she thinks she's going to find a helpless, hunted old man who needs someone to take care of him. I don't think she knows it herself, but she hasn't the slightest intention of seeing him once and then letting him go out of her life. And if they come together, I shall lose her. She'll go off with him. I don't want that to happen.'

'We didn't know you were involved,' the Brigadier said.

'You didn't ask,' Fisher said sharply. 'You've left Paula to get on with the whole dirty mess, just thinking of yourselves. If I may say so, Mrs Ridgeway, you had no right to keep your daughter in the dark about her father. If you'd told her the truth, she wouldn't have this terrible hang-up. God knows what effect it'll have on her if they ever do meet. I want to prevent it. As far as I'm concerned the General can stay hidden for ever. If he does come into the open, I want to be sure that Paula's not anywhere near. He can go straight back where he came from and stay there. That's why I want to find the Salt. If he's going to appear at all, that is where he'll choose, hoping to find her digging it out. I'm not going to let things happen that way. I want to marry her. I hope you get the picture now.'

'I see.' Mrs Ridgeway turned to her husband. 'Darling, this could be the best thing for all of us. How can I help you, Mr Fisher?'

'I know he was in Paris,' Fisher said. 'In June 1944. But I can't find out where he was living. It was naturally kept a secret because the Resistance were after him; he was high on their murder list by that date. Do you know where his quarters were, Mrs Ridgeway? Believe me, everything depends on my finding this out.'

'Of course I know,' Paula's mother answered. She had her arm linked through her husband's; now she disengaged it and made a movement with her hand.

'I know exactly where he was. I spent a weekend with him. Why don't we all sit down?'

'Mrs Stanley? Good morning to you. Joe Dunston here.'

'Oh, hallo,' Paula answered sleepily. Fisher had left her in the early hours. She was tired and depressed after the night they had spent together. For the first time she had been unresponsive, miserable and tense in spite of all his efforts to arouse her. He had failed, and the effect upon him was profound.

He had said very little, sitting up in the bed, apart from her, staring into the darkened room. 'You're not in love with me any more, are you?'

When Paula denied it he didn't seem to hear.

'I know you're not,' he had continued as if she hadn't spoken to him. 'I know it's over for you. You didn't feel a damned thing, did you?'

'I'm tired,' she protested, near to tears. 'Darling, it's the first time it hasn't been wonderful for both of us. Don't make something out of nothing.'

'Nothing,' Fisher had said, throwing back the bedclothes, 'is the operative word. I'll let you go to sleep now. I'll try and call you from England, I'm leaving early in the morning.' And he had gone, letting in a brief shaft of light from the passage outside as he opened her door. Paula had lain awake for a long time. She had cried, but it was more for him than for herself. She was empty, unable to be rushed away on the tide of his sexuality, able for the first time since they became lovers, to resist his assault upon her. It hadn't worked. The thought came to her that it might never work again. When she finally fell asleep it was an uneasy rest, disturbed by dreams of journeys where she was prevented from arriving. As she took Dunston's call, she looked at her watch and saw that it was past ten o'clock. Fisher had caught the eight-thirty plane.

'I didn't wake you up, did I?' The hearty voice broke into a laugh.

'Just as well you did,' Paula said. 'It's terribly late.'

'You must have had a gay evening,' Dunston said.

'Yes,' Paula answered. 'Yes, I did.'

'I know our boy's gone to England today and I wondered whether you might take that shopping expedition with me.' There was a few seconds' pause. 'I'd appreciate it very much, if it wouldn't be a nuisance to you. My taste in clothes is terrible.'

'Of course it wouldn't be a nuisance.' She pushed the hair back from her face and leaned against the pillow which still bore Fisher's imprint.

'I'd be delighted. Where do you want to go?'

'No idea,' he said. 'Somewhere not too cheap, but not exactly Christian Dior. I'd like to leave that up to you.'

'Well, let me think – how about Lafayettes – they have some nice clothes and they're not desperately expensive.'

'Anything you say.' Dunston sounded delighted. 'Where is it? I'd better go direct there, if you don't mind, because I've got an appointment in about twenty minutes. Say about eleven-thirty, quarter to twelve?'

'That would be fine,' Paula said. 'I'll meet you downstairs in the main entrance. A quarter to twelve?'

'Wonderful. And thanks a million. Bye bye.'

Paula got up and went into the bathroom. Under the electric light the dark shadows associated with a night spent making love, were deep under her eyes. The first man in her life hadn't cared enough about her; now she was caught up with one who cared too much. He wanted what she couldn't give him, the full possession of herself. James had complained of her shyness; for a time it seemed that Fisher had smashed through the reserves which kept her aloof. But now the barriers were going up again, and this, more than the failure of one night together, was what he had sensed and what had driven him to leave her in despair. Despair threatened Paula too, the despair of her returning solitude, of the knowledge that she was moving away from Fisher, from loving and being loved, back into the world of lonely waiting. Waiting. That was the right description. She showered and dressed, getting ready for her appointment with Dunston. Waiting for something or someone. And what made her glad to spend the time with Dunston was fear that the someone was not Eric Fisher after all. She hated herself for hurting him. He had told her she was the first woman he had ever loved, and she believed him. And unlike her, there had been no holding back, no reservations.

As the situation was developing, Paula knew she might inflict a mortal wound. And this was inconceivable. She owed him too much; she even owed herself the chance of being happy. She got up, checked her bag for the room key, and made a resolution to be especially affectionate and reassuring when he phoned.

Outside the hotel, seated at a café on the pavement opposite, Dunston watched over a newspaper and saw her come out into the sunshine, hail a taxi and get in. He paid for his coffee, threw his newspaper away and went round the side to the back entrance. He had got her room number from the switchboard when he phoned. There was nobody about when he opened the door and stepped inside a grubby passage; there was a smell of kitchens and rubbish, and a dingy cat fled into a closet as he came upon it. Dunston moved carefully, trying doors. He found the entrance to the service stairs and began to climb them. At the first floor he came out on the main landing and went to the elevator. It was automatic; when it arrived, there were two passengers on the way up. Dunston got in, touched his hat to the couple, and pressed the button marked 3. At the third floor he got out, and he went up the corridor towards room 339. There was no one about; at that hour all the beds had been made. His only danger was the chambermaid coming in to tidy up that particular room. It was a chance he had to take; in less than a minute he had picked the lock of the door.

It was untidy, the bed in confusion; he walked to the window and pulled down the blind. Then he switched on the light and looked round. It was not a very luxurious room; the colour scheme was pastel blue, the furniture mahogany and modern in design. A bowl of roses stood on the writing table. Dunston guessed they were from Fisher. He went over to look at them and open the table drawer. There was nothing inside but some sheets of hotel writing paper, a few envelopes and a laundry list. He glanced at the make-up bottles and the rank of lipsticks. Powder, very expensive scent, in a five-ounce bottle. He wondered whether that were Fisher again. Then he went to the closet and looked through Paula's clothes. He searched everything without knowing yet what he was looking for; he picked up the silk nightdress she had worn, and suffered a qualm of lust.

Then he went into the bathroom. More bottles, toothbrush, paste, combs and a hair-brush. No pills of any kind. Obviously not a neurotic. There couldn't be any accidental overdose. The floor of the bathroom was still wet; on an impulse Dunston pulled back the shower curtain; drops of water spattered him. He looked up and then suddenly he stood quite still. He hadn't gone to look for it; he hadn't even thought it could be found; the idea was so old-fashioned. But there it was. A long-barred electric fire, high up on the wall above the bath. He reached over and pulled the cord. The element began to turn red. It was above eye level, he was tall and he had to tilt up to see it, burning away there on the wall, designed to warm the bather's naked body as they got out of the water. He pulled the cord again and the heat faded. Twice more he jerked at the cord, and each time he used less pressure. Sometimes they could be stiff. This one was loose. He began to whistle softly. He took the end of the cord and slipped the tiny knob under one of the plastic rings holding the shower curtain. Then he switched the curtain round the bath. Immediately the fire turned on. He unhooked the cord. Then he slipped off his shoes and climbed on to the edge of the bath; this brought him level with the fire. He made a careful examination, and stepped down. He would need time, and no fear of being disturbed. His watch said it was already eleven forty-five. She would be waiting at Galleries Lafayette. He had to go. He went out of the bathroom, pulled up the window shade and slipped through the door. As he hurried down the passage to the lift, he saw the maid come through the service door, pushing her trolley for the dirty linen. Fifteen minutes later he arrived, breathless and full of excuses, to meet Paula at the store.

When Fisher telephoned the hotel that afternoon there was no reply from Paula's room. He had lunched at a pub an hour's drive from the Ridgeways' house. The end of the search was only a flight away across the Channel, a matter of making the necessary arrangements and letting the Princess Von Hessel know that she would soon be in possession of the Salt.

Fisher had sat in the pub bar, eating sandwiches and drinking beer, wishing he were able to speak to Paula. He intended breaking his promise; when he told her mother he hoped to prevent her finding her father again, it was a desperate resolve born of his fear that the anti-climax of the night before he left for England was the first sign of Paula moving away from him. She was keeping apart in order to be free, when the moment of choice came. He smoked and sat on, moody and unhappy, despising himself for cheating her and yet convinced that he had no alternative. She wanted love; he could satisfy that need, he had proved that his was more than just a sexual hunger. He wanted her as he had never imagined he could want anyone, she aroused such a dread of losing her, that he no longer recognised his own personality. He had become jealous, obsessed. He would do anything to prevent Paula from escaping on some crazy mixed-up pretext that her father's need of her came first. Fisher had seriously thought of turning the General into the police if he appeared. He had no other way of contacting his daughter, except by waiting till she came to where the Salt was hidden. And she just wasn't going to be there; Fisher left the pub and began to drive to London; she wasn't going to be anywhere near the Salt, and if her father materialised, then Fisher could either scare him off or turn him in. In his present frame of mind he would have preferred the latter course. But if he were caught she would never forgive Fisher. If he never appeared, as far as she knew, then Fisher felt he had a chance of being accepted as a final substitute. As for her claim to the Salt, he was only too anxious to waive that too, if indeed she really had one. Let the Von Hessels have it; let the whole bloody business come to its conclusion and let him get her back. They could get married and start looking for a home. Fisher, the professional nomad, who had never bothered to do more than rent a furnished flat, found himself yearning for a home, with possessions, and a wife. And children. He had even thought that far ahead. He reached his agency's office and put through the call to their hotel. When she was out he banged down the receiver. Uncertainty remained until he could talk to her, and repair the damage. And he had done damage, walking out like that. His male pride had been affronted, and his insecurity had overwhelmed his common sense. He had behaved like a fool. He booked in another call for an hour later and then telephoned through to Princess Von Hessel in Munich. Her response was short but full of excitement; he could hear the tone of her voice changing as he talked.

'When will it be?'

'Tomorrow, if you can fix it with the hotel.'

'Leave that to me. I shall fly down tonight. You've done very well.'

'Thanks,' Fisher said. 'I'm coming back to Paris tomorrow and I'll contact you.' He hung up. It seemed almost unreal that the explanation was at once so simple and so clever. He was a clever man, the General, with an ironic twist of mind. No caves in isolated places, no chilly Swiss lakes, for his treasure. He had hidden it where nobody would ever think of looking, and where it was easily accessible to anyone who knew. Very clever. And not to be discounted even at the end. He would emerge; Fisher was sure of it. At some moment he would step forward out of the shadows, to claim his daughter and the loot he had secreted all those years ago. Fisher was going to make sure that he got neither of them.

The second call came through after a short delay. It was no more successful than the first. Paula had not returned to her hotel.

Dunston gave her lunch after their shopping expedition. They bought a smart coat and dress for his wife; the first of many, he reminded

himself privately, when his assignment was complete. He set out to
be cheerful and amusing; he had a way with women, which had
come in very useful over the years. He had joked his way into
some inaccessible beds, rather to the surprise of the women who
found themselves laughing and seduced at the same time. He would
have given Fisher serious competition with Paula Stanley, if he hadn't
been otherwise committed . . .

'Well,' he said, taking her arm as they came out of the restaurant
into the street, 'now where to? Back to your hotel?'

'No,' Paula answered. 'I'm going to have my hair done, it looks
awful.'

'Not to me it doesn't,' Dunston said. 'You look good enough to eat,
if I hadn't had a good lunch already. Speaking of lunch, what are you
doing for dinner tonight?'

'I'm going out,' Paula said. 'But thanks anyway. I do hope your
wife likes the dress.'

'She'll be thrilled,' Dunston grinned. 'So long as she never knows a
beautiful girl helped me to choose it. Where's the hairdresser's? I'll drop
you off.'

He got out of the taxi, shook hands with her, still showing his excellent white teeth in a friendly smile; he waited until she had gone inside
and he saw her checking in at the desk for her appointment. He told
the taxi to take him to an electrical suppliers. There he bought pliers
with a cutting edge, a screwdriver with an adjustable head for large
and small screws, a yard and a half of cable, and a roll of insulating
tape. He hailed another cab and gave the address of Paula's hotel.

He went up to the reception.

'Mrs Stanley, please.'

'One moment, I'll call her room.'

Dunston waited. Glancing round the hotel foyer, the package with
his purchases under one arm. She just might have used the hairdresser
as an excuse to get rid of him. She might have gone in without booking
an appointment and been told they were full up. He had to make
absolutely sure she wasn't in her room.

The reception clerk looked at him and shook his head. 'There's no
reply, monsieur. Mrs Stanley went out this morning, and I haven't seen
her come back.'

'Never mind,' Dunston said. 'I just took a chance.'

'You wish to leave a message?'

'No thanks. I'll phone this evening.' He walked out into the street
and turned left. He passed a couple of women gossiping; he opened
the service entrance to the hotel and went inside. He reached Paula's
room through the back stairs, avoiding the lift. At that hour in the
afternoon none of the hotel staff was about, and he didn't wish to

be seen by any of the residents. He picked the lock on her door as he had done earlier and went inside, closing it carefully after him. He slipped the catch down; if anyone should come, or Paula herself returned unexpectedly, he would have warning and be able to clear away any tools . . .

The room was tidy; the bathroom was draped with clean towels and there was a smell of abrasive cleaner. He saw a trace of white powder on the shelf above the lavatory. The shower curtain was pulled back. He undid his parcel, laid the cable, the insulating tape and the screwdriver on the lavatory seat, took off his shoes, and climbed on the bath edge to inspect the electric fire above it. He picked up the screwdriver and began to work. Ten minutes later he lifted the fire carefully away from the wall. It came down some six inches and then hung, caught by the cable connecting it at the back. Dunston gingerly let go; the cable was thick and strong and the fire held. He hesitated a moment, making up his mind. Then he gave a slight shrug and pushed it back against the wall, he screwed in two main screws to secure it temporarily, and then got down. Outside he found the corridor empty, and began walking the length looking for the fuse box. It wasn't there. He opened the service door and saw it on the wall. It was too high to reach. He swore unpleasantly. There must be some way of getting up to it. He found a door and turned it. It was a cupboard and inside, among the feather dusters, brooms, tins of cleaning powder and polish, there was a step ladder. He opened the fuse box, and looked at his watch. It was three forty-eight. Nobody was likely to have lights on, or be using electricity on the floor at that hour. And by the size of the fuse box, each floor had its own separate electrical unit, so that failure on one floor didn't mean cutting off the entire electricity supply for the hotel.

Dunston pushed the mains switch to off, quickly replaced the step ladder in the cupboard, glanced into the corridor to make sure nobody was walking down, and went back to the room at a run. Inside the bathroom he worked very quickly. He disconnected the fire from its cable and joined the extra length to the end; this he then reconnected to the fire. Gently he let it hang, and the result satisfied him. Fully extended on the new lead, the fire hung down into the well of the bath. It was directly in line with the shower head. He lifted it up and pushed the extra cable length into the hole in the wall; then he wedged the fire with one hand and fitted two screws loosely into their holes, giving each a couple of turns. The fire held; he caught the cord and pushed the knob through the ring of the shower curtain. He pulled the curtain, the cord jerked, and at the same moment the fire came loose and toppled down. Dunston caught it long before it had reached the end of the cable. He was standing in the bath, and if he hadn't been prepared it would have hit him. As it would hit anyone standing naked and wet who pulled back that shower curtain. The fire would turn on and fall at the same moment. With the extra length of cable it would be as lethal as a bullet. She would be instantly electrocuted. If she were sitting in the bath and touched the curtain, the effect of the fire hitting the water would be the same. And it would be an accident. The hotel would be held responsible for a faulty fitting. He replaced the fire, put in all the screws, and turned the two biggest just enough to give a slight purchase. He fixed the end of the cord into the curtain ring. He stood for a moment looking up. It was high on the wall and the shower curtain itself obscured it. If she was going out to dinner as she said, she would come back and take a shower. And that, Dunston said coolly to himself, would be that. Fisher would be very cut up. But then, breaking eggs was an intrinsic part of making omelettes. She was a nice girl and he didn't wish her any harm. It was just her bad luck to be the price of being very rich. He put his tools, the paper they had been wrapped in, in his pocket, opened the door and went back to the service passage and the fuse box. He switched on the electricity supply, left the steps in their original place in the cleaning cupboard, and ran down the stairs to the side entrance. It had been completed in just under an hour. He went back to his hotel in a taxi, ordered himself a bottle of brandy and lay on his bed to wait. After the second drink, he fell asleep.

'I've been trying to get you all day. Where the hell have you been?'

Paula was undressing when the telephone rang. She had got in, hot and exhausted after the hairdresser's, and then taking a walk through the warm streets, enjoying the atmosphere of the city in the early evening, when the cafés were filling up and the tourists paraded up and down, window shopping and staring round them. She should have gone back to the hotel, but there was something bleak and uninviting about the empty room. Paula avoided it, and in the meantime her telephone shrilled unanswered, until Fisher's call came through again and she was there.

'I went shopping with Joe Dunston,' she explained.

'Not till this hour, for Christ's sake,' he said. He sounded angry. 'What were you doing?'

'We had lunch and then I went to have my hair done and I've been wandering around. Why do you sound so upset, darling? I'm sorry I wasn't here, but I didn't know what time you'd be telephoning.' She lay back on the bed, one arm above her head, listening to Fisher's sharp, accusing voice. The room was hot and still, the light just beginning to fade. She felt tears come to her eyes. This was not what she had planned; this wasn't the mending of the breach. It was opening still wider, and she couldn't stop it.

'I suppose he made a pass at you? He always does.'

'Please don't be silly. He was very nice and we bought something for his wife. I don't know what's the matter with you. Tell me, did you see my mother?'

'Yes, I saw her. What are you doing now?'

'Lying on the bed talking to you. What did she say?'

'Nothing much,' Fisher lied. 'She wouldn't co-operate at all. I wish I was with you. I'd make up for last night. I'm crazy about you, you know that, don't you? I'm even jealous of that bloody fool Dunston.'

'You needn't be,' Paula said gently. 'I wish you were here too. When are you coming back?'

'Tomorrow. I'm not sure what time. Do you still love me?'

'Yes,' she said. 'Yes, of course I do.'

'All right then,' Fisher said. 'Take care of yourself. I'll see you tomorrow.'

'Goodbye,' she said. She put the telephone down and lay still. She should have told him about Philip Von Hessel but she hadn't. And if he were jealous of someone as harmless as Joe Dunston . . . They had parted on a better note; he sounded mollified. And her mother had told him nothing. Paula closed her eyes. She wouldn't help. It had been a wasted journey; the phone was ringing again. She glanced at her watch and sat up. She wanted to have a bath before she changed to meet Philip. But it was Philip on the line.

'Mrs Stanley? I wonder if I could come round earlier. Have you spoken to Mr Fisher?'

'Yes, just a few minutes ago.'

'Then you must be excited. My mother told me; she is coming down late tonight.'

Paula sat up. 'What do you mean, excited. What's happened?'

'Didn't he tell you? He knows where the Salt is. We are going to get it tomorrow.'

'No,' she said. 'No, he didn't tell me. What time do you want to come?'

'It's seven o'clock now. I would like to meet my mother's plane, it arrives at eleven. If I could come to your hotel in about twenty minutes we could have dinner a little early. Would you mind . . . ?'

'No, of course not. I'll be ready by half past seven. Goodbye.' She got up slowly. Fisher had lied to her. Whatever he had wanted from her mother, he had got it. He knew where the Salt was, and he had denied it. She went into the bathroom. The window was open but it was stifling hot. She went to the bath and dropped in the plug, turning on both taps. They were going to find the Salt. Tomorrow, Prince Philip had said. Fisher had alerted the Von Hessels and said nothing to her. Suddenly she felt sick; sick with the sense of his deceit. She had trusted him, loved him. In his way he had been no more true to her than James. Philip had told her; Fisher hadn't counted upon that twist of circumstance when he said he loved her and lied to her at the same time. The Prince would soon be calling for her. There wasn't time to have a bath. Paula shut off the taps and jerked out the plug. She washed at the basin and changed into a dark silk dress. She wore a long string of pearls which James had given her; her hair was burnished and chic, she made up lightly and used Fisher's expensive scent. A glance at her watch showed the time to be seven-thirty. She went out and down in the lift to wait for Philip Von Hessel.

A great number of women had tried to capture Philip. From the time he was in his teens, girls had ogled and simpered in his direction, and their activities became more serious as he grew older and more eligible. There had been flirtations and love affairs; he had a mistress of three years' standing who was already married and had long since abandoned any hope that he might marry her. But he had never fallen in love to the extent of asking any girl to be his wife. Like royalty, the Von Hessels either married cousins or into other families of similar eminence. It was unthinkable that Philip should look outside his own circle or have serious intentions towards a woman of lesser background. As a result he remained an obdurate bachelor, waiting for the improbable to happen, and the appearance of someone suitable with whom he could be in love. Because without love, he rejected all his mother's arguments that he should marry. She had called him a sentimentalist, in some surprise and not with approbation, but once again he had shown a strength of will in parity with her own. He never baulked her except on an issue which he connected with his conscience, and this again baffled and irritated his mother. For her there was no moral code but that dictated by the expedience of the moment. In meeting Paula he had no intention of doing more than enlisting her help in getting Fisher to drop the search for the Salt. The invitation to come to dinner was spontaneous and afterwards he was a little surprised by his action. He was not a man who acted upon impulse, and this had been impulsive to a degree. She was not the most attractive nor the most beautiful woman he had met. His mistress was a magnificent blonde, acclaimed in her wealthy circle as a dazzling example of German womanhood. Paula could not compare in respect of elegance, presence or importance with the women who frequented his circle; they were exotic, pampered, creatures divorced from the reality of ordinary life. He had felt when he talked to her that he was with a living woman, vulnerable, uncertain, dignified and shy.

When he arrived in the foyer of the hotel and she got up to meet him, he felt elated, as if something unusual were about to happen.

'It's very kind of you to make our dinner earlier,' he said. He had taken her hand and kissed it. He looked down at her and smiled; he thought she looked pale and aloof, but after a brief moment she smiled back at him, and suddenly the atmosphere relaxed. In those first moments of a second meeting, much of the future was decided. The success of that evening was assured from the moment Philip took her arm and led her outside to the car. Again, he seldom indulged in physical contact. He had been brought up to abhor the casual pawing which was generally accepted as a social more – the kissing of comparative strangers, the instant use of Christian names, all the debased practices which had once dignified a relationship between two people. He never took a woman's arm and held it on a pretext. He settled into the back of the limousine and offered her a cigarette.

'Thank you,' Paula said. 'Tell me about the Salt. Where is it?'

'I don't know,' Philip answered. 'My mother only had time to tell me she was coming here and the search would be over tomorrow. She was hurrying to catch a plane. I can't understand why Mr Fisher didn't tell you; I thought that's why you were here.'

'I think I understand it.' Paula looked at him. 'The trouble is, I trusted him. Where are we going?'

'To the Grand Vefour,' Philip answered. 'It is quiet, but I think you will like it. I hope so.'

'I'm sure I shall,' she said. 'Let's wait till we get there and then we can talk about it.'

'We don't have to talk about it, if it distresses you,' he answered. 'And I feel it does. You look upset. I want this to be a pleasant evening for us both. After all, you won't accept another invitation if you don't enjoy yourself.'

'I don't suppose you get that many refusals,' Paula said. 'You're not married, are you?'

'No. I am a bachelor and the despair of my mother. She wants grand-children and I want to be happy. So it is stalemate. Here we are.'

It was an elegant restaurant, with the subdued atmosphere of the very exclusive and expensive, a haven for the rich gourmet who wished to concentrate upon the food and the company without distractions. There was no music, only a three-star menu and unobtrusive service that anticipated everything. Paula took her place at the table, and he noticed that several men were watching her.

'May I pay you a compliment?'

'Please do.'

'You are the most attractive woman in the room.'

'Thank you. Why do you laugh . . .'

'Because you have a simplicity that I find delightful, Mrs Stanley. I say something flattering, and you don't simper at me or try to deny it, you just say thank you. Where do you get your blue eyes? I've never seen such a colour.'

'I get them from my father,' Paula answered. 'Are you going to pay me a compliment about that?'

'No,' Philip said. 'I am not concerned with him. But I know that you are. You are no nearer finding him?'

'No,' Paula said. 'And if I depend upon Mr Fisher, I shall never do so. He doesn't want me to find the General. That's why he didn't tell me he had solved the clue about the Salt. He wants me to go back to England and forget about it all.'

'Why should he do that? Why is he involved in your life?'

'He's in love with me,' she answered. He had ordered a fine dry sherry and she sipped it. For some reason which she couldn't explain to herself, she wanted to tell this man the truth. He had a habit of looking very intently at her when she was speaking; it focused all his attention upon her. She found it intimate rather than disconcerting. He had fine eyes, with a serious expression in them that invited confidence.

'And you,' he asked her. 'I can understand him, but surely you are not . . . ?'

'I've been living with him,' Paula said slowly. 'He wants to marry me.'

'He has very good taste,' Philip remarked quietly. 'I am surprised that he appealed to you.'

'I was surprised too,' she said. 'But then he's very much a man, and this was something new to me. Very decisive; I felt so safe with him.'

'And do you love him?'

'I don't know.' She shook her head. He thought how narrow and white her neck was. 'I'm so angry with him and so disappointed. He's tried to cheat me. He knows that finding my father is the one thing in the world I have to do, and still he's cheated me and lied. I can't get over it. He's coming back tomorrow and I don't know how I'm going to face him. I wish I could move out of that hotel and not be there when he gets back.'

'Why don't you?' Philip said. 'Why don't you leave tonight?'

'I'd never get another room. Paris is full of tourists this time of year.

'We have the suite my brother occupied,' he said suddenly. 'Why don't you move in there? That's an excellent idea! It's empty and no one will use it, my mother has her own suite and so do I. It's completely wasted.'

'I couldn't do that,' Paula said.

'Why not? For a day or two, until we have recovered the Salt – then you will be going back to England. It would save you the embarrassment of seeing Fisher in the same hotel.'

'It might be easier,' she said. 'I want to break with him. I've made up my mind.'

'Then you don't love him,' the Prince said. 'And I would suggest that you never did. You were alone, and perhaps unhappy, and he seemed to be the answer. But he wasn't and no doubt you see that now.'

'I don't see anything except that I can't go on, and I don't want a hideous emotional scene,' Paula said. 'I'm so angry with him and so sorry for him.'

'You have a kind heart,' Philip said. 'I've never enjoyed hurting people either.'

'Especially,' Paula remarked, 'when one has been hurt oneself. My husband was an expert at crushing other people's sensibilities. By the time he and I were divorced, I didn't have an illusion left about myself. Eric gave me a lot of confidence. But he's lost his own, that's what has happened. He's afraid I shall find my father and choose him, and that's why he's broken his word to me and gone behind my back. He never thought I'd know.'

'And would you choose your father?'

'If he needed me,' she said. 'I don't know. Nobody could answer that. When you find the Salt, I want to be there.'

'You should be,' he said seriously. 'It may prove to be your property.'

'That's not the reason.' Paula turned to him. 'There may be some message from my father, something to lead me to him – I told you, I don't want the Salt!'

'I know you did,' he answered. 'And I promise you, as soon as I know what is going to happen I will tell you. I promise you. And you will find that unlike Mr Fisher, I don't break my word.'

'You haven't the same motive,' Paula said. 'I've destroyed him. He'll be better off without me anyway.'

'I don't think he'd agree with that,' Philip said. 'I feel sorry for him. If you will excuse me for a moment, I can telephone to the Ritz and tell them you'll be using the suite. It will be very much easier for you.'

'I know it will,' she answered. 'I'll take advantage of your offer; I can move in tonight.'

A few moments later he was back; he looked down at her and smiled.

'It is all arranged,' he said. 'You will be very comfortable. And nobody can trouble you there.'

'You're very kind,' Paula said. 'I do appreciate it.'

'It isn't necessary; I'm glad to help. Now let us enjoy our dinner and forget about unpleasant things. You have a charming smile, Mrs Stanley; I want to see it from now on.'

'You forget,' she said, 'it's the Austrians who are supposed to be gay. I'm straight middle German.'

'So am I,' he said. 'Perhaps that's why we understand each other. I know our temperament; we are the only race in the world who have ever tried to live their legends.'

'But only the sad, destructive ones, the *Götterdamnerung*.' Paula said. 'The awful thing is I love Wagner, too.'

'I hate him,' Philip said and laughed. 'It is Mozart for me. You're fond of music?'

'Very fond. Orchestral more than opera, always excepting Wagner.'

'Then you must come to Germany,' Philip said gently. 'There you will hear our music as it should be played. By Germans, for Germans.' He reached over and for a moment his hand rested upon hers. It was warm and the pressure lasted for some seconds. 'You must remember the good things about our people,' he said. 'The world will remind you often enough of what is wrong with us, of what we did in the past. But my answer to them is that it *is* the past; our duty now is to the future, And it's your duty too, Mrs Stanley. You are a German, and you have a place among your own race. Understand that, and you won't need anyone like Eric Fisher.'

'I was brought up to be ashamed of it,' Paula said. 'It was never mentioned, my father was never mentioned. My name and nationality were changed. And yet I've never felt English.'

'Our blood is strong,' Philip said. 'It isn't easy to suppress. Why did your mother do this to you?'

'Because of her own shame,' she answered. 'Because she hated my father and everything he stood for. And I believe now that she hated me; in a quiet way of course, not admitting it for a moment, but she hated me just the same.'

'Your life has not been happy,' he said. 'I'm sorry.'

'What about yours? What is it like to have so much money and so much power?'

'It is a heavy responsibility which often becomes a frightful burden,' Philip replied. 'But there are compensations, and I don't mean obvious advantages like being able to buy whatever you want, or go anywhere in the world. I mean the opportunities for doing things, for shaping events in the right way. I must sound very pompous to you, Mrs Stanley – a dull man with a sense of mission . . .'

'Not at all,' Paula said quietly. 'I've never been more interested. Please go on.'

'I too have been ashamed of what I am.' He lit a cigarette. 'My family name has been blackened by our association with the Nazis.

And we did associate. My mother tried to resist them, she's proud and she doesn't understand the meaning of fear. But my father wanted to survive. The price was collaboration with Hitler. We collaborated. We used forced labour in our factories; we gave funds to the Party. We protected our interests by participating in their crimes, and as far as the rest of the world is concerned, we were equally guilty. You know this; you know what the name Von Hessel means to non-Germans. Now that my brother is dead, I am the head of the family and responsible for the future. I want to prove that the image has changed. I want to do good with our money and our power. I want to redeem my family name. I want to serve my country.'

'And you'll do it,' Paula said. 'I really believe you'll do it. Do you know what someone once said to me – at a party – if you find a good German, kill him before he goes bad.'

'I know.' Philip smiled briefly. 'But you mustn't mind. We are a new generation, you and I. That is what matters. We're different to our parents; I love my mother and naturally she influences me, but I don't think the same way. I can't; I belong to a new world. And I am determined to help bring Germany into it. That is the only excuse for being as rich as we are, Mrs Stanley, and having this kind of power. To use the money and the power for the right purposes. Otherwise as a family we are damned; and doomed. I am sure of that.'

'I wish you luck,' Paula said. 'You're going to need it. But I think you may succeed. And in a way I envy you, having something to work for.'

'You could work for it too.' He leaned towards her; she thought irrelevantly that he was the handsomest man she had ever seen, and the least personally conceited. 'You should go back to Germany and see what is happening for yourself. I told you before, don't be an exile.'

'And I said I might,' Paula answered. 'But who knows? Who knows where I'll be in three months' time.'

'You could be with your father. Is that what you mean?'

'I could; if it worked out that way. Or I may never see him, and just go back to England, to the same empty life. Anyway,' she shrugged and smiled at him, deprecating her own prophecy, 'who knows? I may well go to Germany some day.'

'And when you do,' the Prince said, 'you will be my guest. I'll get the bill and take you back to the hotel. We can go to the Ritz together.'

'You fool,' Margaret Von Hessel snapped. 'You incompetent, bungling, fool! She's in the Ritz! My son moved her into the suite last night . . .'

Dunston held the receiver a little distance from his ear. He was in the foyer of the hotel, phoning through to the Princess. He had gone to make a report albeit prematurely, because he was feeling very confident. He had tried to call Paula the previous evening at about seven-thirty, judging that she wouldn't have left for any dinner date so early, and got no reply. He had hung up with a mental picture of her lying dead in the bath. He hadn't telephoned again; if she had been found electrocuted, he didn't wish to be remembered. And there would be an inquest, that was normal procedure.

He had assumed that all had gone as he intended. When he phoned through to the Von Hessel suite, he made the mistake of telling the Princess that everything had been taken care of. Her furious retort took him completely by surprise; he held the receiver and gasped. Then he swore obscenely, without caring whether she heard him or not.

'What the hell's your son doing with her!'

'Never mind that,' the Princess snapped at him. 'You leave my son to me and get on with your part. She's here, on the floor above – so much for whatever you thought was happening somewhere else. You damned bungler,' she said again. 'You've had plenty of time to arrange something. Now there's no time left – Fisher is arriving today and he's found the Salt! If you want our agreement to be honoured, you do something at once! Within the next few hours! And don't think you can keep that first payment – the bank will block it on my instructions.'

'You mean this,' Dunston said. 'It's coming to a head today?'

'Tomorrow at the latest. That's what Fisher said.'

'One thing.' Dunston was thinking at speed. 'How much does your son know – about you and me?'

'Nothing,' she said. 'And never must know. *He* wouldn't pay you, he'd hand you over to the police! For God's sake, keep away from him!'

'All right,' Dunston said. 'I'll have to do it somehow. But don't be surprised if it's messy. And you can blame your son for taking her out of the hotel. If he hadn't, it would have all been over!'

'Never mind that!' she snapped back at him. 'Finish it now. Otherwise you won't get a penny!' She hung up. He stood there in the cubicle, looking at the telephone. He'd get nothing; not even the money paid in as a deposit. The old bitch had hemmed him in on every side. He'd tried the accident angle. But if he wanted that money, he couldn't afford to be nice. As he'd said, it would be messy. The floor above, the Princess had said. He glanced up at the ceiling. Three floors. High enough. Bloody messy. But in the time and the circumstances, there wasn't any other way.

8

'I'm sorry, sir,' the receptionist said. 'The suite is occupied.'

He remembered the German gentleman with the white hair and the tinted glasses who had come in a few days earlier with the same query. He appeared to be fixed on that particular suite in the hotel, and the reception clerk was becoming irritated. He had told him already it wasn't available; he appeared not to have heard because he repeated the question.

'You are certain?' he persisted. 'I thought it would be vacant now that Prince Heinrich Von Hessel had died.'

'It is still at the disposal of the family,' the clerk said. 'There is a lady staying in it now. She arrived last night.'

'Oh,' the General said. 'How disappointing. I had counted upon staying here.'

'I have no suites available now, the one I offered you before has been booked. But there is a room on the third floor with private bathroom. That became vacant the day before yesterday because we had a cancellation.'

'On the third floor?'

'Yes. One moment and I will look up the number and I can tell you the position; I believe it faces to the front.'

The General waited; one hand buttoned his top button on his jacket and then unbuttoned it again. Otherwise he remained quite still and calm. A lady. Where exactly was the vacant room in relation to the suite? They were both on the same floor.

'It is number 370, monsieur. And it looks out on to the Place.'

'Thank you.' The General nodded. He buttoned his coat for the last time. 'I will take that. For a week.'

'You will register, please? And your passport.'

'Certainly. Here it is. My name is Weiss.' The Swiss passport came out of his inside pocket and he filled in the details in the register. He gave his address in Spain and signed the name under which he had lived for ten years.

And that was when he saw the name Paula Stanley written on the line above. He paused, underlining his signature, and read the address in England which she had given. It was the same, the place to which he had sent Schwarz. A faint colour showed round his cheekbones and came in a patch on his forehead. He was very pale skinned, the colouring of a pure blond. The flush of excitement faded quickly. She had come. His hands were quite steady, his voice unchanged.

'You have a friend of mine staying here I see,' he said. 'Mrs Paula Stanley.'

The reception clerk glanced down at the register. The Swiss passport had changed his attitude; he had a profound dislike of Germans. He actually smiled at the General. 'Yes, Monsieur Weiss. In fact the lady is staying in your suite – she came last night.'

'What a coincidence,' the General said. 'I shall move out of my present hotel and return in about an hour, with my luggage.'

'I hope you will be comfortable,' the clerk said.

'I am sure I shall.' The General nodded. 'I always used to stay here.' He walked out towards the street, very straight backed, one hand in his pocket. It was a mannerism only too familiar to his subordinates in the days to which he had referred with secret irony, the days when he walked through the foyer of the same hotel and everyone in sight made way for him and his entourage. He was back as he had said, within the hour, carrying a single light-weight suitcase and a heavy canvas duffle bag, which surprised the porter by its weight. He travelled up in the lift and followed the porter to the room on the third floor. His bags were put inside, and he gave a handsome tip. He was left alone.

He looked round the room; it was beautifully furnished, combining taste and comfort to an extent which he had not enjoyed for many years. Even the smell reminded him of the past; it was peculiar to the Ritz, with its fresh flower arrangements in every room, and the scented furniture polish used by the cleaners. He remembered it all. The suite was two doors down the passage. He lit a cigarette and went to the window; it was fastened, excluding the noise and dust of the Place. The air conditioning kept the room a pleasant temperature. There was a handsome bathroom, tiled in primrose yellow. He opened the window on an impulse and glanced down; the sound of the traffic was a steady rumble. He fastened back the catch, preferring the noise of activity to the silence. Then he removed his jacket, folding it over the back of a chair, and lay on the bed. It was the wrong time to go to her; the mornings were busy in any hotel; rooms were being cleaned, guests arriving and leaving. They would need a slack period, preferably during the heat of the afternoon, or the hours between eight and ten when everyone was dining.

Now that the moment had come, he found himself less prepared for it than he had imagined. He had a speech ready; it had been ready since that afternoon in Madrid when he opened the English newspaper and saw her photograph. He had read the cutting so many times and fingered it so much that it was frayed. His daughter. The only link with his past life, his only claim to a future beyond his own shrinking span. He was an old man, with nothing to aim for now but a peaceful death in bed. A sad and feeble ending to a career which had reached such heights of power and touched such depths of failure. He had a sense of the grandiose; it had added a singular glamour to his role; to speed in his black Mercedes on a mission of death like an infernal angel, something beyond an ordinary man. He had fled the débâcle because the prospect of a public trial and a sordid death by hanging offended his sense of what befitted him. Destiny had denied him for nearly thirty years; he had lived the mean, bourgeois existence of a business man expatriate in Madrid, and counted himself fortunate. Now, back in the surroundings of his past, the present day and its realities receded; distant as an echo the trumpets sounded in his brain, the haunted music of a danse macabre played out before a frightened world. He had lost; everything he had believed in had crumbled away and disappeared, leaving nothing but a memory and a huge genetic crime. Nothing was left to him now but obscurity; for his daughter it could still be different. For her there could be wealth and power in the possession of the Poellenberg Salt, and for him the final satisfaction of seeing his blood triumph. She would be immensely rich, sought after, famous – his thoughts ran on, rioting without discipline, breaking the bonds of common sense he had imposed upon himself. Emotion fought with him and won. The fatal German love of sentimental drama seized upon the relationship of father and daughter; it swept him forward, until he had forgotten the need for caution. He lay back with his eyes closed, waiting.

'What the hell's happened?' Fisher exploded. He had returned in the early afternoon, and gone upstairs to Paula's room. The door was open and it was crowded with people. He pushed his way through.

'Where's Mrs Stanley? What's going on . . .'

Suddenly he found himself facing the manager; the man's face was pale and two sweat streaks glistened down each cheek. 'There's been an accident, monsieur!'

'What accident?' Fisher shouted at him. 'Where's Mrs Stanley?'

'One of the cleaners; she was found a few minutes ago. She was cleaning the bath and she was electrocuted – please, monsieur, you must excuse me.'

'A cleaner . . .' Fisher's mind only registered one fact. Whatever the accident, it hadn't happened to Paula. 'Look, where's Mrs Stanley?'

'She left, monsieur.' The manager turned back to him with impatience. 'She checked out of the hotel last night. That's all I can tell you. Now, please – excuse me!'

Fisher could see two men coming out of the bathroom, carrying a limp body in a blue linen dress and a rumpled white apron; he caught a brief sight of a head lolling back, and a blackened face from which two round eyeballs protruded. For a moment he felt sick. Electrocuted, cleaning the bath. He turned away and went to the stairs, too anxious to wait for the lift. He went down them so fast he was short of breath when he reached the reception.

'Mrs Stanley,' he said. 'She left last night. Did she say where she was going?'

'No, monsieur. She just checked out.'

'But you've got a message for me?'

'I don't think so. One moment and I will make sure – no, nothing. There is nothing for you.'

'I don't believe it,' Fisher said. 'She must have left a message. What did she say, why did she leave?'

'I can't help you,' the receptionist answered. 'There was a gentleman with her. They came in, collected her luggage, she paid her bill and she left. I'm sorry, but that's all I know.'

'A gentleman,' Fisher repeated. 'She had a man with her?'

'Yes, monsieur.'

'I see,' he said. 'Thanks. Oh, wait. Did they go in a taxi? Would the porter know where they went?'

'You could ask him,' the receptionist said. 'Perhaps he can remember something.'

But the man only shook his head. Fisher had given him ten francs.

'They didn't take a taxi, monsieur,' he said. 'Mrs Stanley and the gentleman left in a car. A big Mercedes. I just put in the luggage and they drove off. I'm sorry.'

'Never mind.' Fisher turned away and slowly he walked back into the hotel. He couldn't quite believe it. Paula had gone with a man, leaving no message, nothing. Just walked out of the hotel and out of his life. It didn't seem possible. He was about to go back and ask the receptionist to check once more if there was a letter, and then suddenly he thought there might be something in his room. He raced up the stairs again and rushed inside. There was nothing. His bag was on the bed. There was no envelope anywhere. She had gone. Now he did feel sick. He pressed his fist against a sudden cramping in his lower gut, and fought against the pain. It was a real physical fact, a reaction of his body to the volcano bursting in his mind. He had lost her. And somebody else had come and taken her away, somebody she had never mentioned, somebody intimate enough to arrive and drive her off in his car, with her suitcases in the back.

Then Fisher thought of James Stanley. He must have come back to her. But they had spoken on the telephone the same evening; she had been gentle and tender, patient with him when he was jealous. Jealous of Dunston taking her shopping and to lunch. *Dunston!* He grabbed the telephone and gave the number. There was a long pause while his hotel tried to find him and then reported that his key was with the desk and he'd gone out. Fisher swore. He asked to be put through to Mrs Stanley, and was suddenly confronted by a raucous Middle Western voice claiming to be her. He hung up. She wasn't there. Paula wasn't with Dunston. It had been a crazy idea. It was probably the husband. That was the explanation. He got up slowly and went into the bathroom; he washed his face and looked at himself. He looked debauched by the shock.

'You bloody fool,' he said out loud. 'You poor bloody fool. Let this be a lesson to you.' He had bought her a bracelet that morning. It was gold, with lapis lazuli stones and tiny diamonds set between the links. He had looked at rings, but lacked the courage to produce one when they met. Not till he had got the Salt out of its hiding-place and seen the last of the Von Hessels. And the General. He was in the middle of unwrapping the box to throw the bracelet out into the street when he stopped, rocked back by the solution which had come to him. *The General.* That was who she went away with. They'd found each other. And for all he knew, while he sat breaking into pieces, they had gone to get the Salt.

'Mother,' Philip Von Hessel said. 'Mother, where is it? I have a right to know!'

'You have *no* right! How dare you pick up that woman and bring her to this hotel. Have you gone mad?' He had never seen her so angry; she was pallid with fury, her curious yellow-ringed eyes dilated till they seemed black. She stood in the middle of her drawing room, filled with red roses from the management, and shouted at him. It was the first time in his life that Philip had seen his mother lose control. 'You imbecile – you've meddled and interfered from the beginning – now you install Bronsart's daughter in the one place in the world . . . Oh my God, I can't believe it of you!'

'Where is the Salt?' he repeated. 'Fisher told you. Where is it?'

'You really want to know?' She snarled at him like an animal; she moved towards him and for a moment her right hand lifted as if she were going to hit him.

'You want to know where it is? Very well then, I'll tell you; I'll tell you where it is. It's in the suite! It's hidden in the suite where she is staying! Now do you see what you've done?'

'You should have told me,' Philip said. 'You should have trusted me.'

'Trust you? You never wanted me to get it back – you've been

against it from the first. Why should I trust you? This is nothing to
do with you!'

'You are obsessed,' he said. 'You know the risk involved in finding
it. Nothing is worth the ruin and disgrace of us all. Heinrich couldn't
stand against you, God help him. But I'm not afraid of you, Mother.
I love you, but I'm not afraid. The Salt isn't your property; it belongs
to the family. You've pursued this thing in spite of my advice, but you
can't go through with it alone. I brought Mrs Stanley here because she
needed help. I also promised her that when the Salt was found I'd tell
her; I shall keep that promise. If it's hidden in Heinrich's suite that
makes it easier.'

'I see.' The Princess swung away from him. 'I see. You want to act
the nobleman, the shining knight! That's how you see yourself, isn't
it? The man of honour, the good German? You wait, you fool. You
wait until the truth comes out, as well it may, and that woman is a
witness to it! There won't be money enough to buy her off!'

'I don't think she'll be bought,' her son said quietly. 'You haven't
met her or you wouldn't say that. She's promised to give it back to
us, if she has a legal right. And she may have one; we both know that.
I won't stand by and see her cheated. When is Fisher coming?'

'I'll tell you nothing,' the Princess blazed at him. 'Nothing! Get out
of my rooms!'

'Very well.' She turned her back to him; then the door closed. It
was their first quarrel and it had shaken her. She had depended upon
the habit of submission to her will. Since Heinrich's death her son had
altered. He had always been mature, serious; now he had developed
a direction of his own, irrespective of her wishes. He had a different
code, and strength of character as formidable in its way as her own.
For a moment she reflected in mixed rage and pride, that he was not
her son for nothing. But where was Dunston – what was he doing?
It was always possible that he had reneged upon their arrangement
and decided to forfeit the money. But in her judgment the Princess
didn't think so; he was ruthless and cool-headed. Above all he was
passionately greedy. For what she had offered, he would take the risk.
There was nothing she could do, no outlet for her impatience; she had
to wait. To wait for Fisher to contact her upon arrival and for the
commotion in the hotel which would tell her that Dunston had kept
their bargain.

Paula was getting ready to go down to lunch when she heard the
knock on her door. The maids had cleaned the bedroom and brought
a big bowl of yellow and white roses for the drawing room. Paula had
been too tired to inspect the suite when she arrived; that morning she
walked round the lovely little panelled room, looking at the period
ormolu clock on the mantelpiece, and the eighteenth-century bronze

candlesticks that stood on the desk. It was a quiet, sunny room, a blend of delicate autumnal colouring, dictated by the soft honey-coloured wood that covered the walls. The carving and design were exquisite, the work of a master craftsman. She had never imagined that such a unique apartment could exist, even in a hotel like the Ritz. It had an atmosphere of peace and remoteness that reminded her of the country. And yet Philip Von Hessel's brother had been the last person to use it, and from the same idyllic setting he had gone out to take his own life.

She heard the first knock and then the second. She opened the door to the passageway.

'Good morning, Mrs Stanley.'

'Oh, hello, Mr Dunston.'

'Sorry to bother you, but I just wanted a word. Can I come in for a moment?'

Paula opened the door and stood back. 'Yes, of course. Do.'

The General was still lying on the bed when he heard the cry. It came through the open window, high pitched above the traffic rumble from the street below. He sat up quickly. There was a second cry, but fainter, and it stopped, as if something had choked it off. He stepped to the window and looked out. The window of the suite was open; there was a clinking sound of breakage. Instinct impelled him. The muffled scream had been a woman's; the faint crash indicated some kind of violence. He dragged open his door and with a few running strides he had reached the suite. For twenty-five years he had carried a key on his watch-chain. He used it then and flung the door open.

Inside the drawing room, a man and a woman were struggling. The man was big and powerful; the windows were latched back and he was dragging a woman towards them. One hand was pressed over her mouth, the other arm was locked around her, pinioning hers. A small table had toppled over and a china figurine lay in pieces on the carpet. It was a scene in which the silence intensified its menace. The General didn't wait; he sprang, and with the reflex of his military training, his right arm swept up and crashed down on the side of the man's face, missing the vital spot in the neck which would have killed him. But the blow was enough.

Dunston's grip on Paula fell away; for a moment he reeled, blinded by the pain in his cheek-bone. His vision blurred on the sudden apparition of another man. He grabbed Paula by the arms and threw her violently against the General, knocking him backwards. He heard her breathless cry as he rushed to the door to get away. His head was swimming, and there was a warm rivulet of blood dripping down the side of his face where the General's hand had sliced the skin. He pounded away down the corridor, momentarily panicked. Two floors below he found the safety of the service entrance; he slapped a handkerchief against his face and raced on down towards the exit. He'd failed, and with only minutes to go. He'd got inside the suite, chatting amiably and started some story about meeting Fisher. She was alone, and quite off guard. When he opened the windows and made a remark about the view, she actually moved nearer to make it easy for him. He had gone up to her smiling, and seen by her face that she thought he was going to try and make love to her. When he seized hold of her, that was still her impression. She had shouted 'No,' and tried to pull away, before he slammed his hand over her mouth to stifle a second scream, and pinioned her, dragging her across the floor. The windows had gaped in front of them, only a few feet away. He didn't dare to knock her unconscious because the assault would leave marks. But they had never reached the sill. Outside the hotel Dunston collapsed into a taxi-cab. His nerve had been badly shaken. Now it was recovering; he held his throbbing face and swore.

They hadn't got near to the window before the unexpected intervention of the other man. It was just possible that Paula Stanley hadn't realised that his intention was to throw her out. She might still mistake the attack for an attempted rape. In the initial stages of the struggle before he got her arms pinned down, he had handled her breasts. He went back to the hotel and straight to his room. In the bathroom closet he examined his face. There was a two-inch opening and a fleshy bruise. It had been a hell of a blow. He found the bottle of brandy on his dressing table and swallowed a mouthful. Failure. At the best he could expect her to charge him with sexual assault, at worst with attempted murder, if she had realised the connection with the open window. There was a sofa intervening; she might have thought him dragging her towards it. He leaned on the table and steadied himself. So much for the money. There wasn't a chance now. There was nothing he could do but get to hell out. He pulled his suitcase off the luggage stand and on to the bed, flinging back the lid. As he began packing the first of his clothes, the telephone rang. He hesitated. He could always deny it; there hadn't been witnesses. Women had been known to allege that kind of thing before, and the man accuse them in turn of being hysterical, or acting out of pique . . . It went on ringing and suddenly he picked it up.

'Oh Christ,' he said. It was Fisher on the other end.

'I've been looking everywhere for you,' he said. 'What the hell do you do in the mornings?'

'I've been seeing the sights,' Dunston said. He held the handkerchief to his face, took it away and saw that fresh blood had stained it. He needed sticking plaster. By rights it ought to have a stitch. The man had given him a really professional karate blow . . .

'What's doing?' He didn't want to know, but he had to say something to Fisher.

'Plenty,' the reply came. 'Look, I'm going to need your help. I know where the Salt is, and I'm going to pick it up with the Princess today. But there's a complication.'

'Oh?' Dunston said. Every tooth was aching down the injured side of his jaw. 'What's happened?'

'The General,' Fisher said. 'He's with Paula. When we go to get it, he'll be waiting. I don't want her hurt, if there's any trouble. I want you to come along.'

'Where is the Salt?' Dunston said. His mind was far ahead of the conversation; he sucked hard on his lip, seeing again the figure looming at him as he struggled with the girl, delivering that expert blow. It was a killer stroke, aimed at the neck. There had been an impression of a tall man with white hair, now he remembered it. White hair.

'Christ,' he said again, but softly, so that Fisher couldn't hear. That was who had saved Paula Stanley. Of course; he must have been hiding in the suite . . .

'Where is it?' he repeated.

'In the Ritz. In the General's old suite where he lived during the war.'

'Very ingenious,' Dunston said slowly. 'And I believe you're absolutely right. When you go for the Salt you'll find the both of them with it. Don't worry. You can count on me to come along. Just let me know the time.'

'I will,' Fisher promised. 'As soon as I've seen the Princess. And not a word about the General when you meet her. I've a special reason; I don't want the police called in on this.'

'Why should you?' Dunston asked. 'You won't need them. I'll come along and hold your hand.' He hung up. She wouldn't be able to complain. With her father hiding out with her, she wouldn't dare say anything to call attention. He took out the shirts he had packed and put them in the drawer again. She couldn't accuse him of anything, and risk the police coming round. He was safe. And Fisher had called him in. To recover the Salt. He opened the smaller drawer in the chest and took out his Smith and Wesson pistol. He loaded it, and put it in his pocket. He was going to confront a dangerous war criminal, wanted by Interpol. Two birds, he said to himself, and laughed, which changed into a grimace of pain from his swollen cheek.

Two birds with one stone. He might very well earn his money and a medal at the same time.

'Don't be afraid,' the General said. 'I'm not going to hurt you. Look at me, Paula.' She had fallen to the ground when Dunston flung her against him; he knelt beside her, an arm round her shoulders. Her face was streaked with tears; she stared up at him and he saw the expression changing in her eyes.

'I am your father,' he said quietly. 'I am your father.'

'Father?' It was a whisper, for a moment her mouth quivered, and then she put up one hand and touched him.

'It's you?'

'Yes, it is. Don't cry, my darling child. Let me look at you.' He helped her up and for a moment they stood, the General holding her at arm's length. He leaned forward and kissed her on the forehead. Paula took a step forward and threw her arms around his neck. For a long, silent space they stood locked together.

'I can't believe it,' she said. 'It's really you, and you did come . . . That man – he suddenly attacked me . . .'

'I heard you cry out,' the General said. 'He was trying to kill you. Why?'

'Not kill, rape.' She shuddered. 'I know him slightly. My God, if you hadn't come in . . .'

'I should have killed him with that stroke,' the General said. 'But one slows down, one loses the old skills.'

'Father, you shouldn't have taken this risk! Without the glasses, anyone would know you.'

'It's our eyes,' he said and smiled. 'The mark of Cain. You're beautiful, just as I imagined you. Sit down with me, and give me your hand. For twenty-seven years I have dreamed of this.'

'And so have I,' she said. Her eyes filled with tears. It was a handsome face, but lined and tight skinned; the brilliant blue eyes gazed at her with tenderness and triumph. The hand holding hers was gripping hard.

'Smile,' he commanded. 'Smile for me, be happy! This is the most important day in both our lives.' He raised her hand and kissed it. 'Tell me the truth, am I a disappointment? An old man – feeble and white haired? Am I what you expected?'

'I don't know,' Paula said. 'I never even saw a photograph; I hadn't anything to judge by. I just made up a picture of you when I was a little girl, and said, "that is my father, that's what he looked like". I am so happy to find you, I can't think of anything to say. I can't express it, I'm sorry.'

'I knew you'd come, when Schwarz gave you my message. I knew you'd find out where the Salt was hidden. But before we come to that, my darling, I want to know about you.'

'How did you ever find me?' Paula asked him. She slipped her free hand through his arm and clung. There was a fresh, barbered smell about him. Seated so close to him she felt almost childish, as if the years had dropped away from her. 'Oh, Father.' She leaned her head against his shoulder. 'I'm so glad we're together.'

'And so am I,' he said. 'I saw the report of your divorce in the English newspapers. That's how I recognised you, you have a strong family likeness to my mother and my sisters. And I knew that Ridgeway was the name of the man your mother married after the war. So I sent Schwarz. He was a good man, very loyal. But even so I couldn't trust him with our secret. I had to send you the riddle because no man alive could resist the Salt. And Schwarz had seen it.'

'Why didn't you just send for me?'

'I would have done, if he hadn't been killed,' the General said. 'When I was sure that you wanted to find me. I didn't know what your reaction to him would be.'

'Mother never talked of you at all,' Paula said. 'She told me you were killed on the Russian front.'

'She didn't know the truth,' he said. 'She couldn't be trusted with it. She hated me.'

'I know,' Paula said. 'She told me almost nothing, just that you were a general in the German army. They changed my name to Ridgeway.'

'I was a general in the élite,' he said quickly. 'In the SS where the best of our manhood served the Fuehrer. We were gods, Paula. We ruled the earth in those days.' He held her tight and smiled.

'This was my suite during the occupation of France. I lived like a prince; the best food and wines, charming women, people bowing and crawling for favours. They were exciting years, wonderful years. I look back on them now and it's my present life that is the unreality. Mr Weiss from Switzerland, working in Madrid.'

'You don't regret the past?' Paula asked him.

His head was lifted and a proud smile curved his mouth. He looked down at her. 'I regret nothing except defeat,' he said. 'I regret what was lost, that's all. And we came so close, my child, so very close to winning everything. Now the Jews and the Communists run the world. It has no attraction for me any more. Tell me about yourself. Your marriage – what kind of man was your husband?'

'It's not easy to describe him,' Paula said. 'Mother liked him, because he had a snob value. But he wasn't made for marriage. All he wanted was motor racing, sex and excitement. It was disaster for both of us.'

'That doesn't matter,' the General said. 'Next time you will choose better.'

'I'll never choose again,' she said quickly. 'I'm finished with marriage. Now that I've got you, I don't need another man.'

'You are a woman,' he reproved her gently. 'Not a little girl. You must have a man to take care of you. Not an old father in sight of the grave.'

'You're not to talk like that,' she told him. 'I mean it; now I've got you I don't need anyone else. Father, all my life I've wanted someone of my own who loved me. Mother never did, the man I married didn't, now I don't care. To hell with them all. You and I can be together. I can spend my life with you and I shall be perfectly happy. That's why I came to find you. The Poellenberg Salt doesn't mean anything to me. It was you I wanted. And I've got you now.'

'You don't know what you're saying.' The General spoke briskly. He hugged her for a moment and then let her go. He lit a cigarette. 'You've no idea what you are suggesting. It is quite impossible. Believe me.'

'Oh no, it isn't! We're going away together – back to Madrid, if that's where you live. I'll move in with you and we'll just disappear.'

'No.' He shook his head. He puffed out a stream of blue smoke. 'No. You can't ally yourself with me.'

'Why not? What do you expect – we meet here and then you just walk out and vanish? I'm not going to let you!'

'I came to find you for a purpose,' the General said. 'I left Spain, where I've been safe for ten years, and came back to Paris. Not to take you away with me to share my life of exile. A modest flat, a modest income, loneliness, boredom, anonymity! You think that is what I want my daughter's destiny to be?'

'It's what I want,' Paula insisted. 'It's what I've always wanted; to be with you!'

'You are my child,' he said. 'And all those years ago I put something away for you, when I knew that the end of our world was coming and I might well be killed. I wanted to make sure of your inheritance. I have kept one of the greatest treasures in the world to give you. And now, my darling, it is yours.'

'I don't want it,' she said. 'I don't want the Salt. It doesn't interest me.'

'Stop being foolish.' He spoke sharply and he got up, leaving her on the sofa staring up at him. He began to pace the floor.

'The Poellenberg Salt is yours. How can you dismiss it in that way? You've never seen it! You don't know what it means! A huge fortune in gold and jewels, a work of art that could command any price in the world – you will be one of the richest women – you will be powerful, sought after. You'll marry a prince, if you want one! People will fawn after you, as they did with me, anxious for a look or a word!'

'Father, please,' Paula begged, trying to stop the flow. It had an ugly ring of exaggeration, there was a hard, impassioned look on his face which mocked his former gentleness. When he stared at her he was angry, almost hostile.

'I may live like a nonentity, an exile – but you shall not! Come to Madrid and share my life – play nurse to me till I sink into the grave! If you imagine I would let you do it, then it was a great mistake for us to meet at all! No – you have a destiny. I planned it for you and you're going to fulfil it. You're going to possess the Poellenberg Salt. I've come to give it to you.'

'It doesn't belong to me,' she said desperately. 'It belongs to the Von Hessels. And they've discovered where it is – they're planning to get it some time today!'

He stopped abruptly; the hand holding his half-smoked cigarette lowered slowly to his side.

'What do you mean? How can you know this?'

'Because they have a private detective working on it; he contacted me and I gave him your clue. We made a bargain. He wanted to find the Salt, I wanted to find you. They know everything about it.'

'You say they know where it is hidden?'

He was stiff and watchful, completely changed. Paula shivered. The man in front of her was stern and frightening. 'Well,' he said, 'answer me, Paula. Do they know where it is hidden?'

'Yes; I told you. They intend to get it today.'

'I see,' he said quietly. 'That woman is trying to cheat me, it seems.'

'They're entitled to it,' Paula said. 'You took it from them, Father. It was in their family for hundreds of years; you looted it.'

'That's what you think? You think I stole it from them? But they would try and say this, naturally. It is a lie. The Poellenberg Salt is legally mine. And legally yours. As you will find.'

'No,' Paula said. 'I mean this, Father. As far as I'm concerned the past is done with. I'm not your judge for what you did; but the Salt is part of it. I wouldn't touch it. I don't want to be rich or famous because of it. And you've forgotten yourself. You run a risk of being recognised as long as you stay here. An old woman called Madame Brevet recognised you; I went to see her and she spat in my face when I told her who I was. You had her son shot. We won't talk about that part of it, Father, but the Poellenberg Salt *is* part of it. And if you gave it to me now, I'd give it straight to the Von Hessels. I've promised to do exactly that, if I do have any claim.'

'You fool,' he said slowly. 'You fool, to propose such a thing. You know nothing about it. You know nothing of the truth. You'd give it back to Margaret Von Hessel?' He laughed, and it was harsh, contemptuous.

'If you refuse it, one thing I promise you. She will never get it back!'

'Oh please, please,' Paula begged. 'Don't let's quarrel. Father, can't you see what really matters is you and me! Money isn't important to me, I don't want any of the things you want for me, I don't care about treasure or power or anything. I only have you in the world. And you talk about going away, leaving me – you'll break my heart if you do.'

He looked down at her and his expression slowly changed. He went over and held out his hand; she took it and he embraced her. She held him tightly, and for the first time since her childhood the prayer formed silently, please, God, please God . . . Don't let me lose him . . .

'I want you to be happy,' the General said. 'You are the only person I have ever loved. Thinking of you kept me alive, it gave me hope to know you were growing up, away from the ruin that followed our defeat. As a baby I held you in my arms and promised you the world. I am not the world, my darling. I have nothing to offer you – don't interrupt me, let me finish this. I have no future; I am an old man and I'm safe. For me that's enough. If I brought you back with me and saw you condemned to live my life, wasting yourself, then it is my heart that would break. I should lose hope completely. I can live through you, knowing that you are enjoying what I would have given you if we hadn't lost the war. Don't deny me this. Let me gratify my love for you. Take the Salt. At least,' he said slowly. 'Let me show it to you and prove that it is really yours. Then if you refuse it . . .' He lifted her face and looked at her. There were tears in his eyes. 'Don't deny me,' he repeated. 'I have lived for this.'

'Oh God,' Paula whispered. 'Oh God, what am I to do?'

At that moment the telephone rang. He held her, his grip on her tight; suddenly it relaxed and he stepped back. 'Answer it, Paula.'

She lifted the receiver. 'It's me,' Fisher said. 'Don't say anything, just listen. He's with you, isn't he?'

'Yes,' she answered. 'Yes, how did you know?'

'Never mind that. I'm coming up in a few minutes. Has he told you where it's hidden?'

'No,' Paula said. 'Why don't you just leave me alone? I don't want to see you.'

'I appreciate that from the way you walked out on me,' he said. 'But it's not just me; the Salt is in your suite. I'm coming up with a carpenter and Princess Von Hessel. So you'd better get him out of there. I thought I'd warn you.'

'Thank you,' Paula said quietly. She glanced at her father standing waiting, listening without comprehension to the one sided conversation. 'Thank you for telling me. And I'm sorry about what happened.'

'Don't give it a thought.' Fisher sounded curt. 'I always knew if it came to a choice between him and me, you'd choose him.' The line clicked as he rang off.

'They're coming,' Paula said. 'They're on their way up here! Father, you've got to go!'

'The Salt is here, in this room,' the General said. 'I brought something to help us get it out. But now there isn't time. Who told you this?'

'The detective,' she answered. 'He guessed you were with me; he gave me time to warn you. Please, kiss me goodbye, and go *now*! Wait, wait – where can I find you?'

'You cannot,' the General said.

'But you won't disappear, you won't just leave me and disappear?'

He bent and kissed her. 'The Salt,' he said. 'That is what matters. Soon you will see your inheritance. And it is yours. The proof is with it.' He left her and without turning to look back, he went out of the door and through to the corridor. For a moment Paula hesitated, fighting the impulse to break down and cry with the abandon of a child who finds itself deserted. Then she ran to the door of the suite and looked for him, but the corridor was empty. A few minutes later the reception rang to say that Prince Philip Von Hessel was on his way up. 'You've been crying,' he said. She had let him in, expecting to see his mother and Fisher with him.

'What is the matter?'

'Nothing,' Paula said. 'I'm quite all right. I thought the others would be with you.'

'What others? I came to see how you were and to ask you to have dinner with me.'

'Your mother,' Paula said. 'And Eric Fisher. The Salt is here, hidden somewhere in this suite. They're coming to get it. I thought that knock was them.'

'She never told me,' Philip said slowly. 'She never said a word about it. I think it's a good thing I shall be here. You may need an ally, Mrs Stanley, if I know my mother. We'll wait for them together. Is that what made you cry?'

'No,' Paula said. 'Something quite different. Could I have a cigarette?'

'Of course.' He lit it for her, his face grave. Uncharacteristically he touched her shoulder. 'I won't ask about it,' he said quietly. 'But after this business is over, perhaps we could go somewhere and talk?'

'I don't know,' she said. 'I don't know what's going to happen. I want to run away!'

'Not now,' the Prince said. 'You have come to the end; you will face it and for what it's worth, you know I'm here as your friend.'

'Yes,' she said. 'I believe you are. I hear them now, that was the door opening.'

The first person to come into the drawing room was Margaret Von

Hessel. As she saw Paula and then her son, she stopped. She spoke over her shoulder.

'Mr Fisher – what are these people doing here?'

He came in, followed by a man in overalls carrying a toolbag. He looked first at Paula and then, with taut suspicion, at the Prince. Philip had moved close to her; he stood so close that they were side by side.

'Mrs Stanley?' That was the Princess, sharp and imperious. 'Would you be good enough to leave – this does not concern you. And you' – she glared at her son – 'had better accompany the lady!'

'Mrs Stanley stays,' Philip said quietly. 'And so do I.' There was a sound outside and then Dunston walked into the room, one hand in his pocket, an oblong piece of plaster covering his cheek. Paula gasped and stepped back. He looked directly at her and he smiled. He spoke to Fisher.

'I think I'll make sure there's nobody else in here,' he said, and before Fisher could say anything he opened the door connecting with the bedroom and went inside. He came out again, and glanced at Paula. His message was clear. Say one word about what happened and I'll set the dogs on *him*. She turned away from him, helpless before that sly, taunting grin. The memory of his hands on her, of that vicious grip on her mouth and the force of his knee propelling her from behind made her tremble suddenly. He had recognised her father; he knew that there was nothing she could do, that even with Fisher standing a few feet away, she couldn't accuse him . . . He had gone away from the bedroom and moved to the window; she saw him nudge the long curtains to make sure that nobody was concealed behind them.

'Unless you and Mrs Stanley leave, I shall call off the search.' The Princess spoke again.

'They stay, or at any rate Mrs Stanley does. I'm not interested in your son,' Fisher said coldly. He didn't look at Paula. With the younger man standing so close beside her in that intimate way, he couldn't trust himself to do so.

'I'm the only one who knows where the Salt is, and I shan't do another thing about it, unless Mrs Stanley is a witness. There's a question of ownership, and she's entitled to be here.'

'That is exactly my view,' Prince Philip said. 'Please proceed, Mr Fisher.'

'All right.' Margaret Von Hessel swung round to Fisher. 'All right, we'll have it on your terms. For God's sake, get your man to work!'

The hotel carpenter came forward and Fisher said, 'Try the walls. I think that's where we'll find it. Look for any woodwork that's been replaced.'

'Tell me one thing,' Paula said to him. 'Before you start. How did you find out where it was?'

For the first time they looked directly at each other; Fisher felt the same solar plexus pain. She looked different; the habitual poise was gone, there was something distraught about her, the slight dishevelment of her hair, usually so chic and groomed, and the anxious glances round the room, to Dunston standing inmovable and inscrutable, a little away from them all.

'I got it from a friend of Madame Brevet's,' he said. 'A neighbour who knew the family. Jacquot was a master carpenter; that was the clue. Your father picked him out from the hostages because he discovered what his trade was. And he put him to work here that night. In his own private quarters, where he could work without anyone knowing what was going on. And then he picked him out next morning and had him shot to stop him telling anyone. I was sure the General had used him to wall up the Salt or hide it and when your mother told me he stayed in this suite at exactly that date, I knew this was where the master carpenter had been employed. As soon as I heard what Jacquot's trade was, all I had to do was find a suitable place. It wasn't very difficult.'

'Why don't we get on,' the Princess snapped at him. 'You've told all this to me – tell the man to begin looking!'

It took half an hour for the carpenter to find the portion of the wall which didn't ring true. He went over the surface from ground level upwards, tapping, while Paula watched him, and the Princess sat in a chair, her back stiff in disdain of fatigue, one foot swinging in rhythm to the sound of the carpenter's knocking. She didn't look near her son. Then the carpenter turned and spoke to Fisher.

'There's something wrong here. It sounds different to the rest of the room.' They were to the right of the marble fireplace, about four feet from the ground. The panelling was covered with a beautiful tracery of acanthus leaves, with a design of daffodils and ears of corn. Fisher bent over the area and ran his finger down the tracery. It was impossible to see a join. 'You're sure of this?'

The man nodded; a blackened cigarette hung from one corner of his mouth. The Princess had forgotten to object when he lit it.

'I'd say the wall behind this was hollow,' he said. 'There's nothing solid behind this wood panel. But I can't see where it's been cut – one minute, there's a torch in my bag . . .'

The beam of light flashed on and hung over this woodwork. Fisher directed it while the man ran his fingers over the raised carved surface.

'Impossible,' he muttered. 'Impossible to see. Whoever took this wood out and put it back was a master craftsman.'

'Yes,' Fisher said quietly. 'Yes, he certainly was. Can you feel anything different?'

The carpenter was kneeling with his back towards them. His fingers were curled around one large piece of fine scrolling. 'Bring the light in closer. That's right. Ah! I think I've found it. Look, there it is – a hair line right along the curved piece there! And it goes on, smaller, but it's still there. This is where the wood was cut!'

There was a sound from the Princess; before she had sat silent, betraying nothing except through the pendulum swing of that one foot. 'Open it!' she commanded. 'Cut it open!'

The man glanced at her over his shoulder. 'I'm not going to damage this panelling, madame. It's eighteenth century and beautiful work. I'll do a good job and I'll take my time.' Nobody spoke. Fisher stayed beside him holding the torch. Slowly and with great care, he put the point of a fine saw along the carving and began to cut. The sound seemed loud out of all proportion; it was as if the watchers had stopped breathing. Paula couldn't move, transfixed by the yellow circle of light and the motion of the saw, backwards and forwards through the wood. Suddenly there was a movement. The Princess was on her feet.

'Cut!' she shouted. 'Cut through it and for God's sake get on!'

'Do as she says.' Fisher spoke quietly. 'She can pay for any damage. You can't avoid it. Hurry up, let's get the panel out.'

Outside the windows a clock struck; immediately a little ormolu and porcelain timepiece in the room began its sweet chime. There was a foot left to cut through; the wood was gaping at three sides, showing a line of blackness.

'Hah! That's it . . .' The carpenter dropped his saw and slowly pulled. Fisher swung the torch beam into the aperture and there was a sudden brilliant gleam of gold. Because he was nearest the carpenter saw it first. He shoved the panel aside and it fell with a clatter, knocking against a table.

'Jesus Christ!'

Fisher dropped the torch and it rolled across the floor; its light went out.

'Help me,' he said. 'Help me to get it out.'

In spite of herself, Paula moved towards them, her view masked by the figure of Margaret Von Hessel.

The two men reached into the darkness to the yellow gleam, and very slowly lifted. 'Get away from it,' the Princess rasped at them. 'Get away – let me see it!'

It stood on the carpet, shining like sunlight, flashing with diamonds, the huge ruby in the base was red as a wound. Fisher stood upright. 'My God,' he said. 'My God, look at that.'

The photographs had not prepared Paula. They showed something inanimate. The golden ornament seemed to be alive. The leaves of the tree were visibly trembling, the nymphs and the pursuing satyrs were as mobile as gilded flesh. The beauty and the magnificence burned and glittered like a sun.

'At last,' Margaret Von Hessel said, and her voice trembled, with triumph, with passion, with so many emotions that she sounded almost incoherent. 'At last I have it back.'

'No, Princess Von Hessel. You do not!' The words came from behind them; Fisher sprang round and then stood very still. They were all turned, looking at the man standing in the doorway. There was a gun in his hand.

Fisher didn't need Paula's anguished cry, or the gasp of the old woman, who was staring, hands upraised as if to ward off an attack. The General stepped forward into the room. He took deliberate aim at Margaret Von Hessel.

'There is something else in that opening. One of you get it out. If anyone tries anything foolish, I will shoot this woman. You . . .' He gestured at Dunston. 'You – stand with the others. I would especially like to kill you . . .' Fisher went to the opening; there was something in the darkness, something pale that crackled when his fingers touched it. It was an envelope, yellowed and stiff.

'Ah.' The General spoke softly. 'Good. It is all in German. Let me tell you what is in it.'

'No,' Margaret Von Hessel cried out. 'No!'

'On the 23rd of April 1944, you signed the document inside that envelope. It made me the legal owner of the Poellenberg Salt. By deed of gift. Witnessed and binding, legal in any court in the world.' The gun was pointing at her; Fisher calculated that if he made a move, the General would get the first shot through her left chest. There was nothing he could do.

'Father,' Paula cried out, 'Father, don't . . .'

'That is one document.' The General didn't even turn his head towards her. 'The second is another deed of gift, made by me for my only daughter. Giving her the Salt. That too is legal. Anywhere in the world.' He spoke directly to the Princess. 'But that is not what you're afraid of, is it? You could fight those papers; you could use your money and you might even win because I can't defend myself. I thought of that. I knew the end was coming and I thought of everything. There is another paper, Paula. That is what the Princess doesn't want anyone to see.'

He spoke to Fisher. 'Open it,' he said. 'Give the papers to my daughter. And move slowly; otherwise she dies.' And looking into Margaret Von Hessel's face, he smiled. Fisher glanced at Dunston and quickly shook his head. He handed three folded documents to

Paula; he moved very carefully as the General had suggested. He had seen men with that expression in their eyes before. He didn't want to be responsible for the Princess's death.

'General Bronsart.' Philip Von Hessel's voice was calm. 'If you intend to shoot anyone, I suggest it is me. Please don't point your gun at my mother.'

The General glanced at him. 'Your courage is misplaced,' he said. 'Your mother would take a risk on your life; you won't do the same with hers. So long as she is in danger you won't move. None of you will. Paula, the two large documents are your proof of ownership of the Poellenberg Salt. The small piece of writing paper is the reason why no Von Hessel will ever dare dispute it. Open it and read it aloud.'

She did as he told her, slowly, because her fingers were stiff and clumsy with a growing sense of fear. Dunston had been standing immobile beside the Princess. His right arm was crooked slightly against his side; so long as that gun was directed at her, he couldn't move his hand towards his pocket. He was watching the General.

'It's in German,' Paula said. 'I can't read it.'

'Destroy it!' There was a jerky movement from the Princess. She took a step forward, one hand thrust out. The little black eye of the gun muzzle followed her. 'Destroy it!' she cried out. 'I'll give you anything, anything – one million pounds, for that letter!'

'No.' The General smiled, mirthless and implacable. 'No, you can't buy my silence a second time. You bought it all those years ago, and then you tried to cheat me. To cheat my daughter. The Salt belongs to her. Tell me, Prince Philip, when you offered yourself instead of your mother, did you know about that little note she wrote me? I think not.' He shook his head. 'I think she kept that secret to herself. Shall I tell you what is in it, Paula? It's a letter from the Princess addressed to me. Delivered one night in May 1944.'

'It was the only way,' the Princess shrieked at them. 'You found out about Heinrich's marriage, you threatened to denounce him – you threatened to destroy us all!' She turned to her son, standing white and immobile near to Paula. 'I told you,' she went on, 'I told you we had no alternative; Hitler was raving, he would have sent us all to concentration camps, seized our factories, we would have been destroyed!'

'I know this, Mother,' Philip Von Hessel said. 'You told me.'

'Ah yes,' the General said. 'But that's all she told you, isn't it? That she gave me the Poellenberg Salt as the price of my silence. You knew that, didn't you, and you knew the lie told to the world that it was looted? But that's not what she is offering a million pounds to suppress. That's not what is in that letter which my daughter has. I'll tell you what it says.'

'No,' Margaret Von Hessel cried out once again. 'It's a lie, a forgery . . .' She stopped suddenly, as if defeated.

'It gives the name of a village on the Franco-German border, near Alsace, and the address of a small pension. That, it says in the letter, is where you will find them. They suspect nothing and are waiting to be brought to us. I remember the words. I remember the bargain we made, Princess Von Hessel, you and I, when you signed away the Salt to me in exchange for my silence about your Jewish daughter-in-law, and for a further favour you requested. I granted it to you, didn't I? I kept my bargain. I had your daughter-in-law arrested and your baby grandson. I sent them to Mauthausen to the gas chambers as we'd agreed. How old was the child – eighteen months?'

There was a moment of complete silence, as if the people in the room had stopped breathing. Time seemed suspended. Paula heard his voice and that last question, asked in a mocking tone, and thought suddenly that the ground was sliding away and she was going to faint. With a tremendous effort of will she focused on his face and saw the burning blue eyes, blazing in triumph at the stricken woman, saw the smile on his mouth and the horrifying, unbelievable lack of remorse at what he had just confessed. Now the floor was swaying. She felt a hand come out and steady her. It wasn't the Prince, who was only a few feet away. In defiance of the General and his levelled gun, it was Fisher who had come beside her.

'Mother,' Philip Von Hessel said. 'Mother, you *betrayed* them? You *asked* him to kill them?'

'I had no choice,' she answered slowly, gathering strength, straightening herself from the moment of collapse. 'So long as they lived we were vulnerable. He had discovered it. So might someone else. She was a Jewess, an adventuress.'

'And the child,' Philip asked her. 'Heinrich's son – you had him murdered too?'

There was no answer. She gestured with one hand as if to defend herself, and then decided to say nothing.

'Now, Paula.' The General spoke with exultation, with vindication. 'Now you know the truth. Do you still want to return the Salt to her? Look at it! Look at the beauty of it!'

'May God forgive you.' Paula trembled. 'I can't bear to look at the filthy bloodstained thing! The mother and the child – you murdered them, Father!'

'A Jewess and a half Jew,' the General said. 'They were nothing to me. They were dying in millions. Inferior people, polluting the world. What were they compared to that?' In the middle of the floor the great golden Salt glittered and flashed its jewelled eyes at them.

'I wouldn't touch it,' Paula cried out. 'Or you.'

'I see,' the General said. 'I was afraid of this. But I have come prepared. Paula, go to the passage and bring me the bag that's by the door.'

'No,' she said. 'No, I won't do anything for you.'

He looked away from her to Fisher, who had his arm around her. 'You go,' he said. 'Take your hands off my daughter and get the bag. Bring it to me. If you don't, I will shoot the Princess.'

'Steady, darling,' Fisher whispered. He let go of Paula and went to the doorway. A duffle bag was just outside it. He carried it inside and brought it to the General. The thought passed through his mind of diving on him and hoping that the stray bullet wouldn't hit anyone. If it had struck the Princess he wouldn't have cared. But Paula was there, white and stricken, swaying on her feet. He couldn't take the risk. 'Open it,' the General ordered. 'Now give it to me.' There was a small cylinder and a muzzle on a cable. He put the muzzle into the General's outstretched hand. 'Now light it!'

His lighter flicked, there was a loud hiss and a plume of brilliant blue-white flame shot from the mouth. Immediately the room filled with a dazzling light.

'No,' Margaret Von Hessel screamed. 'No, no . . . Oh my God!' The fierce flame of the oxyacetylene licked at the top of the golden tree; in his right hand the General held the gun, with his left he directed the searing fire at the Salt. Already the upper branches were sliced off and lay misshapen and dripping on the floor; the metal began liquefying; as they watched, shielding their eyes against the blinding light, the shape began to blur, the figures of nymphs so nubile in their grace, were mutilated and running rivulets of gold on to the carpet; jewels fell in a glittering cascade.

Margaret Von Hessel was sobbing. There was no noise beyond her choking grief and the fierce hiss of the scorching flame as it devoured and mangled the great golden mass, now so misshapen that it had no longer any recognisable form.

'There is your Salt,' the General shouted. 'Look at it! Now you can have it back!'

For a few seconds he faced Margaret Von Hessel and the hand holding the gun lowered. With a single movement Dunston got his hand to his pocket. He fired through the cloth, and then brought the pistol out and fired again. The General lurched and gave a cry; his gun fell. Dunston's moved round and took a deliberate aim at Paula. The oxyacetylene flame swung in a brilliant arc, a single agonised scream came from Dunston as the fire hit him. The bullet meant for Paula cracked into the wall feet away from her. For a second it seemed that the General stared at her and tried to speak. Then the dazzling light went out and he fell, hitting the ground at dead weight. Paula screamed.

But louder still came the anguished cry of the Princess, directed at the maimed and groaning Dunston. 'You fool! Too late – you fool!'

Fisher turned the General over. The eyes were still open, the mouth ajar for the words he had never spoken. Within reach of his outstretched hand, the mutilated mass of the Poellenberg Salt wept golden tears.

'I'm leaving this afternoon.' The Prince looked older; there were lines under his eyes and a crease running across the fine forehead which Paula had never seen before. He stood in the suite, very upright and dignified; she thought that outwardly, except for the look of bitter strain, he seemed completely unmoved by what had happened. Whatever their enemies said, no one could deny the Von Hessels' self-control.

'I was going to come and see you,' she said. 'I'm going back to England. How is your mother?' The last she had seen of the Princess was when she had been supported out of the suite, suddenly a collapsed old woman in the throes of shock.

'I think she has recovered,' Philip said quietly. 'I haven't been to see her, I'm afraid.'

'I understand how you feel,' Paula said. 'I'm sorry.'

'I hope you will never understand. I knew my brother's wife was murdered. I didn't know about the child. As for my mother – what she did can never be forgiven,' he answered. 'I shall have nothing to do with her now.'

'You may change your mind,' Paula said.

'Would you, if your father had not been killed?'

'No,' she agreed. 'I don't think I would. I want to give you something. I won't be a moment. Please sit down, you look terribly tired.'

'Thank you,' he said. He made an effort and smiled. It only emphasised the misery in his eyes. 'I was worried about you, Mrs Stanley. I hoped you weren't too upset.'

Paula came back; she held an envelope. 'I was,' she said. 'But I wasn't alone, thank God. That made it easier. I'm going to be able to forget the past. You must try and forget it too.'

'It will be very difficult,' he answered. 'I am a German as well as a Von Hessel. I shall have to live with it all my life. I have to live with the knowledge of what my mother did; that will be the hardest thing I have to do.'

'I want you to have these,' Paula said. She gave him the envelope. 'The legal documents and that – letter to my father. You can destroy them and nobody will ever know. Please take them.'

He looked at her. 'I won't thank you. I won't say anything, but you know – I'm sure you know . . .'

'I have to leave soon,' she said. 'I want to go home.'

'To England? Home?'

'Yes,' she said. She held out her hand. He took it and instead of the formal kiss, he held it.

'We're going different ways,' he said quietly. 'But I meant what I said. Will you come to Germany?'

'No,' Paula said. 'No, Prince Philip. Not now. Looking for roots in Germany was like looking for my father. I'm finished with fantasy. I'm not running away any more. I said home, and I meant it. Goodbye, and good luck.'

He bowed, and raised her hand to kiss it.

'Goodbye, Mrs Stanley. I wish it were *auf wiedersehen*.'

The door closed and he was gone. Paula crossed to the telephone.

'This is Mrs Stanley,' she said. 'Please send up for my bags.'

The rasping sound of death was in the room. It rose and fell to the rhythm of the Brigadier's laboured breath. A bright beam of afternoon sunshine poured from the window and fell over the foot of his bed. Uncountable millions of dust motes flickered in it. It was a very hot day, and the windows were open. Sounds of life interrupted the drowning rattle coming from the Brigadier's flooded lungs. He had caught his last cold and suffered his last chest infection. There was nothing his wife could do now but sit beside his bed and wait for him to die. She had refused to leave him, even to let the nurse attend to him.

He was still conscious, although he lapsed into a doze which would be prolonged into death. His hand was held tightly in his wife's and sometimes he exerted a little strength and squeezed, trying to comfort her. People had been very kind over his illness. Paula's mother had never appreciated the sterling qualities of English character until the nightmare of the General broke over their heads, and the façade they had erected round themselves was torn away by Press and television and a brief world interest which flared and then subsided after a few days. Their friends had not deserted them. They had expected to be isolated; instead they were surrounded, comforted and sympathised with in their dilemma with the hungry newspapers, supported upon every issue by the people they had known over the years. There was not a word of reproach or a look which could be construed as criticism. The village stood fast beside the Brigadier and his wife. And then, within a month of it all, he caught pneumonia and she was going to lose him. He was propped high up in the bed, and he turned his head towards her and smiled with blue lips.

'I'm so sorry, darling,' he whispered. 'I can't fight any more.'

'Don't try,' she begged him. 'Don't use your strength – just close your eyes and sleep.'

'I'll sleep in a minute,' he said. 'In a minute, darling.' His eyes had closed and he was drifting. The semi-sleep was restless; he shifted, his head rolling from side to side, and he made little anxious sounds. The rattle of phlegm in his chest was getting louder. Paula's mother lowered her head and wept. She had stayed calm for his sake, reserving the agonies of crying for the hours spent alone in the spare bedroom. Her daughter and the man she was going to marry had come down as soon as they heard from her; they were downstairs in the drawing room. The doctor had told them it was only a matter of a few hours. Certainly not overnight. They had offered to take her away with them, but she had refused.

She appreciated her daughter's sympathy; not that it mattered, because when her husband died, her own life would come to an effective end. She recognised this with the dignified fatalism of her background. It had made no real difference that her daughter had come. But it was kindly meant. The hand which she was holding tightened suddenly and then wrenched away. The Brigadier's eyes were open, staring at her. There was a slight grey film over them which she had not seen before.

'I couldn't stop it,' he rasped at her, choking, 'I tried, my darling, but I couldn't do it . . . I killed him. I followed him from Paula's office that day and I killed him. To protect you. To stop the story getting out . . .'

His wife gazed at him through her tears. She found his hand and clasped it.

'I knew you did,' she said. 'I knew it was you when I realised you'd slipped away to London the first time and there was no committee meeting. You did it because you loved me. And you were right. There's nothing on your conscience, except love.'

'I failed,' he mumbled. 'All your suffering – I'd have done anything . . . You'll be all right, my darling, won't you? You'll be all right?'

'Of course,' she said. 'Of course. I shall do just what you want me to do. And please God we will soon be together.'

'He died very quickly.' The Brigadier was gasping, fighting for the words. 'I burnt my walking stick. I don't regret it, my darling. There's nothing in the world I wouldn't do for you . . .'

'There's nothing in the world you haven't done.' His wife leaned close to him; for a moment her lips pressed against his cheek. His jaws slipped and suddenly there was a harsh, throttled sound coming from the open mouth.

'I love you,' Paula's mother whispered, 'I love you, Gerald. I'll just wait to be with you.'

He didn't answer and he didn't hear. There was a last choking breath and then the room was quiet. His wife put her hand over his eyes and pressed the half-closed eyelids shut. Before she went out of the room she kissed him again.

'I'm very sorry, Mother. I wish there was something we could do.' When her mother came into the room Paula had gone up to her and taken her arm. Watching them Fisher saw the mother flinch. It was a tiny movement, so transient that it had gone as soon as it had registered. She didn't like being touched by Paula. He was not surprised when she disengaged herself. She had come into the room and said simply, 'Your father is dead.'

It was the same flat statement as the one which had brought them down from London. 'Your father is dying. I thought you would like to know.'

And now in the sunny room, with the two labradors settling at her feet, she faced them with the same stoic dignity.

'He was a wonderful man,' she said. 'He gave me perfect happiness.' There seemed nothing more to add; she didn't appear to want sympathy. She had sat down and was stroking one of the dogs. He saw Paula standing in the middle of the room, more forlorn and alone than her mother. He went over to her, taking her hand.

'You're quite sure you don't want us to stay, Mrs Ridgeway? We'd be very happy to stay with you, or take you back with us.'

'No, thank you,' she answered. She even gave him a polite smile. 'It's very kind but I don't want to keep you and Paula here. I would prefer to be alone. I don't want to leave this house; it was our home. He loved it.'

'We'll be in touch tomorrow,' Fisher said.

Mrs Ridgeway got up and came over to them. She held out her hand and Fisher shook it. There was a brief moment when mother and daughter embraced and then Mrs Ridgeway had stepped back.

'Thank you for coming,' she said. 'And I'm very happy for you, Paula. If you have anything like the joy in your life that your father and I have had together, you will be very fortunate indeed. If you don't mind I won't come outside with you. I think I will go and lie down.'

They went out of the drawing room, through the front door into the sunshine. His car was parked in the forecourt. He opened the door for Paula, and then climbed in the other side. He lit a cigarette and gave it to her.

'I'm not going to say anything to you,' he said, 'except I love you very much and I'm going to make you very happy.' He reached over and kissed her. 'It's all over now, my darling. It's a new life for both of us.' He switched on the ignition and the engine throbbed. 'Let's get to hell out of here.'

THE OCCUPYING POWER

I

It was a wide, quiet street, lined with chestnut trees; the houses were protected by walls and wrought-iron gates, and there were few of them. It was a place where the rich lived, but not those who had recently acquired money and wished to make a display. It was a little faded, reserved, very conscious of its status as an address in one of the most status-conscious cities in the world. The taxi cruising slowly down its length came to a halt outside a pair of tall iron gates. There was a gilded crest at the top of them, a circle of oak leaves and a boar rampant, with a coronet above. The driver leaned out and opened the passenger door.

'This is it,' he said. 'Rue de Varenne.' A woman climbed out; she moved clumsily, a heavy-set body on thick legs. She was dressed in a dull coat and skirt and flat shoes, her greying hair showing at the edges of an unflattering felt hat. She opened her handbag and gave the driver the exact fare; after a moment's hesitation she added a very small tip. He took the money, slammed the gears and drove off without thanking her. She stood on the pavement looking up at the gates. A house was visible beyond them, a three-storied grey-stone building with a graceful classical façade, the work of an eighteenth-century architect. There was a small paved courtyard, and two huge stone urns stood at the foot of a flight of steps, filled with flowers. The woman didn't move; she stood as if she were uncertain what to do, looking through the gates. She had arrived in Paris the night before, booked into a modest tourist pension on the Left Bank, and spent a miserable evening sitting in her room. She had never travelled abroad before; her youth had been spent in pre-war Germany where foreign travel was actively discouraged, and then the war had come, binding her to home and a part-time job in a hospital.

While her husband had gone to France, she had kept his letters, all the weekly news sent from his posting outside Paris, full of enquiries about her and the children, prosy, serious letters which she read over and over again to ease her loneliness while he was away. She still had them, yellow and ragged at the edges, tied up in a cardboard box. They had been married thirty-two years and she still loved him. That love and the extreme of desperation had brought her from her homeland to Paris and to the house of a woman she had never seen. A woman who might try not to see her if she knew who she was. Under the ugly hat her blue eyes narrowed. The face was lined and its contours blurred by middle age, but it showed traces of a vanished prettiness; the colour of her eyes and the shape of her mouth were pleasing. When she married she had been a gay and attractive girl of twenty, with a nice rounded figure and a tiny waist. Now she was coarse and shapeless, the result of all the post-war years of hardship, worry and hard work. While the other woman, the one who lived in the elegant house behind her crested gates – how had she survived the onslaught of the years? Was she as beautiful still as she had been when her own husband had first met her – Louise, Comtesse de Bernard.

She said the name under her breath. An aristocrat, smart and spoiled, a prominent figure in Parisian society. On an impulse she opened the gate and went into the courtyard. Her expression was hard, hostile, masking the inward fear of facing the unknown with such a brutal sense of disadvantage. Only for Heinz, her husband . . . for him she would have faced anyone in the world. Even the woman with whom he had fallen in love, all those years ago. She crossed the courtyard and rang the bell.

Louise de Bernard was on the telephone. She used her small boudoir as an office; there was a plain desk and a small filing cabinet, and a telephone with an internal system. A large desk diary was open beside her. Long fingers with beautifully polished nails held a pen and wrote in a name and a time on a day two weeks ahead.

As she talked she smiled. 'Of course Raoul; I'll be delighted. And thank you again for the flowers. Yes. Goodbye.'

The door of the study opened and a girl who somehow looked like Louise de Bernard and was yet completely different in type, put her head round and shook it at her mother.

'Is that the faithful Raoul again?'

'Yes, you know it is; don't be nasty, darling. He's very sweet.'

'He's a stuffy old bore.' She came in and sat on the edge of the desk. She was painfully slim in the modern fashion, casually dressed in trousers and a shirt, her feet in canvas shoes and her ankles bare. Long straight hair hung down past her shoulders and there was no make-up on her face. She put an arm round her mother and kissed her.

'Don't marry him for God's sake! He's a dreadful old reactionary.'

Louise de Bernard glanced up at her daughter. 'He's the same age as me. And I'm not going to marry anyone, as you know perfectly well. Don't sit on those papers, darling, I haven't read them yet.'

Sophie de Bernard slipped off the desk, fumbled in her breast pocket and produced a flattened packet of cigarettes. She flicked at the desk lighter and blew a cloud of Gauloise over her mother's head.

She was thirty but she looked younger, almost coltish. The expression on Louise's face was tender as she looked up at her. Sophie was the younger of her two children, the most physically like her father, and the most temperamentally akin to her. She was unmarried, living with a left-wing writer whom Louise considered an offensive boor, with whom she quarrelled and became reconciled at regular intervals. She was a Maoist who sincerely believed that her mother's generation and all it stood for should be swept away by force. At the same time there was a deep and devoted relationship between them which nothing, neither Louise's disapproval of her mode of life or Sophie's revolutionary convictions, could ever undermine. They loved and understood each other and were far closer than Louise could ever be with her son. Paul was steady, conventional and immersed in his own family life. As Sophie said, and Louise didn't disagree with her, his marriage to Françoise de Boulay had stifled an individuality he might have had. He was a good son, an excellent father and husband and, in his sister's merciless description, a catastrophic bore. Married to a woman whose personality wore a strait-jacket. They were pleasant, dutiful to Louise, who never interfered, and frankly horrified by the antics of Sophie, whose lovers and political activities caused them agonising embarrassment.

'Mother, I didn't mean to disturb you. How's the appeal going?'

'Very well,' Louise said. 'I'm holding a meeting here tonight. I think we may raise more than our target.'

'At least you work hard,' Sophie said. 'But you know what I think of organised charity, don't you?'

'Oh yes,' her mother said. 'I know all about that. Give me a cigarette?'

'Here.' She lit it for her. 'What did Raoul want? Dinner again?'

'The opera; there's a gala performance of *Norma*. I said I'd go.'

'I think it's extraordinary. Half the men in Paris are sniffing round you, and you choose to go out with that pompous idiot. Why don't you take a lover – somebody glamorous and exciting. It would be good for you, darling. Much better than all this committee work.'

'I don't want a lover,' Louise said firmly. 'And I like Raoul; he's an old friend. I also like committee work. Now go away and don't lecture me.'

'You only stick to him because he's safe,' her daughter remarked. 'Papa wouldn't want you to waste your life. You can't go on forever living in the past.'

'Please,' Louise said. 'Don't start all that this morning. I'm happy, Sophie. I have a busy life and I've no intention of having a lover or marrying Raoul. Now let me get on with some work! We can lunch together if you're free.'

'I am,' Sophie admitted. 'I'm furious with Gerard, he can get his own lunch today. And his own dinner!'

Louise, who had heard this threat before, only smiled slightly and said nothing. The bombastic Gerard had a feeble streak, which had so far claimed Sophie's ready sympathy. The day she discovered that it concealed a contemptible character, there would be no more meals and no more relationship. Louise, who had seen the pattern repeat itself, without her daughter suffering any apparent harm, was content to wait upon events.

'I'll go and leave you in peace,' Sophie announced. 'But actually I came up to tell you something – there's a woman downstairs, asking to see you. I told Gaston I'd give you the message.'

'What woman – I'm not expecting anyone this morning. Who is it?'

'I don't know,' Sophie said. She had gone to the door and opened it. 'I've never seen her before. She's a German; she said her name was Minden.'

Louise de Bernard still held the pen balanced between her fingers; the cigarette burned in an ashtray in front of her. Now the pen dropped, spattering ink across the blotting pad. 'Minden?'

'Yes.' Her daughter changed her mind about going out. She pushed the door shut. 'My God, Mother, what's the matter?'

'Minden,' Louise repeated. She got up slowly and turned round. 'Are you sure that was the name?'

'Perfectly sure. Mother, what is it – what *is* the matter?'

'Oh, Sophie – it's not possible, it can't be!' The girl came towards her quickly.

'For God's sake, who is this Minden woman – why are you looking like that?'

Louise didn't answer for a moment. Minden. It wasn't possible after all these years. After so much pain and suffering . . .

'What did she say?' she asked. 'What does she want?'

'To see you, apparently. That's what Gaston said. I saw her waiting in the hall. She looked very ordinary, a dumpy kind of frump . . . Mother, will you please sit down and tell me what this is about? You look as if you'd seen a ghost. Who is Minden, what does it mean?'

'Minden,' Louise said slowly, 'is the name of the German officer who was billeted upon us during the war. Heinz Minden. Now do you understand?'

Sophie de Bernard went up to her mother and put her arm around her. 'I'll send her away,' she said. 'I'll say you're not here. Don't worry; you just stay up here. I'll get rid of her.'

'No, Sophie.' Louise shook her head. 'If it's a woman it must be his wife. I'll have to see her. I'll have to find out what she wants.'

'No you won't,' her daughter said fiercely. 'You're not having the past brought up again – you've gone through enough because of that bloody war. You and Papa! I don't care what she wants – you're not seeing her. I'll go and get rid of her now!'

'No,' Louise repeated. 'No, I'll go. I'll see her. Tell Gaston to show her into the salon and say I'll be down in a few moments. Don't argue, Sophie, do as I say. I don't know what she wants or why she's come here, but I've got to see her!'

'Why?' her daughter demanded. 'You don't owe her anything! How dare any of them come here!'

'I'll come down in a moment. Ask if she wants anything – some coffee – please, go and do as I ask.'

'All right,' Sophie de Bernard said. 'But you're not seeing her alone. I'll be there with you!'

The door closed and Louise could hear her hurrying step go down the passage and run down the staircase to the hall. Minden. She hadn't thought of him for years. There was no association with him in the Paris house. That had been bought after the war ended, when she wanted to escape from St. Blaize and never see it again. He came into the eye of memory and it was as he had been, as a young man in his thirties, neat and efficient in his uniform, with that expression she knew so well in his eyes as he watched her, following every movement she made. And there were other memories, pictures she refused to see, fighting to shut them out. Hands reaching out, words whispered to her in the darkness. Shame and fear and love. Above all, love. But not for him. And not for the father of Sophie and Paul.

That memory, more than any of the others, she had struggled to suppress over the years. Her daughter, sweet, undisciplined, immature at thirty, talked of lovers, without the least understanding of what love itself could mean. But Louise knew. The moment of panic passed; when she was arguing with Sophie her hands were trembling, now they were still. If Heinz Minden's wife had come to see her, then she wasn't going to run away. She paused for a moment, smoothing her hair, steadying herself. If the past had come back then it had to be faced. She opened the door and went downstairs.

Ilse Minden had refused to sit down. She followed the tall French girl into a large room, splendidly decorated in shades of pale green with touches of blue, and some gilt furniture which she recognised instinctively was very valuable. She shook her head when it was suggested that she might like to have coffee, or wait in comfort. She stood in the middle of the carpet looking round her, holding a large plastic handbag in both hands like a shield. Sophie offered her a cigarette. Minden's wife could sense her hostility in spite of an attempt to be polite.

She refused, her tone abrupt because of nervousness.

'Thank you. I don't smoke.'

She couldn't have afforded to smoke, even if Heinz had approved of the habit. She didn't smoke and they lived so sparingly that she had forgotten the smallest luxuries of self-indulgence. It was so long ago since she had been to a hairdresser, or bought new clothes. Everything they had went to their children, who seemed to take it for granted and were busy running as far away from them as possible, now that trouble had overtaken them. Bitterness bolstered her courage. Underneath her timidity there was a worm of hatred, slowly uncoiling as she waited, taking stock of the wealth and good taste in the room, of the casual self-confidence of the young woman, in spite of her mannish clothes and bizarre appearance. Ilse Minden moved towards a table, covered by a blue velvet cloth. There was a small Louis XVI ormolu and porcelain clock on it, and two photographs. One was a studio portrait of a young man, dark and good-looking, smiling towards the camera. The other showed a woman standing with a little boy and girl on either side of her, a fountain in the background. The woman wore the long skirt and clothes of twenty-five years ago. She turned towards Sophie.

'Is that your mother?'

'Yes. With my brother and me. Taken at our home in the country during the war.'

'I see. Does she still look like that?'

'I think so. But you'll be able to judge for yourself. I hear her coming now.' There was something in the German woman's face that made Sophie uncomfortable, a look of sullen menace mingled with uncertainty. And the menace was predominating, as she gained confidence. Ilse Minden turned towards the door. The picture showed a young woman, very beautiful . . . When the door opened she stiffened. A tall woman walked towards her; a beautiful woman in an elegant brown dress, with a silk scarf round her throat and pearls knotted through it. Dark hair and eyes, expensive scent. Hate suffocated Ilse Minden at that moment; jealousy constricted her so that when the woman held out her hand she couldn't move to take it.

'Madame Minden? I am Louise de Bernard. What can I do for you?'

'I have to talk to you.' The woman facing her spoke with a thick accent. She glanced towards Sophie.

'This is my daughter,' Louise said.

'I am Heinz Minden's wife; I've come from Bonn to see you.'

'Please,' Louise said, 'won't you sit down. Did Sophie offer you some coffee, Madame?'

'She didn't want anything,' Sophie said. She walked up close to Ilse Minden. 'Why do you want to see my mother?'

The German didn't answer her. She walked across and settled herself in a chair, clasping the ugly handbag on her knees. She spoke to Louise.

'I don't speak very good French,' she said. 'I would like to speak to you alone.'

'My daughter knows about your husband,' Louise said slowly. 'You can speak in front of her. Why have you come here?'

'She knows about my husband?' The blue eyes turned to Sophie; there was a sarcasm in them now, stronger than the hostility which had been there before. 'All about him?'

'Yes,' Louise answered her. 'There are no secrets in our family, Madame.'

'How lucky,' Ilse Minden said, 'that you have nothing to hide. Please let me talk to you alone. I've come a long way.'

'Sophie,' Louise said quietly. 'Leave us alone, darling. Please.' There were times when it was unwise to argue with her mother. For a moment Sophie hesitated. Her lover said that being a rich American gave Louise de Bernard her authority. But to Sophie that was a superficial lie. Her mother commanded others because she was fully in command of herself. Which was something that Gerard, riotously self-indulgent, would never understand. She got up and went out.

'Thank you,' Ilse Minden said. There was a pause; they looked at each other. Jealousy was rending the older woman's purpose. She was beautiful, she looked young, she would turn any man's head as much now as she had done then ... Suddenly tears came into her eyes and overflowed. She dug into the handbag and brought out a paper handkerchief. She pressed it tight against her face.

'Don't, please.' The American woman's voice was gentle. She felt a hand on her shoulder and took the handkerchief away. She had a speech prepared, rehearsed over and over during the long journey overland from Bonn, repeated in front of the mirror in her dingy pension bedroom that morning. Now she remembered none of it. Old sorrows and present fear came out in a rush of words.

'You've got to help him! You've got to pay back what you owe him – he sacrificed everything for you! Oh God, God help us ...'

'Don't cry,' Louise said. 'Try and calm yourself.' She pulled a chair next to Ilse Minden and sat down. 'I don't understand,' she said. 'How can I help your husband now? I haven't seen or heard of him since the war.'

'No,' the other woman said, using the handkerchief. 'No, you wouldn't. You didn't need him any more, did you? You were safe then because we'd lost – while he ... Do you know what he's suffered for all these years, do you know how we lived after the war was over? How could you . . .' She spoke with angry vehemence. 'You had everything you wanted. You were the victors!'

'Madame Minden,' Louise said. 'I knew your husband many years ago when he was living in my house. You talk about a debt; all right, I owe him a great deal. You say you've come to ask for help. Would you please explain what kind of help you want? And try not to be so hostile towards me; I never did you or your husband any harm.'

She moved away and got a cigarette. She felt disturbed and distressed. There was something ugly about the other woman's tears, something more than emotional turbulence which is always disconcerting to a stranger. There was hatred, and there was a subtle suggestion of threat. For all her tears, there was a determination and a toughness about Heinz Minden's wife which made Louise uncomfortable. She had come to demand something, rather than to plead.

'You say you never did him any harm?'

'Never. If he told you anything different, then I'm afraid he's lying.'

'Oh, he wouldn't describe it that way!' She gave a short, unpleasant laugh. 'Everything you ever did was perfect, Madame de Bernard. You couldn't do wrong in Heinz's eyes – surely you know that?'

'You're talking about years ago,' Louise pointed out. 'About the distant past. None of that matters anymore.'

'Not to you, of course. But it matters to us. It's mattered to me, Madame, knowing my husband didn't love me any more because of you! It may be years ago for you, but it's day to day for me! How do you think I felt, living in dirty back rooms, taking what jobs I could to support us, starving myself and him to give our children a chance, and knowing that nothing I did, *nothing*, stopped him thinking about you!'

'I'm terribly sorry.' Louise looked away from her, from the anguish and bitterness assaulting her from so close. 'Please believe me, I did nothing to encourage this . . .' And then she stopped, remembering. 'I'm sorry,' she said again. She put out a hand to Ilse Minden, who jerked back from being touched.

'Helping you caused all the trouble,' she said. 'When the war was over the organisation which took care of people like Heinz found out about it, and they threw him out. They stopped helping him. We were on our own then, hiding, running from place to place frightened to settle anywhere. We could have been in South America by now if he hadn't compromised himself for you!'

She could have argued with Ilse Minden; she could have pointed out that what her husband had done only reflected credit on him, that it was not because he was in love with her. Any man, anyone with decency or sensibilities would have done the same. But she didn't say anything. To the woman facing her, it was an incomprehensible folly, committed by an infatuated man for a woman he loved. And the knowledge of this made Madame Minden, dull and plain and tearful, a very frightening person.

'Surely by now that kind of thing is over,' Louise said. 'There are thousands of people living in Germany without having to fear for what they did. Or what they were.'

'My husband was a brilliant man,' Ilse Minden interrupted. 'You call working in a pharmacy, selling tubes of toothpaste and bars of soap, living without fear? And that's only in the last five years. Before that he was doing odd jobs, sweeping, digging, anything he could find where nobody would notice him. And now, Madame de Bernard, even that miserable life is over. He's in prison!'

Suddenly the German woman's tears were dried up; she looked calm and grim waiting for Louise to react. In all the years of running a large household, managing her family and the complicated affairs of a large fortune, Louise had never felt as lost and disconcerted as she did now.

'Why is he in prison? What's the charge?'

'War crimes,' his wife said. 'For all these years they've been hunting him; that filthy Jew in Vienna had his name on a list. And two months ago they found him. He was arrested and he's in jail waiting to be tried.'

'It shouldn't be,' Louise said slowly. 'Your husband wasn't like the others – he didn't . . .'

'He did his duty,' Ilse Minden broke in harshly. 'He fought for his country and his Führer as we all did. Then it was patriotism, now it's a crime. The only time he failed was when he put you first.'

'It wasn't me he put first,' Louise said. 'Surely you can see that?'

'Can't see anything but my husband facing a sentence of fifteen or twenty years,' came the reply. 'That's why I'm here. I've used my savings to get here and see you.'

'What do you want me to do?' Louise asked. 'If you need money for his defence . . .'

'No thank you,' Ilse Minden said. 'Money would be easy for you, wouldn't it? I don't need money. There are lawyers in Germany who will undertake a defence for someone like my husband. Someone who's being persecuted by the politicians and the Jews. No, Madame de Bernard, I need a different kind of help. I want you to stand up in court and tell them what my husband did for you. I want you to testify that he saved lives, and risked his own. His counsel knows what happened. He says that if you appear for the defence it will make all the difference. He could get a suspended sentence.'

'I can't give you an answer.' Louise stood up suddenly. 'I've had no time to think about it, no warning. I can't just promise to go to Germany and stand up in a court – I'll have to talk to my family.'

'I see.' She opened her handbag, took out another paper handkerchief and wiped her mouth with it.

'You had a sister-in-law, didn't you?'

Louise stood very still. 'Yes.'

'Her name was Régine, wasn't it?'

'Yes it was.'

'You look upset, Madame,' Ilse Minden said in a quiet voice. 'Why don't you sit down again? I'm not leaving here yet. Shall I tell you about your sister-in-law? Shall I tell you what my Heinz told me about her?'

'Are you threatening me?'

'Of course not; I need your help. Heinz needs it. One thing the defence counsel said to me – there'll be a lot of dirt and scandal when this case comes to trial. People who've been living a lie and pretending to be what they weren't are going to look very sick by the time it's all over. Don't you think that's true?'

'You are threatening me,' Louise said slowly. 'You're trying to blackmail me. Well, you've made a mistake. I won't be blackmailed. I'll show you out.' She stood up and went to the door. The German woman got up.

'Your husband,' she said. 'The Resistance hero. I believe your son is running for deputy for your home region, isn't that so? Before you throw me out of your house, Madame, think carefully. All we need is a few words from you, to save an old man from spending the rest of his life in jail.'

'If you'd put it to me like that first, I might have testified,' Louise said quietly. 'Now will you please leave my house.'

'You're very grand, aren't you, Madame de Bernard? You can turn a poor woman away, and leave the debt you owe my Heinz unpaid? Very well. But here is my address. I'll be there for the next two days. Let me know when you change your mind.' She walked past Louise to the door and let herself out, leaving it open. Her thick shoes made an ugly noise as she crossed the marble hall. There was a snap as the front door shut.

For some moments Louise didn't move; it was as if the presence of the other woman hadn't left the room. Hate hung in the atmosphere like cigarette smoke. She went to the door and closed it. She pulled the chair away from the sofa where Ilse Minden had sat down; she lit a cigarette and deliberately calmed herself. She straightened a cushion and made a note to replace one of the hothouse plants.

'Mother? I heard that woman go out. Darling, what's the matter?'

Sophie de Bernard came towards her. 'What in God's name did she say to you?'

'Not a lot,' Louise said slowly. 'But enough. Her husband's in prison in Germany; he's going to be tried for war crimes. She wants me to go and give evidence for him. She wants me to tell the story in court.'

'That's ridiculous! You're not doing anything of the sort! You can give written evidence, an affidavit and send them that. You're not going near any war crimes trial!'

'Darling, you don't understand. She threatened me. She threatened to make a scandal.'

'And can she make one?' Sophie asked the question boldly. Her attitude was defensive, determined not to care. 'Not that I give a damn,' she said. 'You know that.'

'Yes, I do. But you're not the only one. What about Paul?'

'Don't tell him,' Sophie said. 'Look, Mother, be sensible. She's just trying to frighten you. There's nothing she can rake up now that would matter to anyone. It's over and done with – nobody cares any more. Let her go to hell. And so what if he did do one decent thing? What about the rest of it? Come on, forget about it. I'll take you out to lunch today.'

'She left me her address,' Louise said. 'She said she'd be there for two days and to let her know when I changed my mind. When. Not "if".'

'That's just bluff,' Sophie said angrily. 'You'll never hear another word about it.'

Louise looked at her daughter. She was brave and loyal and loving, ready to battle the world for her mother. Would she be so ready, so trusting if she knew exactly what the woman Ilse knew? Probably; there was a generous spirit there and a capacity for understanding which was rare in the modern *avant garde*.

She held out her hand to Sophie and forced herself to smile.

'You're right, I expect. I won't hear any more from her. Give me half an hour to telephone and finish that wretched report upstairs and then we'll go and lunch together.' Reassured, Sophie preceded her mother out of the salon. She had a capacity for believing the best would happen rather than the worst. Upstairs in the study, with the mechanics of her normal life to be attended to, Louise stared at the telephone and the papers, unable to apply herself to either. Sophie had tried to comfort her, and had succeeded in lulling herself. Louise thanked God for what she felt was only a respite. When you change your mind. Heinz Minden's wife had chosen her words with care. The piece of paper with the address of the pension was on her desk. She had brought it upstairs with her. Subconsciously. She put it away carefully in a drawer, and knew as she did so, that the first part of the battle had been won by Ilse Minden.

There was a three-hour delay on calls to Bonn. She sat in the dreary little sitting room of the pension, waiting for the call, looking through old copies of *Plaisir de la Maison* and a tattered edition of *Elle*, which was six months out of date and featured an article by film stars who had undergone abortions and were championing the cause. She hated the French. Their lack of morality disgusted her. She disliked their food and their fashions, their architecture annoyed her because it was so grandiose and nothing could take away from the people of the country the splendour of its history and the strength of its traditions. She could never forget that they had been beaten; that she had worn stockings and scent and a smart fur coat which Heinz had brought her after his posting to France. For a brief period they had had their hands in the till, fingering the luxuries. Twenty years of deprivation had followed that fleeting indulgence. Defeat and humiliation, shame and fear. She hated her country's enemies, and above all she hated the woman who had received her that morning. It had been a catharsis to go and see her, to spill out some of the venom which had corroded her spirit for so many years. Now she could hate the real woman, not the figment which was all Heinz's unhappy confessions had created for her. Now she knew the colour of Louise de Bernard's eyes, the shape of her face, the gestures she used. The enemy had taken on flesh. When the call came through she hurried to the outer office and dropped into the chair behind the reception desk. She gave a glare at the proprietress who seemed inclined to linger and try to listen.

'Herr Kopner? Frau Minden. Yes, yes I've seen her.'

There was a pencil on the desk and a note pad. She began to draw little lines, crossing and recrossing as she talked. 'Yes, I had a long talk. No. She refused. Well, we expected that. Of course. No, no, I didn't say anything too obvious. Now I will make the next move. I'm sure of it. Certain. How is my husband? He mustn't suspect anything – he wouldn't agree – yes, yes, I've told you, I shall do it immediately. I gave her two days. I will telephone to you as soon as I have any news. Good. *Auf Wiedersehen*.' She hung up. The proprietress came back, her expression curious. 'You wish this call to be put on your bill, or would you like to pay for it now?'

'On the bill,' Ilse Minden said. 'Can you help me please – I need a directory for the Houdan region. Do you have one here?'

'The directories are under the shelf there. Can I get the name for you?'

'Thank you, no. I can look it up myself.' She ruffled the pages, uncertain at first where to look, refusing to satisfy the old woman's curiosity by letting her find the number. She ran one finger down the page; her nail was filed short and the cuticle was rough. She found the name and the number, and wrote it down.

'I want to make another call,' she said. 'Also on the bill. Do I dial direct?'

'For Houdan and that part, certainly, yes. Shall I get it for you?'

'No. Thank you.' Ilse Minden dialled slowly, checking the figures against the number scribbled down on the pad. There was a pause.

'Hello?' She raised her voice unnecessarily, as foreigners do when speaking on the telephone in a different language. 'I wish to speak to the Comte de Bernard. Thank you. Yes, I'll wait.' She glanced at the proprietress, who looked preoccupied and went out of the hallway. 'Good morning,' she said. 'Monsieur de Bernard? You don't know me. My name is Ilse Minden.'

In his office on the Hofgarten Strasse in the centre of Bonn, the defence counsel, who was preparing his brief for Heinz Minden, put back the telephone and lit a cigarette. He smoked the cheapest brand; it was a curious idiosyncrasy and quite out of character; he lived extremely well and bought the best for himself. His practice was flourishing, he owned a smart house in the best residential area, out on the Bahnhof estate; ran two cars and had a well-connected second wife, who was fervently advancing his political ambition. He was a good-looking man of forty-two, just the right age to seek office. Too young for the war and yet old enough to appeal to those who had fought in it, and for whom the old wounds still smarted. His name was Siegfried Kopner. He had visited Heinz Minden the previous afternoon. He found him a pathetic specimen, and Herr Kopner did not equate pathos with pity. Minden was broken, his resignation infuriated Kopner, who had staked his reputation in public upon saving him. And more than him, much more than the liberty of one listless old man who actually looked back on his past with regret. Kopner had been looking for a platform from which to deliver his political viewpoint. The trial of someone like Heinz Minden was exactly what he needed. In the court he could say all those things and ally himself with attitudes which would have been unthinkable as part of an election formula. And yet they supplied a need and expressed the feelings of thousands, perhaps millions of his countrymen. Fortunately, if the husband's spine was snapped, there was plenty of determination in the woman. Kopner thought his client's wife was an unpleasant type, enbittered and sexless, fastened like a leech upon the uncaring corpse of the man she was married to; but she presented him with the weapon he needed. During the long, tearful consultations about Minden's defence, she had told him, little by little and with increasing self-pity, the story of her husband's infatuation for the Comtesse de Bernard, and of the effort he had made on her behalf. Nothing would convince the woman, so blinded by jealousy, that Minden had acted out of anything but a desire to ingratiate himself with the Comtesse. To Kopner it was a gift; the kind of story which properly presented, could diminish his client's responsibility for the crimes charged against him, and show him in the kind of heroic light which the liberals found so satisfactory. And at the same time there in the courtroom would be a representative of the enemy; the old enemy, but still very much a symbol, not only of their own heroism but of the iniquity of their opponents. Louise de Bernard. He had checked on the family after listening to Ilse Minden and in the dung-heap of marital discord and old infringements of international law, he had found a shining political pearl. He had smoked the meagre cigarette down to its buff coloured tip. He rubbed it out in an onyx ashtray. He had sent Minden's wife to Paris. It was too compromising to go himself. Her initial failure had disappointed him but he appeared undaunted by it. She possessed the confidence of the obsessed. She wanted her husband's freedom; that was the reason she gave to herself. But equally, and probably more, if motives were honestly analysed, she wanted her rival humiliated and destroyed in public.

Which was exactly what Siegfried Kopner wanted too. He lit another cigarette and spoke to his secretary on the intercom.

'Telephone to my wife,' he said.

There was a dinner party arranged in his honour that evening; he decided it would be simpler if his wife brought a change of clothes to his office and he dressed there. He had a great deal of work to do and he didn't want to leave early.

His wife was the daughter of a former Admiral; her family were of a higher social class than his own, but the war had deprived them of their Eastern estates and she was eager to marry him. She was a hard, determined woman whose ambitions were centred upon him. She had devoted herself to his comfort and his career from the start of the marriage, and he was very happy with her. He slept at regular intervals with a delightful, amusing little dress designer he had met at a party, and considered himself to have the best arrangement any man could want.

His wife came through on the line. He told her to bring his evening suit; she agreed immediately. 'Any news from Frau Minden?' She knew everything about the case. He always discussed his work with her; she often had valuable comments to make. 'She phoned not long ago,' Kopner said. 'The Comtesse wouldn't agree. I don't think she handled her very well. But she's going to carry out the second plan, and she thinks this will work. I think so too.'

'Excellent,' his wife said. Her voice came through high pitched through the receiver. He held it a little away from his ear. 'They'll give in,' she said. 'I'm very confident. I'll be at the office at six-thirty; that will give you an hour to change. We mustn't be late. I've sent flowers to Hilda.'

'Excellent,' he said, imitating her. 'Until six-thirty.'

A senior member of the Bundeswehr would be present at the dinner. It was hoped to enlist him as a sponsor for Kopner's candidature. The evening would be very important in his career. At about the same time as his wife arrived with the suitcase, carrying his beautifully pressed dinner jacket, Ilse Minden got off the train at Houdan railway station and took a taxi to the Château St. Blaize.

2

Sophie de Bernard was a fast driver; she took the autoroute out of Paris, following the signs to Versailles and swung round past the town onto the Chartres road. For the first twenty minutes Louise sat beside her without speaking. The traffic was always heavy, and although they were ahead of the evening rush, the pace was sluggish; there were few opportunities for Sophie to unleash the Mercedes and drive at her usual speed. Finally they cleared the slow-moving line of cars and lorries, and the car shot forward. Louise looked at her.

'Don't go too quickly, darling. We'll be there soon enough.'

'He makes me sick,' her daughter said furiously. 'You shouldn't have come down; they're only going to make things difficult for you.'

'They won't mean to,' Louise said. 'Besides. I've made it difficult for them. Paul sounded terribly shaken on the telephone.'

'Only because that damned Françoise had been at him. "Think of your career, think what will happen if there is a scandal" – I can just hear her saying it!'

'You've got to promise me not to quarrel with them,' Louise said. 'I've got to talk to Paul and find out what he wants me to do.'

'He'll want you to protect him,' Sophie said angrily. 'That's obvious. He should have thrown that woman out of the house instead of listening to her! I shouldn't have called you to the telephone! Anyway, whatever you say, Mother, I'm not going to stand by and let them bully you.'

Louise didn't answer. Her son's anxious voice on the telephone the night before had been completely unexpected. She had never thought for a moment that Ilse Minden would go direct to him. But she had, and the worried man, trying to seem calm, had begged her to come down to St. Blaize and discuss the problem with him. And with his wife, whose voice she could hear murmuring in the background. They would both be there, frightened and surprised, not knowing how to cope. The unexpected seldom disturbed their lives. She allowed herself to wonder how her son and his wife Françoise would have behaved had they faced the same situations as she had done. And her husband, whose portrait had been commissioned by Paul and now hung in the main hall of the Château. He was very proud of his father, who had been a hero of the Resistance. If she wore her own Legion d'Honneur ribbon, he was visibly gratified. She thought of the coming interview and shuddered. Not for herself. Since the telephone call last night her feelings for herself were numb. All she could feel now was sorrow for the others, the innocent whose safe illusions had been shattered. How much had that woman told Paul – how much would she have to tell Sophie, who might not be as immune as she pretended . . .

They had left the autoroute behind and were travelling fast along the country roads, passing through St. Leger en Yvelines, where her husband Jean used to hunt before the war, on to Houdan, and then across to St. Blaize, down the narrow road she remembered so well. It was a long time since she had been there, almost three years. Visits for the christening of her first grandson, then a grand-daughter, one painful Christmas spent with the family, who hadn't known how to entertain her, because her distress at being in the Château was so obvious. They had meant to be kind, Paul and Françoise, and Sophie, at that time in the first stage of a violent love affair with a popular guitarist, had been in America with him on a tour. She couldn't spend Christmas in Paris alone; it would be too painful. Against her will, and only to please them, Louise had allowed them to persuade her and she had come back to the house which had been her home, and which she never wanted to see again. Now, passing through the wrought-iron gates and turning up the drive, she saw the familiar turret, clothed in ivy and the handsome façade, surrounded by sweeping green lawns, the old trees giving their magnificent shade, unchanged by centuries. Dogs rushed out to meet her, the lean grey Weimaren hounds that her daughter-in-law kept, and which had replaced the spaniels which she and Jean had loved. And then her son, tall and anxious-looking, with his wife's slight figure, suitably dressed in tweed and English cashmere emerging from behind him. They kissed her; he was affectionate and warm, and pretended not to notice his sister's aggressive attitude as she walked into the house. Inside, Louise paused for a moment.

There was the hall, a large room with a Norman ceiling, the sixteenth-century tapestries which had been there since they were woven, and the portrait of Jean de Bernard, with a light over it, dominating the room. Françoise advanced towards her; she had a special tone for her mother-in-law, of whom she was very much in awe. It suggested that whatever happened she had to be humoured, and it never failed to make Louise feel like an intruder.

'Would you like to go upstairs to your room, first, Louise? Then we can talk in the library?'

'Yes, that would be nice. Where am I sleeping? The little blue room?'

'Well, no,' Françoise explained. Her smile was strained and she looked as if she hadn't slept. 'We've had that done for Christiane. You're in the second guest room. It's all been decorated; it's very pretty now.'

Louise smiled back at her and followed her up the staircase. A manservant was carrying her small case. They had insisted that she and Sophie stayed the night. It couldn't be discussed in a hurry. She walked slowly up the winding stone stairs and outside the bedroom door she hesitated. Her bag was inside, the servant stood waiting for her to go in. It was a room she hadn't seen for over twenty years. A room which held memories of such anguish and such longing that she felt her colour fading as she stepped inside it.

Nothing remained the same. The walls were a different colour, the old-fashioned four-poster bed had gone, the armchair, the Empire furniture, the ugly pre-war chintzes. 'Thank you,' she said, not turning round, and the door closed. She was alone in the room which had been Roger Savage's bedroom. She went to the window and looked out. He had done the same, that morning in June, in 1944, drawing back the curtains and looking down. She hadn't thought about him, she hadn't let his memory return to spoil the last few years. Now there was no defence. Suddenly she dropped upon the bed, and found that she was crying. No defence at all. Her daughter-in-law had made the changes, turning the room into a pretty, chic guest bedroom, but she couldn't paint out the past, and it rushed at Louise, sharp and so real that the present seemed to have no substance. Roger Savage. And down the corridor Heinz Minden's room, and the room where Régine slept. They were all there, the ghosts and the living, crowding in upon her, demanding to be recognised. And Savage was the most real of all. She could see him standing by the window, tall and broad, the sun shooting rays of light around him as he blocked it out, looking down at the forty-foot drop below. She put both hands to her face and wiped away the tears. He had hated to see her cry. Even at the end when she was weeping in agony for him, he had been hurt by her tears . . .

There was a knock at the door. It opened without waiting for her to answer, and it was not Sophie, as she expected, but her son Paul.

'Mother,' he said gently. 'I had a feeling you'd be upset. Come downstairs; we're all waiting for you. We'll talk about it and find a solution together.' He put his arm around her, and they left the room.

There had been a row between Sophie and Françoise; she could feel it as soon as she went into the yellow salon. They were apart, the Comtesse de Bernard sitting very upright, her face pink and her eyes bright with anger; Sophie lounging like an urchin, a cigarette dangling from her mouth. Louise looked at them both and gently disengaged herself from Paul's arm. He couldn't support her. He belonged to his wife; he had a family of his own, a life apart from hers. His was the future. Ilse Minden had come into their lives, and the past was threatening them all. She was the direct link with it; the responsibility must be hers alone. But first, before any decision could be taken, there was something she knew she had to do. She had known in that upstairs room, as clearly as if Savage had come back and told her.

'Let's all sit down,' she said. 'Paul, my dear, get me a drink, would you? A whisky and Perrier.'

'Of course.' He looked relieved at having been asked to do something.

'Françoise? Sophie?' Both women shook their heads. Louise took the glass from him and lit a cigarette. For once her daughter-in-law didn't rush forward with an ashtray.

'I don't know what that woman told you,' Louise said quietly. 'But I can imagine you've found a lot of it distressing.'

'We didn't believe it,' her son said. 'We would never believe anything . . .' He stopped, embarrassed. 'We just wanted to discuss what should be done.'

'You're not going to bully Mother into giving evidence to keep that bloody woman's mouth shut.' Sophie turned on him fiercely. 'And that's what I gather you're proposing to do!' She gave her sister-in-law a look of fury.

'No we're not,' Paul de Bernard said. He avoided his wife's anxious glance. 'We're going to behave in a sensible fashion and talk this out. Nobody's going to do anything to upset Mother. So you needn't talk like that.'

'None of you need get angry with each other on my account,' Louise said. 'There's no need. I'm sure Ilse Minden told you she'd been to see me. She tried to blackmail me. As she obviously did to you, Paul. One thing is certain; she doesn't intend to give up. What we have to decide is whether to give in to that blackmail, or whether to resist it.'

'There is another point.' Françoise de Bernard spoke for the first time. There was an expression on her face as she looked at Louise which had never been there before. 'And that's whether, in conscience, Mother shouldn't do as she asks.'

'That's true,' Louise answered. 'And there's only one way to decide. And that is for me to tell you exactly what happened. The truth.'

'Mother . . .' Sophie began, 'we know . . .'

'No, darling,' Louise interrupted. 'I'm afraid you don't. But I am going to tell you. Then we will make up our minds what I must do.'

The Château de St. Blaize lay some fifty kilometres from Paris, and forty kilometres from the great medieval city of Chartres. The village of St. Blaize en Yvelines was dominated by the Château which watched

over it from a slight rise in the ground. It was a small, turreted château
of grey stone with a slate roof, a tower at its north side, approached
from the road by a long gravel drive. For nearly six hundred years it
had been the centre of life for the village, and the same family had
lived there without interruption except for a period of exile during the
Revolution. The bigger houses in the area were under German occupation, their owners quartered in a small portion of their homes, but
St. Blaize belonged entirely to the de Bernards. The village, observing
everything that happened at the Château, congratulated the Comte on
having kept his home intact and admired his facility for coping with
the occupying forces. He showed remarkable tact and foresight for a
comparatively young man, and his lack of false heroics relieved the
citizens of St. Blaize of any feeling of guilt for their own complaisance
towards the enemy.

One experience of German anger had been enough for the most
reckless of the men who sat round boasting and grumbling in the
wine shop. They followed the example of the Comte and showed
their wish to co-operate with the German authorities. As a result,
their lives were undisturbed, and only one German officer, more of
a guest than an intruder, lived at the Château with the Comte and his
family. It was known that the Comtesse held different views from her
husband and had never hesitated to express them, but since she was
an American, her example was ignored. Nobody in St. Blaize wanted
trouble, or to be forced to fight the Germans. They wanted to survive,
like the Comte de Bernard.

One evening at the end of May in 1944 Louise took their coffee into
the salon; for the last three months Jean de Bernard had insisted upon
the German dining with them instead of in his room, and staying for
an hour or two afterwards. Eating with him had been bad enough
for Louise; his presence in her drawing room only increased her
disgust with her husband. There was nothing obviously offensive
about Major Minden. He was a quiet man in his thirties, unobtrusive
and embarrassed by his being billeted upon them. He had gone out
of his way to be self-effacing and when the Comte de Bernard offered
him hospitality, he responded by generous gifts of things which were
unobtainable for the French. He was always polite, tactful, appre-
ciative of everything. He apologised for the situation in which they
found themselves without ever putting his guilt into words, and he
followed Louise with his eyes, mentally fornicating, until she could
have screamed.

The meal this evening had been simple; food was short and luxuries
like butter and sugar tightly rationed. Not even Minden's ingenuity
could get them the rich veal and cream, the pork and game and poultry
which had made the food at St. Blaize famous before the war. The

cook had died in 1941, and now the cooking was done by Louise or Marie-Anne, who showed remarkable skill with vegetables, eggs and an occasional chicken. There was a splendid cellar at the Château, and they bottled a light white wine from their own vineyards in the Loire. After dinner, Minden produced a bottle of fine cognac and offered his host a cigar. Louise looked at him as he pierced and lit it. It was May, but the weather had been wet and cold; a log fire was alight in the wide stone grate, and the light flickered over the face she had loved, and caressed with her hands. He had changed very little in the eight years they had been married. His manner was the same; gentle, courteous, a little aloof but his laugh hadn't lost its warmth or his eyes their charm. She could see Minden responding to it, smiling and talking, leaning a little forward, the cigar jutting through his fingers. For a moment he was concentrating on the Comte and not slyly glancing at her, his tongue slipping over his lips. She hated the way he treated her, the spring to his feet when she came into a room, holding out her chair when they sat at the dining table, always polite, with his head a little on one side as if he were concentrating on every word. And she said as little as possible. She showed him that she resented him and disliked him, but his skin was elephantine. Nothing she said or did to convey her feelings made the slightest difference. He responded by bringing her a large bottle of the most expensive scent at Christmas which was exclusively exported to Germany. She would have respected him more if he'd tried to put his hand down her dress.

He and her husband were talking about the war; the room was full of the smell of cigar smoke; Louise poked at the logs and listened.

'I didn't believe they'd ever invade,' Jean de Bernard said. 'I still can't take it seriously.'

'It's very serious indeed,' Minden said. 'It's said there must be quarter of a million men waiting to leave England and land over here. Of course, it's the Russians pressing for a Second Front that's forced them into it.' He tapped his ash into a silver bowl,

'You don't seem concerned, Major,' Jean de Bernard remarked.

'I can't see them winning,' Minden said mildly. 'I foresee terrific casualties and complete defeat,'

'Aren't you being a little complacent?' They both looked at Louise,

'I don't think so,' the Major answered. His tone implied that it wasn't a topic on which she would have anything sensible to say.

'After all, the British Empire and the United States are a pretty formidable combination,' Louise went on, knowing how Jean hated her to goad the German. 'You won't just flick off a quarter of a million men like a speck of dust.'

Minden nearly smiled. He had to be careful not to show the extent of his confidence but it was so much a part of him now that he

couldn't pretend to be afraid. Invasion didn't trouble him. Victory
was certain. He stared for a moment at the Comtesse's beautiful legs.
American women had the best legs in the world. And the best teeth;
hers were perfect. In spite of her colouring, brown hair and hazel eyes,
she couldn't have been a Frenchwoman. She was too tall, too slim.

'You must forgive me, Madame,' he said, 'I believe our soldiers are
the best in the world. I think we will beat the invasion forces when
they come.'

'And will you be going to fight them?'

His half-smile was still there, the light of admiration in his eyes
as he answered her. Jean de Bernard re-lit his cigar, without looking
at his wife. 'Unfortunately, I shall still be attached to General Brühl.
Believe me, I would like to be a combatant, but someone has to do
the staff work.'

'It may be dull but it's better than being sent to Russia.' Louise lit
a cigarette. Jean de Bernard got up bringing his cup.

'Could I have some more coffee?'

She ignored the warning in his eyes. He was a coward. He was her
husband and now she despised him as much as she had looked up to
him and loved him. Let him crawl to the conquerors; she didn't glance
at him. She poured the coffee which was real instead of the filthy
mixture of acorns and chicory which was all the non-collaborationists
had to drink, and gave it back to him.

'I think I'll go to bed,' she said. 'I'm rather tired tonight.'

Immediately the Major was on his feet, his heels snapped together.
She went out of the room, savouring the small exchange which was
already beginning to look petty and pointless as she thought about it.
Scoring off someone too insensitive to feel it was small compensation
for the misery and shame wlich tormented her every time she saw him.
He wasn't a brute, there was nothing of the strutting Nazi about him;
he was an ordinary man, not remarkable in any way, but he was a
German, the symbol of the disgrace of France and the capitulation of
the man she loved. Jean had collaborated and the village had done the
same. French girls walked the lanes with German soldiers and their
families accepted cigarettes and food. France had lain down for her
conquerors, it was not so much a rape as a seduction. Louise, who
had loved all things French and embraced the culture and even, within
two years of marriage, the faith of her adopted country, watched in
horror as people she respected set about ingratiating themselves with
the invaders, as the homes of their friends were filled with German
officers on social calls, and there were dinner parties and murmurs of
love affairs with women whose husbands had not yet been repatriated.
The first shock had come that summer's day in 1940, four years ago,
when she and Jean had stood together in the Château with his sister

Régine, then a girl of fifteen, and seen the German scout car come skidding up the gravel drive, scattering the stones, and slam to a stop before the entrance. There were black and white crosses painted on its sides and as they watched through the window, three men got out in field grey uniform. He had held her in his arms, and she had gripped him tight, ready to die with him if he asked her. 'Oh my God,' she had whispered to him. 'What are we going to do . . .'

'Learn to live with them,' Jean had answered. 'Live with them and survive. And keep our home.' She hadn't believed him, she hadn't really understood. When the salon door opened and the first German officer stepped inside, she waited for Jean to move, to show resistance. Instead he had disengaged himself from her and walked towards them, one hand extended.

'Gentlemen,' he had said. 'Welcome to St. Blaize.' There were two of them, young men with anonymous faces under their peaked combat caps. Tears had come rushing into her eyes; she had caught Régine by the hand and dragged her past them and upstairs. As she ran into the hall she heard her husband say, 'You must excuse my wife. She is upset. Please sit down.' From that moment the disintegration had begun.

When Louise had gone out, Minden stretched and sat down again. Jean poured some brandy into his glass and offered the bottle, but the Major shook his head. 'I've got some work to do,' he said. 'Brandy makes me go to sleep. I'm glad your wife went up early, I wanted to talk to you in private. You know there was an alert tonight?'

'No,' Jean de Bernard said. 'They must have been on their way somewhere else, nothing was dropped near here.' The Major had come back late; to Louise's irritation Jean had insisted upon waiting dinner for him.

'It was a single plane,' the Major said. 'We've had them come over before. Personally I believe it was a reconnaissance flight. On the other hand it may have been a drop.'

'A drop – what do you mean?'

'Enemy agents. It's not likely but we have to take precautions. There'll be road blocks tomorrow and a search. I wanted to warn you. I didn't want to worry Madame de Bernard.'

'They won't drop anyone here,' Jean said. 'It's two years since they tried that. Nobody at St. Blaize wants any trouble.'

'We know that,' Minden said seriously. 'There's no resistance in this area. Now that the resistance at Chartres has been broken . . .' He paused, regretting having mentioned the incident. 'But I just wanted to ask you to use your influence with the village. If anyone should have landed here – I hope you'll impress on them how foolish it would be to shelter them. As I said, I'm sure it's a reconnaissance plane that probably went astray. It may have crashed somewhere nearer the coast; that's the official view, but we have to be careful.'

'Don't worry,' Jean de Bernard said. 'We're at peace, we get along with you extremely well. The last thing anyone wants to do is to spoil our relationship with the military. You have my personal assurance that I'll go down and speak to the mayor tomorrow. If the Allies have been stupid enough to try and involve us by dropping any agent here, they'll be given up to you immediately.'

'Thank you,' the Major said. He got up. 'I should make sure all doors are locked. I hope your wife won't be frightened; really there's no need to mention it. There'll be a routine search tomorrow, but I'll make sure you're not disturbed.'

'That's very considerate of you,' Jean de Bernard said. 'Louise wouldn't be alarmed but it might upset my father. He's getting so confused so quickly.'

'I'm sorry to hear that. I must go and have a talk to him one evening. He isn't getting any worse?'

'Not physically; age is a sad thing, Major. He's becoming more and more of a child.'

'I'll say goodnight,' the Major said. 'If you should hear any rumours tomorrow you will let me know?'

'You can rely on me,' the Comte de Bernard said. 'Goodnight.' He didn't leave the room after Minden; he stayed on beside the sinking fire, finishing the brandy. Enemy agents. A quarter of a million men waiting on the other side of the English Channel to launch themselves against the coast of France. A rain of shells and bombs falling on French homes and killing the innocent inside them. The giants squaring up for a fight to the death, with his people and his country as their battleground. Above all he didn't believe the Germans would be beaten. Their vengeance upon any who had turned against them would be too terrible to contemplate. Thanks to his efforts St. Blaize en Yvelines had suffered only two casualties since the occupation, and they were the direct results of night warnings like this one, of a parachute drop by the British . . . No more French lives were going to be sacrificed to the ruthless strategists in London. He finished his brandy, and lit a cigarette. He had better follow Minden's suggestion and make sure that every door and window was locked. And then he had to go and see his wife. In his youth there had been fifteen servants at the Château; now there were two, Marie-Anne and Jean-Pierre, husband and wife who had started working in his parents' time as kitchen maid and undergardener. They were in their sixties and Jean-Pierre had a stiff knee. Soon after Minden arrived he pressed his batman, a surly Rhinelander with a milky eye, into helping them and doing odd jobs in the garden. It was part of his plan to ingratiate himself. Jean de Bernard had accepted it as he did everything the Major offered. Cigarettes, the few petrol coupons that were more valuable than banknotes, brandy, cigars; the clumsy ogling of Louise . . . And so St. Blaize survived, his father lived in gentle senility upstairs, his son and daughter played on the green lawns and chased each other through the shrub gardens just as he had done. The village and its people lived in peace. Shortages would not last for ever nor would their occupation by a conqueror. France would outlast the Nazis; the Château with the scars of old sieges on its outer walls would stand intact when the occupation was just a section in the history books. What he was doing had to be done. It had cost him his pride, his self-respect, and the love of his wife.

He smoked his cigarette down and thought about her, his brow furrowed with unhappiness. They were completely different in temperament. She was passionate, impulsive, with the pride he recognised as truly American. Compromise disgusted her; unlike so many of her sex she never lied, or demeaned herself by petty actions. She was a woman of daring and character, bold and fiercely loyal to those she loved. Soon after they met in New York he had teased her that a hundred years earlier she would have taken a waggon out West and fought the Indians. Although it was a joke, he had come to recognise how accurately he had described her. She was truly the child of her New World, and he the product of the Old one. Now she despised and hated him for a cowardice she couldn't understand. She had expected him to fight; expected the people of St. Blaize to rush against the Germans with flails and scythes, like the mobs in a Hollywood movie about the Revolution. After eight years of living among them, Louise hadn't understood the villagers any more than she did him. He threw his cigarette away, placed a wire guard in front of the smouldering fire and fastened the window shutters before turning out the lights. It took a long time to bolt the windows on the ground floor, to lock the back doors and the massive entrance door with its iron hinges. He checked that the little door leading from the cellar was also locked. Jean Pierre always fastened it from habit. Then he began to climb the steep stone stairs that led to the tower, built by an ancestor in the sixteenth century as a fortification for the house and the only means of reaching the upper floors. A nineteenth-century Comte de Bernard had built a back stairs to accommodate his staff, but the massive stone steps, hollowed in the middle by hundreds of years of use, had never been replaced. On the first floor Louise de Bernard slept in what had been their bedroom. At the top of the stairs he paused. In the first few months when Louise kept the door locked, he had taken a mistress. Outraged and bitterly hurt, Jean had turned to the wife of a neighbour who had been considered for him when they were both children, but it had been a tepid affair which died away in mutual disappointment. He wanted Louise; her substitute proved to be a vain and vapid shadow of whom he quickly rid himself.

Since then he had accepted the situation and only once tried to force a reconciliation when he got drunk sitting alone in the library one winter. His need and his loneliness had driven him upstairs to batter on the door. Her rejection of him had been angry and contemptuous. He hadn't tried again. Now she no longer used the key. It was finished for ever between them. He came to her room and knocked.

In London, blacked out against German air attacks, two men were sitting in the coffee room of the Garrick Club, smoking cigars and drinking liqueurs. To one of them the surroundings were familiar; it was a club patronised by the Stage and the Law, famous for its unique collection of theatrical portraits and mementos, for the excellence of its food and service and the quality of its membership. The English Colonel had joined many years ago after establishing himself at the Bar; he hoped that his American guest was impressed by the grandeur and originality of the coffee room, and by the atmosphere of calm gentility which was not altered even by war.

There were a dozen people seated at the side tables, all of them male. The rule excluding women except as guests on Thursdays had not been relaxed, nor the tradition reserving the long central table in the dining room exclusively for men. They had eaten as well as rationing had permitted and drunk an excellent wine, which the Colonel appreciated and the American General tended to ignore. Colonel Fairbairn asked his guest for the third time whether he liked the brandy and the General said he did. He made no attempt to hide his preoccupation with something other than cognac and the history of the eighteenth-century portraits which the Englishman had been describing to him. General Frank Heidsecker was a big man, inclined to fat in spite of rigorous exercise and attention to diet, with a round, bland face, hair so crew cut that he seemed almost bald under the light, and mild blue eyes. He was a third generation American, his ancestors having come over in an emigrant ship to work the Pennsylvania mines. His grandparents had spoken German all their lives, his own mother's people came from Düsseldorf and he had married a girl called Susan Schwartz. In type and attitude, Heidsecker personified the humane, unpretentious American commander whose epitome was Dwight Eisenhower. Heidsecker disliked military pomp, ignored protocol whenever possible, and cared passionately about the men for whom he was responsible.

He was happily married with three sons, and a daughter who was still in high school in St. Paul, and he believed with the simplistic passion of an early Christian in the rightness of his country's cause, and the sanctity of its way of life. He was as completely different from the English Colonel as it was possible for one human being to be from another. The Colonel was tall and thin; his knees stuck up through his well-creased trouser legs, his hands were long and bony at the wrists, with nervous fingers always fiddling with buttons or the buckle of his Sam Browne belt. His face was gaunt and patterned with freckles; he had sandy hair which was receding, and short-sighted eyes covered by horn-rimmed spectacles; he plucked them off and waved them about when he wished to emphasise a point. They were whisked off his nose and began making circles in the air, as the Colonel leaned towards the General, 'You mustn't think about it, you know,' he said. 'Once they've gone, there's nothing one can do.'

'This man is different,' Heidsecker said, 'You know his reasons for volunteering? I damned nearly didn't accept him.'

'With respect, sir,' the Colonel said, 'they made him the best possible choice. We can't afford to fail in this mission. Too much depends upon it.'

'Everything depends upon it,' the American corrected gloomily. 'If our guy doesn't get through . . .'

'Then we'll send one of our chaps,' Fairbairn said. 'I'll have plenty of candidates for you.'

'You don't mind sending your people in, do you?' Heidsecker asked him.

'No,' Fairbairn said mildly, 'I suppose I don't let myself think of them as people. I look at the mission, I weigh up its importance, and then its chances of success. I don't allow myself to get involved. This sort of work would be impossible. Think of when it is a charming young lady . . .' He laughed, which made the General positively dislike him.

'In fact, I think your man was one of the toughest characters I've ever come across. We should be drinking to his success, you know.' He raised his glass, and reluctantly the General did the same. 'He must be nearly there by now – probably landed. I know that part of France, it's very pretty.'

'I doubt he'll appreciate it,' Heidsecker remarked. The Colonel's attitude of callous irony was irritating him into remembering the difference in their rank. There was a short silence, while Fairbairn accepted the rebuke. Heidsecker sucked at his cigar; the Colonel made peace by striking a match for him.

'There are so many damned "ifs" to this whole mission,' the General said suddenly. 'For something as vital as this, the whole plan seems plain crazy. Supposing the Comtesse de Bernard has changed her attitude – all we have is the word of some village priest . . .'

'As a Presbyterian,' the Colonel said, 'I don't exactly rely on Roman Catholic priests as a source of credibility, but in this case, this priest has done some very useful work for us. I'm sure the lady hasn't changed her mind and gone over to the Germans. She'll help our man. That cigar isn't drawing very well – let me get you another . . .'

'No thanks,' Heidsecker said. 'You know what he said when I wished him luck – Come back safe and sound, that's what I told him. He looked me right in the eyes. "I don't give a damn about coming back, just so long as I get in and do the job." And he meant it too. He doesn't expect to get out.'

'Oh Lord.' Fairbairn looked pained. 'Not false heroics, I hope? That's awfully dangerous – he didn't seem that type to me.'

'He isn't,' the General said. 'But if you had his motive, would you give a damn about what happened to you?'

'No,' the Colonel said. 'I don't suppose I would. But I find it difficult to visualise; I'm not a man of action,'

The General's next remark astonished him, 'I'm not a blood and guts commander,' he said quietly. 'I mind like hell what happens to my men. I have to admit that this guy is a certain loser. But it's not just him. There's a much greater responsibility involved. What about the French?'

'The French?' Fairbairn's voice squeaked. 'What about them?'

'If we succeed,' Heidsecker said, 'what the hell do you think the Germans will do to those civilians? Or hasn't that occurred to you?'

'It hasn't,' Fairbairn admitted, 'and now that you mention it, sir, I can't say it worries me. There'll be the usual reprisals.'

'Not for this,' the General said. 'Not if our man gets through and does his job. God knows what they'll do to them. I tell you, Colonel Fairbairn, we're going to have a terrible responsibility for the consequences.'

'Sir,' Fairbairn said with what he hoped was patience, 'at any moment the weather may change and our invasion fleets will set out. Hundreds of thousands of Allied and American lives depend upon that man we sent out today and whether he can get through. Whatever happens to the French civilians, whatever the cost to them or anyone else, the invasion depends upon it!'

'Women and children,' the General said. 'It'll be on our heads.'

'No,' the Colonel said. 'It won't, if we fail, we could lose the war. We must think of nothing but the success of this mission, General. The consequences are no concern of ours.' He raised one finger to the club waiter and ordered the General a large Scotch and water. With ice. The subject was not resumed between them.

'What do you want?' Louise de Bernard was brushing her hair; she turned as the door opened and she saw her husband standing there.

He never came to her room except in an emergency. The last time his father had been taken ill during the night.

'What is it?' she repeated. He came inside and closed the door. He didn't move towards her. 'I want to talk to you.'

'All right.' She put the brush down and got up from the dressing table. 'Come in.'

In the last four years his hair had become quite grey. She remembered how thick and black it used to be. He looked tired and unhappy. She stifled an impulse to be gentle, to ask him to sit down. Their ways had parted. There was no going back.

'Minden told me something tonight,' he said. 'There's been an alert; it was a single plane. It may have dropped enemy agents here.' Louise looked at him. He saw the bitterness in her eyes.

'God help them then,' she said. 'After what happened to the last one. Why have you come to tell me?'

'Because I know you,' he said slowly. 'I know how you feel about what happened before. I have to be sure you won't do anything foolish.'

'Like helping them? With you in the house how could I? – I'd be sentencing them to death!'

'Recriminations are no good,' her husband said. 'I know you'll never forgive me, but that doesn't matter now. What does matter is to prevent another tragedy. I don't want people shot as hostages for some reckless British plan to sabotage or kill Germans round here. I won't stand by and see it happen. I just want your promise that you won't get involved in anything. I'm trying to protect you too.'

'I don't want your protection.' Louise stood up. 'We had this two years ago, when that poor devil came here and the Palliers sheltered him. Was it you who gave them away, Jean? I've asked myself that question and I've never been able to believe you!'

'You know I didn't. You don't choose to believe me.'

'The night the Palliers were executed you had the German commandant to dinner here,' she said. 'That was the night our marriage finished. Two of your own villagers were dragged away and put against the wall and shot in front of everyone. And you did nothing to save them. You say I've never forgiven you. In God's name how could you forgive yourself?'

'He would have shot more,' the Comte said. 'He was talking of fifty hostages. You judged me, Louise, because I disappointed you. You turned me out of your bed and you've kept me out for two years because I didn't behave as you expected! You wanted heroics, didn't you? A grand gesture, flouting the German commander, and fifty people lying dead in the square instead of two!'

'How do you think that Englishman died?' she asked him. 'What do you think they did to him? That Nazi, sitting here with his feet under the table, you eating and drinking with him. Oh no, Jean, whatever your reasons, there was no excuse. As for asking me not to involve myself, you're wasting your time. My country's at war with these brutes. And I'm an American. You've collaborated. You've given the example to St. Blaize and they've followed it. To think I used to be shy about coming from the States! I was so proud of France and her great traditions! God, what a fool I was. If you've finished, then please go away and let me get to bed.'

'Paul and Sophie,' Jean said angrily. 'And Papa. Would you sacrifice them? Would you see your own children and my father dragged off to some concentration camp to be murdered? Is that what you wanted me to do? Was that the price of being loved by you?'

'You've gone all the way with them,' she said contemptuously. 'You declared yourself the first time they came to this house. And then you stood by when that old man and his son were butchered. I've never asked you – what did you and that German talk about over dinner that night? It must have been a charming conversation!'

'We talked about the future of this village,' her husband answered. His anger had gone; a dull despair was in its place. 'We talked about whether the wholesale murder he proposed was really necessary to teach the people to collaborate. I convinced him that it wasn't. I lost two lives and saved many more. And we are all alive and safe, with our homes still standing. That counts with me, Louise. Whenever I walk through St. Blaize and see the people living and working in peace, the children playing, everything normal, I thank God. And I collaborate. You can despise me if you like.'

'Believe me.' She turned to him. 'Believe me, I do. From the bottom of my heart. Now you've delivered your message from your friend Minden, will you please go away? I want to go to bed.'

He didn't answer; he went out, closing the door behind him.

Louise stripped off her dressing-gown, turned off the light and pulled back the curtains. It was a brilliant moonlit night outside. She opened the window and the cold air made her shiver. If anyone had been dropped they wouldn't have a chance unless they reached the woods at Chemire. If they ventured into the village asking for help, the people would give them up. Someone had denounced the unknown Englishman who came one similar night two years ago, and with him had died the two Palliers, father and son. Was it her husband Jean? The informer had never been found but the German commander who ordered their execution had been her husband's guest that night. She shut the window and pulled the curtains.

What had happened to the man she married – why had she never seen the flaw? It was a question to which there was no answer. All she could remember were her mother's arguments against the marriage. 'He's different, he's a European. He doesn't think or feel like us.' And it was true. When total crisis came their priorities had been light years apart. When he left to fight in 1939 she had hoped she might be pregnant, to carry part of him with her in case the unthinkable happened and he didn't come back. But there was no child and she had thanked God for it. Everything in her, her traditions of pride and independence, the fierce American preoccupation with justice and liberty rose up against the rational acceptance of a loathsome enemy and an ignominious defeat. He might learn to live with the Nazis, but she never would.

And yet she ate the food that Minden gave them, used his petrol coupons to drive their car, tolerated him, albeit with hostility. Collaboration was insidious; fighting alone was not as easy as she had imagined. Little by little the corruption of the spirit spread, gaining in little ways over her resolution. She felt weak and filled with self-disgust. The Allied invasion was coming and yet everyone she knew regarded it as doomed. If they were right and the armies of the free world perished, then the future held nothing but darkness and oppression and men like Jean would be responsible. For a moment she had pitied him, seeing the signs of strain, noticing the grey hairs. But she could never afford to forgive him or to try to understand his attitude. If she weakened, she would become a traitor to herself, to her own sense of what was valuable in human life.

She thought of the aircraft which had passed over them that night, its engines throbbing with the distinctive note so different from the German planes. No bombs had fallen; the noise had died away. Enemy agents. Somewhere out there in the cold, clear night, a man or several men might be stranded in a hostile countryside, hoping for shelter. And there was nothing she could do to help them. She turned over, fighting back tears. It was useless to cry; in spite of her conversion to Catholicism she hadn't prayed for years. God was deaf, or dead. Tomorrow would be like all the other days. Routine, helping Marie-Anne with the cooking, looking after her father-in-law and the children, Paul and Sophie. Régine was coming for the weekend; she had forgotten about her. Jean's sister was nineteen, a student at the Sorbonne who lived with an aunt in Paris and occasionally got home to see her family. Louise had never liked her, even when she was a child. She was cold and secretive, resentful of the newcomer whose attempts to win her confidence had failed. Like her brother she was very dark and slight, with a face that was too pale and set to be attractive. The disease of collaboration had been mortal to her. She was passionately pro-German.

If she was fond of her brother she concealed it, only with the children and her father did she show any feeling. She loved the children, and for this Louise tried to tolerate her and avoid a confrontation. And her devotion to her father was a contrast to her indifference to everyone else. She adored the old Comte, and spent most of her visits sitting with him in his room. He was prematurely senile, and Régine was the child of his own age.

He lived on the floor above in a room whose windows had been lengthened to give him a view over the countryside, with a gramophone and a collection of books. He was a beautiful old man, gentle and confused, who played the same record over and over again, beating time to the music, his head a little to one side. His wife had died just before Louise came to St. Blaize and something had gone with her, some spark of life without which he began to wither mentally. His dependence upon his son was like that of a child, loving but intrinsically selfish. He clung to Louise because she was there, but there was no gauge of his real feelings. Food and comfort and security were all he needed. She gave them to him and he seemed grateful. Whenever she came into his room he looked up and gave his charming smile, holding his hand out to her. It was doubtful if he understood what had happened, whether he appreciated the significance of Heinz Minden coming to sit with him, being respectful and polite in order to win friendship in the house. He was a ghost who hadn't died. The night the Palliers were executed and their murderer sat in the dining room below with Jean, Louise had taken refuge in the old man's room, listening to a record of Caruso singing Pagliacci, which the old man played again and again, while she wound up the gramophone. She had cried that night but he hadn't noticed or if he did he made no comment. Like all old people he ignored the grief of others for fear it would disturb his own placidity. There had been a Requiem Mass offered for the Palliers in the village church, a brave gesture by the priest, Father Duval, which Louise had never forgotten, even though she seldom went to Mass.

Jean and his sister Régine had not attended. Louise had knelt alone in the de Bernard stall, with pathetically few people in the body of the little church, and the widow weeping only a few feet away from her. There had been no sermon: not even Father Duval dared preach against the murder of his parishioners. The Requiem Mass itself was a risk, but the influence of Jean and the effect of his conciliatory invitation appeased the military commander and there were no consequences for the priest or the few worshippers. As the wife of a prominent collaborationist, Louise was permitted to strike her attitude and escape investigation. As a woman she wasn't regarded as important in a world so essentially dominated by men. After the executions the village had quickly returned to normal. The troops drove away, business was resumed, the children went back to school and the rumours died.

But Louise and everyone else had heard them. It was said that the body of the elder Pallier was so badly beaten as to be unrecognisable when it was collected for burial. The fate of the British agent could only be imagined. He had been last seen driving away in a car with four Gestapo agents, his wrists handcuffed behind him and a look of despair on his face.

It could happen again. Louise pulled the covers close and tried to sleep. She found herself praying that it was only a reconnaissance plane, and that no second victim had come floating down to torture and death at St. Blaize en Yvelines.

In the village itself all the lights were out. It was a country community and they kept early hours. Only the cats and a single scavenging dog roamed the streets. In the back room of Madame Pallier's bakery, a man sat eating a meal by candlelight. The curtains were drawn and a rug had been pinned over the window to keep any fraction of light from showing through. The heavy-set figure of a woman, dressed in black, was seated in a wooden chair close to the door.

'You have no right to come here,' she whispered. There was a gun on the table, near the man's right hand. He looked at her.

'They killed your husband and your son. You ought to want to help.'

'I never wanted them to get involved,' she hissed at him; her face was grey and her eyes sharp with fear and anger. 'I told them it was madness. I told them you dirty British were just making use of them and nobody would care what happened to them if anything went wrong! But they wouldn't listen – no, they were full of politics and all that wind – and look what happened. Dead, both of them, and me left alone with nobody to help me, running this shop, working just to keep alive in my old age. You get out of here! Go somewhere else!'

'And have you call the Germans?' the man said. 'Like hell! You make a move or a sound and I'll shoot you, understand that? I'm no English gentleman, Madame. I wouldn't hesitate.'

'They'll get you,' she sneered. 'They'll cut your balls off when they find you. That's what they did to the other one, the man who came here. They tore him to pieces making him tell . . . I'm not afraid of you! And I won't help you!'

'You are helping me,' he said. 'And you'll go on doing it, just for tonight. I'll be gone by tomorrow. You be a nice old lady now, and nothing will happen to you.'

'And when you're caught,' she demanded, 'and they make you tell where you were hiding? What becomes of me then, eh?'

'You get shot,' the man said. 'But if you try anything while I'm here,

I'll do it first. So you've got trouble either way. You make good bread. I'm hungry.'

'You're eating my rations,' Madame Pallier accused. 'You come in here and steal my food . . .' She called him an obscene name. He went on eating, watching her. He was in the early thirties, a fair-haired man, with irregular features and blue eyes. He had a small suitcase and a smart leather attaché case with initials in gold. R.B.S. He wore a French roll-necked oatmeal sweater and casual trousers. His shoes were two-tone calf and suède, made pre-war. He looked a well-off member of the professional class who was in the country for the weekend.

At that moment his mind was occupied by the problem of Madame Pallier. London had supplied his chiefs with her name and address in St. Blaize. There was no Resistance in the district, no Communist activity because it was miles from major industrial development.

There was a chance of assistance from the widow of a Frenchman shot for hiding a British agent two years earlier. He could either try her or hole up in the woods at Chemire till the hunt had died down. He had elected to trust the widow. The London-based branch of the American Office of Strategic Services had provided him with the vital contact, upon whom the whole plan would depend.

Fortunately it wasn't Madame Pallier. He poured out some wine; he had to decide what to do with her. The solution was obvious, but being a reasonable man, he tried not to jump to it too quickly. He didn't want to kill her till he was certain that he had to. She had a hard, shrewd face; everything about the way she sat, the tightness of her clenched hands, suggested a desire to rush into the street and scream for help. The moment he left the house in the morning, she would find a telephone and get through to the local army headquarters. He couldn't trust her even if she promised. Her own skin was at risk. Her husband and son she regarded as fools who had thrown their lives away and her remembrance of them was a grudge. He couldn't take the chance.

There was a mental adjustment to be made before you killed a woman. He had been taught this. They had to be depersonalised; you had to get them out of focus, so that it was just a shape, an object. It made it much easier. 'I'm sorry about the rations,' he said.

She didn't answer; she hugged herself and glared at him.

'You'd like me to go now, wouldn't you?'

'Yes!' She spat it at him, coming forward in the chair.

'If I did, how do I know you won't raise an alarm? Would you give me your promise?'

She didn't hesitate. 'Yes, yes, of course I would. I wouldn't tell any-one, I don't want trouble, that's all. You go. I won't say anything.'

There wasn't a hope in hell of trusting her. He had an assignment on which a quarter of a million lives depended. One old woman – he stood up from the table and picked up his gun. 'Okay then,' he said. She was becoming a dark shape in front of him, the embittered face was a blur.' You open the door first and make sure it's clear.' She turned her back on him and he fired.

Heinz Minden had not gone to bed. He liked to work late; he found it difficult to lay everything aside and leave something until the morning. Unanswered questions spoiled his sleep. He was methodical by nature and this trait had been developed by his training into an obsession. He had been on General Brühl's staff at the Château Diane for six months, and it was certainly the most satisfying part of his career. He leaned back in his chair and stretched; his shoulders were stiff from stooping; he shuffled his papers together into a neat pile, fastened them with a clip, stacked them in his briefcase and closed it. It was self-locking. He wore the key round his neck with his identity disc. He had enjoyed the evening. For eighteen months he had been stationed near enough to Breslau to spend weekends at home. The move to France had distressed him; he hated leaving his family. He disliked a mess atmosphere; like his chief, General Brühl, he was not a professional soldier, and his attitude to the rigidity of military life was tolerant but not enthusiastic. He liked privacy and the company of women in the evenings. He missed his own two children badly. He wrote to them both twice a week. Photographs of them all stood in a frame beside his bed. He judged that within another six months, he would be back with them again. 1943 had been a bad year; he remembered the sense of despair that grew in him as the Russian campaign disintegrated and the rumours of collapse crept through the corridors of the informed. Food was short, casualties mountainous, air raids transformed the nights into a hell of modern making. Germans like himself began to tremble. But now he was confident. Now he knew that victory was certain for his people. He carried this knowledge with him and it made him invulnerable. Land, sea, air, blockade, invasion. It would still end with Germany as master of the world. He didn't see this in terms of a Wagnerian triumph, a funeral pyre of subject races presided over by the men gods of the Reich.

To him it was a state of order, a peace and continuity which would envelop Europe and in which the German virtues would be generally adopted. It was a return to his home, a rebuilding of the cities, a life in which the children grew up without fear. And it would come. He knew this now. He thought of Frederick Brühl. He was the son of a Hamburg butcher; Minden's own father had been a solicitor's clerk. They had many traits in common. They were in their thirties; Brühl looked older. He too was quiet, and although a bachelor, untouched by the fashionable smear of homosexuality. He painted for relaxation, and in Minden's opinion showed some talent. He didn't swagger and he didn't shout. He surrounded himself with his own people and, blessed by the personal protection of Heinrich Himmler with whom he was on friendly terms, he carried out his work. He had a weakness, which the upper-class officers derided, but which Minden thought amusing and quite harmless. He was a romantic snob. Grandeur appealed to him, and he surrounded himself with the trappings of greatness which belonged to a vanished age. For this reason he had made his headquarters in the Château Diane, the magnificent house built for the most famous royal courtesan of the sixteenth century, Diane de Poitiers, mistress of Henri II. In many ways it was extremely suitable; it was built in semi-fortress style, with a superb gateway, surmounted by Diane herself in stone, flanked by stags. The General occupied the royal apartments; he took his meals with his officers in the state dining room, at a refectory table twenty feet long, with Renaissance candelabra and superb tapestries; he had insisted on having the original fourposter bed fitted with a proper mattress so that he might sleep in it. There was a large contemporary portrait of Diane de Poitiers which had been moved from the marble hall into the General's sitting room.

It showed her in the guise of Diana the huntress, naked and voluptuous, the crescent moon, symbol of the goddess, gleaming in her hair. The General liked to sit and stare at it, entranced. It was not a picture that aroused any sensual response in Heinz Minden. Nude voluptuaries were not his type.

Whereas the slim and elegant Comtesse de Bernard would have driven him to any folly. When he first came to the Château St. Blaize, she had avoided him, making no secret of her hostility. Being a man of sensitivity he appreciated her resentment and made himself as unobtrusive as possible. He thought the Comtesse the most sexually attractive woman he had met in his life. When she walked into a room or stood near him, he broke out into a fine sweat; his hands, normally so sure and steady, trembled. He lay awake at night, forgetting his pretty wife with whom he had been so happy and dreamed hot, lustful dreams of possessing the Comtesse in unlikely erotic situations. He was a patient man and doggedly determined. He wanted her and as the weeks went by and she was forced by circumstances into accepting him, he felt that one day his desire would be realised.

He set out to be a benefactor; he made friends with the two children, whom he genuinely liked, and was flattered by their response. He even went up and talked to the old Comte; he brought presents for Jean de Bernard, choosing those luxuries which he knew were unobtainable on the open market. Cognac, champagne, cigars. He ordered his batman to help the two servants, he made himself part of the family in spite of themselves and little by little he was taken for granted. When he first arrived, Louise de Bernard used to leave the salon rather than sit in his presence. Now she talked to him over the dinner table, and it wasn't long before he sensed the deep hostility which she felt towards her husband. Minden was not a particularly immoral or ruthless man. He had his own code, which was ethical and middle class. He wouldn't have deliberately put himself between husband and wife. But this wife, whom he wanted to the point of agony, didn't even share a room with her husband. The batman had soon discovered that. The knowledge diminished the stature of the Comte de Bernard in his eyes. No self-respecting man would have allowed his wife to lock him out. Minden, normally mild and considerate, with an exaggerated view of women's frailty, would have soon put an end to the attempt. The situation increased his hope of ultimate success. She must be lonely; she was young and beautiful and living like a nun. He brought her a present of scent at Christmas, and began very carefully to disclose his interest in her. He had to be careful, because she was spirited, and a premature move would spoil his chances.

He treated her with friendliness and courtesy, but he let her know, by a touch against her, a smile when she came into the room, by the scent which was the most expensive and exotic he could buy, that he found her irresistibly attractive, and that the moment she held out her hand, he would be there.

He went to the window, after switching off the lights and opened it wide. He knew the value of fresh air for healthy sleep; for a moment he looked out over the countryside, illumined by the same bright moon Louise had seen two hours before.

There was a red glow to the left, a finger of fiery orange in the middle of it. He leaned out, and on the wind he smelt smoke. There was a fire in St. Blaize. He watched for a few moments and then withdrew. He had no curiosity about the village or its people. They were co-operative and peaceful. If they needed help beyond the capacity of the primitive local fire engine, they would call upon the German military. St. Blaize was a good place for a German. No assassins lurked in the streets or sprang upon them in the lanes. There was no trouble. Which was exactly why Brühl had picked the district to set up his headquarters. Minutes after he was in bed, Minden was deeply asleep.

'Mama! Mama, wake up!' Louise felt her son's arms round her neck, and his mouth pressing excitedly against her cheek.

She hadn't heard the maid come in and draw the curtains back; the room was filled with a pale sunlight. 'Darling, what is it – why haven't you gone to school?' She sat up, and the little boy climbed onto the bed.

'I'm going,' he said. 'Fritz is downstairs.' There was another of the Major's gestures. His batman drove the children to the village school each morning before taking him to the Château Diane.

'There's been a fire,' her son announced. 'A big fire in the village!'

'In the village? Where – Marie-Anne, is this right?'

'Yes, Madame.' The maid came towards her. 'Poor old Madame Pallier's house. They couldn't put it out; everyone was asleep when it happened. She was burned to death, poor old soul.'

'How terrible.' Louise shuddered. She looked at her son's excited face. 'Go down now, darling, or you'll be late. Where's Sophie?'

'Getting her books – you know, Mama, she's always late.'

'Go on.' She kissed him. 'Don't keep Fritz waiting.'

'How awful,' she said to the maid. 'That poor woman. After losing her husband and son like that too.'

'They're an unlucky family, Madame.' Marie-Anne paused at the door. She was fond of the Comtesse, and she enjoyed calamity. Without words the two women understood each other. Marie-Anne hated the German Fritz, and she knew that Madame hated the Major. Yet they could not get rid of either of them. She and her husband had served the Comte's father and mother since they were brought up from the village in their teens. They were glad to survive, but they were not proud of the price the Comte had paid for it.

'Very unlucky,' she repeated. 'Two sons lost in the First War, poor Gaston was the only one left, and then he gets himself murdered by the Germans and *his* only son goes too. Now the place burns down. I heard she was found by the door; she must have been trying to get out. Old people like that shouldn't live alone. There's always trouble.' She shook her head, filled with enjoyment.

'Where's Monsieur?'

'Gone down to the village,' Marie-Anne said. 'He left as soon as we woke him with the news. He's gone to see the Mayor.'

Louise got up and dressed. They had only one car and a tiny amount of petrol. The coupons were another of the Major's gifts. There was no way of getting to St. Blaize. Jean should have woken her and taken her with him. She'd had the courage to go to the Palliers' Requiem while he stayed at home. She wanted to go down, to show herself. She ran down the stairs to the hall, hearing a car come to the front. At the foot of the stairs she almost bumped into the Major. He was dressed in his field grey uniform, his cap under one arm, drawing on his gloves. He was a tall, well set up man, his dark hair cut close to a fine-shaped head.

'Good morning, Madame.' He smiled at her.

'Good morning.' Louise disliked meeting him alone, even in the hall. 'I'm looking for my husband, I thought I heard his car.'

'That was Fritz, I'm afraid,' the Major said. 'Coming back from the school. Is there anything I can do?'

'No,' Louise said, 'Thank you. There's been a fire in St. Blaize and an old widow died, I wanted to go down myself.'

The Major looked at his watch and then at her.

'I'm in good time this morning,' he said. 'I'd be delighted to drive you.'

'Thank you,' Louise said again. 'But it wouldn't be possible.'

'Why not?' He had placed himself in front of her. 'You're looking very charming this morning. Why can't I drive you to the village?'

He was making the first move in the silent game, the first acknowledgement that there was a game in progress. She decided to play it in the open too.

'I can't go with you, because the woman who died lost both husband and her son two years ago. They were shot by your military. I'm sure you realise how inappropriate it would be for me to go to the village with you.'

'If you think so. But please remember they must have done something criminal. We don't shoot people for nothing.'

'A British agent was dropped here. The Palliers sheltered him and got caught. That was their crime. And from what Jean tells me it could happen again.'

'It wasn't necessary for him to tell you,' the Major said. 'I just asked for his co-operation, that was all.'

'And I am sure you got it,' Louise said. 'But don't expect it from me.'

'I'm sure you're very brave,' the Major said gently. 'But please, dear Madame de Bernard, don't be foolish. Leave this unpleasant kind of thing to men. Personally I don't think anyone was dropped round here. It was just a reconnaissance, that's all. If I can't be of service, then I shall go. Until this evening.'

He bowed and gave her a smile for which she could have slapped his face. Then he went out into the morning sunshine.

There was a German patrol on the road junction between St. Baize and Houdan. He watched it through his field-glasses, lying on his stomach in some bushes on a rise in the fields about three hundred yards away. The bicycle lay in an irrigation ditch, covered with leaves. He had spent the night hidden there, wrapped in a thin waterproof sheet, eating some of his K rations, watching the fire he had lit in the Palliers' kitchen grow from a flicker in the darkness to a fullscale beacon. A funeral pyre, he thought, for a heroic mother of heroic France. He bit into the bar of chocolate. Christ, he hadn't any right to judge. Nobody had occupied *his* home town. It wasn't till you heard the tanks rumble past the door

that you could say how you'd behave in the circumstances. It was a
pity about the old lady, but he refused to think about it. The fire must
be attracting a lot of attention. It was only when he scouted the roads
in the morning and saw the improvised check point that he knew they
had heard the plane hovering overhead and guessed its mission.

He swore. His papers described him as Roger Bertrand Savage, Swiss
national, domiciled in Berne, born in Ohio, USA, by profession a company lawyer in the firm of Felon, Brassier et Roule, an internationally
famous company with offices in Geneva, Berne, and a subsidiary in
Philadelphia.

It was an excellent cover, worked out from the New York end
and confirmed by their contacts in Switzerland. Felon and Brassier
had substantial US interests and were secret supporters of the Allies.
Anyone checking with them would get the same information. Roger
Savage was a senior member of their staff, an American who had
graduated at the University of Lausanne and taken Swiss nationality
before the war. He was at present visiting a client in France. It would
hold up against all but the most detailed investigation, and he felt
confident in the role. He spoke excellent French and German; he had
a marvellous ear, not only for languages but for nuances of accent.

He watched the soldiers moving lazily round their road block. He
had a survey map of the district and he got it out and studied it
carefully. He knew all the main routes into the village. The one he
could see through his glasses led in from the north. If that one was
blocked then for a certainty so were all the others. The bastards had
put a net round the area. They had cut off the roads as an escape route,
and that meant they were getting ready for a patrol sweep through the
fields and around the smaller wooded hills. It was eight o'clock in
the morning. At any moment the first group would be setting out. He
turned back to the map. The railway line was a very small branch line
of the Paris to Chartres route which was heavily marked. St. Blaize was
a community big enough to merit a small sub-station. Few trains would
be running. The line was marked to the west, about threequarters of a
mile away. It was hidden by a belt of silver birch trees. He crawled
backwards to the irrigation ditch, dragged the bicycle upright and
keeping in the shelter of the ditch, began wheeling it away towards
the birches. He came out of the shelter of the dip, focused on the patrol
once more, and saw no sign of anyone sweeping the area with glasses.
He jumped on the cycle and pedalled quickly over the edge of the field
towards the trees. When he reached them, he dismounted, walked out
to the other side and reconnoitred again. There was no sign of German
military presence. There was no road, only the undulating fields and
the thin ribbon of railway track. He pushed on, using the cycle when
the terrain was possible, but moving as fast as he could. He slid down

the slight embankment to the track, dragging the bicycle with him. He mounted, carrying the suitcase tied on his back; inside were a change of clothes, the ground sheet folded very small, the handsome leather briefcase embossed with his initials and a radio transmitter set. He carried his gun stuck in the waistband of his trousers. The L pill, that release from torture above bearing, was concealed in his left cuff link. He was a brave man, but he wouldn't hesitate to take it.

He cycled along the edge of the track for a mile and threequarters. It wound and twisted in the way of branch lines. Sometimes he glanced back, listening for the rumble of a train, looking for a pencil of smoke. Nothing came. The morning grew warm, and he hummed to himself, his nerves calm. Sufficient unto the day is the evil thereof. The old tag came into his thoughts and he changed it. Sufficient unto the hour; the minute. The sun shone and the way was downhill. And his mission had begun. By nine-thirty he had reached the outskirts of the station at St. Blaize. He pulled the cycle up the incline and wheeled it slowly towards the first group of sheds and outbuildings. Further on the slope became a platform, with the ticket office and waiting room. He tried the first shed, but the door was locked. He could see nobody about. The second building was a store room of some kind. The door was open and it was empty inside. He slipped in with the bicycle and a moment later came out without it, closing the door. It could be weeks before anyone looked in there.

He walked slowly up the platform and stopped at the timetable board. A printed sheet with pencilled alterations showed that there was a train due in thirty minutes. He recognised his own good luck. It was the only train that day. He went into the waiting room, and then stopped. Two young women were sitting inside, one of them was knitting. They both stared at him. He smiled.

'Pardon,' he said. 'I'm looking for the toilets.'

'Through there,' one of the girls said. Her companion smiled back; she showed an interest he didn't find flattering. He went through to one of two doors, marked with a vague male silhouette. Inside the smell was urinous and stale. He unpacked his bag, and quickly stripped out of his clothes. In underpants and singlet his body was muscled and vigorous, the body of a soldier at the peak of training. He changed into a plain white shirt, Swiss made, like the dark suit and the tie, the calf shoes, combed his hair down and put on a soft black Homburg hat. He looked at himself in the spotted mirror. Herr Savage from Berne. He repacked his sports clothes in the suitcase, slipped the loaded gun into his trouser band, and looked at his watch. The train wasn't due for ten minutes. There was nothing to do but go out and face the two women. He came into the waiting room; they were still there and they both looked up at him, registering surprise. He lifted his hat to them and sat down, folding his hands on his lap and closed his eyes. He could feel them looking at him and he heard them whisper. He shifted a little till his right hand was over the hard outline of the gun. He lifted one eyelid a fraction to see if either of them had moved; they were still sitting, murmuring together. He heard them giggle and immediately he relaxed. Everything was going his way. The open shed, the train timetable, the solution of fire for disposing of the old woman. He suddenly saw her face, the hatred and cunning in her eyes, the downward pull of her mouth as she denounced her husband and son ... He had felt no pity at the time and he felt no remorse now. He had a job to do. He had a primary objective to reach and it was coming closer. There was a clanging of a signal bell and then the rattling roar of the train. The women jumped up, hurrying as women do when they are travelling. He yawned, straightened his hat and got up slowly. They were on the platform when he reached the door. A moment later they had disappeared inside the train. Four passengers alighted. Savage walked through the waiting room door and joined them at the barrier.

He paid for his ticket, explaining that he had come through from Paris without time to buy one. Nobody even glanced up at him. Outside the station he looked round. A decrepit Peugeot with a gazogene waited by the side of the road. He saw two of the passengers hesitating. He took a chance and rushed past them to the motorcar. The driver was inside reading a copy of *La Dépêche des Yvelines*.

'You are a taxi?' Now Savage was speaking like a Swiss. The old man nodded.

'I am the taxi, Monsieur. The only one. I have a limit of four kilometres.' Savage opened the door and got inside, throwing his suitcase ahead of him.

'The Château de St. Blaize,' he said.

'That's outside the four kilometres,' the driver said. 'Sorry, I can't take you.' The other passengers were approaching the cab. Ten francs came at him from behind, held between the finger and thumb of the man in the rear.

'Take me there. Five more when we arrive.'

'What about these people here? How do they manage?'

'I don't know,' Savage said. 'Take the money and let's go. I have an appointment.'

The engine started and the old car bumped forward; Savage lit a cigarette, the first he had allowed himself since leaving the Palliers' house smouldering from coals raked out of the stove onto the carpet.

He checked his passport and papers and sat back, tipping the Homburg a little back on his head. He hated hats.

They passed the first German patrol on the way out of the village. He showed his documents, the taxi driver vouched for his arrival on the train from Paris, and from then on the way to the Château was clear.

3

He rang the old-fashioned iron bell-pull outside the door and waited for what seemed a long time before it was opened to him. Jean-Pierre, garbed in a green baize apron, with his sleeves rolled above knotty elbows, showed him into the salon on the ground floor. Savage presented a business card and asked the old butler to give it to the Comtesse. Left alone, he paced quickly round the room, taking stock of the fine eighteenth-century furniture, and the pictures. Ancestral faces, some simpering, some arrogant, looked down at him, and Savage remained unimpressed. He was more interested in a photograph which showed a very pretty dark haired woman posing beside a fountain with two children. He picked it up. She certainly photographed well. He was still holding it when the door opened behind him and he heard a light step cross the floor.

'Monsieur Savage?'

Louise held out her hand and he kissed it, making a little bow. The room faced south and the sunlight fell directly on her; he had placed himself to be in shadow. It was the right woman, no doubt at all about the large brown eyes and the cast of face which was so palpably American. Even after so many years, she spoke French with a Boston accent. He smiled at her.

'You must forgive me for descending on you,' he said, 'without any warning: I would have telephoned, but unfortunately I arrived very late in Paris, and there was some difficulty getting through here this morning.'

'The lines are terrible,' Louise said. 'Please sit down; let me offer you something. Would you like to sit in here or in the garden? It's quite warm outside.'

'The garden would be very nice,' Savage agreed. Less chance of anyone listening in the open air. She seemed relaxed and friendly. He felt she was excited to see a stranger. Life must be dull, he decided. He followed her out into the sunshine.

The butler brought wine; it was pale and dry, with a slight *pétillance*. 'It's our own,' she explained. 'It makes a nice apéritif. You will stay to lunch, of course.'

'You're very kind,' Savage said. 'You will have had Monsieur Felon's letter, so you know why I'm here.'

'No,' Louise said. 'I've heard nothing. Of course, I know your firm, Monsieur Savage, because of my family trust, but I never received any letter.'

'Oh.' He made a gesture of annoyance. 'How ridiculous – it must be the censorship. It will probably arrive after I've left. I shall have to explain it myself.'

'It's about the trust?'

'Not exactly.' Savage offered her a cigarette. The sun was warm and he watched her close her eyes for a moment, lifting her face to it. She had a fine profile. She opened her eyes and turned to him.

'What do you mean, not exactly?' Her father had died before the war; with America's entry into the conflict, her affairs had been placed in the hands of the Swiss lawyers whom Savage represented. She knew M. Felon personally.

'I haven't come about money.'

'No? Then what is it – is something wrong?'

'No.' He shook his head. 'Can I ask you a question, Madame de Bernard? A very personal question.'

'I suppose so. I won't guarantee to answer it.' Her mother was inclined to interfere. For a moment Louise wondered whether some rumour of her estrangement from Jean had reached Boston, and the repercussions had found themselves at St. Blaize via Switzerland. She gave Savage a hostile look. 'What is your question?'

'What are your feelings towards the Allies?'

Louise didn't answer him. She got up. 'I'm afraid I never discuss the war.'

He didn't move; he blew a smoke ring at her.

'You haven't answered the question,' he said. There was nobody near them; trees, lawns, the fountain in the photograph, but no lurking gardener, no passing maid. He spoke in English, 'Sit down and take it easy, I've got news from home.'

She stared at him. She did as he suggested.

'You're American!' she whispered. 'What is this? Who are you . . . ?'

'I saw your mother before Christmas,' he said. 'She's fine; remarkable woman. You look like her. There wasn't any letter fron Felon. There isn't any trust-busting to be done. I'm here on my own. Now – how do you feel about the Allies?'

London said she was reliable. Their information was gathered through an unlikely source. Father Duval, parish priest of St. Blaize en Yvelines, was a gossip, and priests visiting the area paid a call upon him, which he encouraged because it gave him the opportunity to talk. He was a stubborn man in his mid-fifties, devoted to his parishioners and disdainful of the Germans whom he had fought in the First War. He had given a young curé from Paris a complete picture of the conditions in the area and the attitude of the people of the village. He had mentioned the Comtesse's presence at the Palliers' Requiem, and lamented the colaborationist stand taken by the Comte. Within two hours, the curé had picked up enough information to relay it back to London through a radio operator hiding in Chartres, one of a thin chain of Allied secret communication that stretched across France and was being constantly broken up by German intervention. The operator only worked another two weeks before the detector van caught up with him, and he was killed in a gun battle.

Savage hoped that London and his OSS chiefs had been correct in their assessment. It was one thing to make a gesture from the safety of marriage with a known collaborator. It might be quite different for the Comtesse de Bernard to actively help an Allied agent. Women were fond of adopting heroic poses or just being bloody-minded. Watching her now, he felt more confident. There was nothing exhibitionist about her; she even looked frightened, which was reassuring.

'I hate the Germans,' she said quietly. 'I hate them for what they're doing to the world, for what they're doing to the Jews. I hate their arrogance and I hate their beliefs. If they win this war it'll be the end of civilisation. Does that answer your question?'

'I guess so,' Savage said. 'I need to stay here for a few days. I need to operate from here. I've got a perfect cover story and everything will check. You've nothing to fear from that angle.'

'Then you're not with Felon and Brassier . . .' Louise said.

'I was,' Savage answered. 'For about three years before the war. Now I'm working for a bigger firm. Will you help me?'

He saw emotions changing on her face; she was a woman who showed her feelings. Surprise, fear, hesitancy. And then resolution. It was in her eyes as she looked at him. London had been right about her. For some reason, apart from his own skin, Savage was glad.

'I'll help you. I'll do anything I can.'

'Thanks.' He leaned over and refilled their glasses; when he gave one to her he felt how cold her fingers were. But the resolution was still there.

He raised his glass to her. 'Thanks,' he said again. 'I can't say you won't regret it, because if anything goes wrong you may. How long can you keep me here?'

'As long as you like,' Louise said. She was already seeing Jean in her mind's eye, hearing his questions . . . Why should a Swiss lawyer stay with them – couldn't he finish his business in a day – food was short . . .

As if Savage knew her thoughts he said, 'I'm your cousin. I have all the family data. Your mother was a great help. I'm the son of your father's first cousin, Roger Savage. He married a Swiss girl, Marie Thérèse Fielharben, daughter of a rich glass manufacturer. The family weren't exactly pleased, and after I was born the couple divorced. I was brought up in Berne and I became naturalised before the war.'

'That's right,' Louise said. 'There was a Roger Savage . . . Did my mother know what this was for?'

'She didn't know you were going to be involved,' he said. 'She was asked for details for a cover story and she gave it. She'd no idea we'd ever meet up.'

'What have you come for?' Louise asked him. 'What are you going to do?'

'Sorry.' Savage shook his head. 'No questions; no answers. I'm your cousin from Switzerland and you've asked me to stay a while. Just act naturally.'

He smiled constantly, but it was without warmth; there was an alertness about him even in repose. She started to exclaim out loud and then stopped, suddenly. The plane circling overhead, the German alert. That must have been him . . .

'Oh my God!' she said. 'I forgot – you can't stay here! We've a German officer billeted on us.'

'I know,' Savage said. 'Major Minden. That's okay.'

'How do you know?' Louise said. 'How could you know about him . . . ?'

'No questions,' Savage reminded her. 'How about your husband?'

'He's for Vichy,' she said bitterly. 'He went over to the Germans in 1940. He couldn't be trusted with anything.'

'He'll accept the story; so long as you act naturally,' he repeated. 'Does he come home for lunch?'

'He may not today,' she said. 'He's in the village with the Mayor. There was a fire last night and a poor woman was burned to death. Jean takes that sort of thing very seriously. He does what he can for the people.'

'I'm glad to hear it.' Savage sounded unimpressed. 'Tell me about the Major.'

'There's nothing to tell,' Louise dismissed him; the subject embarrassed her. 'He's at the staff HQ at Château Diane. He doesn't obtrude and that's all I can say for him.'

Not quite all; Savage noticed how that pretty mouth had tightened, the look of wariness in her eyes. Major Heinz Minden. She needn't have warned him; he knew more about the Major than she did. The old manservant appeared beside them, wearing a faded alpaca jacket, and formally announced lunch.

They talked about the weather, about Switzerland and the Marshall

Trust Fund, Savage giving a good performance for the benefit of Jean-Pierre who shuffled in and out of the dining room. He noticed that Louise de Bernard was uncomfortable; she said as little as possible, leaving the major role in the deception to him. He didn't falter in it. Years ago he had been an enthusiastic amateur actor at college; his histrionic talent had taken him to the bar where a peculiarly incisive mind promised a brilliant future in the law if he ever got the chance to go back to his practice. It wasn't a chance he would have bet good money on. He didn't expect to get out alive and he didn't care. He had told as much to his own General who had looked worried and responsible, as if the life of one man were important in their kind of war. Savage enjoyed his wine. He believed in taking what was on offer, like the warm sunshine during his trek across the fields that morning. What had happened hadn't soured him for the good things, for food and drink and women and the pleasure he derived from an ironic joke. Just because you expected to die you didn't have to reject life prematurely.

And for him it would be easy; he carried death in his cuff link like a talisman. But only when he had finished what he had come to do. He hadn't pretended it was patriotism. He had told his worried General exactly why he had volunteered and what made him such a suitable choice to go to St. Blaize. The General had been distressed. Not so much by the reason, Savage suspected; stories like this were not uncommon. But by the hate he had showed the General when he talked about his mission. Personal, burning, obsessional hatred. The same feeling had brought him into the special OSS unit, and made him the most promising trainee of his group. He was rougher, quicker, more ruthless than any of them. He learned to kill with his hands, to silence with a single blow. To use many types of weapons, to handle explosives. His French and German were fluent; like many with a natural acting talent he was also a good linguist, with an ear for dialect. He could pass for a Swiss in Switzerland, after his three years spent working there. They took their coffee in the salon, because it had turned colder outside and clouded over. He glanced at the grey skies through the window. The weather must break soon. Clouds and rain, holding back that fleet of barges, keeping the armies on the leash . . . He looked across at Louise de Bernard and smiled. She had been watching him silently for some minutes.

'You're doing it again,' he said.

'Doing what?'

'Asking questions. I can see it on your face. "Was he dropped last night when the plane came over – what's he going to do here . . ." Stop it. Stop thinking about me as anything but your cousin from Switzerland. Otherwise you'll never make it stick.'

'I'm sorry,' Louise said, 'but it's not easy.'

'Nothing like this is. Tell me about Major Minden.'

She shrugged. 'There's not much to tell. He's been billeted here for six months. He gets on well with Jean, my husband. I see as little of him as I can.'

'I take it he's not the strutting Nazi type?' He had cold eyes; however much he smiled, it stopped at his mouth. There was something about him which made Louise uncomfortable.

'No, he's certainly not that. He's rather quiet. He's a staff officer.'

'I know,' Savage said. 'Reliable, a bit stuffy, tries to show it's not his fault the others are such bastards. I can imagine.'

'He wants to be friends,' Louise said. 'He brings us things – luxuries – my husband takes them. I hate him.'

'That must be distressing,' Savage said. 'Since I guess you're the one he wants to be friends with . . .'

'That isn't true!' She felt herself changing colour.

'It ought to be,' Savage said. 'Unless he's a fag. Married, isn't he?'

'Yes. How did you know?'

'Never mind. Go on talking about him. What happens here in the evenings?'

'He has dinner with us; Jean insisted on it. I couldn't stop him. Then he comes and sits in here; I often go to bed early, I hate sitting with him. Sometimes he goes straight up to his room and works.'

'How much work does he bring back?'

'I don't know. He has a briefcase with him; I never go near his room, I don't know what he does.'

'And he gets on well with your husband. What do they talk about – the war?'

'Sometimes. Books and music. He likes music very much. He gave my father-in-law some records.'

'He sounds ideal,' Savage mocked. 'When does your husband get home?'

'Soon now. It must be nearly three. What am I going to tell him – if he thought for one moment you were . . .'

'Don't even say it.' Savage stood up. 'Don't say it and don't think about it. You don't need to explain about him; I know all about him, so don't worry. You just stick to the story. I'll be up in my room when he gets back. It'll be easier for you if I'm not there. He won't be surprised; the Swiss are hogs for sleep. Just remember I'm your cousin Roger.'

'The real Roger Savage never visited the States,' Louise said. 'How did you know about him?'

'Through contacts,' he said. 'He died in Lausanne two years ago. Motor smash. Actually he was a drunk. We did our homework

The Occupying Power

properly. Nobody can pick any holes. Play it straight and your husband will believe you.'

'I won't have to go into much detail,' she said. 'We haven't much to say to each other any more. He goes one way and I go another.'

'Good,' Savage said. 'That makes it easier. Let's find my room.'

She took him up the broad stone stair, past her room and to the floor above. His suitcase, securely locked, was on a chaise longue by the end of the bed. It was a large room, furnished in old-fashioned floral chintz; it had a Victorian atmosphere, emphasised by a mahogany four-poster bed. There was a faint smell of must and stale air. Louise apologised and opened the window.

Savage went and looked out.

'I'd hate to leave here in a hurry,' he said. 'That's a forty-foot drop. Who sleeps near?'

'I do,' she said. 'On the floor below. My husband's two rooms away from mine; Minden is down the passage, my sister-in-law is next to you.'

'You haven't mentioned her,' Savage said. He sat on the edge of the bed and bounced gently up and down. 'Comfortable mattress. Where is she?'

'In Paris,' Louise answered. 'She's a student at the Sorbonne. She lives with Jean's aunt and she comes home for odd weekends. She'll be here for dinner this evening.'

'Is that nice, or nasty?'

She shrugged, as she had done when he asked about the Major. 'She doesn't bother me. We've nothing in common and we know it.'

'How would you describe her as far as I'm concerned? Friend or foe?'

'Foe,' Louise said slowly. 'I'd say definitely – foe. For God's sake, watch yourself!'

'I will, don't worry,' Savage said. He got off the bed and came towards her. 'I'll unpack now. You go back downstairs and look like somebody with a long-lost cousin.' He closed the door and locked it. He hung his coat over a chair back, and went to the suitcase. The clothes were innocent, the ammunition for his gun was concealed as a box of cigars. Each cigar held four bullets; built into the false bottom of the suitcase was a small two-way radio transmitter set. Savage went to the window again and looked out. The view was so beautiful he paused. Chequerboard fields of green wheat and bright yellow mustard, belts of trees outlined against the sky, bending in symmetry before the wind. Below him the gardens of the Château, hedges and yew walks, flower beds – from above it wasn't possible to see the weeds and the signs of neglect. In the courtyard the stone fountain threw up a meagre spray.

There were no ledges, no windows near him; if anything went wrong he was as effectively trapped in the room as a prisoner in a cell. Transmission from there was impossible. He would have to get on the roof; and for that he would need Louise de Bernard's help. It had been easy to say he wouldn't tell her anything, to pretend she could be kept on the perimeter. It was a glib lie in one sense but a necessity in the other. The less she knew the less she could tell the Gestapo if she were arrested. But without her help he couldn't hope to complete his mission. Frederick Brühl. Savage knew the face as if it were his own. There were few pictures of him, many were pre-war civilian snapshots. The latest showed him among a crowd, wearing his peaked cap, a blurred and grainy image which had lost outline when it was blown up. Spectacles, a stubby nose, small mouth with rather full lips. A most unremarkable man. Savage stood by the window with the panorama of a peaceful countryside below him, and saw nothing but that face. And then another face, laughing and with hair dishevelled by wind, streaked across the forehead. Eyes that were wide and bright, half closed against the sun, a brown hand raised to shield them. And then the image changed. Savage slammed imagination's door. Brühl . . . He could think about Brühl, and his hands curled into fists, he could let the hate rise in him. It was safe to think about Brühl, it was like giving the batteries of his purpose a recharge. If he had been afraid for himself or concerned for other people, like the American Comtesse de Bernard, the old woman in the village he had shot in the back the night before, he had only to think about the reason why he was in St. Blaize. Nothing and nobody mattered but to succeed. He pulled the window shut. His chiefs in OSS had chosen well. They had chosen a man with a personal reason, knowing that the force of motive would send him on when other men might have turned back.

And they had made a wise choice when they picked on Louise de Bernard as his liaison. She was brave and she was honest; would hold up well enough to reasonable pressure. She was reliable. She was also going to help him more than either of them knew. He had been sent to St. Blaize because a member of Brühl's staff was living in the house of a collaborator with an American wife of Allied sympathies. Major Heinz Minden. What he made of his situation was up to him. Time, as the sarcastic English Colonel had impressed on him, was not on Savage's side. He had a few days, a week at the most, to make the invasion safe. A tremendous burden. He could hear the pedantic voice, unmasculine in pitch, repeating the remark. The responsibility was almost too much to place upon one man. If he had any doubts – Savage hadn't believed in the offer; they had told him too much to let him off the hook. It was part of the game, part of the tests applied to agents like him. He had given the Englishman a look of contempt

and not bothered to answer. Major Heinz Minden. Not the strutting
Nazi type; unobtrusive, Louise had called him, anxious to be friends.
He remembered the colour coming into her face when he suggested that
Minden might be interested in her. Which of course he must be. She was
a beautiful woman. Her hostility probably intrigued him. Some men
were like that, He would need her help in setting up the transmitter.
It was to be used once only. To report on the success of his mission.
If he failed there wouldn't be a message. He took his shoes off and lay
on the bed. Somehow he had to use Minden in his plan. Possibilities
flitted through his mind, but didn't stay. Until he met him and could
make a judgement, it was premature. He had a strong intuition that
the part Louise de Bernard was going to play would be a vital one.
He couldn't afford to be sorry about it, but he was. He liked her. But
that wouldn't stop him. He didn't hear the Comte de Bernard's car
come up the gravel drive. He was making up for the sleep he had lost
in the fields the night before.

Jean de Bernard had spent the morning in the Mairie; he and Albert
Camier were shut up in the little office on the first floor, and the air
was blue with cigarette smoke. Camier had sent for wine.
    'We don't want trouble.' The Mayor repeated it again. 'We have
to think of the village. Trade has improved since they came to the
Château Diane; my own business is doing very nicely. We don't want
any Allied agents here!'
    'Even if there is an invasion,' Jean de Bernard said, 'it could fail —
nobody beats them on equal terms. Russia was different. That was
the winter. They'll throw the Allies back into the sea, and who will
suffer then? We will. If we've turned against them, they'll crush us to
pieces.'
    'They haven't taken our men,' Camier said, sipping at his wine.
'We've no Jews here, thank God, so that's no problem. They buy
from us and so long as we obey the law, we're left alone. There are no
more Palliers in St. Blaize, Monsieur, depend on it. If someone's come
to this district to make trouble, they've picked the wrong place!'
    'They've given me this proclamation to put up.' He pulled a roneoed
sheet out of a drawer and handed it to Jean. 'I thought I'd write
something myself and sign it.'
    The sheet of paper informed the inhabitants that anyone found
sheltering enemy agents would be shot; it was signed by the district
commander. A different man to the indignant German who had dined
with him the night the Palliers were executed. He had been very indignant; Jean remembered how hard it had been to calm him. He looked
up at Camier.
    'You put a notice up,' he said. 'Warn the people.'

'Why should we die for the British?' the old man said. 'What have they ever done for us – I remember my father saying, they'll fight to the last Frenchman! If we do have to live under the Germans it's not that bad.'

'The Comtesse would not agree with you,' Jean said. He refused more wine.

'With respect for Madame,' Camier said, 'women aren't the ones to judge. We men have the responsibility. Thank God you've given such a good example; it's made a great difference.'

'We're a tired people,' Jean said slowly. 'Bled white by wars. We need peace, and time to recover ourselves. They won't be here for ever. France will survive them. That is what matters. I must go now. Since Madame Pallier had no relatives, there's nothing we can do.'

'It's a pity about the shop.' The mayor shook his head. 'It was a nice little place, good position. She did quite well. Mind you, it could be rebuilt . . .'

He spoke more to himself; he owned the grocery and wine store, and he supplied the officer's mess at Château Diane. If he were to buy the site of the Palliers' bakery and build – it wouldn't be easy. He'd have to get permits for labour and building materials, but then he was on good terms with the district headquarters; someone there might recommend him. He was known for his co-operation with the Government and the occupation forces. He might open a second grocery store, or else employ a baker. He got up quickly as Jean prepared to leave. He shook the Comte's hand, making a little bow. He was not in such awe of the family as he might have been if the war hadn't changed everything. They held comparatively little power. That was in German hands.

Jean started his car and drove slowly back to the Château. Camier's wine was sour on his stomach; the stench of smoke from the smouldering ruin of the bakery clung to his clothes. He had talked to people, taken council with Camier, who was typical of his class and age. Cunning, commercial-minded, concerned with the realities of survival. Men like him abounded, and they made the task of governing France so easy for the conquerors. He remembered his short war service, the overwhelming numbers and efficiency of the enemy, the sense of being swept away like sand before a tidal wave. Men he had known since childhood had thrown their weapons away and turned for home. His people's spirit waned and died; for some it was not so much a rape as a seduction. They welcomed the German strength as an antidote to their own national weakness. France could be great again, and powerful again; what had revived a crippled, beaten Germany within twenty years might well be the saving medicine for ailing France. He knew many who believed this. He had friends who were more Nazi than the SS whose attitudes they imitated.

The Jews had always been unpopular; now they were hated. When the Germans asked for Jews, their French neighbours helped to round them up. He frowned, deepening the line between his brow, ashamed of his own knowledge. The Comte in his Château, the Mayor in his grocery store, the people going about their work and living their lives in St. Blaize. For what should they fight, at this late stage? For Allies who were their hereditary enemies, and who blamed them for their surrender? For a place in a world which would be dominated by outsiders, by Americans who had stayed neutral until Japan attacked them – by England, the foe of centuries ... He turned into the driveway and slowed down, protecting the loose-laid gravel. Louise thought he was a coward. But then they judged by different standards. The difference in priorities was as fundamental as her desire to fight a war which was already lost and thereby lose the chance of gaining from the peace. She despised him; he didn't blame her. He loved her, as he had always done. He accepted her rejection because he knew she couldn't change. He accepted his own suffering for the same reason.

If it was borne with patience, some good would come out of it. He went into the dark entrance hall, and shivered. It was high vaulted, stone walled, with two large Flemish tapestries hung down one side; the temperature was chill.

'Jean?'

He turned and saw his wife facing him, standing in the doorway of the salon.

'I wanted to come with you this morning. You should have waited.'

'I'm sorry; you were still asleep. There was nothing you could have done. The poor woman was dead long before they got to her,'

'It's horrible,' Louise said. He had followed her into the room and they were both standing. She had a cigarette in her hand, and she found an ashtray at the other side of the room, where she could turn her back on him for a moment. He had a way of looking directly at her, watching her face. She had found it attractive once; he had fine dark eyes, full of expression. Now it made her falter. He was an enemy, not to be trusted.

'I had a surprise,' she said suddenly. 'Do you remember I had a cousin Roger, father's first cousin – Roger Savage?'

'I heard him mentioned, but I can't remember meeting him. Why?'

She turned and faced him. 'His son arrived here this morning. From Berne. He works for the family trust lawyers. He's upstairs. I said he could stay with us for a few days.'

Jean de Bernard took a cigarette from his case and slowly lit it.

'Of course,' he said. 'How nice.' He didn't have to look at her. He didn't ask for explanations. He knew with infallible instinct that she was lying.

'Excuse me,' he said. 'I'm going upstairs to see Papa.'

At six-thirty a car drew up at the gates of the Château. The lodge was empty, its windows shuttered. There was no gatekeeper and the gates stood open. The car was sleek and highly polished; the driver sprang out and stood at attention by the back door. Inside two people turned towards each other. The man was in his forties, clean-shaven, with close-cropped brown hair and high cheekbones, deep-set eyes.

He slid his arm round the shoulders of a girl, much younger, with dark hair down to her shoulders and a rapt expression on her face. He bent and kissed her, opening her lips; one hand closed over her breast. Outside the car, his driver stood at attention, staring straight ahead.

'I shall miss you,' the man said. 'I shall think of you with your family while I'm alone.'

Her face was pale, like a mask, the eyes closed. 'I have to come,' she whispered. 'You don't know how I hate it. You don't know how I hate every minute I'm away from you!'

'One day I shall come up to the house,' he said. He searched her mouth again. 'Let me drive you now. Why should you walk, carrying that bag . . .'

'No,' she murmured, holding on to him. 'No, Adolph, not yet. Give me time to talk to them. Let me talk to my brother first . . .'

'All right.' He drew away and opened the door. 'I won't force you, my darling. I won't embarrass you. Till Monday.'

Régine de Bernard got out. The driver handed her her weekend case and saluted. The rear window of the car was down. She blew a kiss through it. The man replaced his black cap, the skull insignia of the Death's Head division of the SS gleamed above the peak.

'Till Monday,' Bernard's sister whispered. The Mercedes waited till she had gone through the gates. Then it did a U-turn in the narrow drive and headed back towards Paris.

Régine went upstairs to her own room. Whenever she returned to St. Blaize she cried herself to sleep because she could have been with Adolph. She banged her door shut, sighing deeply, and touched her breast where he had caressed her. They must never know, of course. Her brother and her sister-in-law, whom she hated. They wouldn't understand the fire in the loins that drove her mad, when she was separated from him. She was a de Bernard, a well brought up Catholic of impeccable family, and it wouldn't be conceivable that she copulated with a German old enough to be her father. The only person with whom she felt comfortable was in fact her father. He was frail and wandering, a dying child, who asked no questions and was content to sit and hold her hand. Her brother had become a stranger. The world was full of strangers now, of people who wouldn't understand how she could be the mistress of a Colonel in the SS. Privately Régine jeered. She knew friends of her aunt who were having affairs with the upper-class officers of the Wehrmacht.

It was only the black uniform that frightened them. It didn't frighten her. She loved it; she loved the inference of force and cruelty, the way he hurt her when they were making love. She wanted to crawl and kiss his feet. She threw the little case on the bed and began to pull out her clothes. There was a noise from the room next door. She stopped, listening. Nobody slept there; it was always empty. Her fool of a brother, whom his wife had turned out of her bed, occupied the room below. Somebody was staying in the old guest room. She stood still; the walls were very thick, they muffled and distorted noise. There was a faint bang, which she thought must be the window; her own made a similar noise because the frame was heavy and it swung on its weight. Régine went outside and paused by the door. She was tense, curious as a cat. She knocked and then opened it.

A man was inside, knotting his tie in front of the dressing table. He turned round and looked at her. She saw a smile which didn't come from his eyes.

'Hello,' he said. 'You must be Régine. Come in.' She found herself shaking hands. He had taken the initiative away from her.

'I'm Roger Savage, Louise's cousin. I'm staying for a few days.'

'I didn't know anyone was here,' she said. She could feel the colour in her face. 'I heard the window bang. Please excuse me for bursting in . . .'

'That's quite all right.' He smiled down at her. There were deep rings under her eyes and she looked plain and tense. 'What time is dinner? I'm afraid I've been sleeping.'

'Seven-thirty. I've only just arrived.'

'From Paris,' Savage said. 'Louise told me about you. How is it there?'

'How should it be?' Hostility flashed at him.

Foe, he reminded himself. Definitely foe. 'I'm asking you,' he said. 'I haven't been there since the occupation. I hope it hasn't changed.'

'I don't think so; perhaps you ought to go and see for yourself.'

'Perhaps I will,' he said. 'We Swiss are such dull fellows; it would be good for me. I might even take you out to lunch.'

'I'm at the Sorbonne,' Régine said. 'I wouldn't have time.' She made a little movement, awkward and unwilling. 'Thank you.'

'I'll see you downstairs,' Savage said. He opened the door for her.

Louise hadn't misjudged her attitude, but he felt her dismissal of the sister-in-law was a mistake. She reminded him of an animal living on its nerves. It was ridiculous, but he had a prescience of danger. He inspected himself in the glass. Hair brushed down, clothes conservative and neat, expression relaxed. The Swiss were dull fellows; he must remember that. He heard voices in the salon and opened the door to find Louise in front of it.

'Oh,' she said. 'I was coming to call you.'

Savage took her hand and kissed it; he felt her fingers tremble.

'I hope I'm not late.'

'Of course not, come in. We're having a drink.'

She wore a yellow printed dress with a long skirt; the cut was pre-war.

'My husband Jean. This is Roger.'

He shook hands with the Comte; he formed a quick impression of a good-looking dark-eyed man with prematurely greying hair and a firm grip, and then his stomach knotted quickly. A man in grey uniform moved forward.

'Major Minden, my cousin Monsieur Savage.'

Minden. Heinz Paul Minden, Major in the 23rd Infantry Corps, aged thirty-seven, married with two children, home in Breslau. Savage bowed. Nothing remarkable, pleasant-looking in a clean-cut way, tall, well built. They shook hands. Louise handed him a glass of the dry wine he had drunk before lunch. The Major offered him a cigarette; he could see Jean de Bernard watching him. He felt Régine come in, and forestalled an introduction by announcing that they had already met.

She accepted a drink and retreated into a corner seat.

'This is my first visit to St. Blaize.' Savage spoke to the major. 'It's beautiful; it must be pleasant to stay here. Do you work in Paris?'

'No, my office is at the local headquarters,' Minden said. He didn't like the Swiss. He was surprised and irritated to find another man in the house. His eyes strayed from Savage, who was describing the train ride from Paris in tedious detail, and followed Louise as she moved round the room. She seemed restless; her cousin's visit appeared to have unsettled her. He thought she looked very beautiful in the yellow dress. Régine was as quiet and withdrawn as usual. Minden paid her no attention. He was wholly absorbed by the older woman.

The voice of Savage recalled him. 'I was stopped on the way here,' he said. 'It looked like a road block. I must say your troops were very polite.'

'I'm glad to hear it,' the Major said. 'There's an alert on for enemy agents in the area. But it's only a formality. I don't think it's a serious possibility.'

'Roger.' Louise had appeared beside them suddenly; she linked her arm through his and pressed fiercely with her fingers. Savage looked down at her. He gave her arm a friendly squeeze.

The Occupying Power

'You don't know how interesting I find all this,' he said. 'Imagine how quiet it is, living in a neutral country. Enemy agents! That sounds very exciting.'

'I disagree.' Jean de Bernard spoke directly to him. 'The last time these people were dropped round here, they involved a local family and two of them were shot. It was a useless, irresponsible act, and it cost French lives. We don't want any more of it. If I found anyone hiding here and trying to cause trouble for the occupation forces, I shouldn't hesitate to give them up!'

There was silence then; Savage felt Louise stiffen beside him. The Major looked embarrassed. 'And quite right too,' Savage said. 'You French are sensible, like the Swiss. You prefer peace. Just think, if I hadn't become a citizen when I was younger, I could have been fighting in the American Army!' They were all looking at him. He patted Louise's hand; he could feel the German wince. He'd noticed the wandering look that followed her, the contracting of jaw muscles when she held his arm. The Major didn't like the cousin from Switzerland handling what he wanted to touch so badly himself.

'Of course,' Minden said, his voice unfriendly. 'I didn't realise you were American.'

'Only my father,' Savage explained. 'My mother was from Lausanne. I've spent all my life in Switzerland. Do you know it?'

'No,' the Major said. 'I've never been there.'

'We used to ski at Verbier before the war,' Jean de Bernard said. 'My father skied extremely well.'

'How is he today?' The Major channelled the talk away from Savage and Louise led him to a sofa which was set back by the wall. She sat beside him. He lit her cigarette and saw that her hand trembled.

'You must be mad,' she said quickly, 'Talking about enemy agents . . .'

'Mad to ignore it,' he said. 'Why shouldn't I mention it? I've nothing to hide; stop looking frightened or they'll notice something. Smile. And put that cigarette out, your hand's shaking like a leaf.'

'It's terrifying,' Louise whispered, 'There's something odd about Jean, I don't think he believes me. How did you meet Régine?'

'She came into my room; said she heard a noise. I'd watch your step with her. She's sharp as a tack.'

'She's completely wrapped up in her own life,' Louise said. For a moment she glanced across to where her sister-in-law sat, holding a glass of wine in both hands, not drinking it and watching her brother talking to the Major. 'She's just young, self-centred. I don't take any notice of her.'

'Well, I shall,' Savage said, 'and you should. My hunch says she's dangerous.' He leaned against the sofa, one arm stretched out along the back. Louise looked at him and suddenly he smiled. It made him look different.

'I like your dress,' he said. 'Try to relax with me, don't look so strained.'

'I'm sorry,' she said. 'I'll try my best. I won't let you down. Aren't you scared yourself? Sitting here with that man across the room . . .'

'No.' Savage shook his head. 'He interests me. Put me sitting next to him at dinner. I want to make a good impression.'

'You ought to avoid him,' Louise protested, 'keep out of his way. I think you're taking unnecessary risks. I've calmed down now, give me another cigarette. It was just when you mentioned the alert . . .'

'Here.' He lit it for her and for a moment their hands touched. His were warm and steady, There was nothing about him to make her feel protective, and yet she said it. 'Be careful. Please.'

'Don't worry.' Savage got up, and slid his hand under her elbow. 'Your manservant has just come in. And don't forget, put me next to Minden.'

Louise sat at the end of the table, with Jean at the head, candles burning between them, lighting the faces of Savage and Minden and Régine.

Savage was talking; he talked to Jean, to Régine, who hardly answered, and most of all to the Major, who was dour and unresponsive. Watching, Louise felt herself relaxing. He was so confident, so bold in his assumption of the role. And so Swiss that she could hardly believe it was acting. She ate little and only sipped the wine, aware that Jean was glancing at her from the other end, with an expression which she couldn't analyse. Did he suspect anything? It was impossible to tell. She had no practice in lying to him, or to anyone; she had been brought up to tell the truth and to despise evasions. Now she had agreed to live a terrifying lie and to deceive people so close to her that every mood and look was known. And if she failed, if Jean suspected that Roger Savage was not her cousin, that he was in any way connected with the air-raid warning of the previous night, then the man she had promised to help was already dead. 'I'd denounce them immediately', that was what Jean had said, and she knew that the words were directed at her. And he'd do it; she had to remember what happened to the Palliers, to reject the hope that he had been incapable of the final infamy.

And if that happened beyond doubt, then even the chill compromise of living under the same roof would be inpossible for her.

Savage's voice interrupted her thoughts. 'What excellent brandy,' he said, talking to his left to the Comte. 'I didn't know you could still get it in France.'

'Major Minden was kind enough to give it to me for Christmas,' Jean de Bernard said.

'And the cigars too? How very generous.' Savage made the German a little bow. 'And are you stationed near St. Blaize?'

'I am at the headquarters, at the Château Diane,' Minden said. 'About half an hour's drive from here.' He looked up at Louise and his expression softened. 'Even if it were Paris, I should prefer to live here.'

'The Château Diane? Haven't I heard of it?'

'It belonged to Diane de Poitiers.' Jean de Bernard answered Savage's question. 'It was built for her by Henri. It's only a part of the original building; much of it was destroyed after the Revolution. But it's very beautiful.'

'Most of the original furniture is still there,' Minden said. 'Wonderful tapestries – my General uses the State rooms.'

'How interesting – does he like history?'

'I don't think so,' Minden laughed. He had drunk a lot of wine and he felt suddenly bold. The presence of Louise sitting so close, and the faint drift of cologne she wore acted as a delicious goad upon his imagination. He wished she would open his scent and use it . . . 'He doesn't care for history much but he's madly in love with Diane de Poitiers!'

'Really?' Jean de Bernard said. 'You never mentioned this before.'

'It's quite amusing,' Minden said. He felt a moment of disloyalty but suppressed it. He wanted to interest Louise. 'There's a portrait of her as Diana the Huntress – you know the kind of picture, a naked allegory, very voluptuous. He had it moved into his sitting room. He sits in front of it, staring. He's read everything written about her; he even sleeps in her bedroom, in her bed!'

'He sounds as if he's a romantic,' Savage said. 'What's his name?'

'General Brühl,' Minden answered. Nobody had laughed or even smiled at his account of Brühl's obsession. Perhaps he had merely sounded coarse. He looked anxiously at Louise and found her watching her cousin. He felt irritated. He felt obliged to defend his General to these people, for whose benefit he had just held him up to ridicule.

'He's a very talented man,' he said. 'He paints in his leisure time – very well. And apart from this little foible about Diane de Poitiers, he's very interested in antiquities.'

'Then we have that in common,' Savage said. 'I should love to see the Château. I suppose, Major, it wouldn't be possible?'

'Not inside, I'm afraid,' Minden said. 'I'd invite you as my guest, but unfortunately non-German personnel are not permitted. I'm so sorry. However, there's some very fine carving on the out-side, you could see that. The gateway is remarkable; it's Diane de Poitiers again, as Diana. Three times lifesize, supported by a stag.'

'I must certainly go,' Savage said. 'Louise, could you find time to take me tomorrow?'

'Yes, of course. We could go in the morning. But we'd have to bicycle. We have a little petrol but it has to be saved for emergencies. Would you mind that?'

'I haven't cycled since I was a boy.' Savage smiled round at them. 'I'm sure the exercise would do me good.'

'Not at all,' Minden spoke to Louise. She tried not to look away, but the moist brown eyes with their message of desire disgusted her. 'Madame, you can use my car. I'll send it back for you and you can drive over and spend as much time as you like. It will be my pleasure.'

'Thank you,' she said. 'You're very kind.'

'Wasn't there a story,' Savage said, 'that Diane de Poitiers had a skin like a young girl when she was sixty?'

'I read that somewhere.' Régine spoke suddenly, and because she hadn't joined the conversation everybody looked at her. There was a polite little smile on Savage's mouth. 'I read all about her; eternal youth and the rest of the nonsense. Personally I don't believe a word of it. Women like that are just myths. As for being in love – those sort of women aren't capable of it!'

'What sort of women?' Louise asked her. 'Kings' mistresses?'

'Professionals,' Régine said. 'The sort of French woman who only exists in the minds of foreigners. A kind of national whore.'

'Régine!' Jean de Bernard spoke sharply. 'That's not a word for you to use. Please . . .'

'There isn't another,' she said coldly. 'I'm not a child, Jean. Please don't rebuke me as if I were.'

Louise pushed back her chair. 'I think we'll go into the salon.' Before she could leave the table, Minden was beside her, pulling the chair away.

'A wonderful dinner,' he murmured.

Louise brushed past him. 'Thank you. I'm glad you enjoyed it.' Régine followed her; she looked pale and there were dark pits under her eyes. For a moment Louise was tempted to ask her if she were feeling ill. But the eyes looked at her and through her, opaque and hostile, the sullen mouth set in a stubborn line.

'I'm very tired,' Régine said. 'Would you mind if I went to bed now?'

'No, of course not. You look tired.'

'Say good night to Jean and the Major and your cousin for me. How long is he going to stay?'

'I don't know,' Louise said. 'A few days. He's come on business over my family trust.'

Régine looked at her for a moment and then away. It was a way she had of being rude. 'He doesn't look at all like you,' she said. 'If he's a cousin he can't be very close.' She walked out of the room before Louise could answer.

They settled in a little group close to the fire; Louise had a frame of embroidery which she worked on in the evenings; both Minden and Savage looked at her. The fire was alight; the light flickered over her as she sewed, casting soft shadows over her face. Both men examined her, but in different ways. The German's eyes ranged over the line of her neck, down to the outline of her breasts and the curve of one leg crossed at the knee. Before his imagination the yellow dress disappeared and the hair caught up behind her head was loose and flowing over bare shoulders. He shifted in his chair and forced his thoughts away from her. To Savage she was more complicated. Sexually attractive, remote and independent, vulnerable and yet brave. There was no need for mental stripping, for the laboured erotic imaginings of the other man. He looked at her and he was stirred.

She had done well that evening. She had kept the balance between them, hiding the fear which he alone had seen. Her hands were steady as she used the needle; the fingers were long and graceful, the nails unpolished. She looked serene in the firelight, removed from them all, as her husband and the Major talked together, excluding him. Once she looked up and caught him watching her. He left his chair and came over to her.

'What are you making, Louise? Show me . . .'

'It's a stool cover – for Papa's room.' He bent over her.

'That's very nice. It must take a long time.'

'About three months, if I do some every night.'

'I want to talk to you,' he said quietly. 'I'll come to your room later.' He went back to his chair, stretched out his feet and gave a little grunt.

'This is so pleasant,' he said. 'I never imagined life was so peaceful in France.'

'It is peaceful,' the Comte de Bernard said. 'And that is how we want to keep it.'

Louise went upstairs first; she paid a visit to her father-in-law and found him sleeping deeply, his bedside light still on. She arranged the bedclothes round him and switched it off, leaving the door a little open. Jean-Pierre and Marie-Anne slept on the same floor within his call. Then she went downstairs to her room to wait for Savage. She heard Jean and the Major come up; she heard Savage saying good night. The minutes went by until an hour had passed, and then a knock sounded on her door. She opened it and he came in.

'I thought you weren't coming.'

'I gave them time to get to sleep; do you have a cigarette?'

'Over there on my dressing table, help yourself.'

Savage sat on the bed. He lit two cigarettes and passed one to her. Again their fingers touched. She wore a dressing-gown, and he noticed how much younger she looked with her hair down.

'I learned a lot tonight,' he said. 'You were terrific. Come and sit down here.'

'You took so many risks,' Louise said. 'I haven't stopped shaking yet. All that business about enemy agents – I nearly died!'

'It was quite natural to talk about it,' he said. 'A real Swiss would have been indignant as hell, being stopped and questioned. I wanted to be convincing.'

'You were certainly that,' she said.

'That Kraut can't take his eyes off you,' Savage said suddenly. 'Why didn't you tell me it was like that?'

'Why should I?' She was surprised and then angry. 'It's bad enough for me having him here, seeing him looking at me like that. I hate him; I hate myself for even speaking to him!'

'And your husband – how about him? How does he like having that goon licking his lips over you?'

'He ignores it,' Louise said. 'Minden will never try anything and Jean knows it. It's part of the price he's willing to pay. For St. Blaize, for being safe.'

'He'd better make the most of it,' Savage said. 'It may not last long. I'm going to need a lot of help from you. How frightened are you? Maybe I should put it differently. How brave?'

'Not brave at all.' Louise shook her head. 'Thinking about this kind of thing is not the same as doing it. I'm scared to death. But I'll still help all I can. You may think this is funny, but I'm grateful to you for the opportunity.'

'To risk your life? It's a hell of a thing to be grateful for.'

'I've been living this life since 1940; living with capitulation, with people thinking of nothing but their own skins. I came here full of pride in being married to a Frenchman – a fine old family, you know the kind of thing. I thought St. Blaize and the Château were marvellous and I was just so lucky to be part of it. Well, I don't feel that any more. I despise them. I despise my own husband. And I was getting like them, taking that man's food and drink, letting him lend his car tomorrow. At last I've got a chance to do something to help. And whatever happens I can keep my self-respect, I mean it. I'm very glad you came.'

'If things go wrong,' he said, 'you will be sorry. I hope you realise that.'

'I do. That's why I'm scared.'

'It's a good way to be,' Savage said. 'It makes you careful. Do you have any books on local houses here? I want something on the Château Diane.'

'I'm sure we have – there's a huge library. But why there? Surely you're not thinking of getting in there! It's Brühl's headquarters – it's guarded like Fort Knox!'

'That figures,' Savage said. 'What do you know about Brühl?'

'Nothing. He doesn't mix socially; nobody's ever met him.'

'No,' Savage said, 'I don't suppose they have. Can you look out some books for me tomorrow?'

'I wish you'd tell me what you're going to do. I could do so much more if I knew. Why can't you trust me?'

'If you're arrested,' Savage said calmly, 'you can't tell them what you don't know. I do trust you. I believe you'd be brave and hold out as long as you could. I trust any woman to keep her mouth shut except when someone is using an electric probe inside her.'

'And what about you? Are you so sure you'll hold out?'

'Damned sure,' Savage said. 'Because they'll never take me. Within two seconds I'll be dead. That means if I fail to do the job, somebody else can try.'

'Is it so important? Is it really vital, this thing you've come to do?' She shivered; it was past one o'clock and the room was cold.

'Here,' Savage said. 'You're freezing.' He dragged the quilt off the bed and wrapped it round her. 'Keep this on. Okay, I'll answer that question. It is important. It's more important than you or me or anything that may happen to us. It's the difference between winning and losing the war.'

'I won't ask you any more,' she said quietly. 'You know I'll do anything I can.'

'I know,' he said. 'I only hope you don't regret it. But at least I've warned you. You'd better get to bed now.'

He got up and stretched himself. 'Put your light out before I open the door.'

Louise sat in the darkness for some moments after he had gone. He hadn't touched her or said anything, but she knew that there was a moment when he wanted to stay. She got into bed, pulling the quilt into position. There had been something in his face when he wrapped it round her. Some current of communication, sharp and shocking in its implication. Moments before he had talked about her being tortured as coolly as if he were discussing someone far away. Then there was that sudden blaze inside him, which was as quickly dampened down. Something had answered him; sparks had struck between them without words, without touch. If he had stayed she would have let him. The moment of self-knowledge showed her that she had reached a time of total crisis in her life.

4

'You look tired, Régine. Didn't you sleep well?' Jean de Bernard got up and kissed his sister; he was sitting on the terrace in the brief morning sunshine. She took the chair beside him.

'I'm all right. It's this weather, it's so unpredictable . . .' She shaded her eyes.

'Are you working too hard?' he asked her. 'You haven't looked yourself for some weeks. There's nothing wrong, is there?'

She didn't answer immediately. She was tempted to tell him. She had reached the stage with Vierken when she wanted to stabilise the relationship. She wanted to bring him down to St. Blaize and present him to her family. Her motives were not clear; she had plunged into what seemed to be an exciting affair, and found it becoming more and more important to her. Vierken had shown her to herself; she knew now what she wanted and that nothing else would ever satisfy her. It was a discovery which had changed her life.

'No, there's nothing wrong. I've met somebody I like. I just thought I'd tell you.'

Jean de Bernard came forward in his chair. 'Oh? Aunt Pauline hasn't mentioned anyone – who is it?'

'She hasn't met him,' Régine said. Instinct told her to go slowly. 'He's a German.'

'I see,' her brother said. 'Where did you meet him?'

'At a concert.' They had been sitting next to each other at the Conservatoire, and he had picked her up. She wondered what her proper-minded brother would say if he knew that. 'It's nothing serious, Jean. But he's nice and I thought I'd like to bring him home one weekend.'

'Why haven't you introduced him to Aunt Pauline?'

'You know how she feels about Germans. She'd make him uncomfortable. It's different with you.'

'Not when it comes to my sister,' he said. 'I tolerate them because I don't want trouble. But I don't like you associating with them. Who is this man, what service is he in?'

'The army,' Régine said. 'I told you, it's not serious, you don't have to get so worked up about it, I won't bring him here either if he's not welcome.'

'If it's not serious, then there's no point in bringing him down to meet your family. It would certainly upset Louise.'

'And you'd mind about that, wouldn't you? Even after the way she's treated you?'

'I'm not going to discuss that. She's entitled to her feelings.'

'But you're not entitled to yours, or me to mine,' his sister pointed out. 'She won't have you in her bed, because you haven't been out blowing up railway bridges and getting a lot of people killed! Oh, don't look at me like that, we all know how it is here. Everyone knows. You've no courage, Jean. You shouldn't let her get away with it!'

'You don't understand, Régine,' he said. 'How could you? You haven't lived yet; you haven't been in love.' She thought of the afternoons spent in Vierken's suite in the Crillon, of the breathless, frantic violence of their lovemaking; of the sick pain of mental and physical longing to be with him. Oh no, of course she wouldn't understand . . . She looked at him,

'You're saying you still love her, aren't you?'

'I'm not saying anything. I won't talk about it.'

'She's gone off sightseeing with her cousin, I suppose.'

'Yes, Minden lent them his car.'

'How long is the cousin staying?'

'A few days. Not long.'

'Why should he suddenly come here? There's something funny about it.'

'There's nothing funny.' He sounded irritated. 'Her trust is administered in Switzerland and he works for the lawyers.'

'Oh well.' She shrugged and got up. 'If you're satisfied. But I couldn't sleep last night, and I heard him go out of his room and down the stairs. I wonder what he was doing? I'm going to play with Paul and Sophie,' She walked away to find the children; he could hear her voice calling to them in the garden. She loved them as much as she hated Louise. He lit a cigarette and settled back to wait for his wife and her cousin to return.

The Château Diane was half an hour's drive from St. Blaize. Savage and Louise sat in the back; he praised the beauty of the countryside, and spoke Schweizerdeutsch to Fritz the driver, who was not amused and said in French that he couldn't understand a word. Savage was in a good mood. He had slept well the night before, and he was feeling confident. Whenever the sun shone, his optimism grew.

The car drove through the little town of Anet; it was worth seeing in its own right, for the cobbled streets and sixteenth-century houses, many with their original outside gabling. They turned down a hill, and swung left. There in front of them towered an enormous grey stone gateway and a high wall; the turrets of the Château pointed above it like fingers.

The car stopped. Fritz opened the door for Louise. They got out and Savage stood looking at the gateway. Above the door there was the magnificent naked sculpture of Diane de Poitiers, as Major Minden had described. Huge carved wooden gates enclosed the entrance porch; two red and white sentry boxes were on either side of them, and barriers strung with barbed wire surrounded the outer perimeter of the wall. A vast dry moat surrounded the whole building. Louise touched his arm.

'You see what I mean,' she said. 'This is just the outside. Think what the Château must be like. It wouldn't be possible.'

Savage took her arm. 'Let's walk round a bit, make it look authentic. They would grab this, wouldn't they? It's so beautiful. If you do have any books on it, could we find them after lunch?'

'I was thinking about it,' she said. They walked slowly, his arm pressing against hers. 'We can ask Jean. He'd know where to find something. You haven't seen the library; there are over a thousand books.'

'Are you still scared?' Savage asked.

'Yes. Aren't you?'

'Not particularly. By the way, you've got to show me how to get out on the roof.'

'The roof? Why . . .' She paused and he walked faster, pulling her on with him.

'I want to look at the view,' he said. 'When does your sister-in-law go back to Paris?'

'Sunday night,' she said.

'Hell.' Savage frowned. 'I don't like her being around. She worries me more than your husband.'

'She wouldn't like you, because she doesn't like me,' Louise said. 'And she's very pro-German, I know that. But there's nothing to worry about from her. She doesn't care what happens here.'

'She cares more than you think,' he said. 'Let's turn back now; and don't look like that. I'm not planning to vault over the Château wall and take it single handed.'

'But you're going to try and get inside, aren't you?' Louise said.

'Yes,' he admitted. 'No harm in telling you that much. I've got to get into Brühl's little fortress. Nice and snug, isn't it, tucked away here . . .'

'You'll never get out,' Louise said slowly. 'You'll be killed.'

'Maybe. So long as I've done what I came to do it won't matter a damn.'

'Isn't there anyone back home who'll miss you?' They had stopped by the Château wall; the gateway towered above them, casting its shadow over them. Two sentries marched between their boxes; a military car came to the entrance and they snapped to attention. Two more guards approached the car and examined the papers of the driver.

'There's no one,' Savage said. 'This isn't a game for married men.' There was a tensing of the arm linked through hers that made her look at him.

'Have you been married?'

'Yes. But I'm not now. Come on, there's the car over there.'

'I'm not trying to pry,' Louise said. 'I shouldn't have asked.'

'No,' he said. 'You shouldn't.'

They drove back to St. Blaize in silence; his mood of cheerfulness had disappeared. He sat turned away from her, looking grimly and blindly out of the window. His hands were clenched tight on his knee. She leaned back and closed her eyes; tears stung behind the lids and she didn't know why.

Suddenly a hand covered hers. It was warm and it pressed her fingers. 'Stop thinking,' he said. 'And worrying. I can feel you doing it.'

'I'll try,' she whispered. 'I'm sorry; I know I upset you.'

'Not you,' he said. 'Nothing to do with you. You're a good girl.'

He went on holding her hand for the rest of the journey. As soon as they sat down to lunch he was back in his role; he asked so many questions and showed so much enthusiasm for the Château Diane and its architecture, that Jean de Bernard could do nothing less than take him to the library and help him find the books he wanted. The afternoon passed quietly for Louise. She had a headache but was too restless to lie down. The children went upstairs to play with their grandfather after his midday rest; they climbed the stairs with their mother, each holding her hand; Sophie, who had her father's dark hair and large brown eyes, broke away to run to the old man's bedroom first.

She was a true de Bernard, shy, intelligent, affectionate only to those she knew. Her love for the senile old man always touched Louise. They sat together holding hands while the Comte talked to her in his thin voice. By contrast the visits to the upstairs floor bored Paul, who was boisterous, and hated sitting still.

That afternoon Alfred de Bernard was in his big leather armchair, with a rug over his knees, his gramophone on a table within reach, and a book open beside it. He was a beautiful old man, with transparent white skin stretched over his fine bones, black eyes that looked into a past of his own, hair as fine as down, and the smile of the old who are content. He glanced up as Louise came in. She bent and kissed him. He had been a kind and gentle father-in-law, stricken by the loss of a much younger wife; his affection for her had been real, but already he was withdrawing from the world. Within three years of her marriage, Louise was taking care of him. He loved his grandchildren; but had they not come to see him every day, he would have soon forgotten them. He depended upon his son, whom he bullied in a timid way, but he loved his daughter above everyone else.

'Dear Régie,' he said to Louise. 'She spent such a long time with me this morning. She doesn't look well. I wish she'd come home. Pauline doesn't look after her properly.'

'I'm sure she does,' Louise said. The Comte drew the little girl into his arm.

'Sophie and she are so alike,' he murmured. 'Régine was such a beautiful child. She's gone back, hasn't she?'

'No, Papa,' Louise answered. 'Not yet. She goes to Paris tomorrow. She'll come up and see you before she goes.'

'I wish she'd stay.' He shook his head. 'Take care of her, won't you .. ?'

'Of course I will.' She patted his hand, 'I'm going to leave the children with you for a few minutes. Paul, you can read something for Grandpapa. I won't be long.' Outside the room she hurried down the stairs to the floor below and along the passage to the guest room. She knocked on the door and went in.

Savage was lying on the bed, the leather-bound books spread round him. 'I found just what I wanted,' he said. 'Come in.'

'You wanted to get on the roof,' Louise said. 'I've left the children with my father-in-law. Hurry and I'll show you. I'll have to go back to him in a few minutes or Paul will run downstairs. He gets restless after a while.'

She took him up the stairs, past the door of the old Comte's room; pausing for a moment they could near the sound of the little boy's voice reading aloud. Then on down a corridor that twisted; Savage pointed to the closed doors on one side of it. 'Who lives up here?'

'The two servants, Jean-Pierre and Marie-Anne; that first door on the left. They're all staff rooms and there's nobody in them. Here.' She stopped in front of a small wooden door and opened it. Another flight of stone spiral steps was immediately inside. 'Go up there and you'll find the entrance to the roof. It's bolted from the inside. And for God's sake be careful; I've only been up there once, to show someone the view. It's very steep and the valleys are slippery. What are you going to do up here?'

'Set up a two-way transmitter,' Savage said. 'And I can only use it once. We don't want one of their detector vans picking up a signal from here. You go back to the children. I'll go up and look around.'

The view was magnificent; he stood for a moment in a wide leaded valley, looking out over twenty miles or more of countryside. The village of St. Blaize crouched like a stone animal to the left, its church spire fingering the sky. And to the north the roofs and squares of Houdan seemed no bigger than his hand. Further still was Anet with the distinctive pink and grey of the Château Diane on its perimeter. There had been no ground plan available in London. It was not one of the great monuments of France; only a small jewel set in a country full of minor treasures, the tribute of an enamoured king to his courtesan. And now General Friedrich Brühl used it as his headquarters. It had taken British Intelligence a year to discover where he was; a year of careful research into the smallest fragments of information, a word here, a rumour, the tracking down of officers with certain specialist qualifications.

It had sounded such an anticlimax when Louise said it the night before.

'That's Brühl's headquarters,' and the casual reference the Major made to the man who was top on the list of all Allied Intelligence services.

'My General's in love with her. He even sleeps in her bed.' Savage stood looking out towards the Château; at that height the wind went through him. He looked round for the best position, given the slant of the rooftops. The big trees which had worried him because of interference were some distance away. He chose a place near the edge. Heights had no terrors for him; he stepped to the rim and looked down. This was the best place from which to transmit. He went back, down the spiral stairs and to his own floor. There was nobody moving, no sound coming from below. It was the hour between dusk and evening when the upper floors were deserted. He got his suitcase out, and dragged the waterproof covering from the top of the clothes cupboard. Less than five minutes later he was back on the roof, the transmitter in position, covered by the waterproof.

He bolted the roof door shut and slipped down the spiral stairs. On his way to his own landing the old Comte's door opened and Louise came out. Two children followed her; a boy of seven and a smaller, very pretty girl, who reminded him immediately of Jean de Bernard. He shook hands with Paul, and asked Sophie if she would kiss him. Shaking her head, the child hid behind her mother. Savage looked at Louise and smiled.

'She's got the right idea. Never kiss a stranger.' They walked the rest of the way together.

On Sunday the de Bernard family went to Mass. To their surprise Louise accompanied them. Savage found himself alone with the Major. He discovered him reading in the salon, looking quite different in civilian clothes. He glanced up as Savage came in and frowned.

'Good morning.' Savage wore his broadest smile. 'The sun is shining and I'm going for a walk. I hope you will keep me company.'

Minden lowered his book. 'I'm reading,' he said.

'You can read this afternoon,' Savage said. 'It's cold in here. Come and get some exercise.' With a sigh the Major put his book aside. He followed him out into the garden. It was indeed a lovely morning, the sun was exceptionally hot and the first cabbage white butterfly of the season fluttered past.

'Let's go this way.' Savage pointed round the side of the Château. 'There's a pleasant walk through here; I found it yesterday. I find this more beneficial than going to church. You're not a Catholic?'

'I was brought up a Lutheran,' Minden answered. They were walking side by side down a shaded path towards an avenue of lime trees. 'Personally I'm an agnostic.'

'The religion of the scientist,' Savage remarked. 'And the law. I prefer the rational law to metaphysics. One could say our society is substituting pharmaceuticals for prayers.'

'I hope that's not a sneer,' Minden said. His tone was sharp. He didn't like Savage; he hadn't wanted to be dragged away from his book to take this walk. Now he detected a sarcasm at the expense of what he most believed in and he reacted angrily.

'A sneer?' Savage repeated it with surprise. 'My dear Major, why should I sneer at the greatest science of them all? Man is controlled by chemistry. That is a fact, not an accusation.'

'It's not a theory people like,' Minden said. The apology had mollified him. Both men began to quicken their pace towards the avenue of trees. 'Nor to be fair, is it completely proven. Certainly most human reactions can be altered by chemical means, but it's not yet certain how decisive a part chemical balances play in the basic behaviour patterns of man. This will be the study of the future.'

'If there is a future,' Savage said. 'The world has been ravaged by war, and there is still the major battle to be fought.'

'It will be won,' the Major said. 'I have no doubts about the outcome. And then there will be peace for the next five hundred years. Time for rebuilding, for re-shaping Europe.'

'You're very confident that the Allies' invasion will fail,' Savage said. Over their heads the sun broke through the trees, dappling them with light. Minden's face was blotched and leprous, as if he had a skin disease. Then the trees closed over them and the illusion passed. 'How can you be so certain of a German victory? I must tell you frankly, Swiss opinion has begun to veer towards the Allies.'

'Then it is mistaken,' Minden said. He spoke without emphasis, coolly, from a position of knowledge denied to a neutral. He had a profound contempt for Swiss moneymaking and dealing with both sides. Minden didn't need to be on the defensive; Savage recognised the absolute certainty in his answer and the skin on his body pricked.

'You're facing an invasion; a huge Anglo-American army will be thrown against you. And you must admit, your best troops were lost in Russia. It's not the old Wehrmacht defending Europe today. There are unfortunate parallels to be drawn with Napoleon.'

'That's understandable,' Minden agreed, 'but it happens to be the wrong conclusion. Certainly our manpower is not what it was. But this won't be the deciding factor. The invasion will fail. England and America will have to capitulate. If Switzerland backs the Allies she will regret it. Shall we turn back now?'

'Are you suggesting that Hitler really has a secret weapon? I can't see what else would make America and England ask for peace.'

'VIs and rockets are already falling upon England,' Minden pointed out. 'The Führer keeps his word. He's promised victory and we shall have it.'

'Then there must be something else, some other weapon,' Savage said.

'If there is,' the Major answered, 'I wouldn't know about it. I'm only a simple staff officer.'

'You're not offended by this conversation?' Savage sounded concerned. 'I felt we could discuss it openly.'

'And why not? I'm not a political fanatic. I enjoyed our talk. Beautiful grounds, aren't they? It's a pity the gardens have become run down. My batman helps with the vegetables but he hasn't time to do more.'

'They must be glad to have you here,' Savage said. 'You've been very helpful to them.'

'I've done what I could,' Minden said. 'They're a nice family. The Comte is a sensible man; we get on very well.'

'My cousin has become very French,' Savage remarked. They were within sight of the Château. 'I'm surprised; Americans don't usually lose their identity so completely. I have the feeling she resents you. You don't mind my saying that?'

The Major did mind, and his frown showed it. However, he shrugged. 'I suppose so. No woman likes a stranger in her home. I think she's grown used to me. One day we will be friends.'

'I'm sure you will. I met my little cousins yesterday. They're delightful children. I've always heard that American children were monsters; I'm afraid my views on upbringing are very strict.'

'With an American father?' the Major couldn't resist it.

'My parents were divorced. My mother raised me. And she had the old-fashioned ideas. I hear the car; they must be back from church.'

'Ah,' Minden said. 'Yes, they're back. I promised to play with the children before lunch.' He began to walk very quickly towards the Château.

They turned the corner and there was the car, with Jean and Régine, the children and Louise. As soon as they saw Minden the children ran towards him. He went down on one knee and gathered them into his arms. Savage could see him laughing. He looked up and saw Louise watching him; Jean and Régine had gone inside. He went across to her; she looked girlish and pretty in a hat. He put a hand on her shoulder. 'Good morning. Did you say one for me?'

'I couldn't,' she said in a low voice. 'I felt if I mentioned it at all, something awful will happen. Besides, I haven't been to Mass for months. I told you, I was a coward.'

'I know,' Savage said. 'I believe you.'

'Look at the children,' she said. 'He always makes such a fuss of them.'

'So I see,' Minden was standing upright, the children, one on each side of him, swinging from his hands. They were looking up at him and laughing.

'Mama,' Paul called out, 'Mama, Major Minden wants to play ball with us!'

'That's very kind of him,' Louise answered. 'Lunch is in half an hour.' The three of them began to run across the lawn.

'So he's a child lover, is he?' Savage said softly,

'There's nothing I can do about it,' Louise answered. 'They'll grow up thinking the Germans are nice. Why are you looking like that?'

'They're not nice,' Savage said. 'They're a race of bloody schizophrenics, and that bastard is a good example. When can we talk?'

'Not now,' she said. 'Jean will be getting us something to drink. After lunch, go to your room and wait for me. I'll say I've got a headache.'

'I can't find either of them.' Régine faced her brother. 'He's not in the house and Louise isn't in her room, I looked.'

'And what is that supposed to mean?' He looked up at her, his face wary, an expression of anger in her eyes. 'Régine, I warn you, before you say anything, be very careful.'

'All right, I know you want to close your eyes to it,' she said angrily. 'That's the trouble with you. But I'm different. I know there's something wrong with this so-called cousin, coming out of the blue! I watched them together this morning when we came back from Mass. I looked out of the window and saw them; he had his hand on her shoulder and they were looking at each other. And it wasn't like cousins! She says she's got a headache and she's going to lie down, he pretends to go for a walk. He went walking this morning, the Major told me. They've gone off somewhere together!'

'So you went to spy on Louise,' Jean de Bernard said slowly. 'You couldn't find her in her room, so you come running down to me to make trouble.'

'He's not a cousin,' Régine said defiantly. 'He's a lover. I know it. I know by the way he looks at her!'

'You know nothing about it.' Jean got up and suddenly he seized his sister by the arm. 'I told you this morning and I'll tell you now. Mind your own business! Louise is my wife and I won't have you snooping and telling lies. Roger Savage *is* her cousin; I know who his parents are, I know everything about him.'

'He's sleeping with her,' Régine sneered. 'At this moment I expect she's flat on her back under some trees!'

With his right hand he slapped her hard across the face. 'Shut your mouth,' he shouted at her. 'Get out of this room!'

She backed away from him, one hand against her cheek. She had begun to cry. 'I'm going,' she said. 'I'm going back to Paris now!'

The door slammed after her; Jean de Bernard stood for a moment, not moving. Régine was right about Roger Savage. Her reaction to him had been instinctive, her deduction wholly feminine. There was nothing Jean could define about Savage that accounted for his suspicion. His performance, if that was what it was, had been faultless; it was Louise who had failed to convince. He knew his wife and their estrangement hadn't changed her personality. She had the natural frankness of her race. The role of deceiver didn't fit her. He walked across to the window and lit a cigarette, staring out. If they had gone for a walk they would return that way.

Minden was wrong. There *had* been a drop of enemy agents, and the man who passed himself off as Roger Savage was the parachutist. Whatever Savage was planning to do, it could only mean death and destruction, with its attendant reprisals against the French. Everything he had worked for and sacrificed so much of his happiness to preserve was now in mortal danger. He had lost his wife and his self-respect, but he had kept St. Blaize and the village intact. He loved the Château above mere stones and trees and an old heritage. It was the house where he was born, where he had played on the lawns and ridden his first pony down the bridle paths. It had survived the Revolution, watching over the village for six centuries. Everywhere he looked there were reminders of the past and of his responsibility for the future. The portraits of his ancestors, the photographs of his grandparents and parents as children, the large studio study of Louise, by the fountain with his son and baby daughter. Standing by the window, waiting for them to come into view, Jean remembered that day four years ago when he had seen the first German scout car drive to the door, and the first Germans to set foot in St. Blaize en Yvelines walked across the gravel. He had been so disillusioned and heartsick, returned from total military collapse to protect what was left of his family's future. At that moment there had been no middle way, no compromise between the decision to step forward and hold out his hand to the ravishers of France, or take out his army revolver and shoot them dead. He had made his choice and paid the price. Now it was threatened with destruction. His old father slipping peacefully out of life upstairs, loved and protected, his sister whom he had slapped across the face like a slut, because she had panicked him, his children, Louise herself. They would all be taken and questioned, before they were dragged before a firing squad.

Jean knew what happened to the dissenters, to the resisters. He didn't feel anger any more; now fear possessed him, fear for the people he loved. Fear for the wife who had betrayed them all by her blind obstinacy, and whose danger he couldn't bear to contemplate. There was only one thing to be done. He had made one choice four years ago. He made a second then. He went to the bureau and from the back of the drawer he took his army revolver and a clip of bullets which had been hidden there since the capitulation of France. Then he went to find Savage.

Savage had his mouth pressed hard against hers; she had stopped resisting him, her lips were open and her eyes closed. He could feel her heart beating fast under his moving hand. It had happened between them without warning. He had gone upstairs and waited for her; he was sure that his mind was occupied by nothing but the Major. When she came into the room his body moved; it came close to her, one hand pushed the door shut and the other caught her by the shoulder. Without speaking, he leant his weight against her, pinning her against the wall.

He hadn't meant to make love to her; equally he was sure she hadn't expected it. The fact was that it had happened. He raised his head and looked down at her.

'This is breaking all the rules,' he said. 'They didn't teach me about this in training school . . . I want you very much. I feel you want me.'

The muscles pinning her against him were steel knots. And yet there was a warmth in the eyes and for all his strength he hadn't hurt her. 'Oh God,' Louise whispered, 'you know I do. Let me go.'

'No,' Savage said. 'We're going to make love. We nearly did last night. It's going to happen anyway. You know it is.'

'Take your hands off my wife!' Jean de Bernard stood in the open doorway, his revolver pointing at Savage. He spoke in English. Savage moved a step back; his eyes flickered to the door, judging the chance of crashing it shut on the Comte and jamming him against the lintel. The gun was too close. He stood clear of Louise.

'I ought to kill you,' Jean de Bernard said. 'I would have done if I hadn't been afraid of hitting Louise. Get away from him.'

'No,' she said quietly. She moved to Savage and took hold of his arm. 'Put down that gun,' she said. 'Nothing happened between us.'

He didn't look at her; he said slowly to Savage, 'I heard everything. You're no more Swiss than I am. You've come to this house and brought us all into danger. My foolish, romantic-minded wife let you stay. You know what the Gestapo would do to her, don't you? But you don't care! You'll use her and try to sleep with her, and never think of what could happen to her – to all of us!'

'All right,' Savage said coldly. 'So I'm not Swiss. You've found out. But I'm here and I've been made pretty bloody welcome. So what do you tell your German friends?'

'I tell them,' Jean said grimly, 'that I became suspicious. That I confronted you, you admitted you were using false papers; you tried to escape and I shot you.'

'Very tidy,' Savage said. 'But where does that leave your wife? You think she won't be questioned? You'd better shoot us both. Unless you're ready to give her up too.'

'No!' Louise cried out. 'Jean – for God's sake . . .'

'He won't shoot,' Savage said. 'Right now he'd like to, but he knows he can't. He knows you won't alibi him if he does, and he doesn't fancy the boys getting their itchy hands on you. Why don't you put the gun away? There's nothing you can do about me that doesn't give Louise to the Gestapo!' He turned away from them both and dropped into a chair.

'You bastard,' Jean de Bernard said. 'You blackmailing bastard . . .' He turned to Louise. 'You see now what you've done! You see what these people really are!'

'He's a soldier,' she said slowly. 'He's here to do something important. He can't let anything stand in the way. I don't blame him.'

'No good trying to enlist her,' Savage said. 'She's on my side. I tell you something, Comte de Bernard. She's got more guts in her finger than you and forty million bloody Frenchmen like you.'

'You're getting out of here,' Jean said, 'I don't care where you go, but you're leaving here!'

Savage waited; his instinct counselled him to wait, to leave the initiative to the woman. She had been taken by surprise, but he noted with admiration how bravely she had reacted. He looked at her and smiled slightly. Her scent was still on his hands, a faint suggestion of flowery powder and cologne. He would have liked to take that gun away and bring it butt downwards onto the Comte's skull.

'Jean,' Louise said slowly, 'he can't leave here. He's got to stay in this district. If you turn him out, I'll go with him. Then you'll be sure of one thing. We'll be arrested together.'

'I see,' de Bernard said. 'I see how it is. He's seduced you completely. You're putting the children at risk, you realise that? And my father? You're quite prepared to do this, just for him.'

'Not for him, no,' Louise said quietly. 'What you saw shouldn't have happened. I'm sorry it did. It was just as much my fault as his. I'm going to help him because I want to see the Allies win. I want to see your country free of Germans. It's too late for me to turn back. And now it's too late for you too. You'll have to help whether you like it or not.'

'That's sense,' Savage remarked. 'You believe in neutrality, that's okay by us. Just forget you came up here.'

'My wife's in danger,' Jean blazed at him. 'My whole family's in danger because of you!'

'It so happens,' Savage said quietly, 'that they're in greater danger than you think. Why the hell don't you put that popgun away and listen?'

Slowly the gun lowered. 'What do you mean?' Jean said. 'What danger?' Savage took a packet of cigarettes out of his pocket and lit two. He held one out to Louise. Her hands were quite steady.

'I came here to do a job,' he said. 'I was picked for it and trained for it. And I tell you this. Nothing on God's earth is going to stop me. Get that clear first. I could make a deal with you now but I've no guarantee you'd stick to it. All right, you'll protect your wife even if it means helping me. But for how long? You'd think of some way to cross me up and get yourselves in the clear. I can't take that chance. I can't take any chance that could stop this going through. So I've got to trust you. You think you can live with the Nazis and survive, don't you? You think if you keep your nose clean and don't get into trouble they'll let you alone and you can go on living here, bringing up your family?'

'I know I can,' Jean de Bernard interrupted furiously. 'It's people like you – you talk about being trained – trained to kill! To destroy, to come into my country and throw away French lives because of some scheme thought up in London! You may be expendable, maybe you don't mind being killed, but my wife and family aren't going to suffer because of your mission or whatever it is. You say they're in danger – I don't believe you. You're the danger.'

The gun was raised again, pointing to Savage.

'You can shoot me,' he said coldly. 'Go ahead. But first I'm going to tell you why I'm here. Then you can make your choice.'

*

Adolph Vierken had taken a suite at the Crillon. When he came to Paris six months earlier he had been very tired, unable to sleep, suffering from the combat fatigue which was common among men who had served on the Eastern front. His service in Russia had been almost eighteen months. He had come back two stone lighter, suffering from dysentery and exhaustion. He and his men had fought a savage rearguard action against the advancing Russian armies, and performed their function of punitive expeditions against the civilian population with a brutality which had earned Vierken the Iron Cross with oak leaves. He could account for thirty thousand executions and the destruction of a hundred villages with every human inhabitant slaughtered, by mass machine gunning, gassing in mobile vans and public hangings. He was weary and melancholic when he arrived in France after a home leave which hadn't helped his nerves at all. His family were strangers, his wife and children irritated him, the least noise caused an explosion of tension; he had even threatened them with violence. He had applied for and received a non-combatant posting; the plum assignment in France was his reward for duty unremittingly performed. Music was his favourite relaxation. In the first few weeks he went alone to the Paris Opera House or to the Conservatoire and listened to concerts; slowly he relaxed. He began to sleep again, his appetite returned. He brought a ruthless efficiency to his police work which reorganised the SD section and he began to enjoy life. Since his return from the East he hadn't touched a woman. He felt drained, impotent; his manhood was suspended, and the knowledge made him savage. His interrogations were ferocious even by Gestapo standards. He fled the cellars of the avenue Foch and soothed himself with Mozart, Brahms, and Beethoven, with a luxurious suite in the splendid French hotel, with superb food and wines. But it was when he met Régine de Bernard that his cure was complete. She was sitting next to him at a concert and for the first half hour he hadn't noticed her. A concert of Schumann's romantic *lieder* held him rapt, unaware of anything or anyone, until the interval. When he noticed her first the impression was unfavourable. He had always liked tall women with big breasts and Aryan colouring. Stupid, subservient women, like the wife whose docility had almost driven him mad when he came home. This was a girl, slight and dark and not even pretty. He didn't know what made him speak to her. Perhaps it was the nostalgic effect of Schumann's beautiful love songs. He had felt a surge of loneliness. He opened the programme and asked her which of the cycle she liked best.

When the concert ended he took her to supper. They talked, politely and casually about unimportant things. He found her intelligent, intense in a disturbing way. He noticed her small hands and the neatness of her body. Interest began to stir in him. He saw her home, very correct, holding his excitement in check. The next day he sent his car to the Sorbonne and took her out to lunch. By the end of that week she came back to the Crillon with him and they went to bed. She was a virgin; uncertain, eager, clumsy. Desire for her and satisfaction, followed a wild unleashing of the pent-up force of imprisoned sexuality. He found his manhood with Régine; she found with him a self she never knew existed.

Cruelty, force, possession; she wanted love in the terms which most appealed to him. Her intellectual cleverness made her submission all the more exciting. She kissed his hands and worshipped him for being what he was; there was no shame, no inhibition. They were twins in their desires, and out of their sexual sympathy a curious love grew up between them. He had never been loved like that by a woman before. He discovered tenderness, outside of making love; it pleased him to be nice to her, to play records together in his sitting room, to buy her beautiful clothes which she could only wear for him. They liked poetry; she taught him to appreciate the plays of Racine and Molière, she went to museums and art galleries with him. Sometimes they wandered along the banks of the Seine, he in civilian clothes, holding hands and looking at the timeless beauty of the city at night. But most of all they made love. The night she left St. Blaize they were together in his bedroom, exhausted and complete. She had gone to his hotel as soon as she reached Paris. She had taken a bicycle to the station and sat miserably waiting for a train, rubbing her cheek where Jean had slapped her, crying with anger and jealousy. She had disliked her sister-in-law from the moment she came to the house. Her own mother she hardly knew; the memory of a delicate woman, dying upstairs in a room full of flowers, was already dim. Her father's grief and withdrawal had been more of an agony to her than the loss of her mother. The arrival of Jean's wife caused a furious upheaval of adolescent jealousy and the fear of being superseded. Dislike had become hatred, but it was silent, secretive, feeding on imagined wrongs. Nothing Louise had done could expunge the crime of coming into the family and taking the place which Régine believed would have been hers.

She leaned on an elbow and stroked Vierken's chest, playing with the coarse dark hair. And she told him what had happened.

'He hit me,' she said. 'He slapped my face. The first time in my life he's ever touched me. Even when I was a child he never did that. Just because I told him the truth about her.'

'You're jealous, sweetheart,' Vierken told her. 'You shouldn't feel like that about a brother. You have me now, I want all your jealousy.'

'How can he defend her?' Régine said. 'I thought he had more pride. She hasn't slept with him for years! I know that man isn't her cousin, I know it!'

'How?' he asked her. 'How can you know?'

'Because of the way he looks at her,' she said, 'It's like the way you look at me. I know what that means . . . Jean had never met him before, he just arrived, no warning, nothing. There's something wrong about him; I felt it as soon as I saw him!'

'And if he is her lover,' Vierken said, 'what does it matter to you? If your brother were a man he'd know how to deal with them. Why make yourself unhappy? Look at you, your eyes are full of tears . . .'

'Swiss,' she went on obsessively. 'A Swiss lawyer – he didn't look like a lawyer to me!'

Vierken rolled over on his back, his arm around her. He pulled the pillow straight under his head. 'What did he look like then?'

'I don't know,' she said. 'But they were lying, both of them. I'll never forgive Jean for taking her part against me. Never!'

'Hush,' Vierken said. 'Forget about it. I love your little breasts. Come here . . .' Early in the morning he sent her to the Sorbonne in his car. He bathed and shaved, whistling to himself. He had an appointment with the Military Governor at ten o'clock. His dislike for General Stulpnagel made these meetings difficult. He resented the arrogance of the military, their ill-concealed snobbery towards his troops and his officers. A middle-class German from a small town near Cologne, he hated the Prussians and the class they represented. He and his élite had taken the place of the Junkers in the German hierarchy. They meant to keep it. He went to the writing table in the sitting room and made a few notes. Then he put a call through to his office and was connected to his aide.

'This is a Obergruppenführer Vierken. I want a security check run on a Swiss national. Yes. Number one priority. The name is Roger Savage, living in Berne, works for a firm of Swiss lawyers, Felon et Brassier. Find out if he's visiting France. If he isn't, send a message to the SD at Chartres to arrest a man staying at the Château St. Blaize under that name. Good. I'll be in at midday.'

He rang off, crumpled the piece of paper on which he had written the details Régine had told him, and threw it away. Her family quarrels didn't interest him; an affair between her sister-in-law and a cousin was no business of his. But a stranger with a suspicious background story suddenly arriving near to General Brühl's headquarters was very much the concern of the SS.

'I don't believe it,' Jean de Bernard said. 'It's impossible.'

'You don't want to believe it,' Savage said. 'Because if you do you'll have to get off the fence.' Louise said nothing; she looked at them both, Jean stunned and disbelieving, the American contemptuous and bitter. It was incredible. Now that Savage had told them she wanted to reject it. It was too horrible to be true. Not even the Nazis . . .

'You could be lying,' Jean de Bernard said slowly. 'You could be inventing the whole story, just to keep me quiet, to make me help you . . .'

'I could but I'm not. Use your head; nobody makes up something like this. We've known they were working on it. They made the break-through last year; Brühl found a formula. Using concentration camp prisoners for experiments.'

'Oh my God,' Louise broke in. There was something terrible in Savage's face now. Even Jean saw it and was silent.

'Auschwitz,' Savage said. 'He was in charge of the I.G. Farben complex there. He started this project and tested it on men, women and children. My wife was one of them. And my child. She was four years old.'

Jean de Bernard opened the revolver; slowly he took out the bullets one by one. He dropped the gun and the ammunition into his pocket.

'I volunteered,' Savage said. 'I'm going to get that bastard. I'm going to kill him.' He opened and closed his hands. 'But that's nothing to do with you. It's not your problem what happened to my family.'

'It is!' Louise broke in passionately. 'It's the most horrible thing I've ever heard – of course we'll help you!'

'The point is, that what they did to my wife and child they'll do to the population of every French town and village on the coast. As a nerve gas this one's a beauty. It causes panic, hallucinations, convulsions and death. Its effect on children is the worst. They go mad with fear, they tear themselves to pieces . . . This is their secret weapon, not the VIs or the rockets. It's Brühl's formula XV. With this they can wipe out the invasion force in a few days. Killing hundreds of thousands of French civilians is just incidental.

'And we know through intelligence that they're on the point of perfecting the gas. It's not the conventional kind that blows away on the wind. It's a chemical spray that releases its poisonous substance into the atmosphere on making contact with the ground. We don't know how long it lasts, but we do know it's easy to manufacture and can be stockpiled very quickly.'

'How did you discover this?' Jean de Bernard said. 'How did you find out?'

'Coincidence. My General called it the hand of God; he's the sort of man who'd see it that way. A number of Spanish Jews were arrested when France surrendered. They went to Auschwitz. The

Spaniards are a touchy people; they didn't like their Jews being pushed around. So some of them who hadn't died in the camp were repatriated. One went to the American embassy in Madrid with a story. There were rumours of an experimental centre deep in the complex; there was a man called Brühl in charge of it. And prisoners were being taken there and never coming back. The word got out that it was gas. And then this woman saw a burial detail. From the description of the corpses, skin discoloration, self-inflicted injuries, and other symptoms, our people realised the guess was right. It was gas, but not the normal kind. Since then we've been tracking Brühl down from the time he disappeared from Auschwitz. We knew the bastard had gone into hiding somewhere to complete the formula. He didn't need any more guinea-pigs. And then we found him.'

'How?' Louise said. Savage lit a cigarette; he let the match burn for a moment.

'Your friend Major Minden,' he said. He spoke to Jean. 'He's no staff officer. That's part of the masquerade. He's one of Germany's leading biochemists. He was with Brühl at Dresden before the war. When we heard he was here we knew the General Brühl at Château Diane and the scientist were the same man, putting the final touches to his project. There are four airfields within a hundred kilometres of here,' Savage said. 'They'll be able to get the stuff to the bomber squadrons in a matter of hours.'

There was silence then; Savage went on smoking. Jean stared at the ground. 'What do you plan to do?'

'Get into the Château. Find Brühl. Without him they'll never finish it in time. And they can't use it in Germany without slaughtering their own people. So time is vital. Once we push through occupied Europe the gas will be no use to them. I've figured out a way to get inside the Château. But I'll need your help.'

'Jean.' Louise stood up. If he hesitated now . . . She was surprised at the way her heart raced.

Jean de Bernard raised his head and looked at the American. 'Tell me what you want us to do.'

Us. It was a commitment she had never thought he would make. Even faced with the nightmare Savage had disclosed to them, Louise had feared he might try to find some compromise.

'I've got to get past the sentries, and whatever security they have inside the Château,' Savage said. 'If I start shooting I'll never get near Brühl. It's got to be done on the level. And that's where Minden comes into it. He has a special pass; I saw them examining a car when Louise and I went over there yesterday. Nobody gets through the outer sentry post without one. I've got to get Minden's pass. All I need is a few hours, time to get there, go inside and do the job. Then get out and get back here.'

'We'll help you,' Jean said. 'Tell us how.'

'Keep Minden occupied this evening,' Savage said, 'Get him to stay downstairs and give me time to search his room. That's all you have to do.'

'I can do that,' Louise said. 'We all have cold supper on a Sunday night; he often takes his up on a tray and works. I'll ask him to join us. He'll come.'

'Make it a family party,' Savage suggested. 'Bring your father down; we'll all be there. Then I can slip out. If I can get that pass I can put it back during the night and he'll never know it was gone.'

'And if you don't get back?' Jean asked him.

Savage shrugged. 'They'll be here in the morning. If that happens I hope to God you'll shoot Louise and then yourself.'

'Very well.' Jean moved to the door. 'We'll get Minden downstairs and keep him there. We'll give you any help we can. But there's one thing.'

For the first time he looked at Louise; then back to Savage. 'If you touch my wife again I'll kill you. I just want you to know that.' He held the door open for Louise. 'Go and find Minden,' he said. 'He'll come if you ask him.'

He went out of the room and without waiting for Savage to say anything, Louise followed him.

'This is very nice,' Heinz Minden said. He looked round him and smiled; at the Comte de Bernard and his father, sitting with a rug over his knees and a glass of champagne in one frail hand, at Louise whom he thought looked especially beautiful in a simple blue dress and a long row of pearls. Even at Savage who raised his glass to him. The party, so Jean de Bernard said, was really in Savage's honour. It was a pity Régine had been called back to Paris and couldn't be with them. Minden had been surprised and delighted when Louise came to his room. He could hardly believe it when there was a knock on the door and he found her standing there. For a moment he had lost his composure and stammered, wondering why she had come. The explanation was simple and he found her manner charming. The family were gathering and they wanted him to join them. She hadn't given him a chance to excuse himself. She had held the door open and stepped aside to let him follow her. On the way down the stairs he brushed against her and his manhood surged at the contact. In the elegant salon, drinking champagne with the family around him, the Major felt more at home than he had ever done before. He missed being part of a domestic unit. He had a sentimental character which liked to be in harmony with other people. He forgot his contempt for Jean de Bernard and his dislike of the Swiss cousin. He didn't regret the work which was neglected for that evening; he kept his eyes fixed on Louise and enjoyed himself. He moved towards her.

'Madame de Bernard,' he said. 'It is so kind of you to include me in your family gathering. I drink to you.' He raised his champagne glass and Louise did the same. The smile on her face felt as if it were stitched on; she did something she hadn't thought possible. She stroked the seat beside her and said, 'Sit down here, Major, next to me.' She felt Savage's eyes on her but they moved quickly away. He was talking to her father-in-law, who seemed animated and cheerful. He was so cool, so in control of himself. She thought of his wife and the child, of the hate and agony in his face as he spoke about them.

And yet in spite of it he had held her in his arms, hungry and demanding . . .

'My mother,' Minden was saying, 'is a remarkable woman. Do you know I'm one of eight children?'

'Really? No, I didn't know that.' She wrenched her thoughts away from Savage, pinning the false smile onto her lips and turned to give the Major her attention.

'She was so good to us all,' he was saying. 'My father died when we were all young. She went to work, Madame de Bernard. It may seem peculiar to you, but she paid for my education and my three brothers'. She was a hospital matron in Breslau where we lived. We didn't see much of her, of course; my grandmother lived with us, you see, and she took care of us. But I owe everything to my mother.' He finished his champagne.

'I'm sure you must be grateful,' Louise said. She took the glass out of his hand. 'Let me give you some more.' She poured from a bottle on the side table. Roger Savage came beside her.

'Your father-in-law would like some,' he said. His voice dropped to a whisper. 'Keep him busy. I'm going upstairs now.' With their backs to the room he gripped her wrist, just for a moment. Then she was on her way back to sit beside the Major.

'Tell me,' she said, turning fully round to him and blocking Savage out of sight, 'tell me about your father, Major Minden. Do you remember him at all?'

Savage went up the stone staircase at a run. Outside the Major's bedroom door he stopped and glanced round quickly. There was nobody in the corridor; the old servants were huddled in their bedroom on the floor above. He opened the door and went in. It was a similar room to his own, with a solid four-poster bed and ugly chintzes, large and comfortable, with a washstand and porcelain basin in one corner. Minden had scattered his possessions round; family photographs, a shelf of books, a travelling clock. There was a mahogany writing table by the window. Before going downstairs he had stacked his papers into a neat pile; the briefcase was lying beside them. Savage grabbed it, snapping at the lock. Nothing happened. He tried again, pushing furiously at the catch. It held fast. It was locked. He searched on the desk's surface for the keys, but found nothing. A glance at the papers proved them incomprehensible, covered in meaningless synbols. He pulled out the table drawers but there was nothing in them but yellowing headed writing paper and a box of paper clips. No keys. He opened every drawer, felt in the pockets of the Major's uniform jacket and trousers which were hanging, with a twin pair, in the wardrobe. He found a handkerchief and wisps of fluff, a cigarette packet and a box of matches. No key. At last he stopped looking and recognised that any further search was useless. There was no reason for Minden to hide the key. He felt he was among friends. He had left his papers on the table. The briefcase was probably self-locking. Obviously he must have the key on him. Savage looked round quickly, making sure he hadn't left anything disturbed. The room seemed exactly as it had when he came in. He closed the door and hurried back to the salon.

Minden was deep in conversation with Louise; Savage dropped into the seat beside the Comte. When Jean de Bernard looked across at him he shook his head.

A little before ten o'clock the old Comte signalled that he was tired. Immediately Jean de Bernard helped him up, Minden came over to say goodnight and Louise kissed him. 'I'll come up with you,' she said to Jean. Each took him by the arm and guided him out of the room.

'I have enjoyed myself,' the Major said. 'What a delightful family they are – ah, it makes me miss my own!'

'Perhaps you'll be with them soon,' Savage suggested.

'Perhaps,' he agreed. His right hand came up and fumbled with the scarf he wore tucked into his shirt neck. Between his fingers there gleamed a metal chain. As Savage watched he drew it out, playing with it. 'My wife gave me this,' he said. He showed Savage a locket held between finger and thumb. 'I keep her picture in it.' Beside the locket he dangled, hung a key. Savage lifted his eyes slowly from it to the Major's face.

'How nice,' he said, 'to have a memento like that.' Just then Louise and Jean came back into the room. He could see by the Comte's face that his message of failure had been passed on to Louise.

The Major sat on with them for another hour. To Louise the time seemed to crawl; her head ached with tension, the effort to keep up a conversation drained her now that the reason for it was gone. She watched her husband with amazement.

He laughed, he encouraged Minden to talk more and more about himself, he exerted his charm until she felt the German would stay up all night. Yet he was being very clever. It had been a party and parties did not suddenly tail off into embarrassed gloom. Savage avoided her anxious signals; he too was playing his part, only she was failing, overcome by worry and the knowledge of his failure,

'You look a little tired,' her husband said kindly. She had no idea how white and strained she appeared. 'Go up to bed; we men may sit and talk for a while.' Gratefully she followed his suggestion. As she said good night to Savage, his lips formed a single word. Wait. She lay on her bed fully dressed until she heard him come to the door.

'You couldn't find it?'

'No. But I know where it is.' She watched him come towards her. He dropped on the end of the bed, close enough to reach out and touch her, but he didn't move. 'It's round his bloody neck,' he said. 'I saw it tonight. I've got to get it off him.'

'You can't,' Louise said. 'If he's wearing it round his neck it's impossible. Why can't you break the lock?'

'And have him find it had been forced? He may fancy you, but not enough to let something like that pass. You'd have the SS coming here.'

'What are you going to do?' she asked him.

'Try to get it when he's asleep. He may take it off at night.'

'It's too dangerous,' Louise said slowly. 'If he wakes up and catches you . . .'

'I'll kill him,' Savage said. He searched his pocket for a cigarette and swore because his case was empty.

'And that will certainly bring the SS to St. Blaize,' she said. 'You can't do that. There is another way.' She got up and brought the cigarettes from the silver box on her dressing table. Over the flame Savage looked up at her.

'How? How else?'

'I'll get it for you,' she said quietly. 'Go upstairs and wait for me.'

'There's only one way you could get it,' Savage said. 'I don't want you to do it.'

'I'm thinking of the children. Children like Paul and Sophie, dying in agony. Tearing themselves, going insane. I'll get that key for you. Just go and wait.' She got up and began to unfasten her dress. Savage reached out and held her arm. She pulled away from him. 'No,' she said. 'Don't touch me. Do as I've asked you. Go away. I'll bring it to you as soon as I can.'

'You're so beautiful,' Heinz Minden mumbled, 'so wonderful . . . Why did you cry out? I didn't mean to hurt you . . .'

'That thing round your neck,' Louise whispered. 'It cut into me.

Please take it off.' In the darkness he fumbled with the chain and it
slid away; she took it out of his hand, feeling the little key between
her fingers. She let it drop on the floor beside the bed. Then she closed
her eyes as his arms clamped round her. An hour later she stood in
the doorway of Savage's room. She held the chain with the locket and
the key.

'He's asleep,' she said. 'Take what you want. He's in my room.'

'Don't cry,' Savage said. He took the key from her. 'How long can
you give me? How long can you keep him there?'

'As long as I like,' she said. She put a hand to her face for a moment
and then brushed back her hair. Savage saw her hand trembling. 'He
said he loved me,' she said suddenly. 'I feel as if I'll never be clean
again. For God's sake go – I'll have to get back in case he wakes.'

'Wait here,' Savage said. 'I'll bring the key back when I've opened
the case. Then go back to him.'

Five minutes later he had come back. She took the key from him.

'It's one-thirty now,' Savage said. 'Give me till four.'

'Good luck,' Louise said. 'I'll pray for you.' She turned to go back
to her own room.

Minden stirred in the bed, reaching towards her.

'Where were you – darling . . .'

'I'm here,' she whispered. 'I'm with you. You were sleeping. It's
early still; we have all night to be together.'

General Friedrich Brühl had finished dinner. He was not a glutton,
but he appreciated the quality of food. He had developed a taste for
wine and rare liqueurs, which was far removed from the days when
he had lived on sauerkraut and beer as a young man. It amused him
to imagine the pride of his parents, good solid artisans from Munich,
if they could see their son's elevation in the world. He sat at the
head of the long sixteenth-century refectory table, and glanced at his
officers; there were six of them, intimates chosen as his personal staff.
The light from candles in solid gold Renaissance candelabra flattered
their faces and reflected on the General's thick-lensed glasses. Three
of them were scientists, like himself, the others were his aide, a liaison
officer with the military commander of Paris, and his nephew, whom
he had saved from service on the Russian front. He raised his glass
and tasted a mellow Château Yquem. The cellars had been stocked
with magnificent wines; Brühl had ordered their careful removal to
the stable block, where it was cool and the precious vintages wouldn't
be disturbed again. He caught his nephew's eye and smiled. His sister
and he were very close; she wrote regularly and he replied with
affectionate enquiries about the family, details of the weather and
the continued progress of her son, who was proving just the sort of

young man Brühl approved of most. Reliable, obedient, soberminded. In his uncle's service he would have a fine career. Brühl had begun his working life at fourteen as assistant in a chemist's shop, sweeping out, running errands, cleaning the counters and bottles for a few marks a week. In the evenings he studied; he had never been aggressive or athletic, his eyesight was poor and his inclination was solitary. He was a bookish boy, a disappointment to his father, who was a boisterous, lusty man, and one of the earliest recruits to the National Socialist Party. He grew up in the violence and mob politics of Munich in the 20's, saw his father come home with the brown uniform of the Nazi Sturmabteilung stained with the blood of Communists and Jews who had been beaten up. He listened to the exposition of the new philosophy and recognised the superiority of the tough fanatical men who were its prototypes of the new Germans. He couldn't be one of them; nature and undernourishment had prevented that, but he hero-worshipped and admired. It was a party member, a wealthy furniture manufacturer, who heard of his interest in chemistry and science, and paid for his education. Brühl found his *métier* in the University. He excelled at his studies, and he gave his services to the Party who had befriended him, by pointing out Communist elements among the students. He was made treasurer of the Nazi student organisation and he was admired for his administrative gifts. His nickname was the Owl; he emerged with an honours degree in physics and chemistry and went on to achieve a doctorate. When Hitler became Reichschancellor, he was given the post of professor, after its former occupant, an elderly Jew, was bullied into resignation. Friedrich Brühl, the butcher's son, became one of the new élite; a fanatical party organiser, an intellectual whose achievements embellished the Nazi image among a people who worshipped academic titles. He also met, and formed a friendship with another mild myopic, Heinrich Himmler. The result of that friendship was to bring him into brief contact with the Führer himself, an occasion which to Brühl could only be compared with the Beatific Vision to a Christian Saint. He was overwhelmed, enslaved; rational political belief became obsessional faith. There was nothing Brühl couldn't equate with service to his leader and his country. At the outbreak of war he was immediately placed in charge of all chemical research and given full facilities at the I.G. Farben chemical plant at Dresden.

One of his minor contributions was the development of Zkl, which came into use in the gas chambers of Auschwitz; it was quicker and left the corpses less noisome to handle than Monoxide. Exposure to Brühl's gas killed within four minutes.

But the perfection of the ultimate in chemical warfare lay before him; after two years of intensive study and research and highly secret experiments, also undertaken within the concentration camps, Brühl was able to offer to his old friend Himmler a means of repulsing the Allied invasion, of rolling back the advancing Russians, of reducing any country to submission. Victory, Brühl announced to Hitler's personal representative, could be within German grasp inside a year. Hysteria, convulsions, panic and death. Armies, entire populations would be destroyed. Everything he needed was put at his disposal. Brühl himself rejected the facilities at I.G. Farben; he didn't need large laboratories for his work, but he did need absolute secrecy and immunity from Allied bombing. It was decided to establish his research centre in France, in a quiet rural district near enough to Paris to be easily accessible to the defensive bomber squadrons, and in an area where there was no resistance and negligible risk of local curiosity. Brühl had chosen the Château Diane as his headquarters, picked a small, highly qualified staff, and assumed the rank of General in the Wehrmacht. His staff were also given military rank, and the Château was officially designated an Army Headquarters for the areas around Dreux, Houdan and St. Blaize en Yvelines. The security was so efficient that the district headquarters at Chartres had no idea of Brühl's real function or of the existence of his research laboratory in the Château cellars. He had enjoyed every moment of the time spent at the Château Diane; he indulged in romantic daydreams of a vanished age, and lusted over the memorials of a woman who had died four hundred years before. He felt like a king, sleeping in the bed where a Valois had coupled with his mistress, sitting at the same table, taking a mid-morning walk through the gardens where they had wandered together. In the laboratory the perfection of his work was near. He gave the signal and the company of men rose to leave the dining room.

On this night he did not invite them to take coffee with him. He didn't believe in spoiling his subordinates. In the splendid marble hall he said good night, and went to the red salon to have his special brandy and coffee alone. The mess waiters were SS men, in army uniform. Even the chef, specially imported from Germany, was a member of the fanatical Nazi Police. Logs were alight in the fireplace; his coffee and a superb Champagne Cognac waited for him. Brühl relaxed into an armchair, sipped his cognac, and gazed at the portrait of Diane de Poitiers.

Red hair in delicate ringlets, a pale Aryan face and a body like white silk, erotically exposed against a dark background. Brühl closed his eyes for a moment and thought about her. He had never wanted a living woman and his sexual impulses were feeble even in youth. Now he copulated in imagination.

By the time he had finished his brandy, he was thinking about his research. Only one factor remained unresolved. The gas was affected by rainfall. On contact with soil, or any greenery, it became noxious and pervasive. Water, or waterlogged conditions, prevented it from rising. As it had a limited effectiveness on exposure to the atmosphere, this was a serious problem. Bad weather could nullify a gas offensive for some hours; after which the poisonous content would be dissipated. Brühl was a perfectionist. He had to present a weapon without weakness. Its strategic importance depended upon its swift annihilation of the enemy. It could not be subject to the vagaries of weather. The strategy had already been worked out; it was the Führer's intention to offer token resistance to the Allied invasion force, allowing a major advance along the entire front. It was calculated that a quarter of a million men would be in France within a week. When the target was large enough, Luftwaffe squadrons would saturate the area with gas bombs, working from the immediate coastal front inland to a depth of two hundred miles. The result should end the invasion attempt and a massive gas raid on selected cities should cause England to surrender. But the vital elements were surprise and timing. If the enemy were not completely destroyed at a safe distance from the German border, the gas could not be used. Brühl frowned; he had a particularly able assistant in Heinz Minden, who had put forward several solutions to the problem of the gas reacting to water, but unfortunately none of them were viable. Without boasting, Brühl recognised that no member of his team possessed the scientific genius which distinguished his own work. He alone would be able to find the answer. He yawned a little, and squinted up at the massive ormolu and ebony clock which stood on a bracket beside the fireplace. It showed eleven-thirty. He rang a bell and the waiter appeared. The tray was removed and the General went up the marble staircase to the state bedroom on the first floor. There his batman undressed him, placed a glass of hot milk and an apple beside the bed, saluted and went out. By ten minutes past midnight Brühl was asleep.

Savage shut himself up in Minden's room. The briefcase was open and he had taken out the papers, carefully keeping them in sequence and was examining them. All Minden's identification papers were there; the special pass into the Château Diane was a small yellow card, with his photograph on the inside. It was quite different to any form of identification used in any of the German armed forces. His controller at OSS had suspected that a special pass would be issued to the members of Brühl's staff, but there was no way of obtaining a specimen. Savage had to get the genuine article and substitute his own photograph. He carried that photograph, full face and showing the upper portion of a Wehrmacht major's uniform, concealed in the lining of his inner breast pocket. It lay on the table beside him. The size was correct, it would fit over the Major's picture. It was firmly pasted in and there wasn't time to remove it without the risk of damage. But it was the papers themselves that occupied Savage. He had glanced at them quickly; most consisted of scientific data which he didn't understand, but there was a copy of a recent memo, obviously circulated among the staff and signed by Brühl. 'Gentlemen, I have received instructions from the highest authority to produce a specimen of the formula XV for testing before the end of May. I cannot comply with this command until we have overcome the problem of the formula's reaction to rainfall. I urge everyone to apply themselves with increased diligence to this most urgent matter. I have assured the highest authority that we will succeed in our efforts. There will be a meeting in the conference room at four o'clock this afternoon. "Brühl".' Savage looked at the date. It was two days old. The formula's reaction to rainfall. It could mean anything in scientific terms. Practically, it meant that whatever the reaction was, it prevented the gas being tested for final approval. So unless they had found their answer in the last two days, he was in time. There was a green leather notebook; inside it was a meaningless jumble of chemical symbols, with Minden's observations jotted down. But the last two pages were straight notes. Again, much of the language was too technical for Savage to understand in detail, but the sense was clear enough.

Water had a nullifying effect on the nerve gas. The final comment, scribbled and underlined, said simply, *'We must find a solution'*. He shut the book and began replacing everything in its original place in the briefcase. With a pinpoint of adhesive at each corner, he affixed his photograph on top of Minden's. Then he went to the wardrobe and began to dress in the Major's uniform. It was tight and the sleeves were an inch too short, but the greatcoat covered this, and the peaked cap fitted. He paused for a moment, catching sight of his reflection in the mirror, Then he went out and down the stairs. The major's car was in the garage, adjacent to the stables at the one side, and out of earshot of the Château. The batman Fritz slept in the chauffeur's flat above.

Savage slipped behind the wheel and started the engine. He just hoped the servant didn't wake and look out of the window. Minutes later he was through the rear gate of the Château and on the road to Anet and the Château Diane.

5

The two sentries at the main gate of the Château had come on duty at midnight. There was a four-hour rota system throughout the day and night. It was two-thirty and both men were sleepy and unalert. Two cars had turned into the Château since they took up their posts; both contained officers returning from trips to Dreux, where there was a discreet little brothel run by a respectable widow. The lights from another car dazzled them for a moment as it swung into the gateway and stopped. The left-hand sentry approached and as he did so, the window on the driver's side slid down and a hand came out, holding the distinctive yellow card which the sentry recognised immediately. As a matter of form he shone his torch, saw the photograph, glanced in the interior of the car and saw a German officer in the semi-darkness.

Savage's hands were stuck to the wheel with sweat. 'Hurry! Open the gates!' The angry command brought the sentry to instant attention; he saluted, gave back the pass, and ran to do as he was told. Savage let in the clutch; he forced himself to drive slowly. The main courtyard was deserted, but the left-hand side was in deep shadow, overhung by the building. The moon, which had been full the night he arrived at St. Blaize, was now on the wane but the light was bright enough to show him everything. He swung the car round and left it in the patch of darkness, its bonnet pointed to the gate. As he switched off the ignition, he wondered briefly whether he would ever get the chance to drive it out, and then dismissed the thought. There was no time for speculation or for premonitions. He had got in, and that was the first obstacle overcome. The second, and equally dangerous, was the entrance to the Château itself.

Walking across the courtyard, he felt naked and conspicuous in the moonlight. The entrance was level with the courtyard. As a senior staff officer perhaps he should have a key. Cautiously he tried the ring handle. It didn't move. There was nothing he could do but press the modern bellpush on the wooden lintel. It seemed a long time waiting there in full view. When the door swung open it made no noise and Savage jumped as the yellow shaft of light fell full upon him. Two soldiers stood in the entrance, both wore revolvers and one had unbuttoned his holster, his right hand poised over the gun butt.

There was no question of palming the yellow pass in front of them. And if that pass was examined the name and the face wouldn't match. Instinct fired in him like a rocket. He stepped across into the hallway and shouted, 'You idiots! Where the devil have you been – why weren't you by the door?' The guards stiffened immediately. The man who had been about to draw his revolver snapped to attention. Savage swung round on them, scowling. 'Names! You'll be on report for this!'

'Vogel, SS korporal, Herr Major!'

'Schumann, SS Mann, Herr Major!' Neither was looking at him, their heads were rigid, their eyes fixed in front. Savage paused for effect. His heart was pounding.

'You'll hear about this in the morning!' He snarled the threat at them. Both flung up a stiff arm in salute, petrified by discipline. The reaction to an officer had saved him; fear and habit threw them into confusion when he reprimanded them. They were used to being shouted at, abused, even struck, by their officers. Numbed by his accusation of negligence, they never thought of checking on him. The German military system might have its faults but disrespect for superiors wasn't among them. He'd have been a dead man by now if it had been. He was in a huge entrance hall, a lofty ceiling with marble walls. Tapestries and paintings glimmered in the lowered electric light; a massive console table of carved and gilded wood was directly in front of him, with a red tortoise-shell clock that showed the time as 2.40 a.m. The massive marble staircase rose on his left, there was a pair of double doors to the right. For a moment he stood, hesitating; the ground plan he had studied in Jean de Bernard's reference book refused to focus in his mind. He heard the sound of one of the guards on duty moving behind him. He took off his cap, pinned it beneath his arm and turned to the door on the right, opened it and went inside. The room was in darkness; he felt for a light-switch, found it, and an overhead chandelier bathed everything in light. It was a spacious room, obviously in use as a mess; besides some fine period furniture, there were leather chairs and sofas, newspapers and magazines arranged on tables, and flowers by the windows. Savage stayed still, looking round. He pulled at Minden's collar; the jacket was too small for him and it was tight.

'Who the devil are you!' He spun round. A figure had risen from behind one of the sofas; the jacket hung open, the face was red and the eyes peered suspiciously. The man wore Colonel's badges. He must have been in one of the chairs. Savage came to attention and saluted.

'I'm sorry, sir! Excuse me for disturbing you.' You fool, You bloody fool. You won't bluff your way past this one ... He turned back to the door. The German was a big man, thick necked and bald; Savage noticed that he swayed a little. Drunk and sleeping it off.

'Stay where you are!' Savage waited, watching the officer come nearer. He had picked up his holster belt and was taking out the revolver. There was nothing Savage could do; if he tried to leave the room the Colonel would raise the alarm, or even fire. He was not quite sober, and suspicious as an angry bull. He came close to Savage, glaring, the revolver held loosely in his right hand.

'What are you doing here? I've never seen you before! Who the hell are you?'

'Major Friedman, sir.' Savage gave the first name he could think of; his football coach at college had been a man called Friedman. Freddy for short. 'Friedman,' he repeated. 'I've just arrived from Paris.'

'At this hour? What the hell do you mean by coming here in the middle of the night? Friedman – I want to see your papers.' The muzzle of the gun came up and pointed at Savage. Colonel Von Gehlen was sober enough now.

'Certainly, sir.' There was no way out. He had Minden's pass in his pocket and the moment the Colonel saw the name he was discovered. Savage took the pass out, stepped up to the Colonel and gave it to him. There wasn't a hope of grabbing the gun, because it would go off in the struggle. He couldn't afford shouts or noise. The Colonel snatched the pass and looked down at it; not long enough for Savage to move. He breathed in sharply.

'Put your hands up,' he said, 'and turn round. You're under arrest.' Savage raised his hands and turned his back. Once they reached the door he was finished.

'Slowly,' the Colonel warned. 'Go to the door. One move from you and you'll get it in the back!'

'All right,' Savage said. 'I surrender. I won't try anything.' They reached the door. Now. He had one chance, and only one. When that door opened they were in sight of the guards on duty at the entrance. If the Colonel knew what he was doing he would stay just behind out of reach. But his brain wasn't quite clear; he took two steps forward because they had come to a stop by the door. Savage heard him breathing heavily and made a guess. He aimed a violent kick behind him, and caught the Colonel on the shin with his heel. Savage had registered that he wasn't wearing boots. He gave a cry of pain and at the same moment Savage swung round, his right arm curved back from the elbow, his hand stretched out, the fingers rigid. The blow was so fast the German didn't even see it. It caught him across the cheekbone. The revolver fell out of his hand, and Savage kicked it across the carpet. He struck again, and this time the blow was lethal. It hit the Colonel across the side of the neck. He gave a choking grunt and his knees sagged; Savage caught him before he fell. There was an open wound across his face and blood was running down it. His eyes were open but the eyeballs showed white. Savage dragged him across the room, looking for a chair in a corner. He propped him in it; he stood over him for a moment, making sure there was no heart-beat, no breath. But the Colonel was dead. Savage turned his head to one side, hiding the ugly slash across his face. He picked up Minden's pass and found the revolver. He threw it into the chair with the Colonel. Then he remembered that cry when he cracked the German's shin. They had been close enough to the door for some sound to penetrate through to the guards outside. But if they'd heard anything they would have come by now. He rubbed the heel of his right hand. In training they had hardened it by constant hammering against wood. He glanced once more at the dead man. At a casual look he seemed to be asleep. Savage crossed the room, opened the door and switched out the lights. The two soldiers were seated by the door; they saw him and immediately jumped up, standing to attention.

He ignored them and turned to the right. The stairway was a magnificent sweep of marble, with a wide balustrade, curving up from the main hall to the upper floors. Savage had plotted the route so carefully before, that the lapse of memory when he first came into the hall seemed extraordinary. But the initial nervous tension had disappeared. Killing the Colonel had triggered off the reflexes of his training. He was cool and confident, and inside him burned the beacon of hate. He mounted the steps and began to climb. It seemed a long way up. Electric sconces on the walls gave a subdued light. He had reached the first floor; a long corridor stretched in front of him, with more sconces lighting the way on low-watt electric bulbs. Three more doors; there was a thread of light visible under one of them. He crept past it. Diane de Poitiers' bedroom. It was at the very end, exactly as it had been marked on the plan, identifiable by its massive oak doors, gilded and carved, with the initial D and the crescent moon in a cartouche above it. So far, he said inside himself, so far and you have got away with it. He's on the other side of those doors. The face in the blown-up photograph, the murderer of your wife and your child. The handle turned without a sound. He stepped inside, keeping the door ajar, trying to see into the room by the light in the corridor outside. It took some seconds before his eyes became accustomed and could distinguish shapes. The bed towered like a tent directly in line with the doorway. He carried a pencil torch in the greatcoat pocket; the tiny beam picked out a gilt chair, a narrow table with ornaments and flowers on it. And then it crept towards the bed, moving over the draperies; he closed the door behind him and began to follow the small bright light. By the side of the bed he stopped and very slowly moved the torch upward. Brühl's head lay on the pillow, turned a little to one side. No spectacles, more hair than in the photograph where he had worn a cap; a younger man than Savage had imagined him. He slept with the innocence of a boy. The torch moved again, finding a table by the bed. It lit up a glass with an inch of milk at the bottom and a plate with an apple core. And a bedside light. Savage switched it on and sprang. He caught the hair in his left hand, jerking up the head, exposing the throat. As Brühl woke, he died. Savage's right hand smashed down and shattered his windpipe. There was a horrible gurgling sound, and his body threshed about under the bedclothes. Then it collapsed, quivered for a moment and didn't move again. Savage looked down at him. It was so quick, so painless. Patricia had died in agony, torn by convulsions, wrenched out of life in the midst of unthinkable terrors as the gas attacked her nervous system. He couldn't imagine his child . . . He stood without moving for some moments. He had lived for this act of retribution, dreamed of it, longed for it, lain without sleep fighting the pain of his grief with the antidote of hatred and revenge. Now it was done. His personal debt was paid. Hundreds of helpless victims had been sacrificed, the wives and children of other men, husbands, fathers, old and young, the human guineapigs selected to perfect the final infamy against the human race. He looked once more at the lolling head on the pillow; blood was trickling steadily out of the corner of the mouth, staining the white pillow. He had paid his personal debt. Now he was going to settle the others. Quietly he began to search the room.

There was a desk, a modern roll-top in a corner by one of the big windows. It was unlocked; inside were files and papers neatly clipped together, several small leather notebooks, and a letter written to Brühl's sister which had been put aside for posting. In the inside drawer he found what he was looking for. The General's personal oddments, a gold lighter, a matching cigar case and a pencil and a bunch of keys. He took the keys. It was a chance. It wasn't part of his mission but he was going to do what even his superiors had thought impossible.

He was going to find the laboratory. Outside in the corridor he stopped, freezing against the wall. He could hear voices coming up the stairs, they were low, and someone laughed. Some of the staff coming up to their rooms . . . He stepped back into Brühl's room and waited by the door, listening. Footsteps didn't reach him, they ceased further up, doors opened and closed, somebody called out goodnight.

When he came out again the corridor was empty. He put his cap on, pulling it low over his face, brought Minden's revolver out of its holster and slipped it in his pocket. The cellars. The laboratory must be below ground, hidden and well protected. On the ground plan they were reached from the main hall, through the kitchens. It was all too easy to walk down the stairs and out past the guards who had let him in. But to walk through the main hall, and go towards the top security area in the building in the middle of the night – he wouldn't get through without being stopped and he knew it. They had refused to give him explosives; the risk of setting off the gas and killing the French inhabitants for miles around wouldn't be countenanced by his superiors, although the English Colonel had tried to argue in favour of a single sabotage operation in which the Château was destroyed. For this reason they hadn't used bombers. The gas couldn't be unleashed. Killing Brühl, the genius of chemical destruction, was the most that they had hoped for. Savage had nothing but a revolver and his manual skill at silent killing. It couldn't be so simple; down through the main hall, on to the kitchens and down again to the cellars. The Germans would never have left such a primitive arrangement to house their hopes of victory over the world. There must be another, more sophisticated way for Brühl to reach his work. And then he saw the other door. Beside Brühl's bedroom. It was a narrow door, much narrower than the others, newly constructed to the same basic design so that it blended in.

He went and tried the handle. It was locked. The third of Brühl's keys opened it. Savage found himself standing in a three-man lift. There were two buttons, one marked 'ground floor', the second, 'XV centre'. That meant there were two entrances to the cellar by the lift shaft, one on the main floor for the staff and the one above, which allowed Brühl direct access from his room. Savage closed the door, shut the steel grid which came up to waist level, and pressed the button marked 'XV centre'. The descent was soundless; for a moment he had feared the hydraulic whine which must surely have attracted attention at that hour. But there was nothing. German efficiency had anticipated that.

Softly the lift came to a stop. There was a red light on the wall by the buttons and it glowed. Savage was on the level with the laboratories. He pushed back the grill, opened the door and stepped out. He found himself in a short corridor, constructed of concrete blocks, with soundproofed ceiling and fluorescent lighting. There was no other exit that he could see. The entrance to the laboratory was at the end of the passage. Savage left the lift door ajar; so long as the little red eye was alight, the lift couldn't be called upstairs, leaving him trapped.

The door to the cellar was steel. He examined the lock and couldn't see any signs of an alarm system being attached to it. If anything existed like an electric beam, he had already broken it. He began to try the keys on Brühl's chain, and with the second try he was successful. The massive door was on a weight mechanism; it swung open and then closed behind him. He felt for a light switch, found something and clicked it down. Instantly there was a flood of brilliant light. Six enormous strip lights bared what had been the château cellars and was now a single room some sixty feet in length. Savage stood for a moment, looking round him. A part of his brain registered that no alarm had sounded. There were long tables with scientific instruments, drawing-boards, some of the paraphernalia of all laboratories. Along the left-hand wall hung a row of twenty gas-masks, suspended like gargoyles from hooks, under each of them a white overall. He stepped into the room. There were two big steel cabinets down the centre, with rows of drawers. He went to one and pulled; it opened, disclosing a thick hessian file. The other drawers were the same. He wandered round the tables and the drawingboards. He understood nothing which was written on them. Formula XV was in that room; the gas-masks proved it. But where? In what guise? He walked from one end to the other and could see nothing. Back to the filing cabinets again. Records; millions of words, the history of their researches, carefully documented. There must be a safe, a vault below the present level where what they were working on was kept . . . It was in the middle of the wall of steel cabinets. A large square box standing at chest height. There was nothing marked on it to indicate what it contained, only a single word in German, printed on a pasteboard slip inside a slot on the front. *Caution.* The lock was inset into the top, covered by a metal flap. Savage went to where the gas-masks hung, stuffed Minden's hat into his pocket and put one on. For a moment he couldn't see clearly; he wiped the goggles with a handkerchief. There was an odd-looking key on Brühl's chain, a thick key with a stubby snout and two irregular-shaped teeth. It fitted the lock.

And there, sitting squat on a shelf inside the steel box, were two glass containers. The contents looked like water. Completely colourless; he tipped one slightly and the formula moved sluggishly, like oil. A pure concentrate, enough to stock hundreds of bombs, to throw hundreds of thousands of people into the violent paroxysms that preceded death. If he spilt the stuff on the floor it would kill the German garrison at the Château. And it would seep out and destroy the people in the area, spreading God knew how far, carried like the plague. He couldn't do it. Savage put the container down. He didn't think of his own life; frustration brought a sweat of agony out on his body; it ran down his face inside the mask, making his eyes sting. He had the formula there, a hand's reach away. All he had to do was destroy it. But how? How? He almost shouted the word, and it came muffled through the filtered mouthpiece. There was an answer and he couldn't find it – there was something, something he knew . . . And then he saw them, up above his head. A dozen eyes in the ceiling, round and black, at five-foot intervals in two rows. Water. Water neutralised the gas. That was what Brühl's memo said, what Minden's notes had repeated. The formula was still imperfect because rainfall would render the gas harmless. 'We must find a solution.' Minden had underlined those words. And there, right above him, was a sprinkler system, installed in case of fire. He pulled off the mask, slipped the rubber headstrap over his wrist, and began to run to the near end of the room. There was the little glass box, with the lever behind it and the instruction in Schrift printed above in red. *In case of fire break glass and depress lever!* He paused for a few seconds, deciding how best it could be done. Water would destroy the formula. And the records. Two years of work and research on how to murder millions of people in the extremity of agony. All neatly documented in those filing cabinets. He went to the first of them and opened every drawer to its length. He did the same with the second. Then he took out both containers of the formula and stood them on top of the steel safe. He pulled on the gas-mask and went to the emergency lever; lifting the glass flap, and taking the handle, he pulled. Immediately there was a drenching downpour from the system overhead. Water cascaded from the sprinklers. Savage drew Minden's revolver, cocked it and took aim. He fired twice; the glass jars shattered, their deadly contents spurted outwards, lost in the flood pouring from the ceiling. Savage turned and ran to the exit. He locked the steel door and pounded down the passage to the lift. Inside, he slammed the gate shut and punched the button marked 'ground floor'. He tore off the gas-mask, smoothed Minden's cap and pulled it on; he suddenly noticed that his hand was shaking. The lift stopped in its noiseless way. Carefully he opened the outer door; the dimly lit main hall was silent. Nobody had heard the two shots, buried down beneath the floor. If the corridor had been soundproofed, so was the laboratory itself.

He stepped out of the lift and pushed the door closed behind him. If nobody heard anything or went near Brühl till the morning, that laboratory would be under ten feet of water. Everything in it, every record, every drawing, would be destroyed. And the murderous fluid floating in globules on the surface of the water could harm no one. Not even its creators, when they discovered what had happened. The two guards were at the entrance; they were sitting down, one had his head sunk forward, lightly dozing. Savage didn't hesitate. He walked towards them. 'You!' He barked the word. 'Sleeping? Stand to attention!'

They leaped to their feet, rigid; the man who had drifted off for a few minutes gasped out loud with fear. 'Open the door,' Savage snapped. 'Immediately!'

He stepped out into the night and into the courtyard. For a moment he couldn't see the car; it was hidden in a patch of shadow. He slipped his hand into the greatcoat pocket and came out with Brühl's keys.

One quick movement flung them into the darkness. He got into the car; there was a horrific moment when the ignition wouldn't fire. He pressed the starter and there was nothing but a sleepy rattle. Then suddenly it burst into a steady throb as the engine turned; the chassis trembled, and he let in the clutch. He stopped at the gate; two guards came up to him, their torches shining. He fumbled for Minden's card, swearing furiously, thrust it through the window and, on an impulse, punched the horn. The gates were opened quickly, the guards were at the salute as he swept past them. Not until he had turned away from the Château and was on the road to St. Blaize, did he realise he had forgotten to switch on his lights. He also realised something else: the shoulders of Minden's greatcoat were soaking wet. He swore, more from a sense of petty anticlimax than from anxiety. A wet coat was no problem. Nothing was any problem now. He had done the impossible and come out of it alive. So far. He found a cigarette and lit it. Perhaps now he could think about Patricia. Never about his child. That was impossible, the mind couldn't endure it. But his wife, whom he had failed in all that really mattered. Perhaps now he could think about her, because Brühl was dead, and what had killed her was destroyed. He looked at his watch; it was three-thirty. He had told Louise de Bernard to keep Minden occupied until four o'clock. His inclination was to drive fast, but he restrained it. Steady now. No accidents, no stopping, no puncture. The idea almost made him laugh. It was three-forty-five when he glided into the garage under Minden's batman's sleeping quarters, his engine cut off, the car coasting home on its own impetus. The Château was completely dark; he moved very quietly, using the little torch to find his way upstairs. Outside Louise's door he paused; there was a line of light showing under it and he could hear soft voices. He went on upstairs to Minden's room, stripped off the uniform, pushing the wet greatcoat to the back of the cupboard, changing Minden's second coat to its place on the rack. The briefcase was there; he removed his photograph from the yellow pass, put it back in the briefcase and closed it, snapping the lock shut. A look round the room showed everything in place; there was no sign that anyone had been there or that anything had been moved. Savage went out, closing the door without making a sound and slipped into his own room. Four-ten. He lay on the bed, waiting; his body felt stiff, his neck ached with the onset of tension. He tried for a moment to think about his wife, but a strange inhibition closed her image out of his mind. Out of the weariness, the mingled sense of exultation and the inevitable let-down after so much pressure on the nervous system, Savage found that he was thinking of Louise de Bernard as if she were the only woman he had ever known in his life.

*

'I'm very happy,' Minden said. 'I hope you are happy too.' He stood by the bed looking down at her.

'Yes,' Louise said, 'of course. But I really must sleep now.'

'I've tired you.' Minden bent over her, one hand stroked her shoulder. 'I'm sorry. You're the most beautiful woman in the world. I adore you.'

Louise raised her arm; her watch showed four-fifteen. 'Here, your chain. You'd better put it on.'

'It wouldn't do to lose it,' he smiled, fastening the chain with the locket and the key round his neck. 'Let me kiss you once more. Then I'll go.'

'No,' Louise said. 'Please – I'm so exhausted.'

'Good night then,' he whispered, taking her hand in both of his and pressing it to his mouth. He murmured something in German which she didn't understand. When the door closed, Louise lay back and for a moment her eyes closed, and real exhaustion overcame her. The first time he had made love like a pig; the second time, after he woke from sleep, he had decided to arouse her; she didn't know which had been the worst. He had become very emotional; the mixture of sexuality and sentimentality nauseated her. She ran her hands over her body and shuddered. The back of her hand was still moist from his kiss. When she went to his room she had expected some query. He had been in bed reading, when she opened his door and stood just inside it. 'I'm lonely,' she had said. 'I thought you might be too.' He had thrown the bed-clothes off and come to her; immediately excited, he had wanted to take her there, and it was with some difficulty that she persuaded him to follow her to her room. He hadn't asked a question. Four-fifteen. Four-twenty. She got up and put her nightdress on and dressing-gown. She had begun to tremble; the sense of degradation passed into panic as she thought of Savage. Had he come back – if she went to his room and it was empty, would that mean he had been caught, and had he swallowed the lethal pill in time . . . ? Or was he at that moment in the hands of the guards, carrying Minden's pass and wearing Minden's uniform? She hadn't faced the reality before; her decision to seduce the Major was an emotional one, like giving Savage shelter, taken without a proper calculation of the risks involved. If Savage failed, then they were all doomed, she and Jean and the helpless old Comte, even the children . . . Her husband was right. To risk her own life was one thing, but to put Paul and Sophie at risk . . .

When the door opened and she saw Savage she gave a cry.

He didn't say anything; he came and put his arms round her. He could feel her trembling. 'It's all right,' he whispered. 'Everything worked. All thanks to you.'

'I was so terrified,' she said at last. 'I stood here and suddenly realised what would have happened to us all if you'd been caught. To the children too. I must have been mad.' She shook her head. 'Quite mad to do it.'

'Maybe.' Savage lit a cigarette and gave it to her. 'But you've just helped to win the war. Calm down now and listen to me. My job was to kill Brühl, to stop him getting the gas to the production stage. Without him, it would take months. And they haven't got months. The invasion is only weeks away. I did my job and I did more. I wrecked the laboratory and destroyed the stocks. Okay, you've slept with a German and you risked the lives of your whole family. But it was the right decision. Even if it went wrong, it would still have been right. Look at me.' He bent down and kissed her mouth; her lips were cold and they didn't open.

'Quit worrying,' he said.

'You killed him,' she said. 'It doesn't worry you . . .'

'No,' Savage said, 'it doesn't. You forget. He murdered my wife and child.'

'I'm sorry,' Louise said. 'I didn't mean to say that. I'm just not used to people being killed.'

'Let's hope you never have to be,' he said.

'Would you tell me about her?' He didn't answer at once. He drew hard on the cigarette and blew the smoke out with violence.

'I've been trying to think about her tonight,' he said. 'And I can't. I've had a picture of her in my mind, ever since I knew what had happened. We had a boat, a nice thirty-footer, I used to take her sailing round Cape Cod. She loved the sea; it was the only thing I did she really enjoyed. I remember her sitting up in the bows, with her hair blowing all over the place, looking out to sea. She used to tan very dark. She was Belgian. Her name was Patricia.'

Louise took the cigarette stub out of his fingers. 'What happened? Why wasn't she in the States?'

'Because she left me,' he said. 'We'd been married four years, she was never happy in California; I tried moving to New York to practise, but that was worse. I met her in Switzerland. I married her when she was just a kid, straight out of convent school. She didn't know what had hit her. But she tried; goddam it, we both tried. She was sweet and gentle, and full of guts. Your kind of guts, all heart and no head.

'But I wasn't what she wanted and she went home, taking the baby with her. She was two years old then. I don't want to talk about her.'

'No,' Louise said. 'You couldn't. Why did they arrest your wife?'

He turned and looked at her. 'Because she did what you're doing. She got herself mixed up hiding Allied airmen. Someone betrayed the network and she was caught and sent to Auschwitz. With my daughter.

That's all I knew for two years. I tried everything; the International
Red Cross, the American embassy in Geneva, contacts in Spain –
everything. Nobody could get her out. I was in the army in the Judge
Advocate department. I kicked like hell, I wanted to fight. But they
needed lawyers and I stayed at my desk. Then I was sent for; there
was my senior officer, who looked like somebody had knocked all his
teeth out, and another man, a Lieutenant Colonel in the Intelligence
Corps. They told me to sit down, gave me a cigarette and offered me
a Scotch.

'Then they told me about Patricia and my child. The Spanish Jewess
who got out of the camp had got to know her there; they became
friendly. Then Patricia was moved to the special compound. The other
woman didn't see her again for some weeks, till one day she happened
to be on her way to the medical centre and she saw a burial detail going
across the special compound, outside the wall and near the wire fence.
She saw the bodies, and she saw Patricia. She was still holding the little
girl in her arms.'

'Oh God,' Louise said. She put her arm round him. 'Oh God, how
terrible – I'm so sorry . . .'

'I left the JA,' Savage said. 'I joined a special unit attached to OSS
and I told them why. So when they wanted someone to take this on,
they chose me. Just before I killed him tonight, that bastard opened
his eyes. I think I went on living just for that moment.'

'You mustn't blame yourself,' Louise said. 'It wasn't your fault.'

'I didn't make her happy,' Savage said. 'When she wanted to go back
to her family I said Okay. Six months after she left the war broke out.
I should have gone over and brought them both back.'

'You didn't love her, did you?' Louise said. He turned and looked
at her.

'No,' he said. 'That's why I let her go. And that's what's been driving
me crazy ever since. I just didn't love her, and that's why she died like
that. Why they both died.' He put his head down in his hands suddenly.
'I'd like a drink.'

Louise got up. 'I'll get you one.'

She found the bottle of Minden's cognac and brought it upstairs.
She poured some into her own water glass and gave it to him.

'You mustn't cry about it,' Savage said. 'I don't like to see you cry.
Come here and sit beside me.' He put his arm round her; it was a
hard grip.

'What did that Kraut do to you?'

'Nothing that matters,' she said slowly. 'I was sitting here, waiting
for you, feeling frightened and sorry for myself. As if I were so special.
You were right. I just slept with a German, that's all. Don't let's talk
about it. It's what you've done that matters.'

'Yes,' Savage said. He drank the brandy down. 'Yes, I killed Brühl and I wrecked the laboratory. By the time anyone goes down there in the morning they'll need a boat.'

'What are you going to do? You must get away at once.'

'I'll go tomorrow,' Savage said. 'I'll leave quite normally. There'll be a massive security check in the area but my Swiss passport should get me through. I'll go to Paris and on to Berne. I don't want to hang around here. With Jean's record and Minden to back it up, you won't be suspected.'

'You must get out,' Louise repeated. 'Whatever happens you mustn't be anywhere near here. I wish you could go now, tonight!'

'No transport,' Savage said. 'And respectable Swiss cousins don't disappear at five in the morning. Our friend Minden might start asking questions. I'll see him tomorrow and say goodbye. I don't want any loose ends here for you.'

He turned her face towards him and kissed her. Louise shivered and he let her go. 'I'm cold,' she said. 'I'm sorry.'

'You've had enough for tonight,' Savage said. 'Get into bed.'

She lay while he pulled the bedclothes over her and tucked them in, watching him. Her body was cold and her courage suddenly low. She put out a hand and held on to him.

'I'm frightened,' she said. 'I don't know why but I have the most awful feeling – why don't you take Jean's car and go? Now! Please, Roger. Don't wait till tomorrow.'

'You go to sleep,' he said. 'Don't worry.' He switched out the light and left her. Louise lay in the darkness. Everything had gone well; Savage had succeeded and returned safely; there were only a few hours to go through before he left the Château. By that time tomorrow he would be miles away. There was no logical reason for the insistent, strident panic in her which cried out that this was not how it would end.

6

Franz Zerbinski had been Colonel Von Gehlen's batman for two years. He had served with him in Belgium when the Colonel was with the occupation forces, and spent a year in Brussels. When they moved to Paris, Franz was delighted. He sent his wife French scent and silk stockings, and set himself up with a girl he had picked up one Sunday morning at a café on the Champs Elysées. She was seventeen, a plump little tart who cuddled up to him and made him feel at home. His Colonel's posting to the Château Diane had disturbed this happy relationship; he didn't see her so often, and he had an unhappy feeling that she had found another friend.

He had been asleep for an hour, or so he thought, until he woke up feeling cramp in his left leg, and discovered it was after four o'clock. He had been dozing on a chair in the Colonel's bedroom, waiting for him to come upstairs and be undressed. It was a nightly ritual, getting his officer out of his clothes and into bed. He was always drunk and irritable, and sometimes he punched out at Franz, who had learned how to dodge him. As an officer he wasn't too bad; he was generous to his batman. His one disadvantage was his habit of getting drunk every night and Franz having to sit up till he came upstairs. Four-twenty in the morning. He had never been so late. Franz got up and stretched himself; he felt worried. If the Colonel were asleep in the mess, he must have taken on a bigger load than usual. It wouldn't do for him to be found there in the morning when the orderlies came. He hesitated, not knowing what to do. If he went down and woke the Colonel he'd probably get a bollocking. If he left him there, he was sure to be blamed.

There was a little loyalty in him. He didn't want his officer to be disgraced. He decided to go downstairs to the mess and bring him up to bed. Because of this decision, Brühl was discovered several hours earlier than Savage had anticipated. In the confusion that followed, nobody went to investigate the laboratories until much later in the early morning. By which time the water had risen so high it flooded the corridor. But long before this, the SS had arrived at the Château.

By six o'clock that morning, Obergruppenführer Knocken, head of the SS in Paris, was holding an investigation at the Château Diane.

He had brought seven staff officers with him, and Adolph Vierken as his second in command. He chose the dining room, where Brühl had loved to preside over his intimates, and sat at the head of the refectory table. He was an ugly man, his hair so close cut that he was almost bald, with short-sighted eyes further distorted by strong pebble glasses. He held a gold pencil in one hand and at intervals he tapped his teeth with the end of it. Before him stood the two soldiers who had been on duty inside the main entrance during the night. Both stood at attention and their faces were grey with fear. Knocken had taken statements from the guards at the gate; their entry book was on the table in front of him. Vierken sat on his right-hand side, smoking, listening to the interrogation. He had been awoken an hour earlier by the emergency call from the Château. Brühl had been discovered almost immediately after the Colonel's body had been found. Instantly the Château was placed on a full alert, and Knocken was notified. He and Vierken and their officers had arrived within the hour.

As senior officers in the German security forces, Knocken and Vierken knew the significance of Brühl's death and what it meant to the Nazi war effort.

'Now,' Knocken said. 'I want you to think before you answer. I have here the report from the guards on duty at the main gate. Seven officers left the Château between nine p.m. and midnight. All had returned by two in the morning. Then an eighth officer was admitted. He passed through the main gate. You say you let him into the Château at about that time. Is that correct?'

Both men nodded. 'Yes, Herr Obergruppenführer.'

'How long have you been posted here? You . . .' He spoke to the private soldier.

'Five months, sir.'

'And you?'

'Four months, sir.'

'I see.' Knocken tapped his teeth with the pencil. He spoke in a quiet voice.

'This officer that you admitted,' Knocken said quietly. 'You say he arrived back at two-twenty-five. Did you recognise him?'

'No, Herr Obergruppenführer.' The most senior of the soldiers answered; he was a regular SS man with ten years' service behind him and he had been decorated for gallantry in the Polish campaign.

'Why not?'

'He was wearing his cap pulled down, sir.'

'And what was his name?' Knocken had a list in front of him. On it were thirteen names. Seven of these were members of the staff who had gone out after eight o'clock and returned during the night. All had been checked out and in. The six remaining names, including

Minden's, were all officers billeted outside, none of whom had yet reported for duty. 'Well,' Knocken repeated, 'what was his name?'

'I don't know, Herr Obergruppenführer.'

'You didn't check his pass?'

'No sir.' Knocken drew a circle on the sheet of paper and placed a dot in the middle of it. 'Why not?'

'We were slow to open the door, sir. He took our names and said we'd be reported.'

'I see.' Knocken made another dot in the circle. 'So he took your names and you forgot to ask for his pass or for any identification?'

'Yes, sir.' The man's voice croaked with fear.

'What did he do – where did he go?'

'He went to the mess, sir.'

Knocken turned to Adolph Vierken. 'Where he murdered Von Gehlen.' He drew a line through the circle. The stony eyes glinted at the soldier.

'You saw him come out?' The corporal nodded. 'And where did he go then?'

'Upstairs, Herr Obergruppenführer.'

'Exactly,' Knocken remarked. 'He went upstairs. And he killed General Brühl, without anyone hearing.'

'It's incredible,' Vierken said. 'He passes the guards on the gates, he bluffs his way in here, murders two men and gets to the cellars, without anyone stopping him!' The gas-mask had been found in the lift, Brühl's keys were recovered from outside.

'He had a pass,' Knocken said. 'The guards at the gates checked him in, but unfortunately they didn't notice the name. A number of officers go out for the evening and they get careless. Very careless. In fact,' he spoke to the others grouped round the table, 'the security arrangements seem to have been extremely lax.' He looked at the senior SS officer present, whose task had been the safety of Brühl and his project. The man didn't dare to look at him. 'I shall hold you responsible, Gruppenführer Brandt. Entirely responsible.' The officer blanched to a sickly colour.

'Yes,' he said. 'I am responsible. But you must realise we had no reason to think any attempt . . .'

'There was an alert here on Friday night!' Vierken suddenly shouted at him. 'You ordered a search of the area with the regular military at Chartres! You found nobody and you assumed, *assumed* it was a reconnaissance flight! That assumption was wrong, Gruppenführer Brandt! It was careless and slack. Somebody was dropped. And that man came in here last night and killed General Brühl.'

'And lost us the war,' Knocken murmured, too low for them to hear. He addressed himself to the quivering Brandt. He tapped the list with his gold pencil. 'There are thirteen names here. Seven regular officers who have all been accounted for, six who live outside and have not reported for duty. But an eighth man came in and went out again. A man whose name is not on any list. That is our murderer. You let him out again?' He spoke to the corporal.

'Yes.'

'Describe him. Remember everything you can.'

The corporal made a visible effort. 'He was tall, sir, about my height. He wore his cap pulled down; I didn't see his eyes or what colour hair he had. He was a German. I'd swear to that. He had a major's rank on his collar. That's all, Herr Obergruppenführer.'

'He would speak perfect German. That means nothing. So we have a tall man in a major's uniform. Not very helpful.' Knocken looked at the corporal and at the private soldier, who had not spoken a word.

'You're under arrest,' he said quietly. 'Report yourselves.'

They sprang to attention and saluted. 'Heil Hitler!'

'And you, Gruppenführer Brandt, will do the same.'

The officer got up, stretched out his arm and said loudly, 'Heil Hitler!' He was dead and he knew it. He left the room with some dignity.

Knocken turned to Adolph Vierken. 'I am putting you in charge of this operation,' he said. 'I want this man found! You can have what troops and facilities you need, on my authority.'

'Thank you, Obergruppenführer,' Vierken said. 'But first I must point out that the murderer left here at least four hours ago. In my opinion he will have left the area. I can't promise to find him.' Knocken allowed himself a tiny smile. Vierken was no fool; he wasn't going to commit himself to something he might not be able to do. And four hours was a long start. Nobody but a madman would stay within a hundred kilometres of the Château Diane.

'I agree,' he said. 'I agree it's unlikely we'll get him. But I'm convinced of one thing. He was landed here on Friday night. Somebody sheltered him for Saturday and Sunday. Somebody, somewhere in this district, has been hiding him. And that car came from the direction of St. Blaize en Yvelines. Somebody hid him there.'

'I'll find them,' Vierken assured him. 'I propose to close off the entire area. Nobody enters or leaves the district within a radius of fifty kilometres. All telephone systems and transport comes under SS control; the regular military authority is suspended. There will be a complete communications blackout. And I want the seventh battalion to supply me with three hundred troops, and the necessary armoured vehicles. I shall set up my headquarters here and conduct the investigations myself.'

'Very good,' Knocken said. He took up his pencil and tapped it against his lower teeth; he looked round the table at his staff officers. Their faces were stiff and grave. 'Gentlemen,' he said. 'I have to tell you something. What happened here this morning has cost us the war.' There was a murmur from them, a wordless protest. He held up his hand. 'I'm not exaggerating. Frederich Brühl and his work are irreplaceable. Both are destroyed. All that is left to us is vengeance. These people' – he turned to Vierken, grim and scowling beside him – 'these people helped our enemies. We've treated them with softness. Our occupation has been gentle. And this is the result! Weakness, gentlemen, has brought this terrible disaster upon our Fatherland. But they are going to pay for it.' His clenched fist slammed the table. 'You,' he said to Vierken, 'are going to make an example of them that will go down in history! I want them punished . . . I want it to be a punishment to fit what they have done!'

Vierken stood up. 'I promise you that,' he said. 'I promise you the French will pay a price for this that will never be forgotten!'

'Good,' Knocken said. 'Good. I am relying on you.'

'I shan't fail you,' Vierken said. 'I'll think of something really special for them.' The meeting broke up; Knocken gave two orders which were to be carried out immediately. An SS firing squad executed the four soldiers who had been on duty on the gates and inside the Château, and Gruppenführer Brandt was handed a revolver with which he shot himself. A message detailing the disaster was sent direct to the Reichs Chancellery in Berlin. Knocken and Vierken returned to Paris, where Vierken went to his headquarters for an hour to clear his desk. Among the messages and memos waiting for him was a brief note from the German Embassy in Berne. 'Felon & Brassier confirm that Roger Savage has left for France. He can be located at the Château de St. Blaize en Yvelines where he is dealing with the financial affairs of the Comtesse de Bernard. His date of arrival was May 30th: he is expected to return to Berne early this week. He is a Swiss national, resident in the city for the past five years. Message ends.'

Vierken had forgotten about Régine's cousin-in-law. He was still stunned by what had happened at the Château Diane, still struggling to reconcile himself to the disaster of Brühl's murder and the destruction of the laboratory. His rage was mounting, with a sense of frustration which could only find an outlet in savage cruelty. He read the report on Roger Savage twice. For a moment suspicion had reared in him, only to subside regretfully in the face of that confirming evidence. There was nothing wrong with the Swiss staying at St. Blaize. Their source in Berne was beyond question. Felon & Brassier were international lawyers of repute. The address given as Savage's home had confirmed his absence. There was nothing there.

He made arrangements for his Parisian commitments to be looked after and went to the Crillon to collect his belongings. A week at St. Blaize from where the killer's car had come – ten days. Time enough to question and search and then, with an ingenuity which was just beginning to suggest itself, devise a punishment meet for the crime . . . He had an appointment with Régine that evening. He had arranged to collect her from the Sorbonne, and bring her back to the hotel. He thought of her disappointment and was sorry. He telephoned and left a message for her. He had a little time left; just enough to explain, to hold her in his arms. Just as he had decided to leave the hotel, Régine arrived. She was breathless and untidy. He opened the door of the suite and she ran into his arms.

'My darling – I came as soon as I could get away. My tutor was furious . . .'

'Kiss me,' Vierken demanded, pressing her small body hard against him. 'Kiss me!'

Moments later she looked up at him, her face streaked with tears. 'How long will you be gone? I miss you so much – I can't bear it!'

'Not long,' he comforted. 'A week, a few days more perhaps. It won't be too long.'

'It'll be eternity to me,' Régine declared. Sometimes the extent of her passion surprised him. She was so small, so slight and pale. He stroked her hair with tenderness. His wife, that placid, obedient cow, had less fire in her whole body than the frail girl possessed in one of the fingers he was kissing.

'It won't be long,' he repeated. 'Don't cry, sweetheart; I shall miss you too. When I come back we can be together again.'

'Where are you going? Why can't I come with you – I could make an excuse to my aunt . . .'

'No,' Vierken said. 'This is official business. I can't tell you where I'm going. It's police work.'

'You won't be in danger, will you?' The thin arms circled his neck, clutching with desperate strength.

'No,' he assured her. 'I've told you, it's a police operation. Resistance.'

'Give them hell,' she said fiercely. 'But come back safely, that's all I care about. You will be careful, won't you? You know if anything happened to you I should die?'

'Would you?' Vierken asked her. 'Do you love me so much?'

'You know I do.' She leaned her head against him and he kissed her hair.

He thought suddenly that he would never, ever go back to his wife. If the war was lost, as Knocken said it was, then his escape was planned. Spain and then Central America. He had money hidden away against

the treachery of fate. He would forget about his wife. He would take
Régine with him.

'You mean a lot to me,' he said suddenly. 'I want you to know
that.'

'I worship you,' she said simply. 'I couldn't live without you now.'

'You have such passion,' he muttered, holding her against him; the
muscles of his thighs were taut. 'Such fire, for such a little girl. I could
break you.'

'Do it,' she whispered, her eyes closed. 'Do it now – we've got time
. . . Love me, Adolph. Love me . . .' He swung her up into his arms
and took her to the bedroom. Afterwards at the door of the suite they
said goodbye. He held her very close. And he broke the discipline of
twenty years. 'Promise me you'll stay in Paris. I don't want you to go
home to St. Blaize. Stay here.'

'Why not?' Régine asked. 'Why mustn't I go?'

'Because I order you not to,' he said, using the sexual language
which had such power over them both. 'I command you understand
me? I love you, Régine. Promise me you'll stay here, with your aunt,
till I get back?'

'If that's what you want,' she said. 'I'll do it. I'll do what you say.'

'Good,' Vierken said gently. He kissed her eyes and lips. 'Good.
Remember, wait for me. We'll be together soon.' He left immediately
after she did; his chief interrogator, a young SS Captain in his twenties, sat beside him in the car.

By the time Heinz Minden arrived at the Château Diane troops of
the Waffen SS were in command, and since Vierken's first orders had
been issued just after nine o'clock, the area had been completely sealed
off from contact with the outside world.

'I can't understand it,' Jean de Bernard said. 'Half an hour ago I
telephoned through to Louis Malle and now the line is dead.' He
banged the receiver rest up and down. 'This is a real nuisance; Malle
promised to get me some supplies of roofing felt; I told him I'd pay
the black market price but we've got to get the tower roof insulated;
there's so much damp coming in we'll have serious damage.'

He glanced at Louise without really seeing her. He had spent a night
sleeping uneasily, disturbed in the small hours by a nightmare in which
he saw his father and his children choking to death. His temper was
frayed and his nerves on edge. He struck the telephone and swore.
He hadn't noticed how pale his wife looked, or the nervous glance
she gave Savage when he appeared for breakfast; they hadn't had
a chance to speak alone. Last night had been a failure. That was all
Jean knew. But something about her silence irritated him. He looked
round at her.

'They must have cut the telephones off,' she said. They were alone in his study.

He frowned at her. 'What do you mean – who's cut the telephones?'

'The Germans,' Louise said slowly.

'What makes you say that?' He walked towards her. 'What do you mean?'

'Savage got the key,' she said. 'He got into the Château. He did what he came over to do. They must have found out by now.'

'My God,' Jean de Bernard said. 'My God – I thought you said he'd failed . . .'

'He didn't,' she said. 'He killed Brühl and he destroyed the gas.' For a moment there was silence; he didn't move or speak. Suddenly he made a gesture.

'Thank God,' he said in a low tone. 'Thank God. He must get away from here.'

'He's going,' Louise answered him. His reaction had surprised her. She had expected fear, reproach, even though he had tried to help Savage. 'When did he tell you this?' Jean asked.

She answered without thinking. 'When he got back; about four o'clock.'

'He came to your room?'

'Oh for God's sake, Jean! How else could he let us know!'

'He could have come to me,' her husband said. 'Did he touch you again?'

She turned on him bitterly. 'And what the hell does it matter? What do you care about a thing like that when we're all in danger of our lives! No, he didn't make love to me, if that's what's worrying you. He went straight to his own room.'

'I must talk to him,' the Comte said. 'I've got to know what he plans to do. He ought to leave immediately.'

'He's going,' Louise said. 'He's upstairs packing now – someone's coming up the drive.' Louise was on her feet, looking out of the window. 'On a bicycle. It's Camier!'

Jean stood beside her, watching the Mayor of St. Blaize pedal to the front door, dismount and wipe his sleeve across his sweating face. The sound of the bell pealed through the outer hall. 'Why has he come?' Louise turned to her husband.

'We'll soon see. He may have tried the telephone. Ah! Albert – come in.'

'Monsieur le Comte – Madame la Comtesse.' Camier bowed to them both. He was out of breath, and he carried a cap in his left hand. When he shook hands with Louise she felt him trembling.

'You look very hot,' Jean said. 'Sit down; we can offer you some wine.'

'Monsieur, the town is full of SS troops – they've taken over the telephone exchange at Houdan, the railway station is closed, there are road blocks everywhere! Do you know what has happened? Why are they doing this?' He was so frightened that a dribble of saliva appeared on his lips and ran down his chin.

'I have no more idea than you,' Jean de Bernard said. 'We have heard nothing. This is terrible, Albert. Are people staying calm?'

'The Mairie was besieged,' Camier said. 'I was at my shop as usual when I was sent for and this German officer was sitting at my desk in the Mairie, banging a riding whip and shouting. I just stood there, Monsieur. I didn't understand it. There's been no trouble – we've done nothing! People were trying to get in to see me, and the troops were pushing them back and hitting them.' He wiped his face again, all pretence of manners forgotten. He looked incongruous in a blue suit and a tie. The peasant of a thousand years, cunning, stupid and fearful of forces from outside, mumbled and sweated, hoping blindly that help would come from the seigneur.

'Will you come down and see them, Monsieur! That pig in my office wouldn't tell me anything – he treated me like a dog!'

'I'll come,' Jean de Bernard said. 'But I doubt if they'll pay much attention to me.' He turned to Louise. 'Don't worry,' he said. 'Don't worry, my dearest. We've nothing to fear; our consciences are clear. I'll come down with you, Albert.'

'It's a calamity,' the Mayor lamented. 'When I saw those black uniforms I nearly pissed myself . . . Oh, Madame, I beg your pardon – I am so worried I didn't realise what I was saying . . .'

'It's all right,' Louise said quickly. 'I understand. Please don't apologise.'

Even as she spoke the door opened and Savage stood there. He looked at them in turn. 'I've interrupted something,' he said. 'Excuse me.' He gave a very Swiss bow.

'No,' Jean de Bernard said. 'No, come in, Roger. This concerns you too. This is the Mayor of St. Blaize, M. Camier. There's some emergency; the town has been occupied by the SS, the telephones are cut off, and no one is allowed to leave the district.'

'And there's a curfew!' Camier burst out. 'They posted the notice up outside my office . . .'

'How very awkward,' Savage said. He raised his brows at the mayor. 'Does this apply to neutrals? I am a Swiss national.'

'I don't know, Monsieur,' Camier quavered. 'I don't think they'd care what you were – my God, it was like a nightmare! Will you come down, Monsieur le Comte – see what you can do.'

'I think that's a mistake.' Savage spoke curtly, addressing himself to Jean. 'I wouldn't seek them out. They'll come and find you soon enough. After all,' he shrugged at the unhappy Mayor, 'they may arrest you both. You have to go of course, Monsieur, but I think the Comte should stay here with his family.'

'I have a responsibility to the village,' Jean de Bernard said. 'I must see if there's anything I can do. No harm will come to Louise and the children.' He kissed Louise on the cheek; she started to say something in support of Savage, but he left the room too quickly.

'He's a fool,' Savage said. 'He shouldn't draw attention to himself. They haven't wasted any time!' It was the usual German practice to take hostages and shoot them in reprisal for acts of sabotage. The going rate in human life was one hundred French for a single German soldier. He didn't say anything about it to Louise.

'You can't get out!' she said. 'Don't you realise, they've closed the roads – you're trapped here!'

'If the Mayor's right,' Savage said calmly, 'and I expect he is . . .'

'I hate that man,' she burst out. 'Crawling round the Germans from the day they arrived – now he sees what they're really like! And he comes running here, whining for help . . . You don't think they'll arrest Jean?' She turned to Savage and the anguish on her face surprised him.

'I don't know,' he said. 'I don't know what they'll do. My guess is that they'll pay us a visit here pretty soon. You'll need to keep your nerve, Louise. If they see any sign of cracking, they'll have you down to their headquarters. You know your story and all you have to do is stick to it. Don't worry about what I say or Jean says – just keep to your own line.'

'But you can't stay here,' she protested. 'You've got to get away before they come round asking questions! Can't you make contact with London – what can you do?'

'I can radio them,' Savage said. 'If the routes are all closed I can ask for a pick-up plane. That was part of the deal. It's bloody risky but it may be the only way.'

'You should have gone last night,' Louise said. 'Now you're trapped here . . . Oh my God!'

'I couldn't do that,' Savage said. He came and caught her by the shoulders. 'For Christ's sake, I wanted to go normally, catching the early train. If I just disappeared after what had happened, don't you think Minden would have seen the connection? He may be in love with you, but don't think he'd hesitate to turn you in! It's my bad luck they acted so quickly. They must have discovered it very early this morning.'

'If they arrest you . . .' Louise whispered.

'They won't,' Savage said quickly. 'I'll put a call through to London for a pick-up.'

'They can't land here, it's madness,' she protested. 'The plane will be shot down!'

'You'd be surprised,' he told her, 'how many times we've landed people on a field not far from here. It can be done. Don't be afraid.'

'I'm so frightened I feel quite numb,' she said. 'Numb and sick. Aren't you afraid?'

'Not for myself,' Savage answered. 'I've done my job. I'm satisfied. If they catch me I'll swallow my L pill and that's the end of it. But you're different. Your husband's a man, he can take care of himself. But I don't want anything to happen to you. I was thinking about it last night. Get on the plane with me. Come to England.'

'I couldn't,' Louise said. 'You know that – the children . . .'

'They'll be all right,' he insisted. 'It's only a matter of a week or so before the invasion. You can come back to them afterwards. We'll smash the bastards back to the Rhine. They'll be all right till then.'

'No.' She shook her head. 'No, I could never do that. I couldn't leave them behind.'

'I'm not sure you'll hold together,' Savage said. He held her against him. 'If you show any sign . . .'

'I won't,' she said. 'I'll hold together. I promise you that. I won't break down.'

'I love you,' Savage said. 'I'm trying to tell you so. This marriage is over; we could be together. If you won't come back with me, then I'm coming back for you. I want you to know that. We'll take the kids to the States. Kiss me.' His mouth was warm; she felt the strength of his arms around her and for the brief moments while they stood together, fear receded. Escape offered itself, not the flight back to England, leaving her family behind, but the escape of losing herself with him, of letting his desire control them both. I love him . . . The knowledge overcame her, impossible to deny. I love him and, oh God, how I want to be loved by him while we have the chance . . . She never knew what made her think of Jean de Bernard at that moment. He came unwanted into her mind; the grey in his hair and the lines of worry round his eyes, going down to face the Gestapo in the village. Abruptly she pulled herself away from Savage.

'When do you think Jean will come back? How long has he been gone?'

'About an hour,' Savage said. 'If he doesn't come back soon it won't look very good. You care about him, don't you?'

'He's my husband,' she said. 'It's not just the children; I couldn't walk out on him now either.'

'I see,' Savage nodded. 'How about afterwards – when the war's over?'

'That would be different,' Louise said. 'If we get through this, I would feel free to go with you. If you still wanted me.'

'I'll want you,' Savage said. 'Make no mistake.'

It was late afternoon when Jean de Bernard came back to the Château. Louise and the children were at the front door to meet him; Paul, whose ears were tuned for engines, heard the car first. Jean kissed them both. Louise tried to question him with her eyes, unable to speak before the children, but he only shook his head. Louise watched him playing with them for half an hour, listening to their tales of what they had done at school, one balanced on each knee. He looked from one to the other, smiling and calm, the Papa that they expected to find when they came home. 'We saw a lot of soldiers,' Paul informed him. 'They were in black, with skull and crossbones on their caps. We waved to them but they didn't wave back. Why are there so many of them?'

'I don't know,' Jean said. 'Perhaps they're going on manoeuvres.'

'I wish I could watch them,' Paul said. 'I'm going to be a soldier and have a skeleton on my cap.'

When they had gone upstairs to see their grandfather, Jean de Bernard sank back in the chair; he looked old and exhausted.

'The Death's Head Battalion, that's what they've brought in here,' he said. 'The execution squads. Louise, would you get me a drink, please? I waited three hours in the Mairie to see the officer in charge. I'm very tired.'

She got up immediately and brought him some of Minden's cognac. 'Drink it down,' she said. 'Oh my God, Jean, what's going to happen, what did you find out?'

'Nothing. When he did see me, he just took down my name and told me the whole area was under curfew and SS authority. I asked him what had happened – what was the reason for it. He just looked at me. Then he shouted, "Sabotage and murder. Assisting enemy agents. You'll learn what it means to touch German lives and property. You'll pay for it round here, I can promise you that!"'

'He didn't question you?'

'No. He was in charge of the military operation. The questioning will be done by others; professionals. That cognac was good. Thank you. You know it was curious today. I watched those swine taking over the village, I saw the people's faces, white with fear; Camier gibbering like an old woman, and I thought this is what I tried to stop. This is what I've been afraid would happen for four years, and now it has. And I helped to bring it about. I brought the Gestapo here in the end. Ironic, isn't it?'

'*I* brought them,' Louise said slowly. 'It's not your fault. What do you think they'll do?'

'Try to find the saboteur. They were already searching the houses when I left. Then they'll make arrests. Hundreds of men, I imagine. And then they'll shoot them unless the agent is denounced to them. That's what they usually do.'

There was silence between them; he held his hand over his eyes, shielding them and Louise didn't move. When she did speak her voice trembled. 'These hostages – they won't take you, will they?'

'They may.' He spoke calmly. 'Poor Camier is certain to be chosen; they always take the mayor, the doctor, the priest. After that it's indiscriminate. Don't worry about that. Where is Savage?'

'I don't know,' she spoke impatiently. 'I'll go to Major Minden; I'll ask him to protect you . . .'

'I'm sure he would,' Jean de Bernard said gently. 'He's not a bad man. But he has as much influence with the SS as I have. He couldn't do anything.'

'Jean.' She came and knelt beside his chair. She laid her hand on his arm. 'You won't give Savage up to them?'

'If I could save the lives of Frenchmen, yes I would,' he said. 'I'd give myself up with him. But not you. You are the reason I will stand by and see innocent people murdered and do nothing. You and father and the children. We are caught; there's nothing now to do but wait and see what they will do.'

'You hate me for it, don't you,' Louise said. 'You blame me for what's going to happen. I can see it on your face.'

'The gas had to be destroyed. The monster who made it had to be killed.' He put one hand over hers but there was no warmth in it. 'A million French could have died when the Allies invaded. Nothing can alter that; we did the right thing. But seeing what I saw today, I can't feel anything but horror. Horror for the few hundreds in this area who are going to die because of what we had to do. It may sound stupid and sentimental, but I can't help it. I feel like a murderer.'

There was nothing she could say to him; silence continued.

At last she spoke. 'When will we know what's going to happen?'

'By tomorrow – perhaps even tonight. They move very quickly. I wish I could get you and the children away.'

'Don't, Jean,' she whispered. 'Nothing can happen to us. You're the one who could be in danger. Roger was right; you shouldn't have gone down and made yourself conspicuous!'

'That won't make any difference,' he said. 'There have been de Bernards at St. Blaize for five hundred years. They would know where to find me. You mustn't worry; we have to be brave and calm. It's our only chance now.'

He got up, and stretched; as he crossed the room his step was slow. 'I'm going upstairs to see Papa.'

Louise lit a cigarette; she was in control of herself again. The effect of fear was to numb, after a time. She felt cold and tired, with a sense of anger spreading under the dread of what was coming. And yet it seemed unreal. Jean talked of people she knew being taken and shot in cold blood: Camier, Father Duval, Doctor Joubert . . . Intellectually she accepted it, emotionally she resisted. It couldn't happen. Something, somehow, would prevent it. She went and stood by the window, the cigarette in her right hand, watching for the unknown. 'There have been de Bernards at St. Blaize for five hundred years . . . they would know where to find me . . .'

They wouldn't take Jean as a victim. He was a well-known supporter of the Vichy Government and an open advocate of collaboration with the German occupation forces. They wouldn't take him. She rationalised it calmly, unaware that the hand holding the cigarette was shaking and spilling ash on the floor. They wouldn't drag Jean away watched by Paul and Sophie, screaming and struggling to go to their father . . .

She was still standing there when Savage found her.

'They're going to take hostages; Jean thinks it will be hundreds of people. People from the village here, from all over the district.'

'That figures,' Savage said. 'I warned you in the beginning it was going to be nasty. Don't worry about Jean; I think he's safe enough. His record will protect him.'

'I wish you could get away tonight,' she said. She turned round suddenly and clung to him. 'Jean thinks they may come here at any moment. Couldn't you just go into hiding . . . ?'

'No,' Savage said. 'Everyone knows I'm here. If I disappear that puts the finger on me, and I'd be flushed out like a rabbit. And where do you think you'd stand – all of you? Forget it; if they come here and ask questions that's okay. I've got answers ready. I've got to clear my escape with Minden tonight. I'm going to make a hell of a fuss about being kept here.'

'That's him now, I think,' she said. 'I hear a car.' Savage went on holding her; her back was to the window.

'No,' he said and his voice was gentle. 'No, darling, it's not Minden.'

There were two cars, black and long bonneted, with the swastika pennant flying from the radiators. He watched the men in SS uniform spring out, and the rear door of the first car open. A tall man with the insignia of a Standartenführer got out and stood looking up at the Château for a moment. The bell began to peal, and someone was hitting the front door with a pistol butt.

'They've come, haven't they?' She didn't turn to look.

'Yes,' Savage said. 'Yes they have. You've got to be a very brave girl.'

Minden was given his clearance to leave the Château Diane at five that evening. He had no work to do, he and his colleagues were helpless, confined to the Château while the laboratory was pumped clear of water.

Late that day a group of Brühl's staff had stood in inches of water, looking at the destruction of their work. The laboratory was a shambles of broken glass, sodden materials, filing cabinets with their drawers open and the contents reduced to pulp. Electrical failure had followed submersion and they were on emergency lighting from a small generator. There was an overpowering smell of chemicals and damp. Gasmasks were worn as a precaution, both by the pumping crew and the staff; they were discarded when the atmosphere was proved unpolluted. This was done by bringing a junior officer's pet dog into the area. The effect of the gas upon animals was as ferocious as upon human beings. The spaniel stood in the water up to its flanks and sniffed unhappily, its brown eyes rolling with fear, but it showed no reaction. Nothing proved the efficiency of water in neutralising Formula XV more than the immunity of the dog. Minden could have wept; one of Brühl's favourite assistants, a man who had worked with him from the start of the project in Auschwitz, stood with his face hidden in a handkerchief, and sobbed. Nobody was allowed to see Brühl; an autopsy was performed inside the Château by the doctor on the staff. The cause of his death hadn't been announced. Secrecy covered everything, and the rumours multiplied. He had been stabbed, shot, poisoned – a dozen different men were said to be arrested – the saboteur had been caught; it was a team of parachutists who were being hunted throughout the countryside; it was the *maquis* group who had been hiding in the Château – Minden heard it all and didn't care. His work was ruined. But more, much more than a sense of personal loss, was the agony of knowing that the war could not be won. In the flood water lapping through the laboratory, he saw the fall of Germany. There was a terrible incongruity about it which numbed him.

At three he was questioned by a team of two SS officers, a Major and a Lieutenant. It was a preliminary investigation; anyone who didn't satisfy these two was passed on to the man in command, a high-ranking SS officer called Vierken. Minden had vaguely heard of him; he was attached to General Knocken in Paris. He had a reputation for severity. The SS Major was a genial man with red hair, and a face so thickly freckled that it looked brown. He told Minden to sit down. The Lieutenant was pale with a narrow face and a long nose. He gave Minden a glance of chill suspicion.

'Your movements yesterday, Major Minden, until you reported this morning. You may smoke if you like.'

Minden thanked him. 'I went back to the Château St. Blaize on Saturday, where I'm billeted on the family. Sunday was quiet and I spent the evening there.'

'And how was it spent? What exactly did you do?'

'I did some paper work for an hour; then I joined the family for drinks . . .'

'The name of the family,' the SS Major asked.

'De Bernard. Comte de Bernard.'

'Continue please. You joined them for drinks.'

'We had dinner together; I dine with them every evening. We talked and about eleven o'clock we went to bed. I left at my usual time this morning.'

'I see.' The Lieutenant was writing on a pad.

'You never left the house?'

'No.'

The Major cocked his red head on one side.

'Can you prove this?'

Minden hesitated for a moment. 'Yes, I can. But I'd prefer not to go into details.'

'I'm afraid you will have to,' the Major said. 'What were you doing that proves you didn't leave the Château between midnight and, say, four, four-thirty in the morning?'

'I was with a lady,' Minden said stiffly.

The Major gave a cheerful laugh. 'So were a lot of the officers who were out last night! They can produce their witnesses – can you?'

'I'd rather not, for obvious reasons.' Minden looked disturbed. 'The husband – it would be very difficult and unpleasant for her, but of course if it had to be corroborated, then she would have to tell you we were together. Until well past four o'clock.'

'How nice,' the Major smiled. 'The name of this lady?'

'The Comtesse de Bernard.'

'Thank you, Major. Only a formality these enquiries, we know all General Brühl's officers are loyal Nazis, but we have our duty to do. We have to find this murderer.' He turned to the Lieutenant. There seemed to be an unusual rapport between them; Minden smelt homosexuality in the big redheaded man. 'And the people who sheltered him. Don't we, Oberleutnant?'

'Yes, Herr Major. And when we do, God help them.'

'God help a lot of people,' the Major said. He stood up and saluted Minden.

'You can go now. This report will be submitted to the Stan-dartenführer and if he is satisfied, you'll get permission to leave the Château. Heil Hitler!'

Minden snapped his heels together and flung up his arm. 'Heil Hitler!' He went back to his office to wait.

Vierken read through every report; four of them were unsatisfactory in that the officers billeted outside had been absent and maintained that they were in bed but had no witnesses to prove it. He decided not to see them; his expert, Captain Kramm, would quickly uncover any evasion. So far his operation had run with absolute smoothness. The whole area was cordoned off, its communications silenced, its municipal offices occupied, and house to house searches well advanced. His men were experts, as efficient in their duties as the excellent Captain Kramm, who could question a man for hours with patient mildness, and then subject him to tortures which never failed to extract the truth.

They had carried out police operations in Poland, in Holland, in Russia; they could uncover a mouse if it were concealed in a building. Vierken felt by instinct that this part of his plan would produce nothing. The man who got into the Château Diane was a trained expert; personally he believed that the agent had already left the district. His ultimate destination would be the South, to an area strong in Resistance supporters like Marseilles, where he could attempt an escape by sea in a boat, or the even more daring pick-up by an Allied submarine. Vierken didn't think he would find Brühl's murderer in the district or that his apprehension was as important now as the total intimidation of the local population. When the Allies invaded, they must be cowed completely. This act of defiance, the succouring of an enemy who had incidentally done unparalleled damage to the German war effort, must be punished with awful ingenuity.

When he came to Minden's report, he paused. Comte de Bernard, Château St. Blaize. Régine's brother. Régine's sister-in-law. He looked down again at Minden's report. His alibi was a woman. Vierken played with his pencil, sucking at it in unconscious imitation of his chief. Minden had spent the night with a lady. It was common enough; a lot of women had affairs with Germans. But it didn't tally well with Régine's description of the household. He had pictured a conservative aristocratic family, dominated by its traditions, to whom Régine dared not introduce him. He had a clear image of the brother and sister-in-law of his mistress, and the lady mentioned in Minden's account didn't suggest the Comtesse de Bernard at all.

Régine had said that Louise was sleeping with the cousin. Perhaps she was. Perhaps she was also sleeping with Minden. And this was interesting, because Régine had conveyed to him that her sister-in-law was very anti-German. He folded the report and made another telephone call. Teams were out investigating in all the villages. He decided to go to the Château St. Blaize and confirm both the Swiss cousin and the Major's alibi for himself.

'Louise!' Minden found her in the drawing room. The curtains were drawn and the room looked intimate and warm in the light of the fire.

She sat in an armchair, her profile illumined, both hands clasped, and Minden felt his pulse leap. He had seen the SS cars in the driveway, and impelled by an instinctive fear, came rushing into the house to find her. Lust stirred in him at the curve of her neck and the line of her legs under the skirt, but something stronger brought him to her side, dropped to one knee, his hands reaching out for hers. He didn't think to analyse the feeling, or to associate her with the enemy.

'My darling – what are you doing here alone?'

'You saw the cars outside,' she said, 'They've been here since five; Jean has been questioned and they've kept him in the dining room with a guard. Roger is in there now,' She moved her head towards the study. 'They're keeping us separated till the questioning is over.' She pulled her hands away from him. 'I'm next,' she said. She reached into the box for a cigarette and immediately he held his lighter to it.

'Don't be angry with me,' he said. 'Please – it's not my fault. There's been a serious act of sabotage and my General has been murdered. Everyone has to be questioned. Try to understand; and don't blame me. They won't hurt anyone who isn't guilty.'

'Not even hostages?' The look on her face shocked him. 'If they don't find this man they're looking for, Jean says they'll shoot hundreds of innocent people.'

She could smell the cologne he used, and she felt nauseated; his hands, with the dark hairs growing from the wrist, were touching hers again. She resisted an impulse to rip at them with her nails.

'Please,' he said again. 'Don't blame me for it.' Before she could stop him he had brought her hands to his mouth and was kissing them. 'It was so wonderful,' he mumbled, holding them tight against her struggles, 'so beautiful – I've been thinking of you and hoping tonight . . . Don't turn against me, don't pull away . . .'

'Let me go!' She wrenched herself free and got up. 'Don't ever dare touch me again!'

'I understand,' he nodded, controlling himself. 'I understand, I don't blame you. This must have been a great shock. But you mustn't be frightened. When they send for you, just tell them the truth. Don't be difficult with them . . .' He swallowed, anxiety tightening his throat. 'Don't show hostility. Just tell them the truth. They questioned me today, and I'm afraid I have something to confess to you.'

'I don't want to hear it,' Louise turned away from him,

'You'll be angry,' he said unhappily. 'But I hadn't any choice. I told them I had spent the night with you. I had to account for myself between midnight and four in the morning, and I had to tell them I was with you. I'm very sorry.'

'Oh I don't mind,' she said. 'I don't mind being classed with all the other whores who sleep with Germans. Would you please go away and leave me alone now?'

'Don't talk like that,' Minden said quietly. 'Don't use that word. I love you. I've been in love with you since I came to this house. I told you so last night and it's the truth.'

'Love?' Louise turned round to him. 'You talk about love? Coming from a German it's an obscenity! You'd like to go to bed with me, wouldn't you – you'd honestly expect me to make love while your bloody butchers are shooting innocent people in hundreds? You wouldn't even see anything incongruous in it, would you? I think you're mad. All of you. You're mad and evil, and the thought of what I did with you makes me want to vomit. You can go in and tell those swine in there exactly what I've said. I don't give a damn.'

'You're upset,' he said. 'You don't know what you're saying. I understand, I really do. I shan't take any notice. As for reporting you . . .' He shook his head, his expression pained. 'How could you think I'd do anything to hurt you?'

'Oh, for God's sake,' Louise said, 'go away. Leave me alone.' He stood for a moment, looking at her. She had turned her back on him and was standing by the fireplace, nervously smoking. She heard him cross the floor and then the door closed.

When they arrived, the SS officer had introduced himself as Standartenführer Vierken. Saluted them and bowed to her. He was polite, his attitude exaggeratedly correct. His men had made a brief search of the house, and in response to Jean's protest, the old Comte had not been brought downstairs. Vierken had taken the little study as his interrogation room; he phrased it tactfully, suggesting that it would be suitable for discussions with each member of the family. There was a younger man, with a cherubic face and little eyes, mild as milk, who followed Vierken everywhere.

Jean had gone in first: they were not allowed to speak when he came out and passed through the drawing room to get to the hall. Louise had jumped to her feet, but an SS man accompanying her husband had gestured her to stay back. Now Savage was in the interrogating room. She hadn't spoken to him since the SS had come into the house. 'Stick to the story. And don't let the bastards see you're frightened.' They were his last words to her, whispered as the door burst open and Jean appeared, grey and shaken, to announce the Germans' arrival.

Before he had time to announce them, the figures seen through the window were in the room. Black suited them; the skull and crossbones embroidered on their caps glittered with silver thread, their boots shone like glass. The tallest and most senior was dark, with brown eyes; it seemed to Louise that he was looking at her with special interest.

What in God's name was happening in the study . . . ? She dropped back into the chair and threw the butt of the cigarette into the fireplace. Minden had worried her; she hadn't known how to reject him without arousing his suspicion. The invasion of the SS gave her the excuse to expurge some of her own self-disgust by abusing him. She shivered, thinking of the brown eyes moist with sentiment, the hard hands grasping at hers and the greedy kisses sucking at them. Love. He talked of loving her, and the horror was that she believed him. In his own way and within his own definition, he loved her. He had been working on a gas that would have killed her and her children, but he would still have loved her. He was the second man to tell her so that day. I love you. Savage had said it too. There was no sentimentality there; no compromise. Strength and toughness, the kind of sexuality which would completely dominate her if she ever gave it the opportunity. A man with whom she would live a very different life from the ordered, tranquil years of her marriage to Jean de Bernard.

Was he convincing them? How secure was his cover story, how astute was that sinister man with the perfect manners who had stared at her with eyes like stones . . . ?

Behind the study door, Roger Savage sat in front of the desk which had been used by three generations of de Bernards, one leg crossed over the other, facing Adolph Vierken. Physically they were rather similar. Both were big men, powerfully built, in the best of condition; Savage with his cropped Swiss hair-cut could have passed for German. He showed no sign of nerves because he felt none. Nothing could alter the astounding success of his mission; the destruction of the laboratory and the corpse of Germany's premier scientist lying with his larynx smashed. His safety was not important beside that. He hoped to escape if he could, but he had long faced the possibility that his was a one-way mission. He had come to look on those lethal cuff-links as friends. Carelessly he stroked one with his finger, looking coolly into the Standartenführer's eyes, and knew he didn't give a damn about the outcome for himself. And so long as he was in that room, he couldn't think about anyone else, not even Louise. His best weapon was his confidence; he was sending it out to do battle with the German's suspicions and he sensed that he was winning, pity or fear for anyone or anything else, could stem that flow between them.

'And how long have you been dealing with the Comtesse's financial affairs, Herr Savage?'

'I haven't been dealing with them,' Savage said. 'It's a very large Trust, there is a considerable sum of money to be administered for her. Normally Herr Brassier looks after her interests, but he didn't feel able to make this trip so he asked me to come instead. I studied the details for a few days and I believe I am sufficiently knowledgeable to be able to deputise for M. Brassier on this occasion.'

'And you came through from Berne direct?'

'I took the train from Berne and crossed the frontier into France on the 30th at about 9 a.m. After that I proceeded to Paris; it's a very tiring journey and the train was stopped at the station for two hours – then I came direct to St. Blaize.'

'Your documents, please.'

Savage raised his brows. 'I've already shown them to you but if you insist on seeing them again . . .'

'Have you any objection?' Vierken's tone was sharp.

'Only to what seems a waste of time,' Savage said. 'You'll see everything is in order.'

Vierken glanced through the passport, studying the entry made at the frontier; the stamp was dated the 30th and initialled by the frontier official. His entry permit from the German Embassy in Berne was stamped and dated in the same way. He looked at the photograph on the passport, checking the details for the second time with the list in front of him. It contained the information on Roger Savage which the SS had received from Switzerland. They checked. Slowly he closed the passport and replaced the permit in its envelope. He didn't hand them back. Instead he lit a cigarette and let the silence become an awkward pause. Savage shifted his position and gave a little cough to attract his attention. Vierken looked at him.

'You realise, Herr Savage, that you arrived in this district on the day after an alert for enemy agents?'

'No,' Savage said. 'How should I know a thing like that? I came here on business, and now that all this unpleasantness has happened, I am extremely anxious to go home. I must emphasise that I'm a neutral and none of the restrictions apply to me.'

'They apply,' Vierken said coldly, 'to whoever is in the area. Which you happen to be. Doesn't it occur to you, Herr Savage, that your arrival was an unhappy coincidence?'

'Not at all,' Savage said stiffly. 'I arranged the date well in advance – how could I know that there'd be an alert? If there's any doubt about my credentials, why don't you check with my firm in Berne?'

Vierken looked at him, 'I already have,' he said. 'That's why I'm asking you these questions here instead of at my headquarters.'

For a blind second Savage faltered. He couldn't have checked him –
there hadn't been time since his arrival at the Château that afternoon
. . . He decided to attack instead of retreating.

'How could you check my credentials when you didn't know I was
here? I don't understand this.'

'But we did know,' Vierken said. 'I personally knew all about you,
Herr Savage. From the day you arrived. Would you like a cigarette?'

That was an old dodge to show up a shaking hand. 'Thank you.' He
took time to take it out and light it, holding the match flame for longer
than he needed. His hands were rock steady. He glanced straight at the
German. 'How did you know about me? Was it reported?'

'Not officially,' he said. 'Mademoiselle de Bernard is a friend of
mine. She mentioned your arrival to me.'

Savage didn't hide his surprise. 'You know Régine?'

'Very well. She is a charming girl.'

'Very charming. She spent the weekend here.'

'I know,' Vierken said. 'She was very suspicious of you, Herr Savage.'
Savage drew on the cigarette and placed one hand across the wrist of
the other; his fingers pressed lightly against the flat surface of the cuff
link. Pressure would release the metal square which concealed the L
pill. So Régine de Bernard was a friend of the Standartenführer. Such
a close friend that she reported on what happened among her own
family. Charming. Very charming indeed.

'Indeed?' He showed resentment, even a little colour appeared
under his skin. He glared at the Standartenführer. 'Suspicious of
what, may I ask?'

'Not of your credentials,' Vierken said. 'It was your relationship
with her sister-in-law that worried her. She seemed to think that for a
cousin from Switzerland looking after money matters, you were much
too intimate. Are you?'

'If you're suggesting that there's anything improper in my relationship with the Comtesse . . .'

'I am suggesting it,' Vierken said. 'She seems to be a promiscuous
woman who doesn't discriminate. Is she your mistress, Herr Savage?
I know that she is sleeping with Major Minden, who lives here. Does
she divide herself between you? Alternate nights?'

Savage's hands were separated; for a second his fist began to double.
He had a violent impulse to leap from his chair and smash his knuckles
in that sneering face. Minden. They knew what had happened with
him. Now he was sweating and it was cold, chilling his skin under
the clothes. Louise. They were going after Louise. That bastard would
hunt her through a labyrinth of questions, probing, insulting, threatening . . .

'I'll answer your question,' he said. 'Though it seems to me to be irrelevant. I am not Madame de Bernard's lover, and I know nothing about Major Minden. I have the highest regard for her character and as her cousin, I thoroughly resent your imputations!'

'Naturally.' Vierken smiled his sour smile. 'When do you want to leave, Herr Savage?'

'As soon as possible. Tomorrow would suit me.'

'I'm afraid that won't be possible,' Vierken said. 'You will need authority from me, or you won't be allowed to leave the area. And I do hope you won't be foolish and try to leave without my written permission. You'll only be arrested, if nothing worse happens to you. My men are in a resentful mood. They would just as soon shoot anyone who breaks the restriction. Here are your papers.'

'I certainly shan't take any risks,' Savage said quickly. 'This is nothing to do with me. I'm Swiss and strictly neutral. I want to get out of here as soon as possible. Could you please let me have the permit soon?'

'I'll think about it. Thank you, Herr Savage. You can go now.' There was a flash of malice in his look as Savage got up. 'I'll see the Comtesse now.'

Vierken didn't send for her at once. He shuffled his papers and drew patterns on a note pad. Captain Kramm was sitting in the corner; he had taken a record of everything Savage had said. After a moment Vierken spoke to him.

'What's your opinion, Kramm?'

'He seems to be genuine. He's very Swiss.' There was a note of contempt in that last comment. 'He showed no sign of nerves, he didn't hesitate or contradict himself.'

'His story checks exactly,' Vierken said. 'If it weren't for that Swiss report I'd take him back to the Château Diane and let you talk to him. But he's a neutral and we can't afford to get rough with him. His firm vouched for him and gave this address. It can't be faulted.'

'He didn't like the questions about the woman,' Kramn said. 'You got a reaction there.'

'No,' Vierken said, 'he didn't like that at all. But that's not the issue. I thought he was lying when he said they weren't lovers.'

'I'm not so sure of that,' Kramm said. 'If you can't put pressure on him, perhaps you could use the woman against him. If you have any doubts.'

'I wish I had,' Vierken said. 'I wish I could find one hole in his story and I'd have them both face to face in the Château and see which one of them broke first. But there's nothing, Kramm. He came here as her lawyer and he's still here. He wouldn't be, if he was in any way connected with what happened to Brühl. Write out an exit permit and I'll sign it. The sooner he leaves here the better – I don't want any damned neutrals hanging round here, making complaints through the Red Cross.'

He looked down at his papers again. There was Minden's report. Minden's alibi. Vierken would have accepted it without more than a superficial check with the Comtesse, if she had not been Régine de Bernard's sister-in-law. Everything Régine had said about her was becoming emphasised in his mind. It was as if his presence in the Château had given the prejudice of his mistress a new substance.

His mental picture of Louise de Bernard hadn't prepared him for the attractiveness which was so evident. She wasn't the type that appealed to him. She would never submit, like Régine, or fawn in an ecstasy of excitement, when he asserted his supremacy over her. Régine had described a cold, arrogant woman, deluding an indulgent husband, a bitter anti-Nazi who had refused to cohabit with him because of his collaboration. Looking at her, and noting the mingled fear and loathing in her expression, Vierken believed every word of what Régine had told him. And this was the same woman with whom Minden said he had spent the night.

It didn't fit. It didn't fit with Louise de Bernard. Which meant that either Minden was lying or she was acting so completely out of character that it needed an explanation. He looked up; his lips were drawn tight, the pencil in his right hand tapped the desk.

'Right,' he said to Kramm. 'Let's have her in.'

'Why did you go to Major Minden's room?'

'I've told you. I wanted to make love,' He had asked her the question so many times in different forms, that she had no idea if she were repeating herself. Behind the desk he played with his pencil and narrowed his eyes at her. The light shone on the surface of his dark hair.

'I don't believe you. I don't believe he was with you last night. Why are you lying?'

'I'm not lying.' She thought her voice sounded calm, but she couldn't be sure. She had begun to shake after the first few minutes, and now it was part of her, sitting on the little French chair with its aubusson seat and back, wishing to God it had been made with arms. She shook and she answered; she could hear the other man moving behind her. taking notes.

'You hate us, Madame de Bernard, don't you? Why would you sleep with a German officer when you hate all Germans?'

'I don't hate anyone.' That sounded feeble, a hollow protest, made through fear.

'I know that's a lie too. I know you're anti-Nazi; I know you've

The Occupying Power

turned against your own husband because you don't agree with his attitude. I know all about you.'

'That has nothing to do with it.' She glanced over her shoulder; the mild young officer with glasses was watching her, his pencil suspended. He looked like a student at a lecture.

'You were overcome with love for the Major?'

'If you like to call it that.' The sweat was running down between her breasts; the front of her blouse felt damp.

'Why didn't you choose your husband? Or your cousin; he's a well set up man. Why not?'

'I'm not on good terms with my husband.'

'That's right,' Vierken said. 'You hate Germans so much you won't go to bed with your husband because he's a collaborator. I find this very interesting, Madame. Don't you, Kramm?'

Louise glanced back at the young man. He was smiling at his superior. He didn't say anything.

'Are you sleeping with M. Savage?'

'No.' She raised one hand to her face, her fingers were trembling. 'No, I'm not.'

'Only with Major Minden?'

'Yes.' She saw Vierken get up from the desk and panic leaped inside her. Calm. Stay calm. Don't let him see your hands are shaking. Sit still. Think of the children, think of Papa lying helpless upstairs, of Jean and Savage – all their lives depend on you . . . He's coming round the desk to face me. They haven't hurt me yet but I know they're going to; it's coming very near. There's pain and violence in the room. I sense it in that man with the notepad, right behind me. If he moves . . .

'I don't believe you,' Vierken said. He put out a hand and caught Louise by the hair. She winced. He jerked her head back, pulling until the tears ran down her face. Behind them Kramm had laid down his notebook. 'I don't believe you went to bed with Major Minden,' Vierken said. 'Why are you lying?' He gave a vicious jerk that forced a cry of pain from her. It felt as if the hair were being torn out of her scalp.

'I'm not,' she said, almost sobbing. 'I'm telling the truth . . . Oh God, you're hurting me!'

'Kramm – she says I'm hurting her. She hasn't felt your soothing touch yet.' Just as suddenly he released her. Louise fell forward. She kept her balance and clung to the chair. Vierken stepped away; he half turned his back and lit a cigarette. 'Kramm,' he said. 'Take her blouse off.'

'No!' Louise sprang up. 'No! Don't touch me.'

At a signal from Vierken the young officer paused.

'Tell me the truth,' Vierken said quietly. 'Otherwise he'll strip you naked and I shall personally put a match to your pubic hair. You didn't sleep with Major Minden, did you? You're giving him some kind of alibi, aren't you?'

'No.' Louise collapsed back into the chair. She raised a face streaming with tears. 'I did sleep with him. I'll tell you the truth – I'll tell you why I did it! I haven't had a man for two years – I was all right till he came here. Then he started looking at me – wanting me. He'd brush against me, try to touch me. It was driving me mad! In the end I couldn't help myself. I went to his room last night. I went in and begged him to take me! And I hate him! I hate all of you!'

She hid her face in her hands. If they don't believe me this time – if I haven't been convincing . . . Oh God, don't let that creature touch me . . .

'Like a bitch on heat,' Vierken said. 'But then all American women are whores. Do you feel like it now – I'm sure Kramm will oblige, won't you, Kramm? Come and put your hand up Madame's skirt, she'd like that.'

'Please.' Louise shrank back in terror. 'Please . . . I told you.'

'I know,' Vierken said. 'And now I believe you.' His look was full of contempt. Women of her type had always irritated him with their unconscious air of equality, even superiority. She hadn't been too difficult to break; the sight of her miserable weeping gave him satisfaction. He enjoyed seeing her humbled, degraded. And he believed her. So much for Régine's independent sister-in-law, the rich American who had bought herself a crumbling château and a useless title. She sat crying and trembling, revealed as a slut who couldn't control her own appetites. Vierken was content. Suddenly he had lost interest in her. Tormenting her now would be a waste of time. And he hadn't time to waste in letting Kramm play games. 'Go into the cloakroom through there,' he said. 'And wash your face. Don't try and pretend we've hurt you. Hurry up!' Inside the little room Louise held on to the basin for support, seeing her own reflection in the mirror. It was white and her mouth trembled. She cupped some water in her hands and splashed her face. The top of her head felt raw and burning. She shivered. It had been so close, so terribly close. And Savage was right. She wouldn't have held out. If that man had touched her, taken off her clothes . . . For a second the little room reeled. Then she steadied herself. It was over. She hadn't failed them. There was a little ivory brush and comb; she brushed her hair back and composed herself. She came back into the room and waited. Vierken was sitting on the edge of the desk. He waved his cigarette at her. 'You can go, Madame de Bernard. Kramm, go and talk to the servants. Look in on the old man.'

'Oh please,' Louise begged, 'please don't, he'll be so worried – he's senile and he doesn't understand . . .'

'Shut your mouth,' Kramm said. He had an unexpectedly loud, harsh voice. It was the first time he had spoken. He jerked his head towards the door. 'You heard the Standartenführer. Get out!'

Louise stumbled past them through the door, and into the salon. There was an SS man on duty there now. He pointed to the dining room.

'In there. And no talking!'

As she came in, both Jean and Savage sprang up. Another SS man swung his carbine round and pointed it. 'Don't move! Stay where you are!' Louise looked instinctively at Savage. He didn't draw back at the threat; instead his whole body tensed, balancing for the assault. Involuntarily, Louise cried out.

'No – don't do anything – for God's sake! I'm all right.' For a moment Savage and the German confronted each other. Before either of them could move, Jean de Bernard had come straight to her and taken her in his arms.

'Sit down,' he murmured to her. 'Come over here.'

Instantly the guard was standing over them, menacing with his carbine. 'No talking!' he shouted. 'Go back to where you were!'

Jean de Bernard looked up at him. 'I am staying with my wife,' he said. For a second or so the German stared at him; then he turned and went back to his position by the door. Louise found her husband's hand holding hers and his arm protectively round her shoulders. It was a sensation she suddenly remembered.

In the salon Adolph Vierken paused to pour himself a drink of wine from a decanter on one of the side tables. He had discovered nothing. Minden's alibi for the night was genuine; much as he would have liked to find a discrepancy in Roger Savage's credentials, they were faultless. There was nothing to keep him at the Château St. Blaize; he drank the wine, his attention caught by the exquisite engraving on the glass. It was a coat of arms with many quarterings. These were the people to whom Régine had not dared introduce him; the spineless French aristocrat with his armorial drinking glasses and his subservience to the conqueror, the moneyed American wife who had collapsed in frightened tears.

Vierken allowed himself a moment of congratulation. He had put them into their right perspective, these superior people. He felt a sharp regret that nothing suspect had come out in the investigation. Régine was different; she was not one of them. She belonged to his world, to him. On an impulse of spite he aimed the empty glass at the fireplace and smashed it to smithereens. He went into the hall, shouted for Kramm, who reported that there was nothing gained from the old servants or the invalid Comte. Vierken drew out a piece of paper and gave it to the Captain.

'Give that to the Swiss. Tell him to be out of St. Blaize by tomorrow or the pass will be revoked. I don't want any neutral hanging around here. The less witnesses we have the better. Give it to him now, and make sure he understands it's only valid for twenty-four hours!' Kramm saluted and went out; when he came back Vierken was already pulling on his gloves.

'He understands,' Kramm said. 'I made it clear to him.'

'Good. There's nothing more to be done here.'

'Pity about the American woman,' Kramm said.

'There'll be others,' Vierken said. 'Come on.' Minutes later their cars were sweeping down the drive, their headlights scarring the darkness.

'What happened?' Savage was beside her. 'You've been crying – what did they do to you?' He seemed unaware of Jean de Bernard. She felt her husband's arm tighten around her. She got up, freeing herself.

'Nothing happened,' she said. 'Thank God. You were right,' she said to Savage. 'If it had got bad, I wouldn't have held out. I know that now.'

'That isn't true,' Jean de Bernard said. 'You were born with courage.' Looking from Savage to him, she felt an impulse to escape them both, to take the shock trembling inside her to some private place.

'I want to go to the children. I don't want them to be frightened. I'm quite all right. The main thing is, they've gone.' She went out and upstairs to the children's bedroom. Savage turned to Jean de Bernard.

'They've gone, but I'm damned certain they'll be back. I want to talk to you alone.'

'Yes,' Jean de Bernard said. 'I think the time has come for that. He gave you a pass. Why?'

'I have a nasty feeling he wants me out of St. Blaize,' Savage said. 'Me and anyone else who might be able to carry tales.' He took a cigarette. 'That's what I want to talk to you about. He picked out Louise tonight; I don't like it. And there's something else you should know. He's pretty friendly with your sister!'

'Régine! I don't believe it . . .'

'He told me,' Savage said. 'He knows her well; and she told him about all of us; me, Louise – the whole family. You'll have to watch out for her.'

'My God,' Jean de Bernard said. 'With a man like that . . .' "I've met someone – he's a German . . ." He remembered Régine saying that and the expression of defiance on her face. An SS commander. It was unthinkable. As unthinkable as Savage's allegation that she informed upon them. He saw the American looking at him and the contempt in his eyes, for him and for his sister. He turned away. 'Things have worked out very well for you,' he said. 'You can leave tomorrow; with the Gestapo's blessing.'

'I want to take Louise with me. She can't get out on this pass; that means I ask London to send a pick-up plane. I don't want to leave her here. Whatever your sister said about her, that bastard's got it in for her. She ought to go to England.'

'I see,' Jean de Bernard said. 'And have you asked her?'

'Yes, and she won't go. She won't leave you and the children. I hope you'll persuade her.'

'Then you're not going to use your pass?'

'Not if I can take Louise with me. And I tell you, she should go. They won't pin anything on you. If they are going to take hostages, my guess is you won't be considered. You're part of the pro-German establishment here, and your sister has made herself a very influential friend. But Louise is different. She's an American and she's known to be hostile to them. They just might take her. You can manage without her here.'

'Persuade her to leave with you . . .' Jean said slowly. 'You'd like that, wouldn't you? You've wanted her from the beginning. It would suit you very well to have her in England where you could take her away from me permanently. You must think I'm an imbecile!'

Savage felt a rush of anger so intense that it was hatred. 'You stupid bastard! You'd rather she played games with Vierken? I'll take her with me and you won't stop me!'

'You make any attempt to touch my wife,' Jean de Bernard said, 'and I'll kill you. I warned you before.'

'You wouldn't kill me,' Savage jeered. 'You wouldn't bloody dare,' he went on. 'But you'd sneak round to your pals the Gestapo and tell them who I really was – you wouldn't mind doing that, would you? That'd be more in character.'

'I have already thought of that,' Jean de Bernard said. 'Do you think I'd protect you, if I could save French lives and stop them punishing this village? But you've involved Louise; if they got you, that would come out. You think you're so brave and so tough, Monsieur Savage? A big, brutish American who knows all the tricks – you'd be crying like a child after they'd had you for an hour or two. You'd betray Louise and be glad to do it.'

Savage stepped close to him. 'Shut your mouth,' he said. 'Or I'll shut it for you.'

'Violence is your only answer.' Jean didn't move. 'To break and kill. You have more in common with the Germans than you know. I shan't denounce you because of my wife. And I shall do whatever I think best to protect her. Turn out the lights when you leave.' He left Savage standing there.

Louise heard the door of her bedroom open and sat up. 'I want to talk to you,' Jean said. 'Can I come in?'

He sat on the edge of the bed, looking at her.

'I've been talking to Savage,' he said. 'He wants you to go to England with him. I think you should go.' Her hand was close to him, lying on the bed-cover, the gold wedding ring circling one finger. He wanted to reach out and touch it.

'I'm not going,' she said quietly. 'I'm not leaving the children. Or you. He knows that.'

'Would you mind leaving me?'

This was the man I loved, she remembered, this was the man I left my country and my family for, the man who conceived our children in this bed. He's older and tired, and I know he's pleading. If I cry now, I'm a damned fool.

'Yes, Jean. I'd mind very much.'

'I'm glad,' he said. 'I'm glad you don't hate me. We had so much happiness till this filthy war. I love you; I shall never stop. But you're in danger and I'd rather lose you to him, than let you take a risk. Go with him.'

She shook her head. 'No, I'm very frightened; I have a feeling that something terrible is going to happen to us all. And we must all be together. You and I and Papa and the children; here at St. Blaize.' He caught hold of her hand; his was unsteady.

'Don't say that,' he begged her. 'It isn't true. These feelings mean nothing – it's just a reaction from what happened tonight. I heard something, something so shameful . . . I don't know how to tell you about it.'

'Go on.' Her hand had gripped his; she knew its pressure well, as well as she recognised the embrace of his arm when he rushed to her that evening. They had been very close for many years.

'Régine informed on us to the Gestapo.' He spoke slowly, not looking at her now. 'She knows that man Vierken; he told Savage. She must know him very well. He knew all about Savage being here.'

'I can't believe it,' Louise said. 'An SS commander – how could she . . .'

'I don't know,' Jean de Bernard said. 'But I can't deny my own example. I set the pattern; she followed it. You would say it was a punishment, wouldn't you?'

'Not now.' Louise said gently. 'I might have said it before but not any longer. It was easy for me to take the attitude I did. I wanted you to be heroic, the brave Comte de Bernard, shouting defiance from the battlements. I didn't visualise the reality. Now I've seen it. I felt it in our little study. I saw it on their caps; the symbol of death. You tried to keep it away from St. Blaize and from us.

You failed. I wouldn't judge you any more. I only hope you won't judge me.'

He kissed her fingers. 'I admire you,' he said. 'You're brave and you have a proud heart. You were ashamed of me, and I can understand it. One day I shall ask you to forgive me.'

'If you can forgive me,' Louise said quietly. 'We've been enemies, haven't we? Now we're facing God knows what. Jean, there's something I've got to tell you. I want to get things straight between us. I got the key from Minden. I gave it to Savage.'

Her hand dropped out of his.

'Why should he give it to you?'

'He didn't. I got it when he was asleep. I put it back before he left me.'

She watched him turn away; he fumbled in his pocket for cigarettes and lit one, cupping the flame in his hands.

'You slept with him?'

'Yes. It was the only way. I want you to know it was the worst thing I've ever done in my life. It was nauseating, horrible. That's why they kept me so long tonight. He'd given me as an alibi. That man didn't believe I'd been with him. He kept on and on trying to catch me out. He knew I was anti-Nazi; he kept saying – you hate Germans.'

'I see.' Jean de Bernard examined his cigarette. 'I understand. Régine must have told him everything about you.' He sounded calm, but he wouldn't look at her.

'I didn't want to lie to you,' Louise said. 'You came to me in good faith, you wanted to make things up. You won't want to now, but at least I haven't cheated you. I did it, because Savage had to get that key. I thought of the children, children like ours, dying of that gas, and it didn't seem important whether I let one man make love to me or not. I'm sorry, Jean. I know you don't look on it the same way.'

'Savage . . . ?' he asked her, looking at her for the first time. 'Savage and you . . .'

'No,' she said. 'Not Savage. I promise you that.'

He blew smoke upwards, and suddenly he gave the cigarette to her. 'It's my last,' he said. 'We'll share it.' With the half-smoked end between her lips, Louise began to cry.

The following day was overcast; early in the morning there was a shower, brief but heavy. Paul and Sophie de Bernard left for school in Minden's car as usual, wrapped in their oilskins. He stood in the vaulted hall, ill at ease and irritable, while Louise kissed them goodbye and pretended not to notice him.

He wanted to talk to her, to make another effort to convince her that he was not responsible for the SS or for what had happened the night before. He had slept badly, struggling with the ache of his desire to make love to her again. He felt helpless and misjudged; he stood about in the hallway, until the children had gone.

'Good morning.' He had placed himself in her way. 'I hope you're feeling better.'

'Yes, I'm quite all right now, thank you.' Louise moved to step past him, but he blocked the door.

'Don't be angry with me. I couldn't sleep last night, I was so upset about you.'

'That's very kind of you.' Jean de Bernard had come up beside him. He took his wife by the arm. 'My wife is quite recovered now.' As Minden watched him, he kissed Louise on the cheek. In six months, Minden had never seen then touch each other. He saluted, his face turning red, and left the hall. Ten minutes later he was in his car, now empty of the children and on his way to the Château Diane. He couldn't get that proprietary kiss out of his mind.

At St. Blaize itself the day passed quietly; Louise spent the morning with her father-in-law. He was in bed, complaining that he felt too tired to get up and dress; bad weather depressed him. He didn't want to read or play his gramophone, so she offered to read to him. He watched her from his pillows, his eyes changing focus as they slid to objects round the room. She had a soothing voice and her company was a comfort. He felt an atmosphere in the house which he didn't understand, but which disturbed him. The children had babbled excitedly of Germans being in the Château, an SS officer had paid him a visit – already the Comte was confused about its purpose. Old Marie-Anne, who had never been a favourite member of his staff in the old days, insisted on sitting in his room in spite of his request to go away. That morning his son had come to him, and he too seemed different, anxious and more solicitous than usual. The old Comte decided that the reason for it all must be himself, and sank into a fit of petulant despair. He decided he was ill and therefore dying and could not get up.

After Louise had been with him a little while, his mood had changed. He felt comforted and safe, petted by everybody. He reached a thin hand across the bed and squeezed hers, his mouth curved into a smile. When she put down the book she saw he was still smiling and asleep. The room was very still; the smell was a mixture of the slight fustiness of age, and the fresh scent of soap and cologne from his morning blanket bath. Marie-Anne looked after him like a child; she didn't seem to notice that he disliked her and was querulous and petty. He looked very old, his hair so white and thin that it was hardly visible against the linen, the blue veins on his forehead pulsing under the tight skin.

Soon death would come to him; Louise put the book away and sat still for a moment. Death would be dignified and peaceful, he would leave the world in gentleness with love supporting him to the end. A different kind of death would come to St. Blaize. A harsh staccato, bullets tearing through flesh, the crack of pistol shots along the line of fallen figures ... The nightmare came at her in the silent room, and she fought unavailingly against it. When would they make the first arrest? Had anyone been taken from St. Blaize already? In God's name, she asked out loud, why couldn't Savage have gone that day instead of having another day and night to wait ... ?

She got up and the movement woke her father-in-law. He stirred and his eyes opened, filmed with age and sleep.

'Louise? Louise ...'

'I'm here, Papa. You slept for a while.'

She pulled the sheet straight; his eyes watched her.

'Where are the children?'

'They're at school. It's not lunch time yet. Go back to sleep; there's something nice for your lunch.'

'Not an omelette,' he said. 'I had one yesterday.'

'Veal,' Louise said gently. 'Jean Pierre got a small cut specially for you. You'll like that.'

'Yes.' He brightened at the idea of food. He pulled himself upright. 'I'm so sick of eggs. Thank you for reading to me, my dear. The sleep was good for me; I'm feeling better.'

'I'm glad, Papa.' She leaned over and kissed his forehead. 'Perhaps you'll get up this afternoon.'

'I think I will,' he said. 'Then Paul and Sophie can come and play up here. When will they be home?'

'About four o'clock. The usual time. I'll bring them up to you.'

The hours passed and the Comte de Bernard got up and dressed to wait for his grandchildren. Four o'clock came; he matched his pocket watch with the chimes of the bracket clock and they were in unison. He had a poor sense of time, but it seemed a short interval till he looked at his watch again and saw that it was long past five. And still the children didn't come.

There was no work for Minden to do. He and the rest of Brühl's staff were confronted with the wreckage that remained in the flooded cellar; the most cursory examination showed that nothing usable had survived. The worst tragedy from their point of view was the loss of the documentation. A massive filing cabinet, indexed and crossreferenced, containing nearly three years of experimental data and the latest developments on Formula XV had been penetrated by the water, and the contents were a congealed, sodden mess. At a conference called by Vierken at eleven o'clock that morning, it was decided to close down

Brühl's section and return his staff to Germany. The Führer himself had ordered that the work should be resumed under the leadership of another scientist with a headquarters in the Fatherland. It was a useless decision, and Minden recognised its futility. He and his colleagues were given twenty-four hours to pack up, and issued with special passes, signed by Vierken without which not even an officer of the Wehrmacht could leave the area. The atmosphere in the mess at the Château Diane was gloomy; there was little conversation, except among the SS officers, who seemed in excellent spirits. Watching them, Minden supposed that, unlike himself, their activities were just beginning. He was sitting next to the redheaded Major who had questioned him the previous day. The Major was enjoying the food and the splendid wines and he was expansive, trying to talk to the disconsolate army officers and getting little response.

'You're going home, I hear,' he said to Minden.

'Yes. We're all leaving tomorrow morning.'

'Better than sticking around here,' the Major said. 'Nothing for you to do now.'

'No,' Minden answered.

'We won't be here long either.'

'Oh? Have you caught the murderer?'

'Not yet; we've searched all the villages, we've questioned hundreds of people. No doubt he came from St. Blaize – that's where the plane was circling and where the car came from. They haven't turned anyone in. But by tonight they'll change their tune!'

'Why? What are you going to do?' Minden didn't really want to know; he didn't want to talk at all. The question was a reflex and immediately he wished he hadn't asked.

'Operation Herod,' the SS Major said. He laughed; several of the other SS officers joined in. 'I'll give the Standartenführer credit for a sense of humour. He thought of the name for it.'

'What does it mean? Operation Herod . . .'

'Think about it; didn't you ever read the Bible?' There was a general laugh at this; the SS Major tipped his chair back and raised his wine glass.

'We'll teach the swine a lesson! They won't be so eager to help the English after this . . .'

'I don't understand,' Minden said. 'Operation Herod. There were several Herods.'

'It's a riddle.' The Major leaned towards him. 'I'll give you a clue. It's not the one that pissed himself over Salome!'

Minden didn't finish his lunch. He took a piece of cheese and cut it into squares, waiting until the senior officer present gave the signal to leave the table. He went outside and smoked a cigarette; the sun was shining and he walked slowly down a short avenue of trees to a stone seat. It faced a small fountain which no longer operated. The water in the basin was a stagnant pool a few inches deep, and the lead dolphin with two rollicking putti on his back was crusty with dried slime.

Herod. Minden threw his cigarette away. He knew the Bible well. Herod the Tetrarch had cut off the head of John the Baptist. Herod, King of Judea, had ordered the massacre of the children. Operation Herod. He looked at the putti, plump and joyous, riding the dolphin's back, and felt a surge of nausea, so strong that he choked into his handkerchief. The children. The children of St. Blaize. That was what they were going to do. Not hostages, not a few hundred adult males to be shot, but the children. 'By tonight they'll have changed their tune.' Tonight. His hands and neck were clammy, the hair stuck to his forehead. Hostages were logical; an enemy population had to be disciplined or no German soldier could walk the streets. Minden accepted that. He approved of it. If he had seen the mayor of the village and the priest and the doctor and anyone else in authority die he wouldn't have thought twice about them. But children. Sophie and Paul de Bernard.

'Major Minden – come and play ball . . . Major Minden, this is my drawing I did at school today . . .' The feel of a hand clutching on to his; Sophie sitting on his knee with her arms round his neck.

And the boy, the brave, open-natured child that reminded him of his own sons, the boy who didn't look at him with fear or hostility. Who accepted him and admired him. Tonight, that butcher had said, with his pansy laugh. Minden stood up. He wiped his hands and face and fastened the top of his collar. It was two-thirty-eight; by three o'clock he was in the back seat of his army car, the pass signed by Vierken in his briefcase, travelling at top speed towards St. Blaize en Yvelines.

The teacher was a widow; she had been born in St. Blaize, the daughter of the village notary, and married in 1940. Her husband had been killed during the German advance, and she had returned to her job at the school, a woman already old at twenty-six. There were twenty children in class that afternoon headed by the daughter of Camier, the Mayor. She was a clever child of eleven, responsible and studious, the idol of her family. Michele Giffier, the teacher, was in the middle of a geography lesson; she was unwilling to let Paul and Sophie de Bernard leave with the German officer. Her first reaction had been refusal; the officer appeared so agitated that she became afraid. But she accepted his explanation that their mother had sent for them, her reluctance overcome by the children's delighted welcome when they saw him, and at three-forty-one exactly they left the school building and climbed into the Major's car. Both children threw their arms round him; Sophie smudged a kiss on the side of his face. Even Heinz the driver looked over his shoulder and muttered something friendly.

'Why are we going home?' That was Paul, always the practical one. 'What does Mama want us for?' Minden was very pale; he looked grim and the children stared at him, suddenly anxious. 'What's the matter?' Paul said. On an impulse Minden put an arm round each of them.

'Nothing,' he said. 'Nothing's the matter, little ones.' The driver started the car and as it moved down the street there was a harsh engine roar from behind them. Minden looked back. An armoured car, the iron crosses painted black and white on its sides, was pulling up outside the school. SS troops armed with submachine guns spilled out of the back and ringed the building. Minden gripped the children tightly. Minutes; there had only been minutes to spare.

'Home, Heinz,' Sophie called out. 'Home please, Heinz.'

'We're not going home,' Minden said. 'We're going to have a surprise. We're going to Paris to see your Aunt Régine.'

'Cries and lamentations filled the land,' remarked the biblically minded Major. 'It was Rachel mourning her children.' He grinned and lit a cigarette. A ring of SS troops encircled the school; the entrance was blocked by the armoured car. The machine gun mounted in its turret swung slowly round, sweeping across the crowd which was gathered outside the school, kept back by the automatic weapons of the troops. There was a noise, a cry without words, coming from the mass of people, men and women of all ages. Fear, pleading, agony, frustration. The major saw Vierken arrive in a staff car; he spat the cigarette out and sprang to attention. The crying sound stopped suddenly; in silence Vierken stepped out of his car, flanked on each side by SS guards with guns at the ready. It was nearly sunset. He walked to the armoured car and stopped in front of it. There was a rush from the crowd.

The Standartenführer didn't move; he knew his men. They wouldn't be allowed to get near. He saw a small, fat man with a grey head, struggling with one of the soldiers, arguing and begging. The man turned to him and shouted.

'I am the Mayor! Let me speak to you, sir! For the love of God, let me talk to you!' Vierken made a signal. Albert Camier came stumbling forward; his pace suggested that he might fall on his knees. His face was streaked with tears.

'Standartenführer – why have you done this? Why are the children under guard? What have they done?'

'The children, Monsieur Le Maire, are quite innocent,' Vierken said. 'Unfortunately, it is often the lot of the innocent to suffer for the guilty. You are all guilty here.'

'But we've done nothing,' Camier cried out. 'Nothing!'

'You harboured a murderer, a saboteur,' Vierken said. 'He was dropped here and sheltered; by someone. Now you are going to be punished. I'm going to make an example of the people of St. Blaize.' He turned, as if there was nothing more to say. Camier seized his sleeve; his eyes were wild, his mouth slack and quivering.

'My daughter is in there. Let her go. Shoot me; shoot any of us, as many as you like! But for the love of Christ, let the children out!'

Vierken pointed to him. 'Put him back in the crowd. And bring me the hailer.'

When he began to speak there was a shiver and then silence from the crowd. Some of the women had been sobbing hysterically; even this was stilled.

'People of St. Blaize.' Vierken's voice came loud through the speaker. 'Two German officers have been murdered. A serious act of sabotage has been committed. We know that the criminal responsible for this was harboured in your area. He has not been found and no one has come forward. Therefore, it has been decided to punish you. You have shown yourselves enemies of the Reich, and while it would suit you to see a few of your fellow citizens shot for this outrage, this is not enough. You are going to learn that German blood is precious. German property is precious. As precious as your children. As a reprisal for your treachery, the children of this village are going to be deported to Germany. You will never see them again.' He put the hailer down and turned back to his car. There was a scream, one high-pitched shriek from the middle of the crowd; a woman fought to the front and ran at him, both hands outspread, the fingers curved into claws; she was screaming incoherently. Vierken paused for a moment. There was a single shot, and she fell, sprawling face downward. The revolver in his hand had a thin wisp of smoke curling round its barrel.

'Anyone attempting to go to the school building is to be shot.' Vierken gave his order to the Major. 'Nothing and no one is to be allowed inside or out.'

'What about the teacher? She's in there with them.'

'Leave her there. When the transport has come from Paris, she can go with them. Keep the men alert; they may try to attack when it's dark.'

'And if they do, Standartenführer?'

Vierken looked at him as if he had said something stupid.

'Set fire to the school. But let them know what'll happen if they start any resistance. I don't want a pitched battle here. I want an orderly operation, properly carried out. Heil Hitler!'

'Heil Hitler!'

Jean and Louise de Bernard had been waiting at the back of the crowd. Jean had refused to be drawn into the hysteria, reminding himself that Paul and Sophie were inside the building and that shooting or violence must be avoided. He had his arm round Louise; she was silent, glazed with shock. 'They're all right,' he said to her. 'Nothing's happened to them. Nothing will happen.'

Louise turned to look at him. Tears were running down her face. 'You heard him; they're going to be taken away. He said we'd never see them again . . .' She was close to hysteria and Jean had seen one woman die already.

'It's a threat,' he whispered. 'They won't carry it out. It's just bluff. My darling, calm yourself now. This is blackmail. I am going to see him and find out the position. Then we'll make up our minds.'

'I want the children,' Louise said. 'I want the children back. I'll give myself up!'

'Hush,' Jean said gently. 'We'll get them. We'll get all the children back. I'll take you home and then I'm going to the Château Diane.' He had decided to wait, to judge the reaction of Vierken to the crowd. What he saw hadn't reassured him, but he still believed it possible to talk reasonably with the man when they were in private. The SS were putting on a show of strength for the people of St. Blaize. Alone, Vierken would take a different attitude. He stood watching the staff car reverse and drive away. The crowd waited, numbed; no one had moved to pick up the woman who lay dead in the road. 'Come home,' he urged Louise. 'There's nothing to do here now.'

'No. No . . .' She shook her head and pulled away from him. 'I'm not leaving here . . .' He was still arguing with her when a woman came through the crowd and ran up to him, grabbing his coat. She stood in front of him, her face contorted with hate.

'You bastard! You dirty collaborationist bastard! You got your brats out, didn't you?'

'No, Madame Barzain,' Jean said quietly. She was the wife of St. Blaize's carpenter. 'No, I didn't. Paul and Sophie are inside with the others.' Louise was staring at the woman, who didn't seem to see her. She was glaring at the Comte, her eyes wild.

'You filthy liar,' she screeched at him. 'I saw them leave the school – just before the SS came! I saw that German from the Château come and take them away in his car! You knew what was going to happen, didn't you – you saved your own but you never warned us!'

'What do you mean – what German – who took them?' Without realising it, Jean de Bernard seized her by the arm. 'What are you talking about – for God's sake, woman, what did you see?'

'I saw them!' she shrieked. 'That German came to the school and took your children out! Just before the SS surrounded the others! I saw it – I'd come to collect my Pierre and Francine and I saw them go with him! God's curse on you, you filthy collaborationist pig!'

She drew her head back and suddenly spat at him. Louise gasped. Jean wiped his face with a handkerchief; Madame Barzain had begun to cry. He put his arm around Louise.

'If that's true,' he said, 'then my children are safe. But we knew nothing about it. We came down here like everyone else.'

'Minden,' Louise said; she felt dazed, too afraid to hope. 'It must have been Minden . . .' Marie Barzain looked at them and her hate died in her. The Comte didn't know beforehand. He hadn't cheated to save his own and left the rest of the village's children to fall victim to the Germans. She spoke to Louise.

'It was that Major,' she said. 'I know him by sight. He took your children away in his car.' She didn't look at the Comte.

'Before God,' Louise said to her, 'I swear we didn't know. I thought they were in there with the others. You shouldn't have done that to my husband. All he wants is to help you!'

'Forgive me,' Marie Barzain mumbled. 'Forgive me – I didn't mean it – they've got my little ones . . .'

'It doesn't matter,' Jean de Bernard said. He laid his hand on her shoulder. 'We must all do our best to get them out. Where is your husband?'

'In the crowd.' She began to sob. 'He's like a madman . . . Oh my God, Monsieur le Comte – what are we going to do?'

'I don't know,' he said gently. 'But they're not going to take our children away. Somehow we're going to stop them. Go and find your husband and tell him to be calm. I shall go and see the SS commander myself.'

'Oh, go now!' she begged him. 'Go right away – it'll be dark soon, they'll be so frightened!'

He turned to Louise. 'I'm going to talk to Camier and Father Duval. We must keep this crowd calm, or there'll be more shootings. Wait here; I'll come back and take you home.'

He found the Mayor comforting his wife; the priest came up to them. He was a big man, with a coarse peasant face and a heavy paunch. He had been curé of St. Blaize for thirty years, a typical provincial priest, looked after by a spinster niece; what he lacked in refinement was more than compensated by personal courage and a kind heart. He pushed his way through to Jean and the Mayor.

'What are we going to do? They can't do this – we can't stand by and let them take our children!'

'My Caroline,' Camier moaned. 'My little girl – my wife has fainted . . . Why have they done this – why, why? We never sheltered anyone!'

'Be calm,' Jean said. 'This is a punishment, a reprisal. But I don't believe they mean to do it. Father, I am going to see Standartenführer

Vierken. I want you and the Mayor to come with me. We will be able to talk to him in private. I suggest that we offer our own lives and as many adults as he chooses as hostages instead of the children. I am prepared to pay a large fine, as well. We can give them men and money in exchange for the children. I think we will be able to strike a bargain.'

'They can have everything,' Carmier cried, 'everything I've got!'

'They can have *my* hide,' Father Duval said. 'And the church plate. That's all I've got. But you believe this, Monsieur le Comte? You think this is a bluff, to frighten us?'

'I am sure of it,' Jean said. 'What they're threatening is unthinkable. Nobody harms children. If we offer them a high enough price, we'll get the children back. I'm going to take my wife home, and then we should go to see this man. Are you agreed?'

'Yes,' the priest said.

Camier nodded. 'God knows I'm not a brave man. But to save my little girl – he can shoot me if he wants . . . I wouldn't want to live without her!'

'Good,' Jean said. 'Now Camier, tell the people we're going to plead with the SS commander. Tell them to be calm and wait here.'

The priest turned to him. 'Where is Madame? She must be terribly distressed – I'd like to speak to her.'

'She's waiting for us,' Jean answered. 'But she's all right. Our children are not in the school.'

'They're safe?' Father Duval stared at him. 'And you're going to stand as a hostage?'

'My frst duty is to my family, Father. The second is to the people of St. Blaize. The fact that my children are not in danger alters nothing. We should go now.'

Jean de Bernard's aunt had lived in Paris since her husband's death. For twenty-three years she had been mistress of a large seventeenth-century château and an estate in the Loire Valley. Her husband was not concerned with the smart world to which his wife aspired. He was older by ten years and devoted to his home and his life in the country. The Baronne de Cizalle saw very little beyond the Loire valley until his death released her. She had relinquished her château to her son and a stalwart daughter-in-law who was obviously longing to manage it, and bought herself an apartment on the Rue St. Honoré. She didn't approve of Germans, but she was polite when she met them, since only the better connected officers came into her circle, and she ignored the unfortunate weakness some of her younger friends betrayed for handsome members of the Herrenvolk. To her credit, Pauline de Cizalle had never received the SS or actively courted the conquerors herself.

So far as a member of her family was concerned, like Régine, she would have rigidly opposed any close relationship. She was dressing to go out to dinner when Minden arrived at her flat with the children. She heard the voices, and sent her maid to see who it was; the maid was followed by Paul and Sophie who rushed forward to embrace their aunt. Both children were too excited to explain why they were there. The Baroness hurried through the rest of her toilette and came into the salon. She paused at the sight of her niece Régine and a German officer, both looked strained and Régine positively stricken. There was a moment of awkward silence; her niece seemed disinclined to introduce the caller or even to speak at all. The Baroness collected herself and advanced upon the German, her hand outstretched, a polite if chilly smile upon her face.

Minden clicked his heels together and kissed her hand.

'Major Heinz Minden, Madame. Forgive this intrusion.'

'Not at all. I believe you've brought my nephew's children with you. I wasn't expecting them.'

'You couldn't have been told.' Régine spoke suddenly. 'The telephones at St. Blaize have been cut off. The whole area is under siege.'

The Baroness forgot her social manners. 'My God! What's happened?'

Régine looked at Minden. 'You tell her,' she said. 'Tell her what you told me.'

'There's been two murders and sabotage,' he said. 'The SS have moved in and taken control. I brought Paul and Sophie to you for safety.'

'Safety?' Régine watched her aunt's well-pencilled eyebrows raise. She seemed bewildered. 'What do you mean, safety? What have the children got to do with the SS? There aren't any Jews there, are there?'

'No, Madame,' Minden answered her. He felt a pang of dislike, and he didn't know why. 'This doesn't concern Jewish children. It's been decided to punish the people of St. Blaize by taking their children. I don't know whether they're going to kill them or send them to an extermination camp. I just got Paul and Sophie out in time.' He made a gesture with one hand. 'I didn't know where else to take them.'

'Sit down, Major Minden.' It was Régine who suddenly took control. She looked plainer than he had ever seen her; the determination on her face made her look ugly. 'Sit down and tell us everything. Has anything happened to my brother? And my father?'

'Nothing,' Minden said. 'The SS came last night and questioned everybody, but they went away. They haven't found the saboteur, and they don't expect to now. The commanding officer is going to make an example of St. Blaize. I only heard it this afternoon. Operation Herod, that's what it's called. I couldn't warn your family; there wasn't time and anyway they'd have come to the Château to take the children. I just got to the school before the SS surrounded it.'

'Thank you,' Régine said slowly. 'Thank you, Major Minden.'

'This is so terrible,' her aunt stammered. 'I just can't believe it. I can't.'

'Nor could I,' Minden said. 'We've had to do many things, Madame, many harsh, regrettable things. But never this. Never using children as hostages. All I can say is that it's not us, not the German army. It's the SS and this man they've sent to St. Blaize. Adolph Vierken. It's him, not us.'

'Did you say Vierken?' He glanced at Régine; he wondered whether he might ask for a drink.

'Yes. Standartenführer Adolph Vierken.'

'Régine – are we going to stay the night with you?' Paul de Bernard stood in the doorway, behind him Sophie's little figure flitted past as she ran down the passage. Régine de Bernard looked at him. 'Yes,' she said. 'You're going to stay here for tonight and maybe tomorrow. Go and see if there's some cake in the kitchen. Ask Juliette to give you some.' She shifted on one foot and brought herself back to face Minden.

'You're sure it's Vierken?'

'Certainly. I've spoken to him. He's in our headquarters. He came to the Château and questioned your family himself.'

'Yes,' Régine said slowly. 'I see. I suppose he was curious.'

'Régine you talk as if you know this man?' Her aunt was staring at her. So too was Minden. A painful smile appeared on her lips. 'Yes, Aunt Pauline. I know Adolph Vierken. Major, you say they've shut up all the children in the village?'

'That was the plan,' he said. 'I didn't try to find out details. They were surrounding the school with armed guards when I left. Mademoiselle de Bernard, I must leave very soon. I'm on my way back to Germany. That's how I was able to get the children out; I had a special pass allowing me to leave. I made them lie down in the back of the car. They thought it was a game.'

'Your driver knows,' Régine said. 'What about him?'

'He's fond of the little ones,' Minden said. 'I know that. He saw the SS coming to the school. He wouldn't do anything to hurt them.'

'I'd better see what they're doing. Excuse me . . .' The Baroness got up. He had saved the children's lives. She couldn't feel gratitude; she felt only loathing and horror. It was a relief to go out of the room.

When they were alone, Régine said, 'You say the area's closed. No one can get out. Or in?'

'No,' he answered her. 'It's sealed off. How did you know Adolph Vierken?'

'Through music,' Régine said. 'He's very musical. We met at a concert. I'm going to St. Blaize. Tonight.'

'You can't,' Minden insisted. 'You won't be let through. You might even be arrested. For God's sake don't attempt it.'

'I'm going to see him,' she said. 'I'm going to stop him doing this.'

'You? You think because you've met him a few times you can hope to influence . . .'

'I've been sleeping with him for months,' Régine broke in. 'He loves me. We love each other. He won't do this when I've talked to him. Say nothing to my aunt. I'll need your car. Will you lend it to me – just to get me there? Your driver can leave me at the first checkpoint and come back here. I'll make my own way after that. Vierken will send transport for me. Please. I know what I'm doing.'

'I don't think you do,' Minden said. 'I don't think anything you say will make any difference. I don't think he'll even see you.'

'You don't know him,' Régine said. 'And you certainly don't know me. He'll listen. It's the only chance to save the children. If he shoots every man in the village I don't care. It's their own damned fault for meddling. But not the children. That mustn't happen. Lend me the car.'

'Of course,' Minden said. 'If there's any chance at all – Fritz will take you as far as he can. I'll wait at the George V till he gets back.'

The Baroness had returned.

To Régine he said, 'I'll walk to the hotel, it's round the corner. I'll instruct Fritz to drive you. Good luck. And goodbye.'

She held out her hand and he bent over it.

'If you get through, let your sister-in-law know where the children are. And give her my respects. I hope in spite of everything she may think kindly of me sometimes.' For a moment his eyes stung. Truth pierced him through. Louise had never loved him; the impulse which had brought her to his room was nothing but a sexual whim. Now she could only hate him and blame him for the horror which had overtaken St. Blaize. Even his rescue of her children wouldn't atone for what was being done by fellow Germans. He bowed to the Baroness. 'If I might see the children for a moment, Madame? Just to say goodbye.'

'Please,' she said. 'I'll call them.' The sight of him bending down embracing Sophie while Paul hung on his arm made her want to cry and at the same time she felt like dragging them away. He left the apartment, and she went into her bedroom. Régine had a small overnight case already packed.

'I'm going home,' Régine said. 'I think I can do something to help. Now, Aunt Pauline, don't argue with me, please. I'm going. If I can get through to you I will. But don't expect anything. I'll come back when I can. Take care of the children.' Then the door closed after her too. The Baroness telephoned her friends and explained that a violent headache prevented her from joining them for dinner.

'Are you going to give him up?' Louise asked him. For a moment Jean de Bernard hesitated. He didn't want to see the look of anguish on her face, or to admit how deeply she was committed to the other man. He didn't want to see it because of what that knowledge might do to his judgement.

'I don't know,' he said. 'I don't know what I'm going to do; it will depend upon Vierken.'

'I was ready to do it,' she said, 'but that was when I thought Paul and Sophie were shut up in that school. Now – now they're not . . . Oh God, where could Minden have taken them? Why didn't he bring them home?'

'Because the SS would have come and got them,' Jean said. 'He knew that and he's taken them somewhere they'll be safe. He wasn't a bad man, I told you that.'

'I know,' she said. 'I want you to promise me something.'

'Not to betray Savage – is that what you want?'

'Yes,' Louise said slowly. 'I wouldn't have said it like that but that's what I meant. Don't give him up to them.'

'I don't think I'll need to,' her husband said quietly. 'As soon as he knows I believe he'll surrender himself. If he doesn't – and the children are at stake, I can't give you any promise. I'm sorry.'

'We sheltered him,' Louise said. 'We're the guilty ones.'

'I know that,' he answered. 'And I shan't let the innocent suffer. I'm going now; try not to worry.' They were in her bedroom and he came close to her.

'Will you trust me to do the right thing? And before I go will you believe me when I tell you something?'

'What is it?' Louise said. He stood in front of her and his hands moved as if he wanted to reach out and hold her, but they stayed at his sides.

'I didn't betray the Palliers,' he said. 'Will you believe that?'

Suddenly her eyes filled with tears. 'Yes; if you say so I believe you now. Oh Jean, Jean!' She was in his arms, holding tightly to him, weeping with remorse and fear, fear for him and a greater fear for Roger Savage. He held her, soothing and gentle, tortured by the knowledge that the pain he was comforting was on behalf of someone else.

'I'm sorry,' she said. 'I'm sorry for what I've done to you. I didn't understand you and I didn't trust you. But I trust you now. You'll do what's right.'

'I'll do my best,' he said, and kissed her quietly on the lips.

Louise came downstairs to find Savage waiting for her. He had a drink in his hand, which was unusual; he never helped himself or presumed on Jean's hospitality. He looked pinched and dangerous. He came straight towards her. 'I know what's happened,' he said. 'Marie-Anne told me. They have four grandchildren in the school. Don't worry, darling. I'll sort this out.'

'Paul and Sophie got away,' she whispered. She shouldn't have leaned against him but her body was trembling and weak. His was warm and his hold was strong. 'Minden came and got them out before the school was surrounded. I can hardly believe it.'

'Bully for him,' he said. 'He'd have gassed them to death but he didn't fancy the SS having fun with them – the bastard! The lousy stinking bastards! Children – that's about their level. What did they say they're going to do with them?'

'Send them to Germany. They'll never be seen again, that's what Vierken said. He was at the school house. One of the mothers ran out and tried to attack him. He shot her dead.'

'Germany,' Savage repeated. 'That means an extermination camp. Come over here. Listen to me, will you?'

'Jean's gone over to see him,' she said. 'To plead with him.'

'He's wasting his time,' Savage said. 'You don't plead with men like Vierken. He'll take those children out of here and they'll be gassed or machine gunned. Jean knows this.' He lifted her face and looked at her. 'Has he gone to turn me in?'

'I begged him not to,' she whispered. 'I don't think he will. He promised to do what was best. Oh God, you mustn't let then take you!'

Savage stroked her hair, twisting one dark strand round his finger. 'There isn't any other way, sweetheart,' he said gently. 'If they don't get me, those kids at the school are as good as dead. I'm going to give myself up!'

'You can't,' she protested violently. 'You can't do that! You know what they'll do to you . . .'

'I have my exit here,' he said, touching the cuff link. 'Don't worry, they won't have their fun with me. But they'll let the children go; that's all that matters.'

'You have a pass,' Louise said slowly. 'You could walk out of here and go back to Switzerland. You carried out your mission and that's all you were asked to do. What happens after you've left is none of your business. That's what some men would say.'

'And some men could live with themselves afterwards, knowing they'd left a lot of children to die for them? Maybe, but not this man. I love you, you know that, don't you?'

'Yes,' she said, 'and I love you. I don't know what to say . . . Isn't there any other way?'

'No,' Savage said. 'There isn't. And we both know it. I never expected to get out of this anyway. Finding you made me want to survive it – that can't be helped. I wish we'd made love.'

'I wish we had too,' she said.

'Don't cry for me,' Savage told her. 'I hate to see you cry. It's going to be tough for you and Jean, talking your way out of it, but I'll square things as much as I can for you both. I can say I *am* your cousin, but the OSS recruited me in Switzerland and sent me here deliberately. You knew nothing about it. They may believe me. There's no reason why they shouldn't. It could have been the truth.'

She couldn't answer him; she held on to him blindly, overwhelmed by an agony only equalled by what she had felt when she believed her children were in danger.

'I don't care,' she said wildly. 'I don't care if they arrest me too!'

'Don't you say that!' He sounded angry. 'Don't you dare talk that way – I came into your life without any right. I'm going out of it. But there's a future here for all of you; the children growing up – the war will be over and these bastards will be beaten now, I promise you that. You'll have a good life, my darling.' He bent over her and smiled. 'You can name the schoolhouse after me,' he said.

'Aren't you afraid?' she whispered.

'No. In a way I've expected it to end like this. And I've got the pill. They won't hurt me, so you don't need to worry about that. It'll be just like dropping asleep. Snap!' His fingers clicked. 'Like that. I think I'll walk down to the school,' he said. 'They can send me to Vierken from there.'

'No, wait, wait!' Louise begged. 'Wait till Jean gets back – he may have persuaded him to let them go! Oh, please don't leave me! Don't go down there yet!'

It was a useless stay of the inevitable and she knew it; instinct made her plead, the dread of that awful goodbye as he left her and gave himself into the hands of the enemy. He talked smoothly of escaping their revenge, of taking a pill and finding a quick death. But there was no guarantee. If he made an attempt and he failed . . . Her imagination fled from the situation; overcome with horror she caught his arm and held it.

'Wait till Jean gets back,' she said. 'Then you can go.'

And Savage realised suddenly that if the Comte were there it would be easier to leave her. She wouldn't be alone. 'All right,' he said. 'We'll wait together. And you take a grip of yourself. I'm going to get us both a drink.'

It seemed a long time before they heard the sound of the car in the drive. Men's voices murmured outside in the hall. A few moments later Jean de Bernard walked into the room. Louise sprang up and ran to him.

'Jean – what happened? What did he say?'

'Nothing happened.' He spoke quietly. 'I went to see him with Camier and Father Duval; I begged him to let the children go. He refused.' He took out a cigarette and lit it; his hands shook badly.

'He'll let them go,' Savage said. 'I'm going to give myself up. Thanks for not doing it first.'

'You needn't thank me.' Jean looked at him. 'It won't be any use if you surrender to them. The children are going to Germany. Whatever happens.'

'But why?' Savage demanded. 'They want the killer – they said so!'

'They don't expect to get him. What they want is to make an example of St. Blaize. To punish the French civilian population for sheltering the enemy. I asked Vierken if he'd let the children go if they found the saboteur.' Jean looked at Savage. 'I was going to betray you. I'm sorry, but when I saw he meant to take them, I made up my mind. He pointed his pencil at me and said, "Comte de Bernard, if the man stood in my office now, I'd send those children out of St. Blaize. A cattle truck is on the way from Paris. By tomorrow night they leave. And no French village will shelter the enemy again without remembering the children of St. Blaize." Those were his words. We offered everything, including ourselves. Money, our lives, anything. He just laughed. He actually laughed. "Go home and make some more." I am going to kill him. I don't know how, but I am going to kill that man.' He lit another cigarette from the stub of the last.

'There's no use you sacrificing yourself,' he said to Savage. 'They'd kill you and then murder our children anyway. You'd only throw your life away for nothing.'

'Paul and Sophie,' Louise said slowly. 'Just think if they were being held in there!'

'We wouldn't be able to think straight,' Savage said suddenly. 'And by God, that's what we've got to do. A cattle truck, eh? That means they'll go by train. And that's better than by lorry. Much better. Where's the Mayor and the priest?'

'In the library. I asked them to wait. Camier is completely broken down. That girl is his only child.'

'Get them in here,' Savage said. 'Breaking down isn't going to save her. And that's what we're going to do. We're going to bloody well save them all.'

'How?' Louise asked him. 'How can we fight the SS. They'll kill anyone who tries to go near the school. They've proved that already.'

'We've no arms, no ammunition, nothing,' Jean de Bernard said. 'But the people will fight, they'll fight with their hands.'

'They'll have guns,' Savage said. 'I promise you. Call the others in here.'

It was dark and inside the school most of the small children had stopped crying and were asleep, stretched out over their desks. The older ones sat mute, staring at the SS guard who lounged against the door, his carbine slung from his shoulder. Madame Giffier, the teacher, moved through the classroom, checking each child. Some were sobbing and she paused to comfort them, others whispered questions and she did her best to answer cheerfully. There was no heating and towards seven o'clock she had made the children put on their coats. There had been a hideous outbreak of hysteria when the crowd outside began to gather and the children heard their parents' voices. Three SS guards had driven them back, knocking Michelle Giffier to the ground when she intervened. There was an ugly blotch on one side of her face and her mouth had bled. The sight of her bleeding, sprawled on the floor, so shocked the children that they quietened. Fear overcame them all. They cringed in their seats, whimpering and shivering. Several of the smallest wet the floor; one adolescent girl was sick. They had no food and only water from the toilet to drink. Michelle Giffier looked at her watch; it was past eight o'clock. They had been shut up for four hours. She got up and went to the guard at the door. She moved stiffly; the fall on the floor had bruised her back. Shaken but determined she spoke to the guard.

'The children haven't eaten since lunch time. They're freezing cold. Let me go out and get some food for them.'

'Go back and sit down.' The German glanced at her. 'Nobody leaves.'

'But please – please, they'll starve – you can't mean to keep them here without anything!'

He shifted his carbine up on its strap and leaning a little forward he pushed Michelle Giffier in the breast with the flat of his hand. She stumbled and fell. He watched her legs displayed as the skirt rucked up. She saw the look on his face and covered herself, biting back tears. She went back to her desk; it was the daughter of Albert Camier who came and put her arms around her.

'Pigs,' she whispered. 'Don't cry, Madame. We're not hungry. We're all right.'

'I can't do anything,' the teacher wept. 'It's so cold and so long for the little ones. They won't let me out!'

'Never mind,' Caroline Camier said. 'It won't be long. They'll let us go. Don't worry.' She glanced across at the SS man and on an impulse stuck out her tongue. Her properminded mother would have been horrified. By ten o'clock a crowd of men and women had settled down outside the school to wait. This was in defiance of the curfew, but the Major in charge decided that it was useless to enforce it. It would provoke a riot and the Standartenführer had made it plain he wouldn't be pleased if there were trouble. He wanted a tidy operation. The parents were allowed to sit down in the road and keep their vigil. Nobody moved; women wept and prayed, a group knelt saying the rosary, the men sat dumb and helpless, waiting in front of the barred doors and shuttered windows behind which their children were imprisoned. The Major had spoken once over the loud-hailer, warning against any attempt to rush the guards or approach the building. A rescue attempt or any disturbance would result in the school being set on fire. As he told them, his men were pouring kerosene round the outside walls. There was a single shuddering wail from the watchers and then silence. The dead woman, mother of five children held inside, had been taken away and a dirty stain marked the place where her body had lain. It grew colder; a very few of the old were taken away to their beds. The sound of the rosary continued through the night. In the school building itself the children slept, and so did Michelle Giffier. The guards on duty yawned and changed watches. The one who had pushed the teacher over and seen her thighs, occupied himself with lewd thoughts. By the morning the children were crying and hungry. Nothing, not even a loaf, was permitted to come in from St. Blaize.

The guards at the checkpoint had kept Régine de Bernard for three hours. When she refused to be turned back they threatened to arrest her. A particularly aggressive NCO poked her in the side with his carbine. White faced, thin lipped, absolutely determined, she withstood them and demanded to be taken to see Vierken. Her confidence shook theirs; finally it was the NCO, anxious not to make a mistake with someone who claimed to know the Standartenführer, who put a call through on the field telephone to the Château Diane. Vierken was out. Régine settled down to wait. The NCO tried to telephone again. An hour later he was handing her into a Mercedes flying the swastika from its bonnet and saluting her as she left. She sat in the back, smoking, hunched and small inside her coat. It all made sense. Vierken's insistence that she stayed away from home. He didn't want her at St. Blaize. He didn't want her to see what was happening or be caught up in his reprisals. He had tried to protect her because he loved her. And she loved him; in spite of what Minden said he was going to do, she still loved him. But she was going to persuade him to relent. The fools, she said it under her breath. The damned fools, meddling with saboteurs and the West. They deserved to be punished; they deserved to lose hostages and be taught a lesson. She had no sympathy with her fellow countrymen if they fought against the Germans, involving themselves in a useless struggle on behalf of an ally who was their traditional enemy. No sympathy and active hostility. But children. No, that couldn't be contemplated. Vierken must be bluffing. It might do the parents good to suffer, to sweat for their folly. But it must be terrifying to be inside the school; as Minden had described the armoured car and the running SS guards, she had an image of the Barzain boys, of Michelle Giffier, of Caroline Camier, and countless others whom she knew by name, cowering and whimpering in terror. She found she had picked a hole in her cigarette and savagely stubbed it out, only to light another moments later. She leaned forward and tapped the driver on the shoulder.

'I want to make a stop. Go to the Château St. Blaize; it's about eight kilometres from here.'

'I'm sorry, I'm not allowed to detour or stop, Mademoiselle. You are going direct to Château Diane. Those are Standartenführer Vierken's orders.'

Having said this, she felt him deliberately accelerate. She swore at him, not caring if he heard, and threw herself back against the cushion. All right then. He was probably angry; there would be a scene, explanations, a reconciliation. Immediately she felt weak at the anticipation of their making up. He would be fierce and strong, demanding subjection. Christ she whispered to herself her fingers clenching, Christ, I mustn't think of that . . . But she was still thinking of it, pale and moist-skinned with excitement, when they passed the school and she saw the kneeling women, the groups of dejected men.

'Stop!' She shouted at the driver. He braked sharply. Régine jumped out. Faces turned towards her, bodies shifted to make room. An old woman mumbled at her.

'Mademoiselle Régine – help us for God's sake. They've got our children and they're sending them away! They say we'll never see them again!' She recognised one of the estate workers from the Château. He caught at her hand; she gripped hard.

'I'll help you. Don't worry, Jumont, I'll help you.' For a moment she paused, looking towards the school. A temporary spotlight had been set up, to thwart a rush in the darkness. It showed up the familiar one-story building with its jutting porch under which she had sheltered as a child against the autumn rains, the window, shuttered and sinister, and the black uniforms of the guards who ringed it, carbines at the ready. The armoured car was drawn up down the side of a street leading towards the main road. She turned back to the car; the driver was out, holding the door for her. He gave her a look of dislike.

'Please . . .' he said sharply. 'Get in.' She drove away and saw the people watching her. They hadn't connected her with the Mercedes and the swastika pennant. Suddenly somebody realised its significance. A de Bernard was travelling in an SS car. A German had rescued the de Bernard children just in time. There was a howl from the crowd; the women thrust themselves forward and spat after her. She didn't see them. She had her eyes closed, as if it were possible to erase the sight of her village and its people, the school and the children held inside. Half an hour later she was in the Château Diane and face to face with Adolph Vierken.

7

The Mayor, Albert Camier, Father Duval and Jean de Bernard were all seated; Savage stood by the fireplace. Jean-Pierre had brought a bottle of wine; his eyes were red from weeping. When he left them Jean de Bernard spoke.

'My friends,' he said. 'This gentleman is my wife's cousin. He has a plan for rescuing the children. I ask you to listen to him.'

'We'll listen,' Camier said. He blew his nose and rubbed the handkerchief across his eyes. 'We'll listen to anyone, God help us!'

'Right,' Savage said. 'Let's look at the position. M. le Comte learned one very important fact tonight. Vierken wouldn't release the children but he told him how they were going to be taken away. Transport is coming from Paris to take them to Germany. By rail. My fear was that they'd use lorries. But rail means cattle trucks. One truck should be enough. You know what they're like; strongly built, completely closed. No windows. The destination is obvious. One of the extermination camps. I'd say Auschwitz; that's where they send your Jews.'

'God curse them!' Father Duval said. 'God damn them to hell!'

'There's nothing we can do while they're in the school. Any attempt to get them out will fail; we'll be shot down and they'll be massacred. But a train, gentlemen, is a different matter. Before I go any further I want to ask you something. You're not afraid to die?'

'We offered ourselves,' Camier mumbled. 'They could shoot every man in St. Blaize if they'd let the children go.'

'You can speak for the rest — say twenty men?'

'For all,' Jean de Bernard answered him. 'Every man, as Camier says.'

'And the women too,' Father Duval said.

'Good.' Savage drank some wine. 'In that case we've got a good chance. You know how to shoot?'

'With sporting guns, yes. We can use knives, clubs, anything. But we have no weapons. They were handed in after the capitulation.'

'I can get guns,' Savage said. 'I promised the Comte and I can get whatever we need.'

'How?' Camier stared at him. 'How can you do this?'

'That's none of your business,' Savage said. 'I'll get them and I'll tell you how to use them and when. But you've got to realise one thing. I'm running this affair and I know what I'm doing. No arguments and no questions. Agreed?'

They hesitated; both looked towards Jean de Bernard.

'You can trust Monsieur Savage,' he said slowly. 'Personally, I put myself in his hands. I have complete confidence in him.'

'That's enough for me.' Father Duval got up. He held out his hand to Savage. 'These are my children too.' He spoke quietly. 'I'll give my life to save them. Tell us what to do and we'll do it.'

'Anything,' Camier said. 'My daughter . . .' He blew his nose again.

'That's settled then,' Savage nodded to them. 'First I'll need men. Young men, fit. I want them at the Lavalliere airfield at dawn. How they get there and how they duck the curfew is up to you. But there's one condition. No woman is to be told. I don't give a damn how hard it is, but if you tell your wife, Mayor, or you start hinting to anyone, Father – we'll fail. The Germans will see or hear something. All it needs is one word in a village like this and the plan will be out. Let the mothers cry. For tonight. Is that clear?'

'It's clear. We won't say anything. The men will swear silence. But how will you get the guns?'

'By parachute,' Savage said. 'They'll be dropped at Lavallière.'

'Lavallière?' They stared at him, Camier's jaw slackened. 'But that's only ten kilometres away from St. Blaize – how could anything be dropped so close?'

'Since 1941,' Savage said, 'there have been two drops made and one actual landing. A man was rescued and flown back to England. From Chartres. You look surprised? It's perfectly true. That field is isolated, hidden from the road by a thick belt of trees. The road itself is seldom used by anything but farm traffic. And this area has been so thinly policed that it was relatively easy to land a plane on a full moon in a field that size. As for the drop – you had a British agent come here in '42, didn't you?' They nodded. 'He landed at Lavallière. So have others. You needn't worry about that field, it's never been discovered as a reception area. Our supplies will be dropped there.'

'With SS crawling all over the place?' Father Duval protested. 'It may have been thinly policed before but that's because we'd had no trouble. We're under curfew now!'

'Their troops are concentrating on the town and the main roads,' Savage said. 'And most important of all, they're not expecting help from outside. The stuff will get through. It's up to you to see there are men there to pick it up.'

'Do we attack the train?' Jean de Bernard asked him.

'Yes. But not till it's left St. Blaize. Again, they'll be expecting trouble

at the station; a riot, an attempt at rescue. They'll be ready for anything. But not on the track. My guess is the station will be guarded at
full capacity. But the engine and one truck can't accommodate more
than six men at the most. Probably with a machine gun mounted on
the roof of the truck. That's the only place they can place guards –
the roof. Which means we can pick them off and there won't be any
danger of hitting the children. What I need now is a railway map.'

'I have one in the desk here,' Jean said. 'I'll get it.' Camier turned to
watch him; he pulled a handkerchief out of his pocket and ran it round
his face and neck; he looked sick and his plump face seemed to have
fallen in, leaving deep hollows round the mouth. He looked ten years
older since the day began. Father Duval was looking at Savage. Many
years in the parish and listening to the outpouring of human frailty
in the confessional had given him a sound judgement of men. The
Comtesse's cousin filled him with unease. He was a Swiss and the priest
was inclined to equate them with Germans. But there was something
different about this man, something beyond the authority and obvious
military connections which he wasn't troubling to conceal. He was a
dangerous man, a type not normally found in a small provincial village
or a nobleman's château. He moved with the taughtness of a powerful
animal; there was a look in his face which worried the priest. And
then he realised immediately that standing in the room with them was
the man who had got into the Château Diane and murdered General
Brühl. He cleared his throat and looked away.

'Now.' Savage opened the Baedeker. 'From here they'll go to Paris.'
He ran his finger down the line. 'It's the direct route. I take it there's
no transport in St. Blaize except bicycles and the station taxi?'

'My car has no petrol left,' Jean said. 'But Camier has a van.'

'I supply the Château Diane with groceries,' the Mayor said. He
looked embarrassed. 'They allow me a little petrol.'

'How much petrol?' Savage asked him.

'A few litres.'

'Good; then that's what we use to pick up the guns at Lavallière.
Get eight men together and you drive the van. If you're stopped by
patrols, you're on your way to the château with provisions.'

'But Lavallière is nowhere near there,' Camier protested. 'How can
I explain why I'm so far off the route . . .'

'You'll just have to talk your way out of it,' Savage said coldly.
'Unless you're too frightened to risk your neck for your daughter.
If that's so, you'd better stay out of it altogether!' He turned away
from him.

'No! No, no!' Camier grabbed at his arm. 'I'm not backing down
– I'll do it, I'll think of something!'

Savage looked into the pallid face, greasy with sweat, at the trembling hand still clutching his sleeve. With a jerk he pulled free. 'I want you to know this,' he said. 'You talk about your child. She's not the only one. All the children are locked up in that school, and by tomorrow night they'll be on their way to the extermination camp. To be gassed or shot. Now listen to me, Monsieur Camier. You're frightened, yes? All right. But if you get so frightened that you ball this up, and those children can't be rescued, I'm going to kill you. I just want you to know that.' He turned away from the Mayor. 'Now what we do is this. We pick up the guns and go to this point on the railway line. Here; about eight kilometres out of St. Blaize. There's no signal box for another three kilometres and the place is isolated. Then we attack.'

'If we succeed and get them back,' Jean de Bernard said, 'where do we hide them? The SS will come looking for them.'

'The SS,' Savage said, 'won't know the train hasn't gone through for at least a day. If we clear up any evidence of the attack, run the engine and the truck off on a side line and leave them there, they might have pulled out of St. Blaize before word comes through that the children haven't arrived. These transports don't stop at stations, they go on for days; they only stop to refuel and change drivers. We'll have time to hide the children somewhere.'

'There isn't anywhere,' the priest said. 'There are no mountains, no caves. The woods are the only place, but it won't be possible to hide that many; there are children of five and six years old. What can we do?'

'I don't know,' Savage admitted. 'But we'll think of something. First, let's get them back. Now, Father, you'll be the liaison. Go back to the school, move round and select eight men — we haven't transport for more. Tell them to go to the Mayor's house and wait there. And don't give any details. Monsieur Camier, you go home. Check your van to see there's enough petrol. It wouldn't help if *you* ran out. What you must do is keep the men quiet when they get to you and wait till the Comte or I give you the word to move. Have you any questions?'

'No.' Father Duval spoke quickly. He didn't want Albert Camier's curiosity aroused. Fear and misery for his child had dulled his sharp wits and kept the obvious conclusion about the Comtesse's Swiss cousin from occurring to him. Father Duval knew Camier too well to trust him. If he connected Savage with the man the SS wanted, he might well make a deal to save his own daughter, if he couldn't help the rest. 'No, everything is clear,' he said. He took Camier by the arm. 'We will do exactly as you say. God bless you, Monsieur. I will pray for you.'

'Thank you,' Savage said. He shook the priest's hand. Jean de

Bernard took them outside. When he returned Savage was sitting on the sofa, the empty wine glass held between his knees. He stood in front of him.

'Father Duval guessed who you were,' he said. 'I just hope Camier doesn't.'

'Giving me up won't help the children,' Savage said. 'They know that; anyway I've got to take that chance.'

'And will this rescue really work? Can you get arms and ammunition for us?'

'I don't know,' Savage answered. 'But by God I'm going to try. Starting right now.'

It was just dark when Savage came out through the door onto the rooftop. He shone the narrow pencil torch to find his way to the transmitter; a bank of cloud hid the moon and a light wind scurried through it, driving the wisps of smoky vapour away, until the moon hung revealed, the outline of the frozen peaks giving the semblance of a face to the luminous surface. For a moment he remembered his childhood excitement at discovering human features on something so distant and majestic, at being able to equate a planet millions of miles away in space with a mythical old man. Perhaps it was the human need to minimise, to scale down the universe to mankind's pigmy size. Yet men had looked as he was doing, on the ineffable beauty of the cold, dead star, and seen divinity in it. Again the wind came sweeping, rushing the clouds to veil the icy face. Savage uncovered the transmitter.

Once more before he began to use the keys, he glanced upward, watching the progress of the wind, trailing vapour draperies. For a second he paused, caught by a memory of long ago, by the line of a verse learned in his youth which had aroused his curiosity and touched him with a sense of beauty. 'My courses are set on the storm winds, I sail on the Lightning Stream'.

He adjusted his headphones. Like the man in the poem he was struggling against an intangible force of destruction, caught up in events which couldn't be left free to rage and wreck the lives of other people. He had come to St. Blaize and fulfilled his purpose; by right he should be free, free to take the chance of escape the pass with Vierken's signature could give him. Free to leave the village and its people, its children, to perish in the storm of events for which he was responsible. But the lightning stream was carrying him with it to an unknown end. He felt a sense of fatality, which he angrily dismissed. There had to be a future for the children of St. Blaize; he had lost his own child, and the wife who hadn't found her happiness with him. But the innocent were not going to be sacrificed this time.

If he didn't much care what happened to him, he cared for them.

He began to transmit. Deliberately he used the code which meant the message went to OSS rather than British headquarters. He remembered that snide, cold-blooded English Colonel; the request he was going to make wouldn't have an icicle's chance on a hot shovel if it went to him. He used General Heidsecker's code name. 'Geronimo. Geronimo from Apache. Mission completed, total success. Imperative assistance sent prevent reprisal against area. All children in village due extermination. Request drop of small arms, ammunition at Lavallière field by dawn, repeat dawn tomorrow. Reply confirming soon as possible. Apache.'

Huddled against a corner of the roof he settled down to wait. It didn't occur to him to pray; there was no God, no benevolent power somewhere in the arch of night sky above him. Nothing would come on angels' wings to save the children cringing in the school. Nothing had come to save his wife and child.

Only the courage and ingenuity of a few human beings might help them. And the policy decided in London. To send help or to refuse; to risk a plane and supplies for what he knew they would regard as a hopeless enterprise, or to ignore the message. Heidsecker was a good man. Savage used the word without analysing what it meant. It was a negative quality, meaning that the General wasn't a bastard, whereas Colonel Fairbairn was. Heidsecker was a family man, noted for leniency and humanity in his dealings with his troops. Savage smoked a cigarette; his mouth felt dry and stale. If they didn't send help – if they just didn't answer because there was a breakdown and they couldn't get through . . . He rubbed the cigarette out, exploding tiny red sparks on the slate. He looked at his watch again. Ten-thirty. He had been on the roof for an hour. The transmitter was silent. There was a noise behind him, and Louise said, 'It's me. I've brought you some soup.'

She came and sat beside him; her face was clear in the bright moonlight. 'Jean told me what you're going to do,' she said. 'Did you get through?'

'I did; now I'm waiting to get the answer. Sit close to me, keep me warm.'

'It sounds impossible,' Louise said.

'Nothing's impossible if you have the will,' he answered. 'And the luck. And something to fight with.' He looked at his watch again.

'You're a trained soldier,' she said. 'The people here don't know how to fight. They'll be massacred.'

'Desperation makes people do extraordinary things,' Savage said. He put his arm round her. 'You'll be surprised what these peaceful villagers will do when their children are at stake. I'm not worried about them.'

'If they don't answer you,' she whispered, 'or they won't help – what do we do then?'

'God knows,' he said. 'But we'll do something. You know I've been thinking about Vierken. Why did he tell your husband how they were going to move the children? And the time – I don't like that part. And why a cattle truck and a special engine, just for a few children . . . They're desperately short of rolling stock. It doesn't make sense. There's something wrong with it, but I'm damned if I know what it is!'

'There's nothing wrong with it,' she said. 'That's how they transport people to the camps; that's where the children are going.'

'Hundreds of people, yes,' he said. 'But not fifty children. It's not very efficient, and that smells bad to me.'

'I think you're imagining something's wrong,' she said. 'I believe it will be just as he said. Do you know, I feel so guilty because our children got away? I went to Minden's room tonight; nothing's been taken. He must have just picked up the children and run. I wish I knew where they were!'

'He's taken a risk,' Savage said. 'I have to give him that. If anyone finds out, he could be in real trouble.'

'He was always fond of them,' she said slowly. 'He didn't do it just because of me. I told Jean I'd slept with him.'

'Oh,' Savage said. 'Why? Why did you do that?'

'I felt I had to,' she said. 'I think he understood. You're the one he minds about.'

'And you,' Savage said. He turned her towards him. 'Where do you stand – with him or with me? I want you to come back to England with me.'

'I won't do that,' Louise said. 'I won't leave him alone here. After the war's over, it will be different. But I'm not walking out on him now.'

'I have a feeling,' Savage said, 'that you still love him. And you won't admit it.'

'If that were true, it would be easy. It might have been true if I hadn't met you. But you've changed my life. Nothing will be the same again for me, whatever happens.'

'How would you like to live in Mexico?' Savage asked her. 'I've had a bellyful of Europe and I don't feel like settling down in the States. How would Mexico suit you?'

'I don't know,' Louise said. She leaned against him. 'I'll think about it. What is your real name?'

'McFall,' he said. 'Brian Patrick John. I love you very much and I'm not going to lose you. I want you to know that. If you won't come back with me I'll come and get you.' He kissed her quietly. He looked at the luminous face of his watch. 'Christ! It's after midnight – why the hell haven't they answered!'

'It must take time,' she said. 'You've hardly given them time . . .'

'I've given them as much as we've got,' he said. 'If they can't cut through the red tape, then those children are as good as dead!'

'I want to come with you,' she said. 'I want to help.'

Savage shook his head. 'Not a chance, my darling. You're not going to be within a mile of this. It might surprise you, but I don't fancy you getting killed. You stay here and wait. This is for men only.'

'I don't want anything to happen to you,' Louise whispered. Her eyes filled with tears and she brushed them away. 'Or to Jean. Don't let him do anything foolish . . .'

'I wouldn't have thought it was in his character,' Savage said. 'He's not the reckless type.'

'You shouldn't despise him,' she said slowly. 'I made that mistake. I blamed him because I didn't know what we were up against. I know now, I've seen it for myself. He's not got your kind of courage but he's not a coward. And he loves St. Blaize and the people. Don't let him throw his life away.'

'All right,' Savage said. 'I'll look out for him, if that's what you want.' At that moment there was a buzz from the headphones and the answer from London began to come through.

Frank Heidsecker was having dinner at the Savoy when he was called to the telephone. It had been a tiring day, but stimulating. The weather reports were improving and the low cloud and winds which had bedevilled the first days of June seemed to have disappeared. Heidsecker left his office at seven and went back to his hotel to bath and change. He had a date with an attractive Englishwoman whom he had met at a cocktail party the week before. Her husband was serving with the Canadian division, which was at that moment waiting on the South coast for the order to sail. Heidsecker was happily married, but throughout that relationship he had enjoyed affairs with attractive women, and he was looking forward to sleeping with the charming wife of the Canadian Major, if he could persuade her to come back with him after dinner. Instead of going to bed and enjoying himself, the General spent the rest of the evening at his headquarters in St. James's Street while his disappointed guest went home intact.

There were four men round the table in the General's office, and a stenographer in WAC uniform. It was eleven o'clock and the room was thick with cigarette smoke. Of the four men one was in civilian clothes. He had a round, pale face and heavy spectacles. He looked grave and self-conscious.

'In my opinion,' Colonel Fairbairn spoke up, his voice on a higher register than usual as his indignation mastered him, 'in my opinion, this is a ridiculous request and highly improper! This man has no authority to interfere!'

'I don't think we can call it interference,' an American Lieutenant Colonel interposed. 'This message says that our help is needed; otherwise if I get it right, they're going to kill the *children*. I'm not saying there's anything we can do, but I can't go along with your criticism of our operator.' He sat back in his chair and folded his hands on the table. He didn't like the English liaison officer from SOE.

A Group Captain in the RAF glanced up at him and then towards the General. 'If you want our help, sir,' he said, 'I can arrange it, provided we don't take too long to reach a decision.'

'And before we do,' the man in civilian clothes spoke up, 'we have to recognise that this has grave political implications.'

'As I see it,' Heidsecker spoke and everyone turned towards him, 'the issue here is very simple. We sent an agent into France with a mission so important that I can honestly say it has decided the outcome of the war. He accomplished that mission. Intelligence from Paris informs us that he went beyond his instructions and that there are rumours of serious sabotage at the Château Diane as well as Brühl's murder. Our man couldn't have done this without the co-operation of the French. And it's the people who helped him who are going to suffer.' The General looked round the table; Fairbairn pinched his lip between thumb and finger and avoided his eyes. 'Children, gentlemen,' Heidsecker said. 'Children are going to be murdered; that's what that message said. I for one will not refuse to help them.'

The official from the Foreign Office, who was only an observer and not as senior as he liked to pretend, coughed and said, 'I'm sure it would damage Anglo-French relations if the story got out after the war that we'd done nothing to assist them. I'm sure my department would agree with your decision, General.'

'And I'm sure mine wouldn't.' Fairbairn couldn't restrain himself. 'I think the whole idea is insane. We *knew* there'd be reprisals and we knew they'd be extreme. It's happened dozens of times before. People are taken as hostages and shot – we don't rush in with planes and guns to rescue them! It isn't possible. I want it on record that I think we should order this man to do absolutely nothing to draw attention to himself, but to get back by the recognised escape route as soon as he can. Of course it's admirable that he succeeded. Nobody, General, is more delighted than I am. After all, I helped to brief him. But I don't believe we should involve ourselves in French affairs. If I may put forward a practical view, that part of France is notoriously lukewarm towards the Allies, and an atrocity like this might be just what is needed to tip them over to our side!'

Heidsecker regarded him for a moment. 'I've noted your opinion,

Colonel, and it's on the record. I reject it completely. Group Captain
– you can arrange for a plane? I suggest we do the thing properly and
send a transport in with the supplies. Lavallière field is big enough for
it to land. If the operation against the Germans is successful we can
airlift the children out.'

'You're going to take them *out*, sir?' That was the Lieutenant Colonel who had corrected Fairbairn.

'I am,' the General said. 'I'm going to give this rescue everything
we've got! Those kids are going to be saved, and I'm going to be
personally responsible!'

'In that case,' the Group Captain said, 'we've a lot to arrange and
very little time.'

'Colonel Fairbairn,' Heidsecker said, 'we'll need your full co-
operation.'

'Once a decision has been reached,' the Colonel said irritably, 'I shall
abide by it. We will do everything necessary.'

'Good,' the General said. He flexed his shoulder muscles. 'Now,
gentlemen, it's getting on for midnight. Let's get down to details.'

She knelt down beside him as he listened, taking the message down.
Savage pulled the headphones off and swung round to her.

'They're sending everything,' he said. 'And a plane to take the
children back! It's due at Lavallière at first light, around five o'clock.
Come on, we've got to get going!'

They found Jean de Bernard in the library. He got up and looked
at them, anger and suspicion on his face. 'You've been together? You
know it's after one o'clock.'

'They're sending help,' Louise broke in on him. She went up and
caught his arm. 'Jean, don't you understand, we've been on the roof,
waiting – the message just came. They're sending guns and ammunition
and a plane which can take the children back to England!'

'Thank God,' he said. He spoke to Savage. 'Camier and the others
will be waiting. I'll go down on the bicycle; I know a way across our
fields which will bring me to the edge of the village. I can get to his
house from there without being stopped.'

'We both go,' Savage said. 'And then on to the field to wait for
the plane.'

For a moment Jean hesitated. Then he came to Savage and held
out his hand. 'I congratulate you,' he said. 'I didn't believe it could
be done.'

'No more did I,' Savage answered. 'And until we see that plane
take off with every child inside it, I wouldn't congratulate anyone,
if I were you.'

*

'Why have you come here? I told you to stay in Paris!' Régine had never seen him look like that before. His face was grey with anger, the deep-set eyes were burning. He stepped close to her and she saw his right hand twitching. She thought suddenly that he was going to hit her, but she didn't move.

'Adolph, I had to come,' she said. 'Why are you so angry? Why did you send the car and let me through?'

'Because I thought something was wrong,' he shouted. 'I thought you were in trouble! Now I find there's nothing, nothing but an idea that you can interfere! You can go straight back – I'll send you back immediately!'

'Why don't you want me here?' she asked him. 'It's because of what you're going to do to the children, isn't it?'

'Children?' He seized her upper arm, his fingers crushing the flesh until she gave a cry. 'How do you know about the children? Answer me!' He slapped her so hard across the face that only his grip on her arm kept her from falling. Tears rushed into her eyes and streamed down her face. He raised his hand again. This was a stranger, a man she didn't know, a violent enemy prepared to beat her unconscious. But they were lovers. She loved him and he loved her. The ferocity of love was not like this. She shrank away, one arm flung up to protect herself. 'How did you find out?' He snarled the words at her. 'You'll tell me, or by God I'll call Kramm in here and let him get it out of you!'

'Minden,' she gasped. 'Minden told me. He came to my aunt's flat with my nephew and niece . . . He'd rescued them from the school just in time. He told me about Operation Herod . . .'

'Minden . . .' Vierken released her. She stood before him, weeping. 'He snatched the de Bernard children away, did he? By God he'll be sorry he did . . .' Without warning his mood changed. The fury he felt towards Régine suddenly veered away from her. He had another scapegoat. Minden: the brilliant biochemist who was one of Brühl's staff, the lover of Louise de Bernard. They were all the same – Vierken raged at the thought of him. He had completely forgotten Régine. Like all intellectuals, thinking themselves superior to the military élite of the Reich, naturally he could indulge his sentimental whim and flout the SS, thwart them of their vengeance. *He* hadn't fought in Russia . . .

Suddenly he saw Régine, wiping her wet face, the ugly weal where he had struck her darkening on one cheek.

'Don't cry,' he said. 'I lost my temper. I'm sorry. Poor little one, come here.'

'It doesn't matter!' Régine said. Suddenly she threw her arms round his neck. 'Don't hate me, darling! Don't be angry with me! I can't bear it – I love you so much . . .'

He embraced her; she held on to him and sobbed.

It was not her fault; women were more sensitive about these things. He regretted having been unkind to her. He stroked her hair and soothed her. Minden, his mind said, Minden. So he went behind our backs, did he, and robbed us of two of them . . .

'Hush,' he said to Régine. 'No more tears. I'm not angry with you, sweetheart. It's all over. We won't quarrel.' He could feel the warmth of her body and the heat rose in him. He was tired and in need of relaxation. He pressed her against him. 'We'll have something nice to drink,' he said. 'And we'll stay together. I'm not angry you came – I'm glad.'

'The children,' Régine whispered. 'You're not really going to do anything to them, are you? It's only a bluff, isn't it?'

He was unbuttoning her coat, his fingers brushing against her breasts. 'Of course,' he mumbled, seizing the soft flesh, bending to kiss her. 'Don't worry about it.'

He ordered champagne; they drank it sitting on the bed. It was the same canopied bed in which Brühl had been murdered. Vierken was not superstitious about such details. It was the best bedroom in the Château and he took it.

She cried while they were making love; he was too absorbed and excited to see any significance in it. Lying in his arms, Régine stayed awake while he slept. She loved him; he was part of her. But so was St. Blaize; the Château where she had grown up, her father, fading out of life, her brother Jean, the children, who were now, thank God, asleep in their aunt's flat and not shut up in that school, like the others . . .

Nineteen years she had lived in the one place; she knew every villager by name. Jumont, clasping her hand and begging for help outside the schoolhouse. He had two grandsons and a grand-daughter, a great-niece . . . She turned over on the pillow and looked at Vierken sleeping beside her. He had said it was a bluff; he had told her not to worry. Doubt tortured her, an instinct stronger than her longing to trust him urged her not to believe it. She slid out of his embrace and lay on the edge of the mattress, huddled and cold. He couldn't mean to hurt them. He had children of his own; he had shown her a picture of them, two boys in Hitler Jugend uniform. He couldn't do anything to Jumont's grandchildren, to Caroline Camier, to dozens of others she kept seeing in imagination. He couldn't.

She was asleep when the telephone rang. She woke, startled and confused, to find Vierken gone. The ringing continued; she picked the receiver up and as she did so, Vierken answered from the extension; there was a sound of water running. He was in the bathroom. She held the receiver and listened. She had taken German as a major subject for her 'Bacchot'. She and Vierken spoke it when they were alone together. The caller was a subordinate; Vierken addressed him as Major.

'What's the position down there?'

'Quiet, Standartenführer. There was an alert about an hour ago, but nothing happened. We let them stay round the school, and at six this morning we moved them off the streets. A few protested but the rest went home. There were four arrests, three women and a man, and that convinced the rest of them. Everything is under control. The transport has arrived. It came at six o'clock this morning. It's ready for them.'

'Good,' Vierken answered. 'They're not expecting anything to happen till tonight. I told de Bernard we were sending the children out this evening. They won't have had time to prepare anything. You sent the special detail to Chemire?'

'Yes sir. The grave has been dug.'

'Good,' he said again. Régine lay back on the pillow, one hand pressed to her mouth, the receiver gripped in the other.

'I think I'll come down and see them go,' he said. 'Take the schoolmistress with them.'

'Right, Standartenführer.'

'And no trace is to be left, you understand? Nothing!'

'I told Grunewald to find a spot inside the woods,' the Major said. 'He reported an hour ago. Nobody will find them; it's completely hidden. There are no farmhouses anywhere near. Nothing will be heard.'

'Move them out in an hour,' Vierken said. 'I shall be there to watch it. Heil Hitler!'

Very carefully she put back the receiver; her hand was steady and she replaced it without making any noise. She lay back, her arms straight at her sides.

'The grave has been dug.' They weren't going to Germany; the children of St. Blaize were going to be taken off the train and marched into the woods at Chemire and murdered. She gave one cry of choking anguish and then stopped. He came into the bedroom, naked, with a towel over his arm, and stood looking down at her.

'You look pale,' he said. 'Go back to sleep. I'm going out and I'll be back in two hours. Then I'll wake you.' He bent over her and kissed her mouth, biting her lower lip. 'You're so bad for me,' he murmured. 'You take my mind off my work . . .'

'I'm not tired,' she said. She smiled and rolled away from him. 'If you're going out, couldn't I go to St. Blaize? I need clothes.'

'Not for me,' he said. 'I like you as you are.'

'Take me to St. Blaize,' she pleaded. 'I want to look nice for you. Please, Adolph.'

'All right; but not to stay. Just to pack what you want and then the car will bring you straight back here. I don't want you hanging about the village.'

'Why not? Are you expecting trouble?'

He shrugged. 'No, certainly not. But I want you here, waiting for me. I'll come to the Château with you. Get dressed then; we haven't time to waste.'

She sat in the back of the car with him; he reached out and held her hand. She smiled at him. 'I questioned your sister-in-law,' he said. 'I made it very disagreeable for her.'

Régine went on smiling. 'How disagreeable – did you hurt her? My brother?'

'No, no, my darling,' he protested. 'There wasn't any need. I'm a mild man, you know that. I just bullied her a little; to please you!' He squeezed her hand. 'It will amuse me to go there with you.'

'Yes,' Régine said.' It will be most amusing.'

The sound of the plane woke Louise. She had refused to go to bed, but stayed in the salon in a chair. Jean de Bernard had come to her quietly and kissed her goodbye. She had given him her hand and pressed her lips to his cheek. Savage was standing in the doorway. She could sense him watching them, fighting against Jean. She looked into her husband's face.

'Take care; and God bless you. I wish I was going with you.'

'You have a long time to wait,' he whispered. 'Hours and hours before anything happens. Stay calm, and try not to be anxious. I believe we'll succeed.'

'Not if we hang around here,' Savage said. He came to Louise and she gave him her hand too. You love me, his eyes said. He kissed you like a brother.

'We'll be back,' he said. 'Just stay quietly here.'

Then they had gone. She got up, shivering because the fire was almost out, and listened to the sound of the engine. And if it was seen to land . . . She turned and suddenly dropped on her knees. Her prayers were incoherent, helpless. She got up again and went upstairs to see if her father-in-law had awoken. His light was on and he was sitting up when she went in.

'An air raid? Are they dropping bombs?'

'No, Papa. It's just a passing plane. It means nothing. Go back to sleep.'

'I can't sleep,' the old man quavered. 'Jean hasn't been to see me – the children never came – nobody cares about me!'

'That isn't true!' Suddenly she lost her temper with him. 'Don't be so selfish – if you knew where Jean was tonight and what nearly happened to the children . . .' She checked herself. 'I'm sorry, Papa. I didn't mean to shout at you. But you're not being neglected. Go to sleep.'

'I know there's something wrong,' the Comte said. 'What do you mean? Where is Jean? What about the children?'

'You wouldn't understand,' Louise said slowly. 'And you're lucky. I'll go and make you a hot drink. Then you'll sleep.'

'It's the Germans, isn't it?' he said. He pulled himself upright. 'Go to my chest of drawers and get me my revolver. I won't let them hurt Jean. I'm not afraid. Go to the chest of drawers!'

'No.' Louise shook her head. 'Please, Papa, don't get excited. It's my fault for saying anything about it. There's nothing you can do. There's nothing I can do either.'

'I fought them in the First War,' the Comte said fiercely. 'I'll fight them now!' He threw back the bedclothes and before she could reach him he was stumbling to the chest. He pulled open a drawer and turned to her, triumphant. His face was very flushed and his eyes shone. 'There! You didn't believe me – but I've always kept it. Just in case we were in danger! And it's loaded, ready . . .' The long-barrelled revolver hung down in his hand, its weight too much for him. Louise ran forward and took it.

'Papa, for God's sake! Give me that. Lean on me now and come back to bed. You'll make yourself ill.'

He fell onto the bed and it was a struggle to lift him into it. At last he lay exhausted on the pillows; his high colour was receding, his eyes were still too bright. He breathed through his mouth.

'Hot milk,' Louise said to him. 'You'd like a nice glass of hot milk. I'll get it for you.' She took the revolver with her and went downstairs to the kitchen. Even the old had their secrets. Nobody knew of the gun's existence. The old man had kept it hidden in the drawer against some imaginary need. She picked it up and saw that it was fully loaded. She went upstairs and hid it in the bureau in the salon. Jean's revolver was gone; he had taken it with him. When she went back to the kitchen the milk had boiled over.

The Hudson stood on Lavallière field, the dawn light showing it up like a huge primeval bird. Savage ran to it first, followed by Jean de Bernard. The villagers hesitated; they seemed almost afraid to approach. Camier's van was hidden under some trees on the edge of the field. It had been pushed off the road. The trees round Lavallière provided an impenetrable screen of the field from the road. The moon still shone brightly, giving the scene a still, lunar quality. The sun had not risen yet. The pilot dropped down from the cockpit and Savage held out his hand. He was followed by his navigator and his airgunner. All three shook hands with him.

'Right on time. Where's the stuff?'

'Inside. Get your chaps together and we'll get it unloaded. I'm not too crazy about standing out in the open like this.' The pilot unbuttoned his helmet and took it off; he looked around him at the figures of men swarming round the plane. The big American was obviously in charge. And he knew how to organise. Within ten minutes the supplies were on the ground and being neatly stacked into piles. A Frenchman came up to him and spoke in excellent English.

'I'd like to express our gratitude to you for coming here. It's a tremendous personal risk for you, but the lives of every child in our village is at stake. The Germans have taken them and they're going to send them to Germany. Thanks to you, we may be able to stop them.' Jean de Bernard held out his hand. The pilot took it.

'Kids?' he said. 'They've taken your kids?'

'Yes,' Jean said. 'They're being held in the school.'

'The bloody bastards!' the pilot exclaimed. 'You can count me in on this. The Yank's in charge, isn't he?'

'Yes,' Jean said. 'He's coming now.'

'Let's get this stuff into the trees,' Savage said. 'Then we can sort it out; and this plane's got to be hidden. How the hell,' he swung round to the pilot, 'are we going to do it? It's like a bloody battleship!'

'The ops boys thought of that,' the pilot said, 'seeing I've got to hang around. You'll find some tackle inside for pulling her. And camouflage nets.'

It was obvious that there weren't enough of them to move the aircraft, but they tried. Heaving on the ropes attached to the undercarriage, Savage, the crew and the men of St. Blaize strained and struggled, but the load was too heavy. The pilot offered to start the engines and taxi, but Savage refused.

'Too big a risk,' he said. 'Something might pass on the road over there; we wouldn't hear it but sure as hell they'd hear us. Camier — get that van over here! The rest of you, move the guns into the trees. And be careful of that crate, it's full of grenades!'

Camier ran back to his van, his breath tearing through his heaving lungs. Sweat had soaked his shirt, his legs trembled. They had been stopped once on their way out of St. Blaize by an SS patrol. Luckily for him, the check point was at a junction which allowed him to insist that he was on an extra supply run to Headquarters at Anet. Sitting in the van, Camier allowed himself a moment of collapse. He sank against the steering wheel, his head supported on one arm, and closed his eyes.

He would never forget that moment, when the guards surrounded him and the face of an SS corporal peered through the window. He had felt physically sick with fear; at the memory his stomach heaved again. There were eight men hidden in the back of the van, crouched on top of each other. All the SS had to do was open the back doors

... He had his papers ready and the pass which he had been given to enter the Château Diane; he had thrust them at the corporal, and the semi-darkness before dawn hid his livid face and the sweat running in trickles down his neck.

The van was well known at the Château. The pass was signed by the Wehrmacht commander of the Dreux district, General Fielder, and it was stamped and re-stamped for many journeys in the past weeks. The corporal had hesitated.

Camier had found a voice from somewhere.

'I shall be late,' he croaked. 'The Standartenführer wants duck eggs for breakfast. I'm bringing them specially . . .'

They had stepped back and let him go. He had no idea what made him think of the excuse. Duck eggs. He raised his head, drew a deep breath into his aching chest and wiped his oily forehead on his bare arm. Then he started the van, and bumping over the soft, uneven ground, he drove it slowly out towards the plane.

It was an old pre-war Renault; its chassis rattled and its engine protested at the strain being put upon it. But with the human power pulling on the ropes and the van dragging at the tow, the plane began to move across the open field until it came to rest under the shelter of some trees. Camier helped to spread the camouflage nets, instructed by the pilot. Savage ordered some branches to be cut, and these were laid along the wings; the tail was in deep shadow. They gathered to open the boxes of arms and the small wooden crate marked 'Grenades', with a skull and crossbones painted in red on one side. Every man present had experience of hunting. Hate and terror for their children sharpened their perception. Clumsy hands imitated the actions of Savage as he showed them how to use the sten guns.

To Jean de Bernard he tossed one fully loaded. 'Set a man to watch the road for patrols,' he said. 'And tell him for Christ's sake not to open fire on any Germans. Just report back here and run like hell if they look like stopping.'

'If they reckon I've landed,' the pilot said, sounding casual, 'how long would it take them to get here?'

'They'd have been here by now,' Jean de Bernard answered.

'Incidentally,' Savage looked up, 'being in uniform won't protect any of you from these boys. They don't go by the Geneva Convention. They'll kick your balls off and then shoot you. So get yours in first if they come.'

'Don't worry about us,' the pilot said. 'I've got my instructions. I know what to do.' Looking at the clean-cut, pleasant young face, Savage doubted it. Brave, cheerful, typically English. He had as much hope against the average SS soldier as a child threatening a man-eating tiger with a pop-gun.

348 *The Occupying Power*

'Right,' Savage said. The sun was rising; the sky was blushing on the horizon; obstinately, the silver moon still hung above them. 'Let's have a look at the grenades.' He glanced at the faces of Camier and the eight men. They looked gaunt and grim. Poor bastards. He was surprised to feel sorry for them. To him this was a well-practised exercise, something for which he had been trained. These people had lived in peace; their children's lives depended upon their learning skills in a few minutes which he took for granted. He reached in and took out a grenade.

He held it up for them. 'Pineapples,' he said. 'The pin has a ring in it; pull that, release the catch on the side, count to three and throw. I once heard of a man holding one of these in live training and saying, "But I never learned to count, Sarge . . ." There were so many pieces of him nobody else counted *them*. So remember. Pull, release catch, count, throw. I know they're pretty, but don't stop to admire them.' One of the men smiled; some of the tension relaxed. 'We'll use these for the engine,' Savage explained.

'Nobody tosses one near the cattle truck, whatever happens. We don't want any of the children getting hurt. A couple of these well aimed will bring the train to a halt. And get rid of our pals who may be inside the driver's cabin.'

'Would they use a driver from St. Blaize?' That was Jean de Bernard.

'Unlikely,' Savage countered. 'It'll be one of the regulars from Paris. He may be Boche or he may be French. Anyhow we can't worry about him. It's just his bad luck.'

'I'd like a cigarette,' the pilot ventured to Jean de Bernard. 'It's getting very light now. Have one?'

'Thank you.' Jean bent over the lighter flame.

'Have you got children in this too?'

'No,' the Comte answered. 'Mine were lucky. They escaped.' He looked at his watch. 'We've a long time to wait. They're not taking them out of St. Blaize until tonight.'

'Tonight!' The cigarette dropped. 'Christ, I'm willing to wait for an hour or even a bit over, but tonight! There isn't a chance – we're sure to be seen here! Look, it's daylight now . . .'

'Planes have landed here for the last two years.' Savage had come up to them. 'Not a Hudson, maybe, but aircraft carrying agents. Nobody guarded this place or gave it a thought. I landed here myself by parachute. You were told to wait. If we get the children out you'll fly them back to England. If we don't, you can get the hell out yourself. But not till tonight.' He turned away and called out to one of the villagers. The pilot looked after him. He replaced the cigarette and sucked on it.

'Nasty piece of work,' he remarked to Jean de Bernard. His tone was low. 'Typical Yank.'

He dug into the pocket of his flying jacket. 'I've got a drop of something here,' he said. 'Keep out the cold.' He offered a small flask to Jean, who shook his head.

'No thank you. You'll need it for the flight back. Why don't you relax now? Perhaps you could sleep.'

'I might.' The young Englishman stretched his back. 'I think I'll go and take a zizz inside.' He smiled at Jean and stamped on his cigarette end.

He climbed up into the belly of the aircraft and disappeared. Jean de Bernard stood apart, listening to Savage demonstrating and explaining the small-arms. There were pistols as well as the sten guns. He was a good instructor, precise, and patient. It was a side of his character which the Comte had not suspected. He couldn't understand Savage; the type was completely alien to him. But then he was too European. He hadn't really understood Louise either.

He only loved her. With the prospect of fighting the SS in front of him, he faced not only the fact of loving his wife, but of being killed before he could do anything about it. She had forgiven him; he knew that. The moment when he found her kissing Savage had roused him to contemplate murder. He looked at the American and wondered how deep his hatred of him went. Morality, sensitivity, nothing so effete as ethics would trouble Savage. He wanted Louise and he would do his best to take her. Unless, in the heat of the battle . . . Jean de Bernard dropped his cigarette close to the mashed stub left by the pilot, and stepped on it. Savage could have stood aside from what was happening. The children of St. Blaize were not his concern; his job was done. He could have used his permit and left them. Jean knew that there were men who would have done exactly that. He went over to the group and touched Savage on the shoulder.

'Let me help,' he said. The sun was up and it was growing warm. The time was six-twenty-three.

Inside the school Michelle Giffier formed the children into groups. There was a lot of crying, even among the older ones. Waking in their classrooms had unnerved them. The teacher organised the wailing little ones herself, helped by a few of the senior pupils. She took them to the lavatories, where she washed their faces and hoped that establishing a routine would calm them. Her own face was haggard and dirty; tears had dissolved her mascara and the split on her lip was now an ugly swelling. She found a hand-comb in her bag and began to tidy the children's hair, lining them up in front of her. Straggling bows were re-tied, frocks smoothed down, and hands inspected. An atmosphere of false security pervaded them, emanating from the slight young woman they had known all their lives.

She never glanced near the guard; the one who had manhandled her the night before had gone. A sullen robot stood in his place, his eyes staring at and through her and the children. She had a horrible sensation of being watched by a machine. It was obvious that he didn't regard her or them as human beings. The sensation was more frightening than the frank brutality of his predecessor. She beckoned Caroline Camier and Pierre Farrière.

'Get the books out,' she said. She smiled at them both. The boy was twelve, sturdy and dependable, the eldest of five. His mother had been the woman shot outside the school the night before. He and Michelle Giffier knew nothing of this.

'Since we're here, we might as well work. Caroline, you look after the little ones; set them some drawing to do. Pierre, we'll start with history. See that everyone starts at page twenty-seven of book three. St. Jeanne d'Arc. It was always my favourite lesson. Go on now.' Steadily she began to read aloud. The door opened after half an hour; she stopped and got up. The SS Major was approaching. She saw the children's eyes following him as he came to her desk. He saluted her.

'Madame. In twenty minutes you must be ready to leave. Gather any clothes together and have the children ready.'

'Leave?' Michelle Giffier went white. 'Leave for where? What do you mean?'

'You are being taken to a place of safety,' the Major said smoothly. 'You have nothing to fear.'

It was the formula with which he had calmed anxious Jews, awaiting removal to the gas chambers. It didn't work with the school teacher. She supported herself on the desk with both hands and said loudly, 'We are not going to any place of safety. Either you let my children go to their homes or we stay here.'

Her injured lip began to quiver; hate and terror brought the tears and they spilled down her face. The Major gave a little smile.

'The outside of this building has been soaked in kerosene,' he said. 'Within half an hour I shall order it to be set on fire. You may stay inside with the children if you wish. You have twenty minutes. Heil Hitler.' He gave a casual salute and turned away. Outside in the sunshine, he yawned. He had dozed in the back seat of the armoured car, but only for an hour or so and his temper was irritable. The cattle truck had arrived and waited at the station. Already a crowd of parents had returned to the school, reinforcing the group who had remained outside all night. The recitation of the rosary infuriated him. He had ordered his men to break up the kneeling group, but some distance away they had reformed, and the low murmur of voices rose and fell all night. He was waiting for the Standartenführer before he could actually load the children into the truck and take them to the station. He had sent the execution detail on ahead to Chemire, where they were waiting. It was all well organised and ingenious. He took his seat in the armoured car and settled down to wait for his superior.

Louise had fallen asleep; she lay on her bed fully dressed, so exhausted that she didn't hear the car arrive. A hand seized her shoulder and shook her. She woke instantly and saw Régine bending over her.

'Wake up for God's sake!'

'What are you doing here?' Louise blazed at her. 'You filthy little bitch – get out!'

'Where's Jean? Where is he?'

'Why do you want to know? So you can tell your friend in the SS?'

'It doesn't matter what you say to me,' Régine said. 'Nothing matters but to help the children. That's why I've come. And keep your voice down. Vierken is downstairs!'

'You brought *him*!' Louise looked at her in horror. 'You brought him to St. Blaize! Well now you've done it, haven't you!' She turned away, overcome with despair. Jean and Savage were missing. If Vierken asked where they were . . .

'Listen to me.' Régine caught hold of her arm. 'Listen to me for the love of God! Minden came to the flat and brought Paul and Sophie – he told me what was happening! I came down to try and help. To plead with Vierken. He's my lover, I didn't believe he'd do anything to really hurt them.' She let go of Louise and hid her face in both hands. 'They're not going to Germany,' she said. 'They've dug a mass grave for them in the woods. They're going to be taken there this morning and murdered. I listened in on the telephone. He doesn't know I know.'

'They're not taking them to Germany?' Louise stared into the girl's face; her eyes were wild. 'They're going to kill them . . .'

'I told you,' Régine hissed at her. 'This morning. He's going down there now to send them off. For Christ's sake where is Jean? Someone's got to organise the village. They mustn't leave the school!'

'Jean has already organised a rescue,' Louise said slowly. 'He and Roger and Camier and others. But they're not expecting anything to happen till tonight. They're miles away from Chemire. Oh my God!' she cried out. 'What are we going to do?'

'I don't know,' Régine mumbled. 'I thought if I could tell Jean . . .'

'I'm going downstairs,' Louise said suddenly, 'I'm going to talk to him myself.' She stopped at the door. 'You'd better stay here,' she said. 'Keep out of this.' She went down the stairs; she felt calm, but icy cold. A mass grave in the woods. He had his back to her when she went into the salon; he was examining one of the family miniatures. He had taken it off the wall.

'Standartenführer Vierken!'

He turned round slowly, still holding the miniature. 'Madame? I was admiring the fine quality of this painting. Where is Régine? I told her to hurry.'

'Régine is upstairs,' Louise said. She walked away from him. 'You know what I'm going to ask you?'

'No.' He glanced up from his examination of the miniature. 'How should I know? Is this an ancestor? – of your husband's, I assume. Americans can't trace themselves that far.'

'I'll go down on my knees and beg you,' Louise said. 'Let the children go home. Whatever the village has done, punish the adults. Shoot as many of us as you like – but don't murder the innocent!'

'I don't think your kneeling would make any difference,' he said pleasantly. 'It might be amusing to watch, however. I'm usually amenable to pretty women. Like your sister-in-law, for instance.' His eyes considered her, dark with hatred and contempt. 'You don't believe it's going to happen, do you, Madame de Bernard? You think I'm bluffing, don't you? Régine does. Surprising, because she knows me very well. You think you people can kill Germans and sabotage our war effort and we won't punish you as you deserve? You'll know better next time. I'm going to make an example of this place.'

Louise stood with her back to the bureau. 'You must have children of your own,' she said. 'How could you do this thing?'

Vierken laughed. 'My children have nothing to do with it, it's your children who are going to be re-settled.'

'That's a lie,' Louise said slowly. 'I know what re-settled means. You're going to kill them. Put down that miniature – don't put your filthy hands on anything belonging to us!'

He half turned; the delicate seventeenth-century enamel smashed into the fireplace.

'Now,' Louise said slowly, 'either you let the children go home or I am going to kill you!' She held the old Comte's revolver in both hands. Vierken stood very still.

'You're being very foolish,' he said. 'You wouldn't hit anything with that.'

'You send a message,' Louise said, 'releasing them from that school. You've got a car outside. Write the order and your driver can take it. Now.'

'And afterwards?' Vierken asked her. His right hand was creeping inwards towards the holster at his side.

'Don't do that, Adolph,' Régine said from the doorway. 'She means it. She'll shoot.'

She walked into the room; her hair was brushed smooth and she had smeared a crimson lipstick on her mouth. She looked ghastly. 'Don't move,' she repeated.

'Do as she says. Send that note.' She didn't look at Louise, she was staring at Vierken. Her hands opened and closed at her sides. 'She'll shoot you – let them go!'

Vierken looked from her to Louise and then back to Régine. A smile of contempt twisted his mouth. 'Come over here,' he said in German. 'She can't shoot both of us. Be calm, sweetheart. Just take my gun.'

Régine walked up to him, she turned and faced her sister-in-law. 'I'm not going to let you kill him,' she said.

'Get back,' Louise cried out. 'Get away from him – he'll use you as a shield!' Régine didn't answer. She plunged her hand into the holster and brought out his revolver.

'Good girl,' Vierken said softly. 'Now step between us and give the gun to me . . .'

Régine looked at him and shook her head. 'No,' she said. 'No. You lied to me, Adolph.' She had stepped back and the black eye of the muzzle was pointing at his chest. 'I listened in on the telephone this morning. I know what you're going to do to the children. I know about Chemire.'

'You wouldn't hurt me, sweetheart,' Vierken said. 'You love me. You wouldn't shoot.'

'Send the message,' Régine said. Her voice trembled. 'Release them. For the last time, I beg of you . . .'

'Go to hell!' Suddenly his nerves snapped. 'They're going to be shot and buried! Every last one of them – give me that gun, you little whore, or I'll break every bone in your body!' As he leaped for her, the first shot cracked out. Louise screamed. There was a second shot and then a third. Vierken jerked backwards, his body jack-knifing as the bullets slammed into him at point-blank range. He crumpled and fell. Régine stood over him, firing repeatedly until the gun clicked empty. He didn't die at once. He twitched and choked, blood bubbling out of his mouth. His eyes opened, glaring and then suddenly they filmed over.

She stood and pulled the trigger. There was another useless click. Louise ran to her and wrenched the revolver away.

'Stop! Stop it, for God's sake!'

Régine fell on her knees beside him; she was moaning. 'Adolph . . . Adolph – oh God, oh God.' She held herself, rocking with grief.

Louise found the old servant Jean-Pierre standing in the doorway. He carried a little axe they used for chopping firewood. 'Madame – we heard shots . . . What's happened?'

'There's been an accident,' Louise whispered. 'Shut the door . . .'

'I had to do it,' Régine wept. 'I loved him but I had to do it. I couldn't let him murder the little ones . . .' She looked up and saw Jean-Pierre staring down at her in horror. '"They're going to be shot,"' she said. '"Shot and buried." When he said that I killed him.'

Louise caught hold of her. 'There's the driver outside,' she said. 'Get up, come away from here. Jean-Pierre, go and see if he heard anything!' She had half lifted Régine to her feet and was supporting her to the door. For a moment the girl pulled against her and looked back. There was no hysteria left in her; her eyes were dead.

'He called me a whore,' she muttered. 'I thought he loved me . . .'

'Come upstairs,' Louise begged her. 'Don't look at him any more. If you hadn't done it, I would have shot him . . . I wish to God I had!' The old man appeared beside them in the hall.

'The driver's still waiting by the car, Madame,' he said. 'He didn't hear anything.' The walls at St. Blaize were a foot thick. 'Is it true?' he asked her. 'Is she telling the truth – are they going to kill my grandchildren?' His mouth quivered.

'Yes,' Louise answered. 'I'm afraid it is. They're all going to be murdered. Unless I can get to the Comte in time.' She went to the window and looked out. Vierken's Mercedes gleamed in the sunshine; the driver leaned against the bonnet.

'I'm going to get that car,' she said. 'It's the only chance we've got. But you'll have to deal with the driver. There's a revolver in there.' She pointed to the salon. 'It's loaded. I must have dropped it. I'll send him inside. Make sure you don't miss!'

'I won't,' the old man said. 'Leave him to me, Madame. Marie-Anne, come here and take Mademoiselle Régine upstairs!' Louise ran down the steps and out into the sunlight. She went up to the car and the driver straightened himself.

'You're wanted inside,' she said. He turned and ran to the front door. She didn't wait to see what happened. She wrenched open the car door and slid behind the wheel. The keys were in it. She pressed the starter; it fired instantly, and a moment later the car skidded through the gates and swung onto the road to Lavallière.

8

The woods at Chemire were full of birds. At the approach of the execution detail that morning, they had risen from the centre of the wood in a mass, screeching in alarm, streaking off in all directions. About two hundred yards into the wood itself, the SS scout car came to a halt at a natural clearing. A lorry was parked nearby. Above their heads was a circle of open sky, on all sides the massive trees surrounded them; underfoot the ground was soft and black with leaf mould. There were five men. They carried the machine gun in two parts. In the centre of the clearing a rectangular pit had been dug about twenty feet long and eight feet deep. The earth was piled into a huge mound on the far side. A group of men were squatting near the pit, smoking and talking. They were in shirt sleeves, their arms bare; earth stained them.

It had taken them three hours to dig the pit. Past experience made them as quick as professional grave-diggers. They had stacked their shovels in a neat pile, and someone was boiling a metal coffee pot over a fire.

The noise made by the anxious birds continued for some minutes, while the SS NCO shouted directions to his five men. The machine gun was set up in front of a beech tree, its snout pointing at the yawning pit. To the execution squad it was a familiar routine. They had dug mass graves in Poland, in Russia, and in the makeshift camps set up for Eastern prisoners and Jews. They had shot and buried thousands of people of all ages and sexes. The cries of women and children had no meaning for them any more than the shrieks of the birds whose refuge they had disturbed. Some were married men with families; while they waited they joked among themselves and passed the time sharing cigarettes and talking.

Two men were occupied with a crossword puzzle. The NCO inspected the pit, decided on the placement of the gun, and then stretched out under a tree. He enjoyed the pattern made by the sunlight as it filtered down through the thick branches. The railway was about half a mile away. They would hear the train. It would take time to march the children across the fields and into the wood. Depending upon how small some of them were. He closed his eyes and let himself drift. It was a very warm morning.

One of the digging detail brought him coffee. He sat up and yawned, looking at his watch. It was nine o'clock. They were already late. He buttoned his uniform jacket, put his cap on straight and went to the edge of the woods, where he could see down to the railway line. There was no sign of the train.

The Major was also looking at his watch. He stood inside the doorway of the school, looking out onto the silent, sullen crowd. Behind him the schoolteacher and the children were ready. They waited with their satchels and books; a few were crying. He could hear them through the closed door and it irritated him. The Standartenführer was late. He had promised to be there in an hour, and it was already an hour and twenty minutes. The Major hesitated. The train was ready; the truck taking the children to the station was drawn up outside the school, surrounded by armed SS guards.

The longer he delayed in getting them out, the more the news of their removal was spreading through the village. There would be a crowd at the station. The Major smelled trouble. He was used to judging the temper of a crowd. He knew fear and indecision because he had seen it so often in the condemned. He also recognised revolt. He had been in charge of a group of Jewish and Polish prisoners once, when a riot broke out. Just before, he had seen a certain uniformity about the hungry, desperate faces. The same look was spreading through the crowd of men and women outside the school. The moment would come when they'd rush the lorry, regardless of the troops opening fire. And the Standartenführer had stressed his desire for an orderly operation. The Major made two decisions. He put the first into practice by going into the building. He came up to Madame Giffier. She was standing with an arm round two children who were in tears. He saluted her.

'Madame,' he said, 'it's time to leave. Before you go outside I have to warn you. There is a truck which will take you and the children to the railway station. There is also a crowd. If any rescue attempt is made, my men will fire. Not on the civilians but upon you and the children. I'm sure,' he said this with a slight smile, 'that you're not frightened for yourself, but equally you won't want those two you're holding now, for instance, to be shot dead. I want you to go outside and tell those people what I've told you. Warn them not to do anything to interfere with your departure. Tell them that their children will die if they move.' He opened the door and pointed with his cane. 'The responsibility is yours,' he said.

Madame Giffier looked at him. 'Where are you sending us? Tell me, before I go outside. Or I won't go.'

'To Germany,' the Major said. 'To a detention camp. Nobody is going to harm you or the children. But their parents must be punished. After a time you will all be released.'

'You give your word?'

'Of course. Go out and do as I've told you.'

She blinked in the strong sunlight; there was a loud anguished murmur from the crowd, and a movement towards her. It was checked by the SS using their gun butts.

'I've got something to tell you.' She raised her voice. 'For God's sake listen to me! We're going away in a few minutes. We're being taken to Germany but we're not going to be harmed. The children are safe and nothing's going to happen to them! But if you try and stop us going, they'll shoot the children! Don't make a move, don't try anything, for God's sake!'

There was a scream from the crowd. 'Janine – how's my Janine?' 'Pierre, Marie – are you all right!' 'Philippe . . .' 'Raoul . . .'

'That's enough.' The Major came beside her. 'Go back inside and bring the children out.'

'They're all right,' Michelle Giffier shouted. 'They're all all right, don't worry! I'll take care of them!' She turned back into the school. Inside, the ranks of children waited, faces upturned towards her. Tears made her blind and for a moment she faltered. It was Caroline Camier who saved her. She put her arm through the teacher's. 'Don't cry, Madame,' she whispered. 'We're not frightened. We'll be together.'

'You're a good girl,' Michelle Giffier said. She brushed her hand across her eyes and smiled; it was a painful grimace of her swollen mouth. The girl squeezed her arm. Her little face was set and stubborn; she was an ugly child who strongly resembled her father. She gave a look of hate at the Major.

'Children!' Michelle Giffier called out. 'We're leaving now. There's nothing to be frightened of, and we shan't be separated. We're going by train to a place where we'll stay for a few days and then we'll be brought home. File up in twos and do exactly as the soldiers tell you.' She turned to the Major.

'We're ready,' she said. This was the Major's second decision. Vierken had told him to move the children; that was more valid as an order than his remark about coming down to see them off. The Major's men were waiting at Chemire, the crowd were still subdued by the teacher's warning. He couldn't wait any longer and hope to avoid some incident.

'Good,' he said. He opened the school door. 'Outside!'

There was a group of SS about a hundred yards up the road. Louise saw them and for a second she braked. There was a motorcyclist and three men armed with machine pistols. They were at the side of the

road, stationed to stop anything travelling towards St. Blaize. Since
there were no private cars in use in the area and people travelled on
foot or by bicycle, no road blocks were considered necessary on the
subsidiary roads out of the village. The motorcyclist was enough. She
had little time to think; her first reaction of fear made her slow down,
the second was to slam her foot on the accelerator. If they chased her,
she would probably be caught; the way was narrow and she wasn't
used to the heavy car. But they wouldn't chase the Standartenführer's
private Mercedes flying its Nazi pennant, unless they had time to see
that a woman was driving it.

She gripped the wheel tight and pushed the pedal to the floor. All
she glimpsed as she roared past the group was a blur with someone
saluting. She rounded a bend and almost ran into the verge; it needed
all her strength to wrench the wheel back and straighten up. Then she
slowed, listening. There was no sound of a motorcycle. They'd seen
the car, and the driver was as much a blur to them as they had been
to her. Louise let the speed drop for a moment; her body was shaking,
and her hands were so wet that they slipped on the wheel. Lavallière
was only four kilometres away. She picked up speed again, guiding
the car round the bends and twists in the road; it hit a rough pothole
that jerked her out of the seat. Her mind kept trying to switch back
to the Château, to Vierken lying dead on the floor with blood seeping
out of his wounds onto the carpet; Régine, ashen with shock, weeping
for her lover. It was like a nightmare. It couldn't have happened; she
had a sensation of panic, imagining that it was all an illusion, that at
some point while she slept for those few hours, her mind had given
way and she had woken to a hideous hallucination. Panic came and
she fought it off; she opened the window and the rush of air was
calming. Lavallière; one kilometre. Less. There was the encircling belt
of trees that hid the open field. After they were married, Jean and
she drove out there and picnicked once. She suddenly remembered
the smell of the grass and the dappled light above their heads. She
braked, and stopped. When she got out there was complete silence.
She began to walk into the trees. If they had left the field already . . .
Nothing. No aircraft, no sign of life. A hand touched her shoulder;
she wheeled round with a cry. Albert Dumois, who worked in the
butcher's shop in St. Blaize, was standing in front of her, pointing a
sten gun.

'Madame!' He was staring at her. 'When I saw the car stop I nearly
shot you!'

'Where's the Comte?'

'Across the other side! There, under the trees, can't you see the
plane?' Now it was visible, shrouded under the camouflage net. Louise
didn't answer; she began to run.

It was Savage she saw first; he caught hold of her and held her for a moment. She pulled away from him.

'You've got to get to Chemire,' she gasped, breathless from that wild run across the field. 'You've got to go now! They're going to shoot the children!'

By now she was surrounded; Jean de Bernard pushed towards her. He spoke quietly to Savage. 'Let go of my wife. Louise – what's happened! How did you get here!'

'In Vierken's car,' she said. 'He came to St. Blaize, with Régine. Don't ask any questions, just listen! She'd found out they were going to murder the children in the woods; taking them on the train was just a blind. Oh God.' She stopped, and Jean reached out for her. For a few moments she clung to his hands. Then she stood back and faced them.

'There isn't time to tell what happened. They were moving the children onto the train this morning. If we don't get there in time they'll be shot and buried in Chemire.'

'You're certain of this? It's not a trick?' She shook her head at Jean.

'No,' she said. 'It's the truth.'

'How did you get Vierken's car?' Savage asked quietly. 'Where is he?'

'At the Château. He's dead; Régine killed him.'

'That's good enough.' Savage looked round at the group of men. The RAF pilot and his navigator had come to join them; they couldn't speak French beyond a few words and they didn't know what was happening. 'Camier, you and the Comte take four men with you and ammunition. We'll use the Mercedes. How long will it take to get to Chemire?'

'By the direct route, twenty minutes,' Jean de Bernard said. 'But there's a longer way round. It skirts St. Blaize, and crosses the railway line about three kilometres down. There's a little hand-operated crossing gate.'

'There'll be Germans manning it,' Camier burst out.

'Why should there be?' Savage spoke to him quietly. The man's face was contorted; he looked as if he might fall down with a stroke. 'They're not expecting trouble. Who usually operates it?'

'Servard,' the Mayor mumbled. 'Servard. He's over seventy; half the time he sleeps . . . God knows why there hasn't been an accident . . . Caroline . . . Oh Christ Jesus help me!' He dropped to the ground and covered his face with his hands. There was a sound of sobbing, harsh and inhuman in its agony.

Louise went to him and shook him by the shoulder. 'Don't do that,' she said. 'It won't help. We may be in time still.'

Slowly he raised himself; he wiped his face with the back of his hand.

'Pardon, Madame,' he muttered. 'Pardon. I was overcome . . .'

'How much longer by the railway route?' Savage turned to Jean de Bernard. The sight of Camier's collapse wasn't helping the morale of the rest of the men whose children were under sentence of death.

'Half an hour, forty minutes. Louise, how did you get through – weren't there any patrols, check points?'

'Only one; a motorcyclist and some SS I drove past at top speed and they didn't see me. They must have thought it was Vierken.'

'Then that's the route for the Mercedes. Jean, you go with Camier and take half the men with you in the van. I'll go with the Mercedes on the shorter route. If one of us gets stopped the other will get through,' He took a cigarette out and lit it; he handed it to the Comte.

'Camier drives, like last time. Go to the crossing and wait. If you're in time and the train stops to unload the kids, move in on them. If it's already done so, join us at Chemire.'

'And if we're too late?' Albert Dumois asked the question. He looked from Savage to the Comte. 'If they're dead, Monsieur – what do we do then?'

It was Jean de Bernard who answered. 'We attack and we kill every German we can find,' he said. 'None of us will survive, but if this thing happens, none of us will want to. Louise.' He reached out and took his wife's hand. He kissed it. 'God bless you. God bless you for your courage and resource in getting to us. Pray for us.'

'I'm coming with you,' she protested.

'No,' Jean said, 'you are not. You will stay here, with our friends from the RAF. Take good care of her, please.'

'Don't worry about that,' the young pilot said. 'But what's up? What's the panic?' In spite of his attempt at being nonchalant, he looked unhappy.

'We're going to get the children now,' Savage explained. 'The bastards are planning to murder them. Give us three hours, and if we're not back by then, get to hell out of here. And make sure you take Madame de Bernard with you.'

He didn't touch Louise. He raised the sten gun and saluted her. 'We'll get them,' he said. 'And we'll be back.'

Standing with the pilot beside her, Louise watched them running across the sunlit field and into the shadow of the trees. Minutes later, the sound of the Mercedes's engine was followed by the uneven rumbling of Camier's van. Then there was silence. The pilot looked uncomfortable; the woman was crying, and he didn't know what to do. He remembered the hip flask and quickly offered it.

'Drink this,' he said. 'It'll make you feel better – come on, don't upset yourself; there's nothing you can do about it.'

'Thanks.' Louise swallowed; the raw whisky made her cough. She wiped her hand across her eyes using the same gesture as Albert Camier. 'I'm sorry,' she said. 'It's just nerves. I'm all right now.' He had a young, worried face, its lack of comprehension suddenly infuriated her. She turned away from him.

'You're American, aren't you?' He had walked after her. He wanted company; he was personally brave in situations which he understood, but waiting around for three hours in German-occupied France while a group of inexperienced Frenchmen tried to attack the SS was not a contingency for which he had been trained. The navigator and gunner were back at the aircraft. The quiet, sunlit field and the surrounding trees was the most sinister place he had ever been. 'Where do you come from?' he persisted. 'How did you get here?'

'I live here,' Louise answered. 'I'm married to a Frenchman. They should have taken me with them. I can't stand this waiting.'

'It's pretty bloody,' he agreed. 'If the Jerries come I've got orders to set fire to the plane. You'll just have to run for it, I'm afraid.'

'It won't matter what I do.' Louise turned to him. 'One of their top men is lying dead in my house; my sister-in-law shot him. We're finished, whatever happens. And I don't care; I don't care about anything but saving the children. They've dug a mass grave for them in the woods.'

'Christ,' the airman muttered. 'You can't believe it, can you?'

'I can,' Louise answered. 'I can believe anything. Could I have a cigarette?'

'Don't worry,' he said. 'It'll be all right. Couple of hours and they'll be back here. Take the packet; I've got plenty more.' Louise saw him take a service revolver out of his jacket, load it and put it back. Together they sat on the grass under the shadow of the wings, to wait.

The engine sent from Paris was an old-fashioned steam locomotive, manned by a German army driver and two firemen from the depot. A single cattle truck was connected up behind. It was wooden-walled, creosoted black and the sliding door was drawn back. An SS guard stood at the entrance; he carried a whip of plaited leather. The first group of children climbed up unaided; a seven-year-old had to be lifted. The German swung him easily onto the top step. The boy hesitated and began to scream with fear of the darkness inside. The whip cracked as a warning to the rest to hurry up. The boy was pulled inside and only his persistent crying could be heard. Michelle Giffier was kept to the last; she stood near the Major, watching the pathetic file disappear into the black mouth of the cattle truck; she carried a five-year-old girl in her arms. Suddenly she turned to the Major. 'They won't be hurt – you promise?'

'My word of honour,' the Major said. 'Hurry up; we're running late and you have a long journey. There's food and water inside.' He saluted her. 'Heil Hitler.' She had a thin body, her clothes were creased and she looked dishevelled; she reminded him of many other women he had sent on a similar journey. The expendables, the inferiors, weeping Jewesses clutching their children and moaning, sections of humanity marked by nature for disposal by the strong.

The girl mounted the few steps and went inside. He gave an order and the door was dragged shut, its heavy batten secured. The cries coming from within were muffled. Three of his men climbed into the engine cab and stood with the driver. A third climbed to the roof of the cattle truck and crouched by the machine gun mounted on top. The Major gave a signal and the train lurched forward, hissing steam. Behind them, held back by a ring of SS guards, the people who had gathered at the station sent up a cry. The Major turned and addressed them.

'You've brought this punishment on yourselves,' he shouted. 'You know now the price of opposition to the Reich! Go back to your homes! Disperse or my men will open fire!'

There weren't more than twenty men and women; the stricken parents round the school had not had time to get there. Helpless, they began to drift away. Many of the women wept, the men looked back and cursed, a few waved their fists. One of the guards fired a burst over their heads and they scattered. The stationmaster had been locked into his office. Contemptuously they flung the door open; he staggered out. The SS piled into the lorries and drove off; their acceleration was an insult.

Down the line the rear of the cattle truck disappeared from view.

The group of men at the control point heard the car approaching. It was the Standartenführer's Mercedes being driven even faster than when it had passed them not long before. Automatically they saluted; it shot past them and the senior NCO peered after it. 'There must be something up,' he said 'He never drives like that. You, Fritche, go after him and see if everything's all right.' The motorcyclist kicked his machine and minutes later Savage heard the whine of its engine.

'They've seen us!' Dumois shouted. He was staring through the back window. 'He's coming after us! Go faster!'

'He'll catch up,' Savage said. 'Open your window – quick. Be ready, Albert, I'm going to slow down. Let him get close and then shoot him. Now!'

The Mercedes' red brake light showed so suddenly that the motor-cyclist found himself shooting towards the car; he slowed sharply. He saw something glint at him from the nearside window and made an instinctive movement to swerve, but the reflex came too late. A burst from Dumois's sten gun ripped into him; his machine reared up and then went spinning off the road as he fell.

'I got him!' Dumois shouted with exultation. 'I got him!' Savage didn't answer. He snapped his foot down on the accelerator and took the road which branched to the left towards the famous hunting ground and beauty spot, Chemire.

'Lie down, Mademoiselle Régine — I'll make you something hot to drink.'

'No,' Régine said. She sat on the edge of her bed, her hands gripped together on her lap. 'I'm all right, Marie-Anne. Leave me alone.'

'Jean-Pierre said I was to sit with you,' the old woman protested. She had known Régine since she was born; the face looking up at her seemed to belong to a stranger. It was grey-coloured, as bloodless as if she were dead; the eyes were dilated, the lips trembled, but she no longer cried.

'I've told you I'm all right. Go away!'

Régine didn't move for some minutes; she sat on the bed and twisted her fingers together. The first hysterical storm had subsided, leaving her sick and drained. He was dead. She had gone on firing at him until the gun was empty. If she closed her eyes she could see his face, changing to the ghastly hue of death, the jaw falling slack, one hand grasping his side, blood trickling between the fingers. Blood coming from his mouth. She gave a low cry, and then stopped. His body must still be downstairs. An awareness of danger crept into her confused mind; she got up and went to the door. It was an instinctive movement, without real direction. She couldn't go downstairs and see him lying there. She couldn't call Jean-Pierre and tell him to take the body away . . .

She opened the door and hesitated. Her father. Her father was upstairs; she could go to him, sit with him. When she went into his room, he was sitting in his armchair, a book open on his lap. He smiled when he saw her. Memory often deserted him at the first sight of someone, but never with his daughter. He held out his hand, and said, 'Come in, my little one. Come in!'

She bent and kissed him and his hand clutched at hers, like the claw of weak bird. Tears filled Régine's eyes.

'How are you, Papa? How did you sleep?'

'Not well.' He shook his head. 'There was so much noise last night. The Germans are coming but you mustn't be afraid.'

'I'm not,' she said. 'Don't worry about me.'

'I won't let them hurt you,' the old Comte said. 'I fought them once before – I can do it again . . .'

He stroked her hair, his hand tremulous, his attention flitting from subject to subject. Emotion distressed him, anger made his heart race, and he sank quickly back into tranquillity.

'It's very warm Régine,' he said. 'Take this rug away, will you? I don't need it.' She took the rug off his knees and folded it. She turned and looked at him. 'You look pale, my darling,' he said. 'Is anything the matter?'

'No,' Régine said. For a moment she had thought to find a refuge with him. But it was a child seeking a child. She came and kissed him. Love. Love for this gentle old ghost whose body was still earthbound; love that consumed and burned for a man whose brutal sensuality had corrupted everything else. Adolph Vierken. If his body was discovered, they would all be shot.

'I've got a few things to do downstairs,' she said. 'Then I'll come back and read to you.'

'Don't be too long,' he said. 'Come back soon.'

She found Jean-Pierre in the hallway. He was pulling the driver's body along by the feet; the effort was exhausting him. Régine paused, and then looked away.

'Did you do that?'

'Yes,' the old man said. 'The swine – I nearly blew his head off! My grandchildren . . .'

'We've got to get rid of him,' Regine said. 'And of the one in the salon. I'll help you with this one first.'

The driver was a big man, and his weight was too much for them. Régine called Marie-Anne. Blood streaked the stoneflagged floor from the German's shattered skull. The old woman didn't blanch or even turn away. She looked down at the body and spat. Then she seized a leg and began to drag. They didn't speak; getting him out of the house required all their strength. There was a long garden trolley, which Marie-Anne found, and heaving together they managed to get the German's body on it.

'This way!' Régine gasped. 'Down that path . . .' They dragged the trolley to the end of the garden path to the enormous heap of compost and leaf mould which had not been cleared for three years. Occasionally Minden's batman Fritz used to mow the lawns and tidy the kitchen garden, but there hadn't been a young gardener at St. Blaize since the war. The old man who kept the vegetables and weeded along the front of the Château was bent with rheumatism. Moving the compost heap was out of the question. Régine and Jean-Pierre heaved on the trolley and the body rolled off. They pulled it out of sight behind the mound.

Gasping for breath, with sweat running down their faces, the three of them paused. 'Now,' Régine said; her body was trembling with the exertion, and her clothes were sticking to her skin. 'Now let's get the other one. Marie-Anne, go in first and cover the face. I don't want to see it.'

Vierken seemed less heavy; the old woman had wrapped a kitchen towel round his head. Régine helped to half lift, half drag him without looking at him. She didn't realise that as she worked she was crying, the tears running down her face, her mouth screwed up with soundless sobs. Neither of the servants commented, even to themselves. Something terrible had happened to Mademoiselle Régine, but she was in command and they obeyed her.

At last the two bodies lay beside each other at the edge of the heap.

'What are we going to do?' Jean-Pierre mumbled. 'I can't dig a grave deep enough for them, I haven't the strength.'

'We don't have to dig,' Régine said. 'That's why we've brought them here. We'll move that earth on top of them. Three of us can do it. But first we'd better clean up the mess in the house. Marie-Anne, you go back and do that. Jean-Pierre, get two shovels. We'll begin on this.'

'Won't they come looking for them?' the old woman asked. Her husband was still out of breath.

'Nobody knew where he was going this morning,' Régine said. 'He was expected at the school; they're probably still waiting for him. Madame has taken the car. There's nothing to connect him with St. Blaize except me; I can say he went on to the school. They'll think he was ambushed – or kidnapped! Anyway, we've got to do our best. We have the Comte to worry about.'

'They'll murder him,' Jean-Pierre said. 'They'll murder us all, if they find anything.'

'They're not going to find anything,' Régine said. 'What's done is done,' she muttered. 'I've got to protect Papa now. Get the shovels!'

Albert Camier's van rattled along the road; the men crouched in the back were bumped and jolted. It was a narrow country road, not much better than a track, and it wound its way across country until it joined up with the railway line and intersected it at the little crossing. Jean de Bernard was seated beside Camier; he carried his sten gun across his knees, covered by his jacket. His shirt sleeves were rolled up and his tie removed. As they rounded a bend the railway line came into view, not more than a hundred yards ahead of them. The engine stood at the crossing, steam idling from it; the cattle truck was open. A single figure in uniform straddled the roof, leaning against a machine gun.

'Stop!' Jean de Bernard yelled, and Camier stamped on the brake.

For a moment they stayed immobile, staring at the scene; the old crossing keeper had seen the van and was moving slowly towards the gates to open them.

'Oh mother of Jesus,' Camier groaned. 'Mother of Jesus – we're too late!'

'The others won't be,' Jean said. 'They had the Mercedes and they took the short route. We've got to put these pigs out of action. There's three in the engine and one on the roof there. Drive forward and when you get to the crossing, stall the engine.'

The SS guard on the roof watched the van come close and trained the gun on it. Within his view, but hidden from Jean and Camier, a column of children was moving slowly across the field towards the dark lip of the wood at Chemire. It was a brilliant morning; the sun beat down upon the man on the wooden roof, making the metal parts of the gun hot to the touch. His collar was tight and a ring of sweat stained the edge; he ran one finger under it, his right hand crooked round the trigger of the machine gun. The van bumped over the level crossing and then stopped. The old keeper shuffled forward, waving his arm. 'Go on,' he shouted. 'You can't stop there – this train is leaving any minute!'

Inside the van Jean whispered to Camier. 'Get out – he knows you. Open the bonnet and fiddle inside. I'll follow. Don't do anything, just keep your head down.'

'Ah, good morning,' Serard saluted the Mayor. 'What's the matter – trouble?'

'Blasted thing's falling to pieces,' Camier muttered. 'I'll just have a look . . .' He threw up the bonnet and dived under it, pretending to grab at engine parts with shaking hands. He heard the van door open and a moment later Jean appeared beside him.

'I'm going to get the one on the roof,' he whispered. 'Stay where you are and for Christ's sake don't put your head up when it starts . . .' Then he was gone. He went to the rear of the van and opened one door. Inside the men huddled against each other stared at him from the dimness. 'Grenades,' he said softly. Two were passed to him; they went into his jacket pockets. 'A pistol; I can't hide the sten.' It was handed to him and disappeared under the jacket.

When Jean reappeared he saw the crossing keeper leaning beside Camier, looking at the engine. There was a shout from the train; the Army driver leaned out and yelled at them. 'Get that moving! Push it!'

Jean looked up at him and shrugged; the SS guard behind the machine gun was looking directly down at him. He slipped his hand in his pocket and found the sectioned surface of the grenade. He walked round the front of the engine, which placed him out of sight, and then, crouching, ran round the side of it. He pulled the pin on the first grenade, released the side catch and tossed it towards the cab. At the same moment he straightened and aimed his pistol at the man on the roof. The guard was not looking directly at him, his attention was focused on the van. Jean de Bernard sighted him; not daring to aim for the head in case he missed, he fired at the trunk. The sound of the shot cracked out, and he dropped on one knee. The blast of the grenade knocked him to the ground; there was a short stuttering burst of machine gun fire, the hiss and rattle of metal tearing and spinning lethally through the air. By now the van doors were open and the men inside were spilling out. Dazed, with his ears buzzing, Jean picked himself up. Above him the engine was hidden in smoke and blackened fumes; the cabin was shattered and as he watched, a dismembered arm, still wearing a rag of uniform sleeve, fell out and hit the ground. On the roof of the cattle truck, the SS guard lay forward, depressing his machine gun; he moved, and Jean de Bernard shot at him a second and a third time. He fell sideways and tumbled off the roof on the other side. Jean ran back to the van; he called to one of the men standing around it. 'Climb up and make sure they're finished inside that cab! Albert . . . Oh God!'

The Mayor of St. Blaize had fallen backwards; the burst of fire from the machine gun had sprayed the area in front of the train as the dying German pressed his trigger, and instinctively Camier had left the shelter of the van and tried to run. He had been cut down by a dozen bullets ripping into his chest. Serard lay riddled on the roadside a few feet away. Jean de Bernard knelt beside Camier. For a moment his eyes opened and he was conscious. Blood frothed in his mouth. 'Caroline,' he choked, and then his eyes rolled up and he died.

'There they are! Look, over there!' A hand seized Jean de Bernard by the arm and shook him. He looked, following the man's excited gestures.

Across the fields the dark caterpillar crawled, its pace the stumblings of the youngest who were still too big to carry. The man who had seen them burst into tears. 'We're in time, in time . . . Oh my God, my darling, we'll get you!'

Jean de Bernard didn't hesitate. He slapped him across the face.

'Get into the van!' he ordered. 'See if it's been damaged – if you can drive it, back it off the line and onto the road. Go on! Now.' He turned to the others. 'There are our children. Look, they've heard the shooting!' Larger figures could be seen running up and down the lines, and the procession began to hurry, faltering and uneven though it was, they were being made to run towards the woods.

'We've got to stop them!' There was a shout from the men.

'Wait,' Jean bellowed at them. 'Stay where you are, you fools –

you can't shoot it out with them while they've got the children!
Keep calm!'

There was silence then, except for the spasmodic bursts of steam
from the engine. The van suddenly began to rattle as its engine turned
and fired. It eased backwards away from the railway line and pulled
up on the road.

'We can follow them,' Jean said. 'Spread out, and keep low. For
God's sake, I know your children are out there, but you've got to keep
your heads. If Savage has got through he'll be waiting for them in the
woods. If not, then we'll try and pick them off one by one. Separate
now and run; we've a hell of a way to go to catch them up!'

Chemire covered an area of about forty acres; as he approached the
edge of the wood by the road, Savage slowed down. He spoke to
Dumois, who was so excited by the death of the motorcyclist that
he couldn't stop talking about it. 'You know the woods,' Savage
said. 'Where could they bury the children? Looks as thick as hell
to me.'

'On the other side,' Dumois said. 'There's a track about two hundred yards up, it goes through the middle to a clearing. It's a place
for picnickers and courting couples. There's nowhere else which isn't
stiff with trees. Poachers hide in there during the season and nobody
can flush them out. Turn up here – here's the track.' Savage put the
Mercedes into low gear and they began to bump through a rough
pathway between the trees.

'How far?' Savage asked.

'Another five minutes or so.'

'We stop here.' He got out, closing the door quietly. The little group
surrounded him; even Dumois, who was carrying his sten gun at a
rakish angle over one shoulder, was subdued. It was very silent, with
the feeling of oppressiveness and menace which is common to all
woods whose tenure of the land goes back for centuries. The ground
was soft and green with moss; tracks stretched ahead of them, rutting
deep into the friable dark earth.

'They're up ahead of us,' Savage said. 'There are two sets of tyre
marks there; one looks like a small lorry. From now on we don't
make a sound. They won't be expecting anyone but they're no
fools. They're professionals and if they hear anything, we'll never
get within spitting distance of them.' He looked at his watch. 'It's
ten o'clock,' he said. 'We made it in very good time. The children
won't have got here yet. Check your weapons; Dumois, picking off
a motorcyclist doesn't make you a crack shot, so don't get over-
confident. I'll go in front and you follow in file. Walk carefully, and
don't talk.'

'How do you know the children aren't already dead?' That was a heavy-set man whose name Savage had never learned. He looked tough and morose; his hands were huge and coarse and they gripped the sten gun like hams. Misery made him resentful of the stranger.

'I don't,' Savage snapped back. 'And there's only one way to find out. Come on!' He unslung his sten gun and began to walk, treading with catlike care, avoiding the branches which were lying on the path, dry and cracking underfoot. The rest began to follow. The man who had questioned him made the Sign of the Cross and began to mutter. He had three children, two nephews and several cousins among the victims. He hadn't prayed for thirty years.

The SS NCO had posted a lookout on the edge of the wood. He saw the train pull up at the crossing, and the children trickle out of the cattle truck. The men aroused themselves and the machine gunner began checking his weapon. The NCO decided he had time for a cigarette before the distant line of figures reached them. He went back into the wood, leaving his men to report on their progress. He ordered the fire under the coffee pot to be put out, and all uniforms to be properly fastened. He went over to inspect the machine gun. The sound of the grenade exploding and the short stutter of gunfire brought him running to the edge of the wood. Below him the train stood still, smoke pouring from the engine cab. He had a pair of field-glasses; seconds later they showed him the van and the men jumping out of it. Two were lying dead, and the machine gun on the roof of the truck leaned forlornly with its nose down.

He swung the glasses to the file of children. They were running, urged on by three guards, one of whom was using his whip. There was a woman with them, stumbling with a child in her arms; when she slipped there was a moment of total confusion. She was struck and kicked to her feet, the child torn out of her arms. For a brief moment the glasses held her and the scene and then swung back to the train's attackers. They had dispersed and were running after the file of children. The NCO shouted orders; his men came running, their weapons ready.

'They've bombed the train,' he said. 'There's five of them down there and they're on their way up here. Two of you take positions behind the trees. They won't catch the little bastards up, but as soon as you can get them in range pick them off!' He put the glasses up again; the children were within three hundred and fifty yards by now; he could hear shouts and cries. Some of the burial detail came out of the wood to watch. It was the machine gunner, wiping the barrel with an oily rag, who looked up and saw Dumois moving through the trees.

Savage knew they had failed when he heard the guttural yell. He froze behind a tree. They had crept up without making a sound, inching their way through the trees, guided by the voices. The burial pit gaped only a few yards in front of them, and the machine gunner caressed his gun, wiping the barrel with a rhythmic stroke. Then Dumois moved, shocked into forgetting that by now the trees were thinner and anything slipping between them could be seen.

The burst of fire caught him sideways on; Savage saw him spin completely round, both hands flung upwards, the sten dropping away from him. He gave a fearful scream and fell, blood spurting from terrible arterial wounds.

The SS training was superb; within seconds every man in the group had taken cover, the NCO was behind a big beech tree and the machine gunner crouched swinging the muzzle from side to side. Savage picked out a man lying flat on the ground, sheltering behind a trunk of beech with a fissure running down the side of it. He dropped to his knee and took aim.

'Come out!' It was shouted in French. 'You haven't a chance, we've got you all covered. Hands up and come out!' He looked over his shoulder and could see three of the men who had come with him, sheltering behind the trees, pointing their sten guns. They looked amateur and clumsy; Dumois was dying noisily only a few yards away from them. Savage slung his sten gun over his shoulder. He made a gesture to the three of them: stay where you are. Don't move. He felt quite cool, the chill of rage settled on him, as it had done when he killed Brühl. He took a grenade from his pocket, pulled the pin out, slipped off his jacket and held it in one hand. He held his sten by its sling in the other. He raised his voice. 'Kamerade! Don't shoot!'

Then with both hands raised to shoulder level, he stepped out from the shelter of the trees. They saw a big man, blond in the brief sunlight, and as he emerged into the clearing, he threw his sten gun away. The NCO stepped from behind the tree; he held his revolver pointed at Savage. His intention to shoot him was obvious.

'Don't shoot,' Savage cried out. 'I surrender!' Under cover of the jacket, his thumb pressed the three-second release catch on the side of the grenade. As the German pulled the trigger, Savage threw it at the machine gun.

The blast tore the gunner to pieces and dropped the NCO who caught it full on. Almost at the same moment, the three Frenchmen ran into the clearing, firing wildly and indiscriminately; the big labourer leaped over Savage's body and the mangled machine gun, he caught two of the SS in his fire and dropped them. A third killed him, and was exposed in doing so. The other two of Savage's men shot him together. Then they flung themselves behind trees, and the first grenade fell in the direction of the remaining SS composed of the grave-diggers, two of whom had been wounded by cross-fire. Screams followed the explosion; the younger of the two Frenchmen, a chemist's assistant, who had done military service and been wounded in the back and invalided out, yelled to his companion and a barrage of grenades fell into the trees around the area. For three minutes they threw, and the forest was shattered by explosions. Wood splinters and human fragments flew; dust covered the clearing, blotting out vision. Then there was no more sound. The chemist's assistant, who was named Pellissier, and had twin sons, slowly came from behind his tree. There was a groan from the left. He gestured to his companion to follow; moving very carefully he approached the sound. For a moment he disappeared from the other's view behind a clump. There was a short burst of fire and then he stepped out. The two men looked at each other. 'We got them,' Pellissier said slowly. 'They're all dead now.'

He dropped his sten, and went to Savage.

The NCO's bullet had caught him in the chest; its impact had thrown him to the ground just before the grenade exploded. The blast had concussed him, blood was staining the front of his shirt.

'He's dying,' the second man said. 'If he hadn't got that swine with the machine gun . . .'

'I don't know how bad the wound is,' Pellissier said. He had opened the shirt and was swabbing with a handkerchief. 'I've nothing to dress it with. Don't move, friend, for God's sake, you've been hit.' Savage had opened his eyes.

'Get the kids,' he said. 'Never mind frigging about with me.' He spoke in English and neither of them understood. His eyes closed again. Pellissier took off his own shirt and tore it in strips; he bandaged Savage's chest, but within minutes the dressing was soaked through. He shook his head. 'I can't help him,' he said. 'It's no use. We'd better go and look outside the wood.'

At the first sound of firing, the SS had halted the column of children. Michelle Giffier was sobbing, embracing the children nearest her. One of the guards yelled at her. 'Shut up! Shut up, you bitch, or I'll smash your jaw!'

The firing in the wood was suddenly interrupted by a series of explosions. The children began to scream. The senior SS guard, a man in his forties with service in the East and a corporal's rank, bellowed at them to lie down. Michelle ran among them, dragging them to the ground.

'You!' the corporal shouted. 'Come here!' He seized her by the arm, pulling her in front of him. The sound of fighting in the wood had stopped. The children were crying and moaning with fear. The corporal looked back down the field to the train. There was no sign of the men who had attacked it. The ground was uneven; they might well be within range of him and hidden by the terrain. He had twenty children, one trembling woman as a human shield, and only two men. He swore, and jerked savagely at the woman, in his rage. He cupped a hand to his mouth and yelled, 'Comrades! Show yourselves! Are you all right up there!' There was no answer. No one appeared.

Somehow the French had discovered their plan and mounted an attack. The silence showed him that it must have been successful. They were waiting for him in the wood. Behind him, the attackers of the train were moving after him. If he obeyed his common sense and abandoned the brats, he would be shot for cowardice and disobeying orders. Discipline was merciless. His only salvation was to carry out his orders as much as he could and then run for it. He made up his mind. He shouted an order in German to his two subordinates. 'Start shooting the little bastards – then we'll make a run for it!'

It was part of Michelle Giffier's youthful curriculum to know two foreign languages. She understood and spoke both English and German. He flung her aside and she fell. As she watched, he grabbed his machine gun. She gave a wild scream and with a speed and strength that was beyond her frail physique, she sprang up and threw herself on him.

He was a powerfully built man, trained to a high pitch of physical fitness. He would have thrown a man off in one movement. The ferocious woman who attacked him drove her nails into his face, raking for the eyes, the gun went off, and it was a moment or two before he swept her aside and smashed his elbow into her. As she fell, Jean de Bernard came over the rise in the ground and shot him. The children lay sprawled on the ground. The two SS men were on their feet; both were dead before they had a chance to fire, killed by Pellissier and his companion who had come out of the wood above them.

For a moment nobody moved; Jean de Bernard stood with his gun slowly pointing downwards. Michelle Giffier lay in a heap by the dead German. Then he walked forward, joined by the rest of his group; one of them gave a cry and began to run. Jean de Bernard stopped by a small child, who knelt on the ground hiding its face and sobbing with terror. Very gently he lifted him up. It was the child of Dumois, whom he did not know was dead. 'Oh, oh,' the boy wept, and flung his arms around his neck.

'It's all right, little one,' Jean said gently. 'It's all right. You're safe now. You're safe . . .'

The navigator and the gunner were conferring with the pilot. He walked over to Louise. 'Look,' he said, 'it's three hours. There's no sign of them.'

'Please,' Louise begged him. 'Just a few more minutes . . . they'll be here! You can't leave without them!'

'Your chap gave me the time limit; I ought to start the old girl up and get us out of here.' He frowned and looked at his watch again. Louise had taken turns in watching by the roadside from the shelter of the trees. No traffic at all had passed in the last hour.

'I'm not going,' Louise said. 'I'm staying here. What will you feel like if you take off and you see them coming back with the children?'

'Oh for Christ's sake,' the pilot said. 'I'll give them another fifteen minutes and then I'm off. We're going to get the nets off her.'

'Thank you,' Louise said. 'I know they'll come.' She started pulling the camouflage netting down. It had seemed like days while they waited. They had nothing to say to each other; it was a relief to wait, hidden, by the roadside, praying that every motor sound was either the Mercedes or the van. Once a military ambulance raced past her, and she had given way to momentary panic. Chemire was miles away, and nearer to St. Blaize than the Lavallière field. They wouldn't send an ambulance along that route. Twenty minutes later it returned, travelling more slowly. Inside, the dead body of the motorcyclist was strapped to a stretcher. There were so many injuries that the bullet wounds which had sent him spinning off his machine were not obvious on the first examination.

When the plane was free of camouflage, the pilot turned to Louise. He looked awkward but determined. 'Five minutes to go,' he said. 'I'm going to start her up. I'll help you inside.'

'No!' Louise backed away from him. 'I'm going to look again . . .' She ran into the trees before he could stop her. The road was deserted; she leaned against a tree and suddenly all hope left her. They had failed; Jean and Savage, Camier and the others. They had been butchered and the children were already tumbled in the grave at Chemire . . . The Mercedes came into view first. Then a small German lorry, its canvas sides and body marked with the Iron Cross, followed by a small field car and then last of all, rattling as if it were going to fall to pieces on the road, came Camier's little delivery van. Louise ran into the road; behind her there was a roar as the aircraft propellers began to turn in the field. She waved wildly at the Mercedes, tears blurring her sight of who was driving, and then dashed back into the belt of trees, shrieking at the pilot to stop . . . stop . . .

Within the shelter of the trees the cavalcade jolted to a stop. Louise came running back, followed by the airmen. The first person she saw was Jean de Bernard; she threw herself into his arms. 'Oh Jean – Jean, thank God! I'd given up! The plane was leaving . . .'

The Comte kissed his wife. 'Don't cry,' he said. 'We got them all; they're all safe. Come and help get them out.' Children were being lifted down from the inside of the German lorry; they came tumbling out of Camier's van. The men who had rescued them were calling for their own sons and daughters; Pellissier found his twins and knelt on the ground, hugging them, openly crying with relief.

'Papa – papa . . .' The cries were repeated as fathers and children were reunited. Michelle Giffier, her face so bruised and sallow with shock that Louise hardly recognised her, watched the scene, with a wailing toddler by the hand.

'Madame Giffier – what did they do to you? Come here, little one.' Louise tried to take the child. Instantly it clung to the teacher with both hands, its face screwed up in terror.

'I'm all right,' she said. 'Thank God none of the children was hurt. Don't make that noise, Ninie, there's nothing to be frightened about now . . . Oh Madame, I can't tell you what might have happened . . . In the clearing they'd dug a huge pit for us . . .' She turned away and Louise saw her shudder. She spoke calmly but hysteria was very close. Louise put an arm round her. She was a proud, self-contained woman who would have resented the intimacy in other circumstances. Now she burst into tears on Louise's shoulder. 'It was so terrible,' she said. 'The firing, I thought we'd all be killed. And then one of them was going to open fire on us – just at the last minute!'

'Don't think about it,' Louise said. 'You're going to England with the children. They'll be safe there till the war's over. Get them together and we'll lift them inside. Come on; the pilot's got some whisky. I'll get you some.'

The plane stood out in the field, clear of the trees. 'Children,' Jean de Bernard called, 'line up and come over here. You're going in the aeroplane with Madame Giffier.'

Shepherded by fathers and the teacher, the children formed a queue; many were too dazed to understand what was happening to them. Others began to cry and protest. There were heart-breaking cries. 'I don't want to go – I want Maman – Maman!' One boy broke free and had to be caught, struggling and kicking against being lifted into the plane. Jean de Bernard came to Louise.

'It was Savage who saved them,' he said. 'Pellissier told me. He deliberately sacrificed himself.' Shock robbed the scene of reality; she didn't say anything for a moment. Jean didn't touch her.

'He's dead?'

'He's dying,' he answered. 'He wanted me to leave him behind.'

Louise moved back from him. 'And you did?'

'No, he's in the scout car. He's going back on the plane.' She turned and ran, back into the belt of shadow where the car was standing. A man who was the notary's clerk in St. Blaize was bending over someone on the ground. Louise pushed past him. Savage lay with his head on a folded jacket; his shirt had been cut away and Pellissier's blood-soaked bandage replaced. His face was grey and cold with sweat, his eyes closed. The notary's clerk got up and made way for her.

'He's been asking for you, Madame,' he said. 'I was just going to call you.'

'Go away,' Louise whispered. 'Please, go away.' She caught at the slack hand lying by Savage's side. 'Oh God,' she held it tight and her tears fell on him. He opened his eyes; there was a glaze over them which cleared as he recognised her.

'It worked,' he said. She had to bend close to hear him. 'We got every child back. And we killed all those bastards . . . I take it back about the French . . . they were bloody marvellous.'

'Don't talk,' Louise begged him. 'Please, don't say any more. Lie still . . .'

'That son of a bitch knew how to shoot.' Savage grimaced. 'I love you – can you hear me?' '

'Yes, yes, I can hear you.' Louise felt a pressure from his hand.

'I'm not through yet. He's a good guy, that husband of yours; but he made a mistake. He should've left me behind . . .'

'You're going home,' Louise said. 'You're going on the plane and you'll get proper care – oh darling, don't die – I couldn't bear it . . .'

He didn't seem to hear; his eyes had closed. Suddenly she felt his hand tighten on hers. 'Louise . . . I'll be back. Remember that.'

She felt Jean de Bernard come behind her; she turned round to him, still holding Savage's hand, and as he watched she bent and kissed it.

'He must go now; the plane's ready.'

'Be careful,' she said. 'Try not to hurt him . . .' She saw them lift him; he was unconscious and her last sight of him was masked by the navigator who reached down from inside the plane to lift him up.

At the edge of the field she waited in the little group of men, as the propeller turned and then idled, turned and then swung into full power. The noise was a hideous assault, the airstream tore at their clothes and sent them staggering, holding to each other for support. Fathers with children waved and shouted; Jean de Bernard put his arm around her and held her steady. The plane was taxi-ing fast down the field, bumping and lurching over the uneven surface; suddenly its nose lifted, and the clumsy progress became a smooth, miraculous ascent into the sky. The machine rose steadily, easily topping the trees, climbing until it became smaller and smaller and the noise of its engine a distant throb.

Nobody spoke for some moments. Men who had seemed extraordinary, with guns on their shoulders, slipped back into their normal selves. They looked upward, disconsolate and lost without their children. Out of the ten who had started out from St. Blaize, six were left. The notary's clerk blew his nose and found a packet of cigarettes. He came and offered one to the Comte and more hesitantly to the Comtesse. Louise refused. Jean de Bernard inhaled into his lungs. He wiped his face with his forearm and looked round at them.

'Our children are safe,' he said. 'Whatever happens to us, they'll have their lives and they'll come back to St. Blaize when the war is over. That is what matters.'

'What do we do now?' Pellissier asked him. 'Where do we go?'

'Home,' Jean de Bernard said. 'Home to collect money, food, everything we'll need for the next few months. We have two alternatives. We can wait at St. Blaize for the murder squads to come and pick us up, or we can go into the countryside and fight. Thanks to the British we have guns and ammunition. We have the lorry and that car. We may not last long but we'll give some account of ourselves.'

'I'll go with you,' the clerk said. He was a gentle, precise man who usually wore wire-rimmed spectacles. 'And me,' Pellissier said. One by one, with one exception, they came and shook his hand. The lone dissenter also shook it.

'My wife is ill,' he said. 'I can't walk out and leave her. I have to make sure she's all right with her sister. If I can join you, Monsieur, be sure I will. But I have to look out for her first.' He came and shook hands with Louise; the others followed.

'I'll stay here,' Jean de Bernard said. 'The rest of you go back to St. Blaize in the van and take my wife with you. Pick up what you need and come back here as quickly as you can. There won't be much time before they realise what's happened at Chemire. When nobody reports back they'll start searching. We have an hour or two start.'

He threw the cigarette away.

He turned to Louise; they were alone, as the others dispersed and somebody started Camier's van. 'I thought you would have gone with him,' he said.

'No,' Louise answered. 'I'm staying here; with you and Papa and Régine. The children are in Paris, they'll be safe there. But I loved him, Jean. And I'll never know what happened to him.'

'I know you did,' the Comte said. 'Thank you for staying. God knows what the end will be for us all. Will you take care of St. Blaize and Papa and Régine for me?'

'You know I will,' she said. He took her hands and held them. Tears came into his eyes.

'At least now you can be proud of me,' he said.

'I will always be that. God bless you, Jean. Come back to us.' She came close, and for a moment they held each other.

'I don't want to say goodbye,' Jean de Bernard said. 'So just go with them now, my darling. Just go . . .

Louise pulled away and ran to the little van; the passenger door was flung open for her and she jumped inside. She sat, tears running down her face, refusing to look back until they came to the edge of the road. Then suddenly she couldn't bear it. She leaned out of the window, staring back through the trees. It was too late to see him. There was nothing visible but shadow.

They were all silent. Paul was standing in front of the fireplace, looking down at the ground; there was a frown between his eyes; his wife was sitting with her hands clasped on her lap, staring at Louise. Suddenly Sophie got up, flung her cigarette into the fire and went over to her mother. Louise glanced up and felt her daughter's arm slip round her shoulders.

'All right,' Sophie said. 'Now you've told us. What a hell you must have gone through. All of you.' She bent down and kissed her.

Louise's eyes filled with tears. 'Thank you, darling. I hoped you'd understand.'

'Perhaps it's easier for her.' Françoise de Bernard spoke in a strained voice. 'Sophie wouldn't mind anything coming out – she hasn't got a family and a position to think about. But we have!' She faced Louise. 'What about Paul and the election? What in God's name would his enemies make of a story like that? His father was a collaborator who only resisted at the end – his aunt was the mistress of that dreadful butcher . . .' She stopped suddenly, both hands to her mouth. 'Oh my God – under that big rockery – is that where those bodies were buried?'

'Yes,' Louise answered quietly. 'I'm afraid so. They're still there.'

'Oh my God! It's horrible!' Her daughter-in-law was sheet white. She stared at Louise, 'And you lived here – knowing that!'

'Let's keep it in proportion,' Paul de Bernard said. 'Forget about the rockery. After all these years there's nothing left there anyway. What you've told us, Mother, is exactly what that woman Minden hinted at. Only worse. She didn't know that Régine murdered that man Vierken.

'They'll bring it out that you slept with that German, and that's why he risked his life to save your children,' Françoise said. 'They'll make it as sordid as they can. Two of you, you and Régine. Nobody will believe it was only once – you know what people will think . . . We'll be disgraced, Paul's career is as good as over now, if even a whisper of this gets out.'

'I don't believe that,' Paul said. 'They've nothing to gain by dragging mother through the dirt. All they want is a case for mitigating the sentence on Minden, something to prove he was personally humane. Saving Sophie and me is just what they need. They'll concentrate on that. Nothing else need come out in court at all. Don't worry about it, Mother.'

'I think we're trying to delude ourselves,' Louise said. 'That woman threatened to bring every detail out in court. And in telling the story of what Heinz Minden did, she'll see that my part in it, his relationship with your father, Régine and Vierken, everything will be exposed. I believe she'll do it. If she's told the defence council all this, and I refuse to testify, they'll have to make a big drama out of it to emphasise his heroism. But if I go to court, I need only say that he was fond of you both, and risked his own life to save you. My presence there to speak for him will have tremendous impact. That's why not even an affidavit will satisfy them. I shall have to go and give evidence at the trial.'

'No you won't!' Sophie said loudly. 'You're not going near any court! How do you know what they'll ask you when you get up on the witness box – what do you think the prosecution's going to try and make of this? They'll tear you to pieces! As for you, Paul, if you let her do this, I'll never speak to you again! To hell with your political career – Mother's not going to be sacrificed.'

'I shall be sacrificed anyway if the truth comes out,' Louise said to them all. 'I could bear that, but not to see you hurt, Paul's future destroyed. Your father's good name smeared. He was a hero, decorated for his work in the Resistance. To hear him called a collaborator would break my heart. To see your Aunt Régine's memory disgraced . . . I can't do it. I knew that even before I came down here, but I suppose I was hoping to escape. I'll have to go to Germany.'

'No!' Sophie interrupted. 'I won't let you!'

'I think you've made the right decision,' Françoise said. She stood up, and linked her arm through her husband's. 'Paul would never ask you, but I know how much his political career means to him. I know how hard he's worked for St. Blaize, and this would ruin everything for him. The whole family would be disgraced. As it is now, the Comte is a hero, his sister a Resistance heroine, killed fighting the Germans. Please, please let us keep this between us. Go to Germany and speak for this man. Otherwise we're destroyed.'

'No, Mother,' Paul said. 'Don't do it. Not for me. I'll withdraw my candidature. Then they can say what they like. It was a very long time ago. People won't be all that interested if there's no political capital to be made out of it. It'll soon be forgotten.'

'I've made up my mind,' Louise said to them. 'There's nothing else to be done. I'll telephone Ilse Minden in the morning.' She smiled at her son. He looked strained and guilty. His arm was still linked to his wife's, and as she watched, Louise saw them clasp hands. They were in agreement, and she couldn't blame either of them. Paul had built his own life at St. Blaize; whether Louise and she had little in common or not, didn't denigrate the efforts of Françoise to be a good wife and to advance his chosen career. Louise might not like her, but she appreciated her loyalty to her husband. And she even understood the shock and condemnation which the younger woman hadn't been able to conceal. She had been brought up in the post-war world, married into a family with a reputation for heroic resistance in the late war, and had never imagined that all was not exactly as it seemed. In Françoise's conventional world, people did not fornicate and kill, or invite a German into their bed, however patriotic the motive. She glanced up at her daughter, and saw with a pang that the face was pale, the mouth taut. Sophie had been shaken too, although she was too loyal and protective to her mother to reveal it. Not by the infidelity, but by the unconsummated love for Roger Savage. Instinctively Louise knew that to Sophie that love was a betrayal of the father she had loved so deeply, and knowing this had hurt her.

'Thank you,' Françoise said. Her tone was final, discounting any possibility of second thoughts. 'I know you've made the right decision. Now let us go and have some dinner.'

She led the way out of the salon, into the panelled dining room. It was a silent meal, and immediately afterwards Louise excused herself and went upstairs. At the door she turned and said gently to Sophie, 'Come and say goodnight to me.'

'Of course.' Love flowed between them; forgiveness was implicit in the way her daughter squeezed her and the kiss she gave was warm. 'I'll look in,' she said. 'If you're asleep I won't disturb you. Goodnight, darling. And don't worry.'

But when she came Louise was wide awake. It seemed to Sophie that her mother looked much younger suddenly, sitting up in the bed with her hair hanging down like a girl's, her face slightly in shadow.

She must have looked like that during the time when Roger Savage was at the château. She had always been aware of her mother's beauty and elegance; now, with a sense of shock, she recognised the sexual quality that distinguished her. Louise held out her hand.

'I'm glad you came; come and sit beside me. You're hurt and disappointed, aren't you?'

'Not about Minden.' Sophie brought out the Gauloise packet and lit a cigarette. She had chain-smoked throughout the evening.

'You did the right thing. But the American – I was surprised, that's all. I never thought for a moment you'd ever looked at anyone except Father. You seemed the most devoted, loving couple.'

'And we were,' Louise said quickly. 'After the war when he came back, so terribly hurt and helpless, I realised that I had always loved him, And we were happy, right to the day he died. You know that.'

'I know,' Sophie said. 'You did everything for him. I used to watch his face when you came into the room. It was quite something to see. I suppose I knew I'd never be able to affect anyone that way. Maybe that's why I've never wanted to get married. It would never be like that for me. That's what I thought.' She blew smoke into the air. 'I'd like to ask you something. If you don't mind?' She glanced at Louise, awkward and anxious not to hurt her.

'You can ask anything you like,' Louise said gently.

'Did you ever see Roger Savage again?'

'Yes,' Louise answered. 'For months I thought he was dead. Your father was fighting, the Allies were advancing. Régine and I were here with your grandfather. I couldn't forget the last time I saw Roger. I was sure he'd died, even on the journey. I went through a very bad time, Sophie. I wouldn't have left your father while there was any danger, and I'll answer one question I know you won't ask me; I never had an affair with him. But I loved him. I loved him with all my heart.'

'Poor Mother.' Sophie reached out to her. 'How awful for you. Don't talk about it any more. It doesn't matter.'

'Months later I got news that he was alive and recovering. He'd been sent back to America. And then he came to St. Blaize.' Louise paused. 'You wouldn't remember it, but you saw him arrive. I can see you now, running into the hall, calling for me. And he followed behind you. I sent you out into the garden. He'd kept his word. He'd come back for me.'

'And you didn't go,' Sophie said. 'But you wanted to, didn't you?'

'Yes,' Louise said. 'He wasn't an easy man to refuse. When he wanted something he got it. But I didn't argue with him, Sophie. I just took him into the salon and showed him your father sitting in the garden in his wheelchair. He understood why I couldn't ever leave him. He left here and I've never heard from him since. That's many years ago.'

'It's sad,' Sophie said. 'Terribly sad for both of you.'

'I never regretted it,' Louise said. 'Your father was happy. That's all that mattered.'

'Darling,' Sophie said suddenly. 'Don't go to Germany. Never mind about Paul and his bloody silly election. Don't put yourself at these people's mercy. I really mean it. I'm afraid of what could happen to you.'

'Nothing will happen to me,' Louise said. 'I'll give my evidence and it'll all be over very quickly. Then I'll come straight home.'

'I'll come with you,' Sophie said. 'But I have a very nasty feeling about the whole thing.'

On the 3rd of October, exactly two weeks after Ilse Minden had come to the house in the Rue de Varenne, Louise took the Lufthansa flight to Bonn. Normally she found flying peaceful; unlike many women whose nerves objected to the speed and altitude in jet flying, she was relaxed and calm in the air. On this journey she spent the hour and ten minutes in taut discomfort, wishing she had allowed Sophie to come with her. The more she tried to convince herself that the ordeal would be minimal, the more uneasy she became. Minden's wife had been brief and non-committal on the telephone. She didn't thank her for agreeing to help, or say anything but that Minden's lawyer would be in touch with her. The letter, signed Siegfried Kopner, had arrived within three days; it was friendly and courteous and said all the grateful things which Ilse Minden had omitted. Temporarily Louise was reassured. Paul and Françoise accepted the tone of the letter with relief; only Sophie was sceptical. The affair with Gerard was coming to a graceless close; there were rows and mutual walk-outs, and Sophie looked pale, and had lost weight. Louise refused to have her travel to Germany. She had installed her in the Rue de Varenne, where she could escape the importunities and tantrums of her lover, and promised to send for her when the trial began. At Bonn airport she found a uniformed chauffeur waiting with her name written on a card. He bowed and spoke in clumsy French, 'Herr Kopner's compliments and I'm taking you to your hotel.'

The gesture was unexpected. So too were the flowers she found in her hotel room. Welcome to Bonn. Siegfried Kopner. It was a luxurious hotel, the Steigenberger Hof; smartly decorated in modern style without extremes of taste. She dined alone in the large dining room, watched by groups of business men who interrupted their conversations and negotiations long enough to admire the elegance and beauty of the new arrival. She felt lonely and conspicuous, more of an alien in the atmosphere than she had ever felt before, and since Jean's death she had travelled every spring. Her last trip had been to Mexico. She was neither shy nor self-conscious about going anywhere alone; but in the heavy chic of that German hotel dining room, Louise felt a sense of total isolation. The food was excellent, the service impeccable; she ate very little and didn't look round her. A large middle-aged man at a nearby table was staring at her openly. There was an appointment with Siegfried Kopner for the next morning at eleven. If it wouldn't inconvenience her, he preferred the meeting to be in his office.

This country and these people, clean, efficient, polite, were the background of Heinz Minden, who had worked on a project to kill millions, and yet risked himself to save two children of whom he had grown fond. It was the birthplace of Adolph Vierken.

It was impossible to fault them or to explain the feeling of disquiet which was increasing. Perhaps it was the reflex of the war, of years spent equating the sound of German with tyranny and fear. Perhaps the sight of that schoolhouse ringed with armed men, and the huge empty pit at Chemire, which she had gone to see after the Allies took St. Blaize in their advance, had prejudiced her for ever. She didn't know the reason, but she found it very difficult to sleep that night.

The next morning was crisp and sunny; she went for a walk, hoping to admire the city. The charm of the old University City was being eroded, its shape deformed by modern buildings, post-war constructions without beauty or tradition, but there was no attempt to hide its affluence. The cars were sleek and expensive, the shops full of luxuries, priced very high. She found nothing to admire except the weather, which was beautiful. At ten-forty she found a taxi and went to Kopner's office on Hofgarten Strasse.

It was a twenty-storey block, built in granite and glass, and it glittered in the sunshine like an iceberg. His office was on the nineteenth floor; she went up in a soundless lift, arriving in seconds without any sensation of having moved at all.

A smart, attractive secretary showed her into a private waiting room. It was sparsely but beautifully furnished in contemporary style, and there was a fine Klee drawing on one wall. She lit a cigarette and waited. She insisted, almost angrily, that there was no reason to be nervous.

Her watch showed that she was early, by three minutes. At eleven o'clock exactly the secretary came in, smiled and said, 'Come with me, please. Herr Kopner is expecting you.'

He was a tall man, with receding fair hair and bright blue eyes, soberly but expensively dressed, and when they shook hands, he smelt strongly of toilet-water. He made no attempt to hide his admiration. He kissed her hand and gave a little bow. 'This is a great pleasure, Comtesse. Please come and sit over here. Cigarette?'

Louise took one out of the handsome aluminium box and he was beside her immediately with a light. The smell of his toilet-water or after-shave, whatever it was, was overpowering.

'I am delighted to meet you,' Siegfried Kopner said. He had great confidence in his capacity to charm, and he exerted it to the limit. He thought the American woman exceptionally attractive; he had a weakness for good legs, and hers were beautiful, showing discreetly under the dark sealskin coat. Feet also appealed to him; hers were

narrow and high arched, clad in hand-made calf shoes. He looked at
her and smiled. No wonder poor Minden had made a fool of himself.
If she was this striking now, how much more at that time . . .

'Thank you for the car,' Louise said. 'And the flowers. It was very
kind of you.'

'I hope your hotel is comfortable?'

'Yes, it's very nice.'

'I have all the data for the defence here,' Kopner said; he laid his
hand on a thick hessian folder. 'I saw Heinz Minden yesterday and I
told him you would be coming. He was very grateful.'

'I want to help if I can,' Louise said. 'Could you explain exactly
what the charge against him is?'

'Certainly. He's accused of crimes against humanity in that he was
working on a nerve gas, which is a weapon outlawed by the Geneva
Convention. Unfortunately experiments were carried out upon political prisoners in the early stages of testing the formula, but my client
was not concerned with the development of the gas until after this
had happened. Otherwise, I'm afraid we would not have any defence
to offer.'

'No,' Louise said. The image of a woman, clasping a child in her
arms as she died in terrible convulsions, passed through her mind as
he spoke. 'No, you couldn't possibly defend that.'

'Believe me, Madame de Bernard, I wouldn't try.' He leaned towards
her earnestly. 'I assure you, I abhor the crimes committed by the Nazis.
It's because I know that Heinz Minden is an honest man who was
misguided, that I've agreed to take his case. You must believe that.'

'I'm sorry for him,' Louise said. 'He was never a bad man, Herr
Kopner. He had human feelings; that's more than you could say for
some of the others.'

'Adolph Vierken?' He said the name with a slight smile, a suggestion
of sympathy, on his mouth. 'A monster; a psychopath. Every country
in the world has them, but it was just Germany's misfortune to be
ruled by the biggest madman of them all. I must say, Frau Minden's
story is a little hard to believe. Would you mind if I asked you some
questions?'

'No. If you feel they'll be helpful.'

'In order to make the most of your testimony, Madame, I must have a
clear picture of the facts, all the facts, in my mind. Then the prosecution
can't spring any surprises. Not, I assure you, that your evidence will be
contested. Now, may I ask you something very personal – was Heinz
Minden in love with you?'

'Yes,' Louise answered quietly. 'He was.'

Kopner cleared his throat. 'His wife says that you had an *affaire*
with him. Is that true?'

'He made love to me once; that was all.'

'I see.' Again he cleared his throat. He half rose from his desk, holding the cigarette box towards her. Louise shook her head.

'May I ask you how it happened?'

'I'd rather not discuss it. It hasn't any relevance to your case.'

'I understand,' he nodded. The look of friendly sympathy had never left his face. He watched her with caution, even with respect. One night. She didn't want to give the details. She could refuse to answer now, but when they were in court . . .

'And your sister-in-law Régine de Bernard – she was killed fighting for the Resistance, wasn't she?'

'Yes,' Louise said. 'She was acting as a liaison for my husband's group, when she was stopped by an army patrol outside Chartres and shot trying to escape.'

'Yet according to Frau Minden, she told Heinz Minden that she was not only Adolph Vierken's mistress but that she was in love with him. Is this the truth? I have to ask you these things, Madame, because I have only Frau Minden's word, second hand from her husband. He won't discuss any of it, even with me. I have to be sure she's not exaggerating.'

'She's not,' Louise answered. 'It is perfectly true. When Vierken disappeared and Régine discovered what he had planned to do to the children, she changed completely. She became a patriot.'

'His disappearance has always fascinated me,' Kopner said casually. 'But then the Resistance knew how to hide their victims.'

The word victim stabbed at her, sharp with warning. She looked into the blue eyes and saw nothing there but friendliness, good will.

'I'd hardly call Adolph Vierken a victim.'

Kopner mentally kicked at himself. Hard. This was not a woman to be treated carelessly. She was far too intelligent; and not afraid to speak her mind. He was unused to being corrected so sharply and a little colour came up under his well-barbered skin.

'An unhappy choice of words,' he said. 'My English is not as good as I would wish. What was the relationship between Heinz Minden and the rest of the family? Did he get on well with your husband, for example?'

'Very well,' Louise said. She took a cigarette out of her case and lit it, forestalling him by seconds. 'He was very generous at a time when we could get very little of anything; he was friendly and never intruded. My husband liked him. He used to play with the children and even go up and sit with my father-in-law. He was an invalid and rather senile. Everyone liked Heinz Minden in the house.'

Yes, Kopner thought, watching her, everyone except you. You didn't like him and it shows by the way you speak. You're trying to be sorry for him, to be impartial. But you hated him; you used his love for you, and because of that love he endangered his life to save your children . . .

'Would you ever have described him as a typical Nazi? You know the type, arrogant, bullying?'

'No, never. He was a quiet man, anxious to be friendly.'

'Good,' Kopner said. 'Excellent. And you will say all this in court? You will speak of him as you have done to me?'

'If you want me to, yes. Because it's the truth. He was like that.'

'When did your husband die, Madame?'

'Ten years ago. Why do you ask?'

'Just for my file,' Kopner said. 'He was a very brave man, highly decorated, wasn't he?'

'Yes. He was shot in the back during a battle with a German patrol, and he spent the rest of his life in a wheelchair.'

'Heinz Minden thought very highly of him,' he said. 'He often talked about him to his wife. He described him as a man of peace.'

'And so he was,' Louise said. 'He always hoped to find a reasonable solution to any problem. He hated war and he hated the waste of life.'

'So it was really the SS action against the children that changed him?'

'Yes it was. It changed the whole village, overnight.'

'Overnight,' he repeated. 'Naturally. What an unspeakable crime – it's almost incredible that my countrymen could contemplate such a thing. To murder children. Madame de Bernard, I would like to say something to you.' He stood up; it was a little theatrical as if he were facing an audience.

'I think it is wonderful of you to come and give evidence on behalf of a German, after what happened at St. Blaize en Yvelines. It shows a truly generous spirit.'

'I owe it to him,' Louise said quietly. 'I didn't want to come, to open up the past again. But he deserves to be judged on the good as well as the bad. There is one point I would like you to clarify, Herr Kopner. My evidence will consist only of an account of how he took my children from the school and brought them to Baroness de Cizalle in Paris? Nothing else will be mentioned?'

'Nothing,' Kopner said. 'You will be asked for those details and nothing more. Anything else we have discussed is quite irrelevant. You can be assured of that.'

He pressed his intercom button and spoke in German. A woman's voice answered him. 'I have ordered you a taxi,' he said. 'I'll take you down to the front hall.'

'That isn't necessary,' Louise protested. She didn't want to stand about with him, making small talk. 'I know you're terribly busy. Please don't bother.'

'It will be a pleasure.' He took her elbow and walked with her out of the offices into the passage. The same atomic type lift shot them to the ground floor, and there, drawn up by the pavement, a taxi cab was waiting. He took Louise's hand and made the obligatory pretence of kissing it. 'One thing,' he said. 'Would you be prepared to see Heinz Minden before the trial? I can get permission.' She hesitated. The idea of going to a prison to see someone who must now be an old man repelled her. Kopner looked as if he expected her to agree.

Despising herself, Louise said, 'If it would help, but I'd rather . . .'

'Thank you,' he said quickly. 'I think it would help him. I'll arrange a visiting time and telephone you later. This evening – about eight o'clock?'

'All right.' Louise got into the taxi. 'Would you tell him to take me back to my hotel, please.'

He closed the door, made her a little bow, and spoke rapidly, and in a brisk tone, to the driver. He waved his hand a little as she drove away, and then vanished back into the building. She knew, without being able to rationalise it, that agreeing to see Heinz Minden was the first mistake.

At twelve-thirty Siegfried Kopner left his office. He used a taxi rather than the chauffeur-driven Mercedes which was garaged in the basement of the office block.

He had decided to let the Comtesse de Bernard find her own way to the appointment; the same quirk of meanness which smoked the disgusting cigarettes, resented saving her money on taxi fares. Being met at the airport and greeted by flowers in the hotel should surely be enough to make the right impression. His reason for not using his own car was different; he didn't want anyone to know where he was going. Chauffeurs talked; so did secretaries. His appointment was extremely confidential. He arrived at one o'clock at a large house in the Venusberg district, a smart residential complex, with large expensive houses and gardens. He ran hastily up the steps of a big red sandstone house, built within the last ten years, and disappeared inside. Nobody saw him go in; it was the lunch hour and his compatriots were devoting themselves to eating lunch. Meals in Germany were a serious ritual. It was almost more important to enjoy food than to enjoy life.

The house was heavily furnished, mahogany and gilt, ugly pictures, a massive bronze equestrian group in the hall. He was shown in to a study by a manservant, who didn't ask his name. A man, slightly built, with white hair and a proud face, rose from an armchair and came to meet him. They shook hands. Kopner was stiff, deferential. For a moment or two his host kept him standing. They discussed the weather for two or three sentences, paying tribute to some convention that would not allow them to mention their real business immediately. Then the old man asked him to sit down.

'We will have some wine,' he said. 'And we lunch in fifteen minutes. My wife and family are unfortunately not at home.' Kopner, who had not expected anything else, expressed regret. The man he had come to see was one of the most influential politicians in Bonn.

'Well, Herr Kopner,' he said. 'What happened this morning?'

'I had a very useful interview with the lady,' Kopner said.

'And what sort of impression will she make in court?'

'Exactly what we want. She is extremely attractive, very poised. The contrast between her and Minden should strengthen our case. She admitted that they had been lovers. Also that her sister-in-law was the SS commander's mistress. She described her husband, the Resistance hero, as a man who hated war and always sought a compromise whenever possible.'

'That's very encouraging,' the old man said. He had poured a glass of iced Riesling for Kopner and a slightly larger one for himself. He sipped it, showing appreciation. 'I hope she didn't suspect what line your questions will take?'

'I'm sure she didn't. We parted on friendly terms and she has agreed to see Minden. I'll arrange a visit tomorrow morning. She didn't want to go, but I persuaded her.'

'And you think that's wise?'

'I think the newspapers will make a very interesting item of it,' Kopner said. 'After all, here is a man accused of war crimes, being visited in prison by the Frenchwoman with whom he was in love during the war. A wealthy lady with a title, prepared to come and testify for him. That alone will blur the public image of a Nazi murderer.'

'Not the tabloids, I hope. We mustn't have sensationalism at this stage.'

'The *Frankfurter Allgemeine Zeitung*. Very respectable. There will be foreign syndications, of course.'

'I look forward to reading it.' A smile flitted over his mouth and then disappeared. 'I have great confidence in your ability, Herr Kopner. If you can manoeuvre this case in the way that our party wants, your political future is assured. You have my word on that.' Kopner bent forward from the waist; it was difficult to bow when sitting down, but he accomplished it.

'My one wish is to serve my country,' he said. 'I have lived with shame and reproach all my life, and I have refused to deny my pride in being German. It's time what happened in the war was seen in its true perspective. The vindictive hounding of men for doing their duty in defence of their country has gone on unchecked for all these

years. If we can gain an acquittal for Heinz Minden, or a suspended
sentence, there may be an end to these trials. And a political rebuff
to the people who advocate them. It's time we stopped hiding from
the past, and cringing before the world. What happened at St. Blaize
en Yvelines was a military operation, a so-called atrocity, which in
fact never took place, and Germans are vilified while the people who
collaborated and battened off them are described as heroes. There will
be no heroes left by the time this case is over. Just let me get Madame
de Bernard into the witness-box.'

'That, my dear Herr Kopner,' the old man said quietly, 'is what we
are waiting for. Now let us go in to lunch.'

Bonn prison was a dark stone block, situated in the old part of the
city. It was approached by electrically operated gates, and guarded by
armed men. Kopner had collected Louise at nine that morning, and
passed the short travelling time in explaining to her that she would
find Minden very much changed. She was annoyed and embarrassed
by the sympathy in his tone, as if he were preparing her for a reunion
which must by its nature be a painful one. Without saying so, he
conveyed the impression that her relationship with Minden had been
more prolonged than the single incident she had described. Her discomfort changed to dread when they passed through the gates, Kopner
being quickly recognised and admitted, and were actually within the
precincts of the prison itself. It was horribly oppressive, dingy and
impersonal, a dungeon for the mind as much as the body. More
electrically operated gates, more men with dour faces in grey-green
uniforms, horribly reminiscent of men she had known years ago,
with the same harsh look of authority. Then they were in a small
room, with a plain table and two chairs, lit by fluorescent lighting.
The walls were painted a dull slate blue; the effect was chilling and
metallic. She turned to Kopner. 'What a dreadful place – how long
has he been in here?'

'For two years.' The bland face smiled at her. She thought suddenly
that to this pleasant, highly cultured man, there was nothing offensive
about the stone cage in which his fellow men were shut away. A warder
opened the door; there was a brief conversation between him and
Kopner, and when he returned a moment later he brought a third
chair. 'Sit down,' Siegfried Kopner said. 'They've gone to bring him
up. I'm afraid smoking is forbidden.' There was a large notice on the
wall, printed in Shcrift, of which the prohibition of smoking was only
one of the rules.

Louise sat down; the chair was wooden and hard. She gripped her
handbag tighter than she realised, and waited for the door to open.
When it did, she didn't recognise the man who came in, a warder

behind him. He was quite short, whereas her memory of Heinz Minden was of a tall man, well built. His hair was grey and his eyes sunken into his face. Kopner came towards him. He spoke to him in German, and then in French. 'Here is Madame de Bernard. She's come to help you.'

Louise stood up and slowly they approached each other. He looked at her without saying anything. She held out her hand, and after a second's pause he took it. His hand was dry, and it trembled.

'You shouldn't be here,' Heinz Minden said, and the voice was the same. 'This is no place for you.' He let her hand go and turned to Kopner. 'You shouldn't have done this. I told Ilse and I told you. I don't want Madame de Bernard mixed up in this.'

'Sit down,' the lawyer said. 'Madame de Bernard wanted to come. She wanted to see you. For old times' sake.' He turned away and walked over to the notice. His back was to them, leaving them alone as far as he could.

'How are you?' Louise said at last. 'How are you bearing up?'

'We'll sit down,' Heinz Minden said quietly. 'I only have twenty minutes; they don't count this as a legal visit. They're very strict about visitors.' He shook his head suddenly; the hair was very white. 'I won't see Ilse today; I'm only allowed one visit a week.'

Kopner spoke without turning round. 'You'll see her tomorrow. I got special permission for Madame de Bernard to come.'

'I'm going to give evidence for you,' Louise said. 'I'm going to tell them how you saved Paul and Sophie.'

'They told me,' he said. Now the eyes were fixed on her; they were bright in the prison-grey face, and the look in them was the same as it had always been. She had a sudden flash of understanding for his wife. 'You're as beautiful as ever,' he said. 'You haven't changed at all. How are the children – they're grown up now, of course, but I still think of them as they were . . .'

'Paul is married, he has two children. He lives at St. Blaize now. Sophie isn't married; she's very modern about these things.'

'That's a pity,' Minden said. 'The world is changing. I haven't seen my sons since I was arrested. But my wife has been very loyal to me. I wish you'd go home!'

'I can't,' Louise said quietly. 'You need my evidence. I want to give it.' Now, having seen him, it was true. On an impulse she put out a hand to him, 'Don't worry about me,' she said. 'Your wife told me you'd had a very bad time since the war. I was so sorry things turned out like this for you.'

'You shouldn't be,' he said. 'I deserve it. Me and people like me who supported them. I've had years to think about it. I deserve to be punished.' Behind him, Siegfried Kopner's back went stiff.

Minden looked at Louise and smiled slightly. Old and physically broken, he had a strange dignity. 'I am quite resigned to what will happen,' he said. 'It is very kind of you to try to help me. But any human being would have done what I did. I was very fond of your children. And of you. I never forgot you.'

'If you lie down, you'll be walked on.' Siegfried Kopner spoke suddenly. His voice was cold and he looked impatient. 'If you go into that court and hang your head and ask to be punished, you'll stay in here for the rest of your life. One letter a month, one visit every three months. Solitary confinement as a special case. Madame de Bernard! For God's sake, try and convince him that he's got to fight. He wasn't responsible for what he was making – it was a weapon of war!'

'Gas was forbidden under the Geneva Convention,' Minden said. 'You know that, Herr Kopner. It won't do you any good to defend me. You'll be accused of sympathising with the Nazis. Enter a plea of guilty, let Madame de Bernard go home to her family, and leave me in peace!'

'Think of your wife and your sons,' Kopner urged him. He shrugged in Louise's direction. 'He mustn't take this defeatist attitude. He will be his own worst enemy.'

'Try not to give up,' she said. 'What's done is done now. And Herr Kopner said in the car coming here he thought you'd get a suspended sentence. That wouldn't be too bad.'

'Herr Kopner is an optimist,' Minden said. 'Tell me, how is the Comte?'

'He's dead,' Louise said. 'He died ten years ago.'

'I'm sorry to hear that. He was a good man.'

'Yes,' Louise said. 'He was.' They both heard the door open, and the warder come into the room. He spoke to Minden, who got up.

'You have to go now,' he said. He held out his hand, and she shook it. He didn't bow, or kiss it. He was very much changed.

'I am glad to have seen you,' he said. The moist brown eyes gazed at her and the years fled. 'But if you really want to help me, don't listen to Herr Kopner or my wife. Go home. Stay away from this. And God bless you.'

Then he was gone. Kopner came to her side. 'He's been here too long,' he said. He sounded a little brusque, as if he were trying to minimise what Minden had said. 'He's given up hope of justice.'

'Perhaps,' Louise answered him slowly, 'perhaps it's justice that he wants.' They walked out of the main building in silence. As they reached Kopner's car, Louise had an impression of a group of men converging on them from the gates. Seconds later the first photographer ran up and snapped his camera in her face.

Sophie looked at her mother's old friend Raoul Delabraye. She had dismissed him for years as a dull, conventional man, plodding on in pursuit of Louise. She had made fun of him and worried in spasms in case he persuaded her mother to marry him. She remembered that morning when Ilse Minden came to the Rue de Varenne, he had just telephoned to take Louise to the Opera and she had made a slighting remark about him. Now, sitting opposite him in the Ritz lounge, she saw why Louise liked him, and why he was her most regular escort. Grey haired, very well dressed, impeccable manners and a gentle voice; none of these appealed to Sophie who saw them as varieties of stuffiness. But there was strength and reliability; and kindness. She had come to ask his help and she felt ashamed of her intolerance. She carried a copy of *Le Monde*.

'Have you seen this?'

'Yes,' Raoul said. 'There was another photograph in *Figaro* and the story was worse. "Comtesse to defend war criminal." It was almost libellous.'

'It's terrible,' Sophie said. 'The whole slant that's been put upon it is making Mother look like this bloody man's mistress. As if they'd been lovers! I'm very worried for her, Raoul. I felt I had to come and see you – you're such an old friend.'

'What can I do?' he asked her. 'If she'd told me, I'd have done my best to stop her going there. I don't trust these people; a war crimes trial is a very nasty business. I wish you'd come and told me before – why didn't your brother go with her? I can't understand it.'

'My brother is so terrified of being connected with it, Mother wouldn't hear of it. He did offer, I must admit that. But she was blackmailed into going; that's why she didn't tell you. Minden's wife threatened her if she didn't give evidence. And because of Paul and his career, Mother gave it. I'm going to fly to Bonn tomorrow; the trial opens the day afterwards, but I feel she needs a man there with her. I want you to come with me.'

'What was the blackmail? Can you tell me?'

'No,' Sophie answered. 'I'm sorry. But it doesn't reflect any blame on Mother. You must believe that.'

'Knowing her as I do,' Raoul said, 'I couldn't believe anything else. I've been thinking about this story. It must have been a planned leak to the press. Somebody wanted the spotlight to turn on Louise, and show her in a certain light. And you're right, my dear. She is going to need help. Would you pour me some tea – I'm afraid it may be cold. We quite forgot it.'

'I'm sorry, I wasn't thinking.' Sophie poured him a cup and some for herself. Tea at the Ritz was a pleasant ritual, enjoyed by little groups of people sitting in the handsome lounge. Silver, fine porcelain and delicious small cakes; an atmosphere of placid elegance. Sophie lit a cigarette. 'Will you come?'

'Of course,' he said. 'But I don't think I'm the one to help in this. Moral support won't be enough. When she goes into that court she's going to need more than a faithful old friend sitting in the background. Neither of us, my dear Sophie, are what she needs. We weren't at St. Blaize, we've nothing to contribute. She will be at the mercy of the prosecution; perhaps even of the defence. I know this man Kopner's reputation. He's an ambitious politician, a self-publicised lawyer who's putting himself up for election to the Bundestag. He's undertaken this man's defence because it's going to be a major trial and he will be centre stage. The very thought of Louise being in the hands of such people horrifies me. No; I won't be much help to her. But I know exactly who would. And I'm sure he'd come to her, wherever he is, if he knew what was happening.'

'I don't understand,' Sophie said. She had flushed, without knowing why. Even before she heard the name, she had tensed up against it.

'Roger Savage,' Raoul Delabraye said. 'The man who was there at the time. And he is a lawyer too.'

'How did you know about him?' Sophie said. She crushed out her cigarette. 'Why did Mother tell you?'

'Because he is the reason she won't marry me,' he said quietly. 'Or anyone else. She still loves him.'

'She loved my father,' Sophie said. 'That other man was years ago. She can't still care about him. It's not possible.'

'I wish I could agree with you. I've been in love with your mother ever since I met her, but I know I haven't got a hope. I've learned to be content with being her friend. And as her friend I know she needs this other man to help her now. It will be ironic, don't you think, for me to bring them both together?'

'He's probably married,' Sophie said angrily. 'He won't care what happens to someone he knew all that time ago. Men aren't that faithful.' She had a painful memory of Gerard as she said it. He had left her life as abruptly as he had come into it. Without the courtesy of goodbye. She was not hurt, she insisted, only angry. He had also left her apartment in a filthy mess. Then she thought of something. 'You'll never find him,' she said. 'Roger Savage wasn't his real name. It was the name of Mother's cousin, who'd died.'

'It was his wartime name,' Raoul said. 'I have a very good friend in the State Department. I'm sure he could find him for me. He received a decoration for his work against the Germans. I think we'll manage it, between us. And in that case, I should go now. I'll put in a call to Washington when I get home; the time difference is about right.'

'If he does come back,' Sophie said, 'and he isn't married . . .'

'I will lose what little of your mother I have now,' he said gently. 'But if it saves her being hurt in any way, then it is worth it.'

Sophie stood up. She despised the social habit of kissing on the cheek; she held out her hand.

'I take it back,' she said. 'Some men are faithful. I suppose I've been picking the wrong ones.'

'Go to Bonn and look after her,' Raoul Delabraye said. 'And try not to worry. Say nothing to her about this. Just leave it with me.'

The court was full; when Louise, Sophie holding her arm protectively, came in to take her seat, there was a loud hum of interest; people turned to stare at her. The trial had been in progress for four days. On Kopner's advice, Louise stayed away until he decided it was time to call her evidence, and she was only too relieved not to be present. The newspapers and German Television carried daily reports. Minden's chances looked poor; the prosecution had made out a damning case against him. His participation in Brühl's hideous project was established earlier than the six months he had spent on the staff at Château Diane. He had been engaged on research work the previous year, although not part of the team which had operated in Auschwitz. His membership of the Nazi party was lifelong, his record of allegiance to it unswerving. For years he had lived in hiding, fully aware of his criminal record. The prosecutor was a flamboyant personality, who was presenting the court with a picture which Louise herself knew to be grossly exaggerated. The Minden she had known at St. Blaize bore no relation to the callous Nazi fanatic portrayed at the trial. On the morning when her own evidence was to be given, there was an early telephone call from Siegfried Kopner.

'Just to assure you, Madame de Bernard,' his voice said briskly. 'You needn't be nervous. I will see you in the court. My car will come for you at nine o'clock.'

Before she had time to ask any questions he had said goodbye and hung up. The court was a large one, decorated in pale green; the panel of three judges and six jurors sat on a raised platform at the far end. The chair for witnesses was to their left. It was the first thing she saw, apart from the crowded rows of seats. At the entrance to the Criminal Court itself, they had run a gauntlet of photographers; Sophie had swung her shoulder bag at one who tried to block their way. Shaken, Louise hurried into the building, where they couldn't follow her, and was met by one of Kopner's clerks. She took her place in the front of the court on the defence side. It was pointed out, politely, that Mademoiselle de Bernard would have to sit in the body of the court. Louise sat down, and immediately Siegfried Kopner came beside her. The same flowery toilet water smell enveloped her; she leaned a little away from him.

'I open the defence this morning,' he said. 'And you are my star witness. You mustn't be nervous. And answer my questions as fully as you can.'

'It's going badly for him, isn't it?' Louise asked.

'The prosecution has made a strong case,' Kopner said. 'But they've said no more than I expected. You are his only chance, Madame.' For a moment the blue eyes were cold, the look of friendliness was gone. There was a suggestion in his tone that somehow she was to blame for something.

'I'll do my best,' Louise said. The sensation of being stared at was overpowering; she lowered her head for a moment, seeking to hide from it. The feeling increased. She glanced towards the left of the dais, and recognised the prosecuting lawyer from his photographs. He looked at her with hostility. On an impulse, Louise turned round and found Ilse Minden seated behind her. There was no smile, no nod of recognition. She looked thinner, more lined, and there was a tense expression on her face. As her eyes met Louise's glance, there was hate in them. And expectation. Louise turned to the clerk beside her. The heat seemed overpowering suddenly . . .

'Could I have a glass of water? Thank you.'

Two doors at the side of the raised platform opened; everyone stood up, with a regimented unanimity, and the three judges came in. They wore loose black robes and white neckties. The most senior took his centre seat as President of the Court. There was a command called out in German; the spectators sat down again, and through a second door, on the opposite side of the judges, Heinz Minden came into the court and took his place on the right.

He wore a dark suit and a white shirt, the collar of which stood away from his neck; it made him look old and pitiable. Kopner, who knew the value of visual impressions, had told his wife to bring a size larger than the normal. He didn't look at the judges; immediately he searched the front rank, and when he saw Louise, an expression of distress was clearly visible. She smiled at him, trying to show encouragement. In return he shook his head. Then he clasped his hands and stared down at them. Siegfried Kopner got up, pushing his chair back; the court was so quiet that it made a loud rasp on the floorboards.

He faced the judges, one hand tucked into his gown. 'If it pleases you, Herr President, I shall open the defence case for Heinz Minden by calling my first witness. My only witness.' There was a sharp hiss of breath from behind him, coming from the tightly packed hall. 'I shall call someone who has travelled from Paris at her own behest to speak on behalf of the man you have heard described by my learned colleague as an inhuman monster, a man who worked on an infamous weapon without a scruple of conscience for its effect upon helpless human beings. I call the Comtesse de Bernard to come before the court!'

There was a touch upon Louise's arm; one of the court officials had come up to her, and with an outstretched hand was showing her the way to the witness chair. As she walked the short distance, passing under the judges' eyes, there was a low murmur from the crowd. She took her place in the chair, and swore the oath. Kopner advanced towards her. He walked slowly, his gown swinging round his legs, his head thrust forward. He came to a stop in front of her.

'Madame de Bernard, you are the widow of Comte Jean de Bernard, a hero of the wartime French Resistance, are you not?'

'Yes, I am his widow.'

'Would you tell the learned judges how you came to know the accused, Heinz Minden.'

'He was billeted in our house, the Château de St. Blaize, at St. Blaize en Yvelines.'

'During what period of time?'

'About seven months; from November 1943 until June 1944.'

'What was his attitude to you and to your family while he was living in your house?'

'He was very friendly.'

'What does "friendly" mean, in this context, Madame? Describe what forms this friendliness took, if you please.'

'He used to bring us things – things we couldn't get. He got his batman to help in the house.'

'When you say "things" I assume you mean food and drink? Luxuries, perhaps.'

'Yes, that would be correct.' He wasn't looking directly at Louise, although she was impelled to watch him, trying to anticipate his questions. At present their purpose seemed confused. He moved about, shifting from one foot to the other, addressing his questions more to the judges than to her.

'And you accepted these presents from Heinz Minden?'

'My husband did.' It was said before she realised that she had made the distinction. Kopner paused, and looked at her.

'Your husband accepted presents from Major Minden? Can I assume he wasn't in the Resistance at this time?'

'No,' Louise said. 'He wasn't.'

'So up to June 1944, your husband, who was afterwards so heroic, was not engaged in any anti-German activity at all?'

'No.'

'Describe the relationship between you, and your family and Major Minden. Please address yourself to the judges, Madame, and not to me.'

She moved a little in the chair. Nervousness made the judges' faces seem a blur. She had said something which had put Jean in a false light, but how – what . . .

'I will repeat the question.' Kopner raised his voice. 'Did you and your family get on well with Major Minden? Did he take meals with you, for instance?'

'He dined with us every evening.'

'As a person, Madame de Bernard, how would you describe him?'

'He was very quiet; he never intruded.'

'He didn't force his company upon you then?'

'No. He was invited.'

'By your husband – they got on well, didn't they?'

'Yes.'

'The prosecution has described Heinz Minden as an ardent Nazi, a man without humanity. Was that your impression of him?'

'No. He seemed perfectly ordinary to me.'

'Perfectly ordinary,' Kopner repeated, raising his voice. 'A typical German from a middle-class background, serving his country in a war. Would you agree with that description?'

For the first time Louise hesitated. 'I can't say that exactly. I know nothing about typical Germans. I only knew Nazis occupying France.'

'Nazis like Adolph Vierken, the SS commander who was sent on a punitive expedition against your village?'

It didn't seem to need an answer and she didn't say anything. One of the judges leaned towards her.

'Please answer the defence counsel's question.'

'I suppose so.'

'A lot has been written about that incident at St. Blaize en Yvelines. It might be described as one of the most publicised Resistance operations in Europe. The battle with the SS. The rescue of the children who were being deported.'

Deported. Suddenly she was stiff with alarm; her hands gripped the chair seat. He had said deported. It was a deliberate misrepresentation. The face looking down at her was harsh and full of enmity; the mask had been ripped away.

'They weren't going to be deported,' Louise protested. 'They were going to . . .'

'The witness will confine herself to answering questions. She is not allowed to comment.' The President's voice cut across her reply. 'Proceed, Doctor Kopner.'

'Your Honours, members of the jury.' Kopner addressed the judges above him. 'In order to establish the case for my client, I need to elaborate on the situation in which he found himself. I assure the court I have a definite point to put before you.'

'Proceed,' the senior judge said again. Kopner turned back to Louise.

'Heinz Minden was on General Brühl's staff at the Château de Diane when he was billeted with you. Were you aware of the nature of his work?'

'No. God forbid.'

'When did you become aware of it?'

'When I was told what he was doing. In May.'

'Until then he had impressed you as just another army officer? You had no suspicion that you were in fact entertaining in your family a fanatical Nazi scientist, bent on destroying the human race with a nerve gas?'

'No.'

'Up till that month of May, everyone at the Château and in the village itself had lived at peace with the occupying German forces, isn't that so?'

'Yes, it is.'

'Until just before the invasion, in fact. There was no sabotage, no outbreaks of violence against the army?'

'Nothing. But then two years before . . .'

'You have answered my question already,' Kopner interrupted her. 'Nothing, you said, no resistance, no hostility to the German troops. They can hardly have been such brutal Nazis, can they? Any more than Major Minden, who was made so welcome in your house. Would you tell the court what changed this state of affairs, apart perhaps from the imminence of the Allied invasion . . .'

In the body of the court Sophie de Bernard watched her mother. At one stage in the questioning, Louise had flushed; now she was terribly pale. The atmosphere in the court was quivering with tension. It was obvious to those observing that Minden's counsel was treating Louise de Bernard as a hostile witness. And it was even more apparent to Sophie that his questions were taking a completely different direction to the one her mother had anticipated.

'Why did Adolph Vierken come to St. Blaize?'

'To punish the village.'

'And what crime had this peaceful, might I say, collaborationist community committed, to bring the SS upon them?'

'There had been two murders,' Louise said slowly. Her throat felt tight, and she swallowed. Now she was on guard, watching her answers, trying blindly to protect herself from a menace that she didn't understand. He wasn't defending Heinz Minden so much as attacking her. Attacking the people of St. Blaize. And Jean de Bernard.

'Explain, if you please. Who was murdered, and by whom?'

'General Brühl,' Louise said. 'He wasn't murdered, that was the wrong word. He was killed, by an Allied agent. To stop the gas being made.'

'I see,' Kopner said. 'And the village sheltered the killer, isn't that right? They hid a man who broke into the Château Diane and murdered two Germans with his bare hands. And they were not aware that General Brühl was anything but an ordinary serving officer in the Wehrmacht at the time?'

'Nobody knew what he really was,' Louise said.

'So, perhaps understandably, the German authorities were angry. They sent Adolph Vierken with his SS troops to investigate. Was Adolph Vierken known to you?'

'No,' Louise said. Visibly, Kopner sneered. He half turned his back on her, almost addressing the spectators. There was a movement among the prosecutor's seats. She didn't look at them; she saw only Heinz Minden staring at her.

'Not to any of you? To your husband?'

'No,' Louise said. Régine. She knew what was going to happen. She knew now that she had been tricked and lied to, that whatever this man wanted, it was not so much the vindication of Heinz Minden as the ruin of the de Bernard family.

'You did not know Adolph Vierken. Your husband, who was so friendly to the German officer staying in his house, he didn't know him either. But your sister-in-law Régine de Bernard did!'

'I object to this line of questioning!' The prosecutor was on his feet, advancing over the floor towards them. For a moment Louise's vision swam. 'It is completely out of order. It has no relevance to the case!'

'It has every relevance,' Kopner snarled at him. 'Heinz Minden is on trial for crimes against humanity. I am going to prove that he was more humane than the people who accuse him! That in the sordid and despicable story I am going to lay before the court, his was the only honourable, decent action!'

'Your objection is overruled.' The President spoke to the prosecutor. 'Continue, Doctor Kopner.'

'Your sister-in-law, Régine de Bernard, was another Resistance heroine, was she not?' Now his tone was soft, insinuating.

'Yes,' Louise answered boldly. 'She died fighting for her country. And whatever you say won't alter that.'

'But she was still the mistress of Adolph Vierken?' Kopner raised his voice to a shout. 'There we have this typical French household in this typical French village; the aristocrats at the château pretending friendship to Heinz Minden while they battened on his generosity to supply themselves with rationed goods, the sister of the heroic

Comte de Bernard, Grand Cross of the Legion d'Honneur, herself a posthumous heroine, sleeping with a notorious SS commander! And it was to people like these that Heinz Minden showed much more than generosity! But we will come to that, Madame de Bernard. First let me ask you one more question. Was Major Minden in love with you?'

Down in the court, Sophie de Bernard clenched her hands. 'Oh you bastard,' she said out loud. 'You bastard!' A man sitting beside her hissed at her fiercely to keep quiet.

There was a gasp from the crowd; she half rose from her seat to see what had caused it. Heinz Minden was on his feet.

'I wish to change my plea.' His voice rang out, loud and strong. 'I plead guilty to the charges against me!'

Siegfried Kopner opened his arms wide.

'There is no need for you to answer, Madame de Bernard. The officer you duped has answered for you. Even now he tries to shield you! I ask that this interruption be stricken from the record of the trial. The plea cannot be changed except through me.'

The senior judge spoke for a moment to his colleagues. 'There will be a recess,' he announced, 'while you speak to the accused. We will reassemble in half an hour.'

A moment later Sophie de Bernard had fought her way through to the front and seized Louise's arm. Behind them the silence had changed to an excited babble; reporters were struggling to get to the exits and the telephones in the main hall. 'Darling!' Sophie threw both arms around her. 'Come on – we're getting out of here!'

But Louise didn't answer; she didn't seem to feel the pressure on her to move forward. A man was coming towards them. Sophie saw her mother's face and stepped away, letting her go. She knew, before either of them spoke, that Raoul Delabraye had succeeded.

'Now,' Siegfried Kopner said, 'you asked to see me. What can I do for you, Senator?' There were five of them in the little side room. Outside the door a policeman stood on guard. Heinz Minden and his wife were seated side by side; Louise, with Savage near her, sipped a glass of water. Kopner examined the American. He was a tall, strongly built man, middle aged but without a grey hair. Kopner had the card with his name on it in his pocket. Senator Brian McFall. He had come into the room with Louise de Bernard on his arm, and there was something about him which alerted Kopner. He sensed that this was a different type to the suave American politicians of his acquaintance, anxious to ingratiate themselves and prove their lack of bias towards Germans. 'What can I do for you?' he repeated. Savage put a hand on Louise's shoulder.

'You can change your client's plea to guilty,' Savage said, 'and save yourself and him a lot of trouble.' He lit a cigarette and passed it to Louise. Kopner smiled unpleasantly.

'Really? And are you qualified to give me such advice?'

'Better qualified than you know,' Savage answered him. He looked for a moment at Minden, who was staring at him.

'I have no idea why you make this suggestion,' Kopner said coldly, 'but I can assure you there is no question of changing the plea. I shall resume my examination of Madame de Bernard as soon as the court reassembles. Major Minden has been under a great strain. He's not responsible for that outburst in the court.'

'I am responsible.' Minden spoke suddenly. His voice sounded tired. 'I want to plead guilty. And don't keep calling me Major. It was only a sham rank.'

'You should be proud of it.' Kopner rounded on him angrily. 'Proud to have served your Fatherland! I will not change the plea!'

'Then I shall take the witness stand for the prosecution as a special witness.' Savage didn't raise his voice. 'They have the right to call me. And by God you'll regret it when I get up there. I've watched you bullying this lady for the last half an hour, Herr Doctor. I only hope you try to cross-examine me!'

'If that's a challenge,' Kopner said contemptuously, 'then I accept it. But I have yet to see how your testimony could make the slightest difference.' He turned away and lit one of his cheap cigarettes.

'As I understand it,' Savage said, 'your defence will be that your client was a patriotic German, acting under orders, that he was an unwilling subordinate who had no choice but to work on the project, that he showed no enthusiasm for it, and everything about his character confirms that he wouldn't willingly hurt the proverbial fly – right?'

'You should conduct the defence for me,' Kopner sneered.

'You're going to prove he was a humanitarian, aren't you? That's why you brought Madame de Bernard here – to testify to his saving her children's lives? First you show up the French as a lot of self-seeking, double-crossing bastards, turning on the Germans when they thought the Allies were going to win – you crucify Madame de Bernard and her family – then you present Heinz Minden as the true Teutonic Knight, bravely risking his own safety to rescue the children of the woman he loved?'

'Really,' Kopner shrugged, 'I need hardly go into court at all. You have won my case for me, Senator.'

'I'm the one who'll lose it for you,' Savage said. 'Because I saw

Minden's notebook. I saw the work he was doing on Brühl's formula. They were having trouble with it; water neutralised it. It was all there, written out in Minden's own handwriting. And one phrase. I can testify to that one phrase, and how in his anxiety to perfect this filthy weapon, he had underlined it. "We must find a solution". That shoots the hell out of your unwilling subordinate plea!'

'How did you see it?' Kopner asked the question slowly; his look narrowed.

'Because I am the Allied agent who killed Brühl,' Savage said. 'And the people who sheltered me were the de Bernard family. He knows me.' He spoke to Minden. 'You knew who I was the minute I walked in here, didn't you?'

'Yes.' Minden's voice was listless. 'I recognised you. Her cousin. That was a lie then?'

'It was a lie,' Savage said quietly. 'I went to your room, opened your briefcase and read your notes.'

'I did write that,' Minden muttered. '"We must find a solution". I remember it well. God forgive me.' He hung his head again.

'You listen to me,' Savage said. He stepped close to Kopner, who did not recoil. 'Whatever the dirty game you're playing – and being a politician myself I guess it's a nice little job of whitewashing the Nazis for political ends – you might as well give up. I haven't gone to the prosecution yet and offered myself as a witness. But believe me, I'll make a hell of a good one. I'll give them a picture of Heinz Minden and the gas he was so anxious to make perfect that will send him to prison for the rest of his life. And leave a very dirty smell around anyone defending him. Especially when I describe how that gas was used to kill my wife and child at Auschwitz!'

For a moment Kopner fought back, silently, using an intangible force of will, he struggled against Savage and against his own conviction that he faced defeat.

'Change the plea to guilty,' Savage said. 'Otherwise I'll go in there and blow your case and your political future to smithereens!'

'Don't listen to him!' Ilse Minden had leapt to her feet; she confronted Savage and Louise, her face blanched and contorted with hate. 'You swine! You dare to threaten what you'll do to Heinz – you who killed in cold blood! My husband isn't pleading guilty to please you – or to save her! She was just a whore who made a fool of him, and it's all going to come out – she's going to stand in front of the world for what she is!'

'Be quiet!' Kopner shouted at her. 'Hold your tongue! Minden, we have no choice. The plea will be changed to guilty. I'll ask the court for mercy. There's nothing more I can do now.' He flung the cigarette on the floor and trod it to pulp. For a moment he looked at Louise. He seemed as if he were going to say something, but Savage stepped between them. He took Louise by the hand.

'Come on,' he said quietly. 'We've finished here.' With his arm around her shoulders, they left the room.

Sophie de Bernard was watching as they came out of the side room. She started forward to meet them, and then stopped. Neither her mother nor the tall man, unmistakably American, had seen her. They appeared oblivious of their surroundings; he was bending over Louise, with one arm around her, she was looking up at him. A pang of jealousy caught Sophie by surprise; this was the man who had meant so much to her mother that even now, after so many years, there was no place in her life for anyone else. They had paused in the corridor, talking quietly. He had taken his arm away from Louise and was holding her hand, they faced each other. Sophie stayed in her seat, watching them. He was not a conventionally handsome man, but there was power in the way he held himself, authority in the face. Her father had been slim and graceful, elegant even in the captivity of a wheelchair. This man was hard and big boned; there were no fine edges about him. Beside him, her mother looked small. Sophie got up and walked towards them.

'It's all right, darling!' Louise said. 'He's pleading guilty – it's all over! This is my daughter, Sophie. Senator McFall – Roger Savage!'

He had a deep voice. 'The last time I saw you, you were a little girl,' he said. He held out his hand and Sophie shook it. She saw her mother's radiant smile.

'Thank you for coming,' she said to him. She had never felt awkward or inadequate with a man before. Her jealousy retreated in shame, and with it the regret that none of the men she had known would have crossed the world for her.

'I hope you'll have lunch with us,' Roger Savage said. 'Then we can tell you all about it.'

'That's very kind of you. Can I ask you one question?'

'Of course.' He was looking as happy as Louise. She felt he would have gone on smiling whatever she had said.

'Are you married?'

'Sophie!' She ignored her mother.

'No,' he said. 'I'm not.'

'Then in that case,' Sophie said, 'you and Mother had better lunch alone.' She took out a cigarette and lit it, throwing the empty Gauloise packet away. 'I'll join you for dinner tonight.' She kissed Louise quickly on the cheek and walked away.

Savage looked down at Louise.

'It's taken a very long time,' he said. 'But I think you'll be happy to come home?'

'Yes,' she said. 'I think I will.'

THE GRAVE OF TRUTH

I

'You've had that nightmare again, haven't you?'

He was shaving and he could see her reflection in the bathroom mirror. She wore pink pyjamas with a pattern on them; without make-up she was as pretty as a doll, with big brown eyes and marvellous American teeth. Pink was a colour he loathed, yet she insisted on wearing it, and the look of concern on her face irritated him so much that he nicked himself shaving. She had been trying for years to convert him to an electric razor. A little nodule of dark blood appeared on his lower lip. 'Oh, darling,' his wife said, 'you've cut yourself.'

'Ellie' – with a great effort he kept his tone gentle – 'please don't fuss.' The reflection in the mirror shook its head at him; the curly brown hair fluffed round her shoulders.

'I'm not fussing, Max. I know you've had that dream again and it's upset you. Why won't you talk about it?'

He put down the razor, splashed his face and dried it. There was a blood spot on the white towel. Then reluctantly he turned round to look at his wife.

'All right, I did dream the same thing last night. It happens now and again; I don't know why you have to make such a drama out of it.'

'Because of what it does to you,' she said. 'I remember the first time, when we'd just got married. You were soaking with sweat and shaking all over. We talked about it and you felt better. It was a long time before it happened again. We used to communicate in those days; now when anything goes wrong you just shut me out.'

'I've got an early interview this morning,' he said. 'I must get dressed.' They went into the bedroom and his wife sat on the bed; he didn't have to look at her to know that her eyes were full of tears.

'It used to be very rare,' she said. 'Now I know it's happening regularly. You can't fool me, darling. You get moody, withdrawn, you snap at me and the children – you're not yourself for days!' He was dressed, fastening his watchstrap. The watch was a gold Piaget; she had given it to him for Christmas, with a note that overwhelmed him with guilt: 'Just to prove to you I love you.'

'I'm sorry,' he said. 'I don't mean to be difficult. It's probably just a phase – I probably won't dream about it again for months.'

'Max, darling, you've been saying this for years,' she said. 'Why won't you see a doctor, get him to analyse what it is that's worrying you? Dreaming about the war is just symbolic of some inner anxiety . . .'

'For Christ's sake,' he said, 'don't start that psychiatric stuff again. There's nothing symbolic about what happened to me in Berlin. I don't need any half-baked therapist telling me it's because my grandmother took away my teddy bear. I dream about being bombed and blown up because I bloody well was! Now I've got to go – I'm going to be late.'

'Don't forget to kiss the children good morning,' she said. She got up and went into the bathroom, locking the door. He knew she was going to cry. He paused outside the kitchen door; they had coffee in their room in the mornings – Max never ate breakfast since it meant starting the day with a meal with his children. Kiss the children good morning. Otherwise they'll feel you don't love them and they'll grow up insecure. The headache which was there when he woke up intensified suddenly as he went into the kitchen and forced himself to smile at his children and the English student who was giving them breakfast. She was a nice girl, shy and ill at ease. He was ashamed of the way his son and daughter bullied her. 'Good morning, Pat . . . Peter . . . Francine . . .'

Fifteen and twelve were said to be difficult ages, pre-teens and teens; Ellie was always saying how traumatic it was for their children to be growing up and how understanding they both had to be and how careful not to pressurize them.

His son Peter was dark and good-looking like his mother; Francine was small and fair-haired. 'Hello,' she said. Peter didn't speak at all. He was eating cereal and scowling. Max kissed his daughter and, seeing the boy's expression, decided to damage his psyche by ignoring him that morning. Both children were at the local *lycée*, at his insistence, where, in spite of their mother's disapproval, they had to work extremely hard. His son was exceptionally clever, specializing in science and mathematics. His scholastic abilities did not compensate Max for his lack of good manners and consideration for anyone but himself. His father's attempts to impose discipline early on had been successfully frustrated by his mother; by the time he was seven Peter was adept at playing off one parent against the other. His relationship with his father was hostile and competitive; he bullied Francine because he suspected that his father found her more congenial.

'Good-bye, Daddy,' Francine said.

'Peter,' the English girl pushed back her chair, 'you'll be late for school.'

Max had turned towards the door when he heard his son answer.

'So I'm late – so what's it got to do with you?'

Max didn't pause to think, he didn't take a decision, he just lost his temper as he had been losing it inwardly for years. Perhaps the dream was responsible; perhaps he suddenly saw his son through eyes which hadn't been conditioned by modern child psychology and an American wife who had been reared on a deadly combination of Freud and Spock. He turned back, reached the table in three long strides, and hit his son across the left ear with such force that he knocked him off the dinette stool. There was a few seconds pause of shocked silence, and then his daughter shrieked and burst into tears, and his son, crouching in shock and amazement on the ground, suddenly began to roar with rage and pain. Max looked down at him.

'Don't you ever dare to speak to anyone like that again!'

He wasn't aware till he had left the apartment and was getting into his car that he had shouted at his son in German.

It was a glorious spring day in 1970, and Paris was awake early, the shops open, the traffic clotting at junctions and traffic lights. The city had a smell which was exclusive to itself; had he been blinded Max would have known Paris from any capital in the world by that original blending of food smells and street smells, and a thousand varieties of human and artificial scents.

He had lived there for fifteen years and he loved Paris. Ellie loved it too; she hadn't liked London where they had lived when they were first married in 1954. It had been a grey, sad place after the war, pinched by austerity, its people weary and seeking change, as if the conflict which had destroyed Nazi Germany had somehow defeated them too. It hadn't been easy for Max, working in London during the fifties. Anti-German feeling was stronger in Britain than in some countries which had suffered Nazi occupation. The articles he had written on the changes taking place in post-war Britain attracted a lot of attention in European political journalism, and the by-line 'Max Steiner' appeared in leading West German newspapers and prestige political publications on the Continent. When he was offered the post of chief foreign affairs correspondent for *Newsworld*, based in Paris, he was married to Ellie and she was pregnant with their son.

Driving along the rue Constantine, the sunshine roof of his smart new Peugeot open to admit the morning sun, he ignored his headache, concentrated on the traffic, and told himself, as he had done so many times in the past year, that he was an ungrateful bastard who didn't appreciate his family and his job, and it was time he realized how lucky he was. He had no right to criticize his wife: most men were sexually bored after sixteen years of marriage, and, naturally, when sex had ceased to be an urge and become a habit, the critical faculties sharpened and trifles previously unnoticed began to grate. He had been unfaithful to her once or twice, during trips to the States, and formed a brief liaison with an Italian girl who lived in Rome. As a result his sex life at home became guilty as well as tedious, the guilt partially eased by the certainty that had Ellie known she would have sat down with him to analyse his reasons for going to bed with someone else instead of being jealous.

It was unfair of him to resent her intellectual limitations. What had happened to the attractive girl whose frivolity had enchanted him when they first met? Why should the plus have become such a minus that her opinions irritated him until he tried to avoid any serious discussion? . . . Motherhood. He could blame that. Women changed when they had children. There at least he had reason for complaint. She had become obsessed with the children. He had definitely shifted down two places in her scale of priorities. But how much time had he spent travelling, leaving her alone with the children he resented . . . ?

A right turn at the end of the street and along the river. A very pretty girl in a short skirt crossed in front him, threading her way through the stationary traffic. He watched her without interest. His marriage was falling to pieces. He had hit his son. As hard as he had once been hit, so that he fell to the ground . . . the dream again. They didn't speak German at home; he and Ellie spoke English and the children brought up in France were bilingual. Peter wouldn't have understood what he was shouting at him. Why, suddenly, had he lapsed into his own language, except that his wife was right and the nightmare persisted in his mind long after he had woken?

Of course, he *had* been dreaming about it regularly; it had begun after Christmas, bringing him upright in the bed, his heart and pulse rate galloping with fear, full of fire and thunder and the distortion of the dream world, but still real and still horribly recognizable. He hadn't dared to go to sleep again. The first time he had made the excuse that he was tired, that he'd drunk several whiskies after dinner – he'd rationalized it, and remembered everything quite deliberately to disarm the subconscious that Ellie was always talking about. He wasn't hiding anything from himself. He had even written about his own experience in Berlin at the end.

Not everything, though. Was that the thorn embedded in his mind: He drove his car into the car park under the *Newsworld* building in the Champs Elysées, got out, closed it up and locked it.

From January onwards he dreamed about it, sometimes on consecutive nights, sometimes with a merciful gap of nearly a week. He formed a routine: he got up, went into the kitchen, made coffee, had a cigarette, woke himself up thoroughly and then went back to bed. His wife only surprised him twice, and he had lied to her. He couldn't have endured her attempts to comfort him and explain it all away. Because of course she couldn't, because she didn't know the truth. He had told her no more than anyone else when he described the last days in Berlin. And yet although he called her stupid in his private thoughts, bilious and disloyal as they'd become, she'd sensed what was happening and faced him with it that morning.

'You've had that nightmare again.'

It came nearly every night now, sometimes in episodes, at others in rich detail. He walked through the entrance to the lift, pressed the third-floor button, ascended and got out. He had an interview that morning, although it was not for another hour; lying to Ellie was becoming a need rather than a habit. He wanted to look through his notes and fix the line of his questions in his mind. He never wrote anything down when he was talking to people, nor did he produce a tape-recorder. He carried that in his pocket. People said more when they imagined themselves to be talking off the record.

He had a bright modern office, and an efficient French secretary who was too intelligent to try to be sexy. He liked her but he had never even bought her a drink.

'Martine – good morning. Could you get me some coffee and some aspirin? Don't put anyone through to me: I'm going to read over the notes on Sigmund Walther.'

Sigmund Walther was a West German politician who had graduated to politics through industry. His background was well documented: father a naval officer killed during the war, mother a member of the minor Bohemian aristocracy; a bright young man, too young to have fought for Nazism, brought up through the harsh post-war years by his mother and grandparents, his time at university followed by a spectacular career in the industrial rebirth of West Germany. Married to a member of the old *Jünker* military caste; five children, all born close together – unusual for an ambitious man. Joined the Social Democratic Party and began a determined and ruthless campaign to reach ministerial level. Was known to have made a large personal fortune since the war.

Max began writing, underlining points to fix them in his memory. There were stories circulating about Sigmund Walther and his affiliations in East Germany, and rumours of his ambition to form a splinter group inside the Party. He was staying at the Crillon with his wife and two eldest children on a private visit to Paris. If it really was private it had been extraordinarily well advertised in advance, and *Newsworld*'s request for an exclusive interview had been promptly granted.

The aspirin had taken effect, and Max was totally absorbed in his

work. Walther was a challenge: his personality had eluded previous
interviewers; even the television cameras had failed to expose more
than he intended to reveal about himself. Journalists covered themselves by describing him as an enigma.

Max prepared himself as he did his notes. No personal prejudice,
no slanted questions; a man as clever as Sigmund Walther would
detect immediately if his attitude were hostile and defend himself.
Max wanted him off guard if possible. His telephone buzzed; he
frowned and picked it up. Martine's voice reminded him that he was
due at the Crillon in twenty minutes. He put his notes in his desk,
slipped the little transistorized tape-recorder into his outside pocket,
and went out. The secretary looked up at him as he passed.

'Is your headache better?'

'Yes, it's fine.'

'Your wife rang, but I didn't put her through. I said you were out.
I hope that was all right.'

He could imagine Ellie, brimming with outrage because he had
given a Peter a box on the ear, and suddenly the idea made him
smile. At a safe distance he could imagine the scene he had left behind
as hilariously funny. It wouldn't be so funny when he went home.

'Did my wife leave any message?'

'Well, yes.' He sensed Martine's hesitation. 'She asked if you would
come home; she said Peter was too upset to go to school. I told her
you were out all morning at this Walther interview but I'd give you
the message as soon as you came in.'

'Thanks,' he said.

The doorman at the Crillon took his car and parked it for him.
The reception desk was surrounded with people checking in and out.
The service was courteous and efficient and within a few minutes
a pageboy was escorting him in a lift to the Walthers' suite on
the second floor. It was one of the best suites in the hotel, with
a magnificent view over the Place de la Concorde; the door was
opened by a tall slim woman wearing a scent he recognized because
he had given it to Ellie for her birthday. It was probably the most
expensive in the world, and it was his first, misleading impression of
Minna Walther.

'M. Steiner – come in, please. My husband won't be a moment.'

She had an amazing figure for a woman with five children; a long
straight back, narrow hips and elegant legs. She was wearing a very
expensive casual coat and skirt; he noticed the lack of jewellery, the
plain wedding ring on her finger.

'Do sit down,' she said. 'I'll go and call Sigmund.'

'Thank you, Fräu Walther,' he answered in German. She was too
Slavic in type to be beautiful: the cheekbones were too high and the

grey eyes a little too far apart. She had a lovely wide smile that changed her face completely.

'I'm afraid my French is terrible,' she said. 'I'm told I have a very strong accent.'

'No worse than mine,' Max said. 'It's not an easy language for us.'

She hesitated by an inner door, touching the handle. 'How long have you been away from home?'

Home. It was years since he had thought of Germany as home. Or heard anyone speak about it in that way.

'Nearly eighteen years,' he said. 'I moved to England soon after I left university. Then I got married and we lived in England and over here.'

'I'll call my husband,' she said.

He got up and went to the window; sitting down would have placed him at a disadvantage when Walther came in. He stared down at the traffic coiling round the Place below. The breadth and splendour of Napoleon III's concept for his capital had made the site of the guillotine and the Terror into the epitome of civic elegance. Germany had revived the guilotine; those found guilty of high treason during the war were executed face upwards by Himmler's special order. He turned round as Sigmund Walther came through from the inner room. He reached Max and held out his hand.

'Sorry I kept you waiting; I had to take a call. Would you like coffee or a drink?'

'A whisky and soda would be fine.'

'I'll join you.' Walther went to a walnut cabinet and started pouring drinks.

He was shorter than Max had expected, very fit and quick moving; his skin was lightly tanned, as if he made use of a sun lamp. Blue-eyed, hair slightly thinning, impeccably dressed in a dark suit, white shirt and plain tie, he wore his forty-two years lightly. Max tasted the drink and set it down. They faced each other, Walther leaning back on the sofa, legs crossed, very relaxed, Max sitting slightly forward in the armchair. He had slipped his hand into his pocket and activated the tape while Walther's back was turned.

They began with a general conversation, designed to put the interviewee at ease; Max didn't continue for long because he sensed that Sigmund Walther knew the technique and was impatient with it. His questions became more specific. How would Walther deal with the problem of urban terrorists? Did he think de Gaulle's withdrawal from NATO or his resignation would have a significant impact on German policy towards France? Was he in favour of Britain's joining the EEC? Walther's answers showed a mind at once incisive and decisive. 'Tell me,' Max went on, 'what role would you like to see West Germany play in the Community in the next five years?'

'Five years from now? I wouldn't look that far ahead – in a year I'd like to see some sort of *rapprochement* with the East German government, while keeping our links with the Community and NATO as strong as possible.'

'You don't think these aims are incompatible?'

'No. There is one thing about our people which distinguishes us from other Europeans. Our nationhood is comparatively recent. Partition, division, all the punishments inflicted upon us by the Allies and Russia after the war, have not only affected us but are responsible for the atmosphere of confrontation which bedevils the world at the moment: I believe that the principal duty of our government is to try and establish good relations with our people in the East. We must aim at polycentrism, not bipolarity.' He leaned forward to emphasize what he was saying. 'That is the policy I am advocating in Bonn.'

'And this is what you will try to bring about if you are offered a post by Brandt?'

'Yes,' Sigmund Walther said. 'I have considerable support in the Bundestag.'

'Are you really proposing the ultimate reunification of Germany?'

'If Europe is to have any hope of peace in the future our country must become a sovereign state with all our people within our own borders.'

Max gave a slight smile. 'Some might think of the word *Lebensraum*, Herr Walther, when you talk about all Germans being incorporated into Germany.' He was watching Walther's hands for any sign of tension; they were a truer barometer of inner reaction than the eyes. They didn't move from his side, and yet he hesitated before answering that gentle provocation. When he did, it was Max who was taken by surprise.

'I'm not a Nazi, Herr Steiner. I believe the desire of every German is to belong to his country, not to Communism or Western democracy or any other ideological faction. I believe that whatever Ulbricht's dictatorship behind the Wall has imposed upon our people can and will be eroded by that longing to be one nation again. But we in West Germany have to take the political initiative.'

'What makes you think that either Russia or the West would allow this *rapprochement* to take place?'

'As far as the West is concerned, I also believe that Europe has grown up politically in the last twenty years. I believe from personal contacts among senior NATO officers that the reunification of our country would be welcomed by the West.'

'You still have Russia to convince,' Max said. 'Even if France, for instance, could be persuaded to accept a strong and united Germany, is it really conceivable that the Soviet Union would stand by and allow the Eastern territories to escape her? Of course,' he added thoughtfully, 'reunification would be a marvellous platform in the elections.'

Sigmund Walther didn't answer. He picked up his whisky and drank most of it. 'You're not taking any notes,' he remarked. 'But no doubt you have a tape-recorder?'

'Yes,' Max said. 'But I find it puts people off when they can see it. Have you any objection to this being taped?'

'None at all. I just wanted to establish that you weren't relying on memory.' The easy smile came and lingered; Max could see why Walther had been so successful in industry; his reputation had begun as a negotiator. He had a magnetic charm that in no way concealed his considerable authority.

'Let me put my last question to you another way. If at any time in the future East Germany tried to form some kind of federation with Bonn, Russia would act as she did in Hungary – and in Czechoslovakia less than two years ago – to prevent it. Wouldn't what you're proposing lead to a military confrontation with the West?'

'Are you asking that question for *Newsworld*, or do you have any interest in the future of Germany as a German?'

'I'm asking the question,' Max said, 'so that *Newsworld* readers can get an answer; I'm not personally concerned.'

'That's a pity,' Walther said quietly. 'But I'll give you the answer just the same. West Berlin is the parent of the Wall; the division of the capital of Germany into two halves was dictated by vengeance and the Allies' fear of offending Stalin. An island of Western-style democracy in a Marxist sea. The concept is crazy and was very nearly fatal. The world has been closer to war over Berlin than over any other issue since 1945. If it means confronting Russia then I believe the West is strong enough to do it, exactly as America did over Cuba. Russia is not going to embark on a nuclear war with China at her back.

'I believe it will be possible to reunite Germany and not only preserve peace but restore proper balance to Europe and the free world.' He finished his drink. 'That will make a nice quote for the article you're going to write,' he said. 'Now perhaps you would switch your little machine off? Wherever it is – '

Max took the recorder out of his pocket and laid it on the coffee table. He pressed the switch to 'Off'.

'Amazing how small they can make these things,' Walther said.

'Would you like me to play it back?'

'No, thanks. In spite of being in politics, I don't enjoy hearing myself speak. I'd probably ask you to wipe it out and start all over again.

And we haven't got time for that.' He got up, looked at his watch, exclaimed softly.

'I have a luncheon appointment at one – the traffic is so bad in Paris, I've hardly enough time – excuse me, I'll ring down for my car.' He turned, holding the telephone. 'Wait a moment – we can go down together.'

He opened the inner door and called to his wife. She came and stood in the doorway, smiling at him.

'I'll be back at three, my darling. We've had a very good interview. I hope I haven't given Herr Steiner too bad an impression!'

Max said good-bye to her; she kissed her husband on the cheek and shook hands with him. He had forgotten how distinctive that type of German woman was.

Walther and he went down in the lift. As they reached the foyer he turned to Max. 'How long is it since you've been back to Germany?'

'A long time,' he said. 'Your wife asked me the same thing.' They had reached the glass street doors and passed through them into the brilliant sunshine. Walther's car, the chauffeur waiting by the rear door, was drawn up outside. Walther held out his hand to Max. 'Minna feels the same as I do. Germany needs men with talent and courage. You could do a lot for your country. Why don't you come back?'

'I live here now,' Max answered. 'I'm not due to be posted anywhere as far as I know.'

'I have a lot of contacts in German journalism,' Sigmund Walther said. 'Think about coming back. I'm being quite serious about this. Just let me know.' They were still shaking hands as they talked, Walther half turned from the street facing Max, when the first shots cracked out.

There were two of them; Max saw them quite clearly seconds before he realized what was happening. Two men, with dark glasses, standing within a few feet of Sigmund Walther, with guns in their hands. It was a moment frozen in shock and disbelief; Walther's hand gripped his in a convulsion of agony; the smile of a second earlier became a hideous grimace, and still the shots cracked, as bullets thudded into his lurching body and one whined like an angry hornet past Max's head. Walther was falling now, turning a semi-circle as he collapsed, almost in slow motion; people in the street were screaming and shouting; the firing had stopped. Max scarcely saw the running figures disappear into the crowd as he held the dying man in his arms. Blood was streaming over the pavement. Walther's face had turned a deathly grey, his eyes were filming over.

His lips moved and Max crouched close to him, his hands sticky with Sigmund Walther's blood. For a moment the eyes cleared, and by a last effort of will a single word was spoken clearly: 'Janus . . .' Then Walther choked and his head rolled sideways as he died.

*

It was dark and the offices of *Newsworld* were closed up except for the night-watchman and the office where Max Steiner sat alone. He switched his desk light on when the room grew too dark for him to see, and he sat with his elbows on his desk and the little tape-recorder in front of him. The police had played the tape back, while they took a long statement from him. Someone had asked if he wanted to see a doctor himself, if he felt shocked. He had been very calm and refused everything but coffee. He wanted a clear head unclouded by alcohol or tranquillizers. He had seen the killers: two men, one above medium height, the other slighter in build and shorter; the dark glasses had made it difficult to guess their ages but both had dark, short hair and were Caucasians. Professionals, who had escaped through the crowds and been seen leaping into a waiting car. The car had been found abandoned in a Paris suburb. Predictably it had been stolen that morning.

It was a political assassination and the newspapers and other media were blaming the Baader-Meinhof because Walther was a West German politician.

Max had gone over the details with senior men from the Sûreté and then with a couple of investigators from SDECE. He had told them everything he could remember, every fleeting impression gained in those last few moments of panic and horror. Except for the dead man's last word.

He had washed and changed his bloodstained clothes for a suit sent round from his home. He had ignored the frantic messages from Ellie, who was assured by the police that he was quite unhurt. When he was told he could go home he asked to be driven to his office. His editor-in-chief was a Frenchman who had never forgiven him for being German but was too practical to let it influence his judgement. Steiner was one of his star correspondents; he cleared everyone out of Max's office and took the story down himself. 'I'm going to write it,' Max said.

'Eye witness,' Martin Jarre said briskly. 'This is going to be your guideline. Tomorrow it mightn't be so clear. Go home and get your doctor to give you something for a night's sleep. You look clapped out.'

But Max hadn't gone home. He had switched off his telephone so Ellie couldn't get through to him, and sat on, playing the tape back once or twice.

It all looked very straightforward. Not the Baader-Meinhof but assassins from the right wing who didn't want *détente* with East Germany. Or the KGB, who didn't want it either . . . The motives were there on that tape: reunification of Germany through a political understanding with the Communist regime in East Germany. A proposal that would make Walther many powerful enemies. But no more, on examination, than a political ideal to be promoted during an election, by a man who was aiming at power and popularity. Not sufficient threat to have him murdered in a Paris street, with all the attendant publicity and uproar. Walther had been killed for something else, and he had known it, and said so just before he died. 'Janus.'

It was twenty-five years since Max Steiner had heard that word, and the man who spoke it then was just about to die. In the Bunker in Berlin on 25th April 1945, when Adolf Hitler shot himself and the Third Reich came to an end.

For twenty-six days and nights the city had been under bombardment from the air and the advancing Russians, their artillery ranged around the perimeter within fifteen kilometres of the Brandenburg Gate. Within the last seven days Berlin had become completely encircled, and already the first Russian patrols had penetrated the suburbs. All who could get out had taken to the roads and were fleeing to the West and the Allied armies. A massive pall of black smoke hung over Berlin, and through it the fires from bombed and burning buildings licked and spouted jagged flame. The air was thick with rubble dust and sweet with the stench of burst drains and corpses buried in the ruins. The air-raid sirens howled continuously and the thud of explosions from Allied air attacks was competing with the crash of high-velocity shells.

Berliners had forgotten how to sleep; they dozed between air attacks, risked a forage into the shattered streets for the meagre rations which were still being supplied, and huddled underground, waiting for the final assault upon the city. In the heart of Berlin the Führer stayed on in the Bunker below the Chancellory, directing a war which had been lost months before. Berlin, the centre of the Third Reich, its buildings designed by Albert Speer as a monument to the New Order which was to last a thousand years, burned and crumbled under the attacks of the enemies who had so nearly been defeated.

The city lived on rumours; nobody believed the lies broadcast by Goebbels radio, or its hysterical admonitions to fight on to the last and victory could still be won. The war was lost: Himmler and Goering had left Berlin; only Hitler and his few fanatics – Bormann, Goebbels and his personal SS guards – remained to fight on and die with the people and the city. German troops, exhausted and hopeless, were entrenched in the ruins, with orders to fight the Russians street by street.

No surrender. Fight to the death. Those were Hitler's orders, and the veterans and old men and schoolboys of the Hitler Jügend joined what was left of the army and prepared to defend Berlin and the Führer to the last man.

Max Steiner was sixteen; his platoon was due to take up position in the Pichelsdorf district, where savage fighting was holding the encircling Russian troops from driving through the centre. They had been issued with uniforms, ill-fitting olive green, with forage caps and belts, the insignia of the Hitler Jügend on their collars. Max, being the eldest, was the platoon commander; unlike the younger boys he carried a revolver. The others carried rifles and shoulder packs, with grenades. There were stories of children, even younger than the fourteens and fifteens in this group, who had thrown themselves and their grenades under Red Army tanks. Max's platoon had been ordered to the Bunker for the supreme honour accorded those who were about to die for the Fatherland.

Adolf Hitler himself was to review his boy soldiers; he would exhort them to hold back the invader. They had been waiting since dawn, crouching half-asleep in little groups, the tumult of the bombardment muffled below ground. Max's mother was still in her house on the Albrechtstrasse; the adjoining buildings had been wrecked by a bomb but their house still stood and she and his grandmother lived in the cellars and refused to leave. There were no false heroics about Marthe Steiner or her mother-in-law who was seventy-eight years old. Only the quiet logic that countered Max's frantic pleas to join the refugees with the answer that he was all the two women had left, and they weren't leaving Berlin without him. There was no suggestion that he should run away. His father had been killed during an air raid on the Luftwaffe station at Brest, and his elder brothers shot down during the Battle of Britain.

It was his duty to fight for his country, and theirs to stay and give what help they could. His mother helped with the street kitchens and his grandmother sewed bandages for the Red Cross. None of them expected to survive the fall of their city. Max had kissed them good-bye when the order came to report for active duty; his mother was not a demonstrative woman but she had held out her arms and he had run into them, and they were both in tears.

He thought of her, and looked round anxiously in the dull light to make certain no one was awake and watching him cry. The others were silent, some sleeping, some with their eyes closed but awake. He was the platoon commander; he wiped his eyes with his sleeve and tried not to think of his family. Not of his father, or his two brothers who had seemed so splendid in their blue uniforms and were lost over the English Channel within a week of each other. It was his turn now, to prove himself as brave as they were, a German ready to die for the Führer and the Fatherland. He wished his mother and his grandmother had gone, when their friends the Schultzes packed up and left. He wasn't just afraid for himself, because he had been taught that fear was childish and unworthy in a Hitler Youth; he could contain the niggle in his stomach that was becoming a nervous pain at the idea of being shot or blown up. He couldn't bear the thought of his mother staying in that dank old cellar with his grandmother, their personal possessions heaped around them, and perhaps the house being hit by a shell or a bomb and the walls crashing down on top of them . . .

He shifted, and eased his legs to stretch the muscles that were cramped from sitting. Albert Kramer was on the left of him, his back balanced against another boy who was crouching forward, his head on his knees. He and Albert had been at the same school and joined the Hitler Youth at the same time. A few months separated them in age, and Albert had expected to get the senior post in the platoon. They had spent a large part of their lives together, but they were never friends. Albert's father was in the Waffen SS; he had lost an eye and part of his left leg in an ambush in Poland during the retreat. Albert told them how every civilian in the area had been arrested and shot as a reprisal.

Obersturmbannführer Kramer was in an Eastern hospital; nobody knew what had happened to him when the Russians occupied the area, but Albert told everyone his father must have died fighting. The Waffen SS were the best soldiers in the Reich; Albert's eyes glowed when he talked about his father. He didn't seem to mind that he was dead. He only lost his temper when it was suggested that his father might be a prisoner. No SS officer surrendered to those Russian swine. Max could remember him shouting, and how he cried with rage. He had thought, secretly, that he would have been happy if *his* father were somehow alive . . . But then Albert was a fanatical type. He believed in the Führer and the Third Reich the way some people believed in God.

Albert had never had a doubt about the war or about victory. He should have been made platoon leader but Max was picked instead. He knew how Albert hated him because of it. He looked at his watch: it was nearly six o'clock. He was hungry; the boys had been given a bowl of potato soup when they had mustered earlier. They were all as thin as stray dogs; food was rationed just above starvation level; anyone found hoarding or using forged food cards was shot immediately, without even a trial. Max yawned, and was ashamed to see his hand shake as he covered his mouth. He was afraid; he wondered how the other boys were feeling. Otto Stülpner was barely fourteen and small for his age. He was asleep on the ground, his face pinched and sallow in the emergency lighting. There were marks on his cheeks where he had been crying. The rifle lying beside him looked ridiculously big.

Children, Max thought suddenly, and couldn't stop the rush of indignation that followed it. Children sent out to fight against the Russian army, the crack troops specially chosen to reduce Berlin . . . Mongols from the East, if rumours were correct, savages with a licence to rape and slaughter without mercy. The stories from refugees fleeing their advance had filled the Berliners with terror and caused a mass flight of women and children from the city as the threat came closer. Little boys like Paul and Erwin Rapp and Fritz Kluge, who should have been sent to safety not told to go into battle with rifles as big as themselves and the children's oath of loyalty to the Führer as their reason for committing suicide. All right for boys like Albert and himself. Sixteen was old enough when men of seventy were fighting. It had to be; he accepted that, but for most of that little band of boys it was equivalent to murder. He found himself trembling with rage and near to tears. If Adolf Hitler saw them, surely he wouldn't expect them to go to fight in an area which was a hell of shelling and street fighting ... Surely if he loved his people, as he was supposed to, he wouldn't want a snivelling child like Otto Stülpner to get ripped to pieces by Russian bullets ...

'I wonder how long it'll be before we see him?' Albert Kramer might almost have read his thoughts.

'I don't know,' Max muttered. 'Keep your voice down – don't wake the others.'

'I can't wait,' Albert whispered. 'I can't wait to see him face to face. Aren't you excited, Max? This'll be the biggest moment of our lives! I keep thinking what I'll say if he speaks to me. You don't even seem to care – what's the matter with you?' The boy's eyes had narrowed in suspicion; his jaw jutted aggressively. 'Don't you want to die for the Führer?'

Max Steiner looked at him and said the unthinkable. 'No,' he said. 'If I get killed, it'll be for Germany.'

'You dirty swine!' Kramer sprang up, shouting. 'You traitor! I'll report you –'

'Shut up! Come to attention, all of you! Quick!'

Max had seen the two SS officers come into the room; he stood up and saluted. Kramer froze into attention: his response to an order was instantaneous. The boys struggled up and formed themselves into a line. There were twenty of them. The senior SS officer, wearing the flashes of a Standartenführer on his lapels, walked towards Max and raised his right arm stiffly.

'*Heil Hitler.*'

The children responded in unison; Albert's voice was louder than the rest.

'*Heil Hitler.*'

The Standartenführer cleared his throat. He was a big man who had grown thin; the black uniforn hung loose on him and there were heavy pouches of fatigue and strain under his eyes.

'I am the Standartenführer Otto Helms. The Führer sends you his greetings,' he said. 'He regrets that he cannot speak to you in person today, but he reminds you of your oath of allegiance and your duty to him and to the Fatherland.' He paused and his eyes lingered for a moment on Max.

'The Führer has chosen to stay with his people and to lay down his life with us,' he said, and emotion made the harsh voice quiver. 'If we have lost the war it is because of the traitors inside Germany. One of those traitors has been discovered, here, at the Führer's side. It will be your privilege, as members of the Hitler Jügend, as German soldiers, to execute that traitor in the name of Adolf Hitler and the Reich!'

He spoke directly to Max. 'You come with me.'

It was a long narrow passage deep underground; their steps echoed on the concrete floor. The SS officer came to a door, shot back a bolt and opened it. He stood aside so that Max could see in. It was some kind of storeroom because there were boxes stacked to ceiling height in one corner and a fluorescent bar blazed overhead.

A man lay on the bare floor, curled up in the foetal position, knees drawn up, his arms cradling his head. There were splotches of blood on the ground and a sour, sick smell. For a moment Max felt he was going to be sick.

'That swine there,' the SS officer said, 'was the Führer's trusted friend. He betrayed him. The Führer sentenced him to death himself. You're going to form a firing squad.'

Max tried to speak; his throat was constricted with terror and disgust. The man on the ground moved a little and gave a whimpering groan.

'What did he do?' Max whispered.

'Only the Führer knows,' the Standartenführer said. 'We carried out his orders. I would have killed him myself but I have the Führer's own command. He wants him executed and he wants you to carry out the sentence. "The future of Germany depends on the children." Those were his words. "Let the Hitler Jügend shoot him. Let them see what happens to traitors."'

'He's injured,' Max whispered.

He saw the SS officer smile. 'Yes,' he said, 'but if he can't stand up we'll shoot him in a chair. You get back to your squad now; Oberst Frink will take you above ground and show you the place. He'll be brought up in a few minutes.'

He turned back into the room and closed the door. Without thinking Max began to run down the corridor. He found the SS Obersturmführer barring his way; the squad of boys was ranged up behind him.

'Line up!' he shouted. As Max hesitated he pushed him. They moved off behind the SS Leutnant, clattering up the two flights of stairs that brought them to ground level.

The discipline of his training in the Hitler Jügend kept Max Steiner on his feet, made him give orders to the rest of the squad and stopped him giving way to the impulse to turn and run from the whole nightmare. And it was a nightmare, a sequence so horrible that it was almost unreal. He saw a plain chair standing in the enclosed garden where they were waiting; the air was thick with smoke and the cinders of fires floated down on them in a light breeze. The noise of explosions was joined by the rattle of shots from street-fighting in the distance. He glanced over his head and saw a flight of birds high above, winging away. They were not just being sent out to die for their country, the frightened children of Berlin, the Pauls and Erwins and little Fritz Kluge who was clinging on to his rifle and staring ahead like a terrified rabbit. They were being ordered to kill a man in cold blood. The Führer's personal order. The Führer hadn't come to see them, to give lunatics like Albert Kramer something to die happy remembering. He had chosen them to kill a man who hadn't been tried, and whose treason was just a word to be accepted.

He closed his eyes, fighting himself and his panic and revulsion. His family were all National Socialists; his elder brother had won the Iron Cross 1st class for bombing raids on England. As a child he had grown up with the idea of Adolf Hitler as the saviour of Germany, the leader with mystical powers who had brought his people out of the chaos and humiliation of the years after the Great War and set them on their path of destiny. A strong Germany, a pure Aryan super-race whose mission was to rule the world. His father and his mother and his brothers had accepted that, and so had he. The marches, the rallies, the torch-light processions, the marvellous victories, the films glorifying war and sacrifice – nobody questioned that everything their Führer did was right, certainly not Max.

When adversity came, and the war closed in upon them bringing the dreadful air raids which destroyed cities like Cologne or engulfed Hamburg in a holocaust of fire, the people of Germany responded with courage and determination, just as his own family had done when their three menfolk were killed. Max wore the black armband that showed that Steiners had given their lives for the Fatherland, and was proud while he grieved. There had been nobility as well as suffering, and through it all the belief that the Führer would not fail, that the army's reverses were the failure of the generals to carry out his orders. With the shells falling on Berlin itself, part of the myth survived. But the reality was sending children out to die and, now, commanding that they become his personal executioners. They had brought the victim out; he used the word unconsciously.

The Standartenführer and an SS trooper were dragging him between them; he stumbled and staggered till they pushed him into the chair.

'You – cadre leader – come over here!'

Max didn't want to move; he stood as if he were paralysed, and then unwillingly his legs obeyed, and he found himself standing close to the man who was to be shot, with the two SS men confronting him.

'You know what to do?'

He looked up into the Standartenführer's face: it was gaunt and grim, but all he could remember was that brief, hateful smile . . . The condemned man was conscious; his eyes were open. They had wiped his face clean but a rim of blood showed between his lips. Now he had been tied to the chair. He wore civilian trousers and a shirt which was torn and bloodstained.

Max kept on staring at him; he felt his eyes filling with tears.

'You know what to do – answer me, you stupid little clod!'

'No,' Max said, and his voice sounded very loud.

'You give the order: "Take aim, fire." If he's still alive you shoot him through the head.'

Max heard him dimly, as if he were shouting from a long way away. The man in the chair was looking at him. Not a young man, because his hair was turning grey. The eyes were agonized. They reminded Max of the expression in the eyes of a crucified Christ he had seen during a visit to the Kaiser Friedrich Museum. It had haunted him for nights afterwards. Then slowly the bleeding lips opened; the words were spoken directly to him.

'Janus . . . Find Janus . . .'

Max wasn't sure which of the SS men hit the man; he saw the blow, and the fresh blood, and suddenly he was shouting at them.

'No . . . no . . . no!'

The world rocked under his feet, tears blinded him, and a punch to the head sent him sprawling. He saw what happened afterwards as if it were a series of scenes from a film that kept breaking down. He saw Albert Kramer come out of the ranks; he was dragged to one side and somebody kicked him. Then he heard the shots which seemed to go on for ever. The man in the chair fell over. Then Max became unconscious.

He heard the voices from a distance; they came and went at first while he struggled back to consciousness. 'Poor devil – no, he's alive – ' 'Christ, that one was close – here, help me . . .'

Someone was dragging him by the arms, he opened his eyes and saw the sky, rent by scudding clouds, and his ears buzzed from the shell which had just exploded nearby. Then the sky disappeared and there was grey concrete over his head and he was being helped to stand. An SS Scharführer supported him; a uniformed police guard was beside him.

'You all right, son?' The Scharführer asked him.

Max nodded; his head and the side of his face were throbbing. He remembered that savage punch that had knocked him to the ground. He had been kicked too; breathing sent shafts of pain over his ribs.

'We saw you out there,' the police guard said, 'and we thought you'd caught a shell splinter. One of the HJ's going to Pichelsdorf, weren't you?'

'Yes,' Max mumbled. 'They shot the man . . .' He put his hands over his face and began to cry. The SS Scharführer glanced at the police guard.

'Come on, son,' he said. 'You've just got a bit of concussion, that's all. Think yourself lucky you got knocked out and didn't get to bloody Pichelsdorf – suicide squad, that was – come on, we'll take you downstairs.'

'I'm on duty in the watchtower,' the police guard said. 'All I see is the Red bastards getting closer every minute. Take the kid below; he looks green . . .'

Max had recognized his surroundings as they talked; he wiped his eyes on his sleeve and choked back more tears. They were in the porch under the exit from the Bunker. Outside was the garden where the man had been executed.

'Mind the steps,' the Scharführer said. 'You're not going to puke, are you?'

'No,' Max mumbled. 'No, I'm all right.' The stairs seemed to go down and down; they had been comparatively few when he had hurried up them with his squad in the early morning. At the foot of the stairs they were met by three SS officers, headed by a man wearing the insignia of a Sturmbannführer.

'What are you doing?' he shouted to the Scharführer who was ahead of Max, and the man snapped to attention.

'Carrying out orders, sir.'

'All exits into the garden are closed?'

'Yes, sir.'

'What's that boy doing?'

'We found him lying outside – he's all right, just got a knock on the head.'

Max watched the Sturmbannführer's face; it was haggard and the lips quivered; there was a look of frenzy in the eyes.

'Get him away from here – at once! This corridor is to be kept clear!'

The SS Scharführer saluted and grabbed Max by the arm, hurrying him forward. He saw two doors on the right of them as they hastened through a long wide room with chairs and a long table and wall maps. The second door was partly open, and he glimpsed the black uniforms of the SS inside. He had an impression of a blanket-shrouded figure being held by two men, but even as they passed the door was slammed shut, and by now the Scharführer was forcing him into a run.

They came out of the long room which looked as if it were used for conferences and into another room of the same size: it was full of people, men in uniform, women wearing the military-style garb of the female SS staff. Nobody looked at Max or seemed to notice him; faces were dazed and no one spoke. Two women, one of them young and pretty, wept without making any sound or attempt to check the tears which streamed down their faces. Max was hustled through them and to another flight of stairs; his head was quite clear now and he recognized the route he and the squad had taken earlier; through the dining area of the upper Bunker, past the passage and the storeroom where he had seen the executed man for the first time. They reached the bulkhead before a shorter flight of steps, and at the top of these they came into a room which was also full of people.

'Stay here,' the Scharführer said. 'Ilse, come and look after this one; get some of that liquor they've been hiding in the kitchen.'

'You hurt?' The girl was in civilian dress, a brown skirt and a white blouse; she had fair hair severely pinned back in a bun and her face was very pale, with puffy skin under the eyes. Max shook his head.

'No. What's happening? Why is everyone in here – that other room below was full of people . . . I saw some of them crying . . .' He caught hold of her arm. 'Is the war over? Have we surrendered?'

She had a glass in her hand and was pouring wine into it. She drank some herself before giving the glass to him, and wiped her pale lips with the back of her hand. 'Don't say that word,' she said. 'Not till we know for sure he's dead. You must have come up through the Führer Bunker. Did you see anything?' She was watching him closely, speaking very low.

'They were clearing the corridor and closing all the doors outside,' he said. 'I thought I saw somebody dead, wrapped up in one room, but they slammed the door –'

She gave a deep sigh, and suddenly her eyes were filled with tears. 'He said good-bye to us all last night,' she said. 'He came and shook hands with us. We knew what it meant. Somebody started a gramophone in the canteen and we began to dance. It was about three in the morning – I work in the kitchens here, doing the catering. Do you know, one of the senior officers in his bodyguard – a Standartenführer – he danced with me? I knew it was the end then. Everything was breaking up . . .' She caught hold of Max by the shoulders. 'You don't understand me, do you? You don't know what I'm talking about?'

Her hands dropped away from him. 'The Führer's dead,' she said. 'If they're closing everything up like that, and you saw a body – those rooms are his private suite. Him and Eva Braun. She came here to die with him.' She took the glass away from Max and poured more wine into it. Again she drank half herself.

'It's all over,' she said. 'Now we can make peace, while there's anyone left alive – my husband's fighting with General Wenck's army. We kept hoping they'd come to Berlin and drive back the Ivans, but they didn't . . . I expect my man's dead anyway. I haven't had a letter for weeks – ' She paused; it was as if she had been talking to herself rather than him. Now she looked at him as a person, and hesitantly touched the bruised and swollen side of his face.

'That's nasty,' she said. 'What are you doing down here – we haven't any HJ's on our staff – '

'Our cadre were sent for last night,' Max answered. 'We thought we were going to see the Führer, before we went to fight at Pichelsdorf – he didn't come. There was a man shot this morning – '

'That's what we heard,' Ilse said. 'Someone said he was caught with E.B.'s diamonds, getting ready to run. Listen, where's your home?'

'My mother lives on Albrechtstrasse; I want to get back and see she's all right. How can I get out of here?'

'Stick close to me,' the girl said. 'Now that the Führer's dead there's nothing to stay for – not to get caught by the Ivans. The Scharführer's a friend of mine' – she looked briefly sly – 'the one who brought you up here. Josef Franke, that's his name. They're shooting all the SS, as they capture them. Josef's not going to get himself caught by them . . . Some of us are going to try and run for it. I'll ask him if you can come along.'

'I want to get home,' Max insisted.

Someone had come up behind him. He was a tall, thin young man in the uniform of a Luftwaffe staff officer. 'And where's home, cadre leader?'

'Albrechtstrasse, sir. My mother and grandmother are there.'

The thin man shook his head. 'No good trying to get there,' he said. 'The Russians have got control of the whole section. They broke through to the Schoneberg this morning. If you're found on the streets in that uniform you'll be shot dead.' He moved away. 'Albrechtstrasse' – Max heard someone else say it – 'there's not a house left standing. We got a message from the Volksturm commander before they surrendered. Poor old devils, there were just a handful of them left.'

He felt Ilse's thin arm go round him. 'Never mind,' she murmured. 'Never mind – it's the same for all of us. You come with Josef and me . . .' Max leaned his head against her narrow bosom and wept for the loss of his family and his home. By five o'clock that evening, his olive-green Hitler Jügend uniform exchanged for an ill-fitting assortment of civilian clothes, Max Steiner crept out through the vast ruined Chancellory building, with Ilse and Franke, now wearing army uniform, and some of the clerks and domestic staff from the Bunker and the Foreign Office who had taken shelter there. As they left the shattered building, its marble and malachite walls cracked and crumbling from Allied bombs and Russian shellfire, the group of fugitives noticed, without realizing the significance, two thick black columns of smoke rising from the Chancellory gardens. They came from the petrol fire that provided Germany's Führer and his lover Eva Braun with their Viking funeral.

He had fallen asleep at his desk, his head resting on his folded arms, and the tape-recorder shone its red eye unheeded, waiting to be switched off. The window grew lighter, showing the outline of roofs on the opposite buildings, and the sky changed subtly from grey to pink and then to a sulphurous yellow as the sun rose. He woke stiff-necked and aching, with the nightbeard bristling on his chin, and a staleness in his mouth. It was too early for the office staff to have arrived; he heard the distant hum of a vacuum cleaner in the corridors. He needed a bath and a shave and first, some coffee. There was a machine outside his secretary's office, and he got a plastic cupful, so hot and black that it burned his tongue.

He went back to his office and lit a cigarette. The thought of Ellie nagged him; he needed to go home and use his own bathroom, change out of the suit he had slept in. But going back to the apartment meant facing his wife, submitting to the questions and the fussing and the reasoned reproaches. He stretched, loosening the muscles in his back and shoulders. He was behaving badly, like a coward. He was sure she hadn't slept all night; his children must be worried, shocked by his involvement with a violent murder. He switched on his portable radio and caught the eight o'clock news. There were no new developments; the police were conducting a nationwide hunt for the two killers; he listened to the clichés that concealed a lack of fresh news, and then switched the set off.

'Janus.' The nightmare had not come; he had slept deeply and without disturbance. But his memory was running as clear as if he were watching a film of his own past; incidents long forgotten came crowding and jostling for recognition, linked by the dying word of Sigmund Walther, and the whisper of the condemned man in the Berlin Chancellory yard. He had got out of the centre of the city, with Ilse, the girl from the kitchens, and her SS lover, Franke. How clearly he remembered their names. Then an American patrol had picked them up; the Red Cross had arranged his repatriation to his father's sister in Bremen. With her family, he had begun to reshape his life and go to school and then to university. He had kept the secret of his last days in Berlin to himself. There had been no point in returning to Albrechtstrasse to look for his house; it had been destroyed. His mother and grandmother were never heard of again.

As a young journalist he had written of his flight from the doomed city, of the shelling and fighting he had lived through and his arrest by the Americans. But he had never mentioned his presence in the Bunker to a human soul. But whatever the condemned man had known and tried to communicate to him, Sigmund Walther had known about too. He knew exactly what he had to do, and the decision brought with it a sense of extraordinary relief. He picked up the telephone and dialled the Crillon; no calls were being put through to the Walthers' suite. He persuaded them to send up a message, and he waited, holding onto the telephone.

When he heard her voice it shocked him; it sounded thick with tears.

'This is Minna Walther. You wanted to speak to me.'

'Yes,' Max said. 'I'm sorry I had to intrude on you, Fräu Walther. Please believe me, this has nothing to do with my paper. Your husband said something before he died. I didn't mention it to the police. But I'd like to talk to you about it. Will you see me?'

There was a slight pause; he heard her clear her throat.

'Yes,' she spoke slowly, carefully. 'Yes, of course I will. My elder children are here – there are arrangments to be made this morning. I'd rather not see ordinary journalists.'

'That's very natural,' he said. 'What can we do, then – '

'I shall arrange to be alone at lunchtime,' Minna Walther said. 'Come and see me just after one o'clock.'

'Thank you, Fräu Walther,' he said. She hung up without saying good-bye.

2

'Why doesn't she cry? Why won't she let go for once?' Helmut Walther stopped pacing the sitting room and turned round to his sister. He was pale and red-eyed from a night spent weeping for his father; he looked very much like him. He was eighteen, and going to be reading law and economics at Heidelberg University. He faced his younger sister and asked the same angry question. 'She loved him – for Christ's sake, why can't she show what she's feeling?'

Freda Walther shook her head. She too resembled her father, except that she had inherited her mother's tall, slight build. At seventeen she was a pretty girl with the promise of beauty when she matured.

'She doesn't want to upset us,' Freda said. 'You don't understand Mother, you never have. This isn't the time to start criticizing. She's just thinking of us!'

'Oh no, she isn't,' Helmut said. 'It's the shit Prussian attitude – no human feelings, no tears – only the lower orders cry! I remember Grandpa saying that to us, and so do you! I tell you, Freda, I don't know how Papa lived with it –'

He sat down and covered his face; his shoulders moved as he sobbed. His sister got up quietly and went to comfort him. He was a brilliant student, but the most impulsive of the family; he laughed and cried easily, loved and hated on intuition. He would be a great man, Sigmund used to say gently, when he learned to control himself and think first before he spoke. Freda loved him; she stroked his hair and murmured to him. He had worshipped his father; although she was not as clever as he was, she understood that venting his anger upon their mother was only part of his grief.

'Come on,' she repeated, 'come on, Helmut – Papa would not want you to go on like this. He'd want you to be brave and help Mother now. We've all got to stick together and look after Hedda, Willi and poor little Magda – we'll be going home tonight and we've got to think about them.' She hugged her brother close to her for a moment. 'You're wrong about Mother. I was awake last night and I heard her crying her eyes out. Papa absolutely worshipped her, you know he did.'

Her brother slipped an arm round her waist.

'All right,' he said. 'I suppose she can't help it – none of that generation could. Oh God, how we're going to miss Papa! I still can't believe it – '

'Nor can I,' Freda said. 'I keep thinking he'll walk in from the bedroom . . . why – why did anyone want to kill him?'

'Because he was a liberal German,' Helmut said fiercely. 'He wanted to bring us all together. I know who murdered him – the bloody right wing!'

They heard the bedroom door open and together they looked up and saw their mother. She was very pale and though it was a trick of the sunlight through the window, her blonde hair seemed almost white. She stood and looked at them for a moment; Freda moved first. She went and put her arms round her mother.

'How do you feel, Mama: Did you sleep?'

Minna clung to her daughter for a few brief seconds, and then released her.

'I'm all right darling. Helmut – ' She approached her son with hesitation.

There had always been antipathy between them; she had married Sigmund Walther at eighteen and been a mother by her nineteenth birthday. The strong-willed, volatile boy had grown up into an adversary, as close to his father as he was distant with her.

'I spoke to the Ambassador this morning. Arrangements have been made to fly your father home. They've booked us on a Lufthansa flight this afternoon; they're very worried about security, so the Ambassador suggested you and Freda should go round to the embassy at lunchtime, I'll join you later and we'll be driven to the airport together.'

'Why aren't you coming with us?' Helmut asked. 'If there's any danger, you should go to the embassy too. You've no reason to wait on here, Mother.'

'Someone is coming to see me,' Minna said quietly. 'He's coming to the hotel.'

'Who is it?' Her son spoke sharply. 'It's not a reporter is it? I said last night we wouldn't give any interviews or talk to anyone on the media. I thought you agreed to that – ' Minna looked at him. He was the head of the family now that his father was dead; there was a silent confrontation, witnessed by Freda. Then Minna Walther spoke. Her voice was cold and there was anger in it.

'The man who is coming here was with your father when he died. I have a right to see him, and it is nothing to do with you, Helmut, or anyone else. The embassy car will be here at twelve. You'll both go, and I shall join you later.'

She turned her back on her children, went into her bedroom and closed the door. She didn't come out until she knew that they had left. She checked herself in the mirror; it was habit, not vanity. Nineteen years of living in the spotlight as Sigmund's wife had conditioned her to looking right, whatever the occasion. She had not worn black, although she possessed a black suit; but her husband had detested mourning and the ritual of death. He had been a man to whom life was all-important; a man with a personality that radiated energy, optimism and hope. She would never wear black for him.

She went into the empty sitting room; it was full of sunshine. She poured a glass of whisky and water, lit a cigarette; went to the windows and looked out over the Place de la Concorde. The evening they arrived from Bonn, she and Sigmund had stood in front of the window, he with his arm around her, enjoying the spectacular view of the Place at night, jewelled with lights, the traffic flashing diamond head-lights in a glittering moving pattern. He had said suddenly that he felt everything they had worked for was coming closer; he told her how much he owed to her support, and asked her, as he often did, if she still loved him. They had made love that night. She remembered it, not seeing the panorama beyond the window. The cigarette was finished. She stubbed it out and went to the sofa, sipping the whisky. She sat down to wait for Max Steiner.

Max Steiner was right when he supposed his wife hadn't slept; she had spent a long time calming Francine and reasoning with Peter, who was still sullen and hostile towards his father. The more she emphasized the danger he had been in when the West German MP had been assassinated, the more hysterical Francine became and the less her son responded. In the end Ellie took the girl into bed with her, and left Peter dourly watching late-night television with the English girl. Love for her children masked Ellie's own anxiety and hurt feelings until Francine was asleep and she was awake in the darkness. She loved Max, and she was in love with him; she admired his intelligence, his grasp of events, his brilliant journalism. Her role was supportive; to mother his children and care for him, to be lover and companion, and to apply her own brand of simple wisdom in dealing with his difficult temperament. She had never consciously put the children first; they were children and automatically claimed priority over either of their parents. It pained and troubled Ellie that Max had grown so apart from them, and from her in the last year or more. She had accepted the change in him, rationalized her own disappointment and continued to do her best. In the darkness her daughter stirred uneasily beside her. He should have come home; he should have thought first of his family's anxiety and at least telephoned. By the morning, Ellie had recovered her composure; she was pale and her head ached from weariness and tension, but she saw her children off to school, kept up a bright chatter with the English girl, and refrained from telephoning the *Newsworld*

office until ten o'clock. There Max's secretary told her that he had
been called out, and gave her his message. He would be back after
lunch, and she was not to worry. Everything was fine.

She was reading the *Figaro* and drinking coffee in the kitchen when
the doorbell rang. 'I'll answer it, Madame Steiner,' Pat said. Ellie
nodded, deep in the editorial which was devoted to the significance
of Sigmund Walther's murder. A moment later Pat was back.

'It's someone called Durand from the Sûreté,' she said. 'He wants
to see you.'

Ellie frowned. 'Okay, Pat, thanks. Bring us some coffee, will you
please?'

He was a small, square man, holding his hat rather stiffly at his side.
He wore thick-rimmed spectacles. Ellie took him into the sitting room
and sat opposite to him.

'I'm afraid my husband isn't here,' she said. 'I got a message he'll
be back this afternoon.'

'Have you any idea where I could find him, Madame?' The eyes
behind the lenses were small and blue; he had an intent look that
made Ellie feel uncomfortable.

'I haven't. I'm sorry. His secretary said he was called out, that's all
I know.'

'Your husband was very lucky not to have been killed yesterday,'
the Sûreté detective said. 'It's surprising they didn't shoot him too.'

Ellie shivered. 'Don't even talk about it,' she said. 'You'll have
some coffee, won't you?' Pat put down the tray, glanced briefly at
the policeman and went out.

'I was hoping to talk to your husband,' Durand said, 'but perhaps
you can help me. What exactly did he tell you about the killing –
anything, even the smallest detail, could help us find the murderers.'

Ellie shook her head. 'He didn't tell me anything – I haven't seen
or spoken to him since it happened. He was down at the Sûreté
yesterday making a statement. I guessed he was back there this
morning – ' she paused, and then spoke her thoughts aloud. 'I wonder
where he is?'

'Maybe with SDECE,' Durand said. 'They're a law unto themselves;
they don't believe in co-operating with us or anybody else. I'm sorry
I've bothered you for nothing. It's just that sometimes the memory
plays tricks after a shock; your husband might have remembered
something talking to you which he'd forgotten when he made his
statement to us.'

'Can I get him to call you when he comes back?' The detective
stood up. His coffee cup was full; he hadn't touched it. 'No, thank
you, Madame Steiner. We'll contact him.' They were on the way to
the front door when he stopped.

'Has anyone else tried to see him this morning – have you had any telephone calls?'

'No,' Ellie said. 'Only from friends wanting to know he was all right – nothing official. Why?'

The pale eyes focused on her face. 'Your husband was a witness, Madame. He saw the assassins. I'm a family man myself. I would persuade him to get out of Paris and take a trip somewhere. It might be a good idea if you and your children went with him.' He set the soft hat on his head, tweaked the brim till it came down on his forehead, made her a little gesture like a bow, and let himself out.

Ellie stood in the narrow hallway; slowly her hands came together and locked.

'Oh, my God,' she said.

Minna Walther held out her hand; Max took it. It was cool and quite steady. He thought she looked ill; the skin around her eyes was taut, emphasizing the Slav cheekbones; there were black shadows under her eyes.

'Help yourself to a drink,' she said.

'No, thanks,' Max said. He noticed the half empty glass beside her chair. Tension crackled in the air like electricity after a storm.

He had gone to a barber's for a shave, and spent an hour walking along the Seine near Les Invalides, thinking thoughts that had taken him a long way from Paris. As he faced Sigmund Walther's widow, it could have been a lifetime since he had taped that interview in the same room, instead of twenty-four hours. He had a sense of sharp anticipation, a flutter in the stomach, as he waited for her to speak.

'You have something to tell me about my husband,' she said.

'Yes,' Max answered. He found a cigarette, offered one to her, and lit them both.

'Please,' he caught the high pitch in her voice, 'please tell me.'

'I held your husband as he died,' he said quietly. 'He said one word, and it didn't come out by accident. He meant me to hear it. "Janus."' He watched her as he said it. No shade of expression passed over her face. The large grey eyes returned his look. 'Was that all? He said nothing else?'

'No. He died immediately afterwards,' Max leaned a little forward in his chair. 'What did he mean, Fräu Walther?'

'I don't know. Janus was a Roman god – it doesn't make sense.'

'You've never heard him mention it?'

'No, never.'

Max felt suddenly depressed. 'Could I change my mind and have a drink now?'

'Of course; I'll get it for you – what would you like?'

'Don't move, please, I'll get my own. One for you?' He was surprised when she emptied the glass and held it out to him; she didn't seem the type of woman who drank except to be polite.

He poured whisky for them both and his depression deepened. He hadn't expected her to lie. 'Janus.' She hadn't been surprised; he had the feeling that she had been expecting him to say it. He sat down opposite her.

'Your husband was murdered,' he said, not looking at her. 'Janus was the reason, that's what he was trying to tell me. If you want to get the people who killed him, you've got to tell me what Janus means. Before you answer, Fräu Walther, I'd like to tell you something. It's not the first time I've heard it said by a dying man.'

The rigidity went out of her so quickly that she sank back in the chair and closed her eyes. 'Who are you working for?'

'Why should I be working for anyone?' he countered. 'Stop lying to me, Fräu Walther. Who is Janus?'

'A Roman god with two faces,' she said. 'That's all I know. It's a code of some kind. Sigmund was trying to find out what it meant.' She raised her head and looked at him. 'When did you hear it first?'

'In 1945. It didn't mean anything to me then; it was just part of a nightmare. Since then it's become a real nightmare; I dream about it – something in me won't let it rest. Then your husband gets shot down, and it's right back in the present day. You asked me who I was working for – I'm not working for anybody but myself. I want to know who or what Janus is, that it can kill a man like Sigmund Walther.'

'And the other man,' she asked him, 'the one you mentioned who said it before?'

'That's a long story,' Max Steiner said. 'Let me ask you something – do you want to find your husband's murderers?'

There was a spot of colour blazing on each cheek when she answered him. 'I'll do anything, pay anything – how could you even ask –'

'Because I want to be sure,' he interrupted. 'You may prefer to let the police handle it. Their record for finding high-grade political assassins like the two who shot your husband isn't all that impressive. You may be frightened for yourself – or for your children . . . I'm just on the fringe of the thing; you may know far more than you're prepared to tell me. But I'm going to find out what this means, and I came here to ask you to help me.'

She didn't answer. She got up from the chair, wearily, as if she were exhausted, found a cigarette and lit it. The lighter closed with a snap that could be heard, the room was so quiet.

'Sigmund was an old-fashioned man,' she said suddenly. 'He loved his country. It's been fashionable for a long time among certain Germans to reject their race and their history, as if denying them could wipe out what happened in the war. It can't, and Sigmund knew that. We have to forget about the past and concentrate on the future. I'll help you to find out what Janus means. Not just to find the men who killed him, and the people who sent them to do it. But to carry on his work for Germany.'

'And Janus is connected with that work?' Max asked her.

'Yes,' Minna Walther said. She stood leaning against the fireplace, looking down at him. 'You'll have to come to Germany.'

'I was planning to,' he said. 'One thing: we've got to trust each other. You've got to tell me everything your husband knew.'

'I will,' she said quietly. 'I'm flying home this afternoon. I'll go through my husband's files and have everything ready for you to look at. When will you come?'

'When is your husband's funeral?' Max asked her.

'The day after tomorrow. In Hamburg. Our home is there.'

'His family came from Silesia,' he said.

'So did mine,' Minna Walther answered. 'Where were you born, Herr Steiner?'

'Berlin,' he said. He stood and for a moment they faced each other.

'I'm very sorry about about what happened,' he said.

'He had a good life,' she said softly. 'A lot of people loved him. Telephone me and I'll meet you at the airport.'

He took her hand once more and held it. He hadn't kissed a woman's hand since the war, but he did so then. Outside in the corridor, walking down the thick-piled carpet to the lift, he thought suddenly, Christ, Steiner – what's got into you? Then the lift came and he stepped inside, as he had done the day before with Sigmund Walther by his side. He went back to his office and wrote a special article on the murder and the short political career of the dead man, for the end of the week issue. It was easy to do; he avoided sensationalism, and at the back of his mind was the fact that Minna Walther and her family might read what he had written. He gave it in to the editor-in-chief, and waited while he finished it. Martin Jarre put the script down.

'Good. It'll be the lead story and we'll run a cover with Walther's head in a mock-up. You're looking better this morning – get a good night's sleep?'

'No,' said Max. 'I didn't go home. I stayed in the office. I'm glad you like the piece, but it's just the tip of an iceberg. I want to do an in-depth investigation job on this Walther murder.'

'Why?' Jarre frowned. 'What have you held back?'

Max picked up the script. 'Something that could bring his killers after me,' he said. 'But they don't know I know anything. I'm asking you for a *carte blanche* on this one: expenses, time, the lot. If I succeed in finding out what I'm after, you'll have a big story. Very big. If I don't, you can kick my arse. Or pay the funeral expenses.'

Jarre's frown became a scowl, and then cleared suddenly. 'All right, Max. Write your own ticket. Be careful.'

'Thanks, I will. I'm going to Germany on Thursday. I'll report back when I've got something. I'd like a credit account opened in the Deutsche Bank in Bonn, with facilities in West Berlin and Hamburg. Twenty-five thousand marks as a start.'

'I'll make the arrangements,' Jarre said. 'It would help if I knew what you were looking for.'

'It'd help if I knew myself,' Max Steiner said, as he went out.

The men who had killed Sigmund Walther boarded the Swiss air flight to Geneva less than two hours after the murder. They carried Swiss passports, made out in the names of Kesler and Franconi; the elder of the two was grey-haired, wore glasses and carried a briefcase, the younger was blond, soberly dressed, and carried a small handcase and an armful of the financial papers. They were described respectively as a civil engineer and an accountant. The dark wigs they had worn for the killing had been pushed into a rubbish bin en route for the airport. The two handguns, all serial numbers erased and never used before, had been dropped in a paper bag into the Seine. They abandoned the stolen car, picked up the self-drive which had been left parked in the car park behind Les Invalides, and driven to Orly airport to catch their flight.

They didn't sit together on the journey. Kesler took papers out of his briefcase and studied them, making notes, and Franconi read the London *Financial Times*. Kesler ordered a vodka and tonic: Franconi asked for coffee. The flight was uneventful; after a time Kesler put his papers away and stared out of the window at the piercing blue sky. He had been killing professionally since the late fifties; five years in the Foreign Legion had provided him with a hiding place. It was full of people like him, with false names and war crimes behind them, men too unimportant to merit the help of the SS escape organization, Odessa; Poles and Ukrainians and Germans, members of the terrible Einsatzkommandos who had exterminated Jews in the East, concentration camp guards, rankers in the Waffen SS who had thrown away their uniforms and papers and crossed the Italian frontier with the refugees and the army of displaced persons that roamed Europe.

Kesler was a Pole by birth; the Legion accepted him and thousands like him, and sent them to fight for France in Indochina. He had survived the siege of Dien Bien Phu, and returned to civilian life with skills in every kind of modern weapon, and a reputation for ruthlessness that filtered through to people interested in recruiting such men. He went to Marseilles, because he had contacts there through the Legion, and worked for a narcotics ring. That was where he met Maurice Franconi and fell in love. Franconi was an Italian Swiss who had been in petty crime since he was a boy, graduating from male prostitution to theft and extortion from his victims.

Kesler set up an apartment with him, and began to teach him to better himself. He had proved quick and skilful; after a few months he was as good as Kesler with a knife or a handgun. Employment was found for him too, and between them they murdered seventeen people, five of them women, in the next two years. This had been their biggest assignment; the payment was in proportion to the importance of the victim and to the risk involved. After this, Kesler thought peacefully, he and Maurice could retire, buy a little place in Tangier, where they had friends . . . The sexual aspect of their lives was less important than when they had first met; their relationship was tender, at times almost as of father and son. They liked music and the theatre; Maurice had become a keen reader of the classics, under Kesler's tutelage. Kesler's own background had been middle-class in his native Poland; he was a cultivated man and he enjoyed improving his lover's mind and introducing him to the arts. They had a perfectly balanced relationship and, unlike some of their homosexual friends, there were no stormy quarrels, no jealousy. At the end of their first two years together, they had gone through a ceremony of homosexual marriage, and both men wore wedding rings on their right hands.

The plane landed on schedule at Geneva airport; they met in the car park, where the car hired the previous evening was waiting for them. Kesler paused with his hand on the door. 'To be on the safe side,' he said, 'let's just check it, shall we?' Franconi crouched down and opened his handcase. He took out a small pencil torch with a surprisingly strong beam and, getting his knees dusty, inspected the underside of the chassis by both front and rear doors. Kesler said, 'We may as well make sure of the rest of it. No harm in being careful. I'll do the top half if you'll get underneath.'

Franconi nodded and smiled at him. He had fine white teeth, and when he smiled he was handsome. He stripped off his jacket and crawled under the chassis. Kesler checked on everything above; the boot swung open when he was sure the lock was clean; it was empty. The wipers satisfied him, so did the bonnet. He opened the passenger door and checked that the mechanism for opening the bonnet was free of even a hair-trigger wire, and then opened it, so that the engine could be inspected. He was looking inside when Franconi came up from underneath. He had dirtied the back of his shirt and trousers, and there was a smudge on his face. 'Nothing,' he said. 'Did you find anything –?'

'No,' Kesler said. 'Turn round and I'll brush you down. The car's all right.'

'You don't trust anybody do you?' Maurice said.

'That's why I'm still alive.' Kesler helped him put on his jacket. 'I've checked cars ever since we started working for them. I don't say for a moment they'd get rid of us – we're much too useful – but you never know. There was a man used to work for Gabriel – the drug boys got a lead on him and he made a deal. Somebody passed Gabriel the word, and they fixed his car for him. He'd been told to check but he forgot one thing. The cigarette lighter.'

Maurice got in and started the car. 'I'm hungry, aren't you, Stanis? I could do with a good lunch. I suppose the restaurant will be closed by the time we get in.'

Kesler looked at his watch. 'Nearly four – yes, I'd think so. But we'll get something sent up. We can nibble away while we count the money.' He put back his head and laughed. Then he placed his hand lightly on Franconi's knee.

'You were great today,' he said. 'It was a beautiful job. One of our best.'

Maurice frowned. 'They didn't tell us there'd be another man with him,' he said.

'Don't worry about that,' Kesler said. 'He saw the same as everyone else. Two men in dark glasses. We'll listen to the radio and it's sure to be on the TV now. We're out and clear, like we always are, eh? And this time, we've got enough to give up working.'

Franconi glanced at him and flashed the gleaming smile. 'You'd get bored, Stanis. You love working.'

'I love you,' Kesler said. 'I don't want the luck to run out. I want to go and live in the sun with you; you'd love Tangier. We'd be very happy there. And we could always take a trip if you wanted a change.'

'I'd be happy wherever we went,' Franconi said, 'so long as we're together. That's all that matters to me.'

The hotel had a two-star rating; it was comfortable and catered for businessmen and families. Kesler and Franconi had stayed the previous night there and found the food excellent. Franconi parked the car at the rear of the hotel, while Kesler went to the reception desk.

'Good afternoon,' he said to the clerk. 'I'm expecting a package – has anything arrived for me?'

The clerk checked in the pigeonholes and glanced under the desk. He shook his head. 'No, M. Kesler. But there's a gentleman waiting in the lounge for you. He's been here some time.'

'Ah,' Kesler said. 'Thank you.'

There were a number of people in the lounge; tea was being served. Kesler recognized the man sitting alone at a table, and went up to him. His eyes noted that the man was carrying a briefcase similar to his own. He went over and shook hands.

'What's this?' he said under his breath. 'We weren't expecting you – where's the money –?' He gave a wide smile and said loudly, 'How nice of you to wait for me – come on upstairs – '

They went up the two floors in the lift without speaking. Kesler unlocked the door of his room; Franconi had the room adjoining. Then he shut the door and turned to the man who had seated himself on the bed. There was no smile on Kesler's face. 'What the hell is this? I was supposed to get a package – nobody told me you were coming!'

'I've brought the money,' the other man said. He had been their contact for the last five assignments. He was known only as Paul; he spoke French with an accent that suggested he came from east of the Oder, but when Kesler tried him out in German and Polish he refused to talk at all. He was a thin, dour, nondescript human being, with deep-set eyes. Franconi nicknamed him 'the undertaker'.

Kesler held out his hand. 'Give it to me.' The briefcase was passed to him and the man Paul tossed him a key. Kesler put the case on the chest of drawers and opened it. The money was neatly packed inside: Swiss francs, in used notes. Kesler didn't trouble to count the packets. He knew his employers had never cheated on a payment. He shut the case again and turned to Paul. Franconi came into the room; he stared at the other man and looked sharply at Kesler. 'What's he doing here?'

'He brought the money,' Kesler said.

The man seated himself on the bed again and drew an envelope out of his pocket. 'I've got a proposition for you,' he said in his ugly French. 'You've got two hundred thousand francs in there – ' he jutted his mean chin towards the case. 'You could earn three times that.'

'Oh?' Franconi sneered. 'Who's the target – the American President, for instance? How do you fancy ending like Lee Harvey Oswald, Stanis – nice bullet in the belly – ' He said something obscene in Italian. Paul ignored him; there was a natural antipathy between them. He addressed himself to Kesler.

'I've got a list in here – ', the envelope was raised like a torch, and then lowered. 'There are four names on it. No presidents – not even the Pope.' His teeth showed in a grimace trying to be a smile. Kesler matched him.

'Maurice and I are Catholics,' he said. 'I'm glad it isn't the Pope. Four people – six hundred thousand francs. That's a lot of money. And a lot of risk.' He shook his head. 'We're not interested.'

'Wait a minute,' Maurice said. 'Who are the four targets?'

'I can't give you the envelope till you've agreed to the job,' the man said. He put the envelope back into his pocket. 'All I know is there's no one that important.'

'Then why so much money?' Kesler asked. 'Six hundred thousand francs. Nobody pays like that unless it's in proportion to the risk. We've done the Walther job and we want to enjoy the money.'

'Show us the names,' Franconi said. 'If they don't trust us, then get someone else. I'm not going into anything blind and neither is Stanis.'

The thin man hesitated. They were the best in the business. Reliable, efficient: a perfect killing mechanism. He took out the envelope, opened it and handed the sheet of paper to Kesler. There was silence in the room for a minute while Kesler read the list and then read it again. He looked up and frowned at Paul.

'Who are these people?'

'I don't know,' the thin man said. 'What do you care – just find them and get rid of them. You've got a month to do it. But no fuss, no publicity.'

'Don't try teaching us our job,' Franconi snapped. He came over to Kesler and studied the list. He shrugged. 'It's a fortune,' he said softly. 'Just one month, Stanis. Think what we could buy for ourselves with money like that – '

'I am thinking,' Kesler said. He looked at his lover. 'You want to do it?'

'Why not? One month and we've got enough money to have everything we want. There's nothing in this – ' he tapped the paper with his index finger. His nails were manicured and lightly polished. He had sensitive, well-kept hands. 'It's a package deal, that's all. No problem.'

Kesler turned back to Paul. 'Some have no address,' he said. 'Just relatives. This makes it complicated.'

'That's why you're being paid so well,' the man said. 'You find them, get rid of them nice and quietly, every one an accident – that's important.' He waited, looking at Kesler for confirmation.

'We'll do it,' Kesler said. The thin man nodded, gave the grimace which was meant to be a smile, and left them.

Franconi waited for a moment, and then, crossing to the door, opened it suddenly. There was no one in the corridor. He turned back to Kesler.

'I don't trust that little bastard – and I don't trust that list.'

'Then why did you make me agree?' Kesler seldom got angry with Maurice but his face had reddened. 'I didn't want to touch it – we've got two hundred thousand besides the money we've saved! Why did you have to be so greedy?'

'Because it's the biggest chance we'll ever have to be really rich!'

Franconi's voice rose. He hated quarrelling with Kesler: rarely as it happened, it unnerved him and he felt sulky for days afterwards. 'You talk about living in Tangier – yes, all right we can go there and hole up and watch the pennies for the rest of our lives, not being really *in* – if we do this last job we can be *rich* – we can buy a lovely villa, do it up nicely, entertain . . . Oh, Stanis, don't you see it's worth it?'

'I suppose so,' Kesler said slowly. 'But something about it stinks. Come on, let's not row about it. We've said we'll do it and we will. Let's put that case in the hotel safe till we can bank it:, and get something to eat. Then I want to watch the TV news. I have a gut feeling that we'll learn something more about that list.'

For the first time in years, Ellie Steiner surprised her husband. He had the scene rehearsed, every line of dialogue already spoken in his mind, his own attitudes and hers plotted out. He was ready for tears, appeals to his responsibility to her and the children, followed by the patient arguments which so infuriated him because they were full of surface logic. When he came into the apartment, the children were at school, and his wife was alone, watching an educational programme on TV. She got up slowly and stared at him for a second or two, before coming across very quickly and putting her arms round him.

'Oh darling,' she said. 'Thank God you're back.'

She made them both tea and they drank it together in the kitchen. The kitchen was Ellie's kingdom, gleaming with copper and pine, equipped like a spaceship with every gadget that came on the market. She was a marvellous cook. He watched her while she got the cups and a plate of biscuits. He noticed that she looked very pale and tense. He told her about Walther's assassination; without intention, he hardly mentioned the murdered man's wife. She reached out and placed her hand over his. It was a touching gesture, and he squeezed it hard, nerving himself for what had to be said next. That was when she surprised him.

'Max darling, a man from the Sûreté came here this morning. He wanted to talk to you, but your secretary had told me you were out. He said we could be in danger; you and me and the children. He told me to take them and go away for a while. He said you should come too.'

'Why would the Sûreté send someone round here? And, for God's sake, why would you and the children be in danger – '

'Because you saw the killers,' she said. 'He terrified me; he said the people who murdered Walther could be after you. We've got to get away – you've got to go to Jarre and tell him you want leave!'

'Wait a minute,' Max said. 'Wait a minute – this doesn't make sense. I spent hours down at the Sûreté yesterday, making a statement – nobody said anything to me about any risk – as for seeing the killers, so did half a dozen other people . . . Who was this man, do you remember his name?'

'Yes, Durand,' she said. 'Durand.'

'Christ,' he said, 'that's like Smith. I'm going to call Regnier and find out what the hell they're playing at.'

Ellie stayed in the kitchen, setting the cups in the dishwasher; she heard Max's voice and the 'ting' of the telephone. She stood by the kitchen door and listened. He hated anyone by his elbow when he was talking on the telephone; he had his back turned towards her. On the other end of the line, Inspector Pierre Regnier told Max to hold on, while he made inquiries. Certainly, he had not sent anyone to the Steiners' apartment. Max turned round while he waited and saw Ellie in the doorway.

'He's finding out about it,' he said. 'He didn't send a man round himself . . . Yes, hello – '

Regnier's voice was sharp. 'We have no one called Durand on the Walther case,' he said. 'Whoever saw your wife this morning, he wasn't one of our men. Could be some crank – but she says he showed a card?'

'He could have shown her a credit card for all the difference my wife would know,' Max said. 'Someone says they're a policeman, you believe them. I'll call you back when I've talked to her again.'

He saw Ellie's pale frightened face and his heart thumped when he thought of the man she had let into the flat that morning. He listened while she told him what the man had said, and fear began to prick along his skin. Whoever he was, and he didn't accept Regnier's suggestion of a crank, he had tried to prise information out of Ellie which she didn't have, and then tried to panic her so that she in turn would panic him.

'I've booked for all of us on the first flight to London tomorrow morning,' she said. 'I'm not risking keeping the children here. If that man wasn't from the Sûreté, then, for God's sake, who was he? Oh, Max, I'm really scared!'

'You did the right thing,' he said slowly. 'He could have been some nut, trying to frighten you. But it's better you and the children get out of Paris for a while.'

'You're coming with us – you're not going to stay here. If there's any danger, we've got to be together!'

'I shan't be in Paris,' he told her. It was slotting into place, like pieces in a puzzle that was making a picture. 'I'm going away on an assignment for Jarre. It'll take three weeks, maybe a month. Where are you going to stay in London – with Angela?'

'Yes,' She seemed thrown off balance by the question. Angela was married to a solicitor; she and Ellie had been close friends. They had stayed with the Steiners in Paris the previous autumn.

'Max,' she said. 'Max, where is this assignment?'

He didn't lie to her, although he was tempted. 'Germany,' he answered. She kept on looking at him, the brown eyes seemed to widen until they overpowered her face.

'Sigmund Walther's murder – is that what you're going to Germany for?'

'Yes,' he said. 'I'm determined to do it. I want to know who and why, and a whole lot of other things. And it'll help to know you and the children are safe in London with Angela and Tim.'

'And if anything happens to you, are Angela and Tim supposed to take care of us?'

Oh, he said to himself, Christ, here it comes. 'Nothing will happen to me,' he tried to sound reassuring, instead of angry. He didn't succeed because he added, 'Anyway, I'm heavily insured.' She gave him an odd look, and he thought she drew her body back and upright, as if something unpleasant had passed close to her. He felt suddenly alarmed, as if he had taken a step too far in a direction he hadn't intended. 'Ellie, I'm sorry. Try to understand, will you? This is terribly important to me. I have to find out why Walther was killed, not for bloody *Newsworld* but for myself! For my own peace of mind – I know you're scared and upset, and you want me to come with you, but I can't. I can't give up the chance to find out something – '

He stopped, and in the seconds that followed, he tried to retrace that step towards the brink, by telling her the truth. He didn't get the chance. She brushed her skirt with both hands, as if she were dusting off an apron, and her face was small and pale and set tight like a fist.

'I understand one thing,' she said. 'Me and the children come second. I've accepted it for a long while, and I've tried to explain it to them so they wouldn't be hurt. But now we're threatened with God knows what, because of you and your goddamned job, and you have the gall to tell me you're not coming over to protect your family! You're going to Germany instead, while we sit in someone else's house and let them take on your responsibility. Okay, Max, you go and play detective, and I'll think up a good reason for Peter and Francine why their father's gone off and left them.' She swung round and walked away; at the door she half turned. 'They'll be really glad to know you're insured.'

He drove them to Le Bourget at eight o'clock the next morning; his daughter was excited about going to London; his son had been morose and ill at ease the night before. He had muttered provocatively about being happy to miss school, but Max had ignored him. Ellie had been bright and artificial in front of the children, who quickly recognized

that there was trouble between their parents, but when they were alone
she refused to speak to him. At the airport he said good-bye, and it
was forced and awkward. He kissed Francine, who started to cry from
nerves and excitement, embraced his son, who went stiff, and kissed
Ellie on the cheek.

'Safe journey, darling. I'll call you tonight.'

'That would be nice,' his wife said. 'Come on, Peter dear, Francy,
take hold of my hand – ' Then they were gone. He ignored the funny
pang of loneliness that nagged at him all the way back from the airport
to his office. He spent the day in the cutting room, and the reference
library, and at the end of the day he had completed a set of notes. He
did not give them to his secretary to type out. He took them back to
the apartment, where the English girl Pat cooked him dinner, and then
he settled down to read them and the books he had brought with him.
The subject matter was the closing days of April 1945 and the fall of
the Bunker in Berlin.

There was a seven-and-a-half-hour time difference between Washington and Bonn; the telex from the Director of CIA West Germany
reached the Director in Washington a little before two o'clock. It was
decoded and passed straight through to his personal tray, because of
the double prefix TP, which it carried. The Director lunched in his
office; he arrived there at eight o'clock prompt and set no limit on
the hours he worked. He read the telex through carefully:

INTERPOL REPORT PROGRESS NEGATIVE. OUR INFORMATION RULES
OUT TERRORIST RFSPONSIBILITY FOR ASSASSINATION. ANALYSIS OF
MOTIVE AND METHOD TALLIES WITH CONTACTS HERE; UNCLE VANYA
OPERATION PROBABLE TO CERTAIN. REQUEST WASHINGTON LIAISON WITH
APPROPRIATE AUTHORITY AS SOON AS POSSIBLE.

The Director pressed a button on his telephone and spoke into it.
'File on Sigmund Walther, right away.' He lit a pipe and puffed gently
while he waited. They had been keeping a careful watch on the West
German politician from the moment he had first declared his belief in
détente with East Germany. His private telephone had been tapped
and his office in Bonn infiltrated by an agent. There had been no
evidence of complicity with the Russians, or of any motive but the
one he proclaimed publicly: the reunification of Germany.

The Director was a man of boundless cynicism in respect of human
beings and their motives. He believed nothing unless it showed evidence
of venality, and Sigmund Walther was too good to be true. He was
bidding for power, and he had chosen a policy which had the appeal of
patriotism and peace, and *détente* which was fashionable, and stood no

chance at all of becoming a reality. So the Director knew he was a fake. That knowledge didn't satisfy him because it left the true motivation of the man in doubt. Power alone was not sufficient explanation. To become leader of his party, to aim at the Chancellory itself – these were the obvious explanations why Walther projected himself as he did, but to the Director's subtle intelligence they were too obvious. There was a muted trumpet in the dulcet tones of Sigmund Walther's political pronouncements, a faint Wagnerian murmur that caught the Director's ear. West Germany was stable, prosperous and firmly tied to NATO and the Western alliance. She didn't need a saviour. There were no scandals about Walther. His business and private life was investigated over a long period without turning up a single dubious incident that could be used against him. Again it was too good to be true; the Director rejected it and told his people in Bonn to dig deeper and go back further. There had to be something discreditable. They hadn't found anything more heinous than a succession of love affairs with girls in his student days, and there were no pregnancies, abortions, drugs or suicides to make them worthwhile. Since his marriage to Minna Ahrenberg, he had never been involved with another woman. An upright businessman, succeeding through sheer ability and personal effort, a model husband, a devoted father, an incorruptible politician with high ideals. It was all a gigantic lie; the Director was convinced of it and let his counterpart in the West German Intelligence Service know exactly what he thought. And there, strangely, he had met resistance.

The head of German Intelligence had credentials which the West considered impeccable. He had led active resistance to the Nazis and to the SS Intelligence Service, when serving as a young officer under Admiral Canaris. He had been arrested after the Generals' Plot of 20th July, and sent to Mauthausen concentration camp, where he had withstood torture and protected his associates. He had been released by the Americans, held for a long interrogation, during which he helped to track down senior members of the SD, including two of Reichsführer Himmler's aides, and by 1947 he was working for the Gehlen organization against the Russians. He had proved himself an anti-Soviet as well as an anti-Nazi; his name was officially Heinrich Holler, but he had several other names, including the one which he had been given at birth. He had astonished the Director in Washington by defending Sigmund Walther, and insisting that he was exactly the paragon he appeared to be.

The Director was adept at reading files, skipping the irrelevant details, mentally processing the facts. Walther had a lot of powerful friends among the old military establishment; that was a consequence of his marriage to a member of it, but they made odd bedfellows with the new rich industrialists, the lawyers and journalists and Social Democratic politicians who were part of his circle. Now he was dead; murdered with the maximum publicity in the heart of Paris, accompanied by a well-known political journalist. Uncle Vanya, the top man in Bonn had said. He certainly needed a specialist to help unravel this one. The Director closed the file; thought for a moment and then pressed a button on his second desk phone. 'Send a message to Curt Andrews in Houston. Tell him to fly up here and be in my office by nine tomorrow. I have an assignment for him.'

3

Sigmund Walther was buried in the family grave at Ohlsdorf cemetery in Hamburg. His father and mother were buried in the small plot, and he followed them on a beautiful sunny day, with a light breeze stirring his widow's black veil. His eldest son watched the veil covering his mother's face and tried to see if it concealed tears. He was angry with her for now adopting the conventional trappings of a ritual she had earlier said his father had always despised. His own concession was a black armband, though Freda had followed her mother's example and dressed in black, as had their cousins and the few close friends invited to the private burial. A public memorial service would be held later. They reminded Helmut of a flock of black crows gathered round the grave, his mother a little apart, seeming even taller because she held herself so upright. He forced back his own tears as the coffin was lowered. His father had left no instruction in his will; Minna Walther had rejected cremation, which Helmut thought was cleaner than the archaic committal to the ground. He didn't believe in a life after death; Sigmund had derided it. It didn't matter what happened to a body; life was the only important thing, and when that had gone it was a flame snuffed out that didn't rekindle anywhere else. Helmut was returning to university that afternoon; Freda and the younger children would go back to school; his mother insisted that she would be better if normal family life were resumed immediately. There was a lunch at their house for the cousins and the friends, which Helmut, the eldest, dreaded. He would be expected to be the host, support his mother, behave with gravity and self-restraint. All he wanted to do was shut himself in his room and cry his heartbreak out. When it was over, he took his mother's arm and they walked to the car. Inside she pushed back her veil. He saw how white her face was, but felt guilty because he did not understand her.

'The little ones were very good,' Minna said. 'Willi didn't cry – they were very brave.' Her son didn't answer. He had seen his brother's drawn face, and the way he kept biting his lip and fidgeting. Prussians, he thought. Thank Christ there's none of it in me. I'm just like my father . . .

'I don't think the younger ones should go to the memorial service,' he said; he was trying to take an adult view. 'This has been quite bad enough for them.'

'There's no question of it,' Minna said. 'I want them to get back to normal. I just wish the lunch was over too, and I didn't have to see anyone.'

'It was your idea,' her son said. 'It didn't have to be done like this.'

'No.' Minna turned towards him. 'No, your father could have been cremated and popped into the ground; I've seen those funerals. It's the way you bury your pet dog.' Immediately she regretted the harshness of her answer, seeing it had upset him; he would never understand how much his hostility upset her.

She turned towards him, but he was staring out of the window, and he didn't look at her until they arrived back at the house. By four o'clock they had all gone. Helmut was on the train to Heidelberg, Freda and the younger children had flown back to Bonn where they were all at school. The housekeeper brought Minna a tray of coffee, and went out, shutting the door very quietly. Minna poured a cup and then left it to get cold; she smoked several cigarettes. The big room was silent; a small mantel clock ticked like a metronome. There were photographs on the tables and on an old-fashioned grand piano: they showed Sigmund and the children. There was a wedding group in a silver frame. People had sent flowers to her and the family; there were big vases displaying them, and they made the room seem artificial, as if it were a setting for a party. She stretched out her right hand, and looked at the gold wedding ring. She drew it back and forward on her finger; it slipped easily over her knuckle. Her hands had got thinner. She got up and opened the antique cabinet which had been converted to hold drinks, and poured herself a whisky.

Max Steiner was arriving at the airport at eleven twenty the next morning. She had booked him into a modest hotel, and told nobody that he was coming. Steiner knew about Janus. It was the most extraordinary coincidence; Walther would have called it Fate, that sent him to the Crillon that morning. It meant that what her husband had begun could be continued. The men who had killed him were merely instruments, she knew that. They hadn't known why he had to be murdered. Those who sent them believed that without Sigmund, it would all come to an end. She wouldn't be expected to carry on, or even to know the significance of Sigmund Walther's dying word, if she had ever heard it. Janus . . .

They hadn't calculated on the existence of Max Steiner. Minna carried her glass across to the piano, and picked up the wedding group. Nineteen years ago. The clothes were very dated; Sigmund looked self-conscious and her own expression was shy. She looked very young, even for eighteen. Her father was there, tall and straight-backed, her mother in a pale blue hat and dress that matched her eyes. It was a good marriage for her; in his mid-twenties Walther was already successful, and the Ahrenbergs had no money, and no possessions. Ivan had swallowed up the house and the lands in Prussia. His drunken soldiers had looted the furniture and the silver and smashed up what they couldn't load up to steal. Sigmund Walther was a good husband for a penniless general's daughter. She hadn't known what love meant; she hadn't wanted to marry him or not wanted to; it had happened and she accepted it. He had made her love him afterwards. He was an accomplished lover, and he wanted her to enjoy it. Sex meant a great deal to Minna, and he was intuitive enough to develop that aspect of their early life until she was completely in love with him. He had encouraged her to have children; he wanted a large family unit; a beautiful pregnant wife was something a man prized like a decoration on his breast. Her own intelligence earned her the place in his confidence that no one else enjoyed. She held the wedding photograph for a minute and then put it face down on the piano. She took her glass back to the cabinet, refilled it, and went out to her husband's study. It was a businesslike room, with modern furniture, filing cabinets, a tape-recorder and a portable television set. She had promised to show Max Steiner what was in that room. She addressed herself in thought to her dead husband.

He would not be defeated, even in death. The search would go on.

Max flew into West Berlin the following day; *Newsworld* had a leg man in the city who had met Max in Paris, and they were friendly. He was at Tempelhof airport to collect him with a car. His name was Hugo Priem. As they shook hands, a tall man in an American-style suit and buttoned-down white shirt bumped into Max, and excused himself. He carried a suitcase and a Leica camera strung round his neck. Max didn't know it, but he had his first encounter with Curt Andrews from the CIA in the arrivals hall at Berlin airport.

He and Priem lunched together in a restaurant on the Kurfürsten-damm. It was a bright day, and the wide avenue passed under their window, the traffic moving steadily; the ruined steeple of the Kaiser Wilhelm Memorial Church pointing its blunt finger to the sky stayed as a reminder of what war had done to the city.

The restaurant was full, the food excellent; he enjoyed the wine. West Berlin was blooming with prosperity. The luxury shops along the Kurfürstendamm were as opulent as anything in Paris. The women he saw were expensively dressed, well made-up, escorted by men with money. There was a lot of laughter round them. Priem was being a good host, but he was uneasy. If there was a feature to be written about West Berlin, then he didn't see why a man from the Paris office should be sent over his head to do it.

Max leaned forward. 'Have a look at this,' he said. He pushed a folded sheet of paper towards Priem. 'I want to find out where they are.'

Priem read the few names, and then looked up. 'Why – what's the angle? Nobody wants to know about the Bunker now – certainly not in Germany. It's been hashed over till people are sick to death of it. Besides, the Russians caught most of them. These three – ' he put his finger against the names – 'these were released. I remember that. In the sixties. They wouldn't talk to anyone then. The others could be dead or still in prison in Russia.'

'How can we find out?' Max asked him. 'And don't think I'm stepping on your feet. This is part of an investigation into the Sigmund Walther killing.'

'What the hell would the end of Hitler and the people in the Bunker have to do with that?' Priem stared at him.

'I'm not sure,' Max said carefully. 'But there is a link. How good are your contacts in the police?'

'Very good. I make sure they are. I've got an expense account to prove it.' He laughed. 'And there's nothing but praise for the good job they do when I write anything. Which happens to be true. They're a good force, and a clean one.'

'Including the expense account?' Max lit a cigarette.

Priem shrugged. 'Lunch now and then, dinner with the wives, the odd tickets for this and that. Anyway, you want help. And the best way of getting it is to go to the headquarters on Tempelhoferdamm and see one of my friends. He'll know whether you can contact any of these people, and what records we have of them.'

The Inspector took them down to the records office. A computer operated the filing system. The names were fed in one by one. Erich Kempka, SS Standartenführer, serial no. 187738, chauffeur and bodyguard to Adolf Hitler. Herbert Schmidt, valet to Adolf Hitler, Gunther Mühlhauser, SS Obergruppenführer, chief liaison officer with Reichsführer Himmler, serial no. 335150. Sturmbannführer Otto Helm, serial no. 977430. SS Scharführer Josef Franke, serial no. 400896. Fraulein Gerda Christian, secretary to Adolf Hitler. Fraulein Johanna Wolf, secretary to Adolf Hitler. Albert Kramer, Hitler Jügend, last known address Hildebrandstrasse 33, Berlin.

They sat round smoking cigarettes; the Inspector was a large, pleasant man in his mid-forties. He was obviously on good terms with Priem. To Max he said, 'What's the object of this inquiry, Herr Steiner – Hugo says your paper is doing an investigation. It's not another Bormann story, is it? War criminals again?' He stubbed out his cigarette and didn't wait for an answer. He looked hard at Max. 'Personally, I think it's time we Germans stopped rubbing our own noses in the shit. It's a long time ago and we ought to forget about it.'

'It's nothing to do with war crimes,' Max said. 'Or Bormann.'

Priem shouldn't have said it, but he did. He wanted to protect his own interest with the Inspector. 'Steiner's doing a piece on the Walther assassination.'

He saw the disbelief on the policeman's face, and raised his hands in a gesture which was mockingly Semitic. 'Don't ask me what all these dead heads have got to do with it; ask him. He doesn't know either.'

'Just so long as it's not an anti-German angle,' the Inspector said.

'I am a German,' Max said, suddenly angry. 'When will we get those answers?'

'Now,' the Inspector said. The computer assistant came up to them, carrying a sheaf of papers. The policeman didn't hand them to Max; he read through them quickly first. 'Best of luck,' he said. 'Excuse me, I've got work to do. I'll sign you out.'

Max went back to his hotel; Priem offered an invitation to dinner with his wife, said he knew of a nice girl if Max was interested. He wasn't and he refused the dinner. Priem didn't quite conceal his relief, shook him hard by the hand, and drove off.

There was a bar and grill in the hotel; Max found a corner table and ordered a steak. He had brought the computer's answers with him; he wasn't sure why but he didn't want to leave the papers in his room.

Kempka, the chauffeur; Schmidt, the valet; Mühlhauser, Himmler's assistant: all three returned alive from captivity in Russia. Kempka was dead, lung cancer in a Stuttgart hospital three years ago. Schmidt was alive, living at Berchtesgaden, Max noted that: the Führer's favourite 'Eagle's Nest', perched high in the Bavarian Alps, Berchtesgaden was a Nazi shrine. He made a red pencil mark against Schmidt's name. Gunther Mühlhauser. He had served fifteen years in a Russian prison, spent two years in hospital, was now employed in the personnel section of A. G. Hoechst, Hamburg. Address Goethe Allee 18, Hamburg, tel. no. 768029. Married, the second time, Hilde Ploetz, one child, female, aged six. Mühlhauser. There was a red mark against his name. Otto Helm, officer in the elite SS guarding the Bunker. Surrendered to the Americans, tried and was convicted of war crimes, sentenced to life imprisonment, released five years ago on compassionate grounds after two strokes. Living in West Berlin, Apartment 2, Regensdorfstrasse, home of daughter and son-in-law, Dr Heinz Mintzel, tel. no. 967252.

The two women, Gerda Christian and Johanna Wolf, secretaries to Hitler, were no longer traceable by the computer. Both had left Germany for Central America, in 1951 and 1952, and vanished.

But Josef Franke was, by the luckiest coincidence, working in a department store as a security man, also in Hamburg. Franke, who had pulled him out of the Chancellory yard and, together with the skinny girl who worked in the kitchen, guided him through the shattered streets of Berlin away from the encircling Russians. He had very clear memories of Josef Franke, and they were all good. He had saved Max's life. Franke had taken him and the girl out of the Bunker that same night. According to the records Max had been investigating, the main group, including the secretaries and Martin Bormann and Artur Maxmann, had waited until 1st May, when it had been virtually impossible to escape the Russian patrols or survive the bombardment. He circled Franke's name in red.

Albert Kramer was adviser on industrial relations to the Social Democratic government in Bonn. He was a director of one of the largest banks, chairman of a plastics company, on the boards of three major nationalized industries, gas, electricity and the railways. He was married, with two children, and his address was in the exclusive residential suburb of Puppelsdorf, just outside Bonn.

Albert Kramer. The steak arrived, with a bottle of red wine, and Max began to eat. He hardly noticed the food. It was a big steak, popular with tourists, too large to eat before a third of it got cold. Albert Kramer. He could remember him as if it were the day before that they last saw each other. The cropped fair hair, the blue eyes with the aggressive stare, the Hitler worship. He had jumped forward to take Max's place as officer in charge of the execution squad. Half stunned as he was, Max could see him standing over the man lying, still tied to the chair, on the ground, pointing a revolver at him and firing . . .

Albert Kramer was a powerful businessman, and high in the council of the Social Democratic government of West Germany. That was going to be a very interesting interview. He put the paper away in his inside pocket; he had memorized one telephone number. He went to the foyer to telephone; the directory checked with the address on the list in his pocket. Heinz Mintzel, Regensdorfstrasse.

A woman answered him; he sensed the wariness of the doctor's wife against a call in the middle of his supper.

'Is that Fräu Mintzel speaking?'

'Yes; what can I do for you? I'm afraid the doctor's not available at the moment.'

Max smiled, his intuition proved right. 'I'm not making a sick call,' he said. 'My name is Steiner. I wondered if I could call and see your father. I used to know him in the old days.'

There was a long pause; he heard muffled sounds and knew she had covered the telephone with her hand and was speaking to someone. 'My father's an invalid,' she said. 'He's partially paralysed. I don't think it would do any good your coming to see him, Herr Steiner. But I could tell him you called.'

'I'd like to come,' Max insisted. 'I'm trying to trace a cousin of mine. They were together in Berlin in forty-five. If your father could help me at all, I'd be very grateful. There's some family money involved. And I'd like to see him again. Could I come round for ten minutes?'

He waited, while she mumbled in the background. The doctor mightn't be available to a patient, but he was certainly there beside her.

'All right,' she said. 'But I doubt if he'll be able to help you. His memory's very bad. If you can come round in half an hour we'll have finished our supper.'

It was a modest street, tree-lined and the houses built within the last ten years. Each had a small patch of garden in the front and a garage. The house where Otto Helm lived with his daughter and son-in-law was on the corner, and it had been converted into three self-contained flats. Max pressed the bell for the second floor, and the door opened. The stair was narrow, carpeted and the walls were papered in a cheerful yellow. It was a good conversion, and he decided that it must belong to the doctor. He could imagine the type; frugal, honest, very hard-working, a man who had risen by his bootstraps after the débâcle of the war to a profession and a small property. The kind of man who wouldn't let space go to waste when it could earn him money. He had his father-in-law, the war criminal and ex-convict, to support.

He had formed a character in his imagination, and when the door opened he was so wrong that he hesitated. A young man in his thirties stood there; grinned at him, held the door open and offered him his hand. 'I'm Heinz Mintzel. Come in.' He was untidily dressed, in a sweater and a badly tied tie, which he had loosened; his hair was on end. Max realized with a start that his impressions of his countrymen were long out of date. This was not the starched *Herr Doktor* of his youth, whom his patients treated with respect and children with positive awe. This was a young German. 'Trudi! Herr Steiner's here – ' He turned to Max and the friendly grin was rueful. 'I've got to rush out, I'm afraid. I've got a call. My wife'll look after you. I'm afraid the old man won't be much help, but it'll cheer him up to have a visitor.' Trudi Mintzel didn't fit in with his notion of her either. She was about the same age as her husband, a little plump, wearing jeans and a bright shirt, and round spectacles with heavy frames. She shook hands with him; a little frown appeared as she looked at him. 'I thought you'd be much older,' she said. 'You couldn't have known my father, surely?'

'I did,' Max said. 'I was only a boy, but I knew him.'

'He didn't remember you,' she said, 'but then he wouldn't. Half the time he doesn't know who he is himself. Come on in; he's looking forward to seeing you.'

It was quite a large bedroom; the bed was an iron-framed hospital type; there were bright reproduction prints on the walls and a big bowl of greenhouse plants on the table. Sturmbannführer Otto Helm sat in a chair by the side of the bed, with a blue rug over his knees. His daughter raised her voice.

'Dad, here's your friend come to see you. Herr Steiner. Sit down, won't you? I'll bring you a beer, or would you rather have coffee?'

'Nothing, thanks,' Max said. He perched on the side of the bed. Otto Helm looked up at his daughter, and then at Max. He had thin hands, with veins standing out under the pallid skin. One lay palm upward, like a withered claw, in his lap. The hair on his head was white and translucent as candyfloss; it crowned a skull-like face, which was tilted in a frozen grimace on the left side. Then he spoke, the words slurring but still intelligible. 'I don't remember you,' he said. 'Trudi says you knew me in the old days . . . I don't remember you.'

'I was in the Bunker,' Max said.

'They jailed me,' the old man said. 'It wasn't my fault. I only did my duty.'

'Yes,' Max answered. 'I know that.'

A thread of saliva slipped down one side of the old man's mouth. Max felt a sudden nausea. He wanted to get up and leave the room and the pitiful wreck in the chair, telling himself that it was useless, that Otto Helm couldn't possibly help him.

'I forget things,' the sludgy voice went on. 'I had a stroke and then another but I didn't die.' The lips twisted in a terrible smile, showing the teeth and gums on one side. 'They let me out,' he said.

'The Führer died, though.'

Max waited in the silence; there was a smell of antiseptic in the room. He felt he could have heard a leaf fall from one of the plants in the bowl. 'Yes,' he said at last very slowly.

'The Führer died. He had a man shot that day. By a firing squad. Don't you remember that, Otto?'

'No.' The lids closed over the eyes like a tortoise going to sleep.

'Think,' Max said. 'Think about the day the Führer died. There was a man; you said he was a traitor. You told me about him; I was there. With the Hitler Jügend. You can remember that, can't you?'

The eyes opened again. 'He was shot,' Otto Helm murmured, as if Max wasn't there and he was thinking aloud. 'Swine. She tried to get him off, but no – the Chief wouldn't listen. Didn't listen to her . . .'

'Who tried to get him off?' Max leaned close to him, he put a hand on the mobile arm and gave it a little shake. 'Who was it? Tell me . . .'

'E.B.,' Helm sniggered. 'But the Chief wouldn't listen.'

E.B. The girl who had escaped with him from the Bunker had used those initials but they hadn't registered. He'd forgotten them until he started reading the Allied reports and Trevor-Roper's definitive account of the last days in Berlin. *Eva Braun.* Eva Braun had tried to save the man from execution. Adolf Hitler hadn't yielded. He brought himself very near to Otto Helm.

'Who was he?'

'Eh? Who? I don't know – I don't remember things. Where's Trudi – I want the bottle.'

'You can pee in a minute,' Max Steiner said. 'When you think back. The Bunker, the last day – who did E.B. try and save, Otto? Come on, you tell me and I'll get Trudi for you.'

The eyes were looking into his, and there was a clear intelligence in them. 'Fegelein. He was trying to escape – betray us. I never told them about that. They put me away for all those years . . . I never said anything about that.'

'No,' Max said. He felt as if he'd been winded. Fegelein. Herman Fegelein. The man who had whispered to him to find Janus had been Eva Braun's brother-in-law.

He got up, and went to the door. 'I'll get Trudi for you,' he said.

He found her in the sitting room, watching television. She looked up and smiled. 'You haven't been long,' she said. 'Was Dad able to help?'

'No,' Max shook his head. 'I didn't worry him too much. He's pretty confused.'

She stood up and there was something awkward about her. 'He was in prison more than nineteen years,' she said. 'I was eight when he went inside. My mother kept things going till she died. I don't know what he was supposed to have done, Herr Steiner, and I don't care. He's my father and I'm not ashamed of what he was. There are people around here who'd spit on us if they knew he'd been in the SS.'

'He wants the bottle,' Max said.

'Oh, God,' she said. 'Why didn't you say so?' She hurried out. He looked round the pleasant little room. More potted plants, photographs of herself and her husband on a skiing holiday, outside the Mayor's office after their wedding; modern furniture and bright colours. All his preconceived ideas about Otto Helm's family were ludicrously wrong. The house didn't belong to them; they were tenants, not owners, a young couple, not long married, looking after the wife's invalid father. He remembered so vividly that it sickened him the last time he had seen Otto Helm, standing over the bound and bleeding victim in the Chancellory yard. He had been right not to mention that incident to his American interrogators. He might have been hanged instead of going to prison. To his daughter, and probably to her decent young husband too, he was a sick and helpless old man who had been punished for serving his country.

There was nothing he could say to Trudi Mintzel that made any sense now. He let himself out of the flat and began to walk slowly down the road. He was booked on the ten-thirty flight to Hamburg the next day.

Minna Walther had promised to meet him at the airport; it was understood that there would be an exchange of information. He went on walking; there was a tightness in his stomach that followed the nightmare, only he wasn't dreaming now. He took a bus to the sector where his hotel was. A pretty girl sat next to him and smiled; the atmosphere was genial, different from his remembrance of the city where he had been born. But then he only remembered the war, and the grim years afterwards when he had paid a visit to Berlin before taking up his post in London. The people had rebuilt out of the ruins; they lived with the Wall running through the city like a scar, and behind it lay the dead heart of Nazi Germany, the site of Hitler's Chancellory, now razed to the ground by the Russians. The Bunker itself. The dead heart of Nazi Germany. It was a good phrase, and he could use it one day. But that heart was beating still; the murder of Sigmund Walther proved that. He and Fegelein had died because of Janus. Whoever or whatever Janus might be. He went to his room and put through a call to Ellie in London. Tim, the solicitor answered. Ellie and his wife and the children had gone to the cinema. They were all fine and enjoying their stay. He sounded offhand, and Max could imagine what Ellie had told them. He left affectionate messages and rang off.

Hamburg tomorrow. His wife and children, the disapproval of Tim, the good family man – he'd forgotten them as he put the phone down. The tension in his stomach kept him awake; when he dozed images chased through his uneasy sleep. The crippled old man in the chair, Minna Walther by the window in the Crillon with the sunlight on her face, the crack of shots in the Chancellory garden that became the gunfire in a Paris street. Janus. A Roman god. A God with two faces. The symbol of Deceit. . . . At twenty minutes past eleven the next morning, Max Steiner walked through the domestic arrivals gate at Hamburg airport and found Minna Walther waiting for him.

*

Curt Andrews arranged to meet the Inspector who had given Max
Steiner his list of names and addresses in a restaurant in the Old
Tempelhof district for an early lunch. Andrews no longer looked like
an American tourist. He wore German casual clothes and when he took
his table his accent was South German. He ordered beer and waited for
the Inspector to come. There had always been a close liaison between
the CIA and the West Berlin police and Intelligence services. His check
with the Inspector had produced a surprising reaction. Something of
interest had come up, and the Inspector wanted to talk to him urgently.
They had arranged to lunch in an inconspicuous place where they
could discuss their business without interruption. Or bugs, as Andrews
thought cynically. Not even a police station was safe in West Berlin.
It was one of the most sensitive areas in the world, penetrated and
counter-penetrated by agents of East and West. The policeman was on
time; Andrews had arrived early. He liked to look over a rendezvous
before he used it.

He listened quietly while his informant talked. 'What's the information on Steiner – any political tie-ups?'

'Not that we know,' the Inspector said. 'When he gave me this list
of names I thought, Christ, here we go again, another Nazi scare story.
But when he said it was tied in with Walther – then I knew you'd be
interested.'

'We are,' Andrews said. 'That's why I'm here. We want to know who
killed him and why. So does Steiner, if he was telling the truth. It won't
be hard to check. But this list of names – how do you figure them?'

'I don't,' the policeman said. 'But they all have one common denomi-
nator. They're all people who were in the Bunker when Hitler died.
Except for Kramer, the industrialist.'

Andrews lit a pipe. 'So it looks as if the snow-white knight Walther
had some Nazi connections after all? My Director never believed
in him.'

'It could be anti-Nazi,' the Inspector suggested. 'We have a theory
that he was murdered by the extreme right. It could be he had started
to get close to something certain people mightn't like discovered. He
had a lot of political enemies with his pro-East attitude.'

'And German reunification,' Andrews puffed hard. 'The Soviets
wouldn't like that. If you put it all down, pretty near everyone
on both sides had a reason for getting rid of him. The right and
the left.'

How about the CIA, the policeman thought but didn't say. You've
put a few people away . . . He watched the American. He knew the
type. Thorough, cold-blooded, ruthless bastards. But a deal was a deal
and allies were allies.

'Is there anything we can do to help?'

Andrews paused; a waitress was passing their table. 'One of those was a Berlin address,' he said. 'You could find out if Steiner's made contact, and what sort of questions he asked. I'm going over to Bonn. You'll be able to contact me at the Königshof Hotel.'

'I'll send someone round,' the Inspector promised. He left before Curt Andrews, and made no attempt to pay the bill.

The two Swiss businessmen had asked for adjoining rooms. They had flown from Geneva to Munich via Frankfurt, hired a car at the airport and driven to a *pension*. The proprietress looked at the booking, and briefly at them. She was used to homosexuals, although neither of them gave that impression. They signed the register: Stanislaus Kesler, Maurice Franconi. They had booked in for a week. They were shown to their rooms, and when they were alone in Kesler's bedroom Franconi brought out his road map. They studied it together.

'Berchtesgaden – we take the E11, branch off here' – Franconi's finger traced the red line of the autobahn – 'the last exit in Germany at Bad Reichenhall, and we should reach it in about two hours.'

Kesler frowned. 'We could start at the convent,' he said. 'Settle the one at Berchtesgaden and then go on to Berlin.'

'I don't fancy the convent,' Franconi said. 'I was brought up by nuns.'

'She's not a nun,' Kesler pointed out. Franconi shrugged and went back to the map. It had taken exactly twenty-four hours to locate the people they had undertaken to murder. Their contact was a detective agency in Cologne with informants in Interpol and the major European police headquarters. A sum of money substantial enough to satisfy the agency's principal contact in the Federal German police had produced the addresses to fit the names.

'I think we should start at Berchtesgaden,' Franconi persisted. 'It's a nice drive. I'd rather get to hell out after we've dealt with *her*.' The tip of his finger touched a name.

'All right,' Kesler agreed. 'We'll set off as soon as we've unpacked. We can have lunch on the way.'

'I like Bavarian food,' Maurice said. 'But it's terribly fattening.'

'You don't have to worry,' Kesler protested. 'I'm the one with the belly.'

Within the hour they were driving their rented Opel through the centre of Munich and on to the autobahn E11, heading towards the majestic range of the Bavarian Alps. The tops of the mountains were crowned in snow, and they sparkled in the clear sunshine. The countryside was green and wooded; they left the autobahn, drove through picture-book villages and stopped in one at a roadside café to eat a large lunch. At four in the afternoon they arrived in the small hamlet five miles outside Berchtesgaden. Franconi parked the car in the little square opposite the church. They began to walk at a leisurely pace along the quaintly cobbled street with timbered houses on each side. They stopped at the fourth down on the right, glanced at each other, smiled, and knocked on the door.

An elderly woman answered. She held the door open and said, 'Yes?'

Kesler was spokesman. His German was flawless. 'We've come to pay our respects to Herr Schmidt,' he said softly. 'My friend and I have travelled from Munich. Would you tell him we're here?'

'He's not expecting you,' she said. She looked uncertain. Kesler had spoken with authority. 'I wrote to him,' Kesler said. 'Hasn't he received the letter –?' He took a step forward and she let him pass through into the house. Franconi followed.

'I'm his cousin,' the woman said. 'I look after him. If you'll wait in the front room, I'll go and see – What's the name, sir?'

'Fritsche, Colonel Hans Fritsche. I've brought Captain Emden with me. How is Herr Schmidt – not sick, I hope?'

'No, no,' she was becoming more flustered, because Franconi had managed to get in front of her and she didn't like to push past him. 'He's quite well, considering.'

She hesitated. When Schmidt was first released from the Soviet prison camp, there had been a stream of visitors. Newspapermen, sightseers, old friends. And that was after the Allied military authorities had released him from their long interrogation. Those were the days when the controversies about how the Führer had died and whether Bormann had in fact escaped alive were breaking out all over the world. Herbert Schmidt had been the first man to see his master's body. Everybody wanted to hear his version. But that was years ago. Nobody had been near the house for a long, long time.

'Take us to him,' Kesler said. 'Please?'

She passed the young, good-looking man, trying not to brush against him in the narrow passageway. She led them to a small room at the back of the house. The man who had been the personal valet to Adolf Hitler got out of his chair as Kesler and Franconi came in. 'These gentlemen have come to see you, Herbert,' the woman said. 'They wrote you a letter – you didn't tell me about it. I'd have got the front room ready . . .' Kesler saw the bewildered look on the old man's face, and hurried forward. 'Colonel Hans Fritsche. My comrade Captain Emden. We did write, but obviously the letter went astray. It's good to see you, Schmidt.' He reached out and shook the man's hand. Franconi clicked his heels and gave a slight bow. Herbert Schmidt had spent eleven years in Soviet captivity. The frame was that of a big man, with broad shoulders, but the body had shrunk away, leaving the large skeleton in clothes that hung loose. The face was lined and taut, the eyes had a glaze of suffering in them which was a permanent memory. Franconi and Kesler observed this, and Kesler thought quickly that he was very feeble and wouldn't be difficult to kill.

The woman went out, and Herbert Schmidt asked them to sit down. He was embarrassed because of the letter. Kesler offered him a cigarette, but he shook his head. 'Gentlemen,' he said, and the voice was husky and trembled, 'what can I do for you?'

'My friend, Captain Emden, would like to know about your time in the Russian labour camp,' Kesler said. 'And I want you to accept this; your services to our Leader have not been forgotten.' The gold pencil gleamed in Kesler's fingers as he held it out. Herbert Schmidt reached towards it, and Kesler brought it up level with his face and thrust it so close that it almost touched his mouth. The tiny deadly puff of cyanide caught his breath.

Franconi held him as he collapsed and lowered him in to his chair. Kesler counted three minutes on his watch, and kept up a loud monologue in case the woman should be listening. He nodded at Franconi, who felt for a pulse in Schmidt's neck. There was no sign of life. Together they flung open the door and shouted for Schmidt's cousin. She was running down the street to the post office to telephone for a doctor as Kesler and Franconi quietly left the house. She told the doctor, when she got through to him, the same as Kesler had told her. Herbert Schmidt had suffered a heart attack, and she couldn't be sure but she thought he was dead . . .

Kesler and Franconi drove back to Munich, stopping for dinner on the way. The next morning they searched the local newspapers, and Franconi found a tiny item at the bottom of the home news page in the *Münchener Merkur*. It reported the death of Adolf Hitler's former valet from a heart attack. There was no other mention. 'Well,' Franconi said, 'that's one we can cross out. A beautiful job.'

He glanced at Kesler. 'I suppose we'd better get on with the next one.'

'No hurry,' the older man said. 'We've got time in hand. This job can't be rushed; it won't be so easy, getting to her. I want to keep the place under observation for a day or two – see if we can make a contact with anyone who works inside. Find out when she comes out and where she goes.' He folded up the papers and pushed them aside. They were having breakfast in the restaurant. 'You're bothered about this, aren't you?'

'Yes,' Franconi admitted. 'I am. It's just the idea of a nun – I know she's not an actual nun, but it just turns me up a bit.' Under the shelter of the table, Kesler pressed his knee.

'Superstition,' he said gently. 'But I've got an idea. If you don't want to do this one, why not leave it to me? You could go ahead and settle one of the others. How about the one in West Berlin? Old invalid, living with his daughter. It won't be difficult; you know I won't let you take on a heavy job without me, but the one in Berlin is easy . . . Why don't we do it like this? We'll have a few days here, keep an eye on the place and find out what we can, and then you go off to Berlin and I'll see to the business here?'

Franconi covered Kesler's hand with his own.

'I'd like to do that,' he said. 'You're very good to me, Stanis. You're sure you don't mind? You won't need any help?'

'One woman? Don't be silly.'

Minna Walther drove back from the airport. Max had expected a car and driver; the Porsche was a surprise, and so was the speed and dexterity with which she cut through the traffic. He had seen her immediately among the crowd by the arrivals gate, because of her height and the green suit she was wearing. They shook hands and she led him to the little sports car. 'What are you doing in Berlin? I thought you were coming from Paris,' she said.

'I was,' Max answered. 'Then something struck me as worth looking at, before I came here. So I went to Berlin first.'

She didn't turn to look at him; she cut through an intersection in a way that made him clutch his seat. 'Was it to do with Sigmund?'

'Yes,' he said. 'Indirectly. I went to see someone; watch out for that car, it's coming across – '

He saw her smile. 'Don't worry, I can see it. I'm a very safe driver.'

'I'm sure you are, Fräu Walther; you're just a bit positive, if you don't mind me saying so.'

'My husband couldn't bear me driving,' she said. 'Men are nervous passengers, I've noticed that. I suppose it's because they don't think women know what they're doing. Here we are!'

He looked up at the house as she got out her keys and opened the front door. It was not very big, red brick and rather ugly. There were some fine trees surrounding it. He went upstairs to wash, and his journalist's eye noticed the comfort without ostentation. *Newsworld* had done an article on the 'Millionaires of the German Miracle.' The wealth and, in some cases, the almost nineteenth-century vulgarity of the lifestyle of some of the big industrialists had made marvellous copy. But Sigmund Walther had refused to be interviewed. That, as Max remembered, was before he went into politics. As he crossed the landing, he saw a door had been left open. There were draped net curtains and a big bed; Minna Walther's green jacket was lying across it. He hesitated, staring into the room, at the bed, and then hurried on downstairs. Her bed had nothing to do with him.

She was waiting for him in the sitting room, smoking, looking very elegant in a silk shirt that matched the green of her suit. He looked tired, she thought suddenly. Such a different type of man from Sigmund, who always looked glowing with health. Very dark for a Berliner – there must be Bavarian blood in him somewhere. A restless man, keyed up with nervous energy. He lit a cigarette, and she noticed his hands. They were strong, but sensitive, without hairs. She hated a man's hands to be hairy. He wore a wedding ring. She noticed the silence and didn't know how to break it. They were mentally circling each other, seeing the sex and individuality of the other as they hadn't done before. Like animals deciding whether they were scenting friend or foe . . .

She knew that Max was seeing her as a man taking stock of a woman, just as she had noted his hands, the dark colour of his eyes, the way he sat opposite to her, leaning a little forward . . . The moment of mutual recognition lengthened; she felt the colour in her face, and a sensation that was almost panic. Ten days. She'd been a widow for ten days and already she was reacting to a man . . .

'Fräu Walther,' Max Steiner said. 'You have something to show me. And I've got things to tell you. Where do we start?'

Like a stone flung into water, the question dispersed the reflection of themselves which each had permitted to emerge, and each had looked at. The moment was gone and the danger with it. Minna Walther said, 'We have to trust each other. I trust you, Herr Steiner. But I don't know why you want to find out about Janus, if it isn't to make use of it. As a political journalist. I've brought my husband's file here from Bonn, but before I show it to you, I have a right to know what your motives are.'

'Finding your husband's killers isn't enough?' Max asked.

She shook her head. 'No. A lot of other people have that motive. The police, for instance, his friends – I want to find them more than anyone. But it's not just that with you. It's Janus. Why?'

He paused for a moment, and then made up his mind. They were going to be allies, working together. They had to trust each other; she was right. He remembered saying the same thing to her when she lied to him the day after Walther's murder. No secrets, no holding back.

'I was in a Hitler Jügend cadre in April 1945,' he said. 'We went to the Bunker; Hitler was going to shake hands with us and send us off to the Pichelsdorfbridge to get blown to bits by the Russians. We never saw Hitler; we were detailed to act as a firing squad, I was the platoon leader. The man had been beaten up, probably tortured. He spoke to me. He said, "Find Janus." '

'And you shot him?' Her voice was low, shocked.

'No,' Max said. 'I didn't. Something just snapped in me; the whole Nazi mess blew up in my face. My father and my two brothers were killed, my mother and grandmother were under shellfire, we were all going out to die for Hitler. That was enough without being told to kill a man they'd half murdered already; the Führer's order – that's what the SS told us. He couldn't even stand; they'd had to tie him into a chair so we could shoot him.'

'Don't,' she said, and her hand covered her face for a moment.

'I said no,' Max went on. 'So the Standartenführer knocked me flying and laid a few kicks into me, and my squad carried out the execution. Then I passed out. I used to wonder why they didn't shoot me. Still,' he shrugged, 'maybe a few shells started falling near and they took cover. One of the guards picked me up later and brought me down into the Bunker. I didn't know what was happening at the time, but apparently Hitler and Eva Braun had committed suicide and they were going to burn the bodies, so everyone was cleared away from the Chancellory garden and the exits.'

'How did you escape?' she asked. 'Nobody got away from there – the Russians killed or captured all of them – '

'The guard who found me in the garden and his girlfriend slipped out that night, and took me with them. They disappeared together when we got near the American patrols, but I was picked up and sent to a camp. Eventually I got back to my aunt in Bremen through the Red Cross.' Minna got up, and he stood with her.

She didn't say anything, she walked across to the mahogany cupboard and opened it. He saw the ranks of bottles shining inside. She came back with two glasses of whisky. He took one of them. 'I never told anyone about it,' he said. 'But I had nightmares occasionally. I'd dream the whole thing, and wake up shaking like a leaf. It doesn't sound very manly, does it, but I was never the Nazi Superman type – '

'How old were you?' she asked.

'Sixteen. It's an impressionable age. I made my life, got married, got myself a very good job, and I still dreamed about the man who said I had to find Janus. In the last year I've been having the dream nearly every night. I began to think I was breaking up. Then I met your husband. And now you know why I have to find out what Janus means.'

'Yes,' Minna said. 'I see. Thank you for telling me. Bring your glass and we'll go into my husband's study.'

He sat in Sigmund Walther's chair, and she put the thick brown hessian file on the desk in front of him. Then she sat and sipped her drink.

'It was a million to one chance that Sigmund heard about the defector,' she said. 'He'd just got elected to the Bundestag, and he was very friendly with someone in the Ministry for Internal Security. He told Sigmund about the Soviet trade delegate who had asked for political asylum.'

'When was this?' Max had the file open.

'Last year. You'll find it there. He brought a lot of information with him; apparently he was a senior KGB officer who felt he was falling out of favour at home, and took the chance to come over to us.'

'Trade delegations usually have a couple of them, to watch the delegates,' Max said. 'Vladimir Yusevsky; I remember him – ' he was glancing quickly at the first sheets in the folder. 'There was a fight between the British and the Americans as to who got hold of him. The Americans won. But not before our own people had got their hooks into him by the looks of this.'

'I'll leave you for a while,' she said. 'Call, if you want anything.' She closed the door so quietly that Max didn't hear her go. He turned the first page in Sigmund Walther's file and began to read.

There was no complete transcript of the Soviet defector's information; that would have been classified as top security. What Walther had assembled were copies of available Russian documents which had been released long after the events they described, with notes appended to clarify or extend the information. These notes were marked with 'V.Y. deposition' and a date. The first document was written by Sigmund Walther in longhand. No secretary had been trusted with this material. Vladimir Yusevsky had asked for political asylum in the autumn of '69, during a trade delegation visit to Bonn. The Federal government had granted him temporary asylum while negotiations were in progress with the Soviet government for his return. During the negotiations, he had been discreetly interrogated by the West German Intelligence Service, under the personal direction of Heinrich Holler; his co-operation was a condition of the Federal government stalling Russian attempts to get him back. It had been arranged for him to escape to the Embassy in due course, and from there he was flown to the United States.

He had talked very freely to Holler and his team. There were references in Walther's report of a Soviet network being exposed within the Federal government itself, and a link through to Brussels and NATO which caused a spate of resignations, three arrests and a suicide. Yusevsky had blown a hole in his native Intelligence operations, which had been satisfactory for the West. But he had brought something else, as a bonus for his German hosts. A copy of the original Russian autopsy reports on the bodies of Hitler and Eva Braun. The findings had been released by the Soviet authorities in June, three months after the discovery of the dead Führer and his wife in a shell hole grave in the Chancellory garden. Max had already read brief extracts in his initial research in Paris. The reports were accompanied by photographs of the badly burnt corpses, and long, ghoulish descriptions of their teeth and internal organs. The identity of Adolf Hitler had been established beyond doubt by the capture of his personal dentist, complete with his and Eva Braun's dental records. The Soviet doctor in charge had been a woman, A. Kretchinova. She and her assistants had carried out thorough post-mortem examinations on all the bodies discovered in the Bunker itself and in the graves in the garden. Goebbels and his wife had taken cyanide, after poisoning their six daughters. The evidence set out identified the bodies of Hitler and Eva Braun beyond any dispute; the Russians found that the Führer had taken poison, rather than shooting himself. It tarnished the martyr image, and ignored the skull shattered by a bullet wound. It detailed primly that the leader of the Third Reich had only one testicle.

Max Steiner was reading, slowly, concentrating on every word. The autopsy on Eva Braun: her age, her height, her teeth, fillings, crowns, bridgework, the evidence of cyanide in her mouth, tiny glass crystals from the bitten ampoule, the smell of bitter almonds when the body was opened. And the findings of the meticulous Soviet woman doctor which had been omitted from the autopsy report released to the rest of the world. Eva Braun had had a child.

4

'You've found it,' Minna Walther said. She had come into the study, and Max got up slowly, holding the file in both hands.

'Yes,' he said. 'I've been trying to think what this means.'

'It means that Adolf Hitler left an heir,' she said quietly. 'Have you read everything?'

He nodded. 'I want to go through it again. I want to make notes and put together what I've got. My God, I can't believe it – '

'Neither could Sigmund,' she said. 'But it's there, and it's true. The Russians found out, and they must have tried to find the child. That's why they wouldn't let the British or the Americans talk to any of the people they captured from the Bunker. The ones they released didn't know anything. When Yusevsky defected, the secret came with him. American Intelligence knows about Janus.'

'Why that name?' Max said. 'Why did Hitler choose that as a code?'

'Sigmund thought it represented himself and Eva,' Minna Walther said. 'The god at the gate of the city, facing attack, defending his people at one and the same time.'

'The child was never found,' Max said slowly. 'That's why your husband was killed. He was searching for it, wasn't he?'

'Yes,' she said. 'Sigmund knew that if Hitler had a son, he represented the greatest danger to world peace and to the future of Germany. He may not even know who he is, but there are others who do, and they're waiting for the right moment to produce him. Sigmund was convinced that he hadn't been found; Yusevsky was very close to the investigation after the fall of Berlin. He said they'd been unable to trace it.'

'How do you know that? It doesn't say so in here – '

'Heinrich Holler told us,' she said quietly. 'He was trying to help Sigmund.'

'Why should the head of our Intelligence need someone like your husband to do the work for him?' Max asked. 'Surely finding the child was his job?'

'You've been away from home a long time,' Minna answered. 'There are men in positions of power in Germany who wouldn't want Holler to find that child. Men in his own service that he couldn't trust. He was helping Sigmund do what he couldn't do himself.'

'It's twenty-five years,' Max Steiner said. 'You're not telling me there are Nazi sympathizers running Germany today?'

'Not running it,' she corrected. 'But they're there. And memories begin to blur; people forget the horrors and remember the propaganda, the successes. Now we're divided, split down the middle with our capital cut in half by that disgusting Wall ... There are people who could look back to Adolf Hitler and think he wasn't all that bad. I know, Herr Steiner. I've heard those views expressed by sensible, decent people, who wouldn't hurt anyone. That's why my husband believed so passionately in Germany being one country again, whatever the compromise. If once we come together, we'll make ourselves independent and free!'

Max listened to her, and noted the colour in her cheeks and the intensity in her voice. Not so cool and composed now, the Prussian aristocrat had changed into a woman of passionate convictions. There was a lot of fire behind the ice.

'Now that you know,' she said. 'What are you going to do?'

He was sitting hunched forward, elbows on his knees, looking up at her. 'I'm going to find Janus,' he said, 'if you'll help me.' He hadn't expected her to do what she did. She moved quickly and came and sat beside him. She put her hand on his arm. Once again he could smell the scent she used, the one he had given Ellie for her birthday.

'We'll work together,' she said. 'I've got friends who can help. We'll find this child.'

'It'll be a grown man,' Max reminded her. 'And if we do find him, what happens then?' She turned away from him. 'I don't know,' she said.

'Supposing it was a girl?'

'Sigmund was sure it was a boy,' Minna said. 'It makes more sense. It *was* a boy. The Führer's son.'

'It makes me shudder,' Max said, 'just to imagine what could be done with a trump card like that to play.' He lit a cigarette and gave it to her. He noted that she took it and that she let their fingers touch. Sexual excitement rose in him; he fought it down. The time would come for that; he knew it would, just by sitting close to her. 'I made a list of people,' he said. 'I saw one of them in Berlin last night. SS Standartenführer Otto Helm. He was the officer who ordered the shooting in the garden. He told me who the man was. Herman Fegelein, Eva's brother-in-law. He knew about Janus, and that's why they killed him, because he was trying to escape. They couldn't risk the secret getting out. So if he knew about the child's existence, then his wife must have known a hell of a lot more. Her name is down in your husband's notes. But there's no record he ever went to see her.'

'He tried, several times,' Minna said. 'But she wouldn't agree. She wouldn't see or talk to anyone; she lives in a Catholic convent in Munich. She's a lay sister, and the Reverend Mother refused flatly to see Sigmund or discuss Gretl Fegelein.'

'We'll have to try again,' Max said. 'I've another call to make, at Berchtesgaden. Hitler's valet lives there; it's a bit of a long shot if the Russians let him out, but there might be some clue he could give us . . . We can try and get to Gretl Fegelein on the same trip.'

We. Minna Walther questioned. Max looked at her and nodded.

'A woman has a much better chance of getting into a convent than a man,' he said.

They had dinner in the house; his suitcase was still in the boot of the Porsche. Max had gone back to the study and spent the afternoon reading through every item that Sigmund Walther had collected . . . Then he processed the information, discarding the irrelevancies and the dead ends, set out the facts in Walther's file and the facts which he knew himself. The outline was finished by the evening; he gave it to Minna to read. Walther had been painstaking and imaginative in his investigation, helped by the guidance of Heinrich Holler, whose memory of the old Abwehr records was invaluable. Admiral Canaris had kept detailed files on the Führer and all his associates; so had the Intelligence Service of Reinhard Heydrich and Himmler. Both services, outwardly in truce, but in mortal rivalry for control of the internal and external security of the Reich, put their spies into every department and every private house.

Until the failure of the generals' bomb plot in July 1944, Canaris and his successor had compiled a report of the activities and routine of every person who stayed at Hitler's retreat in the mountains at Berchtesgaden. There Eva Braun lived in seclusion, with her two terriers for company, appearing in front of Hitler's intimates only on his command. It was a strange love affair; her role as mistress expanded with the years, until her dances and exhibitions of athletics, loyally filmed by her mentor Heinrich Hoffman, became part of the entertainment offered to the favoured few who shared their leader's relaxation. There was no doubt that she loved Adolf Hitler with a mixture of naïveté and mysticism which submitted without question to a life of loneliness and restriction. She was a simple woman whose appeal lay in her natural prettiness and homely ways, regarding herself as divinely appointed to serve the Leader. The Abwehr spies at Berchtesgaden reported that she was in poor health during the early summer of 1943, and that she had gone to stay with her sister Gretl in Munich after Christmas, returning to Berlin in late February. The agents' report suggested that she might have fallen out of Hitler's favour, and this was the reason for her illness, which seemed to be neurotic in origin, and her return to her sister. If this was the case, then her position was even stronger after she and the Führer became reconciled.

Unfortunately for both the Abwehr agents and their former chief, Canaris, the bomb planted beside Hitler during the conference in July did not achieve its aim. He escaped with cuts and bruises, and thousands of people were executed in a purge that destroyed Admiral Canaris himself and delivered his records into the hands of his enemy the Gestapo. It had seemed to Sigmund Walther, as it did to Max, that the 'illness' from which Eva Braun was suffering was pregnancy, and the stay with her sister had been to cover up the birth of the baby.

The execution of Fegelein and his knowledge of the code-word Janus reinforced this theory. With Holler's assistance, Walther had compiled a long report on Gretl Fegelein, the pre-1945 data taken from Gestapo files. In the early part of 1944 she had entertained her sister Eva; there was no record of anything unusual during their stay together. The sisters were friendly but not intimate. There were few visitors, Herman Fegelein was one of Reichsführer Himmler's most trusted assistants, and he was seldom able to leave Berlin. His wife was a retiring woman, who felt uneasy with the Führer's inner circle and refused to take part in the intrigues and power politics that surrounded him. She was a practising Catholic, and continued to attend Mass in spite of pressure from her husband, who feared Hitler's disapproval.

Walther's report on Fegelein's execution was the official one. He had been caught hiding in a flat in Berlin, having slipped away from the Bunker; Swiss money and his sister-in-law's diamonds were found on him. Hitler ordered his immediate return to the Bunker, where he was interrogated and shot. His body had been buried in a bomb crater and dug up by the Russians. Walther had tracked down the two surviving servants who had lived in the Fegelein household during Eva's stay. One was an old woman, a war widow, who lived on a pension and helped out with a Munich family's washing twice a week. She had seen very little of the famous Eva; what she did see was when she brought her breakfast in bed during the morning. She remembered being sent a message during the visit, that the ladies were going away for the weekend and she wouldn't be needed till the Monday.

The other survivor of the household was an ex-SS man, called by the unlikely name of Schubert, who acted as chauffeur and bodyguard. His story was the same as the maid's; nothing unusual occurred while Eva was staying there, except that he too had been dismissed for the same weekend.

There followed a long and fruitless series of inquiries at hospitals and doctors in the city, none of which yielded any information linking them with Eva Braun or with the delivery of a baby in suspicious circumstances. There had been a private clinic ten kilometres outside the city, but it had been closed down at the end of the war, and the building demolished. There was no trace of the doctor who ran it or of any of his staff. The evidence pointed to Eva having had the child induced over that weekend, the baby itself being taken away by a foster-mother.

Bombing, chaos and disruption followed by Allied occupation had made it impossible to track down anyone who knew anything about the clinic or its medical staff. And there the trail had ended for Sigmund Walther with the refusal of Gretl Fegelein to see him, and of the convent to accept letters or messages for her. He had made a note of Holler's suggestion that the Reverend Mother's reluctance to assist them might be on direct orders from her superiors in Rome. There was nothing to be done officially, since the investigation was a private one, and Gretl Fegelein had not committed any breach of the law.

'We've got to see her,' Minna put the report down. 'She helped to arrange the birth and she *must* know who took the child! Her husband knew, too. That's what he was trying to tell you – find Janus!'

'It must have been kept secret from everyone else,' Max said. 'Somebody would have given it away, at Nuremburg, or tried to do a deal to help themselves. Read the rest of it; there are one or two people left on my list who just might be able to lead somewhere.'

He watched her reading, a slight frown drawing the fine eyebrows together.

'There are two in Hamburg,' she said. 'Mühlhauser and Josef Franke. Why don't you see them first – then we can fly to Munich. She's not going to disappear out of the convent.'

'I didn't know what Janus meant when I drew up that list,' Max said. 'But Mühlhauser was a very important man, the last liaison between Himmler and Hitler in Berlin. The Russians got him, and what bothered me at the time is how he got released. It bothers me even more now. He and Fegelein were Himmler's men. And Himmler was trying to make peace behind Hitler's back. Fegelein knew about the child, and I'm beginning to think he told Himmler. And if Himmler knew, then Mühlhauser would have known too. Maybe we should see Mühlhauser first. Josef Franke was the guard who got me out; he can't tell us anything, but I'd like to see him again anyway. I owe him a drink, at least.'

He saw that she wasn't listening; she was looking at the list again and this time the frown deepened suddenly, and then disappeared.

'Albert Kramer – why is he on this list?'

'Do you know him? – of course, you would do,' he said. 'He's a powerful man in Germany today; he's got a finger in everything, including government policy.'

The coldness in her eyes surprised him. 'He is one of our closest friends,' Minna Walther said. 'What could he have to do with this?'

He felt suddenly angry; the last person he had expected to find ranked with Minna Walther and her husband was Albert Kramer. He wanted to shock her, to repay the snub with the truth about what her oldest friend had done in the Chancellory garden that day. But he didn't. Instinct stopped him, and he obeyed it.

Albert Kramer, and a patriotic idealist like Sigmund Walther, with a wife of Minna's integrity and devotion. Albert Kramer must have changed a lot from the boy who emptied his revolver into the dying Herman Fegelein. He would have another motive now for meeting him again.

'I'd better go to my hotel,' he said, 'it's getting late. Can I phone for a cab to take me there?'

'Where are you staying?'

'The Parkhotel.'

'It's not a very comfortable hotel, I'm afraid,' she said. The eyes were innocent; there was no subtle invitation in them. 'It *is* late; they'll be closed except for a night porter, it's that sort of hotel. Why don't you stay here tonight?'

'That's very nice of you, Fräu Walther. I don't want to be a nuisance,' he said.

She smiled, and the strain which had arisen between them was gone. 'It's no trouble at all. I always have a room ready; we never knew when someone would call and need a bed. I left my car keys on the table in the hall; if you get your case, I'll take you upstairs.'

He followed her up to a room on the first floor. It was some distance from the bedroom he had seen that morning. She opened the door and switched on the lights; it was a warm and pleasant bedroom, impersonal as all guestrooms are.

'I hope you'll be comfortable,' she said. 'What would you like for breakfast?'

'Just coffee, I never eat anything,' he said.

'Nor do I,' Minna said. 'Goodnight.'

'Goodnight, Fräu Walther.'

He picked up his case, dropped it on the bed and began to unpack. The sight of his pyjamas reminded him of home and the room he shared with Ellie. She seemed so insubstantial that it shocked him; she and his children were receding like shadows into the background of his life. Time was running backwards; with every hour spent in that house, immersing himself in the world of the war, he was losing his identity as Max Steiner, French-domiciled with a wife and children and a bright career in political journalism. The past was closing in on him, seizing him and dragging him back into it. His youth, his lost family, they were taking shape and becoming more real than the living. He could see his mother as if she were in the room with him; her face was lined with tiredness and grief, the brown hair prematurely grey. His father, and the dimmer figures of his brothers, killed in the war which was to make Germany the ruler of the world.

He went to the washbasin and, instead of cleaning his teeth and making preparations for bed, he spent a long time staring at himself in the mirror. The man started dissolving into the boy, the member of the Hitler Youth since he was eight years old, the youngest son of a proud National Socialist family. Adolf Hitler, the saviour of his people. Somewhere in the world outside, a man carried within him the seeds of that supremely evil genius, and only an optimist or a fool would imagine that the heir to the Fourth Reich was not being nurtured and prepared to claim his inheritance, under some other guise. He had a clearer picture of Sigmund Walther after the hours spent reading his work and seeing into his mind. He had a vision of Germany which was based on his faith in the people themselves. He saw them united in peace, their talent for hard work, self-sacrifice and honesty overcoming the ugly dogmas of the left and the narrow hysteria of the right. He saw their vulnerability through partition, and recognized that a moment of frustration might emerge which could be seized and turned to all advantage. He knew his country's weakness. Germans needed a hero to reflect their ancient culture and the deep-seated racial myths which were a part of the Teutonic ethos. If Germany was to be safe for the future, the heir of Adolf Hitler had to be found. Walther had set himself this mission and he had died because of it. The responsibility had fallen on Max Steiner; it was no longer a selfish quest, or a journalist's coup of the decade. It was a mission.

He fell asleep quickly.

In her big lonely bedroom across the passage, Minna Walther stretched out to the empty pillow beside her, and began to cry for her husband. And for herself, because she knew she wasn't going to be faithful to his memory.

Maurice Franconi had bought himself a puppy. It was a black and white terrier, and it gave him the excuse over the last few days to walk up and down the street where Otto Helm lived with his daughter and son-in-law. Nobody commented on a man walking his dog; he lingered by the house, saw the doctor leave on his morning calls, worked out a routine for the family. Otto Helm's daughter went shopping in the morning, but she didn't leave the old man alone. Maurice had telephoned when she and the doctor were both out, and put the phone down with the excuse of a wrong number when a woman answered. Probably there was a neighbour in one of the other two flats who stayed with the invalid till his daughter came back. It wasn't going to be quite as easy as Kesler had imagined.

There was a limit to the number of times he could appear with his terrier in that street when he wasn't a resident. Otto Helm would have to be dealt with at night. Franconi had a room in a small *pension* not too far away. He bought himself a can of petrol and a plastic bag of polystyrene filling for cushions.

The little terrier licked his hands, and Franconi patted it. He liked animals, but Kesler was allergic to dogs and cats. He wouldn't be able to take the puppy back with him, but he enjoyed her company while he laid low between visits to Regensdorfstrasse, trying to teach her tricks she was too young to pick up, though she played enthusiastically, licking his face and responding to his voice.

He had dinner at a café, paid his bill at the *pension* and said he would be leaving very early in the morning. He walked the dog past the house at just before eleven o'clock; there were lights in the first-floor windows. Otto Helm and family were at home. The doctor's car was parked outside.

Franconi went back to the *pension*; he had hired himself a little VW under the name of Hubert, with one of the forged driving licences he and Kesler kept in reserve. He packed his case, shushed the terrier, who was scampering by his feet, and packed the petrol and polystyrene in a big holdall. He had provided himself with matches and a long twist of rag. He looked round the bedroom, making sure he had forgotten nothing. Kesler had taught him to pay attention to detail; even a book of matches left behind could help identify a man. Nothing. Nothing but the terrier. He opened the door, picked up the case and the holdall and called it softly. 'Hella – come on . . .' A single light burned in the narrow hall below; he checked his watch. It was nearly twelve-thirty. Everyone had gone to bed. There was a pay telephone in a cubicle near the desk. He slipped inside, paid two pfennigs, and dialled the doctor's number. It rang for nearly a minute. Then a man's voice answered; it sounded sleepy. Franconi spoke rapidly, urgently. There had been a bad accident, three cars involved; one of the victims had given the doctor's name. Come, please, at once – it's too terrible down here – he gave the location about two miles away at a well-known junction near a shopping centre. Then he hung up, grabbed his cases, and ran silently through into the street and got into his VW. The terrier bounded in after him. He parked outside the house on the other side of the road. He saw the doctor come out of the front door carrying a surgical bag. He jumped into his own car and drove off, swerving at the corners. Maurice got out, carrying the holdall, and went to the entrance. He pressed the bell marked 'Mintzel'. The buzzer sounded and he went up the stairs. He saw the door open and a slant of yellow light cut across the dark landing.

'Heinz?' Trudi Mintzel called. 'What have you forgotten – '

He reached the door and threw his weight against it. He had a brief sight of a young woman in a short nylon nightdress with her mouth opening to scream. He hit her so quickly that she didn't have time to make any noise. She fell backwards, and he had a glimpse of her thighs and lower body exposed; he looked away. Women disgusted him.

He opened the doors till he found Otto Helm's bedroom. The room was in darkness but the old man's snoring rattled. Franconi switched on the light, but he didn't wake. He was propped up on the pillows like a dummy, white-haired and waxen, his paralysed face twisted into a sleeping grimace. Franconi brought the holdall into the doorway; he piled the polystyrene into a heap by the bedside, and poured petrol over it, sprinkling the rest round the curtains and the furniture. Then he went back and picked up Trudi Mintzel. The blow had broken her neck. He laid her down by the bedside, near the heap of polystyrene. He backed out of the room, lit the twist of rag with a match. It was nylon and highly inflammable. It flared immediately and he stepped forward and threw it on to the mound of plastic fibre. There was a thump and a bright flash as the petrol exploded. Franconi shut the bedroom door and waited outside for a minute. The crackle and hiss of the fire was joined by wreaths of deadly smoke seeping under the door. Polystyrene gave off lethal fumes. Franconi thought he heard a faint, gurgling cry from inside the bedroom, then he left the flat, slipping the latch on the front door as he left. He hesitated in the entrance, but there was no one in the street.

He didn't look back until he was in the VW, with the engine switched on, and the terrier Hella was trying to lick his hand because she was pleased to see him. Flames were shooting out of the first-floor window. Franconi let in the clutch and drove away. The first flight back to Munich was not till eight in the morning. He drove to the centre of Berlin, parked the car, and went to an all-night movie showing sex films. He slept through them until six o'clock. He felt tired and dirty and his head ached. The terrier was curled up in the passenger seat, waiting for him. He climbed inside, and picked up the little dog to break its neck. She whined and struggled, licking joyously at his face.

Franconi hesitated; she had bright, button brown eyes and a short tail that wagged and thumped against him.

'Good Hella,' he said. 'Good girl, then . . .' He opened the door and put her out. 'Someone'll find you,' he said, and drove off. In the driving mirror he could see her racing after him, until he outdistanced her. He caught the plane to Munich and had lunch with Kesler. He told him everything, and Kesler complimented him warmly. He had been working hard on his assignment at the convent, but there hadn't been an opportunity yet. Franconi looked disappointed. He had hoped to find it settled.

He let Kesler reassure him, while he sulked. He didn't mention the terrier Hella.

'There's a pattern,' Curt Andrews said. He laid a long finger on the paper in front of him, and looked at the head of West Germany's Intelligence Service. Heinrich Holler, the legend. Andrews wasn't impressed by reputations; he liked to make his own judgements. Holler was small and slight, with grey hair, and a limp, the legacy of his imprisonment by the Gestapo. He had pale, clear grey eyes in an intelligent face and the kind of mouth that is described as humorous. He made Andrews feel big and clumsy, which he wasn't. The two men didn't like each other, but it was a well concealed hostility, invisible to anyone else. Their personalities were at variance: Holler, the intuitive intellectual, with his crippled leg and European education, was the mental and physical opposite of Curt Andrews. Andrews stood over six feet two inches and weighed two hundred pounds; he was built like a fullback, which he had played in college; he was a veteran of the US Intelligence Service in Vietnam, had gravitated to the CIA after discharge, and proved himself one of its most ruthless and able operators. Vietnam had dehumanized him; it was a pitiless war, distinguished for its corruption, failure and brutal disregard for human decencies.

Andrews had no illusions about his fellow men when he returned to America. Years of negotiating the labyrinth of Washington political life had confirmed his opinion that humanity was shit, and the only important thing in life was power. He had a keen, fierce intelligence and an instinct for deception in others; he was inordinately brave, and quite without scruple. He would have been surprised to know how much he reminded Holler of certain members of Himmler's infamous Black Knights. But he was the Director's man, and Holler worked very closely with the British and American Intelligence Services. He had considerable reservations about the reliability of the French, and carefully monitored information destined for Paris.

'Two deaths,' Andrews said. 'Both connected with Hitler, both present in the Bunker.'

'One accident, one natural death,' Holler murmured. 'A fire and a heart attack. Hitler's valet, and one of Himmler's top liaison officers. Not to mention his daughter, who was in the bedroom when it caught fire!' He offered Andrews a cigarette, and accepted a light in return. 'I wouldn't see any connection if both Schmidt and Helm weren't names specifically asked for by this man Steiner from *Newsworld*. Our people gave him the information he wanted, and within a few days two of the people on that list are dead. According to the woman who looked after Schmidt, he was visited by two men, and died suddenly while they were with him. Helm's son-in-law, Dr Mintzel, said the old man had also been visited; his description of the man fits Steiner, but doesn't tally with the two who went to Berchtesgaden.'

'And Steiner was with Sigmund Walther when he died,' Andrews pointed out. 'This isn't just coincidence, Herr Holler. Walther is murdered – ' He saw the pain on the older man's face, knew they had been close friends, and went on more forcefully. 'Steiner comes to Germany, digs up information about a list of people who have only one thing in common – they were all with Hitler in Berlin at the end. He goes to see one of them; right. Somebody else goes and sees another on the list. Within a week, both men are dead. In my book that makes a pattern, starting with Walther.'

Holler tapped his cigarette ash into a metal bowl; he was a heavy smoker and it was full of stubs. 'I had an autopsy done on the valet, Schmidt,' he said, and the light eyes glanced up at Curt Andrews. 'Very discreetly, of course. He died from cyanide poisoning. Probably fired from a pen or pencil. You know the kind of thing.' Andrews knew very well. He had used them and authorized their use. His department called them 'toys'.

'Then it was a professional job,' he said.

'So was the fire,' Holler said. 'The place was practically gutted, but we found traces of polystyrene in the bedroom, and there was no furniture with that filling in the room. And one other thing – I have a feeling they're connected, but it's no more than that. A stray dog has been running round that street since the night of the fire. People the police contacted said it belonged to a man who walked it round the street, but he hasn't been found and nobody recognized him.'

'Where is it?' Andrews asked.

'I have it at home,' Holler said. 'My wife likes it – it's a nice terrier puppy. I think that the man who walked it near Otto Helm's house, and then abandoned it, had something to do with killing him. And his daughter. Polystyrene is just like a poison when it's lit.' He was speaking reflectively and so low, that he might have been talking to himself. 'But examination showed she had a broken neck. There were traces of urine on the sitting-room carpet; she was killed there and put in with her father afterwards. Very professional again.'

'Why haven't you pulled in Steiner?' Andrews demanded. 'He's the one link we've got – the killing of Walther and these other people are all connected. It looks to me like Uncle Vanya.'

'If it is the Russians,' Holler said, 'we have to know why. They had political reasons for killing Sigmund. His reunification policy was gaining support. But why the tie-in with Hitler and the Bunker?'

'Maybe Walther was a neo-Nazi.' Curt Andrews tipped up in his chair and beamed his hard stare at the German. 'Certain people at home suspected it.'

'They also suspected that he was working for the Russians,' Holler said. 'They were just as wrong. I knew Walther well. He wasn't a Nazi and he certainly wasn't a Red. He was a man who loved his country.'

'If you say so.' Andrews set the chair back on its four legs. 'But whatever he was, he got killed for it. And this reporter is nosing around among the corpses. I'd like to talk to him. I'd like to ask him why he went to see Helm, why he wanted to interview these other people.' He waited, silently exerting pressure on Heinrich Holler. A man who loved his country. He had never heard such crap said seriously before. A smart-ass politician, loaded with money and ambition, aiming for the top . . .

'You'll have the opportunity,' Holler said. 'When I decide to ask him myself. But he wasn't in Berlin the night Helm was murdered, and he didn't see Schmidt. He is certainly a link but he's not the killer.'

'And where is he now?'

'In Hamburg. Where two more names on his list are living. Both are being watched by our people. He's staying with Walther's widow. His investigation seems to have her blessing.'

'What's the run-down on her?'

'Old Prussian military family, married at eighteen, five children, very happily married. I know her quite well, though not as intimately as her husband. She was always a great help to him. There's no scandal or political ties there.' He seemed to say it to irritate Andrews. 'Just a woman in love with a fine man.' He didn't allow himself to smile, but the shift in Andrews's expression showed that he had scored. It was odd, Holler thought, that a man as young as Andrews should dislike human nature so much that he couldn't bear hearing virtue ascribed to man or woman. Perhaps it was the only way he could do his job. Holler had known a number of men with the same attitude. They had big offices in Gestapo Headquarters in Prinz Albrechtstrasse, and in a later generation they had surrounded a president of the United States.

He had to co-operate with Curt Andrews and what he represented, but he wasn't going to let him touch Max Steiner, or cast his shadow close to Minna Walther. He smiled, and got up from his desk. 'Let me take you to lunch, Herr Andrews. Then you might like to fly down to Hamburg with me. I think it would be useful to see these two men on Steiner's list. Just to find out what questions he asked them.'

'Thanks,' Andrews got up, aware that he towered over Holler, and it didn't give him a feeling of power. Just size. 'Let's hope we find them alive to give an answer.'

Max had gone to call at the address where Josef Franke and his wife Ilse lived. He had spent the day studying Walther's notes again; Minna had met him with an excuse the next morning, asking if he could entertain himself as she had made an appointment for lunch that couldn't be broken. She looked pale and her eyes were strained. He guessed that she had been crying before she went to sleep. The housekeeper brought his lunch into the study. He was hungry and the food was excellent; there was a superb chocolate dessert topped with whipped cream and walnuts. He had forgotten the richness of German cooking; when he was a little boy just before the war, there had been no shortages. In the early years of war, too, the fruits of victory were shared liberally among the German civilians. They had the guns and the butter too; French cognac, scent, silk stockings and underclothes, furs, all the luxuries looted from the countries under occupation flowed into Germany, and everyone lived better than ever before.

He could remember the family dinners when his brothers were on leave. They had a Polish girl to help his mother; Max hadn't understood why she was always red-eyed and sullen. He hadn't heard of forced labour, whether it was digging trenches or washing the floors for a German family. He was reminded of those meals, of the beer and wine that he was allowed to share, while his brothers sat on either side of his mother, looking like young gods in their Luftwaffe blue.

Ellie had weaned him away from what she called unhealthy eating. She made him lose weight, which was a good idea, and introduced him to the delights of low-cholesterol cooking and American salads. He had never equated her distrust of rich Continental cooking with the fact that his children were allowed to stuff themselves with biscuits and rot their teeth with Coke and sweets.

He sat in Walther's study and wondered how Ellie was and how his children were, and ended up thinking of Minna Walther instead. She had not wanted to spend the morning with him; he sensed that the lunch was an excuse. She had seemed tense and uneasy, and he didn't know what to do to reassure her. Except to keep out of her way. He had decided to go and see Josef Franke that evening, when the store where he worked was closed. He had telephoned, but there was no reply. Probably the wife worked too. If they'd had children they were probably grown up by now. Minna came in during the afternoon. She looked better; there was a faint colour in her face, and he thought suddenly: She hasn't been to lunch, she's been walking . . .

'I hope you've been all right,' she said. 'Did Paula look after you?'

'She certainly did,' he said. 'I nearly fell asleep after lunch. Did you have a good day? Enjoy your lunch?'

'Yes, yes, very much.'

He tried not to look at her; he hated it when she lied, even though it was so innocent a lie. There was a quality about her which made him associate her with honesty and truth, even in unimportant things like an excuse.

'I'm going round to see the Frankes tonight,' he said. 'They won't have anything to tell me, it's just for old times' sake.'

'For saving your life,' Minna reminded him. 'Of course I needn't come with you. Getting into the convent is different.'

He looked at her, and let the moment lengthen.

'I want you to come with me to see Franke,' he said. 'I want you to go every step of the way with me.'

'Why?' She said it quietly, and the question floated between them, full of meaning. Because I love you. He could have said it then, because it came straight into his mind and almost escaped into words. And you want me. I know you do; I feel it every time you're near me. But 'I need you' was what he said.

'Sigmund wouldn't let me get involved,' she said suddenly. 'I wanted to so much, but he said no. It wasn't a woman's business to get mixed up in something so – so dangerous. I'm glad you want me to help. I'll be glad of the chance. Glad to have something to do. Thank you, Herr Steiner.'

'Max,' he corrected. He reached out his hand to her and she took it. He saw the shame in her eyes and the flash of desire it extinguished. He kissed her hand as he had done that day in the Crillon, the morning after she was widowed.

'We'll do it together,' he said quietly. 'We'll find Janus.'

He got up quickly and went out of the room before he ruined everything by taking hold of her and kissing her on the mouth. She sat very still and watched him go; she covered the back of her hand with the other and gripped it tight until the fingers lost all colour. The telephone rang; it shrilled until she went to answer it. The voice was deep and familiar. She held the receiver close as she heard it, as if it could bring her comfort.

'Minna? My dear, how are you?'

'I'm all right,' she said slowly. 'Thank you for your letter; it was wonderful. I shall always keep it.'

'I want to come and see you,' Albert Kramer said. 'If you feel ready to see anyone.'

'Yes,' she said. 'Oh yes, Albert, I'd love to see you.'

'This evening,' he asked her, 'just for half an hour?'

'Please do; I'd be so happy to talk about Sigmund – you were such a friend – '

'I'll be with you at seven,' he said.

The Frankes lived in a big post-war block of flats just outside the centre of Hamburg; Max took the lift up to the twelfth floor, and rang the bell of apartment 27. It was opened very quickly, and a woman stood framed in it, looking up at him, her expression changing from expectation to surprise. He had last seen her in 1945, her body hidden in a mannish white shirt and brown skirt . . . His memory of her was so vivid that it seemed to Max he was looking at two images, blurring and separating the girl Ilse in the Bunker from the older Fräu. She was still thin, but her hair was short and curly and she wore a bright coloured dress with flowers.

She stared at him. 'Yes?'

'You're Ilse Franke, aren't you?' he inquired.

She nodded, and her eyes were wary. 'That's right. Who are you? – what can I do for you?' She had closed the door so that she could slam it instantly.

'I came to see you and your husband, Josef,' he said. 'You won't remember me, it has been such a long time. Is he in?'

'Not yet,' she said. 'I thought it was him at the door. He forgets his keys sometimes . . .'

'Can I come in and wait, please?'

'What's your name?' she demanded.

'Max Steiner,' he said. It meant nothing to her. She had never known the name of the boy in the Bunker. 'All right, come in then. Josef won't be long.'

He glanced round the sitting room; it was comfortably furnished, the colours too bright, and a garish reproduction of Tretchikov's Chinese woman glared at him from the main wall. There was a TV set and a trolley laid out with bottles and glasses.

He sat down, and she asked him if he would like a beer. 'Or gin, maybe? We've got some Bols, if you'd like that.'

'No, thank you,' Max said.

She seated herself on the chair opposite, her hands clasped primly on her lap. 'Where did you meet Josef? – I don't place you at all, Herr Steiner. How long ago did we meet you?'

'We were in Berlin,' he said. 'The last day of April, 1945. I was the Hitler Jügend troop leader you helped escape from the Bunker.'

She was a sallow-skinned woman, and when the colour drained she looked a pasty grey; her eyes opened wide in horror, and she brought both hands up to her mouth.

'Oh my God! My God – it's you? It can't be – Oh, Jesus Christ!'

'Why be so upset?' Max said quietly. 'You saved my life; your husband certainly did. I've come back to see you both and thank you. There's nothing for you to worry about.'

'Oh no? Where the hell have you been all these years then? – nothing to worry about! After we've got ourselves settled and Josef's in a good job . . . Listen.' She got up and glared at him. 'You get out,' she said. 'We don't know anything about the Bunker and we don't know you.'

'What's the matter, love?' Josef Franke was in the doorway; he wore a dark brown uniform, with the insignia of a well-known security force on his shoulder. He was still a big man, though smaller than Max remembered, with broad shoulders and a powerful neck. His hair was cropped very short and completely grey. He stared hard at Max. He would have been a match for most men, in spite of his age. 'Who are you?'

His wife answered. 'It's the kid we brought out of Berlin.' She hurried over and caught his arm. 'You remember – tell him to get out, Seff; we don't want anyone like him coming round, making trouble!'

'I'm sorry,' Max said. 'I didn't mean to upset your wife. I've just come back to Germany and I wanted to look you up. Just to say thank you.'

'Well, you've said it,' the woman snapped at him. 'Now go away and leave us alone.'

'Ilse,' her husband said. 'Ilse, shut up!' He went over to Max and held out his hand. 'Don't mind her,' he said. 'We had a rough time after the war. I'm always glad to see an old comrade. Sit down and have a beer; I often wondered what happened to you.'

'The Americans picked me up,' Max said. 'I was sent to my aunt in Bremen. I live in Paris now. I'm just here on a visit. What happened to you?'

'The Americans arrested both of us,' Franke said. 'They found the serial number I'd had tattooed under my armpit. I had to admit to being SS, but I said I was a deserter from the Eastern zone. I went into the bag for a couple of years; they didn't hold Ilse and she waited for me.' He glanced at her and his expression softened. 'Kept me going with food, got herself a job cooking for an American colonel. Robbed the bastards right and left and they never caught on – when I came out we got married. And it was rough. No jobs for people like me, after the war. Nobody wanted to touch us with a ten-foot pole. And I wasn't a bigwig so Odessa didn't bother with the likes of me. We scraped by; Ilse had a baby but it died.' He shrugged and reached for the glass of beer Ilse had given him. 'Never mind, we're all right now. I got this job with the security force and we live very well. Nice little place, this, isn't it?'

'Yes,' said Max. 'Very cosy.'

'What's your job?' Josef asked. 'Why do you live in Paris? I never liked the French – crawl up your arse one minute and stab you in the back the next!'

'I work for a news magazine,' Max said. 'I'm on a story at the moment, as a matter of fact. I'm doing a story on the last days in the Bunker.'

'Oh?' For a moment the older man's face darkened with suspicion. Max saw it and recognized the same sensitivity to anti-Nazi propaganda that he had found in the police inspector in West Berlin. He decided to make good use of it.

'It's about time,' he said, 'that people knew the truth about us; all the world's been fed is horror stories, concentration camps, six million Jews killed, all the old anti-German stuff that keeps on turning up. I'm going to write about it as it *really* was. About my mother and my grandmother being killed, about the old men of the Volksturm and the children in the Hitler Jügend going out to face Russian tanks to defend their city and their homeland. That's what I'm going to write!'

Josef Franke's face had reddened. He leaned forward and slapped Max on the knee. Beer breathed over him.

'About time! It's about time someone put over our side of it. The Yids have been yelling their dirty heads off ever since the end of the war! I'd like to see an article like yours – telling the world we weren't all swine and sadists, just patriotic Germans fighting for our country against the bloody Reds! Isn't that so, Ilse?' She had come behind him, her hand resting on his shoulder. Her pale eyes burned.

'My God, I'll say it is! They've got their Russians now, haven't they? Breathing down their necks! Serves the bloody Western world right – they destroyed us when we were fighting Communism! Now they can get on with it. I hope you say the lot!' She came and sat beside her husband. 'I'm sorry I was rude,' she said to Max. 'But if you knew what we went through because Josef had served in SS . . . Another glass of beer?'

Max shook his head. 'No, thanks. I'm going to do quite a piece on the Bunker itself. The way people stayed with the Führer right to the end. I won't mention ourselves, just generalities. I want to convey the atmosphere at the end. It was a real "Twilight of the Gods".'

He had won them completely; he felt a qualm of guilt about deceiving them when he owed them so much, but it jarred him to find that neither had changed their old attitudes, or faced the reality of what they had brought upon their country and themselves. The *Heil Hitlers* were vibrating in the air.

He turned to Ilse. 'You remember they shot Fegelein that morning,' he said. 'You said something about it to me. Didn't he have Eva Braun's diamonds and a lot of money stacked away?'

'Those were the rumours,' she said. 'But Josef would know more about that.'

'I was in on the interrogation for a bit,' Franke said. 'Standarten-führer Helm was in charge. I thought he'd kill Fegelein the way he was going at him.' He grinned, and the last twinge of guilt at his deception left Max as he saw it. 'He had her jewels all right, and money. But what Helm was really giving it to him for was something he'd told Obergruppenführer Mühlhauser. He punched Fegelein in the charlies, and yelled at him that he'd betrayed the future of Germany. I didn't know what it was all about.'

Max finished the last of the beer. Fegelein had betrayed the future of Germany. That meant he had told Gunther Mühlhauser about the existence of Janus. Or where he was hidden. Josef looked at him, and shook his head. 'You're not going to mention that, are you?'

'Why should I?' Max said. 'I'm interested in the heroes of Berlin and the Bunker, not the rats like Fegelein.' He stood up and shook hands with them. They came to the door with him, and as he turned to say good-bye again, Josef Franke straightened and brought his heels together. '*Heil Hitler*, comrade. I know you'll do us justice.' He raised his right arm to shoulder level, in the old salute.

Max didn't answer. He nodded at both of them and hurried out into the passage and the lift. He breathed in the cool air, and began to walk at a fast pace as if he were trying to leave something behind. Franke had given him a clue, when he had chanced a question without expecting an answer. Herman Fegelein had passed the secret of Janus on to Himmler's aide and confidant; that was why Hitler had ordered his death and Eva Braun had at last accepted it. He had told Mühlhauser about Janus, as part of the package Himmler was assembling to make peace with the Allies and divide the West from Soviet Russia. Only no one had considered making peace with Himmler, and he had fled, only to be arrested by a British patrol and commit suicide like the leader he had at last betrayed. But Gunther Mühlhauser had been captured in Berlin. By the Russians. He went on walking, making his way back to Minna Walther's house; he had lost the sense of time. A clock chimed midnight, and he stopped suddenly, checking his watch. He had been walking through the city for almost two hours.

He found a cruising taxi-cab and gave the address. He felt tired and jaded, and his spirits were low. Mühlhauser knew about the child. He could well have been told where to find it. And it was beyond reason to hope that he hadn't passed that information to the Russians, in exchange for his life and ultimate release.

Albert Kramer had kissed her hand and then her cheek. She disliked the smell of his aftershave; it was musty and rather strong. It lingered wherever he had been, advertising his presence. She had mentioned it once to her husband, who laughed and said it was supposed to attract women. Minna had wrinkled her nose and said it had the very opposite effect on her. It was the only fault she could find with Albert Kramer; he was a loyal supporter of Sigmund in politics and a charming, intelligent friend of the family, who exerted himself to win her affection. Sitting in the pleasant drawing room, sleek and blonde and handsome as ever, he looked at her and shook his head.

'You're pale,' he said gently. 'And a little too thin. You mustn't grieve, Minna; Sigmund wouldn't want that.'

'I'm all right,' she said. 'You mustn't worry about me.' He had been married and divorced in the ten years she had known him. His wife was a bright, hectic girl, with a doting father who had made a fortune out of textiles since the war. She had a child by a previous marriage, and a dubious reputation which Albert chose to ignore. He had waited six years and had a three-year-old son before he divorced her. By that time he had become one of the richest and most influential industrialists in West Germany. His enemies attributed his forebearance towards his wife with the use he made of her father, and its sudden ending with his emergence as a power figure in his own right. Minna didn't listen to gossip; she hadn't liked his wife because they had little in common, but she had accepted her because she was a part of Albert. He had been very tactful when he arrived; his mention of Sigmund was brief and gentle. He talked about the children, asking after her eldest son Helmut, and she knew this was an effort, because Helmut was opinionated and abrasive, and Albert instinctively reacted against him.

'He's a clever fellow,' he said. 'Remember, Minna, I've got interests all over the world, and if Helmut wants to start with any of my organizations, I'd be only too delighted. I mentioned this to Sigmund before.'

She smiled in gratitude and shook her head. 'It's very sweet of you, Albert, but I don't see my son settling down to capitalism for a long time. His head is full of notions and ideals, and he thinks making money is a crime.'

'I wonder how he came to terms with his father's fortune, then?' He lit a cigarette, and offered one to her. He carried a heavy gold case, long out of fashion.

'Everything Sigmund did was perfect,' she said. 'If he made money it was only to finance his political career and advance his plans for Germany. Helmut worshipped him. He wants to go into politics, and before that, he's determined to be a journalist. He was terribly upset by his father's death; it was harder for him than any of the other children. Unfortunately, I'm no substitute; we've never been close.'

'That's surprising,' Albert Kramer said. 'I hoped he'd be a support to you. Do you want me to talk to him ?' She saw the hard line of his mouth and the glint in his eyes, and imagined the furious confrontation that would take place if he tried to lecture her son.

'No, thank you, Albert. Helmut will settle down in time.'

'And you,' he asked her, 'what will you do now, my dear?'

She didn't answer immediately; she hesitated. Sigmund had often spoken of Albert as one of his closest friends. She didn't know whether that friendship extended to telling him about the secret of Janus.

'I shall go on with Sigmund's work,' she said, and she watched his face for a sign. There was none. Only a faint surprise that irritated her.

'You're not thinking of politics, surely – Minna, that kind of world isn't suited to women, at least not to ladies.'

'I don't see why not,' she said. 'Women have to live with political decisions made by men; why shouldn't they have a say in what affects them?'

He smiled, and there was a gentle condescension in it, which made her suddenly very angry. 'I never thought of you as a feminist,' he said. 'Or a militant.'

'How did you think of me?' she asked him. 'As some kind of ornament?'

'Not at all,' Albert said. He thought how desirable she looked, with the angry colour in her cheeks. 'I thought of you as a perfect wife and mother, and Sigmund as the luckiest man in Germany. How *do* you intend to carry on his work? – please, I'm being quite serious. I'd like to know, and maybe I could help.'

'I'm going to commission a biography,' she said. 'And there's a journalist who wants to do a series about him. I've got to keep his name alive, until someone comes forward to take up his work for the reunification of our country.'

'Have you someone in mind?' He was taking her seriously, as he'd said; there was no male chauvinism in his attitude now.'

'Sigmund had a lot of colleagues with the same ideas. But the man has got to be politically reliable. He's got to have authority in the world outside Germany, like Sigmund.'

'With friends in the right places,' Albert Kramer said. 'Yes, a man with a sound political record, and independent of the party machine. Rich, like Sigmund, so nobody could buy him.' He stood up, brought out his gold case and lit another cigarette. He had a good figure; he and Sigmund used to play squash together. She sat still and watched him; there was tension in the atmosphere and it was growing.

'Minna,' his voice was low, but emotion made it deeper, 'Minna, I want to ask you a question. A very important question, and very personal to me. I loved Sigmund as much as I admired him. I believe in his ideals and I want what he wanted for my country. A united, free Germany. If I offered myself as his successor, would you give me your support?'

'You mean go into politics full time? Give up your businesses?'

'I've done all I can do,' he said. 'I want to serve my country now, out in the open. I'll seek election to the Bundestag next spring, on the same platform as he did. *Détente* with the East German government and ultimate reunification. I can do it, Minna; I've been thinking about it for a long time. I can gather his supporters together and I've a lot of influence in the government itself. I'd be a force to reckon with. But I need you to give your blessing. And more than that, I'd need your help in co-ordinating Sigmund's policies through his personal papers. I'd have to think through his brain to start with.'

'Yes,' she said, 'I see. I think I'd like a drink. Will you have one with me?'

She got up and went to the trolley, and poured herself a whisky. Albert shook his head and frowned.

He didn't approve of women drinking spirits like that. And she hadn't answered his question. He came and stood close to her, so that she was looking up. It gave him an advantage. 'What do you say, Minna? Can I count on you?'

He had hot blue eyes, and there was something besides ambition and urgency in them; she knew that he was bidding for more than her dead husband's political career. He wanted her, too, and she had always sensed that, even when Sigmund was alive. She had a flash of memory, and the hand holding the glass of whisky tightened. Sigmund saying to her one night as they undressed for bed after a party, where Albert Kramer had been the host, 'Such a pity he won't join with us – we could do with his influence and his brains. But he says politics bore him. I had a good go at him this evening to try and make him change his mind, but not a hope of it . . .' That had been only a few months ago. She put down the glass and stood up slowly; they were face to face and he was close enough to touch her.

'Let me think about it,' she said. 'Give me a few days. I'll telephone you, Albert. Now, please forgive me, but I'm rather tired.'

He held out his hand and she had to take it. His lips pressed hard against her skin and they were moist.

'I'll wait to hear from you,' he said. 'And I shall hope. Goodnight, my dear.'

She closed the door on him, and waited until she heard the sound of his car starting outside. Then she went back to the room and sat down, with the glass in both hands. His name was on Max Steiner's list. He hadn't told her why.

She was still sitting there when Max came in, and she called out to him. He looked tired and downcast. He came and sat in the chair Albert Kramer had used.

'What happened?' she asked him. 'You've been such a long time.'

'I was walking,' he said. 'I saw the Frankes; they didn't give me good news. I had to think out what it meant, that's why I went on walking.'

'What did it mean?'

'Fegelein was shot for telling a man called Gunther Mühlhauser about Janus. Josef Franke was in the room during the interrogation. He didn't know what it was all about, but I believe Fegelein told Mühlhauser that Hitler had a child. Mühlhauser was Himmler's personal aide. And he was captured by the Russians. You know, his name's on my list and he's living here in Hamburg. If the Russians released him, he must have told them what Fegelein told him. Which means, if the boy is alive at all, he's in Russian hands.'

Minna Walther shook her head; the light behind gleamed in the blonde hair, turning it into a halo.

'They got their information from the autopsy on Eva Braun,' she said. 'They may have got confirmation from this Mühlhauser but I don't believe for a moment that they got the child.' Max raised his head and looked at her; he felt weary and pessimistic. He didn't recognize it but the pessimism stemmed from that moment in the Frankes' flat when he heard once more the words *Heil Hitler* spoken in modern Germany.

'Why?' he said. 'Why are you so sure?'

'They never found him,' she said. 'Sigmund knew it too. And not just Sigmund. I had a visitor tonight. Your friend Albert Kramer.'

'*Your* friend,' he corrected.

She nodded. 'I want to ask you something. Why is he on your list of people connected with the Bunker?'

'You won't like this,' Max said. 'He may have been a friend of your husband's, but he wasn't always one of the bright lights of German liberalism. He was in the Hitler Jügend with me. We grew up together, and he was one of the most fanatical bastards in the unit. His father was in the Waffen SS, and Albert Kramer was just like him. He took over the firing squad when I refused; I saw him standing over Fegelein, pumping bullets into him as he lay dying.' He saw the look in her eyes, and said, 'Maybe he changed after the war. People can change. But that's how I knew him.'

She got up and stood by the fireplace, facing him. 'He *was* a Nazi?' she said. 'He's kept that hidden very well. Sigmund trusted him and liked him. He came here and said he wanted to go into politics and carry on Sigmund's work for Germany. He asked me to help him.' She leaned against the mantelpiece, one foot balanced on the fender.

The line of the thigh was provocative; Max forced himself to look at her face.

'He talked about loving my husband and wanting the same things for Germany. He was very convincing. Except that only three months ago Sigmund asked him to join him and he refused. Now he wants to take his place. Which is a lot of nonsense; he wanted an excuse for going through his papers. He said that – "I'll need to co-ordinate his policies through his personal papers." That's why he came here and told a pack of lies. He wants to see the file. He knows what Sigmund was looking for, and he's trying to find it too. I realized that, suddenly, tonight. I didn't know his background. I didn't know he'd been a Nazi.' She stepped away from the fireplace and stood in front of Max. 'Don't you see – that boy has never been found by the Russians or anyone else. But people know he exists. Albert Kramer knows, and he saw a chance to follow up on Sigmund's leads. And he was ready to throw everything in the balance to get his hands on the information Sigmund had collected.'

'He hasn't changed,' Max said slowly. 'He's just gone under cover for the last twenty years.'

'If he's a neo-Nazi,' Minna said, 'that means *they* haven't got the boy. I don't think you should wait to see Mühlhauser; I think we should fly to Munich tomorrow and see Gretl Fegelein in that convent. I believe she has the secret.'

'All right,' he said. 'We'll go to Munich. Why don't we go to bed now?'

She didn't step back when he put his hands on her shoulders; she didn't move when he brought his body close and bent down to her mouth. 'Don't hold back from me,' he said. Her lips were open and her eyes were shut. He kissed her slowly at first, and then harder, his hands bending her in to him. He felt her nails digging into his neck. There was a moment when he was undressing her when she broke free and said, 'I hate myself . . . I hate you . . .' He put his hand over her mouth.

5

It was the first time Maurice Franconi had seen Kesler despair of an assignment.

'We've tried everything,' he exploded. 'I've spent a small fortune bribing the tradesmen who deliver to the convent, I've hung about for days on end in case she came out, they hung up on me when I phoned and said I was a relative! There's no way we can get to her!'

When in difficulty Maurice favoured what he called a blanket operation. 'We could set the place on fire,' he suggested. He had a weakness for this method.

'Don't be a fool,' Kesler snapped irritably. 'With our luck, she'd be the one to get rescued. I don't know how to tackle this – I really don't.' He slumped down on the bed and swore in Polish. Maurice put an arm round him.

'Come on,' he said. 'Cheer up. We've never failed yet. And anyway we can't afford to fail on this one. Think of all that money!'

'I am thinking of it,' Kesler said. 'It was your bloody greed got us into this in the first place!'

'Oh, all right, blame me – ' Franconi turned away.

'If you're going to bite my head off, I'm going out!'

Kesler threw up his hands. 'I'm sorry,' he said. 'I didn't mean to take it out on you. But this one's getting on my nerves. It's not like any ordinary woman working in a convent. They're not an enclosed order, she could come and go and see visitors. They've built a wall round her. If we do get inside, we're not going to be able to fake an accident like the other two. And the orders specified that. Make them look accidental. No police, no investigations. You realize we won't *get* the money unless we carry through the whole contract?'

'I know that.' Franconi still sulked. 'I had an idea, that's all.'

'Tell me, for Christ's sake,' Kesler said. 'What have you thought of – come on, don't be sulky. I said I was sorry.'

'They must have a priest who hears confessions,' Franconi said. Kesler looked up. 'Yes, they must. So?'

'So we find out who he is,' Maurice said, 'and we make a substitution.'

'That's very clever,' Kesler said warmly. 'Very clever thinking. Something happens to the regular priest and a strange one goes instead. He asks to see Gretl Fegelein and, because he's a priest, she'll come. Maurice, you're a genius!'

'I'm a Catholic,' he grinned. 'I know a bit about convents and the way things work. So do you, you old sinner. I'm surprised you didn't think of it.' He was delighted by Kesler's praise. 'It shouldn't be difficult to find out who the regular chaplain is. I think we should try the nearest parish church.'

Kesler got up. 'We will,' he said. 'starting today. I'm sick of this place. I want to get it over as quick as we can, and move on to the next one.'

Franconi nodded. 'Bonn,' he said. 'I've never been there.'

'I have, once,' Kesler said. 'It's a dreary hole – we won't want to hang around there for long. Now, let's get a street directory and find the nearest church.'

Twenty-five minutes later he circled the Church of St John the Apostle with a green biro pen. 'There we are. Two streets away from the Convent of the Immaculate Conception. We'll try there first. Then this one – St Gabriel – that's about a block away. Look up the telephone number, Maurice. We can call through from downstairs.'

They went out and took the lift to the hotel foyer, and while Kesler slipped into the half cubicle and dialled the presbytery of the first church they had chosen, Maurice pretended to read a copy of *Die Süddeutsche Zeilung*, and watched the reception to see if the woman clerk was taking any notice of them. She wasn't.

Kesler came out and shook his head. 'No,' he said. 'They don't serve the convent. Give me the next number.'

'I'll try,' Franconi said. 'I'm feeling lucky today.'

When he came to join Kesler a few minutes later, he was grinning. 'You got it?' Kesler asked.

'They don't go to the convent either,' he said. 'But they told me who did. He's a retired priest, and all he does now is say Mass for the nuns and hear confessions. He lives in a hostel on the Burgstrasse.'

'How did you get all that?' Kesler asked. He was genuinely pleased when Maurice showed initiative and skill in his work.

'I said I had a sister who wanted to become a nun. I wanted to talk to a priest with experience of convent life, because the family was worried. The man I talked to went out of his way to be helpful. I had a feeling he wasn't too fond of nuns and convents. Probably one of the new "progressive" priests – '

'Huh,' Kesler snorted. 'I know the kind. Folksongs and guitars on the altar, and no celibacy. I don't know what's got into the Church these days.'

'I quite agree,' Franconi said. 'No wonder we don't go any more.'

They went out of the hotel into the morning sunshine, and took a bus to the Burgstrasse and the hostel for retired and aged Catholic priests.

Albert Kramer got the telephone call at seven in the morning. He was shaving; in spite of being fair he grew a tough beard, and he preferred the old-fashioned method of lather and blade to the electric razor. He wiped the soap off his face and picked up the phone in his bathroom. There was no preamble from the caller. 'Two comrades are going to have visitors,' the voice said. 'The day after tomorrow.'

'Who are they?' Kramer said.

'Josef Franke and Gunther Mühlhauser. The Chief and a CIA visitor; very senior, all stops being pulled out for him.'

'Thank you,' Kramer said. 'I'll warn our friends.' He hung up. He went back to the mirror and resoaped his chin and shaved himself. The old ties of loyalty still operated, even in the heart of Holler's Intelligence kingdom. A schedule had been seen and the warning phoned through. Kramer had been an active member of the Odessa organization since the end of the war. He had run messages for them during the early days of the Occupation; his house had been used as a refuge for fugitives, and he himself enrolled under the most solemn oaths when he was eighteen and a student.

He had helped Odessa channel wanted Nazi officials of the SS through to Italy and Spain, where they took ship for South America, and in return Odessa had financed his education and his first business venture, as an importer of copper from Brazil. That early business had been a cover for the activities of the underground SS escape route, but his natural flair for making money expanded it and added to it, until he was doing Odessa a favour rather than the other way round. Then he had married the nymphomaniac daughter of one of post-war Germany's most important industrialists, ignored her activities and made all possible use of his father-in-law. Now he was free of all but his old associations, and he held fast to them. His belief in the ideology of National Socialism was absolute; it had never wavered at any time throughout his boyhood or his adult life. He believed in the supremacy of the Aryan people and the truth of Adolf Hitler's political creed that Germany was destined to overcome her enemies and rule the world. He hated the English, the Americans and the Russians, and he had a profound physical revulsion of the Jews.

The core of his personality had not altered since his indoctrination in the Hitler Jügend; it was concealed so effectively that no one suspected him of being anything but a contemporary German of the best kind: brilliantly successful in business and widely consulted on government financial policy. A sportsman who sponsored promising young athletes, a patron of the arts, a close friend of one of Germany's most liberal politicians, Sigmund Walther. He was all these things because they were the hard shell that concealed the crab. He was a Nazi and he was waiting for the rebirth of National Socialism in another guise. And because the old links still existed and were strong, the information passed to Sigmund Walther by Heinrich Holler had been whispered to him. Eva Braun had borne the Führer a child. Walther was trying to find it. So he had set out to win the politician's confidence and become his friend. When Sigmund suggested that he join the Social Democratic Party as a candidate he had refused. He didn't want political office; he had enough power as an outside adviser. He wanted Sigmund to tell him about Janus, but Sigmund never did. So he had gone to see the widow, to offer his help and insinuate himself into her trust.

He didn't think Walther would have confided in her, because he personally considered women inferior, and took it for granted that Walther felt the same. He wanted to go to bed with Minna Walther very badly; she was the cool, Nordic type that appealed to him. He suspected that she was very sexual; he had an instinct for women and a lot of success with them. He wasn't deceived by the well-bred airs and graces of that Prussian lady, with her five children, and a husband like Sigmund who hadn't even been unfaithful to her once in nineteen years. He wanted Minna but he wanted to lock himself up with Sigmund's investigatory notes, and when she spoke of a successor to her husband, he had grasped the opportunity and offered himself.

He was confident of success. Not immediately; she might take a little time to convince. And seduce into sleeping with him. Once she had done that, she would be quite amenable to the rest of his desires. He had ordered flowers to be sent the morning after he had called on her. He didn't expect her to telephone; he was prepared to make a second approach, more personal than the first. He patted the aftershave on his cheeks and jaw; it stung pleasantly, and he liked the musky smell.

Mühlhauser and Josef Franke. Fifteen years in a Soviet labour camp for Mühlhauser and he was still being persecuted. Kramer didn't know him personally; he had merely given him a job when he was asked to do so. The same for Franke, who applied to the security service; the personnel officer had been given notice of his application and asked to view it favourably. He got the job through the network, although he didn't know it. Kramer kept a special diary with names and addresses and telephone numbers. He unlocked his dressing-table drawer and took it out, looking for Gunther Mühlhauser's phone number. He dialled it, and waited. It rang for some time, before a woman answered. Kramer asked for Herr Mühlhauser and the former Obergruppenführer came to the phone. Kramer didn't give his name.

'You're going to have a visit, the day after tomorrow. The top man and an American. Be ready for them.'

'Yes,' the voice said. 'I will.'

'Contact a Josef Franke, security services. Warn him.'

'I will do that. Anything else?'

'Just be careful,' Kramer said; 'I'll call you after they've been. Try and find out what they want.' He hung up. Why would Holler and some senior CIA operator bother with a played-out old war criminal like Gunther Mühlhauser? He'd been debriefed until there was nothing left to analyse but the dirt under his fingernails. Fifteen years in Soviet hands had made him less of a wreck than most, but he couldn't be of any use to any Intelligence service after all this time.

Kramer frowned, locked the little diary away, and began to dress. What did the CIA hope to gain from talking to Gunther Mühlhauser? Least of all, why bother with a former SS man more renowned for his brawn than his brains? And then, as he got into the back of his car and directed his chauffeur to drive him to his office in the city centre, Albert Kramer saw the connection. He knew the records of the two men in every detail, though he had never met them face to face. The personal aide to Heinrich Himmler and the non-commissioned sergeant had one thing in common. They were both in the Bunker at the end. Sigmund Walther's murder had stirred up the ashes of the Führer's funeral pyre and that meant that the phoenix of National Socialist Germany was stirring in the flames which the world had thought put out for ever.

The child of Hitler and Eva Braun was still alive, and the reason the CIA had sent one of their top men to Heinrich Holler was to try and find him. Albert Kramer swore under his breath. If Mühlhauser or that numbskull Josef knew anything, Holler and the American would get it out of them. Nobody would have interrogated Mühlhauser about something which nobody in the Western alliance knew. If he had any knowledge of Hitler's heir, he had kept it from the principals of Odessa as well.

Kramer had made a mistake in alerting Mühlhauser and the other man. Neither must be allowed to talk to Holler, who was a traitor and a renegade, in Kramer's eyes, or to the highly skilled and ruthless operators employed by the United States Central Intelligence Agency. He picked up the telephone in his car and began to make arrangements.

Minna woke while it was still dark. She lay quietly, listening, and then reached out with her hand. He had gone to his own room. She switched on the bedside light, blinking against it, and then sat up. Her hair was loose and tangled, cold sweat had dried on her naked body. She leaned her head back, and a tear seeped under the closed eyelids and ran down her face and neck. She didn't blame Max Steiner; she blamed herself, and she cried with shame and self-disgust. He was different from Sigmund, rougher, less sentimental. He had made her aware of passions which her husband hadn't aroused, and she had loved her sex life with him and been deeply satisfied. Now a new man had come, and, instead of easing the pain and the loss, he had created new longings which she couldn't sublimate in grief.

She threw back the sheet and went to the bathroom; her reflection in the glass was wild looking; she stared at herself and called the woman in the mirror bitter names. He was a stranger, a man who had come into her life because of Sigmund's death, and in the moment of self-knowledge, Minna admitted that from the first meeting she had felt attracted to him, and known that he felt the same about her. She had been able to stave off men while her husband was alive; she had never even been tempted, and opportunities to be unfaithful were always presenting themselves. Albert Kramer's hungry stare was easy to ignore; the tentative moves from friends and other women's husbands had been shrugged off with tact and determination. Her vanity had been satisfied because she knew she was still very desirable to men and this was important to her, but she had all she needed in her marriage. What had happened was not adultery, because she was a widow and her body was her own. But it was crude and disloyal, and she didn't love the man. She said that aloud. 'I don't love him. I don't even know him.' It wasn't possible to feel love for someone else so soon after her husband's death . . .

And he hadn't said he loved her. She was grateful for that: hypocrisy would have made it worse. She stepped into the shower and soaked herself in hot water, as if she were carrying out a cleansing ritual. She dried herself, and rubbed her wet hair.

The bed looked cold and uninviting; half the bedclothes were on the floor. It was six o'clock and light was showing through the curtains. She put on a dressing gown and went downstairs through the silent house to the kitchen. There was a gleam of electric light under the door. He was making coffee. He turned quickly and saw her there. 'I couldn't sleep after I left you,' he said. 'Do you want a cup?'

'Yes,' Minna said. 'No sugar.' They sat on opposite sides of the table, and he lit two cigarettes and handed one to her.

'I'm not going to say I'm sorry it happened,' he said abruptly, 'because I'm not. And you shouldn't be either. We're very good together.'

'Yes,' she said. 'We are.'

He held his hand out to her, palm upward, and after a moment she put her hand in it. Their fingers locked tightly. 'Drink your coffee,' Max said. 'It'll get cold.' Lying beside him in bed afterwards, Minna thought that he had said he loved her at one stage, but she was too close to sleep to be sure.

'I have been thinking of becoming a Catholic for some time,' Stanislaus Kesler said. The elderly priest looked surprised. He was a round, bespectacled little man, with a circlet of white hair round his bald head. He had come down to the priests' parlour to see the unexpected visitor. It was a bare little room, sparsely furnished with hard-backed chairs and a polished table. The floors were polished wood and they were as slippery as glass. There was a strong smell of beeswax. A garish statue of the Sacred Heart rested on a plinth in one corner, with a little red devotional lamp gleaming at its foot. The place reminded Kesler of his youth in Poland. He had been to a convent school as a child, and he recognized the smell and the spartan surroundings. He smiled encouragingly at the priest.

Father Grunwald had been retired for five years; he was nearing his seventieth birthday, and he had a peaceful life after his years as a parish priest during the turbulence of the post-war period. He said Mass for the nuns in the Convent of the Immaculate Conception, heard their confessions and acted as spiritual adviser to the Reverend Mother, who frightened him to death. He suppressed a most un-Christian resentment at being called in at this late stage to instruct a stranger in the Faith.

'That's very good,' he said. 'But I think you should go to your local parish priest. He is the proper person to instruct you. May I ask why you came to see me? I'm retired now, you know.'

Kesler took a gamble; 'Reverend Mother suggested it,' he said. 'Her family and mine were old friends.'

'Really?' Father Grunwald's white eyebrows lifted; the tufts peeking above the horn-rimmed spectacles made him look like a little barn owl. 'Yes, well, that's very kind of her . . .'

'I gather she thinks a great deal of you, Father,' Kesler said. 'It must make quite a change, looking after nuns. How often do you visit the convent?'

'I say Mass three times a week, and on Sundays, of course.'

'Do you hear confessions?' Kesler asked. 'That's the one thing about the Church that worries me. What would a nun have to confess, for instance?'

'They're not all saints by any means,' the priest said. 'People tend to forget that nuns are human beings with human weaknesses. You mustn't worry about confession; most non-Catholics find it difficult to accept at first.'

'I would very much like to talk to you about it, and about the Catholic Faith in general,' Kesler said. 'But you might not have much time to give me. When do you go to the convent, Father?'

'Tuesdays, Thursdays and Saturdays. And Sunday, of course. I'm there all day Sunday with Mass and Benediction, and most of Saturday morning, hearing confessions before Mass.' He grasped quickly at the excuse Kesler had offered him. 'I don't think I could possibly instruct you; you really need to visit a priest every day and it usually takes at least three to four weeks before you could make up your mind to the preliminary stage. Becoming a Catholic takes time, you know. I really think you'd do better to go to your local parish priest.' He heaved himself up from the uncomfortable chair, and Kesler stood, with his hand held out. Father Grunwald shook it briefly. He had never been happy with middle-aged converts; he believed that the Faith took a stronger root in the young.

'May God bless you,' he said, 'and guide you. I'll remember you in my prayers.'

'Thank you,' Kesler said. 'I shall need the gift of Faith. Goodbye, Father.'

Outside in the street he walked to the car where Franconi was waiting. He slipped into the passenger seat. 'Tuesday, Thursday, Saturday and Sunday,' he said. Franconi started the engine.

'Good,' he said. 'Which day will you go?' 'Thursday,' Kesler answered. 'I don't want him talking to the Reverend Mother about me. I said she recommended me.'

'That's tomorrow,' Franconi said. They were cruising along the street, and he turned right towards the centre of the city. 'You'll have to get some clothes.'

Kesler frowned. 'Not clerical clothes,' he said. 'The first thing the police will do, if they suspect anything, is go to the clerical tailors and the theatrical costumiers. That could give them a lead. I've got a dark suit, and I'll buy a black silk muffler and a black homburg. That'll get me into the convent.' Franconi looked at him, and then back to the road ahead.

'You don't think you can make it look like an accident?' he said. 'That's worrying.'

'I'll do my best,' Kesler said. 'I'll use the pen again, but you've got to get right up close to them. If there's any difficulty, I'll just have to do what I can. Don't worry,' he added. 'I won't take any risks. If I could persuade her to leave the building, all the better.'

'I don't like this at all,' Franconi said. He shuddered suddenly, as a nervous *frisson* quivered up his spine. 'You're quite sure she's not a nun?'

'Frau Gretl Fegelein; works as a lay helper. That's what it said on the paper,' Kesler reassured him. 'And you're not to be superstitious. Nothing will happen to me just because it's done in a convent. Let's go out and treat ourselves to a nice lunch. That'll take our minds off it. Bear left here; there's a very good restaurant down the next street. I looked it up in the Michelin guide last night.'

Gunther Mühlhauser had come back from a labour camp in what was later known to the world as the Gulag Archipelago. The camps were full of Germans, prisoners of war, civilians captured during the Russian advance into Germany, SS criminals who had escaped the death sentence. Like himself. Mühlhauser hadn't expected to survive when he saw the conditions in which the prisoners were condemned to live and do hard manual labour.

They froze and they starved, and they died in their tens of thousands. The suicide rate was nearly as high as that for deaths from hunger and mistreatment. Men went mad, and were shot down like dogs; others died at their tasks, breaking the iron-hard earth to build roads which never ended, or mumbled their lives away in delirium. Mühlhauser was a very strong man and physically fit. He determined to live, because his sentence had a limit. That was the deal he had concluded with his Soviet interrogators. They wouldn't hang him, but they would send him to the slow death of the labour camp and it was up to him to survive if he could. He became a model prisoner; he co-operated with the guards and made it easier for them to supervise the other prisoners. He informed on three escape attempts, and consequently his rations were improved. He became so useful that the commandant withdrew him from work on the roads, and gave him an administrative job in the records offices of the camp. There Mühlhauser kept a tally of the dead, and of the pitiful few who managed to escape and were brought back and shot. He was gaunt and cold and underfed, but by comparison with those who resisted or failed to grovel to their guards, he lived well enough. At the end of fourteeen years he was suddenly summoned to the commandant's office and told that he was being sent south. They shook hands, and the Russian gave him some cigarettes for the journey. He packed his few rags of clothing into a bundle, and marched for two days with a group of Russian civilians who were going to the railhead. Nobody told him anything.

The journey took a week, and four people died of cold. Mühlhauser divided up their clothing between himself and the remaining five men; he persuaded the guards to continue the original ration. Otherwise, as he pointed out in fluent Russian, they would have nothing but corpses to deliver at the end of the journey. They arrived in Moscow, and all but Mühlhauser disembarked from the train. He was locked into the compartment, and it was the following day before they moved out of the station. Nobody would tell him where he was going, but he was given more food, and a change of clothes, including a heavy army greatcoat, and boots. Mühlhauser had tried hard to forget his experiences in the years that followed his arrival in what was now East Germany, but he couldn't stop odd incidents floating like jetsam to the surface of his mind. Most persistent of all was the meeting face to face with his principal interrogator when the train crossed the Polish frontier. He had opened the compartment door, and the two soldiers guarding him had jumped to their feet at the sight of the red flashes on the colonel's collar.

He hadn't changed much, except that his cropped hair had tinges of grey in it. Mühlhauser knew by his expression that he himself was almost unrecognizable. The Soviet colonel had sat opposite to him, given him a cigarette and said simply, 'So you survived. I thought you would.'

'Yes,' Mühlhauser mumbled. 'Where am I going?'

'Home,' the Russian said. 'As I promised you. I always keep my promises.'

That was when Mühlhauser broke down and began to cry for the first time in fifteen bitter years. The colonel had got up and gone out of the compartment. He said nothing, and Mühlhauser never saw him again. He wondered whether the Russian knew that he was crying for shame as well as relief. He knew why he had been released. And the oath he had sworn, and violated to save himself, haunted him for many years. Until he married a second time, and his young wife had a daughter. He was settled in Hamburg; his name and background and his sufferings in Russia brought financial help and he knew very well where it came from. Also the offer of a job in a firm of textile importers.

His second wife was fifteen years younger, a secretary in the Customs and Excise; she knew nothing about his past. She accepted him as a returned German prisoner of war, and he married her within a year of meeting her. He loved her and she was an excellent wife. He liked her gay spirits; they made him feel young again. When she gave birth to Beatrix, he was so overcome with happiness and gratitude that he felt tempted to confide his past in her. But fortunately he resisted the temptation. The less was known about his capture in Berlin and what followed afterwards, the safer he would be. He gave himself up to his happy life and his infant daughter, and began to forget about the old days. Sometimes his memory was rudely jogged. Newspaper articles, books, discussions on TV ... They wouldn't let the past die. The Jews were hunting for his old comrades. He read of the trial and execution of Adolf Eichmann; there were other trials in West Germany of men he had known and served with. He was safe, but only just. His association with Himmler was known, but he had been purely an administrator; he had never been involved in the camps, or the liquidation of Jews in Russia. He had served his sentence in the snow-white hell of Northern Siberia, and he was left alone.

When he received the telephone call warning him about a visit from the police and an agent from the CIA, he had felt sick with apprehension. He couldn't eat his breakfast, and he snapped irritably at his innocent wife. He kissed Beatrix good-bye with extra tenderness and wondered what he could do, how he could avoid seeing anyone.

He remembered there was someone else he had to warn, and he did so from his office; he was trying to decide whether to pick up his wife and daughter and take the first train to her grandparents in Bavaria, when his secretary announced that a man was in the outer office demanding to see him, and refusing to give his name. Mühlhauser went grey with fear. He came out, and there was a man in a belted mackintosh and a brown felt hat, his hands stuck aggressively into his pockets. Mühlhauser had never seen him before. 'Yes? What can I do for you?' He heard the tremor in his own voice. 'You can go, Fräulein Huber.'

He was a young man, and suddenly he took off his hat. 'I'm afraid I have bad news for you, Herr Mühlhauser,' he said. 'I'm from the police. Your daughter had an accident at school this morning. You'd better come with me.' Mühlhauser gave a choked cry of anguish. He didn't ask to see the man's identity; he followed him blindly out of the building and down into the street. He got into the car which was waiting, and was taken to a house in the suburbs.

They let him see Beatrix through a crack in the door. She was sitting reading a comic book. There was a man in the room; Mühlhauser could just see his trouser legs. Then the door closed and he was facing the two men who had abducted him and a third who was sitting in an armchair. It was an unusual setting for kidnap and interrogation. The room was on the ground floor, and it was an ordinary sitting room, with a sofa and chairs, a TV set, ornaments and a plant in bloom on the table. Mühlhauser tried to swallow; fear had dried up the saliva in his mouth and he couldn't do it. The young man who had come to his office was standing a few feet away, with a gun pointing at him. The gun moved whenever Mühlhauser did. Albert Kramer looked up at him; he leaned forward in the armchair.

'We want some questions answered,' he said. Mühlhauser nodded. They hadn't hurt him or threatened him.

'Why is Beatrix . . . why have you – ' he stammered and stopped. Kramer's eyes were as fixed and malevolent as a snake's, about to strike. Mühlhauser knew what it meant when a man looked like that.

'Your child hasn't been hurt, or frightened. And she won't be, if you tell the truth.' Kramer paused deliberately. When he spoke again his voice was empty of emotion. 'If you don't co-operate, you'll never see her again. We won't do anything to you, Gunther Mühlhauser. We will kill Beatrix instead. Sit down.'

Mühlhauser felt his legs giving way. A tide of blind fury swept over him, and then receded before an even wilder panic. He knew the blond man in the chair meant what he said. Beatrix . . .

'Let her go,' he said. 'I beg of you, let her go home. I'll do anything you want.'

'She goes home with you, if we're satisfied.' Kramer answered. 'Or not at all.'

Mühlhauser bowed his head. 'What do you want from me?'

'You were in the Bunker at the end, weren't you?' Mühlhauser sensed the other two men, the one with the gun and the driver, leaning closer towards him.

'Yes,' he said. 'I was captured; I spent fifteen years in a Soviet labour camp.'

'We know that,' Kramer said. 'We looked after you, when you came home. You must have realized that?'

'I suspected,' Mühlhauser muttered. 'I was very grateful.' Now he knew whom he was facing. Certainly they would kill Beatrix.

'Why didn't they hang you, Mühlhauser? They hanged or shot everyone in the SS. Why not you?'

'I was an administrator,' Mühlhauser said. 'I had no part in the Einsatzgruppen, or the selection of foreign labour . . . I hadn't been involved in action against Russian troops or civilians. You know all this already. I don't understand what you want from me . . .'

'The truth,' Kramer said. 'I want you to tell me what you told the Russians, that they let you live. Because you bought your life, didn't you, Mühlhauser? You saved your neck by betraying something to them. What was it?'

The room was very quiet; Kramer sat motionless, waiting. A car droned past the house. They'll kill me, Mühlhauser thought. But I don't care. So long as they let Beatrix go . . . He raised his head slowly and squared his shoulders: He had betrayed his sacred oath. 'Blood and Honour' – the words floated through his mind. He wasn't afraid for himself.

He spoke to Kramer. 'I told them about the Führer's son.'

Minna placed one hand over the telephone and spoke to Max.

'It's Heinrich Holler,' she said. 'He wants to come and see me this afternoon.'

'We're going to Munich,' Max reminded her.

She spoke into the phone. 'I was going away this morning,' she said.

'Is it very urgent, Herr Holler? I see. Yes, of course I'll postpone it. At three o'clock then. Good-bye.'

Max put down the overnight case. The car was outside, waiting to take them to the airport.

'We can go this evening,' he said. 'I'd like to meet him. If you don't mind.'

'It won't be up to me,' Minna answered. 'He may want to talk to me alone, or he may talk to you too. You can be sure he knows you're staying here.'

Max put the cases in a corner; she had gone into the sitting room. He hesitated; a few hours earlier they had made love with feverish intensity. He knew everything about her body; he had explored it like a map. And he had lost his head completely at one moment and told her that he loved her. She had said nothing. The greater their physical intimacy, the more it disturbed him that he knew even less about her as a person. The woman in his bed was a separate entity from Minna Walther. It was almost impossible to connect the cool, self-contained personality that had come down and said good morning to him with the passionate, demanding creature he had held in his arms through the night. He had said he loved her; she had said she hated him and herself . . . He had a feeling of emptiness, standing there in the hall. He wanted to go to Munich to be alone with her, away from the house and the bed she had shared with Sigmund Walther. Perhaps then he could break through the barrier which restricted her response to sexuality alone. He went out and put the car into the garage.

He walked round the garden, as it was a beautiful morning, and there was nothing else for him to do. It was colourful with flowers and shrubs. He lit a cigarette and wandered through the paths between the flowerbeds. There was a tennis court and a swimming pool. He could imagine the parties given in the summer, with barbecues and iced drinks. Liberals and journalists and politicians. And Albert Kramer.

He came to the edge of the pool and stopped. His own reflection shivered in the bright blue water. He had a wife and two children. He hardly remembered their existence. He found it difficult to visualize their faces; he couldn't think of their Paris apartment in connection with his home. He should have telephoned Ellie, reassured her and talked to the children. The truth was he didn't want to; his disinclination was stronger than his guilt. He was in love with Minna Walther, that was part of the reason, but not the whole of it. His life pattern was changing even before he met her. The past kept coming up like a boil, plaguing him with the nightmare; his sex life with Ellie was stale, his children irritated him or bored him, and he felt increasingly restless. He didn't dream any more, because he was facing the implications of the dream in real life. He had stopped running away from himself. The time would come when he and Minna would come to terms with their relationship; when she would have to choose between her contempt for her own weakness and her dependence upon him. And he would have to choose too. But first their search had to be concluded. He began to walk back to the house.

Heinrich Holler was ten minutes late; he came in apologizing to Minna. 'I'm so sorry, but I had to make a call and it took longer than I expected. How are you, Fräu Walther? You're looking well.'

Max got up, and stood waiting until Minna introduced him. Holler and he shook hands. 'Ah, yes,' Holler said. 'I always read your articles, Herr Steiner. They often tell me things I ought to have known and didn't!' He had a charming smile; he chatted to Minna for a few minutes, accepted a cigarette, and asked Max how long he was staying in Germany. 'You're writing an article on my friend Sigmund, I believe?' he said. Max didn't look at Minna; he hadn't discussed what he should say with her because, until he met Holler, he hadn't been certain himself. He made up his mind.

'That's what I'm supposed to be doing,' he said. 'But in fact I'm looking for the same thing that Sigmund Walther was looking for, and which he tried to tell me about before he died. I want to find Janus.'

Holler examined his cigarette and then glanced at Minna. 'You've given him access to Sigmund's papers?'

'Yes,' she said. 'He knows everything. And he had something very important to contribute.' Holler turned back to Max.

'I hope you'll confide in me,' he said. He listened without interrupting while Max talked. At the mention of Fegelein's dying words, he looked up quickly, but he said nothing. When Max had finished he let out a deep breath.

'Thank God I got rid of my American colleague,' he said. 'He was trying to come with me today. You wouldn't know, of course, but the CIA are also investigating Sigmund's murder. They believe it was Russian-inspired. But they don't know, and I pray they never find out, that he was involved in the search for Janus. They have given that up; there was a lot of activity when we first heard of the child's existence, but there were as many people here who *didn't* want to help the Americans as there were like Sigmund and myself, who felt it was a German problem and should be solved by us.'

'Why did they stop searching?' Max asked.

'Because they believed the Russians had found the boy and killed him,' Holler said.

'And you don't think so?' Max said.

'No. Because our information is that they're still looking,' Holler answered.

'And that's why they killed Sigmund.' Minna spoke for the first time. 'Because he was getting close. But if they were searching for the same person, why not *let* Sigmund find him and then step in!'

'I've tried answering that point, and I can't,' Holler admitted. 'Except that they couldn't risk the man's identity coming out; rather than chance Sigmund succeeding and alerting me, they preferred to go on looking themselves.'

'I keep forgetting,' Max said. 'We're looking for a grown man.'

'You have a list of names,' Holler said. 'How many people have you seen?'

Max hid his surprise. Of course Holler knew about the list. The West Berlin police would have passed it on.

'Otto Helm, Herbert Schmidt, Josef Franke. We're going down to Munich to try and see Gretl Fegelein this evening.'

'Helm and Schmidt are dead,' Holler said: 'The deaths were meant to look like accidents, and if they hadn't been on your list, nobody would have questioned it. But I did, and both men were murdered. So it seems that someone else is treading in your footprints, Herr Steiner. Or else, by some incredible coincidence, these people are on *another* list. So far, nothing has happened to Josef Franke.'

Minna had been standing by the fireplace while they talked; she often leaned against the marble chimneypiece, one foot on the fender. Max remembered the erotic effect of her long thigh under the skirt. She came and sat down facing both of them. She had lost colour, but her composure was like a mask through which no feeling of alarm or even surprise was evident.

'If nothing *does* happen to him,' she said. 'Then there is another list. Probably my husband was the first name on it. Max seeing the other two may have been sheer, incredible coincidence, as you said.'

'And if it is, and someone is killing off the people who were in the Bunker,' Max said slowly, 'they're going to get to Minna and me, because we've talked to them.'

Holler didn't answer. He changed the subject. 'What did Franke tell you?'

'He told me that Fegelein was shot for betraying the future of Germany. He didn't understand the significance of it. But I did. And that led to Gunther Mühlhauser, who was Himmler's confidant and liaison with the Bunker. That's who told him about Janus, Fegelein. And my guess is, Herr Holler, that he told the secret to the Russians.'

'Who had it confirmed by the autopsy report on Eva Braun,' Holler said. 'But if he only knew of the child's existence, that wouldn't be much use to them. He had to know where it was hidden. And he can't have known, because they're still looking . . . I don't want to depress you, but you won't see Gretl Fegelein.'

'Why not?' Minna asked. 'Why is she so immune? I've never

understood how that convent has been able to defy someone like you, Herr Holler, and refuse to let you or Sigmund talk to her. That woman was with Eva when she had the baby; her husband knew where it was being hidden, and she must have known it too!'

'You underestimate the power of the Vatican,' Heinrich Holler said. 'Gretl Fegelein went through the denazification courts and was acquitted. She took refuge in that convent as soon as she was released from custody, and I have it on the best authority that the Vatican undertook to protect her for the rest of her life. It was made clear to me, and to others, notably the CIA in the early days, that any violation of Gretl Fegelein's sanctuary in the convent would cause a major diplomatic rupture with the Papacy. So she cannot be made to answer any question. And she certainly won't be persuaded. We've tried, as you know very well, Fräu Walther.'

'This time, I'm going to try,' Minna said.

It was Curt Andrews who discovered that Gunther Mühlhauser was missing. Holler had politely but firmly refused to introduce him to Sigmund Walther's widow; as a sop to the American's professional pride he suggested that he arrange a meeting with Mühlhauser. And Andrews, aware that he was being sidetracked, decided to pay Heinrich Holler back in kind. Instead of telephoning and making an appointment for himself and Holler, he went direct to Mühlhauser's office. His secretary seemed flustered, and Andrews detected uncertainty when she said he had left his office. He could be very engaging when he chose and he asked his questions so gently that she answered without realizing that it was none of his business where Mühlhauser had gone.

'I don't know,' she said. 'Someone called here this morning, a young man, not very pleasant looking – he refused to give his name – he was quite rude to me, in fact, and when Herr Mühlhauser came out to see him, he sent me away. The next thing I knew Herr Mühlhauser was rushing out after this man – he didn't even put his hat on – and when I tried to ask him when he'd be back, he didn't answer! He looked terribly upset. He hasn't phoned in or anything. I did telephone his wife, but he hadn't come home. I really don't know what can have happened.'

'Well, don't worry,' Andrews said kindly. She was a woman in her middle fifties, plain and efficient, but unused to coping with the unexpected. So a young, tough-mannered man had called on him, and Mühlhauser had gone rushing out – Andrews smelled conspiracy; whether on the part of Heinrich Holler, whom he didn't trust an inch, or someone else he wasn't sure. But he was sure that Mühlhauser wasn't going to be around to be asked questions. Whoever had killed Otto Helm and the ex-valet Schmidt wasn't going to make the same mistake and get to his victim too late.

'I think I'd better go and see Fräu Mühlhauser,' he said. 'Could you give me the address?'

The secretary hesitated: 'I'm sorry, but I'm not supposed to give Herr Mühlhauser's private address or telephone number to anyone, sir.'

'I do understand,' Curt Andrews said. 'But I think you can give it to me.' He took an ID card out of his pocket and handed it to her. It appeared to be issued by the West German police in Bonn. Curt Andrews always carried ID cards when he travelled; he had British, French, Italian and West German cards, and even one from East Germany. The secretary looked at it, and said, 'Oh, oh dear. Yes, of course. I'll get the address for you.' Andrews put the card back in his pocket. Languages were another of his talents. His German was fautless, so was his French; Italian was more difficult but he could manage well in the regions, where local dialects made every outsider sound different. He had never mastered the long English vowels; the forged Scotland Yard Special Branch ID had never been used.

'Here, I've written it down, and the telephone number,' she said. He took the piece of paper, and thanked her. 'Don't worry,' he said again. 'I'm sure everything is all right. I'll get Herr Mühlhauser to call you, when I see him.'

Holler had given him a car and a driver; Andrews swung his big body into the back seat, and gave the driver Mühlhauser's address.

Albert Kramer was back in his office. He told his secretary he was taking no calls and didn't want to be disturbed for the next half-hour. He needed time to think; he lit a cigarettte and noticed that his hand was unsteady. He wasn't surprised. He couldn't imagine anyone who would have been unmoved at the end of Gunther Mühlhauser's interrogation.

He smoked rapidly, staring ahead of him through the cigarette haze, not seeing his surroundings. The others had wanted to kill Mühlhauser and the child. One of them, Brandt, who was too hotheaded and rough for his own good, had smashed the old man in the face and knocked him to the ground. Kramer had stopped them hurting him. His brain was working at top level, clear and calculating, refusing to be hurried into anything that might prove to be a mistake. And murdering Gunther and Beatrix Mühlhauser was exactly the kind of unpremeditated act of vengeance which could destroy them all. He would have liked to shoot Mühlhauser; it was the little girl, calmly reading comic books in the next room, who saved her father's life. A vanished father and daughter would entail the biggest manhunt West Germany had seen for years.

She had been taken from school on the same pretext as Gunther; an accident at home. The man who was amusing her had got her out of school. His face would be remembered; so would Brandt, who had tricked Mühlhauser into going with him. Albert made his decision, and Mühlhauser, who had been expecting death, burst into tears.

He had walked out of the house, holding his daughter by the hand, bound by Kramer's final threat. Beatrix was the hostage for his silence.

Kramer opened his cupboard and poured himself a drink of cognac. It was incredible; he kept going over the facts to himself, trying to see any way in which Mühlhauser could have lied. But he hadn't been able to fault him. And instinctively he knew that what he heard was the truth. A truth so fortuitous that it was no wonder his hard hands were shaking. With excitement. With a fierce joy and expectation. Now, more than ever, he needed to get hold of Sigmund Walther's papers.

'Gunther! What have you done to yourself?' He saw the expression on his wife's face and put a hand to his cheek. It was throbbing and obviously the bruise was coming out. He said gently to his daughter, 'Go and play, darling. I want to talk to Mummy.'

Hilde Mühlhauser put her arm round him protectively. 'What happened? Did you fall – and why have you brought Beatrix home so early –?'

'Come into the kitchen,' he said. 'I've got things to tell you.'

She didn't interrupt him; he watched in anguish the dawning horror in her eyes, and felt her draw away from him.

'You –' she said, 'you were one of *them* – oh, my God!' Hilde had been terribly distressed by a recent television programme about the extermination of the Jews. He had tried to dissuade her from watching. Now he saw his wife's love shrivel and die as he told her what he had been and why he was sent to Siberia. He blinked back tears, but he didn't falter. He told her everything except the secret which had bought his life from the Russians. And done the same for Beatrix and himself that afternoon. The blow had shaken him badly; his face throbbed and pain scorched up and down his neck and shoulder, where he had fallen on the floor.

'Something happened today,' he said. 'It involved Beatrix.'

She gave an angry cry and started up. He said, 'It's all right, she didn't know anything about it.' Then he told her about the men from Odessa.

'I'll never forgive you,' Hilde Mühlhauser said. 'Never. You brought your child into this filthy business – I want to know exactly what happened. Otherwise,' she looked at him and he saw real hatred in her eyes this time, 'otherwise I'm going to the police!'

'You can't,' he said. 'The people who threatened us were Nazi sympathizers. They're very powerful still. One word about this afternoon and they'll harm Beatrix.' He didn't dare say 'kill' although that was the word Kramer had used.

'Oh, you swine,' Hilde said. 'You swine!' She suddenly began to cry. He tried to put his arm round her but she jerked away.

'We've got to decide what to do,' he said slowly. 'I was thinking about it on the way home.'

'I don't care what you do,' his wife said. 'I'm taking Beatrix home with me. You can do what you like. I'll get a divorce.' She sobbed into her hands.

That was when the doorbell rang. Beatrix was nearest the hall; she put down her doll and opened the door. Then she went to the kitchen door. She saw her mother crying and her father standing looking oddly helpless, with a horrible blue and yellow mark on his face. Behind her stood Curt Andrews.

'Take my advice, Fräu Mühlhauser,' he said a little later. 'Don't do anything in a hurry.' He had listened to the almost hysterical accusations of the young woman against her husband. Andrews didn't sympathize with either of them. To him the human tragedy of broken trust and fear was merely a nuisance, because it took up time. He pacified the wife and defended the husband, not because he believed his own arguments, but to defuse a potentially dangerous situation. He didn't want Hilde Mühlhauser grabbing her child and running off to Bavaria. He didn't want any attention drawn to the family.

'You mustn't judge your husband,' he said. 'If you'd been born a few years earlier you might have had to face the same decisions as he did. A lot of patriotic Germans joined the SS because they believed they were fighting for the survival of their country.'

'Don't tell me *he* didn't know what they were doing? About the concentration camps, and the gas chambers!' She swung round on Mühlhauser, her face contorted. 'I feel sick to my stomach,' she said. 'The thought of touching you makes me sick!'

Andrews saw Gunther Mühlhauser flinch and sag; a young wife had certainly got him by the balls, he thought. But not as much as the kid had got them both.

'You may be angry with your husband,' he said, 'but you don't want to risk anything happening to your child, do you?' That cut her short, he noted. She went a ghastly grey colour. 'I thought she looked pretty upset when she saw you and her father quarrelling in the kitchen,' he said coldly. 'That kind of thing is very bad for young children. And, after all, it's her safety we're really worried about; not whether your husband was a member of the SS administrative staff a hundred years ago. I should take a hold on yourself, Fräu

Mühlhauser, and go and calm her down, while I talk to your husband.'

Mühlhauser poured him some beer; the sitting room was stuffy and full of cigarette smoke.

'You're in a mess, aren't you?' Andrews said. 'Your Nazi friends have caught up with you, and you've nowhere to run. They've found out you talked to the Russians, and you're scared they'll fix a nice accident for you.' He watched Mühlhauser as he spoke. He hadn't believed the story and he was just waiting to smash it to pieces. Mühlhauser didn't answer. He had recovered himself while he talked to the American; he put his wife's reactions aside, because there was nothing he could do about them. It would take a lot of time and patience to win her back. If he ever could, after what she had learned. He had been thinking rapidly while he talked to Curt Andrews. This was the CIA man he had been warned about; only the West German counterpart was not with him. The more he remembered Kramer's voice, the more sure he became that it was he who had telephoned the warning. So the man sitting opposite was one of the CIA's top men. A man with authority, able to carry out promises if he made them . . .

To Mühlhauser his release from the interrogation had seemed a miracle at first, but while he travelled home with Beatrix he recognized it was only a reprieve. They wouldn't kill him without killing Beatrix too. He would be punished for his betrayal later, when he imagined himself safe. Or, worse still, the threat to murder his child would be carried out, in the guise of an accident, if they thought he had betrayed his oath a second time . . . Even if it wasn't true, there was no guarantee for Beatrix and none for him. He made up his mind at the same moment as Andrews exposed his story as a lie.

'How do you explain your release from Siberia?' he asked. 'You say you gave details of the events in the Bunker to the Russians and they let you off hanging?' He didn't give Mühlhauser time to answer. 'And you say the people in Odessa didn't figure this out until now? *Now* they reckon you betrayed them and they're out to get you – '

'I wasn't a war criminal,' Mühlhauser said. 'They knew that – the Russians couldn't find anything against me.'

'Except membership of the SS and intimate friendship with Himmler,' Andrews sneered. 'That hanged lesser men than you, Mühlhauser, right here in the West!' He snapped his fingers contemptuously. 'Your life wasn't worth that! You made a deal, and it's just catching up on you – '

'Yes,' Mühlhauser answered. 'Yes, I did. And I want to make one with you, Herr Andrews. But I want to know whether you can protect me and my family.'

510 The Grave of Truth

Curt Andrews didn't show surprise. 'I can protect you,' he said. 'But only if it's worth my while.'

Mühlhauser tried to smile; it hurt his face and became a grimace. He had survived once, when all the odds were against him. He had survived Soviet Intelligence, the labour camps and, today, the merciless vengeance of his own kind. And now that his daughter's life was at stake, survival was all that mattered.

He faced Curt Andrews steadily.

'I can tell you,' he said. 'Not just what I told the Russians, but what I didn't tell them. And that's what I'll give in exchange for a refuge in the United States and the protection of the CIA.'

'Tell it then,' Andrews said.

Mühlhauser shook his head. 'No. I've got one card and it's an ace, Herr Andrews. I'll put it on the table for you, when Hilde and Beatrix and I are safe in the American Consulate.'

Andrews didn't hesitate. 'Good enough,' he said. 'Call your wife and daughter. I have a car outside.'

6

It was easy to waylay Father Grunwald on his way to the convent. He kept an ancient car at the rear of the hostel in the Burgstrasse and, as he walked towards it, Maurice came up behind him, and rabbit-punched him in the back of the neck. He toppled and fell without a sound. 'Take the wallet,' Kesler said. Franconi turned the priest over, and robbed him in seconds of his money and pocket watch. They left him there, the victim of a violent theft, and hurried to their own car which was parked some fifty yards away, near the main road. Franconi took out a few marks and put them in his pocket; the watch was stainless steel and worth nothing to anyone. They drove to the nearest street litter-bin, and dropped the empty wallet and the watch inside.

'Good,' Kesler said. 'We'll go to the convent now.'

Franconi parked at the side of the building; it was an ugly red brick, with a short flight of steps leading up to the entrance porch. 'Be careful,' he said to Kesler.

'Don't worry, I will.' He got out and walked to the convent. He wore his dark grey suit and a black homburg; a black silk scarf concealed his ordinary collar and tie. He carried a small black leather attaché case.

He rang the bell and waited. He felt very calm and alert; he always reacted to a difficult job with extra coolness. Danger steadied his nerves. The door was opened by a woman in a grey skirt and blouse; she wore a grey nun's headdress.

He knew he was going to succeed when she said immediately, 'Good morning, Father. Come in, please.'

He glanced quickly round the large bare entrance hall, taking stock of the doors and the staircase to the upper floors. The smell of wax was overpowering. He wondered for a second why the holy orders had such an obsession with polished floors. His leather-soled shoes skidded on the glassy linoleum.

He spoke to the nun. 'I've come in place of Father Grunwald,' he said. 'I'm afraid he had a nasty accident this morning. He was robbed in the street.'

'Oh,' she said. 'How dreadful. Is he hurt? The Community will be so upset.'

'I'm Father Rittermann,' Kesler said. 'I was asked to come and say

Mass for you. He's all right, just shaken. There's nothing to worry about. You'll have to show me where the chapel is, and the vestry.'

'Yes, of course, Father,' the nun said.

'But first,' Kesler said, 'I'd like to go into the parlour, Sister. I've got a message for one of your lay helpers.'

'Certainly.' The nun walked across to a door on the right, and held it open. 'This is the parlour. Whom do you want to see, Father?'

He gave a gentle smile, and removed his hat, placing it on the table. 'Fräu Fegelein,' he said. 'It concerns one of her family. If she could come quickly, so that we don't start the Mass late . . . ?'

The nun nodded, and went out, closing the door. Kesler took the pen out of his pocket and checked its mechanism. He had a sheet of paper prepared; it was a printed will form, and it looked official enough to deceive anyone for the necessary minute or two while he produced the lethal pen. He had his story well rehearsed. A man named Philip Fegelein, the brother of one of his former parishioners, had left a will and he was helping to trace the beneficiaries. If Fräu Fegelein would be good enough to read through it and see whether she was in fact one of the persons named . . . and then to sign . . .

The door opened and he turned round. A tall woman came into the room. He saw with surprise that she was dressed like the nun who had let him in. Franconi was right; their victim had taken the veil.

'Fräu Fegelein?' he asked, and he stepped forward to shake hands.

'I am Reverend Mother Katherine,' she said. 'Sister Aloysius told me the horrible thing which had happened to poor Father Grunwald. I gather he isn't hurt?'

'No,' Kesler's smile had faded, 'just very shaken. He'll be quite himself in a day or two.'

'And you are Father Rittermann,' the tall nun said. 'You're going to say Mass for us. We shall all offer it up for Father Grunwald.'

'Yes, indeed,' Kesler nodded. It was not going right and he knew it. Adrenalin was flowing through him, sharpening his responses, making him bold.

'I asked to see a Fräu Fegelein,' he said. 'I have a family matter to discuss with her. Is it possible for her to come, Reverend Mother? This is very important.' He drew himself upright, expecting the authority he remembered of the priests in his youth.

The nun had dark eyes; they were very penetrating, and they considered Kesler without any trace of the deference nuns normally showed towards a priest.

'I'm afraid it is quite impossible, Father,' she said, 'because there is no such person here. We have half a dozen lay helpers, and they've all been with us a long time. There is no Fräu Fegelein. I'm sorry, but you've been misinformed.'

Kesler knew that she was lying. He knew that the nun who had let him in had gone straight to the Reverend Mother with his request, when she would herself have known if there was no woman called Fegelein among the six lay helpers. He had no alternative but to bluff it through, and get out of the convent as quickly as possible.

He shook his head. 'Well, that's very odd. I had this letter from one of my old parishioners, his name was Fegelein, and he told me he had this cousin who was living in your convent.' He shrugged. 'What a mystery – I suppose I did read the address right.' He frowned. 'Anyway, Reverend Mother, there must be other houses in Munich.'

'Not of our order,' the nun said. 'If you'll come with me, Father, I'll show you the vestry and the chapel.' He thanked her, and they went out into the hall.

There he stopped, clapped his hand to his head and said, 'Oh dear, how forgetful of me – I've left the keys in my car. Excuse me, Reverend Mother, but in these days when everything gets stolen – I shan't be a moment!'

'What can we do now?' Franconi asked. They were driving back to their hotel. Kesler had taken off the black scarf; he had left the homburg behind in the convent but that couldn't be helped. There was nothing to identify him with it.

'I don't know,' he answered Maurice. 'I'm sure the woman's being hidden there, but there's no way we can get to her. Not unless we go in and stage a massacre and we're certainly not doing that!'

'What about the money?' Franconi said. 'They can make this an excuse not to pay – '

'I'll put a call through to that wretched Paul,' Kesler said. 'I'll tell him she's not in the convent, and that's that. If they cut the fee, I don't mind. I have a very nasty feeling over this one; I think it's much more complicated than they let us know. Besides, I've been seen in the convent and by the priest. They're going to connect my appearance with his being robbed, and link it up with this woman Fegelein. Whoever or whatever she is, those nuns are standing guard, and they'll know that an attempt has been made to get to her.'

'You're not going to tell Paul this,' Franconi interrupted. 'Let him find out for himself . . .'

'Leave Paul to me,' Kesler said. 'I know how to manage him. We'll ring through at once. I'm going to suggest we go ahead and finish the contract with the man in Bonn.'

'I never liked this business,' Franconi said. 'Nuns are unlucky to me. You go and book the call through, and I'll park the car. I can start packing.'

'Yes,' Kesler said. 'I want to get away from here as soon as possible. I'll ask about the trains to Frankfurt. We can go on to Bonn from there.'

Heinrich Holler looked at Curt Andrews. He made no attempt to conceal his anger.

'You've overstepped the bounds this time,' he said. 'I'm going to demand that Mühlhauser and his family are handed over to us. You had absolutely no right to take charge of German nationals.'

'It happened so fast I had no alternative,' Andrews explained. He had scored heavily in the game Intelligence services play with each other, ostensibly on the same side, and he could afford to be conciliatory. He had come back to meet Holler after two hours spent taping Mühlhauser's account of the interrogation by the Russians, and he had already sent a telex prefixed *most urgent* to his Director in Washington. But he didn't want an official row with Holler's West German Intelligence Service, and he had prepared himself for accusations and demands to give Mühlhauser back.

'I was bored, and I thought I'd see Mühlhauser while you were busy with Fräu Walther. Okay, I should have waited and gone with you, but I didn't, and it was just as well. He was scared out of his mind, and getting ready to run. He *asked* for American protection because he was convinced he was going to be murdered. And he convinced me. So I drove the family to our Consulate. He's quite ready to see you, and answer any questions, but he won't come out. He wants to get to the States where he feels he'll be safe.'

'You realize that we could have caught the men who abducted him, if you'd called in our police? By now, they've disappeared.' Holler glared at him. 'Neo-Nazi thugs prepared to kidnap a child, and threaten her life! But you don't care about that, do you.' He made such a gesture of disgust that Andrews reddened. He called the German a string of obscene names in his mind, but beyond the slight colour his face showed nothing. 'We'll go to the Consulate,' Holler snapped. 'Immediately. I hope we'll get some line on these people, but thanks to you, I doubt it!'

They drove to the Consulate in silence; the atmosphere was hostile, and when Andrews offered him a cigarette, Holler just said, 'No,' and looked out of the window. Andrews's presence, however, secured Holler an interview with Mühlhauser.

'Now,' Heinrich Holler said, 'you've given me all the details of the men who held you this afternoon? There's nothing else about them you can remember? No detail you've overlooked – I want you to think very carefully.'

Gunther Mühlhauser shook his head. 'I've told you all I can,' he said.

Andrews was not in the room; only Holler and a police stenographer taking notes. Holler didn't use tape-machines; they could be falsified, but the notes were transcribed and signed and on the record.

'The house was probably broken into,' Holler said. 'Finding it won't lead anywhere unless they left fingerprints we can match up.' He seemed to be musing, rather than talking to Gunther Mühlhauser. To the stenographer he said, 'I think that's all then. Transcribe that stuff and bring it back for Herr Mühlhauser to read and sign, will you?'

He took out a cigarette packet, offered it to Mühlhauser, who refused, and then lit one for himself. He seemed quiet, reflective; Gunther watched him anxiously. He knew all about Holler, who had been one of the Abwehr's brightest young men, before the service got involved in the plot to kill Hitler . . . He wasn't lulled by the other man's calm. Holler puffed smoke into the air; it formed a neat circle and then gradually enlarged until it lost its shape and disappeared.

'I want the truth, Gunther,' he said. 'Otherwise I'll apply for you officially on a criminal charge, and they'll have to hand you back.'

'What criminal charge?' Mühlhauser started up. 'I've done nothing – '

'I'll think of something,' Holler murmered. 'Don't worry about that. Are you going to answer my questions? Truthfully, just as I'm sure you answered everything the American asked you . . . You'll never get to the United States unless I let you go. Andrews knows that perfectly well. And when I get you out, I'll release you, so your Nazi friends will have plenty of opportunity to find you.'

'I thought you were a man of honour,' Mühlhauser said. He had sunk back into his chair. He looked old and very tired.

'I am,' Holler answered. 'Where ordinary people are concerned. But not people like you, Gunther. You're a special breed of men, remember? The Black Knights of the Third Reich. "Blood and honour." The concentration camps, the extermination squads, the guardians of the gas chambers and the execution yards. I spent some time with your people; they broke my right leg in three places, and then made me try and walk on it . . . It would be ironical, wouldn't it, if they were to kill you? One of their own kind who betrayed them? What did you betray, Gunther? Why did they come after you when you've been home for so many years?'

'Can I change my mind,' Mühlhauser said, 'and have a cigarette?'

'No,' Holler said. 'You can't. You can just answer my question.'

'If I tell you everything,' Mühlhauser said, 'will you promise to let us go to America? Andrews gave his assurance we'd be protected there.'

'Yes,' Holler nodded. He stubbed out his own cigarette. 'Yes, the CIA can have you. I wouldn't want anything to happen to your little girl. Or your wife; I saw her outside. She's a pretty girl. Begin from the beginning, Gunther. Take your time.'

He sat and listened.

'I was caught by the Friedrichstrasse bridge over the river Spree,' Mühlhauser said. 'A few of us had changed out of our SS uniforms, and we were dressed as civilians and hoping to escape through the Russian line to the north. We didn't have a chance. The Russians took the bridge and there was no way through. I was picked up, and taken to an interrogation centre they'd set up near the Wilhelmstrasse. I couldn't produce papers or a story to cover myself. There was a Soviet colonel in charge. He accused me of being an SS officer and said I was going to be shot. So I played for time. I told him who I was and that I'd been in the Bunker. They sent me to the rear, to a special camp, and the proper interrogation began. The same man was in charge. I told them everything I knew about the suicide of the Führer and Eva Braun, I gave them names of people who were with us in the Bunker, I told them Himmler was trying to negotiate a separate peace with the Western Allies, but it wasn't enough and I knew they were going to hang me.'

He looked at Holler and then at his own hands as if he expected to find something had changed in them.

'So I made a deal with the colonel,' he said. 'I told him what Fegelein had told me, for Himmler's use. Eva Braun had a child by Hitler. It was a boy, and it was two years old. I told him where it was being kept. They sent me to a labour camp as a reward.'

'Where was the child?' Heinrich Holler asked.

'With a foster-mother in Munich. Her name was Brandt, and Eva's sister Gretl Fegelein had made the arrangements. Brandt thought it was the bastard of a high Party official. It was called Frederick, after Frederick the Great, Hitler's hero.'

'And what do you think they did with this information?'

Gunther Mühlhauser clasped his hands together and looked up. 'I think they killed the boy,' he said. 'Just as they took the Führer's body out of Berlin. They wanted to wipe out all trace of him. To leave nothing, not even a grave. They would have seized the child and murdered it.'

'Munich was occupied by the Allies,' Holler said.

'That wouldn't stop the KGB,' Mühlhauser said.

Heinrich Holler nodded slowly. 'No,' he said, 'it wouldn't. And you didn't cheat, did you, Gunther? You didn't give them the name and address of someone else so they could murder the wrong child?'

'I wished I had,' Mühlhauser confessed. 'I wished I'd been cunning enough to make up a story, but I didn't. I told them the truth. Otherwise I wouldn't be alive now.'

'Yes,' Holler said, 'that seems to make sense. And this is what you admitted to the men from Odessa today?'

'I didn't tell them I knew where the boy was hidden,' Mühlhauser muttered. 'I kept that back. I just admitted telling the Russians he existed.'

'And they let you go free? I find that very hard to understand.'

'Not really,' Gunther Mühlhauser sounded bitter. 'They couldn't have killed Beatrix and me without causing a huge police hunt. They didn't want that. They pretended to let me go. I would have been punished later; maybe through Beatrix. Some accident would have happened to her and I'd have known but never been able to prove anything – That's why I must get her and my wife to the States. You couldn't protect us, Herr Holler, even if you wanted to.'

There was a knock on the door, and the stenographer came in.

'Here's the transcript, sir,' she said. Holler glanced at the pages and then handed them to Mühlhauser. 'Read those, and sign them if they're what you said.'

Mühlhauser did so, and handed them back. Holler stood up, and limped across to the door. He turned to face Mühlhauser before he opened it.

'So the mystery of Janus is solved,' he said. Gunther answered firmly, 'Yes. And you'll let us go?'

'The CIA are welcome to you, Gunther,' he said. 'Just remember to tell them the same lies that you've told me.' He opened the door and went out.

In Geneva the man known to Kesler and Franconi as Paul put down the telephone at the end of the call from Munich. He sat and tapped a pencil against the edge of the table. So far they had disposed of two of the four people designated with expertise and speed. Helm and Schmidt were dead. But the woman Gretl Fegelein had eluded them. The convent denied all knowledge of her, but the men who employed Paul and professionals like Kesler and Franconi didn't make mistakes. He didn't know what to do; he had told Kesler to call back in three hours, and he hoped to have fresh instructions for them. Kesler had sounded irritable and on edge; Paul guessed that his attempt to get to Gretl Fegelein had involved him in some risk of being recognized. He was leaving Munich in the hour, and couldn't guarantee to make the call until the evening.

There was nothing Paul could do but contact his superior and relay whatever orders he was given. He got up and locked the room behind him; it was a dingy office at the back of a shop selling cheap men's shoes. He told his assistant, an elderly man who helped him three afternoons a week, that he was going out for an hour, and then made his way on foot to the bus stop. He bought a ticket to the Rue du Rhone. It was only a hundred yards to one of Geneva's smartest hotels. He went round to the service entrance, and asked to see the under-manager, M. Huber. He was kept waiting for ten minutes, and then shown up in a lift to the ground floor and into a bright, well-furnished office. Huber came forward and shook hands. He was a man in his mid-forties, with sleek fair hair and an ingratiating smile. 'Good afternoon, Raymond,' Paul said.

'Good afternoon, Paul. Sit down, and have a drink. What would you like?'

'Nothing, thank you.' Paul had never got over his nervousness of the smiling Raymond Huber. His courtesy was full of menace. There was nothing Paul needed more than a drink at that moment.

'What's your news?' Huber asked.

Paul told him. He nodded when the names of Helm and Schmidt were mentioned, and murmured, 'Excellent, very good,' as if he were praising a member of his staff. The smile was gone when Paul had told him about Kesler's failure to reach Gretl Fegelein. 'He says she's not at the convent,' Paul finished; he hesitated and then said, 'There couldn't be a mistake, could there, Raymond – it's certain she's at that address?'

'We don't make mistakes,' Raymond said. 'She's never left that place in more than twenty years. He blundered, that's all and he's trying to cover it up.'

'What shall I tell them to do?' Paul asked. 'They're calling back tonight for instructions – do you want them to try again? It could be dangerous; I got the impression Kesler would be recognized. He seemed very anxious to leave Munich.'

'Then he certainly did blunder,' Raymond said crisply. He walked over to his desk, lit a cigarette and pulled out a bottle of cognac from the drawer, with a little glass. He poured himself a drink, sat down behind the desk and sipped it. Paul didn't interrupt him. He had been working for them for five years; like Kesler and Franconi he had begun with the rackets in Marseilles and graduated through the school of narcotics, blackmail and murder to the rarefied heights of political assassination.

The money was very big; Paul had two large bank accounts in Switzerland, one in Zurich and the second in Berne. He was a rich man, and if Raymond ever allowed him to retire he owned a luxury villa in the beautiful Seychelles Islands, far enough away from his old life and associates. He had a woman he had been living with for years, and two teenage children. She only knew him as the owner of the shoe shop. She was not part of his plans for retirement to the Indian Ocean.

'I shall have to take instructions from higher up,' Raymond said suddenly. He frowned and Paul quailed inside; the blue eyes were like dull stones and he knew that meant Raymond was angry. 'She was the most important target. I hope those two are not getting past it.' He didn't address his remarks to Paul, more to himself. 'You say they're leaving Munich? Where are they going?'

'Frankfurt and then to Bonn,' Paul answered. 'The last name on the list. What shall I tell them to do?'

'Carry out the assignment,' Raymond said. 'And no mistakes this time! This has become very important. Emphasize that. At all costs this man must be eliminated as quickly as possible. Tell Kesler if he completes this part of the contract satisfactorily we may overlook his failure in Munich.'

'Shall I mention the fee?' Paul said.

'Yes; it's what motivates them, after all. Say they shall get the full payment. Good afternoon, Paul. Thank you for coming.' He walked over and shook hands with the older man; the bright smile was back and the eyes were no longer opaque and dangerous. Paul hurried out of the room and down through the service entrance.

Raymond Huber went back to his desk and picked up the house telephone. 'I'm not to be disturbed for the next hour,' he said. 'Reception can deal with complaints, and please don't let them ring through and say somebody has made a double booking and will I come down and sort it out. Thank you, Janine.'

He was a restless thinker; he roamed round the office, looking out of the window, and back to his desk, lighting cigarettes and occasionally sipping brandy. He had worked at the hotel for ten years. First as a trainee, then through the various departments, and now as under-manager. It was the perfect cover: no one who was welcomed by him would connect the charming young Swiss in his formal jacket and striped trousers, a fresh flower in his buttonhole, with the man who had been born in a village on the Russo-Polish border and served several years in the foreign sector training department of what was then the NKVD in Leningrad. Raymond had lost both parents during the war; he had memories of burning villages and corpses, and a sky which was darkened by smoke and burning ash that floated on the wind. He had been taken with the refugees into central Russia to escape the German advance; his brilliance at school was noted, and he was sent for higher education to Moscow. His progress was steady; he left Moscow University after only two terms to study at what was said to be a technical institute in Leningrad. Here he was enrolled in the Soviet Intelligence Service. When he arrived in Switzerland he was bilingual in both French and Schweizerdeutsch, and was equipped with the identity of a genuine Franco-Swiss who had died after a motor accident. Raymond Huber was the key controller for the assassination department of the Service in Western Europe. The higher power to which he intended referring the problem of Gretl Fegelein was visiting Lake Lucerne on a Norwegian passport.

Huber had used Kesler and Franconi for a number of political murders, and this was the first time they had not accounted for their target. Their killing of Sigmund Walther was a classic. There was not a clue left for Interpol or the Sûreté; the newspapers had ceased to speculate, and interest was already fading. That was why it was so important that the others should appear as accidents. There must be no chain of connection to alert someone like Heinrich Holler, for instance. And yet Raymond knew, because a trusted agent had told him, that Holler was involved.

He had received the news over his private telephone line only a few hours ago; it was the last information that particular agent would impart for some time, but it contained another and even more disturbing revelation. Time was running short for Kesler and Franconi's contract. The last person on it could have been killed at their leisure, but not now. He damned the Convent of the Immaculate Conception to a place in their own hell. One bastion too strong for the inquisitors of Western Europe, too secure for his expert killers, protected by a power which he personally resented because it was not based on a political reality. Fegelein's wife had sought sanctuary with the Roman Catholic Church, and the power of that Church had protected her and her secret as effectively from his agents as from those of Holler and the CIA. Something very drastic would have to be done about the Convent of the Immaculate Conception.

He locked his office, and went through to the main foyer; he paused at the reception desk. 'I'm going out for a few minutes,' he said to the clerk. He pulled on a light raincoat to hide his formal clothes and buttonhole, and was soon one of the crowd wandering along the Rue du Rhone. Raymond went to the nearest post office and entered a telephone booth. He dialled the number in Lucerne direct and spoke to his superior officer. The conversation was short and mostly one-sided. Raymond came out of the post office and strolled back to the hotel. It was a beautiful evening, with the sun still spreading a pink and purple haze over the sky, in which the stars were twinkling prematurely.

He went back to his office; there had been no crisis, no messages. He asked for an outside line and telephoned Paul at his home number. 'Has our friend called yet? No? Good. Now listen. Tell him to forget Munich, you understand. But there are two more people I want him to visit. Yes, take a note of the names.' He spelt them out clearly, and gave the city, but not an address. At the other end, Paul copied them out. His common-law wife was watching television, and his two sons were arguing over the programme.

'I've got that,' Paul said. 'I'll give the instructions. Right, yes, I'll tell them to get it done as quickly as possible.'

He hung up and went back to his chair. He memorized what was written on the piece of paper, and then crushed it into a little ball and burnt it in the ashtray. His elder son sniffed and made a face. 'What are you burning, Pa? It stinks.'

Paul was fond of his children. He had made handsome provision for them when he retired to his villa. 'Just a bit of scrap paper,' he said. 'An old bill.'

The boys' mother looked round at him without interest. She had been pretty when young, but she had lost her looks and her figure after the second baby was born. She cooked well and was a careful housekeeper, but he hadn't slept with her for years.

'Do stop talking a minute,' she complained. 'I can't hear what's going on . . .'

'Turn up the volume, then,' Paul said. At that moment the telephone rang again. He had refused to have an extension, pleading the extra cost. But with only one phone, nobody could pick up the second and listen in.

'Oh, for God's sake,' the woman grumbled. 'It's never stopped all evening! Just when this quiz programme is on, it rings and rings . . .'

Paul got up and answered it. It was Kesler. 'Oh,' Paul said. 'Yes, I've got the orders for you. Don't bother sending any to Munich, but take two extra samples. Yes, that's what I said. Two. I'll give you the names they're to go to – are you ready?'

'I'm ready,' Kesler said. Franconi was by his elbow. 'Pencil, quick,' Kesler hissed at him. 'Write it down.'

'Wind up the business as quickly as you can,' Paul instructed. 'The profit is just the same without the Munich sale. But you've got to hurry. And don't be too particular about your sales methods. It's the results that count. Call through when you've got the final figures.'

Franconi leaned over Kesler's shoulder and read what he had written. He looked at Kesler. 'Walther's widow, and isn't that the journalist who was with him?'

'Yes,' Stanislaus Kesler answered. 'We've got a contract for them both. And this original one. He says we're to leave the convent alone.'

'Thank God for that,' Franconi said. 'The same money?'

'Yes. He said so. He wants it all done as soon as possible. Come on, Maurice dear, let's start getting the plan worked out. We must decide which one to go for first and then make our travel arrangements. One thing that makes it easier, they don't mind whether it's accidental or not.'

'That puts the contract into the high-risk category.' Franconi frowned. 'We should have asked for more.'

'Don't be greedy,' Kesler admonished. 'It'll be fast and easy. Then we're retiring. Just be content with that. Now, get out the schedules and the map and let's make up our minds where we go first.'

'It's funny,' Max said, 'to think that it all started here. Munich's such a gay place.'

Minna smiled at him. 'You sound like a tourist,' she said. 'Light-hearted Bavaria, all drinking songs and *lederhosen*. There's more rubbish talked about South Germans than there is about Prussia. We're all militaristic brutes, and the Bavarians and the Austrians are delightful. The irony of it is that the Nazi Party really started in the South.'

'You've really studied the subject, haven't you?' he said. They were dining at the Künstlerhaus, with its courtyard garden. She wore a pale green dress which suited her, and he almost told her how beautiful she was. He said many extravagant things when they made love but she maintained her aloofness outside the bedroom. The duality of her nature confused him; he was deeply in love with her, but no closer to understanding her than when they first met. They had arrived in Munich, booked into a quiet hotel on the outer perimeter of the city centre, and he had resisted the urge to go to bed and stay there. While he hesitated, Minna suggested they dined at the Künstlerhaus. 'It's wonderful food,' she said. 'And I love the atmosphere. Sigmund and I always went there when we came to Munich.'

He watched her now across the table; she was smiling at him over her glass of wine. He loved her so much that it was as much pain as joy when they were together. She spoke quite freely about her husband, as if he and his memory were on a different plane from her relationship with Max. He had begun to feel jealous of Sigmund Walther. 'Yes, I suppose I have become quite an expert,' she said. 'When I was very young, nobody mentioned the Nazis. It was just as if they hadn't existed as far as my family and our friends were concerned. I had quute a shock when Sigmund told me what they were really like.'

'I think we all wanted to forget it,' Max said. 'That's why I left Germany; I wanted to escape the war and everything that went with it. Looking back, I think I deliberately tried to shed being German. You know, neither my wife nor my children speak a word? We talked French or English at home.'

'Where are your family? You've never mentioned them before.'

'There didn't seem to be much point,' he said. 'They've gone to stay with friends in England. I ought to telephone; I just haven't got round to doing it.'

Minna Walther said quietly, 'Tell me about your wife, Max. And your children.'

'Why?' he asked her.

'Because I'm curious,' she said. 'I knew you were married, but it was all quite vague. What's your wife like?'

'Ellie?' He was surprised by his own reluctance to discuss Ellie with Minna Walther. He was suddenly on the defensive about his silly, irritating wife, and the way he was neglecting her. 'She's American,' he said. 'We met in London, and we've got two children, a boy and a girl. We've been married almost seventeen years.'

'Is she pretty?' Minna asked. 'I'm sure she is.'

'Yes,' Max said, and there in his mind's eye was Ellie as he had last seen her, hurt and chillingly aloof as she took their children to the plane. 'She's very attractive indeed,' he said. 'Now let's talk about something else, shall we?'

'You mustn't feel guilty,' Minna said gently. 'So long as she never knows what's happened, it won't matter.'

Max leaned back in his chair; candlelight enhanced her beauty, softening the Prussian bone structure. Her eyes reflected the green of her dress. Ellie and his children. It was the wrong moment, but he couldn't help himself. What had to be said would have no meaning if it was just part of their sexual relationship. 'I'm in love with you, Minna,' he said. 'And my marriage is finished. You didn't break it up, it was over anyway before I met you. That's why I don't want to talk about my wife, or my children. And if I feel guilty, that's too bad.' He reached down the ice bucket and poured wine into her glass.

She didn't look at him. 'You mustn't love me, Max,' she said suddenly.

'No? Then what the hell am I doing with you every night?'

'Making love,' she said. 'That's different.'

'Different for you, you mean.' They were facing each other now, and he was very angry. He thought for a moment that there were tears in her eyes and then dismissed it as a trick of the candlelight.

'I'm sorry,' she said. 'I didn't mean to hurt you. I need you so much, and everything we have together is very valuable to me. But I don't want to interfere in your life. I don't want to involve you too deeply. Please, don't be angry.'

'You don't want to involve me? Minna, from the first moment we met, we were *both* involved. I don't know what you're running away from but it's time you stopped. You're trying to be two people: the woman I make love to, and the wife of the hero Sigmund Walther. You're his widow, darling; he's not there any more. You couldn't sleep with his memory, could you?'

'That's cruel,' she said. 'But I deserve it.'

He nodded. 'Yes,' he said, 'you do. You need to be loved, and you need a man who loves you. Otherwise what we're doing is having a marvellous screw.' He saw her wince at the crudity, and he went on, 'That's what you're pretending, isn't it? That's why you put up the barriers with me as soon as you step out of bed. I didn't mean to force the issue now; I wanted to get the other business settled first and then say all this. But it's done, so we may as well face it. I love you, and I want to know if you love me.'

She wanted to cry out to him to stop, stop before it all went wrong . . .

'I can't tell you that,' she said. 'I don't know the answer myself.'

'All right,' Max said. 'That's honest, for a start. I'll be satisfied with that. It's up to me to make you love me, isn't it?'

She shook her head, and the lights danced in her hair, 'I wish you wouldn't,' she said. 'I wish you'd leave well alone.'

He laughed, but it was not a happy sound. 'It isn't well for me,' he said. 'Do you want coffee, or shall I get the bill?'

'The bill,' she said. She took a mirror and looked at herself; it was the first time he had seen her do so, and he knew it was a ruse to avoid saying any more.

They found a cruising taxi and went back to the hotel. He took her hand and she didn't resist. They didn't say anything until he brought her to her bedroom door. He turned her towards him. 'Do you want me to come in?'

He saw the defeat in her face, and then the lowered eyelids and the parted lips. Her arms went round his neck.

'You know I do,' she said.

Curt Andrews got a reply to his telex late that night. Gunther Mühlhauser was safe in the Consulate, with his wife and child. The wife had tried to leave, taking Beatrix with her, but without actually putting her under guard Andrews managed to dissuade her from doing anything in a hurry. She had looked at him with hatred, her eyes red from crying.

'I don't want to stay with that murderer,' she said. 'I'm going back to my mother and I'm taking Beatrix with me.'

'You've no right to accuse your husband, Fräu Mühlhauser,' Andrews reproached her. Inwardly he damned the vehemence of the young German conscience. If she was going to be a nuisance then he would get really tough . . . 'You haven't heard his side of the story. I can promise you, many of the SS were perfectly decent men. They're all painted as sadists and killers by persistent Jewish propaganda. You owe it to your daughter to give her father a chance to explain himself.' He had sounded sanctimonious enough to turn his own stomach, but at least it quietened her for the time. His Director's telex was terse; typical of the man's economy of mind:

*Congratulations on discovery of extreme importance. Deal with it
personally.*

Deal with it personally. That was the kind of instruction Andrews
liked. He could tell Heinrich Holler to take a running jump at himself
with that telex in his pocket. He made arrangements for Mühlhauser
to be flown out with his wife and child on the first flight available the
next morning, then he checked out of the hotel without telling Holler,
and set out for Munich. There was no internal flight till the morning
and he didn't want to wait that long. He hired a car and began the
long journey by road.

But if he was anxious to avoid Holler, the chief of West German
Intelligence was equally determined not to be found by him. After
leaving the Consulate, Holler had driven back to his hotel, and there
to the city police headquarters where there was a series of messages
waiting for him. One posed an urgent question about the influx of
terrorists from France in the guise of students: two had already been
detained as a result of information, and were found to be carrying
grenades and plastic explosive. The target was an Israeli orchestra
making a tour of the major towns. Holler dealt with that quickly,
and skimmed through the rest; a leak through Norway which was
bringing one of the Embassy staff under suspicion, and armed robbery
which became his province because one the criminals had been linked
to the Baader-Meinhof . . . and a report from Munich concerning an
incident at the Convent of the Immaculate Conception. Holler stopped
leafing through the reports and began to concentrate. Munich police
were instructed to contact his department if that particular convent
was involved in anything out of the ordinary. He was reading very
carefully; the priest attached to the convent had been knocked out
and robbed; he was recovering in hospital. The Reverend Mother had
reported a priest arriving in his place, who simply walked out and
disappeared. Holler knew the reputation of the Reverend Mother of
the Convent of the Immaculate Conception. If she had felt the need
to go to the police, then there was something seriously wrong . . .

Unlike Andrews, who was busy making arrangements for the reception of Mühlhauser in New York, Heinrich Holler caught the evening
plane to Munich.

Early the next morning he was going through the reports in a private
office in the central police station. He listened quietly as a nervous
officer gave an account of his interview with the Reverend Mother.
The black homburg hat lay on his desk with a tag stapled to it.

'Father Rittermann, eh? And you've checked with all the Catholic
parishes on any priest of that name?'

'Yes, sir. We did that straight away. There were two Rittermanns,
but neither corresponded with the man who went to the convent.

One was about twenty-five, and the other was in hospital after an operation. There was no trace of any priest called Rittermann or anyone knowing about the attack on Father Grunwald and being sent as his replacement. In fact, the timing makes it impossible, unless the so-called priest was responsible for the assault and robbery.' Holler looked down at the typed page. 'I see you found a wallet and a watch belonging to Grunwald. No fingerprints?'

'Nothing, sir, just a lot of smudges. He wore gloves.'

'Very professional for a backstreet mugger,' Holler said. 'And of course the priest didn't see who hit him. Is he well enough to interview? Check with the hospital. And telephone Reverend Mother Katherine. I'd like to see her. And don't take any nonsense; this is a criminal charge.'

He went to see Father Grunwald first. The older man was in a side ward in the Augsburg Hospital; he looked pinched and grey. Holler sat down with a police inspector to take notes. He recognized the signs of shock in the bad colour and the quick breathing. He apologized very gently to the priest for troubling him with questions, but the convent was also concerned. He did hope the Father would be able to help.

'You didn't see your attacker, or notice anyone near before you were struck down?'

'I don't think so,' Father Grunwald muttered. 'I was just going round to my car to go to the convent as usual, when the next thing I felt was a terrible blow and then I knew nothing till I woke up in the ambulance . . .'

'And there was nobody about before it happened? Try to think, Father.'

The old man's forehead creased in the effort to concentrate. 'I think there was someone getting out of a car . . . I can't be sure . . . But there was no one else in the street.'

'What sort of car – did you notice the colour or the make?'

Father Grunwald picked fretfully at the top sheet. 'Yes, I did. I'm interested in cars, you know. I've had mine for ten years and there's never been a thing wrong with it . . . It's a Volkswagen, and they're so reliable'

'They are indeed,' Holler nodded. 'Was this car you saw a VW?'

'Oh, no. It was an Opel; dark green.'

'And a man got out of it?'

'Yes, he did, I'm sure he did.'

'And what impression did you get of him – old, young, fat, thin – anything that struck you?'

'I don't know,' the priest mumbled. 'I didn't look at them properly, you see. I just noticed the car.'

'You said, "them",' Holler reminded him. 'Were there two men, perhaps?'

'Yes, one on the street and one inside,' Father Grunwald answered. 'I couldn't see the one in the car . . . I didn't look at them, I was in a hurry.'

'Yes, of course you were. But you've been a great help already. You noticed the car, and the colour and the make, and now we are sure you were attacked by two men, not one. Don't you see how much that helps us?'

'I hope so,' the priest said. 'This has been a dreadful experience. I'm not able to stand shocks like this. Why would anyone want to rob *me*? I'd nothing but a few marks and my old watch . . .'

'I don't think they did want to rob you,' Holler said quietly. 'I think they wanted to get someone into the convent in your place. The theft of your wallet and your watch were just done to hide the true motive.'

'Why?' Father Grunwald's eyes rolled from Holler to the inspector, who hadn't spoken. 'Why would anyone want to go to the convent instead of me? Maybe they wanted the chapel plate – there are some very valuable silver-gilt candlesticks and a chalice . . . How did they know I went to the convent on Thursdays?'

'Perhaps you told them,' Holler suggested, 'without realizing there was any harm. Who did you see that week, apart from the people you see normally? Did anyone telephone you, or call on you – '

The old man frowned again; he had been sedated to take the edge off the shock. He didn't know but his blood pressure had dived as a result. He felt sleepy and frightened at the same time. But also angry. Very angry with whoever had knocked him down and taken his few marks . . .

'Only a man wanting instruction,' he said at last. 'I sent him away; I'm too old for converts now. I told him to go to his own parish priest.'

'Do you get many inquiries like that?'

He looked at Holler's grave, sympathetic face. 'Why, no. No, I don't think it's happened to me since I retired there . . . But this man said Reverend Mother had recommended him . . .' He didn't finish the sentence and his eyes opened wide with alarm. 'You don't think it was him who – '

'I think it's very likely,' Holler said. 'Now you can really help us. What did he say to you. Did he ask questions about the convent?'

'Yes, yes,' the old man nodded. 'I didn't think about it, but he asked me when I went there and whether I'd have enough time to look after his instruction and I saw I could make an excuse and I told him . . .'

'Now tell me what he looked like?' Holler said.

'He had grey hair,' Father Grunwald said. 'He was rather ordinary, middle-aged and he could have come from the East. He wasn't a Bavarian, not with that accent . . . I didn't like him much. I didn't want to instruct him. People have made up their minds about religion by that age, I think . . . Glasses? No, he didn't have glasses – or a moustache or anything. Rather a heavy man, and quite tall . . .'

'But not the man you half noticed in the street, getting out of the Opel?'

'No, no, I'd have remembered him. That one was young with fair hair.'

Holler stood up. 'Thank you, Father Grunwald,' he said. 'I won't tire you any more. You've given us a great deal to go on. I'm sure we'll find whoever did this to you. Take care and get well soon. Good-bye.'

The Munich police started with the cheap boarding houses and then the commercial hotels; they were looking for two men, one grey-haired, well-built and tall, his companion young and blond. The registers revealed nothing, until they came to a modest *pension*. The detective found two names on the register, both having left on the day of the attack on Father Grunwald. The proprietor, a middle-aged woman who ran the place with her married daughter, described the two men.

'Very nice gentlemen, both of them. They kept to themselves and they only ate breakfast with us. I told them we did a nice evening meal, but they always went out. Then the older one paid the bill on Thursday and they left about about – oh, four o'clock, I think.' The register was made out in the names of Kesler and Franconi. Nationality Swiss, with two addresses in Geneva. The detective produced a small folder and laid it on the reception desk. There were sections of the human face, all interchangeable. 'I'll put one together and you tell me what's wrong with it,' he said. The woman shook her head. 'No, the nose is wrong. It wasn't hooked, it was a bit blunt.'

Twenty minutes later the Munich detective had assembled two identikit pictures of the men who had stayed at the *pension*. Holler set off with them to see Father Grunwald. When he came into the ward he stopped; there were screens round the bed. A young doctor came out and Holler went up to him. 'Is anything wrong with the priest? Here's my card.' The doctor glanced at the police ID with its photograph of Holler in a little plastic window. He shook his head. 'He had a heart attack about half an hour ago. We've tried everything, but I'm afraid it's no use. He's dead.'

'I'm sorry,' Holler said. He spoke to the Munich inspector who accompanied him as they ran down the steps into the street. 'That was our best witness. Now the only person who can really identify him is Reverend Mother Katherine.'

'She'll be better than poor old Father Grunwald,' the policeman said.

'I'm not so sure,' Holler said. 'But at least I'll get a chance to see her and ask some of the questions . . . Let's get back to the office.'

He settled himself behind a borrowed desk, lit a cigarette and began to make notes. He wrote at random, setting down whatever came into his mind. He made no attempt yet to arrange the interview with the Reverend Mother. There were other points he wanted to clear first. The cigarette burnt down to its filter in an ashtray. The page became crowded with items, and names. Holler read them, adding here and there or sometimes crossing out. Herbert Schmidt. Otto Helm. Two men had visited Schmidt, and one of them had killed him. One man had been seen in the vicinity of Helm's house before it was set on fire. He reached for the telephone, and spoke to his office in West Berlin.

'Give me a description of the man seen walking his dog – that's right, three separate people came forward. Yes.' He listened, writing it down. Young. Fair-haired. Medium height. His pen scored underneath each word. 'Good now get the Schmidt file. The two men who were with him when he died . . . No, I'll hold on.' The minutes went by; he sat with his eyes closed, thinking.

'Hello – yes, you have. Good. Give it to me.' There followed a description of the two German gentlemen, said to be army officers, that Herbert Schmidt's cousin had let in to see him. Grey-haired, heavy-built. Younger, blond hair.

He hung up. In Berchtesgaden they had passed themselves off as Germans. In Munich they registered as Swiss. The old priest had detected an accent in his caller which placed him well to the east of Germany. The picture was taking shape, like a finished section of a larger jigsaw puzzle. They had identified Father Grunwald and the older one had substituted himself to get into the convent. From what Heinrich Holler knew of the Reverend Mother, she would never have called the police unless she felt her community was threatened. The chain of coincidence was too long to be credible except for the one, vital link between the men who had murdered two survivors of the Bunker and the imposter who had run out of the convent. Gretl Fegelein. Holler had a feeling of exhilaration when he wrote that name down and read it aloud. The men who had killed Helm and Schmidt were also trying to get to Eva Braun's sister.

And so were Max Steiner and Minna Walther. He had the address of their hotel, which Minna had given him. He put a call through and asked to speak to Max.

'This is Holler speaking. I'm in Munich. Listen, I haven't time to explain but I don't want Fräu Walther going to the convent. What?

She has! Damnation – No. Never mind. Call me when she comes back later.'

A shaft of sunlight had settled on the picture hanging above the fire-place; it was a sentimental reproduction of the Sacred Heart. Minna studied it while she waited in the convent parlour. The Christ was a beautiful Aryan, with blue eyes and softly waving chestnut hair, one sensitive hand pointing to the allegory of his love and suffering on account of mankind, a heart surrounded by a crown of thorns, enclosed in a nimbus of light. She wondered whether the artist had realized how anti-Semitic he was being when he painted the original. Jesus, of the House of David, had never looked like that. She heard the door behind her open and she turned. The nun came towards her, one hand resting lightly on the silver cross she wore round her neck. She wasn't as tall as Minna but she gave the impression of height.

'Fräu Walther?' The accent was the twin of Minna's East German pronunciation, with the clipped Prussian vowels. Minna stared at her; at last she found words. The formality gave her time to recover from the shock of recognition.

'Reverend Mother Katherine. It's very kind of you to see me.'

The nun smiled and sat down on one of the stiff little chairs. 'I'm only too delighted to see General Ahrenburg's daughter,' she said.

Minna thanked her. The two women were facing each other across the polished table where Kesler had left his hat.

'But you wouldn't see my husband,' she said. 'He wrote to you many times.'

'I know he did,' Mother Katherine nodded. 'But there was no way I could help him. I don't think I will be able to help you either. Before you come to the point of your visit, how are your family?'

'My mother is very well; my father died four years ago. And you know what happened to my husband.'

'I do. We had a special Mass said for him.'

'That was very kind,' Minna answered. 'But you could have seen him and helped him, Mother Katherine. He was a good and brave man, and he loved Germany. As the daughter of Baron von der Stein, don't you feel responsibility towards your country any more?'

'I have another identity,' the nun answered. 'I have a new name, and new loyalties. What happened to my father is perhaps a little worse than what happened to your husband. If I have come to terms with that, I know the real meaning of patriotism. You're not a Catholic, but I'm sure you understand the principle of obedience to a higher power.'

'There is no higher power in this convent than you,' Minna said. 'I know enough about Catholics to know that. Why are you protecting Gretl Fegelein? You, of all the people in the world.'

'I have never heard of Gretl Fegelein,' the Reverend Mother said.

'You're not supposed to lie,' Minna said. 'It's a sin, isn't it? And you can't lie to me, Freda, because we've known each other too long.'

'Don't call me that,' she interrupted. 'My name is Katherine Ignatius; there is no such person as Freda von der Stein.' She made a movement as if she were going to get up, and Minna leaned towards her quickly.

'We were friends once,' she reminded her. 'When we were children – you remember how my mother and father comforted you and your mother? You stayed with us until the Russian advance, didn't you – then we all fled together. Your father and mine were close friends. So close that he wouldn't involve Papa in the bomb plot because he felt it was going to fail, and he knew the penalty.'

She paused; Mother Katherine had stayed in her chair; under the grey nun's veil, her face was very pale.

'I remember your father very well,' Minna went on. 'He was always so kind to me. They strangled him with piano wire, hung up on a meat hook. Hitler watched the cine film. Maybe Gretl Fegelein was there. Have you asked her, Freda?'

'What do you want?' The nun's voice was low. 'Why does anyone want to bring up the past?'

'Why do you and your Church want to hide it?' Minna countered. 'Other people are looking for that woman, not Germans, but our enemies.'

'I know they are,' Mother Katherine answered. 'One of them came here, posing as a priest. He asked for her, and I told him I'd never heard of her. Then I knew that there was danger. Danger to my community. That's why I agreed to see you, Minna. I can't have my nuns put at risk. Why, after all these years, should Eva Braun's sister be of interest to anyone?'

'If you'll let me see her,' Minna said. 'I'll tell you. Or she can tell you.'

The Reverend Mother stood up. 'Come with me,' she said.

Albert Kramer poured himself a Steinhaeger. He liked a schnapps when he came back from his office, and he experimented; he decided that the old favourite, a Manhattan, was the one he liked the best. He was in a buoyant mood; he examined himself in the mirror above the fireplace in his drawing room, and felt satisfied.

He had spent a long afternoon with certain members of the Bundestag discussing his proposal to stand for election; he dropped hints that Fräu Walther would endorse him as a candidate to take her husband's place. The idea was very well received. He was encouraged and assured of support. He had remembered to send flowers to Minna,

as part of the campaign, but he was surprised when she didn't acknowl-
edge them.

He wasn't a man to be rebuffed easily. He rang the house in
Hamburg and was told she had gone away. Yes, the flowers had
arrived, and Fräu Walther had been there, but the housekeeper didn't
know the date of her return. She had gone to Munich. Kramer felt
annoyed, and then dismissed it. Minna would come round; it added
spice to his pursuit of her. She was unaware that she was his quarry
in more than a personal sense. She didn't know that he knew what
was in those papers of her dead husband and, thanks to Mühlhauser,
he had information of his own.

The immensity of the secret had made him reckless. He dreamed
dreams of power and greatness, and the echoes of salutes shouted from
ten thousand voices in one uniform cry rang through his memory and
brought a flush of excitement to his face. He felt tuned and fit like an
athlete before a race, and his sexuality was at a high pitch. He needed
women regularly, but he had been careful not to get involved in an
affair in his own social circle. He didn't want scandal or attachments.
He used a reputable agency to supply him with girls. He had found
one in particular very pleasing; she matched his exultant mood. He
had made a call when he got home, and arranged for her to come. His
staff were discreet; they knew when he entertained a lady to dinner,
that they were not to gossip if she stayed the night. Or left in the small
hours. Kramer didn't usually give the girls dinner until he was sure
they were amusing companions. Then he liked to play the host. It
made the sex more enjoyable if he could dominate the girl as a person,
rather than an object who took her clothes off, pocketed her fee, and
left. That annoyed Kramer because it was impersonal, and he felt it a
reflection upon his masculinity. He liked to play with the girls over
the dining table, miming the seduction agreed beforehand. The girl he
had booked for that night was ideal for the purpose. He had showered
and changed, ordered a good dinner with some of his better wine, and
was drinking his cocktail in self-admiration before she arrived.

When the door opened he came forward, and as his man-servant
withdrew, he lightly kissed the prostitute's hand.

'*Gnädiges Fraulein* – this is a pleasure.'

'Herr Kramer,' the girl responded, 'how kind of you to invite me.'

She was a well-educated girl, who worked during the day in the
sociology department of the Ministry of the Interior. She had brown
hair and large blue eyes, with a delightful smile; she was expensively
dressed in navy silk, with pearls round her neck and in her small lobes.
She had big breasts, which made her slim body look top-heavy, but
Kramer found the imbalance exciting.

He offered her a schnapps, and she pleased him by accepting. They talked and drank, and she played her part so well he almost forgot she would cost him three hundred marks at the end. He wanted to touch her, but it would have spoiled the charade. He wondered how much he would have to pay if he ripped her dress later, and decided it would be worth the money. He allowed himself the titillation of stroking her hand. She smiled delightfully into his eyes.

Outside in the tree-lined avenue Kesler and Franconi walked past the entrance. Franconi looked at his watch.

'No one else has come,' he said. 'She's been there over an hour.'

'I'll drive the car round,' Kesler said. 'You keep strolling along on the opposite side, and make sure no one else goes in or the girl comes out.'

Franconi nodded. It was a mild evening, dark but warm. He wore a hat, which was unusual, but Kesler insisted. He had become quite nervous after the debacle in the convent. Franconi did as he was told. He strolled, very slowly, along the opposite side of the road from Kramer's house. There were lights on the first and ground floors. He had seen a man open the door when the girl arrived, and it wasn't their target. There was no kiss or handshake. So there was a male servant in the house. Kesler didn't want to confront him; he was trying, in spite of their last set of instructions, to keep the accidental aspect of their contract. Franconi saw the car nose ahead of him and pull up. He walked to it and slipped inside.

'Nothing,' he reported. 'It's past nine. They must be having dinner.'

'We'll wait,' Kesler said. 'I don't think he'll come out tonight. If we're clever we'll catch them in bed.'

Franconi made a grimace. He had a real horror of heterosexuality. 'Supposing they don't go to bed?' he said. 'They may be going on somewhere else.'

Kesler lit a cigarette. 'Then we'll follow them. We'll get him one way or the other, don't worry, Maurice. I have instinct for a job that's going to go well. I'm very confident about tonight. We'll take this turning and come back up again. We can park near those trees; we can see the front door perfectly from there.'

He smiled encouragingly at Franconi. His own nerves had been shaken by having to run from the convent. That nun was no fool; she'd give a very crisp description of him. But Munich was far enough away from Bonn, and Bonn in turn from Hamburg, where the last two on their contract lived. Then a flight to Geneva, to collect the money, and afterwards Tangier ... He switched on the radio, and tuned into some disco music, because he knew Maurice liked it. He preferred classical himself.

Kramer's companion was called Heidi; she was twenty-four and she had been supplementing her income since she was twenty. Her family lived in the country some hundred kilometres from the capital city itself; her father had retired from medical practice after a heart attack, and he and her mother lived a quiet rural life. Heidi was their only daughter, and the family were very close. She was educated and a proficient typist, but the job with the Ministry was only adequately paid.

Heidi enjoyed good clothes, skiing holidays, and was saving for the day when she got married. She had always known she was attractive to men, and being a practical girl, when she heard that it was possible to make a lot of money doing what she had so far done for nothing, she didn't hesitate. She looked at Albert Kramer across the dining table, and toasted him in his own champagne. He wasn't her type, and she didn't particularly enjoy the ugly display of masculine aggression which he called making love. But she obviously suited him and the money was exceptionally good. He leaned across and ran his hand down her arm. She responded with a sensuous giggle. His eyes were slightly red from drink, but it didn't impair his performance.

'Coffee?' he asked her. 'Here, or upstairs?'

Heidi played her part perfectly. She wet her lips with her tongue, and said, 'Upstairs.'

It was a quarter to midnight when Kesler and Franconi opened the door into the entrance hall. Franconi's early criminal background included picking locks, and this one had been easy. The security lock had not been used, in view of Herr Kramer's lady friend upstairs. The servant had gone to bed. There was a single light on in the hall.

Kesler went first; although he was the heavier of the two, he never touched a loose board. On the first floor they paused; there were no lights under the doors. Kesler beckoned Franconi and they started up the stairs again. There was a light on the landing. They switched it off. A streak of dim light showed under one of the three doors on the landing. The two men stood side by side, absolutely still and quiet, listening. It was a thick door; the house was well built. It was a little while before they could distinguish the muted sounds of a male voice. Kesler looked at Franconi in the gloom and nodded. 'I'll deal with him,' he whispered. 'You see to her.' He slipped a gun out of his pocket; Franconi did the same. Then Kesler closed his gloved hand round the doorknob and very slowly eased it round until the door was open.

Kramer didn't see them. He had his back to the door, and the girl was kneeling in front of him; they were both naked. She saw nothing either; her eyes were closed and she was concluding the first part of the ritual dictated by the client.

Kesler came up behind them, and laid a hand on Kramer's shoulder. Kramer gasped and swung round; the girl toppled over, caught off-balance. Kesler shot him through the right side of his head, close to the eye. The girl Heidi managed one sharp cry of fear before Franconi cut it off. He dragged her to her feet, one hand round her mouth; her eyes rolled upwards in terror. Franconi changed his hold on her, and Kesler stepped close and shot her twice in the heart. Maurice let her fall quickly; she sprawled on her stomach, blood collecting on the carpet underneath. Kesler needed help with Kramer's body. Together they managed to lift it on to the bed, and the big mirror on the opposite wall reflected the scene of death as it had done the gymnastics of sex. Kesler fitted the gun into Kramer's right hand, crooking the index finger round the trigger; he brought it up level with the bullet wound and then let the arm fall naturally. The gun slipped out of the dead hand on to the floor. Kesler looked round him quickly.

'Murder and suicide,' he whispered to Franconi. 'Come on, don't forget to shut the door. Hurry!' They flitted down the stairs, into the hallway and out through the front door. The porch was in shadow and for a few seconds both men sheltered, making sure no one was in the street. They left at the same time, keeping close to a line of ornamental bushes, slipped through the gate and were in their car in less than a minute. Kesler switched on, and took care not to gun the engine. They moved off silently and without undue speed. Franconi lit a cigarette and passed it to Kesler. Kesler smiled; he was in excellent spirits. Release from tension after a job always made him elated.

'Wasn't that a classic?' he asked Franconi. 'Perfect. Now we're on the autobahn. We can pick up a bit of speed.

'You think anyone heard the shots?' Franconi asked.

'No,' Kesler said. 'Very unlikely. The servants would be on the top floor. They won't be found till the morning. And we'll be having a nice big breakfast in Hamburg by then.'

'She's dead,' Minna Walther said. 'I saw the grave.'

Max didn't say anything; he felt numbed with disappointment. The feeling changed to anger and he swore.

'That was our banker,' he said. 'The one person who could have told us where that child was, and what had happened to it!'

'She was buried in the crypt under the chapel,' Minna said slowly. 'I just stood there and knew we'd failed. We've come to the end, I'm afraid. My God, I feel exhausted suddenly.' He came and put his arms round her; she leaned against him.

'Holler's waiting for us to call him,' he said. 'I'll do that, darling. But I'm going to get you a drink first.'

She surprised him by shaking her head. 'I don't feel like anything,' she said. 'You talk to Holler; tell him what I found out.'

'I will,' Max stroked the top of her head; the hair was very fine and soft. She sat on the sofa in their hotel sitting room, with her eyes closed. She heard Max go into the bedroom and ask for Holler's number at Munich police headquarters. She opened her eyes and turned her head to listen. He came back and said, 'He's coming over right away. Albert Kramer's been found dead. Holler thinks it's another murder.'

He saw the colour rush up into her face, and wondered why she should blush rather than turn pale.

'Albert? It's not possible – oh, my God!'

'It looks like suicide,' Max said. 'There was a girl with him; she'd been shot and apparently he'd killed himself. Holler's certain it was a double murder.'

'But why? Why Albert?'

'God knows,' Max said. 'Except he was a Nazi. And he'd headed the firing squad in the Bunker.' He looked up at her. 'But nobody knew about that – except ourselves and Heinrich Holler.' A few minutes later reception phoned to tell them Holler was on his way up.

'So Gretl Fegelein is dead,' he said, looking at Minna and puffing jerkily at his cigarette. 'Five years ago, is that right:'

Minna nodded. 'Yes,' she said. 'There was a date on the stone.'

Holler nodded. 'Five years, I see. So that source of information has gone for ever. Taking the secret of Janus with her, we must presume.' He glanced at Max.

He liked Max Steiner; he recognized the type, and saw a little of himself so many years ago in the younger man. Brave without being flamboyant, independent minded; not a man who gave up easily. He was so much in love with Minna Walther that Holler didn't even speculate whether they were lovers. He had always admired her; she had dignity and composure as well as good looks. He admired her a lot less for taking Max into her bed so soon after Sigmund Walther's death.

'Are you sure Albert Kramer was murdered?' Minna asked the question.

'Not sure,' Holler answered. 'Certain. We knew Kramer; he used a call-girl agency, and the one who was killed with him was a regular. There was no motive for her murder and less still for him to commit suicide. His manservant says he was in great spirits that evening; his secretary confirmed that the day was just as usual: he made appointments for the rest of the week – he was exceptionally cheerful. Nothing about his actions or appearance point to a man who is going to murder a prostitute and then kill himself. Besides, we Germans don't go in for that kind of crime. Kramer was murdered, with the girl, and then set up to look like a suicide.'

'But why?' Max asked.

'For the same reason as Helm and Schmidt,' Holler answered.

'Because he knew something connected with Janus and the Bunker. I believe the same people tried to get to Gretl Fegelein in the convent. Not knowing she was dead, of course. The point is, where will they go next?' He stubbed out his cigarette, rubbing the butt to fragments of paper and tobacco. He spoke to Minna. 'I believe something else,' he said. 'I believe the men who killed Sigmund are picking off a list of people. Herr Steiner – you told me a man came to see your wife in Paris, and frightened her so much she left the country. Posing as a Sûreté man, isn't that right?'

'Yes,' Max said. 'He wasn't; as I told you, I checked. It could have been a crank, but I didn't think so.'

'Did your wife describe him to you?'

'Yes, she did. I passed the description on to the Sûreté. It didn't fit any of their men.'

'Tell me what he was like,' Holler said.

'Medium height, thin, very dark hair, blue eyes. Certainly French.'

'Not the same as the one at the convent, then, but undoubtedly connected. The object was not to threaten your wife particularly, but to find out if you had told her anything Sigmund had told you. Fortunately for you, Herr Steiner, your wife knew nothing, because you hadn't had time to tell her.'

'I wouldn't have told her anyway,' Max said. 'I never discussed my work with her; she didn't take much interest in what I was doing.' He didn't look near Minna when he said it. He banished the memory of Ellie's frightened face, because his conscience was stirring while Holler talked. They had been threatened, his family, and he had sent them to friends while he pursued his own objective, and then fell in love with another woman.

'The question is,' Holler went on, 'why anyone is bothering to kill these people if the Russians actually found and disposed of Hitler's child?'

There was a moment of silence and then Max said, 'But you said it wasn't true, they never found him . . .'

'I didn't think they did,' Holler answered. 'But in the last twenty-four hours I've changed my mind.'

'Why?' Minna had got up; now she was pale, unlike the moment when she blushed at the news of Kramer's death. 'Why have you changed your mind – you've got to tell us!'

'I don't have to tell you anything,' Holler replied gently.

'Yes, you do,' Minna said. 'You got Sigmund to do your work for you, looking for the child. That's why he was killed. You owe it to him to tell me why you think Hitler's child was found and murdered.'

Holler didn't answer. He hadn't visualized her as an opponent. He got up and stretched himself, buttoning his jacket. 'What I owe

Sigmund,' he said quietly, 'is to protect you. Your visit to the convent
and what you've discovered makes you as dangerous to these people
as any of the others they've murdered. You're to forget about Janus,
Minna and you too, Herr Steiner. From now on, it's a matter for my
department. For your own safety, I would like you to get out of the
country, and stay out until this business is over.'

He held out his hand to Max. 'You can't get any further,' he said.
'Take her away till it's safe.' He took Minna's hand and bowed
over it.

'I'm not going,' she said.

'You may change your mind,' Holler answered. 'I hope so. For both
your sakes.' Then he was gone.

Curt Andrews found what he was looking for in the files of the
Munchener Merkur. They were old and yellow, and the newspaper
was dated September 1945. It was a small item low down on an inside
page devoted to unimportant home news of a non-political nature. The
paper operated under the guidance of the Control Commission. It was
headed TRAGIC ACCIDENT. Andrews read it, and took down the name
and address supplied. 1945. It was a very long time ago, but there
was just a chance that the family were still living there . . . He drove
to the modest suburb, and his hopes began to fade as he saw the new
houses and the evidence of extensive rebuilding. But the street name
hadn't been changed, and there it was, right at the end of the road on
the corner, a double-fronted house with a small garden. He parked
the car, went to the door and pressed the bell. It chimed instead of
ringing. Nobody came and he pressed again, longer and harder so that
the maddening little tune repeated itself. The door opened so quickly
that he was taken by surprise. He put on his ingratiating smile and
said, 'I'm looking for a Fräu Inge Brandt. Does she still live here?'

The woman was in her early forties, her dress was neat but drab
and she wore no make-up. 'You didn't have to ring like that,' she said
aggressively. 'I was round the back. Yes, my mother's still here. Who
are you?'

'I'm a reporter from the American *Daily News*,' he said. 'I'm doing
a story on your city and its growth since the war. Seen from the human
angle. I'd like to get some impressions from your mother of what it was
like after the war. I was told she'd been in Munich right through. We're
paying very well for information,' he added.

She didn't hesitate. 'Come in,' she said. 'My mother's in the back
garden. She's old, you understand, but her mind's very clear. We could
do with some extra cash – everything's got so expensive these days!'

The old woman was sitting in a garden chair with a rug spread over
her knees; she had white hair done up in a bun, and a wrinkled, sharp

featured face which made Andrews think of a bird with spectacles balanced on its beak. Her daughter bent down and spoke quickly to her; the mother glanced over to him, and nodded. 'There's a chair over there,' the daugher said. 'I'll bring out some coffee. My mother wants to know what you're prepared to pay.'

'Two hundred marks,' Andrews said. Inge Brandt had the broken voice of old age; it was throaty and masculine. She was very clear in her mind, just as her daughter said. Andrews guessed that she must be close to eighty. He spent the first fifteen minutes asking questions about the wartime conditions she had lived through, making notes, meaningless scribbles masquerading as shorthand. He was sympathetic and interested as she described the hardships of the last years of the war. Bombing, food shortages, living in shelters, the terrible casualties on the Russian front.

'And then,' he said. 'I heard you lost your little boy. Was that due to the war in any way?' The eyes were bright and they darted a shrewd look at him.

'No,' she said. 'It was a terrible thing; we were out shopping and he got knocked down by a man running past him; there were crowds everywhere, it was so quick I never even saw what happened. But my boy fell over, and when I picked him up he was dead. He'd broken his neck in some way. They never found the man who bumped into him.'

'How terrible for you,' Curt Andrews said. He knew exactly the blow the Russian agent had used to kill the child.

'In fact,' the old woman said, 'he wasn't really mine. Irma is, and I've a son living in America now, but Frederick was a foster-child. I took him in, you see, during the war. I think he was the son of someone high up in the Nazi Party. Not that I had anything to do with them myself. You must be sure to say that.'

'Oh, I will,' Andrews assured her. 'Of course.'

'I was sorry for the little fellow,' she said. 'People had no morals in those days. Children were being born all over the place. He was a lovely child, big blue eyes, and very bright. Quite a mischievious little boy . . . I was very upset over it.'

Curt Andrews put his notepad in his pocket and pulled out his wallet.

'I'm sure you were,' he said. The bright little eyes were fixed on his wallet, and the withered lips moved as he counted the notes. 'Thank you, Fräu Brandt,' he said. He laid the money on her knee, and she fastened a hand like a claw over the notes. 'This will make excellent copy. Especially the part about you taking in children. People love the human interest. Did you have any others besides Frederick?'

'No,' she said. 'He was the only one. A lady brought him to me when he was a few weeks old. I don't think he was hers, though. You can tell a mother when she handles her own child. Very well dressed, she was, I remember. She had a lot of fox furs.'

'And you never saw her again?' Andrews was on his feet. He shook hands without waiting for the negative answer. 'Good-bye, and thanks again. I'll send you a copy when it comes out.'

'She'd like that,' her daughter Irma said. 'She reads a lot.'

He waved good-bye to her as she stood at the front door. He got into his car and drove to his hotel; he was whistling. The first part of Gunther Mühlhauser's story was true. He had to decide what to do next, and he rejected the idea that he could handle the problem alone. Or even with CIA assistants, who could be sent to join him. He needed Heinrich Holler. He went upstairs to his room, opened the fridge and took out two miniature bourbons, and mixed them with ice and soda. He kicked off his shoes and stretched out on the bed, sipping the drink. It was all so obvious once you knew where to look. A monument of lies marked the grave of truth. The phrase appealed to him, and he couldn't remember where he'd heard it. He was a trader in lies, as adept as any of his colleagues in the game of secrets. He saw no moral dilemma in twisting facts into fiction, any more than in killing a human being to achieve a political end. It was the idealists he disliked, with their moral overtones intact; they could be bloody to the elbows, and still look down upon the pragmatists like himself. He hadn't forgotten the jibe of Heinrich Holler that he, Andrews, didn't care about the life of Mühlhauser's daughter Beatrix. He was going to enjoy squeezing the German until it was *his* finger on the trigger this time.

In his office Heinrich Holler issued instructions.

'I want copies of those indentiphotos given to every hotel and boarding-house in the city. And the same in Hamburg. All proprietors are to report to this office if anyone answering the descriptions takes a room. Circulate to Immigration at the airports.' He put down the phone. It was possible that the killers calling themselves Kesler and Franconi had already left the country, but he didn't think it likely.

The pieces were fitting together but the picture was not complete. The murder of Albert Kramer proved that. He was not even known as a former member of the Hitler Jügend; there was nothing to connect him with the Bunker, or with the mystery of Eva Braun's child. Unless he had been one of the men who kidnapped Mühlhauser, and spared his life because of the information Mühlhauser gave him. That information had sentenced him to death. But who knew that he was in possession of it, except the betrayer himself? And the betrayer had betrayed again, and sent a warning to his Russian masters. No wonder they had freed Gunther Mühlhauser from the labour camp.

And now, by some brilliant opportunism, he had settled himself among the enemies in Washington, the protégé of Curt Andrews and the CIA. He was going to enjoy telling Andrews that he had actually put a Soviet agent into place.

The pattern that was emerging made sense to Holler now; he had been quicker to follow the lead given him by Mühlhauser than Curt Andrews. He had checked the accident to Inge Brandt's foster-son with the Munich police, and the details were hall-marked Soviet Intelligence. So Hitler's son was dead. Janus was solved. He had said that to Mühlhauser and known by the readiness of his agreement that he was lying. Minna Walther had seen Gretl Fegelein's grave in the Convent of the Immaculate Conception. She believed it was the end of the search. No doubt the Reverend Mother intended her to think so. He lit another cigarette; smoking was bad for him. He was always told to stop when he had his regular medical check-up. Unfortunately it helped him to concentrate; also he enjoyed it. There was nothing he could do about his crippled leg, the result of Gestapo beatings, or the scars left on his mind by what he had suffered. At least his lungs were his own affair. He drew a pad towards him and began to draw a circle. He added details and the circle changed its shape. When he finished he sat and looked at it. Two heads, back to back, united. Janus, one of the oldest gods of mythology . . . Janus . . . Janus . . . And suddenly he understood. He pushed his chair back in excitement and struggled awkwardly to his feet. 'My God,' he said out loud. 'My God, that's what it means – not Hitler himself, but the twin forms of Janus and Jana!'

Not one child, but two. Eva Braun had given birth to twins. The boy was dead, but there was a daughter that Gretl Fegelein had separated from her brother as a precaution. And she was still alive.

That was what Mühlhauser had told Kramer and his undercover Nazis; because of this they had forgiven him his betrayal of the boy to the Russians. And then Mühlhauser had warned his Russian contact that he had been forced to reveal the boy's death. Kramer's knowledge of that was the reason for his elimination. And that meant that the chain of murders beginning with Sigmund Walther and anyone else who might have known what Janus represented had been a Soviet operation aimed at concealment, not discovery. Men and women had been killed, not to find the heir Hitler had left behind him, but to hide the fact that he had already been found and was dead.

Holler sat down again; he crumpled the drawing of Janus into a ball. Now the puzzle was coming into frightening focus. The Russians had a candidate of their own, primed and ready to step on to the stage of European politics as the puppet of the Soviet Union who had manufactured him. The evidence they had suppressed all those years ago would be produced as proof of his authenticity.

They weren't trying to find Eva Braun's daughter by the Führer, because Mühlhauser had withheld that last piece of information. He had bought his life by telling them about the boy, holding the girl in reserve for just the emergency which arose when Kramer questioned him. Very clever; Holler had underestimated the man's cunning and will to survive. Now the knowledge of Hitler's daughter was possessed by the neo-Nazi movement in West Germany . . . Mühlhauser had lied to him, passing the information of the boy's fate as if it were the only secret left. He had withheld the truth not only from the Russians, to whom he was bound by treachery, but also from the democracy of Western Germany. Holler could follow the twisted motives of a man who had been the friend of Heinrich Himmler; he knew from terrible experience, the power of the Black Knights' oath. Mühlhauser had tried to keep faith with it by hiding the daughter of his Führer until she could be of use to those who were working for a resurgence of National Socialism. The threat to his own child Beatrix had forced him to protect her at all costs, and by making a deal with Curt Andrews he had placed himself and his family in safety, and averted Russian vengeance by giving them Kramer as a victim. He would be very valuable to his controller when he was established in Washington as the protégé of the CIA.

The Vatican had taken Eva Braun's sister under its protection because she was seeking shelter for Eva Braun's child; the significance of a direct descendant of Adolf Hitler had brought the considerable diplomatic power of the Papacy into operation. They wanted to keep her hidden from the world, and the solution was so obvious that Holler couldn't forgive himself for being blind to it.

The girl was never coming out; the Reverend Mother of the Munich convent and her predecessor had instructions to keep her beyond the reach of outside contact. She could never be allowed to marry, produce children – it didn't need much imagination to see that she had been persuaded to become a nun.

Holler sighed in relief. The political acumen of the Vatican had seen the problems many years before they could become reality, and found a wise solution. He couldn't have wished for a better one himself. Let her stay in peaceful anonymity; nuns were happy people, possessed by a childlike trust in God and His goodness. He didn't need to fear her any more. His duty was to inform his Chancellor of her existence; it might be advisable to approach the Vatican with the object of moving her to a less vulnerable place and obliterating the links between her and the convent. Kramer's people could search for her in vain. The possibility of a Russian imposter posing as her brother was far more serious. Only the highest authority in Bonn could authorize the action Holler wanted to take to frustrate the Soviet manoeuvre. He would have to consult with his government about the plans he had in mind. There was plenty of time; evidence had to be collected and prepared for public scrutiny; the timing was vital.

He thought of his old friend Sigmund Walther, murdered to perpetuate a lie that had still to be told, and he remembered Minna and the journalist. Their danger was acute. They had followed the killers without knowing it, and their involvement with the search for Janus must sentence them to death. He reached for the phone to call their hotel and order them to leave, when there was a knock at his door. It opened and he saw Curt Andrews; the American looked bigger and more menacing. Holler put the phone down.

'Curt? I thought you were in Hamburg, nursing the Mühlhauser family.'

'And so I was,' Andrews said. He walked to the desk and stood looking down at Holler. 'But I felt it was time you and I had a meaningful discussion about the special relationship between our Agency and your Service. Before it gets to a higher level.' He pulled a chair forward and sat down without being asked.

'You've been holding out on us, Holler,' he said. 'Washington isn't going to like that.'

7

It was Kesler who made the call to the Walthers' house in Hamburg.

'My name is Aaron Levy,' he said. 'May I speak with Fräu Walther, please?' Franconi was beside him in the public booth. He saw Kesler frown. 'Oh, she's not? Oh, dear. She told me to call her about some jewellery. Can you please tell me where I can get in touch with her? It's very important, I have a client who won't wait.'

At the other end of the line, Minna's housekeeper hesitated. Jewellery – surely her lady wasn't selling anything? But Levy was a Jewish name and all the dealers were members of the Chosen Race, as she described them to herself.

'Hello, hello,' Kesler shouted into the phone; he grimaced and whispered an aside to Franconi: 'She's not there. I think we've been cut off – oh, yes, yes, I thought we'd been disconnected. Thank you. Hotel Kaiserhof – you don't know when she'll be back – I'll contact her there then. Thank you. Good day.' He turned to Franconi. 'She's in Munich – the last place I wanted to go. The woman didn't know when she was coming back.'

'What about Steiner?' asked Franconi.

'Paul said he'd be with her,' Kesler scowled, and shouldered his way out of the booth. 'I want to get everything finished as quickly as possible,' he went on. 'But I don't fancy going back to Munich. I've been seen and I could be recognized.'

They began to walk along the sunny street, two sober-suited men in earnest conversation. Franconi still wore the hat, which bothered him. He hated having his head covered. They drove their rented car out of the public car park, and set out for a drive. It was a warm day, and they took a route that brought them in sight of the sea. They stopped and watched the shipping in the great seaport.

'I'll go,' Maurice said. 'I'm not known. I'll settle the two of them and get out on the first flight. We'll meet in Geneva.'

'No, no, I won't do it like that,' Kesler said. 'I wouldn't have a moment's peace worrying about you. We'll go together and I'll stay low and wait for you. And promise me you won't take any risks.' He put his hand on Franconi's shoulder. 'Remember how much you mean to me.'

'I will,' Maurice Franconi said. 'Don't worry, Stanis. We're going to have our money and our house in Tangier. Leave the two of them to me.'

They decided not to check into a hotel together in Munich. Kesler went to a guest-house, and Franconi, armed with his briefcase and hand luggage, booked into a businessman's hotel where he merged perfectly into the background. Both used aliases and forged passports. The boarding house registered Mr Levy, resident in Antwerp, and the hotel accepted Maurice as an Italian from Milan. They didn't meet for dinner that night, and neither slept properly for worrying about the other. In the morning, Maurice telephoned Kesler. 'I've checked with the Kaiserhof. They're both there.'

'What are you going to do?' Kesler asked.

'Go in tonight. They have rooms on the same corridor.'

There was nothing Max could do about it; Minna had refused to go to West Berlin. He had tried persuasion, even resorted to the ruse of making love to her. She had surprised him by the vehemence of her refusal to listen to his arguments or to let him touch her. 'I'm not leaving Munich now,' she said. 'Holler knows something, that's why he wants to get rid of us. I said it and I meant it. He used Sigmund to do his investigating for him, and Sigmund died because of it. He's not going to fob me off now. I have as much right to know whether the child was really murdered or not – and if he was, why isn't the investigation over? You have a right, too; you came here to find out the truth and you're being frightened off because Holler wants to keep it to himself.'

'I'm not being frightened off,' Max interrupted angrily, 'because I believe Holler when he says we're in danger. He told me to take you away for your own safety. And it makes sense. Sigmund, Helm, Schmidt, Kramer – they can't leave us alive if they had to kill the others. We know too much, darling, don't you see? We've been following Sigmund's lead, and we've got even further than he did, because you found out that Gretl Fegelein was dead. It's the end of the road – you said that yourself, when you came back.'

'You want to give up?' she asked him. 'You've had your question answered, so now you'll sleep in peace – is that all it meant to you?'

'Stop trying to needle me, Minna,' he said. 'I'm not worrying about myself. I'm ready to stay behind and get what I can out of Holler, if only you'll go. I don't care if bloody Eva Braun had triplets, if it means you're in danger!'

He stopped and they stared at each other; he realized what he had said a few seconds later than she did.

'Not triplets.' She came and caught hold of him. 'Not Hitler and Eva

Braun,' she said. 'But a son and a daughter, Janus and Jana. That's what the code Janus means.'

They stood locked together. He felt her tremble, as if from excitement. 'And the girl is still alive,' Max said.

'She must be,' Minna said slowly. 'That's why Holler has taken the initiative.' There was something in her eyes which Max had never seen before. 'I've got to find her,' she said. 'Sigmund gave his life for this. I've got to carry it through for him.'

'I thought you loved me,' he said. 'But it's still him, isn't it?'

'No.' She shook her head, then reached out and touched his cheek; it was cool now. 'But what I feel about you doesn't change my love for him and what he tried to do for Germany. There's been so much treachery, so many lies. Albert Kramer, his great friend – the people Holler knew would try to stop him finding anything detrimental to the Nazis, the men who killed him and the people who sent them. If you really love me, you'll help me now.'

'Oh, Christ,' Max said desperately, 'I'd go to hell and back if you asked me. But think, my darling. What good is a girl to anyone? She'd never be a focal point for people like Kramer – they wouldn't follow a woman.'

'She could have a child,' Minna said. 'And the world has changed; you're thinking of the old Germany, but the Nazi attitude to women doesn't apply any more. Children, Church and Kitchen. What kind of a woman is she? What kind of monster does a monster breed?'

He didn't answer. He put his arm around her and tried to draw her close again. Her body was stiff, unresponsive.

'Will you help me find her?' she asked him.

Max Steiner had never believed in premonitions. He was impervious to superstition. But fear swept over him as he looked at Minna and knew that because he loved her so much, he was going to act against his instincts.

'If that's what you want,' he said. She put her arms round his neck and kissed him. They made love, and for a time he slept. When he woke she had gone to her own room. He had a feeling that what she had done was a reward.

Maurice Franconi had booked a table for dinner in the hotel restaurant. He had a drink in the bar first; he seated himself in a corner where he could see the doors. He felt unaccountably nervous, infected by the alarm of Kesler. He had worked out his plan, taking care of the smallest detail. He had gone up in the lift to the second floor and marked out the rooms numbered 47, 48. There was no one in the corridor; it was the hour when most people were in their rooms before going down to the bar or going out. He had noted the type of lock, and felt confident of picking it without any difficulty. And the weapon he carried was Kesler's deadly cyanide pen. He had come down by the stairs, so that route was familiar to him; washed his hands in the cloakroom, and bought a newspaper from the books tall in the foyer.

He drank one vodka and lime, making it last; he watched the couples who came into the bar, looking for a tall blonde woman and a dark man. He saw several who might have been his target, but didn't quite fit the description. He recognized Minna Walther and Max Steiner in the dining room. They had a table by the window, and he was across the room from them, sitting close to the serving door at a table allotted to non-residents when the restaurant was full. He ordered a light dinner; drank some white wine, and watched the man and woman he was going to murder. His observation was completely impersonal. As human beings they held no dimension for him beyond a target that had to be assessed and sighted correctly. He didn't form an opinion of Minna as a woman; he didn't like women on any level, even the most superficial. Max he judged in terms of strength and alertness, should anything go wrong. Their relationship was obvious; he saw the way the man reached out for her hand, and lit her cigarettes. They might well be in the same bed when he broke in.

'I've cabled my Director,' Curt Andrews said, 'so there's no way you can keep this under wraps. It's not a West German problem any more.'

Holler had hardly spoken; Andrews found his silence disconcerting. The air was hazy with cigarette smoke, and the ashtray in front of him was full of stubs.

At last he looked at Andrews. 'The daughter of Adolf Hitler is a world problem, not an exclusive for your department to use for American advantage. That is, if she really exists.'

'Don't try and bullshit me,' Andrews snapped. 'Mühlhauser told me the boy was killed, but nobody's found the girl. Or even knew she existed. It's my guess Gretl Fegelein kept her with her and took her to the convent.'

'And what possible problem can she represent if that is true?' Holler asked. 'I believe she's become a nun, and that, Herr Andrews, is the best possible solution for us all.'

'Oh, sure,' Andrews sneered. 'A bride of Christ, eh? What happens if she jumps over the wall sometime – maybe she doesn't know who she is, and she finds out and decides she's had enough of convent life ... If we've figured out what Janus means, then so will the Russians. And just how long do you think she'll stay behind that wall?'

'As long as I decide to keep her there,' Holler said. 'I give you my word, and I'll say the same to your Director, that the woman will never come out into the world. As for the Russians – you can leave that to me.'

Andrews shifted one big leg over the other. 'I might be content to do that,' he said flatly, 'but my Director won't. Nor will the Intelligence services of the other NATO countries. And we're duty-bound to inform them of what we've discovered. Just as you should have informed me, Holler, under the terms of our mutual aid agreement.' He shook his head. 'You withheld information, and that's an official complaint. I have an instruction from Washington. You'd better see it.'

Holler picked up the telex. He read it, folded it and handed it back. 'And will this satisfy you?'

'I won't know until I can judge the situation for myself,' Andrews said.

'And supposing,' Holler said quiety, 'I tell you to mind your own business and get the hell back to Washington?'

Andrews grinned contemptuously. 'You can try, my friend, but I don't think your Chancellor will be very happy when he hears about it. You're tied up pretty tight with us, Holler. Either you go along with the official request in that telex or I take the first plane to Bonn. I personally don't mind which way it plays.'

Holler appeared to be considering. He watched Curt Andrews's foot, in its polished slip-on shoe, swing backwards and forwards while he waited. He was trapped and he knew it. He would have to accede to the request made in the telex. Andrews had played it very cleverly. But not as cleverly as Holler intended to do. No trace of resentment showed on his face as he looked at the American.

'You have a right to the information; but I'll have to get authorization from my government to protect myself.' He stood up in dismissal. Andrews didn't move.

'How long will that take?'

'I should have an answer within twenty-four hours, maybe sooner,' Holler said.

Andrews got to his feet. 'Just so long as we don't find the lady's disappeared,' he said.

'We haven't yet established that she's there,' Holler reminded him.

'Then the sooner we find out the better,' Andrews said. 'I'll call you tomorrow.'

They didn't shake hands; Holler came to the door and opened it for him, and they nodded to each other like adversaries. Holler came back to his desk and sat down. He reached for the telephone and made the call to Max Steiner which Andrews had interrupted. There was no reply from his room or from Minna's; Holler checked with reception. Yes, they were still in the hotel and hadn't given notice they were leaving. Holler murmured a rare obscenity to himself. He knew who had refused to take his warning and his advice. Minna Walther wouldn't leave; he remembered her determination and the reminder of how he had used her husband, and how as a result Sigmund had died. There was no mistaking the loyalty and the strength of purpose in her; stronger than fear for her own safety and for the safety of the man she had taken as a lover. Yet not strong enough to keep her faithful to her husband's memory for a decent interval. Holler had married when he was in his twenties. His wife had saved herself when he was arrested by applying immediately for a divorce. He had never trusted a woman enough to marry for a second time.

He made an internal call. He had to protect Minna Walther and Max Steiner in spite of themselves. Then he put through a call to the Chancellor's office in Bonn and activated the scrambler.

The community of the Immaculate Conception were in the chapel for Benediction when the message came through for Reverend Mother Katherine. She knelt in the front pew, with two senior sisters on either side of her; the twenty-two sisters and three novices were ranged at her back, the six lay helpers last of all. The replacement for Father Grunwald was slightly older, and much less agile. He went through the service very slowly and reverently, and the morning Mass took ten minutes longer. Mother Katherine bowed her head at the Elevation of the Host for adoration, and the silvery tones of the nuns rose in the traditional hymn of praise. O Sacrament most Holy, O Sacrament Divine. For the first time in many years, Mother Katherine was unable to stop the tears filling her eyes. Love of God had blotted out pain and softened hatred into understanding; in time it would finally emerge as forgiveness. The penance she had chosen for herself had become harder as time passed; she tried to repress the memories awakened by the visit of her childhood friend that morning. No one had spoken her real name or reminded her of her father for many years. His image swam through the tears; a stern but gentle man, a tender husband and father; her mother had adored him, her elder brothers had both been killed with Rommel's Afrika Corps, and the family, reduced to three, had clung closer together in their grief. She was said to resemble her father; in the days when she looked in a mirror, she had tried hard to find him in her own reflection, but without success. And if she searched too long, then that other image would surface in her imagination, as it had done in nightmares as she was growing up. The struggling figure on the end of a wire noose . . . Hatred had nearly unbalanced her mind; the Roman Catholic faith had offered sanctuary against a world where materialism was the new religion. The doctrine of reparation for the sins of others by a life of prayer and service showed Freda von der Stein where sanity and purpose lay. She had taken her final vows in the Mother House in Salzburg. Ten years later she was sent to Munich and found that the past she had tried to escape was locked in with her. She blinked back the tears and concentrated on the hymn.

God was the arbiter of her fate; she had made Him a gift of her life when she became a nun. It was His will that she should find herself protecting what she hated most. When the moment came that she could look on the face of a certain novice and feel pure sisterly love in Christ, then her vocation was fulfilled. She prayed for that moment, as she did every day of her life. When Benediction was over and the last hymn sung, she led the way out of the chapel. In spite of herself she glanced at the back row of nuns, and then as quickly looked away. She could feel those other eyes upon her, watching, the head turning slightly till she was out of sight.

Sister Aloysius hurried up to her as she came out of the chapel into the main hall. 'Reverend Mother, excuse me, there was a telephone message. A Herr Heinrich Holler called. He asked you to telephone him as soon as you came out of chapel. He said it was most important. I've written the number down and put it on your desk.'

'Thank you, Sister.' She went into her private room, closing the door.

The scrap of paper with the number of the Munich police head-quarters lay like a white feather on the wooden desk. The Sister's rounded writing looked as if a child had taken down the message. Heinrich Holler. She knew well who he was, and what the message meant. The convent had kept him out, the power of diplomatic relations with the Vatican as its shield. She had been a young woman when she first came to the convent in Munich; she hadn't known who the woman and the child were; that secret was entrusted to her when she became the Reverend Mother.

And it was she who kept vigil beside the deathbed of Eva Braun's sister and promised to protect the girl from the evils of the world outside. Her hand had closed Gretl Fegelein's eyes when she was dead. But now the walls were breached. Poor, aged Father Grunwald had been struck down, and a man posing as a priest had got into the convent, asking for a woman who was dead. She had known then that the outside world couldn't be held back any longer. She had sent a message to Rome, and taken her childhood friend Minna down to the little crypt where the sister-in-law of Adolf Hitler had been buried. It was Mother Katherine's only hope of keeping the promise made by her Church, and when Holler telephoned she knew that it had failed. Gretl Fegelein's grave had not been proof enough that there was nothing left to hide. She dialled the number and asked to speak to Holler. He had known her father well.

He didn't ask for an appointment; she noticed that in spite of his courtesy. He arranged a time to call upon her. He was bringing a representative from the United States security services with him. She sat quietly after the conversation, one hand plying with the silver crucifix on its chain round her neck. Rome had given her instructions. She would obey and carry them out, but above all she must resist the cry of her own heart to be relieved of her responsibility. She had no right to hope for that, because the love Christ asked of her had still to conquer antipathy and fear. She closed her mind to everything but prayer. When she went to join the community for supper, she was serene. She had placed tomorrow in God's keeping.

'I'm tired tonight,' Minna said. 'Would you mind, Max?'

'Of course I mind,' he answered. They were holding hands, and he squeezed her fingers gently. 'I like making love to you, or haven't you noticed – don't be silly, darling – of course you're tired. That damned bed's too narrow for two to sleep comfortably. Let's have something with our coffee, and then we can go upstairs. Brandy?'

'No, not tonight. You're very good to me, Max. Why can't you be a pig sometimes?'

'Why should I be?' He played with her fingers; they were long and thin, with pale varnished nails. He found her hands exciting.

'Because then I wouldn't love you so much,' she said. The waiter came and took the order for coffee in the lounge. Max pulled back her chair and followed her out of the restaurant. He saw a man watching her as she passed his table; he was young and good-looking, and Max glared at him. She chose a corner table. He lit a cigarette and gave it to her.

'You know you've never said that to me before, out of bed.'

'That I loved you? How funny; I thought I had, many times.'

'No,' Max insisted. 'Never. Tonight was the first time. That makes tonight rather special, doesn't it?'

'Yes,' she said gently, 'I think it does. And you still don't mind if we don't sleep together – maybe I'm not as tired as I thought.'

'Oh yes, you are,' he said. 'A good night's sleep for you, and who knows I might just wake you early in the morning. I've been thinking about something. Here's our coffee.'

'What have you been thinking about?' He saw the intense look that changed her face and made it gaunt and watchful.

'About ourselves,' he said. 'You and me, for a change. Relax, my darling, we're not going to think or talk about anything else.'

'All right,' she said. She sighed. 'Just about us. Tell me what it was you were thinking.'

'Only that if you married me we wouldn't have to take separate rooms in hotels,' he said.

'Max,' Minna said, 'Max, please. You *are* married. You're not a man who can throw his responsibilities aside and be happy. I can't think of anything permanent yet; it's too soon after losing Sigmund. And I keep thinking how unhappy your wife must be.'

He leaned back in the chair, cradling the glass of brandy in his hands. He didn't feel angry, because he felt she was evading the issue. She had said she loved him. After that, in his mind, the other obstacles simply melted away.

'Minna,' he said firmly, 'let me tell you about my wife and family. And before I start I want you to understand one thing. If I'd never met you, I don't think I would have gone back. I've been unhappy and frustrated for years, and I haven't been faithful to my wife either. You imagine a sad, neglected woman, and fretful kids worrying because they haven't heard from Daddy.' He surprised her by laughing; it was mocking and angry. 'I married Ellie in England in the fifties. It wasn't exactly pleasant being a German in London at that time. The English hated us; I was very lonely and very guilty because of being German. It was a time of national self-disgust for most of us who were abroad. The concentration camps, the Gestapo, the murder of millions of Jews. I didn't know where to hide myself. Ellie wasn't just a pretty girl, she was friendly and understanding, and she loved me. We had a son and then a daughter and by this time I was with *Newsworld* and doing very well. I had my job. And Ellie had the children. She didn't need to mother me any more because there were Peter and Francine to look after, and her whole life revolved around them. They're not nice children, Minna. Maybe it's because she spoiled them, or maybe the mixture of her and me doesn't work very well. My son is a lout who's never thought of anything or anyone but himself since he was old enough to think at all. Francine whines and wheedles because he's a bully to her, but she's as selfish in her way as he is. My wife thinks that Freud and Spock rule the world, and the only function she and I have is to pamper and pander to our children. My work doesn't interest her; I don't interest her, except as Peter and Francine's father. Maybe I'm being unfair but that's the kind of marriage we have, and I don't want any more of it.'

He offered her the glass of brandy. 'I promise you one thing. If you walked out on me tomorrow, I wouldn't go back to Ellie.'

Minna sipped the brandy and handed it back; the glass was warm from his hands.

'My son Helmut,' she said. 'He's not selfish or anything like that. And he worshipped his father. He doesn't like me very much. And if I'm honest, I don't really like him. I've never admitted that before.'

'It's not an easy thing to face,' Max said. 'The world is full of misconceptions; one of the biggest is that you automatically love your blood relations.'

'Sigmund did,' she said. 'He loved me and his children and it didn't matter how different we were from each other. He loved his friends, and they loved him. I'm making him sound like a prig, aren't I – but that's not true. He was very much a man.'

'He must have been,' Max said, 'for you to be what you are. He wouldn't grudge you happiness – not the man I talked to in the Crillon. I've interviewed a lot of men and women with façades that fooled the outside world. I know what's real and what's fake. Your husband was the real thing. I wouldn't want to take his place, because I'm not like him. I'm just an ordinary man who loves you and wants to spend the rest of his life with you. Think of it like that.'

She smiled, and he thought she was truly beautiful at such a moment.

'I will,' she said. 'But you're not ordinary, not in the least. I'll go upstairs now. You finish your brandy. I won't lock the door – if you do wake early . . .' She leaned across and kissed him lightly on the mouth.

He sat on in the lounge, drinking slowly; the good-looking man with sleek blond hair who had ogled her in the restaurant was sitting at a table on the left. He was reading a newspaper, and it lowered for a moment as Minna walked past him. He left the lounge not long after she did, but Max Steiner didn't notice. He had made up his mind to so something that night which had been nagging at his conscience, and which his talk with Minna had made imperative. He went to reception and asked them to put in a call to Ellie in London.

Minna had undressed and, following a lifelong routine, she was brushing her hair. It was fine hair that crackled with static electricity and flew out in fine gold strands under the brush strokes. It soothed her when it was done by someone else. Sigmund used to brush it for her before she went to bed. It was often a prelude to making love. He liked her hair long, and she compromised to please him. It swept down past her shoulders when it wasn't held in place. She watched herself in the dressing-table mirror; how familiar and yet how alien the woman looked, gazing back at her. It was a young face, and the long hair was deceptive. She had always been tall, even as a child, with long limbs and an athletic body which rounded as she grew up. Rather like a boy, some of her aunts had said, not with approval. She had been dressed in an old suit of her brother's with her hair hidden under a cap when they were refugees from the Russians. The advance guard of the Soviet army were picked troops; picked for their savagery and Asiatic origins. Women in their eighties had been raped and left for dead by them. They had never seen a woman in a short skirt; the stories of atrocity and horror harassed the thousands fleeing to the safety of the Western Allied armies, their homes and possessions abandoned to the Russians. Be brave, her mother and father had told Minna, be a brave girl, whatever happens. How brave was she now, she asked herself . . . The brush was laid aside. Her son didn't see the courage in her, only repressed emotions. He reproached her for being Prussian, as if it were her fault. But Sigmund often told her she was brave, and kissed her on account of it. And Max Steiner loved her. She had told the truth when she said she loved him. She wanted him to know and remember that.

She switched out the dressing-table light and left the latch up on her bedroom door. She lay with the bedside light on for a few minutes, then she reached out and turned it off. She had said she was tired, too tired to take him into her bed. It wasn't the truth. She was restless and she wanted him. It was a deliberate act of self-denial. She was coming close to Sigmund, lying alone in the dark. She repeated the words spoken by her mother as they fled through bombed and burning villages with the noise of battle close behind them. 'Be brave, Minna. Be brave whatever happens.'

At last she fell asleep.

Franconi took the lift to the second floor; two women went up with him, a mother and daughter, overweight and well dressed, chattering in Dutch. He stood back to let them pass out at the first floor, and the younger woman gave him an interested smile. He ignored it, and continued up. When the doors opened three people were waiting. He hurried out into the corridor and they got inside; the red eye on the lift indicator travelled downwards. There was no one in the corridor as he walked along it, and he opened the door to the stairs and lightly ran down to the floor below. Room 47. Adjoining Room 48. The woman had gone upstairs early and alone. He checked his watch. It was still only eleven. She could be having a bath, reading, waiting for the journalist to come and join her. It was too early to do anything. He knew there was a cubbyhole on every floor where the laundry baskets and cleaning materials were stored. He slipped inside and perched on a basket lid with the door just ajar. It gave him a clear view of the corridor and the two rooms.

In the next hour people came up and went to their bedrooms; there was a lot of talk and closing of doors, the lift was busy. It grew quieter and his watch said it was after midnight. Max Steiner had not appeared. Franconi had slight cramp in one calf, and he got down and moved outside the cubbyhole. It was very quiet. The red eye of the lift was stationary on the indicator for the ground floor.

She must be asleep by now. But what was the lover doing? A quarrel, perhaps – he didn't think so. He had seen her kiss him good night. It was twelve twenty-five.

He looked up and down the corridor once more and again to make sure that the lift was still at rest. Then he slipped the piece of cellophane out of his pocket to pick the lock of room 47, and moved towards the door.

Max was not quite sober when the call came through; he had ordered two more brandies, making the tedium of waiting an excuse. He heard the operator on the line. 'Mrs Max Steiner take a personal call from Hamburg . . .' And then Ellie's voice, sounding higher than normal, her Midwest accent stronger.

'Is that you, Max?'

'Yes,' he said. 'How are you? How are the children?'

'We're just fine,' came the answer quickly. 'How are you?'

'I'm fine too.' The stilted exchange continued while she told him about Peter and Francine. They liked London; their friends had taken them sightseeing, to the Tower and the waxworks at Madame Tussaud's. They were going to take a picnic and visit Windsor Castle the next day. He had a vision of the family party going down in the car with sandwiches and flasks of coffee, and the inevitable cans of Coke for his son and daughter. Ellie driving them before her on the tour, determined to improve their minds, while they squabbled and she refereed, being as always scrupulously fair . . . It was like a scene from somebody else's boring home movie. He cut it short because the brandy had made him tactless.

'Ellie – listen, never mind the children for a minute. I want to talk to you about something important.'

'So far as I'm concerned, the children *are* important.' The reply was curt.

'I know they are,' he despised himself for placating her, but he wanted to tell her and get it over. 'It concerns them too. Ellie, I've been thinking while we've been apart.'

'Funny, so have I.'

'I think we're in a mess,' he said. 'It's probably my fault, but I can't just go back and take up the old life.' There was a pause, and then she said,

'I can't either, Max. That's what I've been thinking too. I've talked it over with Tim and Angela and they agree with me. Peter and Francine are so much happier than they were in Paris.'

He didn't mean to lose his temper but he did. 'To hell with Peter and Francine! That's all you ever think about – the children, the children – I'll bet they're happy, doing just what they like and running circles round you. I called you to tell you something.' He took a deep breath to calm himself, and wished he hadn't lost control.

'You've met someone else,' his wife said. 'That's it, isn't it? That's why you've rung exactly once since we left, and now you have the gall to wake me up and disturb my friends at this hour – you're drunk, too, I can tell – '

'Ellie, please,' he begged in desperation; it shouldn't have developed into a row. If he hadn't said what he did about the children she wouldn't be so angry . . . 'Ellie, I'm terribly sorry. I should have called or written but I couldn't. Can't you see I didn't want to spring this on you, when you came home? I wanted to warn you about the way I felt . . .'

'You didn't have to warn me. I knew it was over when you walked out on us and went off on your own. I hope you do a great piece for your magazine. I hope you'll find it's worth losing your family. I'm going to get a divorce. If you can't be a father to the children, I'll find someone else who can!'

He felt a horrible mixture of anguish and relief.

'If that's what you want,' he said. 'Don't be angry, Ellie, please . . .'

'Oh, go to hell! Go back to your Kraut girlfriend!' The line went clear.

Kraut. She had never used that word before, even when they quarrelled seriously. Kraut. Hun. Boche. The scornful epithets of enemies; he was more drunk than he realized, because he looked furiously at the telephone and said loudly in English, 'To hell with you, too.' The lounge was empty; or nearly so; two men were still sitting drinking beer in a corner table. He supposed they were residents. Reception was closed, and a night porter sat in a cubicle reading a paperback. Max began to walk to the lift. His anger had disappeared, leaving a sick unhappy feeling in which there was more guilt than regret. He'd done it so badly, so crudely, just because he wanted to make sure of Minna and tear down the last obstacle to full possession of her. Because he had never possessed her, except in sexual climax. She had eluded him, keeping some part of herself in reserve. Even when she said she loved him, he sensed an area of privacy that excluded him. He weaved a little on his way to the lift, and one of the two residents in the lounge watched him and frowned. Max went into the lift, and the man hurried across to go up with him. 'Which floor?' he asked.

'Second.' Max scowled at him. He wanted to go to Minna, to take her in his arms and tell her his wife wanted a divorce, there was nothing to stop them – but she hadn't wanted him to come. She was tired, she said. In the early morning if he woke . . .

The lift stopped, and the doors opened. He stepped out. The lights were dimmed slightly in the long corridor during the night. The man watched him walk towards his bedroom door and, satisfied, pressed the button to descend. Room 43, room 44, 45, 46, Minna's room, 47. Max stopped suddenly. The door was ajar.

Maurice Franconi found that the bedroom door was not locked. The latch had been put up; all he had to do was turn the handle. He wore cotton gloves, easy to pull on and off. Very gently he eased the door open a crack, and saw there was no light inside. A glance over his shoulder showed the corridor empty. He pushed the door and eased himself inside. It took a minute or more before he became accustomed to the faint light showing from inside, and could distinguish objects in the darkened room and move towards the bed. He had a very acute sense of another human being's presence; he could tell in the pitch dark if a place was occupied, like an animal prowling for prey. He didn't hear Minna Walther breathing, but he knew she was there before he could see the outline of her body in the bed.

He walked carefully across the floor, testing it for loose boards at every step; there was one creak and he froze. Nothing changed; the woman didn't stir. Franconi reached the side of the bed. He could see perfectly by now; her head was dark against the white pillow. She was lying on her side, one arm outside the covers. He smelt gardenias, and recognized the scent she was wearing. He made a little grimace of disgust. Sickly, cloying smell. Women turned him over; much more than they did Kesler, who didn't seem to mind them. He put his right hand in his pocket and found the pen. He brought it out slowly. He would have to lean across to get it close to her face. Then he heard the sound of the lift doors opening in the corridor. He hesitated; he had left the door of the room wide enough to give himself light. If anyone passed and saw it – it only needed a few seconds to puff the deadly gas into the sleeping woman's face, a few more to close the door and keep it shut till the latecomer had gone. If it were the journalist come to visit his lover, Franconi would be ready for him. The pen would dispose of him too. He moved very quickly, leaning over and towards Minna, and that was when she brought her arm up to rest above her head.

Franconi started back and dropped the pen. He saw the door push open and knew that he had no chance to hide. He didn't carry a gun, and the pen was gone. He was across the floor in seconds, and as Max Steiner stepped into the room, Franconi crashed against him, and sent him reeling sideways with a savage elbow chop. He didn't wait to strike again and kill him, because he heard Minna's scream behind him. He swerved into the corridor, and ran for the stairs. He cursed in breathless Italian, skipping down the flights to the ground floor, and there he stopped and waited. He had to get out of the hotel, but not to be seen. To be seen would identify him as the attacker. He had to walk out unobserved, or hide until he could slip out in the morning.

He opened the door leading into the lounge and heard the telephone at the porter's desk ringing. He saw two men in the lounge race towards the lift, and he flattened himself in the shadows. From the office behind the reception desk, two more men appeared, and Franconi broke out into a sweat of fear. They were detectives; the hotel was staked out, and he had walked into the trap set for him. The exits would be closed; he couldn't get away. He opened the door again and peered out. He couldn't stay where he was, the stairs would be searched immediately. He had to place himself somewhere that didn't excite suspicion. His initial panic was fading; his sharp intelligence raced through every possibility and settled on the one that Kesler had always taught him to use in an emergency. Never run. Never draw attention to yourself. Blend into the scenery.

The scenery was the residents' TV lounge, which was in semi-darkness and close enough to the stairs exit for him to slip through to it. He bent low and hurried across the little space to the big, dimly lit area with its sofas and tables and chairs. He made his way to a far corner, and stretched himself out in a deep armchair in front of the set. He peeled off the cotton gloves, cursing them for their loose fit and the loss of the cyanide pen. But leather gloves were difficult to use delicately, and a man wearing them in a hotel at night would be instantly suspicious. He rammed the gloves down the side of the chair. There, with his hands folded across his chest, and his mouth ajar snoring, he was found by Holler's security men twenty minutes later.

In the bedroom upstairs Max held Minna in his arms. She was trembling; he could feel it, but apart from her extreme paleness, she was calm. Holler was expected at any moment; a detective was on guard outside the door. The hotel was being searched and the registers checked for anyone resembling Max's muddled description. He had the vaguest impression of a man, glimpsed as he lay half dazed on the ground. Not too tall and not very big. Dark or fair, old or young – he couldn't tell them anything more. No weapon had been found, nothing but a fountain pen which had rolled under the bed; it didn't belong to Minna but it could have been lost by the previous occupant of the room.

'Oh God,' Max kept saying, 'if I'd been a few minutes later – '

It was Minna who comforted him. 'But you weren't,' she said gently. 'And nothing happened to me. I'm quite all right, darling. I was just shaken, that's all. It might have been a rape – someone who'd seen the door wasn't locked, I may not have shut it properly, and they came in and saw a woman in bed – '

'It was the man who killed Kramer and the others,' Max said. 'He was going to kill you. Just like Holler said. I'll never forgive myself for letting you stay here and not taking his advice.'

'You couldn't have made me go,' Minna said. 'I make my own decisions, darling. And there's one thing we can be thankful for; they'll catch the man. Then we'll know we're safe.'

'We're leaving first thing in the morning,' Max insisted.

She shook her head. She disengaged herself and moved away from him. 'No,' she said quietly. 'I'm staying to the end. Nothing can alter that.'

There was a knock on the door and, before Max could reply, Heinrich Holler came in.

In the sitting room of her friends' Putney house, Ellie Steiner sat and cried. There was a cup of tea beside her which she couldn't drink, and Angela had an arm round her shoulders and was trying to calm her.

'Try to be sensible,' she was saying. 'You said he was drunk – you can't take that call seriously. He'll probably ring tomorrow full of apologies.'

'Oh no, he won't.' Ellie blew her nose and wiped her eyes. 'He wasn't drunk when he wouldn't come with us after we'd been threatened. He's a bastard, Angela. The more I think of the way he's treated me and the children, the more I see what a bastard he is! I think he got drunk so he'd have the courage to tell me – '

'But you've been thinking on these lines yourself,' the other woman pointed out. She was a practical girl, and she had never seen Ellie's marriage to Max as a permanent relationship. He was too volatile, too obviously irritated by his family; she personally didn't like him much, whereas she was deeply fond of Ellie. She liked Ellie's earnestness and sense of responsibility; she shared the same enlightened views on child rearing and the priorities of motherhood. She would never have admitted to prejudice, but she didn't like Germans.

'You haven't been happy,' she said. 'Never mind him, think of yourself. Now face it, Ellie, you said so the other evening to Tim. That's what matters – how you and the children feel. I think this may be a blessing in disguise.'

'I don't want to lose him,' Ellie Steiner said. She blew her nose again. 'A broken home is terribly bad for children – '

'Not as bad as parents' quarrelling,' Angela said firmly. 'If he wants to go, then let him. Only you see that you get what's due to you and he provides properly for Peter and Francine. We'll find you a nice little flat, near us, and you'll meet lots of people – ' She was working herself up to anger and ignored the mumbled admission from Ellie that she still loved him. 'You're a damn sight too good for him,' she said. 'You'll meet someone else, and be really happy. Now drink that tea, and come up to bed. I'll give you a Mogadon, and you'll sleep right through.' Angela had a square little English face and her jaw set aggressively. 'If he rings again, you let me answer him. He won't do this sort of thing in a hurry when I've had my say. Come on, Ellie dear. Upstairs.'

She led Max's wife up to her room, and made her swallow a sleeping pill. Then she tucked her in solicitously, and went back to her own bed and her husband.

'Bloody Germans,' she said, settling down beside him. 'The sooner she gets rid of him, the better for all of them.' Her husband made a sound of agreement.

There were 218 people staying in the Kaiserhof; apart from the guests there were twelve men who were not registered and had been in bed with lady guests or were on their way out when they were stopped by the police, one drunk found snoring in the TV lounge, who turned out to be staying at another hotel, and the night staff of thirteen men.

Holler interviewed every male considered physically capable through age or proximity of making the attack upon Minna Walther. The married men registered with their wives were excluded. That left the twelve who had remained in the hotel surreptitiously, four homosexuals staying in adjoining rooms, who immediately attracted Holler's interest, the drunken Italian found in front of the TV, and the night staff. The thirteen night staff were all in their late middle age, all with *bona fide* backgrounds as residents of the city and established employees of the hotel. He interviewed the remaining suspects in the manager's office; the hotel remained closed and no one was allowed to leave.

The description of the two Swiss, Kesler and Franconi, did not fit any pair of individuals. The homosexuals were ruled out as soon as he saw them. An elderly businessman and a teenage pimp with a record of soliciting – the man's embarrassment was pitiful when he was questioned – and two antique dealers, both so effeminate and slight that from behind they could have passed as women. Neither could possibly have thrown Max Steiner off his feet. But there were five men of medium height with blond hair, and another three whose colouring didn't fit but whose age and physique did. Every one of them had identification which at first check seemed genuine. Of the eight suspects, Holler mentally reserved three. There was a Bavarian musician, who had picked up an elderly woman staying at the hotel and, according to the woman herself, had not gone to bed with her as he had indicated. He had sat up talking and suddenly excused himself. There was a young engineer from Basle who had booked in for the night en route to Prague. His papers were in order, but it seemed an expensive choice for a man of his age for one night, and there was something ill-disposed about him which alerted Holler. The last was the textile dealer from Milan who had gone to sleep in the TV lounge. His story checked out easily. His hotel confirmed that he was staying there; the Milan address was authenticated by a telephone call, and his passport was in order. What worried Holler was his eagerness to help. All the other suspects had complained in varying degrees; some became very abusive. But the fair Italian was complaisant about being kept in the hotel and investigated; he was a shade too co-operative, and Holler didn't equate that with the Italian temperament. He thanked everyone and dismissed them, promising to release them from the hotel as soon as possible, and when they had gone he began to think and chain-smoke.

The killer had not got out of the hotel. The time factor made it impossible for anyone to have left because the main exit in the front, the service exits and the fire escapes were guarded by his men, and as the alarm was raised all the doors were locked. This time it was one killer, not two, and from Max Steiner's vague impression it could be the younger and smaller of the two men who had killed Schmidt in Berchtesgaden and stayed in the *pension* together at the time Father Grunwald was attacked. And he was there, in the hotel, hidden behind a false identity and a well-documented background which would take more than a few days to break down. Holler had nothing on which to arrest any of them; unless he could find some piece of evidence or identification he would have to let them go in the next few hours. The man he was hunting would never be found again once he left the Kaiserhof and slipped into the Munich streets.

It was possible that a new assassin had been employed and the others withdrawn, since the Reverend Mother had seen one of them at close quarters. But Holler didn't think so; if his instinct was right and it was one of the original pair who had begun the chain of murders with the killing of Sigmund Walther then the proprietress of the *pension* would certainly be able to point him out. An identity parade could be held in the hotel, with Minna and Max Steiner to reinforce the principal witness. If she were unable to see one of her clients in the line-up then he would have to release the suspects.

He looked the number up in the telephone directory and dialled. It was very early in the morning and he had to wait some minutes before it was answered. The daughter took the call; no, her mother was not at home. Yes, she supposed she could come to an identity parade, but she didn't think she'd be much help. She sounded rather breathless, as if she had been running to catch the telephone before it stopped ringing. Really, she couldn't remember all that much about the Swiss gentlemen. They had a lot of guests staying a few nights and already she wasn't too sure what either of them had looked like. She didn't remember saying one of them had fair hair . . . No, it didn't come back to her at all . . . Holler put the telephone down. She wasn't going to get involved; he knew the type of person who regarded any contact with the police as a social stigma. If she or her mother did recognize the younger of the two men they wouldn't say so. Then he paused, the lighter aflame, the cigarette in his lips waiting to be lit. He made a second call.

At the other end of the telephone line the woman replaced the receiver with shaking hands. Her eyes were wide with terror, and she whimpered as Kesler brought the gun to her breast. 'I didn't tell, I didn't . . .' He nodded at her encouragingly and shot her through the heart. Her mother lay dead in her bed upstairs. He looked at her as her body slid down, buckling from the knees, and collapsed in a ragdoll heap at his feet. 'You didn't,' he said softly, 'and you're not going to now.' He left her there and slipped out of the back entrance into the street.

When Franconi didn't contact him Kesler knew that the plan had gone wrong. He walked through the empty streets in the pre-dawn and passed the entrance to the Kaiserhof Hotel. He walked on past the police cars parked outside and closed his eyes against a rush of tears. Maurice had been caught. He didn't even think of his own safety. His lover wouldn't give him away; he didn't consider that as a risk. But if Maurice were cornered and alive then he, Kesler, had to protect him as much as he could. He caught an early bus, filled with workers on the first shift, and hurried to the *pension* where they had stayed before.

He got in through the rear door; he knew where the mother and daughter's bedrooms were; there were only ten bedrooms in the place. He shot the older woman as she slept, and caught the younger on her way down to answer the telephone. Nobody else would recognize Maurice. He went back to his small boarding house, let himself in and sat on the bed, his shoulders sagging, his head cradled in his hands. He wept for the man he loved, then he packed his clothes and left some Deutschmarks on the dressing table. He caught the first train out of the city travelling to Salzburg. From there he would fly to Zurich and then on to Geneva.

He bought a newspaper at the station and scanned it, sick with anxiety, and suddenly he began to hope. There had been an attempted assault on a woman staying at the Kaiserhof. No names were being issued for the time and a number of suspects were being questioned by the police. He hadn't got away, but he hadn't been caught outright. Maurice always kept his head; hope surged in him. As his plane took off and thrust upwards through the brilliant sky, Kesler said a prayer to the patroness of his youth in Poland, the Miraculous Virgin of Cracow, for Maurice Franconi's safe return to him. He would never have abjured his atheism and prayed for himself.

Everyone was informed of the identity parade; the hotel staff and the twelve men selected for the initial investigation, were politely asked to wait in the closed cocktail bar. Coffee and sandwiches were served, and Holler's chief subordinate apologized for the delay, and assured them that it was merely a routine. But the hotel remained closed, and nobody was allowed to leave. It was nearly lunchtime when Minna and Max Steiner saw Holler again. He had decided to hold the parade in the main hall, where his witnesses could watch from the lounge. 'I'm afraid it'll be a waste of time,' Max said to him. 'I didn't see anything but a shape in that half darkness. Minna saw nothing at all, she just woke up with the crash when I fell.'

'I know that,' Holler nodded. He knew that Steiner resented Minna being brought into the identification; he had tried to resist the suggestion, but Holler insisted. Holler sympathized with Max Steiner; he didn't want her to be upset by trying to pick out the man who had attempted to kill her. Holler had listened, and apologized, but Fräu Walther was needed; someone would come and bring them both down to the lounge. Privately he thought that Minna Walther was not nearly as fragile as Max Steiner thought.

When they came downstairs Max had his arm round her, and Holler thought again: He's in love and he's a fool. She doesn't need protecting: she's not afraid of anything . . .

'You stand here, Please.' He positioned them in the archway leading to the lounge. They could be seen from the main hall.

In the cocktail bar Maurice Franconi tried to eat his sandwiches. The strain was affecting his stomach, which was revolted by food. He was glad of the coffee. He didn't join in the complaints of the others; he and the Swiss engineer kept themselves apart. The Swiss was taciturn, and to Franconi he seemed very nervous.

'What's the good of locking us up here?' somebody demanded loudly. 'It happened in the dark, didn't it? That's what I understood – so how could anyone be identified?'

'It's a police trick,' someone else answered, 'just to keep us here. I'm going to take this up with my lawyer when I go home. It's disgraceful; I've missed an important business meeting this morning.'

Franconi listened and said nothing. Who could they have found, apart from the woman who was asleep and the man he had flung aside in a dark room – it was all nonsense, just as that idiot had said, moaning about a business meeting – if only he could have got word to Kesler. He must know it had all gone wrong and be frantic with worry. Franconi wondered what Kesler would do. The sensible thing

The Grave of Truth

was to get out as fast as he could and go to ground in Switzerland. That was what he, Maurice, would have done, and yet part of him, which was afraid, hoped that perhaps Kesler was still in Munich . . . He reproached himself for letting his imagination take a morbid trend; nobody could identify him, and the police would have to let them all go for lack of evidence.

They'd be asked to stay in the city for the next twenty-four hours, and they'd all give that assurance, before they started telephoning lawyers and making furious complaints. He'd be out of Munich within an hour of walking through the hotel doors. They couldn't prove anything against him, or the parade wouldn't have been necessary. He urged himself to keep calm and appear confident. It was funny how guilty some of the men were looking; Kesler always said most human beings had something to hide . . .

Holler's assistant appeared at the door of the cocktail bar. He opened it and stood aside. 'So sorry to have kept you waiting, gentlemen. Come through this way, and line up over there. That's right. Thank you.'

Franconi saw them standing inside the archway; the tall blonde woman and the journalist. His heartbeat steadied. Just those two, as he'd expected. Neither of them had seen anything they could identify. He took his place in the line-up.

Holler had come to stand beside Max: 'Do you see the man who attacked you last night?'

'No,' Max said. 'It could have been any of them.'

Holler turned to Minna. She shook her head. Franconi had been watching them, and he gave a slight smile.

'That's what I was afraid of,' Heinrich Holler said. 'It was just too dark. But we have one more witness. Let's see what she thinks –' He turned and snapped his fingers. The little black and white terrier bitch was slipped free of her lead. She had been travelling on a special charter flight from Holler's home in West Berlin. Franconi stood rigid as the little dog scampered through into the main hall. His nerves were screaming as the terrier trotted forward and then stopped, her head cocked to one side, her bright eyes like buttons. He hadn't killed her because she'd looked at him and licked his hand. Suddenly she saw him, and she bounded forward with a happy bark of recognition and leapt round his legs, wagging her tail in delight and trying to jump up into his arms. He didn't kick her away; he just stood motionless, until Holler came towards him. He smiled at Franconi. 'The little dog seems to know you,' he said. 'I think I may have something else that belongs to you, too.' He brought his right hand up very quickly, and the gold pen was pointing its lethally charged tip an inch from Franconi's face. He reacted involuntarily, with the instinct for danger that had several times saved his life. He leaped backwards and shielded his face with his arm.

'Yes,' Holler murmured, 'it is your property. You will accompany the officers to police headquarters. The rest of you gentlemen may leave now.' He didn't see his men take Franconi. He swung round and turned his back on him.

'It sounds as if you're trying to blackmail me,' Heinrich Holler said. 'If so, Herr Steiner, you're making a stupid mistake.'

'I was sent here by my magazine to write an investigation of Sigmund Walther's murder. I'm living on an expense account, and doing an assignment I asked them to finance. I owe them the story. That's all I'm saying.'

'Not quite,' Holler interposed. 'You're suggesting that unless you and Minna see this woman for yourselves, you're going to write the story of Adolf Hitler's children for *Newsworld*. Which may or may not be desirable from my government's point of view. If that isn't blackmail, what is it?'

It was Minna who answered him. 'It's a fair exchange,' she said. 'If you don't mind the story being printed, then there's nothing more to say. If you want Max to give up something which could make him the best-known political journalist in Europe, then you owe him a favour in return. And you know very well what you owe me. My husband's life.'

'Sigmund knew what he was doing,' Holler said. 'Now you're blackmailing, Minna. I told Sigmund that he was going into something dangerous, and that I couldn't protect him. He understood the risks and accepted them. Nobody regrets his death more than I do.' He stared at her and then at Max; his expression was contemptuous. 'What good will it do Sigmund if you see a woman for a few minutes? – she'll never be interviewed or seen by anyone again.'

'What harm is there in seeing her?' Max asked. 'Minna has suffered a lot; you may not approve of us, Herr Holler, but you've no right to judge. I'll give up the story if you'll show us what we've been looking for. And I'll give you a sworn undertaking that I won't mention anything that could embarrass you or the West German government.'

Holler didn't answer for some moments. They were silent, watching him. He couldn't let Steiner write the truth; premature exposure would forewarn the Russians. The revelation that Hitler's son was killed had to be made by Holler, and when it was authorized by Bonn. There would be no mention of a twin sister.

'If you do that,' he said at last, 'and I want the same from Minna, then you can be present when I see the woman. On the condition that neither of you attempts to talk to her. Is that understood?'

'Yes,' Max said. 'If you draw up what you want us to sign – '

'It'll be ready this afternoon. Come back here at three, and we'll go to the convent. I shall have an American colleague with me.'

'She's there?' Minna said. 'You're sure?'

Holler nodded. 'I can't think of a better place to hide a girl, can you? I'll see you at three o'clock.'

They began to walk back to the hotel; Max held her arm linked close to him. 'What's the matter, darling? You seem upset.'

'He thinks she's a nun,' Minna said. 'I can't believe it; it's too ironical. I am nervous, Max. I want to see her for myself, and at the same time' – she turned to him – 'I dread it.'

'But why? Don't you see it's the best possible solution? She'll never know who she is, and she'll never pose any threat to anyone. There won't be any legacy from Hitler now. The Catholic Church will have seen to that.'

'I can't imagine it,' she said. 'Do you suppose she'll look like him?'

'I don't think so,' Max replied. 'Probably take after Eva.'

'She was a very stupid woman,' Minna said slowly. 'Hysterical, neurotic . . . Girls tend to be like their mothers, don't they – my daughters look more like me than Sigmund . . . A nun – I just can't imagine it.'

'I bet she's a perfectly ordinary woman,' Max insisted. 'Convent-reared, pumped full of religion and living a nice celibate life. No grandchildren, darling, no chance for anyone to make political capital out of her. Come on, let's take a taxi and I'll buy us both a drink before lunch. You mustn't be worried about seeing her – it's what you wanted, isn't it?'

'Yes,' She managed to smile at him. 'Yes, of course it is. I'd like that drink. What are you going to write about, if you can't tell the truth? And do you mind too much – giving it up for me?'

'I don't give a damn,' he said. 'All I want is for you to be happy, and put everything behind you. So we can start afresh. As for the story, it's going to be all about Sigmund Walther and how he tried to unify and help his fellow Germans. I've thought of the heading: "Death of a patriot." Do you like it?'

'It's wonderful,' she said softly. 'And so are you.'

'Children,' Ellie Steiner said, 'we're going home.'

'Oh no! Why – we like it here! I don't want to go back to Paris – ' Peter's face flushed, and he scowled. He noticed that his mother looked red round the eyes and seemed to be nervous.

Francine made a face. 'I don't want to go either,' she said. 'I like it better here. Why do we have to go back?'

'Don't you want to see Daddy?' Ellie asked.

'Not much,' her son said. 'Why can't he come here – '

'Peter, you don't mean that. I know you've missed him, just like I have, and Francine too. And he misses us.'

'He doesn't phone up and he doesn't write,' the boy pointed out. 'I don't call that missing us. I'm not going.' He threw himself backward into one of the chintz armchairs; his mother had explained how this would damage the springs, but he went on doing it.

'Ask Daddy to come here,' Francine insisted. 'Tell him we don't want to go back to Paris. I hate the *lycée* – they make you do so much homework – English schools are much better.' Ellie looked at them in turn, begging for co-operation. They were seldom united about anything, but she saw their resistance as a proof that Paris was perhaps not the best place for them, since they disliked it so much. It was their home, and surely if children were well orientated and secure they would want to go back to it. Admittedly they were temporarily going to a progressive school where there was less emphasis on work and more on personal initiative, and of course nobody frustrated them – but even so, it was an indication of how badly she and Max had failed to make them happy at home . . .

'Please, Mummy,' Francine coaxed. 'Let's wait for a little while longer – wait till Daddy sends for us?'

Which he won't, was Peter's silent response. With any luck, he's left. He won't hit me again, anyway.

'I can't do that, darling,' Ellie said. Angela believed that absolute honesty was best with children. They only suffered through lies and treating them as inferiors. But Ellie couldn't tell them the truth because she had a miserable feeling that neither of them would care. Whereas she did, and nothing her friends could say could alter her unhappiness at losing Max. She felt bitter, and angry, but this was defensive. She didn't hate him as much as she loved him, and she was honest enough to admit this.

'Don't you love Daddy?'

'No,' said Peter.

'Yes,' Francine hesitated. 'But I'd rather stay here.'

Then she began to cry; Peter, to his astonishment, felt like doing the same. He didn't love his father, he insisted to himself, biting his lips to stem the tears. He didn't, he didn't . . . When Ellie put her arms round them both, she was crying too.

'All right, all right, darlings,' she murmured. 'Don't get upset, now, please . . . we won't go back then, we'll stay here – '

She didn't understand, and nor did he, why Peter suddenly wrenched himself free of her and raced upstairs to lock himself in his room. He had been fighting his father so long, and suddenly he was frightened and miserable because at last he'd won.

By teatime, their mother had recovered her composure. She was cheerful and made plans for the weekend. There was no mention of Paris or going home. She told Angela that evening that the children had decided for her what was best for all of them.

She would very much like Tim to handle the divorce.

Curt Andrews had put a call through to Washington the previous evening; he had gone to the American Consulate, and waited through until 1 a.m. to speak to his Director. It was a longer call than the Director normally tolerated with a subordinate; Andrews talked for most of the time. The Director listened, interposing a question or two, and then told Andrews to stay where he was and wait for a decision. Andrews dozed in the office, until the call came through at 4 a.m. His instructions were brief; he was smiling when he hung up. He went back to his hotel, showered and went to bed, without any intention of sleeping. He rested physically, and began to work on his plan of action. He had been trained to present himself with likely problems and then set about solving them; so far as he could see, the real initiative didn't rest with him or Heinrich Holler. But the directive was clear, and it had come down from the White House. Nobody who could be used as a focal point for German unity must fall into the hands of the Soviet Union. Assurances from Heinrich Holler were not sufficient guarantee to allay American anxiety. Andrews could hardly wait for the coming confrontation. He fell asleep in the early morning, and woke at nine; the appointment Holler had made was for late afternoon. Andrews had a large breakfast, and went back to the Consulate. There were no further messages and he had lunch with the Consul and his family. An official car drove him to the Convent of the Immaculate Conception at exactly three forty-five; he waited in the parked car until he saw Holler arrive and get out. To his astonishment he saw that a man and a woman were with him.

'Reverend Mother?' Sister Aloysius came into the Superior's private room.

'Tell Sister Dominic that Sister Francis should come to the parlour at four o'clock.'

'Yes, Reverend Mother. I'll tell her so now. If she asks me why, what should I say?'

Mother Katherine smiled at the little nun; she was a sweet-natured, simple woman who had spent most of her adult life in the convent. If she had a fault it was curiosity. 'She won't ask you,' Mother

Katherine said gently. 'Just give Sister Dominic the message. Thank you, Sister.'

The Mistress of the Novices was far from simple; long experience of the different types who either had, or believed that they had, a true vocation to the religious life, made her difficult to mislead. She had spent a long time talking to Reverend Mother Katherine about the novice Sister Francis. It had not been a happy conference. The Reverend Mother had never known the older nun to be so disturbed; several times she was near tears. 'I try to be fair, Mother, I try to see everything she does through Our Lord's eyes, but there's something so different about her – the other novices think she's a saint. But I . . . oh dear, even trying to describe it is so difficult.'

'I know it is,' Mother Katherine had said. 'I know exactly what you feel.' But she hadn't put that feeling into words. Sister Dominic was upset and confused for the first time in twenty years of guiding young women before they took their final vows. Mother Katherine reassured her and said nothing. She had deliberately delayed the girl's entry into her novitiate, on the grounds that she must be sure of her vocation and not misled by her convent breeding; but even her impeccable novice years had not relieved Mother Katherine's mind. She was waiting for Heinrich Holler to come that afternoon in the hope that he would have a solution to the problem of Sister Francis which would relieve her and her community of the responsibility.

She heard the doorbell, and knew that he and the others had arrived. She didn't wait for Sister Aloysius to knock on the door; she went out into the hall. She saw the little nun's face bright with curiosity; so many questions and nobody to answer them; it was a true penance for her. Not like the one she had endured for so long. But then God made the back for the burden. They had an Irish nun in the community when she first came, and she had taught them that saying from her native land. It didn't translate well into German. She opened the parlour door and went in. Holler stood up, so did the man he introduced as Max Steiner and the big American. She came and took Minna's hand.

'I didn't expect to see you,' she said. 'But I'm very glad you're here.'

Max Steiner watched her; it was interesting to see how her personality dominated them. She radiated authority and self-assurance; even Curt Andrews seemed hesitant until she sat down and spoke to them.

'I assume that you all know we have a novice here called Sister Francis. She has been in the convent since she was a child. She took her novice's vows two years ago. I understand from Herr Holler that you wish to see her. She will be with us in a few minutes.'

'And she is the child that Gretl Fegelein brought into the convent?' Holler asked.

'Yes,' the nun answered. 'She is the same person.'

Curt Andrews cut across Holler's next question. 'And this Sister Francis is the daughter of Adolf Hitler and Eva Braun?'

Mother Katherine glanced at Holler, and he nodded. 'Yes,' she said to Andrews. 'That is what I understood when I was made Reverend Mother.'

'Before we see her,' Heinrich Holler said. 'I think that Herr Andrews, who is representing United States interests, would like to be reassured that Sister Francis will take her final vows and remain in the religious life?'

Max saw Minna leaning forward. She hadn't spoken since they sat down; she had been watching the Reverend Mother with tense concentration.

'I can't answer for her,' the nun said. 'She can't be forced to remain with us.' Andrews's look of triumph was noted by Holler.

'Naturally,' he said quickly. 'But a person who has never known the outside world and is within three years of her final vows – '

'Does she know who she is?' Max asked.

The nun shook her head. 'No,' she said. 'Thank God.'

'Why do you say that?' Andrews said. 'What sort of a person is she?' Minna saw that suddenly the old Freda von der Stein was looking at them under the nun's veil.

'That's very difficult for me to answer,' she said. 'All I can tell you is that we have lost three vocations since she became a novice herself; all of them were influenced by her. The nature of the influence is not exactly what it seems. She is devout, scrupulous in all observances of our Rule, faultless in her behaviour. Many in the community talk of her as a saint.'

'But you don't think so, Reverend Mother?' Andrews said.

'There is no sanctity that brings doubt and confusion to those in contact with it. Sister Francis pervades the community; her presence is felt even by those of us who are in authority. But if you asked me to accuse her of any act of disobedience or irreverence, I couldn't do it.'

'What would you say about her?' Minna asked the question. 'As a human being, what do you think of her?'

The Reverend Mother hesitated. 'In the name of charity I shouldn't say this; but equally I have to tell the truth. I have tried very hard not to be influenced by knowing who she is. But I felt it even when she was just a child. The Mistress of Novices, who is responsible for her, feels it too and is terribly distressed. I think she's wholly evil.'

Nobody spoke; Curt Andrews was crouching forward on the hard little wooden chair; he reminded Max of an animal in sight of its prey.

There was a little tap at the door, followed immediately by another. Mother Katherine rose to her feet. 'Come in.' The door opened and a girl in the grey dress and white veil of the novice hesitated on the threshold.

'Come in, Sister Francis,' the nun said.

She was tall; that was Max's first impression, the second was the sweetness with which she turned to her Superior. 'You sent for me, Reverend Mother?' She had a deep, warm voice.

'Yes, Sister.' Mother Katherine turned to Holler, and asked a silent question. He gave a slight nod. She turned to the young nun. 'Thank you, Sister. You can go back to the community now.'

The girl's disappointment showed for a brief second, and then submission took its place; she bowed her head slightly. 'Thank you, Reverend Mother.' She gave them a look that seemed to touch on each of them personally; Max saw Holler's reaction. He recoiled, as if he had been given a shock. It was Curt Andrews who held the nun's gaze; she had large blue eyes, and they were brilliant, as if there was a light behind them. Max had never seen such eyes in anyone before. 'One moment, Reverend Mother,' he heard Andrews say. 'I'd like to hear Sister Francis answer that question – the one you said you couldn't answer for her.'

'I don't think that's advisable,' Holler interrupted sharply. He had turned very pale.

'You promised me a guarantee,' Andrews said. 'The young lady is the only person who can give it. I have the President's authority to speak to her myself.'

Minna had got up; Max saw her move slowly out of her chair, and step back, as if she didn't want to be part of what was happening. And he knew now what Andrews was going to do, and he also saw from Holler's face that the Intelligence Chief had been taken by surprise.

'Sister Francis,' Andrews said. 'I'd like to ask you a question.'

The girl was still looking at him; the sad submission had been replaced by an expression of intentness. Max had the feeling that the controversy had excited her.

'I'll answer it, if I can,' she said.

'Do you intend to spend the rest of your life as a nun?'

The pause before she answered seemed interminable. The transformation that came over her was gradual; visibly, it went with a mental calculation. She seemed to straighten, the blue eyes roved over their faces; Max was again aware of their unusual colour and luminosity. One hand reached up to the veil that covered all but a line of dark hair at her forehead. Long, sensitive fingers touched it; he thought she was going to tear it off. But the gesture was enough; its significance was obvious.

'No,' she said. 'Not if I have any choice.'

She turned to face Holler as he spoke. His eyes were narrowed, and the look on his face shocked Max. He heard Minna draw her breath. She had come to stand just behind him.

'You have no choice,' Holler said. 'Understand that. You'll stay in the custody of the nuns for the rest of your life. And be thankful for it!'

'Custody?' Sister Francis said. 'I've always felt I was a prisoner. Now I know it. And, of course, I know why.' She faced the Reverend Mother; her voice fell to a soft, almost gentle tone. 'I don't blame you, Mother. You had to make me join the community. My aunt helped to persuade me, even though it was against my will.' She gave Curt Andrews another long, communicative stare. 'My aunt was very religious; she wanted to save my soul. She told me who my father was because she thought I'd spend my life as a nun in reparation for his sins.' She gave the Reverend Mother a slow smile. 'I thought it was silly at the time. But she was dying, and I wanted to make her happy. But I knew someone would come and rescue me.'

'Sister Francis,' the nun said, and anger had made her breathless, 'you are free to leave this House at any time. I, personally will be delighted!' She said furiously to them all, 'No one ever put pressure on her to enter religion. She has been perfectly free to go or stay.'

'Sister Francis,' Curt Andrews said, 'if you want to leave here, I am authorized to offer you the protection of the United States government.'

'I would be glad to accept it. From today.' The hand came up again and slowly drew off the white cap and the floating veil. Her hair was almost black and it formed a smooth helmet to a striking face. When you knew what to look for, the resemblance was incredible, even to Max who had only seen photographs. Not Eva Braun, with her round, dimpled face and fair hair, but the features, the colouring, and the eyes of Adolf Hitler. Holler had seen it when he looked at her; the magnetism had been passed to her too. She dominated the room. She was more effective and evocative precisely because she was a woman and not a carbon-copy male.

'No,' Holler said loudly. 'No, Andrews. You won't get away with this.' He spoke in English.

'She's too potentially valuable to our enemies,' Andrews said, 'and she can't be kept against her will. The story will get out . . .' He paused to emphasize the point. 'And if anything happens to her, to a simple nun, dedicating her life to God – it could bring your government down, Holler. The best place for her is safe with us. The Russians aren't going to get their hands on this stick of dynamite.'

Sister Francis took a step towards him. 'Please take me with you. One day I shall have something to offer my country. I've always known it.'

Curt Andrews saw it first; Max heard a movement behind him, and then Andrews shouted and sprang forward. But he was too late; Minna Walther had fired twice before he reached her, and both bullets struck the smiling figure, bareheaded in her nun's dress. The third went wide, smashing the little red glass lamp that glowed in front of the Sacred Heart picture. There was a cry as Andrews struck, and the gun skidded across the floor. Max acted instinctively to protect her, but she had already crumpled to the ground, her right arm smashed from the savage open-handed blow. He held her against him, and she whispered to him, before she lost consciousness. 'I had to do it – forgive me, darling –' He saw Holler and the Reverend Mother kneeling beside the girl, Andrews bending over her. It was Holler who spoke first. 'She's dead,' he said to Andrews. 'You can take her with you now, if you like.'

Afterwards, when he was trying to remember what had happened, Max could isolate certain incidents with clarity; the rest merged into confusion. He knew that the Reverend Mother had come to help him lift Minna, and he remembered the whiteness of her face and the expression in her eyes as she looked up at him. 'Thank God for her courage. That brute has broken her arm . . .' He kept seeing the dead girl, the triumphant smile frozen on her mouth, the nun's headdress still grasped in her right hand. The Reverend Mother had blood on her skirt. The American was coming over to Minna, and Max stood to bar his way. He had a clear recollection of the fury on the other man's face, and the way he clenched his hands into fists as if he wanted to hit her again and again . . .

'She'll be put away for life!' The words were snarled at him. 'We'll make sure of that –' The door had slammed behind him so hard that the furniture shook.

Then Holler, very pale, but with a strange look of calm about him. He had taken charge; the Reverend Mother was advised to change her clothes, gather her community into the chapel and stay there for the next hour. She had seemed to understand when he spoke to her in a low voice; Max heard only the words, 'Leave everything to me.' Then Holler began telephoning. Minna regained consciousness when they moved her. She cried out in pain before she fainted. They wouldn't let him go with her in the ambulance. Holler's men had arrived, efficient and silent moving; they barred his way. The dead woman was removed, and someone was cleaning the bloodstains off the floor. Then Max too was taken; there was a gun in his side when he started to protest. He was pushed into a car outside and driven through the city. He was hurried up the steps into the police headquarters and shut up in one of the interview rooms. Somebody brought him a cup of coffee, but

when he tried to ask about Minna they went out and locked the door.
It was late at night when Holler came to see him.

He walked into the room and when Max tried to speak he held up
his hand. His eyes were cold. 'Before you say anything, you'll listen
to me. Sit down.'

'How is she? What have you done with her?'

'She's in hospital. I told you to sit down. I don't want to be unpleasant, Herr Steiner, but I shall ring this bell for my assistants, and you'll
soon do as you're told. That's sensible of you. Cigarette?' He took one
and lit it; Max shook his head. Holler set one of the chairs in front of
Max, and sat down. He drew deeply on his cigarette.

'Did you know she was going to do this?'

'No,' Max said. 'For Christ's sake, if I'd had any idea, I'd have
stopped her going near the place!'

'That's what I thought,' Holler said. 'She used us both very cleverly.
You're her lover, aren't you – did you think Minna was capable of
killing anyone? No, of course you didn't. Nor did I. But I should have
seen through it. I should have known why she wanted to see the other
half of Janus.'

'She said she had to do it,' Max mumbled. 'She said she was sorry
. . .' He raised his head; Holler saw the total weariness and despair
in his face. 'What's going to happen to her?'

'We'll come to that in a moment,' Holler said. 'I'd like some coffee
– have you had anything to eat?'

'I'm not hungry,' Max answered.

'You may change your mind, when you see food. I'll get some sent
in.' Holler pressed the call bell. Max closed his eyes and waited for a
moment. Minna. Minna. He could have cried her name out loud. He
drank the coffee when it came, but he couldn't bring himself to eat.
Holler smoked and ate sandwiches. The silence seemed interminable
to Max.

'Tell me something,' the Chief of Intelligence said at last. 'Did you
see the resemblance, or was it my imagination?'

'I saw it,' Max answered, 'the moment she took her headdress off.
I was looking for it, I suppose, but there was no mistake.'

'She had the same eyes,' Holler said. 'The same colour blue, the same
power to draw you . . . I used to watch him subduing other people,
men of intelligence and education, generals, staff officers, people who
should have seen through him at once. They couldn't withstand his
power, whatever it was. She had it too. The nun recognized it.'

'She said it was evil,' Max said.

'She was right,' Holler said quietly. 'The Americans thought they
could use her – Hindenburg and the army thought they could use
her father. Who sups with the devil needs a long spoon.' There

was a curious, twisted smile on his face. 'I'm having trouble with my American colleague. He's threatening to expose the whole story unless I take action against Minna. Not official action, of course. And I can't let the story come out.'

'What are you going to do?' Max asked him. 'You can't punish her – '

'I wouldn't have let that woman leave Germany alive,' Holler said. 'Minna forestalled me, that was all. She saw what could happen if Adolf Hitler's daughter came on to the political scene, masterminded by the politicians. If she'd been a fool, or even an ordinary woman, it would still have been dangerous for Germany. But his genes had passed to his child; his capacity to lie and to mesmerize. Andrews didn't even realize how she was working on him. Minna Walther did the best thing possible for us all. I hope you realize it. I hope you still love her, Herr Steiner, because she's going to need you. Now I've got work to do. You won't mind staying the night? They'll give you a bed.' He got up and stretched a little, nodded to Max and went out. The room was hazy with his cigarette smoke. A uniformed policeman came and escorted Max to a cell, where he was given pyjamas and asked if there was anything he wanted.

He shook his head. In his ears were still the words 'Minna Walther did the best thing possible for us all. I hope you realize it.' He dropped down on to the cot, and lay staring at the bare ceiling. Nobody had locked the door. She was in hospital somewhere in the city, under sedation. She had carried the gun in her bag, knowing that she was going to use it.

Holler said he hoped that he still loved her . . . Her own whispered words to him before she fainted: 'I had to do it. I'm sorry, darling . . .' He fell asleep, exhausted, without having answered his own question. The sleep was black and empty, like an abyss into which he had fallen.

'You put her up to it,' Curt Andrews said. 'You knew you couldn't hold the girl if she decided to come with me, so you fixed Walther's widow up with a gun and a guarantee if she had to use it. Very clever; no one can accuse you of acting against US interests, and you'll keep the whole mess under wraps. But you're not getting away with this, Holler. I'm going to string you up by the guts!' Andrews didn't shout; he had a powerful enough voice, even in a low key, to convey that he was capable of any threat he made. Prisoners in Vietnam Interrogation Centre 3 had learned to fear the anger in Curt Andrews's voice. It presaged dreadful pain. Holler hadn't spoken; he listened to Andrews with a lack of expression that was infuriating in itself. He didn't even light one of his intermitable supply of cigarettes. Andrews was so angry that the muscles on his thick neck were standing out; he had taken up a fighting stance as he towered over the West German, balanced on the balls of his feet, ready to strike. He had always resorted to violence as the ultimate solution, and the habit had never died. The knowledge that all through he had been in contention with a brain even keener than his own increased his frustration. 'I've been watching you at work,' he said. 'You're no friend to the Western alliance: you're a Red, Holler, and you always have been – we had our suspicions about your friend Walther, right from the start – *détente* with East Germany, reunification – all the idealistic crap that you people have always fallen for . . . It wasn't the Russians who killed him, your Department were just trying to mislead us! He was killed by the right wing, because they knew he was looking for Hitler's children, and exactly what would happen if he found them – only he was dead, so you got the widow to do it for you!'

'And is this your personal opinion, or is it the view of your State Department?' Holler asked; he sounded disinterested.

'You'll find that out,' Andrews snapped back at him. 'I'm going to put in a report about this whole business, and if there's anything left of you and your Communist-infiltrated service, it won't be my fault. We've had enough bullshit from people like you, Holler, trading on the goodwill of the United States – this time, you've tried to give it to the wrong man. I smelt out Reds for two years in Vietnam, and I've had you and the Walther set-up in my nose ever since I got here!' He glared at Holler. 'I'm going to root you out,' he said. 'And none of you are going to like it.'

'I see,' Holler said. 'You wanted her very badly, didn't you, Andrews? What a coup for you and your service, eh? Adolf Hitler's daughter, carried off to the safety of the United States, where none of us wicked Europeans could try to make use of her. And she would have been useful, wouldn't she – the world is getting used to women in high places since the war. Golda Meir, Indira Gandhi, Mrs Bandaranaike. A son would have been the best, but that was quite an unusual woman, didn't you think so? She had a certain magnetism about her – I wonder how powerful she could have become in the future, with the right kind of backing –' He tossed aside his calm, and his eyes blazed hot with anger. His contempt was savage. 'You wouldn't give a damn what happened to us, to the German people, would you? If it brought some rotten political advantage to your service, you'd promote her and if we got ripped to pieces because of it that would be just too bad, wouldn't it? Well, I'll admit something to you, so you can put it in with the rest of your report. I wouldn't have let her go. If Minna Walther hadn't shot her, my people would have killed her, and you too, if they had to.'

'That's great,' Andrews said. 'I've got that on tape, Holler. Just go on talking.'

Holler shrugged. 'You can put it on the table as far as I'm concerned. Then you can edit out the bits you don't like, when you get home.'

'I won't be editing anything,' Andrews said grimly. 'I'm going to blow the whole stinking conspiracy up in your face. You tried to hide the existence of a daughter from me, but you didn't reckon on Mühlhauser – he told me the *whole* story. When you realized I couldn't be kept out, you primed Minna Walther to act as assassin. I guess when the pressure is on her she'll nail you, Holler, to save herself. You've got enemies in Bonn; they'll know what to do with this report when it comes back as an official United States note to the Bonn government. They'll dig you over like dogs in a boneyard – and you Krauts have a great way of cutting each other up. And it won't help to send Minna Walther on a nice convalescence where she can have an accident before anyone gets to question her. I'm putting that possibility in too; you won't be able to get rid of the chief witness without proving you were guilty with her.'

'It may surprise you,' Holler said, 'but murder isn't my favourite solution. If it wasn't necessary to bury this story forever, I would have Minna Walther tried for what she did. But I can't, because nobody must know that Hitler's daughter ever left the convent. As you said, if we discovered her existence then eventually so will the Russians; secrets as big as this always leave a trail behind them. Only it won't lead them anywhere. My friends in the Vatican will see to that. As for the accusations you've made against me, make them official by all means. I'm sure you think it will lead you a little nearer to your Director's chair . . . But I doubt if this will.'

He reached into the drawer of the desk, and threw a blue folder on top of it.

'The originals are in safe keeping,' he said. 'You can take that away with you. You may want to use it as part of the famous report that you're compiling.' He walked to the door, opened it and went out, closing it quietly.

Curt Andrews was alone in the office. He picked up the blue file, and flipped open the first page. He lowered himself slowly on to the edge of the desk as he began to read.

'I want to make a deal,' Stanislaus Kesler said. He blew his nose; he had cried during the night, and his nasal passages were blocked. He was sitting opposite Paul in a cheap café on the outskirts of Geneva. They had a bottle of wine between them. Paul watched him carefully; Kesler looked haggard and heavy-eyed; he seemed to have aged suddenly.

'What are you talking about?' Paul said. 'You're lucky to be here in one piece. The best thing you can do is take what's owing to you, and disappear.'

'I'm not walking out on Maurice,' Kesler said.

Paul made a grimace of impatience. 'Don't be such a fool. If he keeps his mouth shut, they'll put him away for a few years. If he talks, or they connect him with the other murders, he'll be in jail till he drops dead. Forget him, there's nothing you can do.' He saw the expression on Kesler's face, and wished he'd been more tactful. 'I know how you feel,' he amended, 'but it's no use thinking you can help him. What happens if he trades you in to help himself?'

'Maurice won't shop me,' Kesler said. 'You don't understand us. We really care about each other.'

'All right.' Paul sighed. 'But what can you do?'

'I can put the West Germans on to you,' Kesler said. He poured himself a glass of wine. Paul had his glass in mid-air; the wine slopped out of it on to the table.

'Me! You'd set them on me – '

'Why not?' Kesler said. 'You know who pays the bills. And you'd soon tell them. You're not the courageous type. You would be a very useful bargaining point.' He finished his wine. 'I think that's what I'll do. If you run, you won't get very far.' He watched the other man lose colour, and the sweat begin to break out on his forehead and turn into little beads. Paul's mouth was slack with fright.

'I'll kill you,' he blustered feebly.

Kesler smiled. 'You couldn't swat a fly,' he said,

'You bastard,' Paul mumbled. 'You dirty pederast.'

Kesler kicked him under the table, catching him on the edge of the shin-bone. 'Be careful when you call names,' he said.

Paul couldn't speak; his face was twisted in pain. Kesler waited. He was very calm, as always in moments of crisis. He had spent his emotions in the last day and night, imagining Franconi being interrogated. He was going to save him if it was possible, and the frightened go-between was just the bait he needed. But if Paul was a coward, he wasn't a fool. He had a quick brain and a rat-like sense of survival. Kesler let him work out the problem for himself. It took him a few minutes. If Kesler betrayed him, he wouldn't have a chance. Raymond would have him silenced before he had time to identify him as the paymaster. Raymond wouldn't be pleased about Franconi's arrest either. And he was sick of living with danger, of dealing with killers like the one sitting opposite him. He felt sick with fear and his leg was on fire from the kick. The thought of Raymond terrified him no less than Kesler. Only Kesler was here and Raymond was safe in his office in the luxury hotel. He decided that Fate had made the choice for him; the time had come to escape it all and enjoy himself in the distant paradise of the Seychelles.

'I'll tell you who pays,' he said to Kesler. 'I'll tell you enough to get Franconi out with a suspended sentence.'

Kesler nodded. 'I thought you'd see a way out for yourself,' he said. 'And it's all the same to me as long as it helps Maurice. I'll order some more wine. Or maybe you'd rather have a cognac. You look a bit pasty-faced.'

'How are you going to do it?' Paul asked. He had begun to calm down; he even felt relieved. Kesler could do the negotiating; if he was quick he could make his travel arrangements and be on airplane out of Switzerland by the evening. He could get the details settled later, when Raymond was out of the way . . . The Seychelles, and the villa, waiting for so long to be occupied, and the big-breasted girl he'd picked out to take with him. He took a deep breath. 'Who are you going to contact?'

'You're going to advise me,' Kesler said. 'You know all the crooks in the police here; you'll get hold of one of them for me. I'll talk terms with him.'

'Me?' Paul's spirits fell as suddenly as they had risen a moment before.

'Yes, you,' Kesler said. 'You're going to ring one of your contacts and get him down here. I'll talk about money. And you'll tell me all I need to know before he gets here.'

'All right,' Paul said. He wouldn't get away before the morning.

'You'd better write everything down.'

They drove Max Steiner back to his hotel the next morning; the man who had taken him from the convent at gunpoint was very friendly. He suggested that he and Max have a drink at the bar, and he insisted on paying.

'How is Fräu Walther?'

The detective had been expecting the question. 'She's well,' he said. 'They set her arm and she's under observation for a few days. Nothing to worry about.' He smiled encouragingly at Max. 'Herr Holler wants you to stay here for a bit; at our expense, of course. And enjoy yourself – Munich has a lot to offer. He'd rather you didn't telephone your magazine, or talk to anyone outside, just till everything's settled.' There was a glint in the brown eyes that was at odds with his smile.

'When can I see her?' Max said. 'I won't promise anything until I've seen her.'

'I'll ask Herr Holler, and let you know,' the detective said pleasantly. 'In the meantime, just do as he asks, won't you?' He paid the bill for their drinks, and stood up, waiting for an answer.

'I'll stay here till he contacts me,' Max said. 'I won't be talking to anyone.'

Holler's agent held out his hand. 'Good,' he said. 'Herr Holler will be in touch with you.'

Max watched him go. There were a number of people in the bar, drinking before lunchtime. He remembered sitting there himself, getting drunk enough to ring up his wife and say their marriage was finished. And Minna trying to tell him that they didn't have a future, only he wouldn't listen. She had known from the beginning what she was going to do when they found the other half of Janus. When they lay in each other's arms and he told her how much he loved her she had kept a part of herself intact, because of what she was going to do. But in the end she said she loved him. In the hotel lounge, at a corner table, now occupied by another couple. Two businessmen, deep in conversation. That had given him the courage to desert Ellie and his children. That and the brandy he drank after Minna had gone upstairs.

She had so nearly been killed that night. He thought of the cyanide pen Holler showed them, and the young, good-looking man who had been betrayed at the identity parade by a little black and white terrier. He was the one who had watched Minna in the restaurant and in the lounge afterwards. Max had thought he was trying to make a pass at her. He had been jealous ... He thought of his anxiety for Minna after the experience, how he had tried to shield her, and how Holler had insisted that she was quite strong enough to look at the suspects. 'She's not quite as fragile as you think,' Holler had said. And he hadn't known that a few hours later she would take a gun out of her bag and shoot another human being.

Max signalled the waiter, and ordered a beer. He didn't want to drink too much; he wanted a clear head to try and answer the questions that were poised like daggers, aimed at his heart. Had she used him, as Holler said? Had she ever loved him, or only seen him as a means of completing what her husband had begun? If he hadn't known about Janus, would she have responded when he first made love to her, or was that part of the campaign she was conducting? There were no answers to the questions, and he knew there wouldn't be until he came face to face with her again.

Reverend Mother Katherine was in the chapel, praying. There were half a dozen nuns kneeling in private adoration; they were scattered, and the Reverend Mother knelt at a distance from them. She had made the announcement in the refectory the previous evening. Her bloodstained grey skirt was in the furnace; the shattered devotional lamp before the picture of the Sacred Heart had been replaced, and there was no trace on the newly polished floor of the grim stains that had been scrubbed away. She had made the announcement after grace was said, and before the meal began. Sister Francis had left the convent. That was all; the buzz of comment went on until the supper was finished and the community prepared for evening prayers. The Mistress of the Novices had come to her. 'May God forgive me,' she said. 'But I'm glad she's gone from us. I shall pray for her.'

'I'm glad too, Sister,' Reverend Mother Katherine said. 'We both knew she didn't belong here.'

'I never said it before, because I couldn't bring myself to pass such a judgement on any of our Sisters.' Sister Dominic hesitated. 'Sometimes I thought she was an evil influence. Pretending to be good. No doubt it was my imagination because I couldn't understand her.'

'No, Sister,' Mother Katherine answered. 'You imagined nothing. She was a lost child. But we will pray for her just the same.'

And she had tried to ask mercy and forgiveness for the dead girl, but there was no sincerity in the prayer. Her own hatred made a mockery of the *De Profundis* and her thoughts swung obstinately backwards, to the father who had been strangled to death without a trial, to her mother and herself, fleeing the vengeance of the tyrant they hadn't been able to kill. She couldn't pray for the soul of his daughter without knowing it was hypocrisy. That afternoon, in the quiet period reserved for private meditation in the chapel, Mother Katherine tried again.

She thanked God first, for the deliverance from evil which she believed had threatened her own small community, and then posed a danger to her country and its people.

She thanked God for Minna Walther's courage, and prayed earnestly for her. And then she set her mind upon her duty, and began the *De Profundis* for the child of Adolf Hitler who had murdered the person she loved most in the world. And at last she was able to finish it, and mean it as she said the last line under her breath. 'Eternal Rest give unto her, O Lord.'

'I've brought you your file back,' Curt Andrews said. He dropped it deliberately on Holler's desk. His face was set and expressionless; only the muscles under the jaw were tense.

Holler drew the blue folder towards him. 'Don't you want to use it? Sit down; I'll send for some coffee.'

'No, thanks,' Andrews said. 'I shan't be making a report. If you're offering hospitality I'd rather have a scotch and ice.'

Holler smiled. 'I'm sure we can manage that,' he said. Sunlight radiated through the big plate-glass window, shedding a nimbus of light around his small figure, with uncountable millions of dust motes floating gently downward through it. The office was high above the city, and there was a fine view from the window. Holler didn't like looking out; ever since his arrest by the Gestapo he had been afraid of heights. His own office in Bonn was on the first floor. He studied the American; he wore his well-cut suit and the blue shirt with buttoned-down collar; he looked like a man in transit. He gave no sign of hostility; he was as neutral as a machine-gun with the cap on its muzzle. Andrews nodded towards the file.

'Why did you hold this back?'

'I had to be sure it was right,' Holler answered. 'We didn't have time to investigate very deeply, but we found the first clues in the flat. Mühlhauser had an address book, and we checked out on the names. One of them didn't exist, nor did the address. But the phone number given was real enough. We traced it to a firm of contractors with business connections in Leipzig. That was his East German controller. My guess is, he was recruited soon after he was repatriated. And the fact that the Odessa helped get him settled in a good job here was just a bonus for them.' He waited while a tray of coffee, whisky and ice was brought into the office. He poured a strong drink for Andrews and filled it with ice. 'Odessa were told we were going to question him,' he said quietly. 'I knew it was an internal leak. We haven't traced it yet, but we will. So Kramer took a second look at the good Party member Mühlhauser, and decided to ask him a few questions. Your arrival was a godsend to him. He'd saved his life by telling Kramer what he hadn't told the Russians; and not just for that reason.'

'Why then?' Andrews asked.

Holler sipped his coffee. 'Because he was a Nazi deep down,' he said. 'He'd kept alive, but he consoled himself with the idea that he hadn't betrayed *everything*. And when he told about the twin, he hoped she'd be used by the right people. Either Kramer's friends or else a third party, like the CIA . . . Someone who'd see a use for her in Germany's destiny, and he probably believed that her heredity would do the rest. And of course he was going to feed his Russian masters everything he picked up while you were nursing him in Washington . . . Anyway, now you know.'

'Sure,' Andrews said. 'Now I know I've personally recruited a Soviet agent and sent him to the bosom of the family. That makes me all set for promotion.'

'I thought the report you were submitting about the incident in the convent was going to do that,' Holler said gently. 'But if you were to forget about that, and unmask Mühlhauser yourself when you get back – '

'Or use him to pass disinformation,' Andrews said. 'That's the way I thought of playing it. On the understanding that you don't pass that file on to Washington before I have a chance – '

'My memory for sending in reports is no better than yours,' Holler said.

'I've forgotten mine,' Andrews said.

'That's good,' Holler nodded. 'When are you leaving for home?'

'I'm catching a flight this evening.'

For a moment they sat in silence; each looked at the other. Neither showed any emotion, each made a private vow not to present the other with a chance of balancing the score. Andrews had lost out, and it would always rankle. Holler would need to be very careful in the future. He got up and held out his hand. Andrews hesitated for a second and then took it; the handshake was brief.

'Safe journey,' Holler said. Andrews gave him a slow, hard look.

'Thanks,' he said. 'I won't forget this trip.'

Holler waited till he left the office. Then he picked up the telephone. His conversation was sparse; mostly he asked questions. 'You're sure this contact is genuine? No, no deal for Franconi. All right – it'll have to be a very big fish, if they want him let off the hook. No, I don't intend to, but play it along and see what you get. Right.' He set the receiver back, and took out a cigarette; he poured himself more coffee and drank it; it was no longer very hot. The ends were tying up; Andrews was disarmed, at least on this occasion. And the capture of Franconi had produced a very interesting offer from a source in Switzerland. The name of the top Soviet agent and head of the European assassination department of the KGB. It was very tempting; Franconi had given nothing away under interrogation. It was obvious to Holler that he was protecting an accomplice as well as himself. And it must be the accomplice who was bargaining for Franconi. He could be released through lack of evidence: intelligence was a game in which the scales of justice were adjusted according to what was most politically valuable. Holler had adjusted the scales many times before. He was going to do the same for Minna Walther. What happened to the multi-murderer Franconi was a different problem. He had silenced Curt Andrews and he could protect the widow of his old friend. It was time to let Max Steiner leave the hotel and go to see her.

'I've sent her home to Hamburg,' Holler said. 'Her arm is healing well; there's no reason to keep her in hospital any longer.'

'Then you're not going to take any action against her?' Max asked.

Holler shook his head. 'No. She did Germany a service. Fortunately I don't have to admit that anything happened, which makes life easier.' He gave Max a slight smile. 'It needed a little negotiating, but it worked out. So Minna is safe from prosecution. And you can see her now.'

'Why didn't you let me know before she left Munich? Why wait to tell me after she's gone home?'

'There was a reason for that,' Holler admitted. 'You don't act on impulse in my kind of work. There always has to be a reason. And this one was quite simple, really. Now she's gone home, you don't have to see her if you don't want to. You have been her lover; it would have been difficult to refuse to go to the hospital. Now you have an easy exit if you want one.'

'What kind of a bastard do you think I am?' Max demanded.

Holler pursed his lips and shook his head. 'I don't think you're a bastard at all,' he said. 'Minna wound you round her finger like a piece of ribbon. She has a way of making people love her. Sigmund worshipped her for nineteen years. I'm a little cynical about women, Herr Steiner, and it probably colours my view of the best of them. But Minna Walther is different. The women I've known have all been sensible, pragmatic; that's the new word, isn't it? They're supposed to be such impulsive creatures, ruled by the heart not the head –' Max saw the smile again, and this time it was a little sour and twisted. 'They're the most cold-blooded, the most calculating of the species. All they want is to survive, to protect their children and maintain the status quo. I speak from experience, but that's not important. Now and again history throws up the exception to the rule. Women prepared to die for an ideal. Or to kill for it. Do you still love her, Herr Steiner? That's why I sent her back home, because I owe her something. I wanted her to feel secure in her own house, among the people and the things she knows. If not –' He left the sentence unfinished. 'Her eldest son is with her.'

'Does he know?' Max asked.

'No,' Holler said. 'I told him she'd had an accident. He's very like Sigmund, but he has the strain of Prussian fanaticism dressed up as modern Liberalism. He's never understood his mother because he's got too much of her in him.' He paused. 'Do you want to go to Hamburg? Please understand; there's no obligation.'

'No,' Max Steiner said, 'there isn't. I can walk out of here and catch the plane back to Paris; I can write a long article about her husband and mention her in passing . . . I can probably persuade my wife and children that I didn't mean it when I said I was finished with them and in love with someone else – no, there's no obligation on me to see Minna. I can file and forget, as the saying goes.'

'I haven't heard that before,' Holler said. 'There's a flight to Hamburg at eleven o'clock. I'll send a car if you want to catch it.'

'Thanks,' Max said. 'I'll be ready in half an hour.'

The memory of the first time he came to the house in Hamburg was so strong that for a moment he hesitated before going up the steps to the front door. Minna had met him at the airport, driving a fast car. He had remarked on the way she drove; there was an indication of the hidden side of her nature in the single-minded determination of her driving. It was an unusual trait in a woman. He remembered feeling uncomfortable as they cut through the traffic. So much had happened, and so quickly, since they entered her house together. He had been powerfully attracted to her even at that stage, going forward deliberately into a situation which was dangerous, because whatever Minna Walther was, she wasn't the type for a casual affair. He stopped at the front door and pressed the bell. Waiting there he felt as if he were going to see a stranger. The door opened and the housekeeper let him in, standing aside as he came into the hall.

'Good evening, Herr Steiner. Fräu Walther is in the sitting room. I'll go and tell her you're here.'

The house had a smell of lavender polish and Minna's distinctive scent; he glanced at the staircase. Her bedroom was on the landing facing the stairs. The big draped bed, and the chill of linen sheets. The changing tempo of making love to her. He would know in a few minutes whether it had meant as much to her.

'Come in, please, Herr Steiner.' The housekeeper held the door open for him and he went inside. There was a fire burning, in spite of the warm weather, and Minna was sitting close to it. Her right arm was in plaster and it was difficult for her to get up. He came quickly to her, and caught her outstretched hand. She looked very white and drawn, the grey eyes seemed larger, and the smile was uncertain. He couldn't put his arm round her because of the clumsy plaster; he saw tears swimming in her eyes, and felt the prick of them himself. He kissed her hand and held it. 'Oh, my darling,' he said. 'My darling.'

They didn't talk about anything for some time; he sat beside her, holding her hand. The fire flickered hypnotically and Max let himself drift, knowing only how much he loved her and that nothing else mattered. She had recovered herself; she was very still, leaning against him, gazing into the fire. There was an idyllic quality about the time they sat there together, not breaking the silence. He didn't want to question her; he didn't want to spoil the harmony between them. He felt closer to her than ever before. But it was Minna who spoke of it first.

'Do you still love me, after what's happened?' She didn't turn to look at him.

'You know I do,' Max said. 'More than ever.'

'I wasn't sure,' she said. 'I saw the look on your face immediately afterwards. There were times when I was certain you'd never come back. That you couldn't accept what I'd done.'

'I've got to accept it,' he said. 'Because I love you. Perhaps I don't quite understand it. Why you, Minna? Why not leave it to Holler –'

'I couldn't take the chance,' she said slowly. 'I'll admit that at one moment I hesitated. Before she came into the room, I thought that perhaps if she was a nun it wouldn't be necessary. But as soon as I saw her I knew that Sigmund was right. He loved Germany, but he understood us all too well. We have a streak of self-destruction in us; it's in our culture, our ancient legends; part of us wants to triumph and then perish in a real Twilight of the Gods. That was the secret of Hitler, and why he overcame the reason and humanity of millions of decent, intelligent people. He had the dark side in himself, and he knew how to appeal to it in our nation. He didn't just offer us victory and world conquest – the alternative was always death and dissolution. I saw it in my own family and their friends; it's a kind of insane philosophy that insists on breaking ourselves before we bend. Duty, tradition, military honour – they're all fine words, Max, but they can be made to excuse the worst kind of crimes. You know that too. Nazism was the ultimate expression of the German sickness. That's what Sigmund called it, and that's why he started looking for this heir of Hitler's. Because he intended to kill it.

'He knew, and so did I, that what we had done once to the world, we could not do again, and that the child of Adolf Hitler, man or woman, mustn't be left alive. Germany has had a wonderful rebirth; we've become a proud, respected people, and all we need is to be united as a nation. That will come in time. So there was no doubt in my mind at all. I decided to go on, after Sigmund was murdered, and to do what he would have done. I took his gun with me to the convent.' The grey eyes looked into his; their expression was steadfast, almost serene. 'She was truly evil, just as her father was. I shall never regret what I did.' She laid her hand tenderly against his cheek. 'I love you very much,' she murmered. 'Nothing can change that.'

'I want you to come away with me,' Max said.

She shook her head. 'I can't,' she said. 'My life is here, with my children.

'Ellie's getting a divorce,' Max Steiner said. 'The first time you met me, you asked how long I'd been away from home. Well, I'm home now. I want to marry you, Minna. I'll get a job in Germany, and we'll live in Hamburg if you like. Where's your son? I'd like to meet him.'

'He's upstairs,' Minna answered. 'But he won't accept you, Max. He won't have anyone take his father's place.' He helped her to her feet.

You'll be surprised,' he said, 'how people accept what they can't change. And nothing is going to change me. When does that plaster come off?'

'Six weeks,' she said.

He leaned forward and kissed her on the mouth. 'That gives me time to make friends with your son. Let's go and find him.'

Interrogation was an art as well as a science; Heinrich Holler was skilled in that art but the man known as Raymond to the clientele of a luxury hotel in Geneva was proving a difficult subject. He resented his kidnapping; his furious protest made Holler smile. It would take a long time to undermine him, patience and skill, no violence. Holler knew very well that that only hardened a certain type of man, and Raymond was a true professional. His defence would crumble when they proved him to be Russian, which Holler knew he was. He hadn't seen the Swiss, Maurice Franconi; he disliked that part of the negotiations too much to see him again before he was put on a plane for North Africa. All he had done was alert the Tangier police to the arrival of a dangerous international criminal. What they did about it was not his concern.

'I hate cocktail parties,' Helmut Walther said; Holler looked at him over the rim of his glass and smiled slightly. 'So do I. But this was a special occasion.' They both looked in the same direction: Max Steiner in the centre of a group of people, Minna beside him. They were smiling, Steiner was talking animatedly to a very important West German editor. There were rumours that the editor was making Max an offer to join him that could not be refused.

Holler turned back to the young man. 'They're saying that Steiner's articles on your father are the best political journalism published in the last decade. What do you think of them?'

Helmut hesitated. He liked and respected Holler, not just because he was such a friend of his father, but because the older man treated him as an equal. He did not patronize Helmut; he did not hesitate to disagree with him either. 'They're marvellous,' he said at last. 'I was very much against the idea at first; I didn't want my father to be fitted into any *Time* type biography – you know the kind of thing – the journalist being clever at the expense of the subject. But Max was not at all what I expected. He spent a lot of time with me, asking my personal impressions. I got to like him very much.' He nodded again, emphasizing his point. 'I'm very pleased with the articles. Mother says they're going to be published as a book.'

'So she told me,' Holler said. He saw Minna, smiling and talking to someone close to Max. She looked very pretty, with colour in her cheeks. The broken arm had mended well; you had to look very closely to see that it was slightly crooked.

He turned again to Helmut. 'And how do you feel about the marriage?' he asked.

'I was against it to start with,' Helmut answered. There was an engaging innocence about his serious young face as he looked at Holler. 'But Max took me into his confidence; his wife was set on a divorce and determined to bring up the children in England. He told me how much he loved Mother and wanted to make her happy. He was working in the house here and we saw a lot of each other in the past year. He convinced me that I should go into politics after two years in Paris; he arranged for the introduction for me in *France Soir*. He was very helpful.' He shrugged slightly. 'I couldn't help liking him. That's when I began to accept the situation.'

'Yes,' Holler said gently. He forced back a yawn. He was very tired indeed.

Helmut Walther was still talking. 'He's changed Mother,' he was saying. 'She seems so much less inhibited now, more relaxed. When they do get married, it'll be very good for her. Father was so different – so warm and spontaneous. You knew him, Herr Holler, you knew what sort of person he was.'

'Yes,' Heinrich Holler said. 'He was a man you couldn't help loving, when you knew him. You remind me of him, in many ways, Helmut.'

'You couldn't say anything that meant more to me,' the young man said. 'I just hope I'll be worthy of him. I'll certainly try.'

'And don't underestimate your mother,' Holler said gently.

'Oh, I don't,' Helmut protested. 'We get on so much better now. Thanks to Max; she never could show her feelings, you know. I found that difficult. I think marrying him will be very good for her.'

'Yes,' Holler said. 'I'm sure it will.' He nodded at the young man, and saw suddenly the same steadfast, immovable quality, bold and untrammelled by the shadows of the past. He was very much Minna's son, although he didn't know it.

'She deserves to be happy,' he said quietly. 'Your mother is a very remarkable woman.' He laid a hand on Helmut Walther's shoulder, and then he had slipped away among the crowd.